WARRIOR
JENNIFER FALLON

Was that what had woken him? Had they already killed his bodyguard? Any assassin worth his fee should be able to take out a single guard silently, Damin knew. It also meant there was little point in trying to raise an alarm. His room was large – a suite fit for a prince – and the nearest guards would be out beyond the sitting room in the hall. Even if a palace patrol was in the vicinity and they heard him on his first cry, the chances were good he would be dead long before they were able to get through the outer room and into his bedroom.

There was no help from that quarter. Damin was going to have to deal with this himself. Alone.

Forcing his breathing to remain deep and even, Damin cautiously brought the knife down under the blanket and ever so carefully changed his grip so the blade lay against his forearm. He flexed his fingers and wrapped them around the hilt again, to make certain he had a good grip. Then he froze as the faintest sound of leather on polished stone whispered through the darkness.

It was close. Very close.

BY JENNIFER FALLON

The Hythrun Chronicles

The Demon Child Trilogy
Medalon
Treason Keep
Harshini

The Wolfblade Trilogy
Wolfblade
Warrior
Warlord

The Second Sons Trilogy
Lion of Senet
Eye of the Labyrinth
Lord of the Shadows

WARRIOR

JENNIFER FALLON

THE WOLFBLADE TRILOGY: BOOK TWO

www.orbitbooks.net

ORBIT

First published in 2005 by Voyager,
HarperCollins*Publishers* Pty Limited
First published in Great Britain in 2008 by Orbit
Reprinted 2009 (twice)

A CIP catalogue record for this book is available
from the British Library.

ISBN 978-1-84149-653-5

Typeset in Adobe Garamond by Palimpsest Book Production Limited,
Grangemouth, Stirlingshire
Printed and bound in Great Britain by CPI Mackays, Chatham, ME5 8TD

Papers used by Orbit are natural, renewable and recyclable
products sourced from well-managed forests and certified
in accordance with the rules of the Forest Stewardship Council.

Mixed Sources
Product group from well-managed
forests and other controlled sources
www.fsc.org Cert no. SGS-COC-004081
© 1996 Forest Stewardship Council

FSC

Orbit
An imprint of
Little, Brown Book Group
100 Victoria Embankment
London EC4Y 0DY

An Hachette UK Company
www.hachette.co.uk

www.orbitbooks.net

For Sue Irvine,
who understands the
true meaning of courage

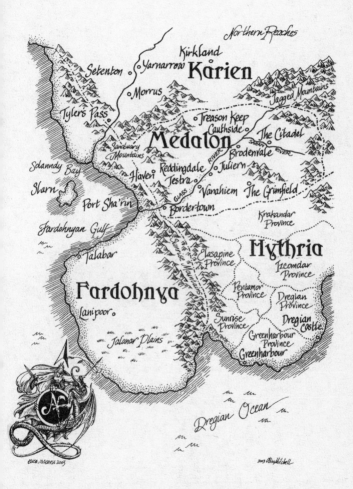

PART I

STRANGE ALLIANCES

PROLOGUE

Damin Wolfblade wasn't sure what had woken him. He had no memory of any sound jarring him into instant wakefulness; no idea what instinctive alarm had gone off inside his head to alert him that he was no longer alone. Straining with every sense, he listened to the darkness, waiting for the intruder to betray his presence. He had no doubt it was an intruder. Uncle Mahkas or Aunt Bylinda had no need to sneak around the palace. Any other legitimate visitor to his room at this hour of the night would have announced themselves openly.

It might be one of his stepbrothers, Adham or Rodja, looking for a bit of sport, Damin thought, as he inched his hand up under the pillow, or even his foster-brother, Starros, trying to frighten him. Maybe his cousin, Leila, or one of the twins had sneaked into his room via the slaveways, hoping to scare him. It wouldn't be the first time they'd tried. There was a great deal of amusement to be gained by sneaking up on an unsuspecting brother and making him squeal like a girl. Then again, it might not be one of his siblings. It might be an assassin.

It certainly wouldn't be the first time in Damin's short life someone had tried to kill him.

Damin's fingers closed over the wire-wrapped handle of

the knife Almodavar insisted he keep under his pillow, the hilt cool and reassuring in his hand. There was still no betraying sound from the intruder, a fact that made the boy dismiss the idea the trespasser was simply one of his friends looking to play a joke on him. There would have been a giggle by now; a hissed command to be silent, a telling scuff of a slipper on the highly polished floor. But there was nothing. Just a heavy, omnipresent silence.

Not even the sound of someone breathing.

Damin opened his eyes and withdrew the dagger from under his pillow with infinite care, the thick stillness more threatening than the shadows. There should have been a guard in the room. For as long as he could remember, Damin had slept with subtle sounds of another human presence nearby. The faint creak of leather as a watchful guard moved, the almost inaudible breathing of the guardian who stood over him as he slept – they were the sounds he associated with the night. With safety. With comfort.

And they were gone.

Was that what had woken him? Had they already killed his bodyguard? Any assassin worth his fee should be able to take out a single guard silently, Damin knew. It also meant there was little point in trying to raise an alarm. His room was large – a suite fit for a prince – and the nearest guards would be out beyond the sitting room in the hall. Even if a palace patrol was in the vicinity and they heard him on his first cry, the chances were good he would be dead long before they were able to get through the outer room and into his bedroom.

There was no help from that quarter. Damin was going to have to deal with this himself. Alone.

Forcing his breathing to remain deep and even, Damin cautiously brought the knife down under the blanket and ever so carefully changed his grip so the blade lay against his forearm. He flexed his fingers and wrapped them around

4

the hilt again, to make certain he had a good grip. Then he froze as the faintest sound of leather on polished stone whispered through the darkness.

It was close. Very close.

There was no longer any doubt in Damin's mind. There was an assassin in the room and his bodyguard was probably dead.

How he had got into the palace was a problem Damin had no time to worry about right now. He judged the man to be almost at the bed, which meant he had only seconds before the assassin's blade fell. *Do the unexpected,* a voice in his head advised him. It was one of Elezaar's infamous Rules of Gaining and Wielding Power, but the voice sounded suspiciously like Almodavar, the captain of Krakandar's Raiders, his weapons master, instructor and mentor.

Where is he now? Damin wondered. *When I actually need him?*

Another barely audible scuff of leather against stone and Damin realised he had no time left to wonder about it. He felt, rather than heard, the intruder raise his arm to make the killing stroke. With a sharp, sudden jerk, Damin threw back the covers, tossing them over his assailant, blinding him. Then he rolled, not away from the assassin and his blade, but towards them, slicing the man with all his might across where he thought his midriff might be, before kicking his legs up and ramming them into the space where he thought the assassin's head was located. It was impossible to tell if his aim was true between the darkness and the man fighting to get clear of the bedcovers.

The pounding of his pulse seemed loud enough to be heard in the hall.

Damin's blade had sliced across hardened leather and made little impact on his assailant's chest, but the boy was rewarded with a satisfying grunt as his heels connected with something solid, presumably the assassin's head. He sliced with his arm again, this time a little higher, hoping to wound the man. The intruder leaned back to avoid Damin's blade and momentarily lost his balance.

His blood racing, filled with a strength born of desperation and fear, Damin threw himself at the assassin, knocking the man off his feet. He landed on top of the killer, slamming the man's head into the stone floor with one hand as he changed the grip on his knife with the other and raised it to plunge his dagger into the throat of his assailant. He drove the blade downward, his heart hammering . . .

Then he stopped, a whisker away from killing his attacker. '*Almodavar?*'

The man beneath him relaxed, smiling as Damin recognised him in the darkness.

'Not bad,' the captain said.

Lowering the blade, Damin sat back on his heels, breathing heavily, still astride his would-be assassin, and grinned broadly. 'See, I told you . . . I could look after . . . myself.'

'Aye, you did, lad,' the captain of Krakandar's guard agreed. 'Pity you're so damn cocky about it, though.'

As he spoke, Almodavar gathered his strength beneath him and threw Damin backwards, his blade slicing across the boy's throat as he lashed out. Damin landed heavily on his back and skidded on the polished floor, coming to rest against the wall. He scrambled to his feet, blade at the ready, stunned to discover blood dripping from his wounded neck.

'Ow!' he complained, gingerly touching the long, thin cut across his throat.

'That was a stupid mistake, boy.'

'But I beat you!' Damin protested.

'I'm still breathing,' Almodavar pointed out, as he

climbed to his feet. 'That's not beaten, lad. It's not even close.'

'But I'd won! That's not fair!'

'What's not fair?' a voice asked from the doorway.

Damin turned to find his Uncle Mahkas striding into the room holding a large candelabrum, his face shadowed by the flickering light of half a dozen candles. Mahkas was still dressed, so he hadn't been called from his bed, nor had the room suddenly filled with guards, as it should have done following an attack on the heir to the throne.

Which meant Mahkas knew about this little training exercise, Damin realised; had probably sanctioned it. It might have been his uncle who had suggested it. Mahkas did crazy things like that sometimes.

'Almodavar attacked me!' he complained. 'After I'd won.'

'If you'd *won*, Damin, he shouldn't have been *able* to attack you,' Mahkas pointed out unsympathetically. 'Always finish your enemy, otherwise he'll finish you. You should know that by now.' He turned to the captain of the guard with a questioning look. 'Well?'

Almodavar sheathed his knife and nodded. 'He'll do, I suppose.'

His objections about his unfair treatment forgotten, Damin glanced between his uncle and the captain as he suddenly realised what this meant. 'I'll do?'

'You'll do,' Mahkas told him, with a hint of pride in his voice. 'If you can take down Almodavar, there's not much else that's a threat to you around here.'

'*Really?*' Damin couldn't hide his grin. 'You mean it? No more sleeping with a bodyguard in my room?'

'No,' his uncle agreed. 'You're almost thirteen and I promised we'd dispense with the guard when you could prove you were able to look after yourself. If Almodavar is content you can, then I'm happy to accept his word on it.'

'Just wait 'til I tell the others!'

'You can tell them in the morning,' Almodavar informed him. 'After you've done forty laps of the training yard. Before breakfast.'

Damin stared at him in shock. 'Forty laps? For *what*? I took you down, Almodavar! I won!'

'You hesitated.'

'You think I should have *killed* you?' Damin asked, a little wounded to think Almodavar wasn't thanking him for staying his hand; instead he was punishing him for it. He'd come awfully close to killing the most trusted captain in Krakandar's service, too.

'How did you know I hadn't *really* come to kill you, Damin?'

'You're the senior captain of the guard.'

'That doesn't mean anything.'

'There's a comforting thought,' Mahkas muttered with a shake of his head.

Almodavar glanced at Mahkas, a little exasperated that Damin's uncle was making light of his point. 'He needs to understand, my lord. I might have been subverted. For all any of you know, my family has just been taken hostage by your enemies and I came here willing to kill even the heir to Hythria's throne to save them.'

'But you don't have a family, Almodavar,' Damin pointed out. 'Except for Starros.'

The captain ignored the comment about Starros. He always did. 'You have no way of knowing the mind of every man in your service, Damin. And any man who can get near you is a potential assassin. You shouldn't hesitate just because you think you know them.'

'I *could* have killed you,' Damin insisted. 'If I really wanted to.'

'Why didn't you?'

'Because I knew you weren't really trying to kill me.'

'How?'

8

'You sliced the blade across my throat. If you were serious about killing me, Almodavar, you would have stabbed me with it. Straight through the neck. Up into the brain. Splat! I'm dead.'

'He's got a point,' Mahkas agreed with a faint smile, and then he glanced at the thin cut on Damin's throat. 'Although you came close enough.'

Almodavar shrugged. 'The lad needed a scare.'

Mahkas squinted at Damin in the candlelight, shaking his head. 'Let's hope that slice has healed without a scar before his mother gets here. Seeing Damin with his throat almost cut is a scare I'm not sure Princess Marla is ready for.'

'He'll be fine,' Almodavar promised Mahkas. 'Anyway, it'd take more than a cut throat to put Laran Krakenshield's son down.'

A part of Damin wished he'd had a chance to know the father Almodavar spoke of so admiringly. All his young life, he'd heard nothing but great things about Laran Krakenshield, so much so that Damin sometimes wondered if he would ever be able to live up to his father's legacy.

'That's true enough,' his uncle agreed with a fond smile. 'For now, however, I suggest we try and get some sleep. Well done, Damin.'

'Thank you, sir.'

Mahkas left the room, taking with him the only source of light. It took Damin's eyes a few moments to adjust to the darkness again. He turned to Almodavar, grinning like a fool, his blood still up from his close brush with death.

'I *could* have killed you, you know.'

The captain nodded. 'I know.'

'So do I really have to do forty laps?'

'Yes.'

'I *should* have killed you,' the boy grumbled.

Almodavar smiled at him with paternal pride. 'If you've worked that out, lad, then you may have learned something useful from this little exercise, after all.'

I

Selling off the slaves she had known all her life was the hardest thing Luciena Mariner had ever had to do. Watching them being loaded into the wagon from Venira's Slave Emporium, chained and forlorn, was the most heartbreaking scene she had ever witnessed in her meagre seventeen years.

Some of the slaves had been with her family since before Luciena was born. Young Mankel, the kitchen boy, was born in this house. He had never known another home. Her voice quivering with emotion, she turned away from the boy's distraught sobs and instead tried to explain for the hundredth time since her mother had died how much better they would fare in Master Venira's exclusive showroom than if she'd simply sold them on the open market.

Her words were little comfort. The slaves weren't fools. They all knew the chances of finding a household as good as the one they were leaving were remote.

What choice did I have? Luciena asked herself bitterly, as she climbed the stairs once the wagon had left. The heavy purse she carried made her feel worse, not better, even though it would go some way to reducing her debts. The big house echoed with loneliness, the blank spaces on the walls where paintings had once hung glaring at her like blank, accusing faces. On the first-floor landing, the pedestal where her father's marble bust had always taken pride of place stood empty now. It had been one of the first things to go, sold to help pay the huge debts her mother's death had revealed.

Luciena made her way along the tiled hall towards the small study where her mother had spent so much of her final days, trying to conceal the seriousness of their desperate position from her daughter. Her slippers hissed softly against floors that had been covered with expensive rugs. Luciena had sold them to pay the livery bill. The upkeep on the coach-and-four hadn't been paid for months. She'd sold the coach and the four matched greys without much emotion, but parting with her horse, Wind Hunter, had almost gutted her.

And I'm not out of the woods, even yet, she thought as she pushed open the door to her mother's study. To maintain their lifestyle, her mother had mortgaged the house, her jewellery, even the furniture and the slaves. Luciena would be lucky if she could keep the clothes on her back by the time the debts were paid. She stopped in the doorway, looked at the pile of paper on the small table, and felt tears welling in her eyes, yet again. It didn't seem to matter how much she sold, how much she sacrificed – that damn pile never seemed to get any smaller.

'Luciena?'

She turned to find Aleesha standing behind her with a tray bearing a tall glass of something gold and sticky and several slices of flatbread and cheese. A year or two older than her mistress, Aleesha was the only slave Luciena had not been able to bring herself to part with. The young woman was more than just a slave. She was Luciena's best friend.

'I'm not hungry.'

'You have to eat.'

12

'I can't afford to eat,' she sighed, holding the door open to allow the slave through with the tray.

Aleesha walked past her mistress and placed the tray on the side table by the window before turning to face Luciena, hands on her ample hips. 'I'll hear none of that, my girl. I know this is difficult, but we'll find a way to survive it.'

Luciena smiled wanly at the slave's determined enthusiasm. 'How, Aleesha? I'm running out of things to sell faster than I'm running out of creditors.'

'Is there nothing left of your father's money?' the slave asked, obviously puzzled by how easily their fortune had evaporated.

Luciena knew how she felt; she had trouble believing there was nothing left, too. 'Mother wouldn't have mortgaged the house to that leech, Ameel Parkesh, if there was any money left.'

'But she always claimed your father had made generous provision for you,' Aleesha insisted. 'When he married the princess . . .'

Luciena's expression darkened at the mention of her father's only marriage, very late in life, to the High Prince's sister. 'That was a marriage of convenience, Aleesha, and the only one who seemed to do well out of it was Princess Marla.'

Aleesha shook her head, even now refusing to believe someone so powerful had robbed Luciena of her inheritance. 'Your mother believed Princess Marla would take care of you, lass. I *know* that's what your father promised.'

'Then more fool my mother and father.' Luciena walked across the room to the table and dropped the proceeds of the slave sale onto the desk. The purse landed with a dull thud. 'Her Royal *bloody* Highness refuses to even acknowledge I exist. She married my father, extorted his fortune and his shipping business out of him with false promises of a grand future for his only child and then drove him to an early grave, leaving his bastard daughter and her *court'esa* mother to fend for themselves.' She stared down at the pile of debts still left to pay. 'That's why we're in such a mess, you know. Mother kept waiting for a summons from the palace. She had us living like lords, waiting for an invitation that was never going to come.'

'Perhaps the princess doesn't know—'

'Princess Marla knows *everything* that happens in Greenharbour,' Luciena scoffed, turning to look out the window. The street outside was deserted now. It was the hottest part of the day, and although it wasn't officially summer yet, the heat was enough to drive people indoors until the sun passed its zenith.

'I'm sure your poor mother only did what she thought was best,' Aleesha insisted, obviously disturbed Luciena was speaking ill of the dead.

'I know,' Luciena sighed, leaning her head against the warm glass. 'But what's it got us besides a pile of debts I can't jump over? Or repay?'

'Isn't that the same thing?'

Luciena shook her head, looking over at the letter that lay on the top of the pile on the desk. It was that letter, more than any other, that burned a hole in her gut. 'There's a difference between owing money and owing a debt, Aleesha. I can live with owing money, but to be unable to help my father's only brother . . . that hurts more than anything else I've had to deal with lately.'

The slave glanced at the desk, and the letter from Fardohnya to which Luciena was referring, and shook her head. 'You can't be expected to take on the woes of every poor sailor in the world, Luciena.'

'The poor sailor you refer to is my uncle.'

'The uncle who fought with your father with every breath he took and never spared him a kind word in twenty years,' Aleesha reminded her mistress unsympathetically. 'I don't care what your father promised him, Warak Mariner had his chance to be a partner in your father's business and threw it all away for some Fardohnyan fisherman's daughter. If he's in trouble now, it's not your fault. Or your responsibility to make it better.'

'But the boy he wants me to help is my cousin.'

'Second cousin,' Aleesha corrected. 'And he's a Fardohnyan.'

'But he's still family.'

Aleesha sighed heavily and placed her hands on her hips, frowning at her mistress. 'Your uncle fought with your father, Luciena, before you were born and pretty much every day after. When he ran off with that woman, your father warned him he'd never have anything else to do with the Mariner family. He ran off with her anyway. That was his choice and, to be honest, I always secretly admired the man for throwing away so much for love. But now I'm starting to wonder about him, because here he is, with your poor mother barely cold in the ground – and when you can least afford it – suddenly in need of your help.'

'I'm sure the two events are unrelated.'

'Really? Convenient, don't you think, that this urgent need for money to send his grandson to Greenharbour coincides with your mother's death?'

'My uncle claims his grandson has some sort of magical talent; that he needs to be apprenticed to the Sorcerers' Collective.'

'And I'm the demon child,' her slave scoffed.

'You think he's lying?'

'I think any man who writes to a niece he's never met the day after her mother dies in the mistaken belief she's inherited her father's fortune, asking for money to save a cousin she doesn't even know exists, is suspect.'

'Then what do you suggest I do?'

'Eat,' the slave ordered firmly. She took Luciena's hand

and led her to the table before making her sit with a firm push. Aleesha shoved the pile of bills aside, along with the letter from Fardohnya and the full purse from the slave sale, and placed the cheese and the flatbread on the desk in front of her. 'And forget about your uncle.'

'That's easy for you to say, Aleesha. But not as easy to do. Do you know what they do to sorcerers in Fardohnya?'

'All sorts of terrible things, I'm sure. But I don't care, and neither should you. This Cory—'

'Rory,' Luciena corrected. 'The boy's name is Rory.'

'Whatever.' The slave shrugged. 'The point is, he's not your problem and you shouldn't try to make him one. Now eat something. I'm sure everything will look better on a full stomach.'

Luciena did as the slave demanded. It was easier than arguing with her. She brushed her dark hair back behind her ears and picked up a slice of the stale flatbread. It tasted like parchment.

'Why?' Luciena asked through a mouthful of bread.

'Why what?'

'Why do things always look better on a full stomach?'

'People think better when they're not hungry.'

'Do they? I wonder what magical properties are contained in bread and cheese that open one's mind to giant leaps of intuitive thinking.'

Aleesha stared at her for a moment and then frowned. 'Just eat,' she said after a moment of puzzled silence.

'I'm sorry, Aleesha. I don't mean to tease you. Do you have any idea about how I can buy us out of this mess, help my cousin and still manage to keep a roof over our heads?'

'You could marry.'

Luciena laughed at the very notion. 'Marry who, for Kalianah's sake? I'm baseborn, Aleesha. My father was a

16

commoner, for all he was a wealthy man. And my mother was a *court'esa*. I have no dowry. Any money I might have inherited from my father is either spent or in the hands of the Wolfblades. No rich man would have me, and it sort of defeats the purpose to marry a poor man.'

'Perhaps you could get a job?'

'I suppose. I've an education rivalling a Warlord's heir,' she agreed. 'Of course, I can't imagine who would hire me, or what they'd hire me for. All the jobs I'm qualified for are the kind they reserve for sons and heirs. And even if I found a job tomorrow, it would be too late to help Rory. Do you think I should try to get an audience with the High Arrion? Maybe she could speak to the Fardohnyans?'

'And tell them what?'

'I don't know,' Luciena replied uncertainly. 'But surely, if the High Arrion intervened on his behalf . . .'

'Then she'd be signing the child's death warrant, I suspect. Advertising your magical talent by having the High Arrion of the Sorcerers' Collective in Hythria asking after you isn't a terribly bright idea in Fardohnya.'

'See! You think he's in danger, too,' she accused.

Aleesha shook her head. 'Even if I did, it doesn't matter. You've got as much chance of getting in to see someone like Lady Alija as I have of marrying the High Prince. And even if you could get in to see her, there's no guarantee she'd be willing to help you. You're not the sort of person she usually associates with.'

'Couldn't you *try* to be a little optimistic, Aleesha? Just this once?'

'I'll embrace optimism, my lady, as soon as you start embracing reality,' the slave suggested tartly. 'Eat the crusts, too. We've not the money to waste these days that you can afford to throw anything away.'

'What's *embracing reality* supposed to mean?' Luciena

17

demanded, munching determinedly through a mouthful of tasteless bread.

'I mean,' Aleesha scolded, 'you need to get over these strange notions you have about your relatives, my lady. Or the lack of them. You're the only child of a nameless slave and a man who cut himself off from the rest of his family. All the wishing in the world isn't going to alter that. There's no big family waiting to embrace you, Luciena, and you've got to stop hoping there's one out there somewhere, looking for you.'

'But—'

'Face the truth, lass. There's no point trying to find a way to help some boy you've never laid eyes on in the hope it'll give you what you're looking for. You need to deal with *our* problems, not the problems of some cousin you hadn't heard of until a few days ago. For that matter, if Warak Mariner kept his promise to never mention your father's name again, your cousin probably doesn't even know *you* exist.'

Luciena sighed, wondering if her childish secret dreams really were interfering with her judgment. Aleesha was making a frightening amount of sense. 'I suppose the timing is a little suspicious.'

'Damn right, it is.'

'It just doesn't feel right to do nothing.' She swallowed the last of the bread, her mouth dry. 'Is that cider?' she added, indicating the glass on the tray.

'Aye,' Aleesha said, walking to the side table to pick up the glass. 'It's the last of the barrels your mother bought before . . .'

Luciena looked up as Aleesha's voice trailed off. She was staring out of the window. 'Aleesha?'

The slave didn't move.

'Aleesha! What's the matter?'

'Are you expecting visitors?' she asked, her eyes fixed on the street below.

18

'No.' Luciena leaned back in her chair and sighed wearily. 'More debt collectors, I suppose?'

'Not unless you owe someone at the palace money,' the slave replied.

'*What?*' All thoughts of her long-lost uncle and her Fardohnyan cousin forgotten, Luciena jumped to her feet and hurried to the window, pushing Aleesha aside to see who was out there.

To her astonishment, there were three horsemen dismounting in the cobbled street in front of her house. They wore the gold and white livery of the Wolfblade House. Palace Guards. Or, to be more precise, the High Prince's personal guards. Luciena was dumbfounded.

'Maybe that summons is going to come after all,' Aleesha suggested, glancing at her mistress.

'I seriously doubt that,' Luciena replied. 'More likely they've been sent here to warn me.'

'Warn you?'

Luciena's expression hardened. 'To keep my head down. I imagine the last thing Princess Marla wants is the world reminded she has a stepdaughter born of a *court'esa* living not three blocks from her townhouse.'

'Look on the bright side,' Aleesha suggested. 'That makes her family.'

Luciena smiled sourly. 'The irony's not lost on me, Aleesha.'

There was a pounding on the door as the officer in charge of the small detail announced their arrival with his gauntleted fist.

'Shall I open the door?'

Luciena thought about saying no. She wanted to. She wished she had the courage. But in the end she knew that even if she denied these men entry, it just meant that more of them would be back later. Three Palace Guardsmen she could probably handle.

'Let them in, Aleesha,' she ordered.

'Are you sure?'

She nodded. 'I'm sure.'

The officer in charge of the palace detail left his two companions in the hall and saluted smartly as he stopped before Luciena, who was standing near the fountain that trickled cheerily into the near-empty pond at its base. It had been full of exotic fish once. Luciena had sold them not long after the horses to pay the butcher. Now just a few lonely goldfish swam in lazy circles around the pool.

The officer was young. Very young. Luciena judged him barely older than she was. Yet he wore the insignia of a lieutenant of the Palace Guard, a rank of no small responsibility. He was dark-haired, and quite tall with a not-unpleasant face; probably the son of some wealthy nobleman who'd bought him a commission in the Palace Guard to keep him out of trouble.

'You are Luciena Mariner?' he asked, looking around the reception hall on the ground floor with open curiosity.

Luciena had ordered Aleesha to bring her guest here. It was an imposing room with its Harshini-inspired fountain and its high-domed ceiling painted with a mural dedicated to the Goddess of Love, her mother's favourite Primal God. Because of the murals, the reception hall didn't look quite as empty as the rest of the house. The young man wasn't fooled, however; she could see him taking a mental inventory of what must be missing from the room.

'I am,' Luciena replied with as much poise as she could muster.

'I have an invitation for you, Miss Mariner.'

'From whom?'

'Her Royal Highness, the Princess Marla,' the young

man replied. 'She requests that I pass on her sincere condolences for the loss of your mother, and asks if you would join her for lunch tomorrow, at her home, so she may discuss your future with you.'

Luciena had to bite her tongue to prevent herself screaming at the sheer gall of the invitation. 'Shall I arrive at the front door?' she asked with icy dignity. 'Or would it be more appropriate if I sneaked in through the slaves' entrance at the back?'

The officer seemed rather startled by her reply. 'I *beg* your pardon?'

'Her Royal Highness has not seen fit to so much as acknowledge my existence until now, Lieutenant,' she told him. 'I can only assume her shame at my baseborn status is the reason she ignored the vow she made to my father when they wed. I believe I can therefore confidently make the further assumption that the only reason she has chosen to acknowledge my existence now is because of the potential embarrassment I pose to her.'

Luciena expected the officer to be offended by her words, but inexplicably he smiled. 'Maybe that's something you should take up with Princess Marla, Miss Mariner.'

'And maybe I choose not to,' she replied stiffly. 'What's your name?'

'Lieutenant Taranger.'

'Well, Lieutenant Taranger, you may return to the palace and inform Her Royal Highness, the Princess Marla, that I am otherwise engaged.'

'You're *refusing* her invitation?'

'You're very quick, aren't you?'

'Are you sure you wouldn't like some time to think about this?'

'Thank you, but no.'

'Very well,' he said, as if he wasn't really surprised by her refusal. 'I shall inform her highness of your reply.'

Without waiting for her to answer, the young man saluted sharply and turned on his heel, his highly polished boots echoing through the hall as he crossed the tiled floor. Luciena held her breath, half expecting him to turn around, half expecting him to order the house torched for the insult to the High Prince's sister, but the young officer did nothing but order his men to fall in behind and left the house without another word.

2

Jarvan Mariner, Luciena's father, had been a commoner –
a rough, ill-mannered, but essentially decent man. Elezaar
the Dwarf hadn't thought much about him since Jarvan
had died more than six years ago, leaving Marla a widow
for the third time, but now, as he waddled across the broad
paved courtyard towards Marla's office, he found himself
thinking of little else.

It's this business with Luciena, the dwarf decided, tugging
on his jewelled slave collar as he walked. He must have put
on weight recently. It felt tighter, more restrictive than
normal, and the sweat trapped beneath the polished silver
left an unsightly green mark on his neck.

A *court'esa's* baseborn daughter was about to be welcomed
into the palace as a member of the High Prince's family,
and the dwarf wondered how the young woman would react
to her sudden change in fortune. It was a scandal that would
be the talk of Greenharbour for months. Which was probably the reason Marla was taking this unprecedented step
at this particular time. Any day now she would be forced
to announce where her son, Damin, was to be fostered. If
people were busy talking about Luciena Mariner's adoption,
the announcement about Damin's fosterage might slip by
unremarked.

It was Elezaar who had identified the elderly (and conveniently unmarried) shipping magnate as a likely consort for the princess more than eight years ago – not long after the tragic and unexpected death of Marla's second husband, Nashan Hawksword. With limited power as a widow, Marla was anxious to remarry and had set her *court'esa* the task of finding someone suitable.

The marriage had been laughably easy to arrange. No man in Hythria was going to turn down an offer from the High Prince's only sister, and Jarvan Mariner was no exception. Despite his status as a confirmed bachelor, the owner of nearly a quarter of all Hythria's shipping fleet was quite prepared to entertain the idea of a union with the newly widowed princess – especially when he learned the offer included a promise to legitimise his only child, arrange a noble marriage for her (an unheard-of boon for an illegitimate child born of a *court'esa*) and to ensure his daughter inherited his considerable fortune. The old man had been well past sixty when they married. Slender and bald, with an unfortunate tendency to drool when he was tired, he had died peacefully in his sleep less than two years after the wedding, leaving Marla with a tidy bequest and, more importantly, control over his vast shipping empire, which the princess now held in trust for his daughter, until Luciena reached an age where she could marry and take control of the fortune herself.

That age had now come and Marla had set in motion the necessary steps to introduce her into the family. Her adoption was to be a wedding present to the girl, conditional, of course, on her choosing a husband Marla approved of.

'Elezaar!'

The dwarf stopped, shading his eyes against the sun, and turned to find Xanda Taranger hurrying along behind him, his hand on the hilt of his sword to stop it banging against his thigh.

Xanda Taranger and his older brother, Travin, were the sons of Marla's long-dead sister-in-law, Darilyn. Orphaned as small boys, both of them had been raised in Krakandar by their uncle, Mahkas Damaran. Travin was still in Krakandar, preparing to take over his father's estate in Walsark when he came of age. Xanda, as the younger son with no estate to inherit, had been invited by Marla to Greenharbour to take up a commission in the Palace Guard, an opportunity the young man had jumped at eagerly.

'So, how did your little excursion to the Mariner house go?' Elezaar asked as Xanda caught up with him. He resumed his waddle towards the main house with Xanda at his side. The townhouse courtyard was quite busy this afternoon, filled with the departing guards who had just escorted Marla back from the palace, several hawkers waiting for the head steward to inspect their wares near the kitchen gate, and a couple of slaves beating a rug from one of the upper rooms with lazy, uninterested strokes.

'She refused the invitation,' Xanda told him, panting a little from the exertion. It was hot this afternoon. And humid. In his smart dress uniform, Xanda would be feeling the heat even more than Elezaar.

The dwarf wasn't surprised. 'Just as your aunt predicted she would.'

'You'd think . . .' Xanda began, then he hesitated and looked across the walkway to where the Palace Guards were remounting in preparation for their return to the palace.

The captain in charge of the detail, Elezaar noted with interest, was Cyrus Eaglespike. Alija's son.

'I'd think what?' he prompted, doubtful Cyrus could hear them.

The young man shrugged. 'I don't know . . . that she'd be a little more grateful, I suppose. I mean, it's not every day Aunt Marla offers to take in someone's baseborn child and give them a name.'

25

Elezaar smiled. Xanda had a rather romantic outlook on life that no doubt had much to do with the fact he was only seventeen. 'I'm not sure Luciena Mariner would see your aunt's actions in quite the same generous light, Xanda.'

They had reached the main building. Xanda opened the door for the dwarf and then followed him to Marla's study on the ground floor. Elezaar knocked on the door and opened it without waiting for a reply.

Marla was sitting on the cushions by the low table, sipping a glass of chilled wine, a thoughtful expression on her face. She was twenty-nine years old now, in the prime of her life, confident, beautiful and sure of her power. Her fair hair hung straight and trimmed to shoulder length, a fashion the princess had inadvertently set last year when, in a fit of pique on a particularly humid day, she had chopped off her long hair, annoyed by the time she wasted having it dressed each morning. Within a month, there was barely a woman in Greenharbour who hadn't followed suit.

Looking at her now, at how she had grown from a foolish girl into the most powerful woman in Hythria, the dwarf felt a surge of affection for his mistress. He had never been so fortunate in an owner and knew he would never be so lucky again. For that reason alone, he would have committed cold-blooded murder for her, if it meant staying by her side.

'How did it go?' she asked Xanda as he and Elezaar crossed the large room to the table where she sat. Marla's townhouse was barely a stone's throw from the High Prince's palace and his garden on the roof of the west wing, where he indulged in most of his perverse pleasures. There were no murals here, or statues of couples caught in improbable embraces. Just a long, carved and gilded table where Marla worked, a stack of documents awaiting her signature and the comfortable

26

low table with its bright cushions where Marla was sitting. The only item in the room that gave any hint of the power this young woman wielded was the High Prince's seal, which sat on the table next to a candle, and a half-used stick of red sealing wax.

'Luciena Mariner refused your invitation, your highness,' Xanda told her, sounding a little peeved. 'She was pretty snide about it, too.'

Marla was unsurprised. 'I imagine she thinks I broke my promise to her father. How did she seem?'

'Angry.'

'Was that all?'

Xanda took a moment to reply. 'I think she was frightened, now I come to think of it.'

'Of you, Xanda?' Marla asked with a smile. 'Good gracious, boy, what did you say to her?'

'It wasn't anything I said, your highness. I think she has other problems. I only saw one slave in the house and the walls were missing a number of paintings. Most of the rugs and quite a bit of the furniture were gone too.'

'Debt problems?' the princess asked, turning to Elezaar.

'I'll look into it,' the dwarf promised.

'Do that,' Marla said, taking another sip of wine. 'And if she is in debt, find out who holds the promissory notes. How did your meeting go with Tarkyn Lye?'

Tarkyn Lye was the *court'esa* belonging to Alija Eaglespike, the High Arrion of the Sorcerers' Collective, and the most senior member of the High Arrion's household. As Elezaar's counterpart in the enemy camp, the blind *court'esa* could be relied upon to provide as much misinformation about his mistress's movements as he could possibly manage.

'He assures me the High Arrion will be leaving for her husband's estates in Dregian Province at the beginning of summer, along with the rest of his retinue.'

'Do you believe him?' Xanda asked.

'No.'

'Neither do I,' Marla agreed. 'Have a message sent to the High Arrion inviting her to accompany the High Prince in the public parade through the streets of the city when he also departs for the Retreat Season. Inform the High Arrion that Prince Lernen firmly believes such a gesture will reassure the citizens of Greenharbour of the close and abiding goodwill between the High Prince and the Sorcerers' Collective and that his highness would be further honoured to have her accompany him to the border.'

'You'd have the High Arrion accompany the High Prince to the border?' Xanda asked, sounding a little surprised. He was a member of the family and, on principle, trusted nobody who wasn't.

Marla shrugged. 'Alija either agrees to accompany my brother to Naribra before heading home to Dregian so I can be certain she's left the city, or she refuses and publicly insults him.'

Xanda smiled. 'That's rather sneaky of you, Aunt Marla.'

Elezaar nodded his agreement. 'Alija's too good a politician to do the latter over something as trivial as a street parade. Once she's gone, Tesha Zorell will effectively be in charge of the Collective until the end of summer and we can breathe a little easier for the next three months.'

'You're lucky we have a Lower Arrion you trust.'

Marla laughed sceptically. 'I don't know that I trust Tesha all that much, Xanda. I just know she's not as ambitious as Alija. That makes her much less trouble.'

Marla's restraint in her dealings with Alija Eaglespike never ceased to amaze the dwarf. Alija had been the lover of Marla's second husband, Nash Hawksword, right up until he died. She may even have been involved in the first attempt to assassinate young Damin when he was barely four years old (and who knew how many attempts since then). A man would have called her out, demanded an opportunity to defend his honour, gone to his grave rather than stomach such an insult.

But not Marla Wolfblade.

In all the time Marla had been here in Greenharbour, effectively ruling the country in her brother's name, the dwarf had never seen her falter; never seen her give even the slightest hint she knew of the affair or suspected Alija of being behind any plot to kill her son. The High Arrion assumed she and Marla were friends, that the princess relied on her counsel. Nobody but her closest family and allies knew Marla was simply biding her time, waiting with the patience of a spider for Alija to falter.

When the blade falls, Alija won't even see it coming.

And neither, Elezaar fretted, would *he*, because of Marla's admirable, but infuriating, willingness to wait. It sometimes drove Elezaar to distraction. He often wished he could find a way to prompt her into action. Marla had plenty of reasons to seek revenge, but every time he reminded her of it, she would calmly remind Elezaar that Damin was still a boy. Marla Wolfblade was prepared to wait and do nothing about Alija Eaglespike until the day he turned thirty, if it ensured her son grew up to be the High Prince she was hoping for.

Which is a fine and noble sentiment, the dwarf thought, except it robbed Elezaar of the only thing he wanted out of life – with the possible exception of staying close to Princess Marla. *Revenge. For Crysander. For my brother.*

'Speaking of Tesha,' the princess added, 'I need to talk with Wrayan when I get to Krakandar. Tesha's looking to retire soon and I'd like his opinion on her replacement.'

Elezaar shook his head, frowning at the notion. 'You're going to consult the head of the Krakandar Thieves' Guild about who should replace the Lower Arrion of the Sorcerers' Collective?'

'Wrayan Lightfinger was the High Arrion's apprentice for ten years, Elezaar. He knows the likely candidates better than anybody. And he has no vested interest in who gets the job. His is about the most reliable opinion around.'

'And has it occurred to you, your highness, that *you* have no say over who replaces Tesha when she retires, either?'

It was Marla's turn to smile. 'Of course I have a say. I'll just take Alija aside and ask her to promise me that whoever I have privately chosen for the position of Lower Arrion doesn't get the job, because I believe they have hidden loyalties to the Patriot Faction.'

'How does that help?' Xanda asked.

'Alija will promise to do her best to keep my candidate out of the job, Xanda. I'll pretend to be pathetically grateful. Alija will make certain the candidate she now believes is secretly one of her Patriots is appointed, and then she'll come to the palace and apologise profusely for not being able to prevent it. I'll accept her heartfelt apology and assure her that I know she has the best interests of the High Prince at heart, and thank her for everything she tried to do for me. She'll go away thinking I'm an idiot and we'll all be happy.'

'I don't think anybody in Hythria makes the mistake of thinking you're an idiot, Aunt Marla. Not any more.'

'I miss that, actually,' she said, placing her wineglass on the low table. 'I used to get things done with much less fuss when people didn't stop to wonder why I was doing what I was doing.'

'Ah, the good old days, eh?' Elezaar chuckled.

Marla smiled. 'Will you follow up on Luciena's debts, Xanda? Elezaar will be able to tell you what the problem is in a day or so. I'll leave you to take care of it as you see fit. You have my permission to use the Palace Guard if things look like they're getting out of hand. I have rather a lot invested in that girl. I really don't want anything to happen to her.'

'I'll take care of it, your highness.'

She smiled and offered him her palm. Xanda kissed it with a bow and let himself out of the office.

'He's growing into quite a charming young man,' Marla remarked with satisfaction.

'At least, you hope Luciena Mariner thinks so,' the dwarf amended.

'I'm sure I don't know what you're talking about, Fool,' she sniffed, quite offended by what he was implying.

He stared at her with his one good eye. 'You're not hoping the notion of the dashing young lieutenant coming to her rescue will prompt Miss Mariner into looking favourably upon your nephew as a potential husband, then?'

'That's a wicked thing to suggest!' the princess replied, full of wounded indignation. 'As if I would ever try to manipulate people like that!'

Elezaar smiled fondly at his mistress. 'Of course not.'

Marla looked at him, concerned. 'Do you think Xanda sees through me as easily as you do?'

'I wouldn't worry about your nephew, your highness. He's seventeen, which means he's far too full of raging lust and bravado to take much notice of anything you're doing.'

The princess laughed. 'Well, that's a relief! Have you made arrangements for my meeting with Corian Burl?'

'Everything is as you requested, your highness.'

Corian Burl was the High Prince's chamberlain, but he belonged, heart and soul, to Marla. Originally a *court'esa*, he was one of the men who had trained Elezaar and his brother Crysander in their youth. Too valuable to waste, when he reached the end of his useful life as a *court'esa*, Corian had been sold to a family in Pentamor Province, where he served as the estate's Chief Steward until the owner died and the son inherited the estate. Anxious to make his own mark on the world, the son had sold off a number of his father's older slaves, Corian Burl among them, around the same time Marla Wolfbade had realised she needed somebody she could trust implicitly to run the palace and the High Prince's affairs when she returned to Krakandar each year for three months to spend time with her children.

Hearing his old master was up for sale, Elezaar had brought Corian to her attention. That was the day Elezaar realised just how much the pupil had exceeded the master. Rather than buy him outright, Marla had left Corian to sweat in fear in the slave pens of Greenharbour's markets for nigh on a month. It was only at the last moment, as the hammer was about to fall, that her agent made a bid for the old man. Concerned by her heartless disregard for the old man's welfare, Elezaar had asked the princess why, if she was planning to take his advice and purchase Corian Burl all along, had she left the old man to suffer in the slave pens.

'Because I want him to be grateful to me,' Marla had replied. 'And I want him to remember what awaits him if he crosses me.' Then she had smiled thinly and added, 'Besides, if I'd expressed an interest in him any sooner, the price would have gone through the roof at auction. I have learned *something* being married to a common trader, you know.'

Yes, Elezaar thought, *you have long ago surpassed your teacher, your highness. You even scare me sometimes.*

'I can't wait to get this business with Luciena settled and get home to Krakandar,' the princess was saying as Elezaar dragged his attention back to her. 'I miss the children so much. Whoever came up with the idea of the Retreat Season really was a thoughtful soul.'

'It was Damin,' Elezaar told her.

'*Damin?*'

32

'Damin the Wise,' he explained, unable to break the habit, even after all this time, of falling into the role of her tutor whenever the opportunity arose. 'Or Damin the First, depending on who you ask. The High Prince your son was named after. Apparently, he was concerned the Warlords spent too much time at court and not enough time seeing to their own estates, so he banned them from the capital over summer. It got them out of the city and back to their own provinces in time for the harvest; meant nobody could really move on anybody else politically for a few months of the year – although he wasn't averse to the odd border skirmish to keep his Warlords on their toes, I gather; and it gave him a perfectly legitimate excuse to retreat to his own estates in the Naribra Valley and escape Greenharbour's humidity during the rainy season.'

'A wise ruler, indeed,' Marla agreed.

'Let's hope his namesake proves just as astute.'

'Well, he's certainly proving inventive,' Marla reminded him with a frown. 'According to Mahkas's most recent letter, between Damin, the twins and the Tirstone boys, they managed to convince their last tutor the Krakandar Palace is haunted. He fled the palace a gibbering wreck, by all accounts.'

'A situation Lord Damaran apparently did nothing to prevent,' Elezaar pointed out disapprovingly. He distrusted Marla's brother-in-law for no reason he could ever pin down. There was just something about him that hinted at dark secrets Elezaar would dearly like to discover.

Marla recognised his tone and shook her head. Over the years, they had arrived at a point where they now just agreed to disagree about Krakandar's Regent. 'Mahkas has never let me down, Elezaar.'

'Not yet.'

'I can't understand why you don't like him. He's doing a fine job as Regent. The province has never been in better shape.'

'So he claims.'

She smiled at his scepticism. 'I'm far too wily to merely accept Mahkas's word for it that he's doing a good job, Elezaar. I do have other sources, you know.'

'Did your other sources tell you about the raid into Medalon last year that almost cost us another war with the Defenders?'

She sighed. 'If you mean the raid in which several of our men were ambushed, killed and then cremated in a deliberate act of provocation by a gang of Medalonian thugs, then yes, I heard about it. Mahkas did what he had to in order to deter such foolishness in the future.'

'He crucified a whole family of farmsteaders, your highness, including the children.'

'He got his point across, Elezaar. Just because his methods are not those you or I would employ doesn't make them any less effective.'

He shook his head, frowning. 'I can't believe you're willing to defend such barbarity, your highness.'

'The Medalonians cremated our dead,' she reminded him. 'They burned our men like rotten sides of beef. Surely you're not suggesting such a sacrilege should have been let go unpunished?'

'Surely you're not suggesting his punishment was just?'

Marla sighed wearily. They'd argued over this so many times. 'I'm not trying to defend him, Elezaar, nor do I like what Mahkas did. I'm simply saying there's nothing I can do about it. Mahkas is Regent of Krakandar and he protects my son and his inheritance as if he were Damin's own father. I'm not going to jeopardise that arrangement because he does the odd thing I disapprove of.'

'If he'd done it ten years ago, when Palin Jenga was on the border in command of the Defenders, we'd never have got off so lightly,' Elezaar warned, wishing the princess could see past her brother-in-law's devotion to her son and recognise some of his faults as well. 'That we're not at war with Medalon over that incident has more to do with their own internal problems than fear of Mahkas Damaran.'

'That may well be the case,' she conceded. 'But we're not at war with them, so I'm not going to make an issue of it. Anyway, you'll have your chance to watch Mahkas closely for a while, seeing as how he concerns you so much. I've decided you're going to be the next tutor I send to Krakandar.'

Elezaar stared at her in shock. 'Have I done something to displease you, your highness?'

'On the contrary, you've done nothing *but* please me.'

'Then why are you sending me away?'

The princess smiled reassuringly, as if she'd only just realised the fright she had given him. 'Dear gods, I'm not sending you away, Elezaar! I'm entrusting you with the most important job in the world. I want you to teach my sons the same things you taught me. I want you to teach them your damn Rules of Gaining and Wielding Power. Make them understand the responsibility that comes with their birthrights. Narvell will rule Elasapine some day and Damin will be the next High Prince of Hythria. I intend to see he's the best High Prince I can make him.'

'But you need me here.'

'I will miss your counsel, Elezaar,' the princess admitted. 'But I have three of my own children and three stepchildren riding roughshod over the entire staff of the Krakandar Palace, apparently doing whatever they please. No matter how much I might enjoy your advice, I owe it to my country to ensure the next High Prince is not a spoiled brat.'

'But, your highness—'

Princess Marla smiled at him, shaking her head. 'I might need you here, Dwarf, but Hythria needs you in Krakandar.'

3

It was hard sometimes, being the youngest. Even harder when you were the youngest and a girl. You never got to go first at anything. You had to fight for every little thing. And you had to stand up for yourself or you'd be left behind playing girly games while the boys had all the fun.

Technically, Kalan Hawksword wasn't the youngest child in the Krakandar nursery. Her twin brother, Narvell, was twenty minutes younger, but it seemed his gender gave him an edge that outweighed the scant few minutes' head start she had on him.

There were two other girls in Krakandar Palace, but they just made things worse. The eldest was Kalan's stepsister, Rielle Tirstone, a raven-haired beauty who had just turned sixteen, whose only interests in life seemed to be planning her wedding, wearing out her *court'esa* or flirting with the palace Raiders. The other girl was her cousin, Leila. She was eleven, a bit less than a year older than Kalan, with long golden hair and smoky dark eyes.

Unlike Kalan, Rielle and Leila actually liked being girls. They were much prettier than Kalan (it was rather irritating how everyone kept remarking on that) and they could make the boys do anything they wanted just by smiling at them. Kalan didn't care about that. She wanted to be one of the boys and was annoyed that she wasn't.

And things were about to change in a way Kalan couldn't anticipate. There was another girl on the way, older than Kalan, Leila *and* Rielle.

Princess Marla had written to them about the newcomer several weeks ago. Aunt Bylinda had come into the nursery to tell them the latest news, the way she always did when a letter arrived from Princess Marla. She had read the announcement with a slight frown. Luciena, the daughter of Marla's late husband, the shipping merchant Jarvan Mariner, was coming to Krakandar with Marla when she returned for the summer.

There were already more than half a dozen children in Bylinda's care. Another one added to the mix was asking a great deal of the eternally patient young woman, particularly as she only had one child of her own and had never been able to carry another past the third month. But as usual, Aunt Bylinda had smiled and put on a jovial face and declared with entirely forced enthusiasm that it would be wonderful, having another sister in the palace.

The boys – Kalan's twin, Narvell, and her stepbrothers, Rodja and Adham – didn't seem to care one way or the other when they heard about it. Her stepsister, Rielle, was much too enchanted with the *court'esa* her father had given her for her birthday to care about anybody else at the moment. Kalan's older brother, Damin, was at that age where girls were a nuisance, and Starros, the oldest in the group, would probably just ignore her. He was fifteen and had very little time for any of the girls these days. Almodavar was too busy trying to make a warrior out of him.

Thinking of the boys, Kalan looked wistfully out of the window at the gardens, wondering how long it would be before they got back from the training yards. It was such a glorious day, too.

Much too nice to be cooped up inside doing boring, girly things.

Damin, Starros, Narvell, Adham and Rodja were training with Almodavar and her cousin, Travin, which was how they usually spent the mornings, learning interesting things in life, like swordplay, and knife-fighting, and how to use a bow, and all the other stuff Kalan wasn't allowed to learn because she was a girl. With a scowl at her needlework, she stabbed at the linen in annoyance. *Why didn't boys have to learn how to sew?*

'It's quite dead, Kalan.'

She looked up at Lirena, their long-suffering nurse. She had thought the old slave asleep in her armchair. 'What?'

'The linen, dear. It's quite dead. You don't have to stab at it like that.'

Leila looked up from her own embroidery and smiled at the slave. 'Kalan's just mad because she's in here and not outside with the boys.'

'It's too hot outside,' Lirena informed the girls. 'You'll get all freckly and look like a peasant if you go outside in this heat.'

'Why don't boys look like peasants if they have freckles?' Kalan asked.

'Don't be silly, Kalan!' Leila laughed.

'I'm not being silly,' Kalan replied, a little put out. It seemed a perfectly reasonable question to her. 'If freckles are what make you look like a peasant, then why doesn't anybody care if the boys get them? I mean, it might be all right for Starros and Rodja and Adham, 'cause they're not highborn, but Narvell is the heir to Elasapine. And Damin's a prince. Don't princes have to worry about things like that?'

'It's different for boys,' Lirena informed her, as if that was all the explanation she needed.

'Why?'

'Why what?'

'Why is it different for boys?'

'Because it is.'

'But why should it be?' Kalan insisted.

'Because women are supposed to look beautiful and have babies and men are supposed to do everything else,' the slave replied uncomfortably, ill equipped to argue the issue of female emancipation with a well-read ten-year-old.

'That can't be right,' Kalan pointed out. 'Mama rules Hythria, and she's a girl.'

Leila rolled her eyes at her foolish young cousin. 'Princess Marla does no such thing, Kalan. And you really shouldn't say such things. Uncle Lernen is the High Prince. He's the one who rules Hythria.'

'But Grandpa Charel called Uncle Lernen a perverted waste of time and space,' she announced, thinking of a conversation she'd heard between her grandfather and her Uncle Mahkas, a few months ago when Charel Hawksword had come to Krakandar to visit his grandchildren. 'He said if it wasn't for Mama's level head, Hythria would be in ruins.'

'Leila's right, lass,' Lirena said with a frown. 'You really shouldn't repeat such things. Anyway, you probably didn't hear all of it. It can be confusing when you hear only half a conversation.'

As far as Kalan was concerned, she'd heard more than enough to glean the gist of the discussion between her grandfather and her uncle. And she knew her mother was involved in important business. That was why Princess Marla lived in Greenharbour and Kalan lived at the other end of the country with her Uncle Mahkas and Aunt Bylinda. It was safe here in Krakandar. Marla had important work to do. Every time her mother left Krakandar after a visit, Marla hugged her and told Kalan so. *I love you, darling,* she always said as she was departing. *And I miss you desperately. But I have to go back to Greenharbour. I have important work to do there.*

Kalan wanted to have important work to do, too. And she was fairly certain, even at the tender age of ten, that it didn't involve embroidery.

'Mama's very, *very* important,' Kalan insisted.

'Of course she is, dear,' Lirena agreed soothingly. 'Now finish that row of knots and I'll have some morning tea brought in, shall I? Some nice little tea cakes, perhaps? Or some nut bread? You like nut bread.'

I like not being treated like a three-year-old even more, she grumbled silently, but knew better than to say it aloud. Kalan looked out of the window again, at that perfect sky, and sighed. She had to get out of here. Now. Otherwise, she'd go mad.

'I suppose if I eat enough nut bread I'll get fat,' she declared, turning on the slave argumentatively. 'And being fat means I won't look like a starving peasant, either, I suppose?' Kalan pulled a face and added in a falsely high voice, 'Oh, look at Lady Kalan Hawksword . . . we can tell she's highborn . . . just look at how bloated and podgy she is . . .'

The old slave was not amused. 'Just you watch that tone, little miss. I put your mother over my knee more than once. Don't think I'm too old to do the same to you.'

'She could do with a good spanking, if you want my opinion,' Leila said.

Hugely offended, Kalan jumped to her feet. 'Well, nobody asked you for your stupid opinion, Leila Damaran! You're always picking on me! I hate you!'

Kalan threw down her embroidery and stormed from the nursery. Leila winked at her on the way past and then lowered her head over her embroidery to hide her smile, knowing full well her comment had given her cousin the excuse she needed to flounce from the room in high dudgeon. Leila was a pretty good sport when you needed to escape being cooped up doing embroidery lessons in the nursery on a perfect spring day. All Leila had to do was say something to which Kalan was sure to take offence and, for the sake of peace, the old slave would do nothing to stop Kalan storming off in a huff.

Once that happened, Kalan was free to storm all the way down to the yards where her brothers were training.

Slamming the door with a resounding thump, Kalan strode past the guards outside the nursery, who hurriedly stood to attention as she passed. Taking a shortcut through the glass-roofed solar, Kalan ran out into the gardens and headed for the gate that led down to the barracks. With luck, Almodavar wouldn't be there. It might be Raek Harlen who had charge of the boys' training today – after all, Damin had almost killed Almodavar last night. He might need a rest. Raek would usually let Kalan stay and watch. He might even be in a good mood and let her have a turn with one of the wooden practice swords.

Slipping through the gate at the bottom of the garden, Kalan headed down the gravel path at a run, thinking the only thing that could ruin her day now was finding out that her brothers had been sent inside to study.

Despite the forty laps of the training yard Almodavar had insisted her brother run for not killing him last night, Damin looked to be in high spirits when Kalan climbed the fence to watch him and their stepbrother, Rodja Tirstone, go through their paces with quarterstaffs under the watchful eye of Raek Harlen. The air was dusty where the boys had scuffed the loose dirt during their bout, and it hung over the training yards like a dry, brown mist. A few feet away, Kalan's twin brother, Narvell, was locked in a similar bout with Rodja's younger brother, Adham. Beyond

41

them were her foster-brother, Starros, and her cousin, Travin Taranger. The last pair was being watched over by another Raider, who stopped the boys occasionally to correct their technique.

Tall, dark-haired, and very handsome to Kalan's eye, at nineteen, Travin seemed all grown up now. Six years as a fosterling in her grandfather's household in Byamor had changed her cousin beyond recognition – not that she remembered him much from before; Kalan was only four when Travin left Krakandar and her contact with him since then had been sporadic at best. But he was home now and he had lots of stories about Grandpa Charel's court and didn't seem to mind Kalan asking him about it, so she figured he was just about the most perfect boy she'd ever met (not counting Wrayan Lightfinger).

If she'd been the type who wanted to get married, Travin would have been her first choice. If not Travin, then his younger brother, Xanda, might do just as well. Kalan missed Xanda since he'd left for Greenharbour and she wondered if her mother would allow him to come home for a visit when she returned this year.

The problem of marriage bothered Kalan a great deal more than it did most ten-year-old girls. She knew these things were arranged well in advance. She also knew alliances sealed by marriage were more than just social arrangements. Travin would one day inherit his father's title as the Earl of Walsark and be a lord in his own right. He would be a vassal of Krakandar, which her brother, Damin, would one day inherit, so it seemed perfectly logical to keep it all in the family, except Damin was going to be High Prince one day, too, and she wasn't sure quite how that worked, because if Uncle Lernen died, then Damin would have to go to Greenharbour. *How could he be Warlord of Krakandar if he was living at the other end of the country?*

Thinking about it gave Kalan a headache. Anyway, Uncle

Mahkas was always saying how Leila would probably marry Damin when they both grew up. *They* were cousins, so it didn't seem in the least bit strange that if Kalan was going to be forced to marry somebody, she couldn't have the cousin of her choice, too.

Of course, the entire issue was moot, Kalan reminded herself, because she wasn't going to get married. She had decided this some time ago. All she needed now was to figure out what she wanted to do with her life, a problem that was looming larger every day as she realised how limited her career options were.

The captain spotted Kalan at the same time as the boys did and frowned at her disapprovingly. 'Are you supposed to be down here in the yards, my lady?'

'Lirena didn't say I *couldn't* come, Captain Harlen,' Kalan replied truthfully, lifting her skirts as she climbed over to sit on the top rail. 'Who's winning?'

'Who do you think?' Rodja asked, sucking on his bleeding knuckles. The boys were practising with weapons scaled to their height. Although Damin was two years younger than Rodja, there was little difference in their size. If anything, Damin was a little taller. And he was almost unbeatable. Certainly her stepbrothers, Rodja and Adham, rarely got the better of him. She'd even seen Damin give Xanda a run for his money before he left, and Xanda was five years older than Damin. Being perhaps the smartest of the boys, Starros simply refused to fight him any more.

'You're letting Damin win,' Raek Harlen told Rodja unsympathetically. 'Instead of striking at his shoulder, you could have changed your grip on your own weapon and taken a strike at Damin's neck.'

Rodja rolled his eyes. 'Now why didn't *I* think of that?'

'Because you fight like a girl,' Kalan told him with a laugh.

'*I* fight like a girl?' he asked, turning to her with a

43

wounded look. 'I'd like to see you do any better, Kalan Hawksword. And does anybody actually *care* that I'm bleeding?' When nobody answered him immediately, he threw his hands up in disgust. 'Apparently not.'

'A few bloodied knuckles won't kill you, Rodja,' Damin assured him with a friendly poke of his staff. 'Again?'

'You really do think this is fun, don't you?' Rodja said, blowing on his stinging hand before turning back to face Damin and resuming a fighting stance.

Waiting for Rodja to attack, Damin assumed a similar pose, but for him it seemed natural, whereas Rodja had to consciously think about it. As Rodja moved to strike, Damin grinned at his stepbrother. 'Don't *you* think it's fun?'

In reply, Rodja struck hard, his left leg forward and his left hand at the centre of the staff. As soon as he moved, Damin, with his right hand placed between the centre and the butt-end of the staff, rotated his weapon too fast for Rodja to counter and brought it up with a whack on his stepbrother's already bruised and bloodied knuckles.

Rodja yelped with pain, dropped his staff and jumped back out of Damin's reach. 'Right! That's it! I've had enough of this! You did that on purpose!'

'No! *Really*?' Damin asked with a laugh.

'Always hit a man in his weakest spot,' Kalan added cheerily. 'Isn't that what Almodavar's always telling you?'

Rodja didn't appreciate the reminder. He nursed his sore hand against his chest and glared at his stepbrother. 'That's all right for you, your *highness*. You're going to be High Prince some day. I don't need to know how to fight. I'm planning a nice safe career as a spice importer like my pa.'

'And you think "always hit a man in his weakest spot" isn't the first bit of advice your father's going to give you when it comes to dealing with the competition in the spice trade?' Raek asked, picking up Rodja's discarded staff.

'Mercenaries and merchants have more in common than you imagine, lad. Here, let me look at it.'

Reluctantly, Rodja held out his hand for Raek's inspection. The captain studied it for a moment and then nodded. 'Perhaps you should get Lady Bylinda to dress it for you.'

'*Thank* you,' he said impatiently, snatching his hand back.

'You still fight like a girl, Rodja Tirstone!' Kalan called after him, as her stepbrother turned and headed for the gate. He didn't reply, but he did make a rude gesture at her with his bloody finger, which made Kalan laugh. If Lirena or Aunt Bylinda caught any of the children making a gesture like that around the palace, they'd be on bread and water for a week, but down here in the training yards, things were much more relaxed.

'You shouldn't taunt him, my lady,' Raek warned. 'Rodja's actually not that bad. And Damin did hurt him.'

'I know,' she shrugged. 'But he gets all red in the face when you tease him. Haven't you ever noticed that?'

'It's still not very nice, Lady Kalan.'

Kalan cocked her head to one side curiously. 'Captain, don't you think it a little odd to be lecturing me about being nice while you're teaching my brothers to hit each other with big sticks?'

Damin laughed. He could see the irony, but Raek Harlen wasn't nearly so impressed. He opened his mouth to say something; but fortunately Damin came to her rescue before the captain could order her from the yard. 'Am I finished for the day, Raek?' he asked. 'Now I don't have a sparring partner?'

'I'll spar with you!' Kalan volunteered.

Damin laughed outright at the suggestion. 'Why do you need to know anything about a quarterstaff, Kal?'

'Because the quarterstaff is an extremely useful weapon,' she quoted smugly. Kalan had a good memory for stuff like this. She could overhear something once and repeat it back, even months later, verbatim. 'A staff can be used any way a man – or *woman* – wants to use it. You can strike like a sword, or hit like an axe. Or you can thrust it like a spear and you can do it from either side of the body and you can change quickly from side to side, which makes it very difficult for your opponent to respond to an attack.'

Damin recognised the speech. He shook his head at his sister. 'It's creepy the way you can do that, Kalan.'

Raek relented a little. He smiled at her. 'And even if you *can* quote Captain Almodavar word for precious word, there's more chance of a Fardohnyan invasion this afternoon, young lady, than me letting you spar with your brother and a couple of quarterstaffs.'

'Are you afraid I'll hurt him?'

'Yes,' Raek agreed, taking the staff Damin held out to him. 'That must be it.'

Kalan glared at the captain, then crossed her arms across her body with a scowl. 'I hate being a girl.'

'Some day you might find you like it,' Raek suggested.

The captain turned to Narvell and Adham and told them they could finish up. Overhearing the order, the Raider supervising Starros and Travin signalled them to finish as well. Travin helped the Raider collect their weapons and headed back towards the armoury with Raek Harlen, leaving Kalan with her brothers. Sitting on top of the fence looking down at them all, she felt like a queen overlooking her court. The illusion lasted right up until Narvell poked her in the side jokingly and she almost lost her balance.

'You and Leila have another fight?' Starros asked with a knowing smile as he walked to the fence, tucking in his shirt.

Kalan nodded. 'I was really convincing. Lirena probably

won't send anyone to look for me for hours yet. She thinks I'm in a right old sulk.'

'I can't believe the old girl falls for it *every* time,' Adham said, wiping his dusty, sweat-stained face on his shirt. With his fair hair and slender build, he looked more like Starros's brother than Rodja's.

'She's getting on a bit,' Kalan shrugged. 'You're not all going back to the palace, are you?'

The boys looked at each other questioningly. Apparently, they had no plans beyond this morning's training session. Their more formal lessons were temporarily suspended, since their last tutor had left over a month ago claiming he couldn't bear to work under such trying conditions. As he was the fourth tutor in as many months to quit the palace, *another* letter had been sent to Princess Marla in Greenharbour about the need for yet *another* scholar and she had written back to say she would be bringing the new tutor with her when she brought Luciena to Krakandar. That meant they had another few days before their lessons resumed. These precious moments of freedom were not to be wasted on things like history or mathematics.

Kalan looked at Damin expectantly. Although neither the eldest nor the biggest of the Krakandar children, he was their natural leader and the others would usually go along with whatever he suggested. Except Starros. He was probably the only one among them who didn't follow blindly wherever Damin led.

'We could go fishing,' the young prince suggested after a moment.

'Only if Uncle Mahkas doesn't find out,' Starros warned. 'He told Rodja we weren't to go near the fens without an escort.'

'We'll take Travin,' Kalan declared. 'Then Uncle Mahkas can't say we didn't have an escort.'

That seemed to satisfy even Starros. The others looked

at each other and nodded their agreement. Kalan jumped down off the fence with a satisfied sigh. *It's a perfect day. I'm going fishing in the fens with the boys and Travin is coming along as my escort.*

Life didn't get much better than this.

4

In the poorer sections of Talabar, particularly among the hovels belonging to the free labourers of the city, life had plenty of room for improvement. For Rory, son of Drendik, son of Warak, life could take a turn for the better any time it was ready, as far as he was concerned.

Now would be good.

Yesterday would have been better.

Rory's troubles all started when he began to suffer unbearable headaches, which at first both his father and grandfather had put down to hunger. It wasn't an unreasonable assumption. Things had been bleak recently, work harder and harder to come by. It had something to do with the completion of a major undertaking far from Talabar, Rory knew, somewhere in the Sunrise Mountains. According to Grandpa Warak, once the construction of the Widowmaker Pass was finally completed, all the workers formerly employed on the project had suddenly flooded the market. There was a glut of able-bodied slaves available for purchase and they were going cheap. Ship owners across Fardohnya were snapping up bargains, crewing their ships – in some cases almost entirely – with slave labour. That meant free sailors like his father and uncles couldn't find work unless they were willing to sign on as bondsmen, which was just a polite way of signing yourself into slavery.

Everyone went hungry as Rory's father and uncles tried to scrape up enough to put food on the table for their large clan, and the headaches got worse by the day. It wasn't unreasonable, he knew, to think the two events were connected. He even stopped complaining about them after a while. The look of despair his father wore most of the time made his own pain seem insignificant.

And then Rory's cousin, Patria, came home one morning, after staying out all night, with enough money to feed the family for a week.

Older than Rory by three years, Patria was fifteen and Uncle Gazil's only daughter, a pale, fair-haired, waiflike girl with a shy demeanour that hid a will of iron. She claimed the money came from working in one of the taverns along Restinghouse Street, washing tankards and cleaning up after the drunks. Rory didn't understand why all the grown-ups had seemed so upset. To Rory and his six younger siblings, any food on the table was welcome – they weren't too concerned where it came from. But his father, his uncles and even Grandpa Warak all wore dark looks for days afterwards and Patria cried a lot. They were no longer going hungry, so Rory couldn't understand why everyone was so upset.

Thinking it would blow over after a while, Rory was distressed to discover the situation getting worse as time went on. The whole house grew more and more tense, to the point where even the youngest children could feel something was amiss. Nobody said anything, though. They just stormed around the house and ate the food they could suddenly afford and never mentioned Patria's unexpected wealth or what she was doing when she left the house each evening in her one good dress and why she didn't come home until daylight.

Determined to get to the bottom of the mystery – and in the hope of maybe somehow fixing whatever it was that was tearing apart his formerly happy home – Rory decided to find out what was going on for himself. He had followed Patria one night as she made her way through the muddy streets of the slums on the outskirts of Talabar until she came to Restinghouse Street with its countless taverns and music halls and houses of ill repute. He almost lost her when she turned into the street. It was Fifthday evening and tomorrow was Restday, which meant the taverns were full of men who didn't have to work in the morning. Pushing through the crowd, Rory hurried in Patria's wake. As she passed one tavern after another, he began to worry. Perhaps she wasn't working in a tavern at all. Perhaps she'd found work cleaning one of the brothels, or worse, one of the music halls. That might explain why everyone was so upset. It would certainly explain why Patria was lying about her job.

Just as Rory came to the conclusion that Patria had betrayed what little decency the family could lay claim to by working in a music hall, his cousin stopped on the corner of Restinghouse Street and the inaptly named Victory Parade. There were a number of other girls standing around, who greeted the newcomer with suspicious eyes and then turned away, intent on their own business.

Rory stopped across the street and waited, curious to see what Patria was up to. If she had a job, surely she didn't have time to hang about on the corner with these girls? None of them seemed to be doing anything useful.

Rory was still puzzling over it when a man walked up to the brunette standing on Patria's left and said something to her. The girl replied, coins changed hands, and the two of them moved off down Victory Parade, arm in arm.

After she was gone, Patria moved a little to the right, as if laying claim to the space just vacated by the other girl.

A moment later, another man stopped and started talking to Patria. He was a big man, his bare arms covered in tattoos, his beard threaded with tiny glass beads. Rory frowned as the man placed several coins in Patria's outstretched hand and then she walked off with him in the same direction the other girl and her companion had gone.

Rory was streetwise enough to realise what the transaction must mean, but still innocent enough to think his cousin incapable of selling herself for a few measly copper rivets. If she'd wanted a career as a *court'esa*, she should have said something sooner, he reasoned. It wasn't unheard of for a girl from the slums to be accepted into one of the *court'esa* schools, provided she was pretty enough and willing to give up her freedom. Many young men and women signed up gladly, because a *court'esa* school meant an education and a pampered life if you were lucky enough to get a good master. To willingly become a working *court'esa*, however – untrained, unsupervised and unprotected – wasn't so much wrong, to Rory's way of thinking, as it was stupid.

He followed them, of course. There was no way he could just turn around and go home now, not without knowing for certain. Patria had no idea he was behind them. As she turned into a rubbish-strewn lane beside a tannery just around the corner in Victory Parade, her customer was already unlacing the front of his trousers. Patria turned to face him. The man shoved her against the wall and pushed up her skirts.

As he watched the brute manhandling his gentle cousin, Rory's anger began to build and with it came a headache of monumental proportions. Patria didn't complain as the man guided himself into her with a powerful thrust. Abandoning any pretence of stealth, Rory stepped into the lane behind them and stared at his cousin, his head pounding in agony. Patria just stood there, her face turned to the side, her expression one of blank resignation. The man grunted as he pressed himself inside her, pushing her against the rough wooden wall of the tannery, his other hand groping down the front of her dress. She winced as he rhythmically slammed her against the wall, but whether from the rough way he was kneading her breast or the careless way he was using her, Rory couldn't say. All he could feel was the pain in his head, like a dam swelling to bursting point with spring melt. The look on Patria's face hurt more than what she was doing. It was the desolation that made Rory's temples want to explode. The anguish, the hopelessness in her eyes . . .

Rory couldn't remember what he did next. All he remembered was the feeling that his head was going to explode . . . Then the pain went away as an anvil burst through the tannery wall behind them, striking the man a glancing blow on the side of his head. He dropped like a sack of wheat at Patria's feet. She stared at him for a moment in shock, then saw the blood on his head and screamed.

Rory was too shocked to know or care if the man was dead. He ran forward, grabbed Patria's wrist and dragged her from the lane before her screams brought someone to investigate. Towing his cousin behind him, he ran down Victory Parade, away from Restinghouse Street, not stopping until the noise from the taverns had faded to silence and they were among the silent warehouses of the wharf district.

'Are you all right?' he panted, when he felt it was safe to stop for a moment.

Patria leaned against the wall of the warehouse and stared at him, her face pale in the darkness, her chest heaving. 'Rory . . . what happened back there?'

'Nothing . . .'

'*Nothing*? Someone threw an anvil through a wall at my customer!' She shook her hand free and rubbed her wrist where he'd been holding her. 'For all I know, he's dead.

And it's your fault! You've ruined everything, you inter-fering little fool! I won't be able to go back to Victory Parade again and it took me weeks to find that corner.'

Rory looked at her in shock. 'Go *back*?'

'Of course I have to go back.'

'But that man—'

'That man was putting food in your belly, Rory,' she informed him coldly. 'You might not like how I'm doing it, but at least one person in this family is capable of earning a living.'

Rory shook his head, unable to believe Patria was a willing participant in this awful trade. 'Maybe . . . if you spoke to Grandpa . . .'

She swore softly at him. 'Grandpa! What good is he?'

'He knows people—'

'Grandpa knows nothing, Rory,' Patria scoffed. 'All his tales about his rich family, and how we're cousins by marriage to the royal house of Hythria, are just stories he makes up to keep our minds off our empty stomachs. When I was little, he used to tell me my great-great-grandmother was a Harshini, too. Do you really think he'd be down here starving with the rest of us in the Talabar slums if even one of his tall tales was true?'

Rory couldn't really answer that. When she saw him hesitate, Patria smiled sourly. 'See, even you can't defend him, can you? Well, I'm sick of being hungry, Rory, and if opening my legs to a stranger is all it takes to fill my belly and the bellies of my family, then I don't care how many drunks have their way with me. Not so long as they're paying me up front.'

Without waiting for him to answer, Patria pushed her way past him and headed down the lane. When she reached the end she turned right, heading back towards Restinghouse Street.

*   *   *

It was much later before Rory got home and, as usual, the only one still awake was his grandfather. The old man sat by the window, as he did every night, staring out into the darkness. When he was small, Rory used to wonder if he was waiting for someone to come walking down the street.

'Bit late for a stroll, isn't it?'

Rory turned to his grandfather, hoping there was nobody else awake. 'I had to do something,' he replied softly in Hythrun as he closed the door. Despite almost a lifetime spent in Fardohnya, Warak Mariner spoke the language like a newly landed tourist. It was always better and easier to speak to him in Hythrun.

'How's your headache?' Only his grandfather seemed to appreciate the pain Rory had been suffering of late.

'It's gone.'

'Has it now?' his grandfather asked, suddenly curious. 'How?'

'I don't know.' The small house reverberated with the snores of its sleeping occupants. Rory's younger brothers slept in this room. His father and uncles slept in the small bedroom at the rear. Patria, when she was home, occupied the small lean-to out back. Rory sat on the edge of his grandfather's pallet near the window. The significance of his headache disappearing hadn't really sunk in yet. 'I followed Patria tonight.'

Warak shook his head sadly. 'That was something you probably didn't need to see.'

Rory stared at his grandfather in surprise. 'You knew?'

The old man's face was etched with sadness. 'No fifteen-year-old girl brings home that sort of money sweeping tavern floors, lad. Why do you think your uncles and your father are so upset? They know what she's doing, and it burns them to allow it.'

'They could stop her.'

'And watch the rest of you starve?'

Rory shook his head, wishing life wasn't so full of unpalatable choices. 'There must be some other way, Grandpa.'

'Your father would've found it by now if there were, Rory. Or her father. Did you want to tell me what happened?'

Rory nodded, glad of the chance to unburden himself. His headache might be gone, but he was still in pain. 'I followed her. She was working the corner of Restinghouse and Victory. A man came up to her, gave her money, and they went into a lane . . . and . . .'

'And what?'

He shrugged, still not sure he believed what he'd seen. 'And then an anvil came through the wall and knocked the man down.'

Warak Mariner sat up a little straighter on the pallet and stared at his grandson. 'A *what* came through the wall?'

'An anvil.'

'I see.'

Rory frowned. 'Why are you looking at me like that?'

Warak didn't answer his question. Instead, for no apparent reason, he asked about the headaches again. 'And now the pain in your head is gone, you say? Did that happen before or after this stray anvil came flying through the wall?'

'I don't know,' he shrugged, wondering what the old man was on about. 'I guess it happened around the same time. Why?'

Warak placed a weathered old hand on his grandson's shoulder and frowned. 'Unless there was an anvil-chucking contest going on behind that wall, my guess is that you've inherited some of the family talent, Rorin, my lad.'

Rory smiled sceptically as he recalled what Patria had said about their grandfather's far-fetched stories. 'The only talent I have, Grandpa, is finding trouble. You ask my pa.'

'That may be truer than you think, lad. Did anybody besides Patria see you in that lane?'

Rory shrugged. 'I don't know.'

'Then you're not to admit you were there. I'll speak to your cousin when she gets home. Hopefully, there'll be no more trouble about this.'

Rory shrugged uncertainly. 'You make it sound like it was my fault, somehow.'

'If it was, Rorin lad, then we're in way more trouble than your cousin turning tricks.'

'I don't understand.'

Warak smiled at him sympathetically. 'I know you don't, Rorin, but that's all right. You just forget about flying anvils and what your poor cousin is up to, eh? In the meantime, I'll write a letter to your cousin in Hythria.'

'The rich one?' Rory asked, humouring the old man. Patria might think his stories wild and unbelievable, but they were often the only escape Rory had from the drudgery of his existence and he wasn't quite as ready to dismiss them as flights of fancy.

'Aye,' the old sailor agreed.

'Why?'

'Because if what I think happened tonight is true,' the old man replied, 'you may need to get out of Fardohnya.'

That night, several weeks ago, still burned in Rory's brain as if it had happened yesterday. Patria had come home a few hours later with tales of the unexplained death of a sailor in an alley off Victory Parade as if she was just repeating gossip and not intimately involved in the incident. The manner of his death had everyone talking, too. He'd been hit with an anvil, they claimed, and it had taken three men to lift it back into place. Already there were rumours flying through the slums, claiming the anvil could only have been moved by magic. Patria studiously avoided

Rory's eye whenever the subject came up and refused to discuss the matter.

Rory had listened to her tale and then looked at his grandfather questioningly, but the old man shook his head and warned the boy to silence. It was their little secret. They had to wait, Rory knew, until they had an answer from his cousin in Hythria, because if the rumours were true, and he really had moved that anvil by magic, then the only chance he had of getting out of Talabar, out of Fardohnya, before someone discovered his ability, was if some girl in Hythria that he'd never even met agreed to send the money for his passage.

Rory wasn't nearly so dubious about his grandfather's stories any more. If he could accidentally throw an anvil through a wall with his mind, then the stories of their family having a Harshini ancestor might not be so silly, after all. And if that was true, what was to say all the other stories Warak Mariner told them weren't just as real?

And if they were real, if Rory really had inherited some sort of magical ability, it made him more than just an object of suspicion.

It made him guilty of murder.

5

Of all the debts her mother had left Luciena, the largest was the mortgage on the house, a sum of some one hundred and eighty thousand gold rivets. The debt itself was bad enough. What made it intolerable was she'd be lucky if the property was worth half that, so even selling it wouldn't get her out of trouble.

And just to make matters worse, the money was owed to the most notorious moneylender in Greenharbour, Ameel Parkesh.

Ameel Parkesh was the sort of moneylender respectable people didn't do business with and, for the life of her, Luciena couldn't understand why her mother had been dealing with the man. Luciena's father had left them with a healthy stipend. He'd arranged for his daughter and her *court'esa* mother to be kept in the manner they had become accustomed to while he was alive. Even Princess Marla, although she'd stolen the rest of Jarvan Mariner's fortune the moment he drew his last breath, hadn't attempted to interfere with the arrangements.

Or had she?

Perhaps that's why the money had dried up? Perhaps they were in debt because her mother hadn't wanted to tell her the truth? Perhaps that scheming bitch at the palace had decided she wanted it *all*, and even the relatively small amount it took to keep Luciena and her mother housed, clothed and fed had become too much of a temptation? Was that what had prompted the sudden invitation to the palace? Was Marla finally asking to meet with Luciena just so she could gloat?

There was really only one way to find out, so Luciena set out on foot for the financial district of town, several days after her visit from Lieutenant Taranger and the Palace Guard, to visit her father's business manager, Farlian Kell. She allowed herself a private smile of triumph as she pushed through the crowded streets, wondering what Princess Marla's reaction had been when her lackey had delivered Luciena's message. She had visions of the princess in a towering rage, smashing priceless pieces of Walsark porcelain in her fury when she learned that even though she controlled almost unlimited wealth and probably most of Hythria, she had no power over the common, baseborn daughter of a slave.

Serves her right, Luciena thought. *Let her see what it feels like to have all her illusions shattered.*

It took Luciena the better part of the morning to reach the financial district and then another hour of waiting around before she was allowed in to see Farlian Kell. He had never kept her waiting before and she was hot, sticky and quite out of sorts by the time she was shown into his presence.

The old man rose to his feet as she entered the room, clearly suffering from the gout that had plagued him for much of his adult life – certainly as long as Luciena had known him. He smiled wanly and bade her take a seat, before lowering himself back down to his own seat and lifting his swollen foot onto the padded footstool under the desk.

'This is a pleasant surprise,' he said, as he shifted his

foot into a more comfortable position. 'I didn't really expect to see you so soon, Luciena. Shouldn't you still be in mourning?'

'I am in mourning, Master Kell,' she said. 'Mostly for my inheritance.'

Farlian seemed a little put out by her tone. 'Is there a problem? Surely, anything your mother had was left to you? I know your father made excellent provision for you.'

'Well, that's the problem, you see. My mother had nothing. If my father left me anything, I see no sign of it.'

Farlian shook his head. 'That's not possible.'

'Not only is it possible, it's happened. My inheritance is substantial, Master Kell. The problem is, I owe it, rather than having it owed to me.'

'But how could this happen?' Farlian asked, clearly confused. 'There was more than enough put aside for your living expenses.'

'I was hoping you could tell me,' Luciena replied. 'I thought maybe Princess Marla decided to—'

'Absolutely not!' Farlian declared emphatically.

'How can you be so sure? You said yourself, the monthly stipend my father left us was more than enough to cover our expenses. Yet according to the household accounts, two years ago the stipend simply ceased. We've been living on borrowed money ever since.'

'Then it must have something to do with your mother's investments, Luciena,' Farlian told her. 'I can promise you, Princess Marla has never once attempted to interfere in the provision of your upkeep.'

'What investments?' Luciena scoffed. 'My mother was a *court'esa*, Master Kell. She knew about keeping a man satisfied and she was a very proficient linguist, but she had no notion of finances and certainly no clue about investing money.'

'Be that as it may,' Farlian shrugged, 'she obviously

fancied herself a little more knowledgeable about money than you give her credit for.'

'What do you mean?'

'I mean, Luciena, the monthly stipend your father left you stopped two years ago because your mother asked for the remaining money to be paid in a lump sum. She said she had some investments she wanted to make and believed the return on her money would be significantly more than the allowance your father had left her to run the household.'

'And you just gave her the money?' Luciena gasped, appalled her mother had been able to ask such a boon. And, what was worse, had been given it.

'Your mother was very determined, Luciena.'

'But she was a slave! Surely it's illegal to hand that sort of money over to a slave?'

'Normally, yes,' Farlian agreed. 'But your father had specifically granted her control over your stipend in his will, to allow her to maintain your house and provide for you. I certainly couldn't have given her any other money, but there was nothing to stop her taking what was legally left in her care.' He sighed, seeming to take pity on her. 'Is there nothing in the accounts indicating the type of investments your mother made?'

'Nothing,' Luciena sighed, shaking her head. 'Just debts. Even the house is mortgaged to Ameel Parkesh.'

'I wish I could help, my dear. Parkesh is not a man to be trifled with.'

'Is there some way of borrowing the money?' she asked, beginning to feel truly desperate. 'I could pay it back, Master Kell. You know me to be a woman of my word. I could find work . . . I could work here, for that matter, to clear the debt, if need be. You know I have a head for figures.'

'How much do you need?'

'One hundred and eighty thousand gold rivets. And that's just to clear the debt on the house.'

The old man shook his head, clearly sympathetic, but powerless. 'I can't loan you that sort of money, Luciena. Not without going to Princess Marla for permission.'

She sat back in her chair, the bitter taste of defeat on her lips. 'Princess *bloody* Marla. It always comes back to her, doesn't it?'

'Perhaps if you explained your dilemma to her—'

'I'd rather sell myself into slavery than accept help from that woman.'

Farlian was obviously puzzled by her attitude. 'Has her highness done something to you, Luciena?'

'On the contrary, Master Kell,' she corrected, rising to her feet. 'She's done nothing. Nothing at all. That's the problem. Thank you for your time.'

She turned to leave, but Farlian's voice stopped her at the door. 'You should go and see her, you know.'

Luciena glanced over her shoulder at him. 'The only thing I have left is my pride, Master Kell. I'm not going to sell that just to get out of debt.'

'Pride won't keep you fed, lass. And it won't put a roof over your head.'

'No,' she agreed bitterly. 'But it will allow me to sleep at night, even if I *am* sleeping in the streets.'

If Farlian Kell had an answer for that, Luciena didn't wait around to hear it. She closed the door on him and strode past the rows of scribes and secretaries in the outer office with her head held high, looking neither left nor right. It wasn't until she was back out in the street, now deserted as the midday heat drove everyone indoors for a time, that she allowed the tears to blur her vision. She turned and headed in the direction of the house that she would, very soon, no longer be able to call home.

Luciena was three streets away from the house when she remembered she wasn't the only one with problems. No matter how desperate her own situation seemed, she had a cousin in Talabar in far worse trouble. Although she wasn't able to explain it to Aleesha, Luciena didn't have much in the way of family and it seemed a crime to turn her back on the one cousin she knew of. Assuming, of course, her uncle's letter wasn't just a very clever ruse to extort money from her, as her slave suspected.

Still, you can't get blood out of a stone, Luciena reminded herself, thinking Warak Mariner sorely misinformed if he thought there was any of the Mariner money left for his niece to squander. But that didn't mean she couldn't try to help. Rory had exhibited signs of magical talent and Warak wanted money to send him to the Sorcerers' Collective in Greenharbour.

Maybe, if Luciena couldn't help him, the High Arrion could.

Luciena didn't even get past the gates of the Sorcerers' Collective before they turned her away, not in the slightest bit interested in her tale about her magically gifted cousin in distant Talabar. Infuriated, although not really surprised, by the Collective's careless dismissal of her petition, footsore, weary and bowed down by the weight of her problems, it was midafternoon before Luciena turned into the street where she lived, only to find the day had just plunged from bad to infinitely worse. Parked outside the house was a litter with four muscular slaves leaning against the outer wall of the house, making the most of what little shade there was on the street.

'Whose litter is this?' she demanded of the nearest bearer as she approached the door.

'Master Parkesh's,' the slave informed her in a bored voice. He didn't bother to stand up straight or even offer a 'my lady'. His insolence scared Luciena. These men knew she was only one unpaid debt away from joining their ranks.

Luciena pushed the door open and hurried through the tiled foyer and into the reception hall. There was no sign of Aleesha but there were two men in the hall, one of whom clutched a wax tablet and seemed to be reporting to the other on the various vintages stored in the cellar.

'Which one of you is Ameel Parkesh?' she demanded, her depression rapidly turning to anger. Clearly, they had been taking an inventory of the remaining contents of the house. How dare these men come in here and start cataloguing her possessions!

'I am,' the taller of the two men answered, as they both turned to look at her. He was a thin man, with a goatee beard and a heavy gold earring in his left lobe. His vest was embroidered and sleeveless, revealing powerful arms that undoubtedly got that way by beating defaulting debtors to a pulp. He dismissed the clerk with a wave of his arm and smiled as Luciena approached. 'And you must be the lovely Katira Keyne's daughter. I'm delighted to see you didn't take after your father in looks, Luciena. He was an ugly old bastard.'

'Where is my slave?'

'The chubby one? Ran out of here howling as soon as we arrived. She was yelling something about going for help.' He smiled coldly and looked around. 'Can't see she's had much luck so far.'

'Get out of my house.'

Parkesh seemed amused rather than intimidated by her order. 'Don't you mean *my* house?'

'It will be your house, Master Parkesh, *if and when* I default on the debt. As I believe the debt is not due to be settled until the end of the week, you have no right to be here.'

'You have my money then?' he asked with a raised brow.

'We'll discuss that at the end of the week.'

65

He took a step closer to her. She could smell the sweat on him, the leather of his vest, and the faint hint of olive oil he used to slick back his hair. She hoped he couldn't smell her fear just as easily. 'And what shall we do with you, my dear, if you can't pay me?'

'I'm sure we can come to some sort of arrangement,' she replied, wishing even as she uttered the words that she hadn't.

Parkesh smiled and reached out to run his finger gently down the side of her face. 'Oh, I'm quite sure we can come to an *arrangement*, Luciena.'

'I was referring to some sort of *financial* agreement,' she snapped, jerking her head away from his touch.

'So was I,' he chuckled. 'Did your mother teach you *all* the skills she was so famous for, I wonder? I hear she could make a man lose his load just by blowing in his ear.'

'I am a free woman, sir, not a *court'esa*,' she reminded him stiffly, dismayed by his insinuation, although hardly surprised. Luciena knew well the few options left open to her if she defaulted on this debt.

What were you thinking, Mama, to leave me in this mess? What did you do with that damned money?

'You're Katira Keyne's daughter,' Parkesh replied.

This time, he ran his hand along her throat and then down towards her breasts, his fingers leaving a greasy mark on her sweaty skin. Determined not to flinch, determined not to give this man any reason to think she feared him, she held her ground and pretended she didn't notice.

'In her heyday, your mother was the most sought-after *court'esa* in all of Hythria,' he added, moving even closer. His breath was hot and rank and all Luciena wanted to do was run away screaming. But fear as much as pride kept her rooted to the spot. There was no point in screaming anyway. She was alone in the house. Even Aleesha was gone and Luciena didn't know what would happen if she rejected this man. He literally held the power of life and death over her. 'That's why she was Jarvan Mariner's mistress, you know,' he told her, his lips hovering over hers. 'He was the only one in the whole damned country who could afford her.'

'Well, I hope you'll not be too disappointed that you've missed out on both the mother *and* the daughter.'

Ameel's head jerked up at the unexpected voice. Luciena nearly collapsed from relief as he pushed her aside. She turned to discover a Palace Guardsman standing in the doorway. Aleesha stood next him, her hands on her hips, looking terribly smug.

'Who are you?' Ameel demanded. As the officer stepped into the room, Luciena realised it was the same young man who had delivered Princess Marla's invitation the other day.

'I am Xanda Taranger. And you, sir, are trespassing.'

'I own this place,' the moneylender announced. 'You're the trespasser here, boy.'

The lieutenant snapped his fingers. Immediately the room began to fill with Palace Guardsmen. More of them ran up the stairs behind him to check the upper levels of the house. There seemed to be scores of them. How had Aleesha managed to get them here?

And why, of all the people in the entire world she could have called on for help, did she go running to the damned Palace Guard?

'You own this house, do you?' the young man remarked, pulling off his gauntlets as he stepped further into the hall. 'Then you must be part of the plot.'

Ameel Parkesh looked uncertain for the first time. 'Plot? What *plot?*'

'The plot to assassinate the High Prince that I've just discovered going on here. My informants tell me this house is the hub of the whole conspiracy. If you own it, Master Parkesh, then I can only assume you are one of the ringleaders.' He turned and waved a couple more of his men forward. 'Arrest this man on charges of treason and plotting to assassinate the High Prince.'

'This is absurd!' Parkesh protested, as the guards closed in on him. 'You're making this up! There is no plot!'

'There is if I say there is,' Lieutenant Taranger insisted. 'And it'll be your word against mine.' He was only a few steps away from Ameel now. He stopped and leaned forward a little, adding, 'Care to wager on who the High Prince is more likely to believe if I tell him I've uncovered a conspiracy?'

To Luciena's astonishment, Ameel Parkesh held his hands up in defeat. 'All right! You win. For now.'

Xanda Taranger smiled. 'Perhaps your involvement in this heinous plot against the High Prince deserves a little more investigation after all,' he conceded. 'Let him go.'

The soldiers stood back as Ameel straightened his vest angrily and then glared at Luciena. 'Your friends at the palace can't protect you against what's legally mine, Luciena Mariner,' he warned. 'You have that money by the end of the week or this house and everything in it is mine. And trust me, I do mean *everything*.'

'Sergeant, escort Master Parkesh off the premises, please.'

Parkesh shook off the sergeant and strode out of the hall without another word, although he did stop as he passed Xanda Taranger and made some comment that Luciena couldn't hear. Then he left the house, the hollow boom of the door slamming shut announcing that, for the moment at least, she was safe.

Luciena felt faint. Aleesha ran to her but she shook her off, trembling so hard she was afraid she might fall. But she was determined not to let her tears of relief at her narrow escape be witnessed by anybody, least of all some lackey in the pay of Marla Wolfblade.

'Luciena . . .'

'Leave me alone, Aleesha,' she said. Pushing past the slave, Luciena ran from the hall and out into the courtyard where nobody could see her give in to the overwhelming despair that threatened to bring her completely undone.

6

Luciena looked up and hurriedly wiped her eyes as the young officer stopped in front of her. She was hiding in the small grotto dedicated to Kalianah that her mother had loved so well. The grotto was screened by a tall hedge but the courtyard wasn't that large. It wouldn't have taken much effort to find her.

'Are you all right, Miss Mariner?' he asked.

'I'll be fine,' she snapped, and then smiled weakly to soften her words. This young man really didn't deserve such anger. She was angry with herself mostly – and the fact that she had needed saving in the first place. 'Really, Lieutenant, I am.'

Without asking her permission, he took a seat beside her on the marble bench. 'Ameel Parkesh won't be back to bother you.'

She snorted sceptically at his optimism. 'Your arrival was timely, I'll grant you, but I don't think you've scared him off for long.'

'You misunderstand me,' the young officer explained. 'Ameel Parkesh won't be back because he has no reason to bother you any longer. By now, Princess Marla has taken over the debt on your house. You no longer owe him anything.'

Beyond surprise, Luciena shook her head and sighed with resignation. 'So I'm delivered from the clutches of one ruthless despot and into the hands of another.'

'Ruthless *despot*?' he repeated with a puzzled look. 'What has Princess Marla ever done to you, Luciena, to engender such feelings? You don't even know her, yet you seem to have this insane notion that she's some sort of evil-spawned monster whose sole purpose in life is to torment you. Why?'

'Why do you care?'

'She's my aunt.'

Luciena stared at him in surprise. 'But you're not a Wolfblade, are you?'

He shook his head. 'My mother was Darilyn Taranger, the sister of Laran Krakenshield, Princess Marla's first husband.'

Ameel Parkesh's inexplicable capitulation suddenly made sense. *Care to wager on who the High Prince is more likely to believe if I tell him I've uncovered a conspiracy?* What Xanda Taranger was really saying to the moneylender was: *Who do you think the High Prince will believe – a common-born moneylender or his sister's nephew?* No wonder Parkesh had given in so easily.

'You've met the princess, I suppose?'

'Well, of course.'

'And doesn't she strike you as being manipulative and cold?'

'Certainly not!'

Luciena rose to her feet and glared down at the young man, angered by his irrational defence of someone so heartless and cruel. She was angry that Princess Marla had paid her debt, too. She was now effectively a slave to the princess, just as she would have been Ameel's slave if she'd defaulted on him. Suddenly, the moneylender didn't seem so awful. At least, with him, she'd know when the rape was over. This way, she might be paying for the rest of her life.

'Princess Marla left us to starve, Lieutenant. Your precious aunt married my father, stole his fortune and left my mother no choice but to borrow money from men like Ameel Parkesh, just so we could eat. She promised my father the world when she married him. She promised I'd be adopted into her family. That I'd *have* a family. But she lied. She waited until he died and then turned her back on every promise she made. That's the *real* Princess Marla. The one you don't see across the dining table.'

She turned on her heel and walked across the small gravelled clearing, the pain of her disappointment still raw, even after all these years. And she was furious with herself for trying to defend her position with somebody as stupidly loyal as the princess's own nephew. *I knew he was too good to be true.*

'Do you know why Princess Marla never tried to keep her promise to legitimise you before now, Luciena?' he called after her.

She hesitated, wondering how Xanda Taranger had known about that, then turned back to look at him. He was still sitting on the bench, watching her curiously.

'Because she's a liar and a thief?'

Xanda smiled. 'Other than that.'

'I was too much of an embarrassment to her, I suppose.'

'Legitimising you meant adopting you into her family,' the young man explained.

'I know that—'

'Which meant taking you from your mother,' he added, cutting her off before she could object. 'You were nine years old when your father married my aunt and barely eleven when he died. Princess Marla held off keeping her promise because you'd just lost your father and she didn't think it fair to take your mother from you, too. And make no mistake about it, Luciena. Adopting you into the royal family would have meant you never laid eyes on your

72

court'esa mother again. Katira Keyne was a slave. The insult to the princess would have been unconscionable if she'd openly remained in a position of privilege as your father's mistress or the mother of his child. Your mother only kept this house because you lived here. If you'd been taken from her, she would have been sold, the house would have been closed up and you would never have seen her again.'

'So Her Royal Sweetness and Light let us fall into ruin out of the goodness of her heart? Is that what you're telling me?'

Xanda shook his head impatiently. 'Your father left you nothing, Luciena. You're his illegitimate child. And he couldn't leave your mother anything. She was a slave. Who do you think arranged the stipend you've been receiving since your father died?'

'Nobody,' Luciena pointed out tartly. 'That's how we fell into ruin.'

'There was plenty of money coming in, Luciena. Marla made certain of it. She merely siphoned it through Farlian Kell so it couldn't be traced back to her. And it was more than enough to keep you in the manner to which you were accustomed. Your mother's gambling brought you undone, not anything Princess Marla did.'

'My mother's *gambling*?' she sputtered indignantly. 'Is that your excuse? Suddenly my mother has a gambling problem?'

'If you want proof, go ask your good friend, Ameel Parkesh. He didn't get the papers on this house because of his charm and wit, you know.'

Luciena shook her head in denial, more than a little annoyed that he seemed to know so much about her private family matters. 'I don't believe you.'

'It's the truth, Luciena. Whether you believe me or not won't actually change it.'

'I spoke to Farlian Kell this morning. He said nothing about any money coming from the princess. In fact, he insisted it was part of my father's will.'

'You seem to forget Kell works for my aunt. He'll tell you anything he's told to.'

'But I've known him all my life. Why would he lie to me?'

'Given a choice between keeping you happy and keeping Marla Wolfblade happy, I know which one I'd choose.'

She glared at him, incensed that he could sit there so calmly while he shattered every delicate myth Luciena believed in. She knew her mother liked to gamble, but then so did most of the adult population of Greenharbour. Now she was forced to wonder if the chips her mother gambled when she played cards with her friends were simply wooden tokens, as Katira always insisted, or did they represent real money – real money they didn't actually have? Was that how the papers on their house had wound up in the hands of Ameel Parkesh?

'What do you want from me?'

'I want you to meet my aunt. Give her a chance.' He rose to his feet and took a step towards her. 'And stop jumping to conclusions.'

'There's nothing you can say to me that will change my mind,' Luciena warned, knowing she had little choice but to agree. She'd been sold along with her debts and, for all intents and purposes, she belonged to Princess Marla now, a slave in fact if not in name. But she wasn't going to be hurt twice by the lure of a bright future full of false promises.

'I'm not trying to change your mind, Miss Mariner. I'll be content if you just come along quietly.'

'She sent you here to bring me to her, didn't she?'

'No. This time, the Palace Guard came in response to your devoted slave's panicked insistence that the house had

just been overrun by scores of evil, hairy brutes all determined to ravish you both.'

Despite herself, Luciena smiled. 'Aleesha does have a
tendency to exaggerate.'

'I'm glad she did. It's nice to be asked to rescue a pretty
girl every once in a while.'

To her horror, Luciena discovered she was blushing. She
turned away from him, the compliment so unexpected she
was left speechless.

'Of course, seeing as how I *did* rescue you,' he continued,
'I think I deserve a boon, don't you?'

They're all the same, she thought, squaring her shoulders
angrily as she turned back to face him. Just because he was
younger and marginally better looking, it didn't make him
any nobler than Ameel Parkesh. *In the end, all men wanted
the same thing*. Her mother had warned her about that.

'Let me guess?' she asked scathingly. 'You want a kiss, I
suppose? Or did you also wish to discover if my mother
taught me *all* the skills for which she was so rightly famous?'

Xanda seemed more than a little amused by her ques-
tion. 'Well . . . um . . . I probably wouldn't *refuse* a kiss, Miss
Mariner, if you felt that strongly about it. And I'd be lying
if I said I wasn't more than a little curious to discover what
your mother taught you, but I actually had something a
little less . . . physical . . . in mind.'

She felt the blood rush to her face once more, as she
realised how badly she'd misjudged him. 'What . . . what
did you want from me then?'

'I want you to come back to the palace with me. To
meet Princess Marla.'

'Suppose I refuse?'

'Then . . . I'll arrest you.' Xanda laughed, as if he knew
how embarrassed she was. 'And deliver you to the princess
in chains.'

'Arrest me for what?' she asked warily, not entirely certain he was joking. 'Plotting against the High Prince like you threatened Ameel Parkesh?'

He shrugged. 'Maybe. If not, I'm sure I'll have thought of something else by the time we get back to the palace.'

What must it be like, she wondered for a moment, *to be so damned sure of yourself? To be so certain of your place in the world, as Xanda Taranger seems to be? So secure? So certain the world can't change from a dream to a living nightmare in the space of a mere day?*

'I'll come,' she conceded with a great deal of reluctance. 'But I am doing this under protest. You may inform Princess Marla that I want no part of her plans for me or my future.'

'You can tell her yourself,' Xanda replied, stepping back as he raised his arm and pointed to the path heading back to the house, indicating she could go first. 'After you.'

It wasn't chivalry, Luciena knew, that prompted his elegant bow. Xanda Taranger wasn't trying to be a gentleman. He was simply making sure she couldn't run away.

7

Marla Wolfblade rose to her feet as the door to her private sitting room opened. The whole house was stuffy this afternoon, the humidity almost unbearable. Greenharbour was always like this just before the rains settled in. The princess was counting the hours until she could leave the city and head north to Krakandar, where at least it cooled down at night and one wasn't constantly bathed in perspiration.

As her visitor approached, Marla smiled warmly. She didn't need to rise. Marla was a princess and the young woman being shown into her presence was a commoner, but she wanted to make a good impression. Marla wanted the girl to like her.

The princess stepped forward as the young woman reached the low table surrounded by brightly coloured silk cushions, looking her up and down with the same considering look the girl gave her. Neither of them spoke.

Dressed in a modest but well-cut gown of pale blue silk, Luciena Mariner was pretty rather than beautiful – the prettiness of youth and vitality, rather than the result of good breeding or a particularly fine bone structure. She was a little exotic-looking, Marla thought, with dark eyes and dusky skin that betrayed her Fardohnyan heritage. The girl's mother had been a *court'esa* of Fardohnyan ancestry, and reputedly a very beautiful one. Marla had only rumour and gossip to rely on for that opinion. Although the woman had lived barely three blocks away in the house provided by Luciena's late father, it was inconceivable that a slave who'd borne one of Marla's husbands a bastard would ever be allowed in the presence of the princess.

'Your highness,' Luciena said eventually, with a graceful curtsey. Although common, she'd had the best education Marla could arrange, and that included the social niceties as well as the more traditional subjects.

'Luciena.'

'Is "your highness" the correct form of address?' the girl enquired. 'Or would you prefer that I call you "mother"?'

Marla smiled. The girl was either very brave or very foolish to declare herself with such hostility within a moment of meeting the person who could make or break her. 'Did you *want* to call me mother?'

'I am at your highness's mercy,' she replied in a tone that was anything but subservient.

'Yes, Luciena,' Marla agreed. 'You are.'

Marla let that sink in for a moment as she reached across to the side table and rang the small silver bell resting there. The chimes had barely faded before the doors opened and a legion of slaves hurried into the room with refreshments stacked on several delicately wrought silver carts. They laid out the sliced fruits, the jellied meats and the chilled wine on the table in the centre of the room and then retreated silently, closing the door behind them.

'Please,' Marla invited with a sweep of her arm. 'Won't you join me?'

Luciena took her place on the cushions opposite Marla, studying the princess warily.

'Help yourself,' Marla suggested.

'Thank you, your highness, but I think I'd rather know what I must do to repay the debt I now seem to owe you.'

Marla reached forward and picked up a slice of melon. It was sweet and beaded with condensation, kept cool in the deep cellars of the palace with snow brought in from the Sunrise Mountains during winter.

'Think no more of the debt. I have no need or wish to be repaid. I simply thought it was about time you and I got to know each other.'

'You never felt the need while my father was alive,' the young woman pointed out stiffly. 'He's been dead for six years and you have taken another husband. I can't see that I matter to you at all.'

'On the contrary, Luciena. You matter to me a great deal.'

'You have an odd way of demonstrating your regard, your highness.'

The girl's self-righteous manner was rather irritating. 'You must understand, Luciena, it was protocol that dictated we could not meet before now. There was enough of a scandal when I married your father. The High Prince's sister married to a commoner? There were dowager ladies fainting all over Greenharbour at the very thought of it. Acknowledging his baseborn child would have been going too far, even for a court as supposedly open-minded as this one.'

'Then why *did* you marry my father? You never loved him.'

'Your father owned nearly a quarter of the entire Hythrun shipping fleet, Luciena. Common-born or not, he was one of the richest men in Hythria.'

'So you admit that you married him for his money?'

'I tried marrying for love once. It was an unmitigated disaster.'

'But . . .' Luciena stammered, obviously taken aback. 'I . . . I don't understand.'

'You are your father's heir, Luciena.'

'I'm baseborn,' she reminded Marla. 'I can't inherit anything because you broke your promise to legitimise me.'

'I broke nothing,' Marla corrected, taking another slice of melon. 'I'm simply working to my timetable, not yours. And, if I so choose, I can still arrange for you to inherit your father's fortune. On three conditions.'

'What three conditions?'

'The first is that I adopt you, obviously,' she explained. 'As your father's only legal wife, I can adopt his child and legitimise her, even though he's been dead these past six years, making you his heir.'

Luciena smiled, but it wasn't pleasant. 'I see. *Now* you decide to keep your promise to adopt me, and because I'm only seventeen you'll get to manage my affairs for the next thirteen years as my guardian, strip me of my fortune in the process, all to prop up your brother as High Prince, no doubt. The rumours about your ruthlessness really don't do you justice, your highness.'

Marla was rather taken aback. 'There are *rumours* about my ruthlessness?'

'As you are no doubt aware, your highness, I've had an excellent education. Please don't insult me by treating me like a fool.'

'Then don't insult me by not hearing me out,' Marla countered. She was staggered. *There are rumours about my ruthlessness?*

Luciena had the good sense to realise she'd overstepped the mark. 'I'm sorry, your highness.'

'As I was *saying*, the first thing we must do is formally adopt you. The second is to arrange a marriage for you.'

'To whom?' the girl bristled. 'Some scabby old man to whom you owe a favour? One of the High Prince's sick, twisted friends, perhaps?'

Luciena's meekness had lasted barely more than a few

seconds. Marla was privately glad. She would have hated it if the girl were all simpering timidity and no spine.

'I'm sure we can find somebody acceptable.'

'And why does it matter who I marry?'

'It doesn't,' Marla told her. 'Not *who* you marry, at any rate. Just that you *are* married. You see, here's the thing, Luciena. We are women in a world ruled by men. In some respects, we have less freedom than a slave. When we marry, we become the possession of our husband. What is his is his, and what is ours becomes his when we marry him. Now, because it was men who made the rules, and there's no point in taking a sixteen-year-old bride if you have to wait until she's thirty to inherit her father's fortune, they left themselves a loophole. A woman might inconveniently die in childbirth long before she reaches her majority, and then what happens to all that money and property you married her for?'

The girl was quick. It took her hardly any time at all to understand what Marla was driving at. 'Do you mean that as soon as I am married, I can inherit my father's estate?'

'If I've adopted you, yes.'

'Who has it now?'

'I do, of course.'

'But if *you* inherited my father's estate, doesn't that mean it now belongs to your current husband?'

'But I didn't inherit it. I'm simply holding it in trust. It doesn't belong to me, therefore my husband can't touch it. And you needn't fear for your fortune, Luciena. I've kept a very close eye on it. When your father died, he owned a quarter of Hythria's trading fleet. Now you own about a third of it.'

Luciena stared at Marla, her expression thoughtful.

'You said three conditions,' she reminded the princess after a moment.

'The third is that you swear allegiance to the House of Wolfblade.'

The girl seemed puzzled. 'You want me to swear allegiance to the High Prince?'

'I want you to swear that you'll do everything in your power, bring the entire weight of your fortune to bear if need be, to secure the throne for the High Prince's heir.'

'You want me to swear allegiance to your son, then?'

'No,' Marla said carefully. 'Asking you to swear allegiance to anyone other than the incumbent High Prince would be treason. I merely insist that you swear an oath to his House. That's not the same thing.'

'Suppose the next High Prince turns out to be as useless as the one we have now? Or worse?'

'You can decide that for yourself when you meet him.'

Luciena was looking completely baffled now.

'If I'm to adopt you, Luciena, you're going to have to meet the rest of the family.'

'You'd have me in your *house*? Me? A baseborn commoner?'

'My husband and I are leaving for Krakandar Province the day after tomorrow. If you're willing to consider my offer, you may come with us to meet your new brothers and sisters, including the High Prince's heir. You'll find Damin inflicted with a degree of obnoxious self-confidence common to most twelve-year-old boys, but we trust he'll grow out of it soon.'

'And if I don't agree to your offer?' she asked warily.

'Then I shall find some likely lad and claim *him* as Jarvan Mariner's long-lost son, adopt him and arrange to manage his estate until he comes of age. It will be a little harder to prove but I do have considerable resources at my disposal. And your father was a sea captain for a long time, you know. With a *court'esa* or two in every port, he's bound to have fathered more than one bastard.'

Luciena thought that over for a while before asking, 'Who do you want me to marry?'

'We can decide that when you agree to my offer.'

'Why?' Luciena asked suspiciously.

'I beg your pardon?'

'What's in this for you, Princess Marla? Is it because you want control of my fortune?'

'I already have that.'

'Then I don't understand why you're doing this for me.'

Marla smiled, thinking she would be just as suspicious of the offer she had just made this child. 'I'm *not* doing this for you,' she admitted. 'You're right about that much. I'm doing it for my family. It's no secret the Wolfblade House has been self-destructing for generations. I intend to see it restored through my son. But thanks to his predecessors, Damin is going to have to fight to win his throne and work even harder to keep it. To do that, he'll need the backing of more than a few sentimental Royalists determined to cling to the Wolfblade line for old time's sake. You'll have control over a third of the trading ships operating out of Hythria. And you *will* have control of them, Luciena. I didn't waste all that education on you just to have you hand the responsibility over to someone else.'

'You're serious!'

'As you get to know me better, Luciena, you will learn this is not my joking face.'

'How much time do I have to think this over?'

'Do you have a better offer to consider?'

'That depends on whether or not I'm willing to sell my soul to the Wolfblades, I suppose,' the girl replied defiantly.

'You have a gift for the dramatic, I see, Luciena.'

'Actually, your highness, I thought I was merely stating an obvious fact.'

'Then allow me to state another obvious fact, my dear. You have a choice before you between a life of privilege and wealth or one of poverty and obscurity. If you are as intelligent as my informants have led me to believe, you will choose the former.'

'Do you think I'm so fond of material wealth that I would place myself in your power for the promise of a roof over my head? Do you think I'll stand by and let you marry me off to one of your sycophants just to aid you in propping up the High Prince's throne? And why should I believe your offer is genuine at all? I've made it plain how I feel about you. What reason have you to trust me? Or is it that you don't *need* to trust me? Maybe all you need to do is adopt me, marry me off to someone you *do* trust, and have the Assassins' Guild take care of the rest.'

'You're not actually worth the price of an assassin. If I was that anxious to dispose of you, I'd do it myself.' Marla smiled at the girl's shocked expression. '*That* was my joking face, Luciena.'

Warily, the girl nodded. 'Yes, your highness.'

Marla smiled even wider, hoping to put the girl at ease. 'We'll have three weeks in a carriage on the way to Krakandar to test each other's mettle, Luciena. I'm sure it will be an enlightening time for both of us. Now, do you accept my offer or not?'

'Must I give you an answer immediately?'

'What could you possibly need to consider?' Marla asked impatiently.

'One of your conditions is that I swear allegiance to the House of Wolfblade, your highness. You say you want me to use my father's fortune to aid your son's ascension to the throne some day. Don't I have a right to see what sort of a prince you would have me swear my allegiance to, before I take such an oath?'

Marla stared at her in surprise. Part of her was quite offended by the girl's manner. Another part was thinking: *This girl is going to be formidable when she gets her hands on her father's business.* 'You've more cheek than a street urchin, Luciena.'

'And whose fault is that, I wonder? Wasn't it *you* who paid for my education?'

Marla frowned. 'Very well. You may accompany me and my husband north to Krakandar. We will discuss your future further once you have met Damin and made up your mind about him. Speak to Xanda on your way out. He'll make arrangements for your slave to have your trunks delivered to the palace. I assume you'll want her to accompany you?'

'Yes. Thank you, your highness.'

'I'll see you the day after tomorrow then.'

Realising she was dismissed, Luciena rose to her feet and curtseyed. 'As you wish, your highness.'

Luciena turned and walked to the door. Marla waited until she was almost there before adding as an afterthought, 'One other thing, Luciena.'

The girl turned to look at her. 'Your highness?'

'Don't get any ideas about my nephew.'

'I *beg* your pardon?' Luciena asked, quite shocked.

'He's young, handsome and completely out of your class, Luciena. I will find a suitable husband for you when the time comes. Someone less . . . exalted. Don't presume to think I will allow you to make such a decision for yourself.'

'I'm sure I don't know what you mean, your highness.'

'I'm sure you do,' the princess corrected. 'Good day, Luciena.'

The young woman curtseyed again without speaking and fled the room.

Marla leaned back against the cushions and smiled with satisfaction. Behind her, the curtain rustled softly and Elezaar stepped out of his hiding place, where he'd listened to the entire exchange.

'What did you think of her?'

'Interesting young woman,' he remarked, waddling around the piled cushions to face his mistress.

'Interesting indeed,' Marla agreed.

'One thing I don't understand, though. Why warn her away from Xanda?'

'Because she's seventeen and she thinks she hates me, Elezaar. What better way to give voice to that hate than to openly defy me?'

'You think that by forbidding her a relationship with Xanda, she'll deliberately set out to have one? Does Xanda have any idea that you're using him so blatantly?'

'Of course not.'

'Don't you think he'd be upset?'

'Wasn't it you, Elezaar, who pointed out that my nephew is too full of raging lust and bravado to notice what I'm up to?'

'Still, you might want to warn him of your plans.'

'I will. When the time is right.'

'Before or after the wedding?' Elezaar asked pointedly.

'After he's in love,' Marla told him with a smile. 'It won't matter what I tell him then.'

'How can you be so sure?'

'Because I know for a fact that people in love don't listen to anything but their own hearts,' she replied, her smile fading. The pain of her own lost love was still a raw wound Marla carefully concealed from the rest of the world, even after all this time.

'Perhaps that's a good thing,' the dwarf shrugged. 'Love is supposed to be blind, isn't it?'

'Perhaps that's why we never see the truth,' Marla agreed. 'Even when it's right in front of us.'

Elezaar offered no reply. He didn't have to. He knew her well enough to understand she was no longer talking about Xanda and Luciena.

'See that she's taken care of, Elezaar,' she ordered when the silence started to become tense. 'And make sure Xanda knows I want him to look after her, for me.'

'Was there anything else, your highness?'

'No,' she said, a little surprised to find herself choking back memories of what it was to be young and innocent and desperately in love. 'Leave me.'

The dwarf bowed and then waddled to the door, leaving Marla alone. Impatiently, she wiped away an unexpected tear and took her wineglass from the table, downing the remainder in a single swallow.

'Don't be a fool,' she muttered to herself.

Never regret anything. Never look back and wonder. Was that one of the dwarf's damned Rules of Gaining and Wielding Power? It ought to be. Because who would have thought the memory of Nash Hawksword would still hurt so much after all these years?

8

It was several days after Damin almost managed to kill Almodavar that the captain sent for Starros to discuss the young man's plans for the future. Starros wasn't sure if the two events were related.

They might have been. Since he was five years old, Starros had been a fosterling of the Wolfblade family. It was the custom in Hythrun highborn families to attempt to confuse potential assassins by surrounding the heir to the house with other children. The theory was that if an assassin could not identify the real heir, he might leave all the children alone.

To Starros's considerable relief, the theory had never been put to the test in Krakandar. Mahkas Damaran, Damin's uncle and Krakandar's Regent, was vigilant to the point of being obsessed with his nephew's safety. The palace was too well guarded, the staff too well vetted, to present a danger to Damin or anybody else in the household.

But Damin had now proved capable of defending himself against a fullgrown man. What need was there for a decoy any longer for a boy so skilled in the martial arts? For that matter, it was almost a year since the boys had even shared a room. When Starros turned fifteen, as was the custom among the nobility, he had been given access to the palace *court'esa*. As this milestone meant he was, while not considered a man, then at least no longer a child, Starros had moved in with Xanda Taranger, Damin's older cousin, until he left for Greenharbour last winter. Damin was still only twelve and it wasn't considered appropriate for a boy so young to be introduced to a *court'esa's* special skills. It was then that Damin begged his uncle to get rid of the armed guard who had stood over him while he slept since the first attempt on his life when he was four years old.

Mahkas had agreed, on the condition Damin could prove he was capable of looking after himself. The young prince had proved it resoundingly.

Perhaps Almodavar isn't sending for me to tell me I'm no longer needed as a decoy, Starros mused, as he neared the barracks. *Perhaps Almodavar is sending for me to tell me I'm no longer needed at all.*

'How many times do I have to tell you, boy?' a familiar voice barked behind him. 'Don't slouch!'

Starros stopped and turned to face Krakandar's most senior captain. Almodavar's face, while not exactly fierce, wore enough nicks and scars to be well on its way to earning such a title. Starros knew the rumours that Almodavar was his father as well as anyone in Krakandar, but there was no family resemblance that Starros could see. He was slender and fair; Almodavar was big and dark, and he certainly never treated Starros like a son. For that matter, Almodavar never treated Starros any differently to the way he treated Damin, or Narvell, or Damin's stepbrothers, so perhaps his gruff, impatient manner didn't prove anything one way or the other.

'Sorry, sir,' Starros replied, straightening a little. 'Travin said you wanted to see me?'

'Aye.' Almodavar fell into step beside Starros and they continued walking through the training yards. The day was clear and crisp. The captain's hands were clasped behind his back, his expression thoughtful, as if he was carefully considering his words. After several moments of strained silence, which took them past the yards and out towards the stables, Almodavar finally spoke again. 'You've been here a long time, lad.'

'Since I was five,' Starros agreed, although Almodavar hardly needed reminding of that. He was the one who had brought Starros to the palace. 'Ten years.'

'And have you given any thought to what you want to do, once you leave?'

Starros looked at the captain curiously. 'I wasn't aware I *was* leaving, Captain. Is there something I should know about?'

'Princess Marla is due back soon,' Almodavar reminded him. 'She mentioned on her last visit that you should start giving some thought to what you want to do with your life.'

'I have a choice?' Starros asked, a little surprised.

'The most powerful woman in Hythria thinks of you as her foster-son, Starros. You have been raised as a member of the family of the next High Prince of Hythria. Young Damin treats you like a brother and, most importantly, you can make him see reason when he gets his head full of some of the more harebrained schemes he's becoming famous for.'

'He's not a bad lad, sir. He just likes to test his limits.' Starros smiled. 'A lot.'

'And you are one of the few with the ability to rein him in. The princess knows this.'

'She's never said anything to me.'

'It wouldn't be appropriate. She mentioned it to me, though. You've a rare chance to make something of your life, you know.'

'I assumed if I had any future here at all, it was as a

member of the Palace Guard. Isn't that usually what happens to fosterlings?'

'You're too well educated for a life in the barracks.'

Starros stared at the captain, surprised to hear the warrior suggesting anything *other* than a life in the barracks. An avid follower of the God of War, for Almodavar there was simply no more noble profession than being a warrior in the service of your prince.

'What did she have in mind?'

'Every High Prince needs a steward.'

Starros stopped dead and stared at the captain. 'You think I'm capable of becoming Damin's steward some day?'

'It's not an unlikely scenario,' Almodavar replied. 'You're a bright lad. Damin trusts you. With the right training, you could be anything you want.'

'I'm a bastard fosterling, Almodavar,' Starros reminded the captain. 'That sort of limits my options a little, don't you think?'

'Hablet of Fardohnya's chamberlain is a slave *and* a eunuch,' Almodavar pointed out. 'And yet Lecter Turon is one of the most powerful men in Fardohnya.'

'Is losing your balls a job requirement?' Starros asked, a little alarmed.

The captain smiled. 'Not unless you're planning a career in Fardohnya.'

'Then I think I'll stay right here in Hythria,' he replied with a shudder. 'With all of me right where it belongs, thank you.'

'But you'll give it some thought?'

'I suppose,' Starros shrugged, seeing no harm in agreeing to this. He couldn't imagine himself ever being offered such a powerful position, despite how highly the princess thought of him. The best Starros thought he could really hope for was to become an officer in the Raiders, albeit one with very important and influential friends. 'What sort of special training would I need?'

'I don't really know. More lessons in economics, I guess. And history. Probably diplomacy. And protocol. Princess Marla has it all worked out, I don't doubt.'

Starros smiled. 'All the stuff Damin can't sit still for.'

The captain nodded his agreement. 'He's going to have to learn to sit still some day,' he warned. 'Damin has the makings of a formidable warrior, but he's not going to make much of a High Prince if he can't get his head around the things that really matter.'

'I thought the only thing that really mattered to a warrior was getting into a good fight?'

'Aye,' Almodavar agreed solemnly. 'And I'll grant you this – Damin is going to be an awesome fighter some day. But before you can tell if it's a good fight, you have to know *what* it is you're fighting for, Starros. That's where you come in. A prince needs to know more than how to spill blood efficiently. And that's what Damin has yet to learn.'

'Do you think Damin will make a good High Prince?' Starros asked curiously.

'He's only twelve,' Almodavar shrugged. 'Ask me again when he's thirty.'

'It'll be a bit late by then.'

'Then we'll just have to surround him with people like you. People we can trust to serve Hythria well.'

'Cover for him, you mean,' Starros suggested with a canny smile. 'The way Princess Marla covers for High Prince Lernen.'

'You mind your tongue, boy. It's not up to you to speculate about what Princess Marla is or isn't doing.'

Their walk had taken them past the stables towards the riding yards where Damin's stepsister, Rielle Tirstone, his cousin Leila and his half-sister Kalan were doing a circuit of low jumps under the careful watch of Krakandar's Master of Horse, Jozaf Pasharn. Starros and the captain stopped to watch, leaning on the rail as, one after the other, the girls rode the course.

Rielle, the tall, flirtatious, sixteen-year-old sister of Rodja and Adham Tirstone, was riding a spirited grey mare but handling her well, guiding her over the jumps with the sure hand of an experienced horsewoman. Leila followed on a handsome gelding with a golden coat and deep chest that hinted at a touch of the prized sorcerer-bred bloodline in his ancestry. By contrast, Kalan's piebald pony had the rugged look of a stock horse, which rather matched the way she was riding it.

'For the gods' sake, Kalan!' the Horse Master yelled, as Kalan dragged her pony around for another go at the second jump when it shied from it. 'Think of that poor beast's mouth!'

'Of the three of them, Leila's the better horsewoman,' Almodavar remarked.

'Why do you say that?'

'Look at them,' the captain ordered. 'Rielle rides like a mistress commanding her slave.'

'It's not just horses she treats like that,' Starros remarked with a grin.

Almodavar smiled, nodding in agreement. 'I've noticed she's rather unconcerned that her stepbrother will one day be her High Prince.' The captain pointed at Kalan then, his smile fading. 'Kalan's fearless, but she rides like she's at war with the beast. Now Leila,' he said, pointing to Damin's cousin, 'she's at one with that horse. They're a team.'

Starros nodded, thinking it was Leila's gentle nature that made her so attuned to her horse. 'She has plans for them too, I suppose.'

Almodavar glanced at Starros curiously. 'Who has plans for whom?'

'Princess Marla. For the girls. She has plans for me. I was just thinking she probably has plans for all of us.'

'Probably,' Almodavar agreed. 'But it's really none of your business, lad.'

'She wants me to study to be a High Prince's steward,' Starros replied, ignoring the captain's warning about it being none of his concern. 'She's arranged for Rielle to marry Darvad Vintner. Travin is being groomed to govern Walsark and I'll bet you all the midges in the fens that Princess Marla didn't invite Xanda to Greenharbour for the good of his health. Luciena Mariner is about to be adopted into the family, undoubtedly with the intention she takes over her late father's shipping empire. Narvell's future is pretty set, I suppose, because he's Charel Hawksword's grandson and therefore the heir to Elasapine, but I'll wager you a month's pay Princess Marla has plans for Rodja and Adham when they're grown. I wonder what she has in mind for Leila and Kalan.'

'It's not your place to speculate about such things, Starros.'

'I know,' he shrugged. 'But one can't help but wonder about it, can one?'

'Actually, one can,' Almodavar announced brusquely, pushing off the rail. 'And you'd be well advised to mind your tongue on the issue, my lad. Diplomacy is the first skill needed by a steward.'

'Assuming I *want* to be Damin's steward.'

Almodavar stopped and looked back at him in shock. 'For the gods' sake, lad! Why would you refuse such an honour?'

'I didn't say I was going to refuse it. I just think it would have been nice if someone asked me first.'

'I'm asking you now,' Almodavar pointed out.

'And if I refuse?'

'That wasn't discussed.'

'Because a bastard fosterling wouldn't dare refuse?' he challenged.

Almodavar shook his head at the young man's tone. 'Because Princess Marla thinks you have more sense. Maybe she was wrong.'

'And what do you think, Captain?' *Are you proud of me? If I do this, your bastard son might one day be counted among the most powerful men in Hythria. Isn't that enough to make you own up to me?*

'It doesn't matter what I think.'

Starros stared at the captain for a moment, wondering what he had ever done to this man to earn a lifetime of denial. He wasn't even sure if he was hurt or just puzzled by it. Leila's theory was that Almodavar took his job as Damin's bodyguard so seriously, he refused to admit to any familial ties that might weaken his resolve; a theory that she was convinced was proved when Almodavar made Damin do forty laps around the training yard for not killing him.

'No, Captain,' Starros agreed eventually. 'I don't suppose it does matter what you think.'

Maybe Leila's right, he told himself silently. *Maybe Almodavar is as proud as any father, just unwilling to admit the fact for fear of exposing a chink in his armour and weakening the circle of protection surrounding the next High Prince of Hythria.*

9

Corian Burl was waiting for Marla when she arrived at the palace. He was a tall man and had been a handsome *court'esa* once, a fact which even old age was unable to disguise. His hair was white, his face a craggy testament to his years, but his eyes were bright with intelligence and he walked with an indefinable air of confidence that seemed rather inappropriate in an old slave.

The chamberlain bowed low to the princess as she entered Lernen's study and waved his arm to encompass the table behind him, laden with scrolls and ledgers. 'We have a lot to get through this evening, your highness.'

Marla nodded. 'I know. I would have been here earlier, but I was meeting with my stepdaughter.'

'Ah, the Mariner girl. Did you find her satisfactory?'

'Better than satisfactory, actually,' Marla replied thoughtfully. 'She seems very astute.'

'Then your plans for her future are progressing as intended?'

'I think I'll wait until she gets to Krakandar before I pass judgment on that.'

'I am pleased for you, your highness,' Corian said with another short bow. 'Perhaps that will leave time to solve the dilemma of what to do with your son.'

Marla nodded in agreement. 'You speak of Damin's fosterage arrangements, I assume?'

'In some circles little else is spoken of these days, your highness.' Corian glanced at the table with concern. 'A good half of the letters the High Prince has received this past month have been either asking for the opportunity to foster the High Prince's heir or complaints about who they think is going to receive the honour. You must make a decision soon.'

'I know.' Marla walked past Corian and took her seat at the table. It was hot and muggy in the room. Normally a breeze picked up late in the afternoon, cooling the city and offering some relief, but the sheer curtains over the long windows facing the bay hung still and lifeless and the candle flames burned steady and even. Not so much as a hint of a breeze lifted off the water to offer a reprieve from the heat.

As usual, Marla avoided looking at the walls. Lernen had decorated his office with a series of lewd murals ranging from the bizarre to the truly disgusting. Even after coming here on an almost daily basis for the past eight years, Marla wasn't used to looking up from her work to be met by them. She still found it disconcerting to be confronted with the agonised face of a young man being taken against his will by a fantastical beast that looked like a cross between a bull, a man and a goat. The creature, depicted in life-sized colour, stood almost eight feet tall. His head was that of a horned bovine, his body that of a man, but his legs ended in cloven hooves. Marla could never define exactly what it was about that particular panel that disturbed her so much. She was neither prudish or easily shocked. Perhaps it was the notion her brother could imagine such a thing and call it entertainment. Or worse, that someone else had shared his vision so comprehensively they had been able to recreate it vividly on a fresco.

'Do you have any thoughts on the subject, Corian?' Marla asked, fixing her attention on the chamberlain in order to avoid having to look at the murals.

Corian noticed her determined focus. He knew what she thought of her brother's taste in decor. 'We could meet in one of the other rooms, your highness.'

Marla shook her head. 'Everything is here, and I really am pressed for time. I do, however, frequently daydream of having these damn walls painted over.'

'It would be foolish in the extreme to even contemplate the idea,' Corian advised. 'Prince Lernen is High Prince of Hythria and even though much of the country either knows or suspects it's really his sister who keeps a steady hand at the helm, they pretended it isn't the case. There is no other way for the Warlords to accept a woman in such a position of power and still maintain face.'

'They don't seem to mind that the High Arrion of the Sorcerers' Collective is a woman,' Marla pointed out.

'The Sorcerers' Collective has no direct control over them, so they're willing to let a woman rule, bow to her wisdom on occasion – even allow her to perform the rites that make the Convocation of the Warlords a place where they can meet in peace. However—'

'*However*, to openly admit their High Prince is a figurehead and that Hythria's prosperity is a direct result of the competent and efficient governance of a woman is more than their misogynistic little hearts can deal with,' Marla cut in with a shake of her head.

Corian smiled faintly. 'Something like that.'

'And if I redecorate the High Prince's private study to suit my own tastes, I'd be rubbing their noses in the fact that Lernen hasn't done much more than screw around in his garden and get drunk for the past eight years.'

'Exactly, your highness.'

'I know. Truly, I do.' Marla sighed and picked up a sheaf

of paper to fan herself against the unbearable heat. 'It's just sometimes . . .' She closed her eyes for a moment, then opened them again and turned to Corian decisively. 'Let's get back to the business at hand. My original thought was to share the fosterage around. You know – six months here, six months there.'

'But?' Corian prompted.

'Before she died, Jeryma made me promise I would do nothing of the kind.'

'Lady Jeryma Ravenspear?'

Marla nodded, feeling a little guilty. She'd not spared her late mother-in-law a thought in more than a year. Jeryma's death last year, like so many other important events in her life, had passed almost unremarked, overwhelmed by all the other crises clamouring for her attention. 'She went to some trouble to remind me that the whole purpose of a fosterage is to give the fosterling something to learn. Jeryma contended that the only thing the Warlords will do if they get access to Damin for a few months each is attempt to outdo each other trying to show him a good time.' Marla smiled in remembrance. 'I believe her exact words were: "Damin will learn nothing, be spoiled rotten, and there's a good chance one of them will try slipping a daughter into his bed, and before you know it, my grandson will be married at fourteen to the pregnant and uneducated get of some unscrupulous Patriot and everything I've worked for will be destroyed!"'

'Your mother-in-law was a wise woman, your highness,' Corian agreed.

She looked at him curiously. 'Do you have an opinion about who I should allow to foster Damin?'

'I can tell you who you mustn't choose.'

'Who?'

'Charel Hawksword of Elasapine, for a start.'

Marla nodded in reluctant agreement of the slave's

assessment. 'Because he is the grandfather of my youngest son and already has unfettered access to Damin?'

'Partly. Remember, your nephew, Travin Taranger, was fostered in Elasapine until recently, too. Then there is the certainty that Narvell will go to his grandfather when he turns thirteen.'

'You're suggesting the other Warlords already think Charel has too much influence over Damin? You might have a valid point.'

'Nor can you allow Chaine Lionsclaw to have him.'

'I suppose my mistake there was allowing Xanda to be fostered in Sunrise Province?'

Corian shook his head. 'Not just that. Chaine Lionsclaw is only recently elevated to power and the bastard son of a Warlord,' he reminded her. 'He's competent, I'll grant you, and loyal to the Wolfblades, but he's barely been a Warlord for ten years. The others would take placing your son in the care of someone so inexperienced as a grave insult.'

'Anyone else?'

'That narrows the field down to four, your highness.'

'Three,' Marla corrected. 'Dregian Province is out of the question. Sending Damin to Barnardo Eaglespike would be as good as passing his death sentence.'

'I don't think anybody would dare—'

'It wouldn't be murder, Corian,' Marla told him with absolute certainty. 'It would be some terrible accident that couldn't be avoided; some tragic set of circumstances which only the gods could have predicted. There would be no blame. Alija would see to that.'

'Surely you're not suggesting the High Arrion of the Sorcerers' Collective and her husband would deliberately seek to harm the High Prince's heir, your highness?'

'She's done it before, Corian. I'm quite sure she's capable of doing it again.'

Corian looked quite horrified. 'But, your highness, if you have proof of such treachery—'

'I don't have proof.'

'Then such an accusation—'

'Would be foolish in the extreme if I made it publicly,' Marla finished for him with a smile. 'Don't panic, Corian. I've taken precautions.'

'Precautions?' he gasped. 'What precautions can you take against such seditious gossip leaking out?'

'Do you remember when you first came to the palace? It was just after my second husband died.'

Corian's expression darkened, a clear indication that he had not forgotten his time in the slave pits. 'Of course I remember, your highness.'

'Do you recall meeting a young man the very first day you were here? Tall, dark-haired, quite good-looking in a rough sort of way? His name was Wrayan Lightfinger.'

'I remember him vaguely, your highness. You said he was an agent of yours. I've not seen him since that day. I assumed he was a spy of some kind.'

'He's more than that,' she informed him. 'He was Kagan Palenovar's apprentice.'

'I see,' the old man said cautiously.

Marla's smile widened. It was patently obvious that he didn't see at all. 'Wrayan is a magician, Corian. A very capable one. He shielded your mind that day. Just as mine is shielded, and Elezaar's mind, and the mind of anyone else close to me. Alija Eaglespike cannot penetrate my thoughts or the thoughts of anyone around me. She has no idea I suspect her of anything.'

'But surely, your highness, if she is able to read the thoughts of others, the mere fact that she cannot read your thoughts is, in itself, a warning.'

'I thought so too, but according to Wrayan, Brakandaran the Halfbreed showed him how to shield a mind without a lesser magician being able to detect it's been tampered with.'

'Brakandaran the *Halfbreed*?' Corian echoed, clearly sceptical. 'Even if the stories about such a legendary figure were true, surely he'd be long dead by now. Old age would have taken him, if not the Sisterhood.'

Marla shrugged. 'I know. It sounds too fantastic to be true. Elezaar suspects Wrayan's just a scoundrel who makes up these stories because it amuses him. But the truth of the matter is this, Corian: I have no idea if Wrayan Lightfinger knows the Halfbreed. What I *do* know is that Wrayan was instrumental in uncovering a plan to destroy my son. He came to me when he could have walked away. He risked exposure and the wrath of the Thieves' Guild to bring that information to me. I cannot discount his value simply because I don't like what I'm hearing.'

'But the *Harshini*, your highness? They're long gone. And if they are still out there somewhere, why choose a common thief as their envoy?'

'I have no idea. All I know is that Wrayan is able to prevent Alija from reading my mind.'

'But how do you know he has?' Corian insisted, clearly not able to accept her belief that their minds were magically protected. Or that the Harshini might still be among them. Or perhaps he didn't like the idea that his mind had been tampered with, without his knowledge or permission. 'You have only this Wrayan Lightfinger's word that Alija can read minds. And only his word that this spell of his prevents it.'

'True.'

'Then surely your trust in him is misplaced?'

'Perhaps.'

He looked at her in confusion. 'Then why . . . ?'

'Because it doesn't matter, Corian. If you're right and Wrayan has no power, then what harm is done by letting him believe that I accept his story? At best, I have protection against Alija. At worst, all I have is a valuable ally in the Thieves' Guild and a source of intelligence to which I would never normally gain access.'

Corian shook his head. 'You play games within games, your highness.'

'I don't have much choice, Corian.' Marla shrugged as she turned back to the pile of work on the table. 'I'm not a man. I don't have the easy option of going to war to protect my son.'

Corian nodded in understanding. 'And it is that which drives your every action, I suspect.'

Marla smiled thinly. 'Corian Burl, you've been working with me every day for eight years. I would think, by now, you would know me well enough not to *suspect* that it's the protection of my son that drives me, but know it for a certain fact.'

'Which is why you're having so much trouble making the decision about who should foster him, isn't it? You're afraid to let him go.'

'I'm afraid he won't come back,' she amended. 'In Krakandar I can protect him. But once he leaves? I have no chance. And it's not so much his physical safety. I can send him anywhere in Hythria with a whole army of bodyguards. Besides, no Warlord other than Barnardo Eaglespike would dare allow any harm come to the High Prince's heir. Not while he's officially in their care, although there's more than one who'd do it covertly if they thought they could get away with it. It's all the other things that could go wrong. Suppose some girl seduces him before he's had a chance to be *court'esa* trained? Suppose – as Jeryma feared – he inadvertently fathers a bastard on some Warlord's daughter? Or worse still, some peasant girl? Suppose he falls in with bad company and they lead him astray? Suppose he turns into a drunken wastrel?'

'Suppose Damin turns into his uncle?' Corian interrupted softly. 'That's what you really fear.'

Marla fanned herself with the sheaf of papers again. The heat was getting worse. Unbearable. 'It's something I have to consider, Corian.'

'Then send him somewhere he's not likely to be led astray.'

'And where is that?'

'Send him to Rogan Bearbow.'

'The Warlord of Izcomdar? Are you mad? He's Alija's cousin.'

'So nobody will be able to accuse you of playing favourites.'

'He does have a son a few years older than Damin,' she remembered.

Corian nodded. 'Rogan. He's named after his father. He's currently being fostered in Pentamor. Only the elder daughter remains in his household and she's been promised to Terin Lionsclaw of Sunrise Province. I believe they're to marry next year sometime. I doubt she will be a problem.'

'Izcomdar does border Krakandar,' Marla said thoughtfully. 'Damin would still be close enough that Mahkas could get to him if there was a problem.'

'There are many advantages, your highness.'

'I will give it some thought, Corian. What else is there that I need to take care of before I leave?'

Corian turned to the table and picked up the first of the neatly stacked piles. 'We should start with these, your highness.'

Marla sighed. Sweat trickled down her back. Her skirts were damp against the leather of the chair where she sat. The air hung heavy and thick and there was still no sign of a relieving breeze.

Even with a possible solution about Damin's fosterage on the horizon, Marla knew it was going to be a long, long night.

10

'Why do I have to wear this damned coronet?' Cyrus Eaglespike demanded of his mother impatiently as he burst into her sitting room. 'I look like a fool.'

'You look like a prince,' Alija corrected, glancing up with a frown from the letter she was writing. She hadn't expected to see her son until later, having sent the coronet to the barracks with Tarkyn Lye earlier this morning, along with instructions that Cyrus must wear it this afternoon during the parade out of town.

'But I'm *not* a prince, Mother,' her son pointed out testily. 'And all your posturing isn't going to make me one. I should be riding with the Guard, in any case, not sitting in an open carriage like an invalid. For that matter, why do I have to go home to Dregian at all? Why can't I stay here in the city over summer with the Guard?'

'You are riding in the carriage because you are the cousin of the High Prince, son of the High Arrion and the heir to Dregian Province. Under the Retreat Season laws, heirs are not permitted to stay here over summer any more than Warlords. You know that.'

'It's a stupid law.'

'But the law, nonetheless. What are you doing here at the house, anyway?'

'Complaining about your taste in accessories,' he responded with an insolent grin. 'I would have thought that much was obvious.'

'You'll be a prince soon enough,' she assured him with a smile. 'When you're heir to the High Prince's throne.'

'Ah, but that singular honour falls to my distant cousin in Krakandar,' he reminded her, snatching the coronet from his head. He flopped inelegantly onto the cushions surrounding the low table in the centre of the room. 'Or had you forgotten that minor but rather important detail, Mother dear?'

It was obvious Cyrus wasn't going to let her finish the letter so Alija put aside her quill and looked at her son. Cyrus had been in Greenharbour for over two years now and had already been promoted to the rank of captain in the Palace Guard. As he was the son of the High Arrion, Alija could easily have placed him in the Sorcerers' Collective Guard until he was old enough to take over his inheritance – the lordship of Dregian Province – but she had thought it more prudent to keep him close to the High Prince. Nobody would ever accuse *her* son of not having any experience at court.

He was nineteen, still a little self-conscious and gangly, the way most boys of his age were, caught between childhood and manhood and not entirely certain, from one moment to the next, exactly where he stood in the general scheme of things. Cyrus was not a handsome young man. He favoured the High Prince in looks, which was a mixed blessing. It would have been better if he'd looked more like a classic Hythrun. They tended towards the blond stereotype; the fair, handsome specimens of which the Harshini artisans had been so fond.

Thinking of the Wolfblades set Alija wondering what Marla's eldest son, Damin Wolfblade, looked like these days. Marla had wisely kept him away from Greenharbour for the past eight years. *He'd be twelve, almost thirteen years old by now*, Alija calculated. She knew remarkably little about him. Getting spies past Mahkas Damaran and into Krakandar palace had proved next to impossible, so she'd had to rely for her intelligence on those few people who'd visited the northern province and actually laid eyes on the boy. It was scant at best.

Has he inherited the fair looks of his ancestors, or does he share his uncle's pinched features?

Perhaps he favoured his father. Laran Krakenshield had been a big man, but not a particularly handsome one. The child Alija remembered was an appealing little boy with fair curls and a winning smile, but cherubic beauty rarely followed its owner into puberty. She smiled to herself, thinking the lad was probably an unruly mess of pimples and embarrassing bravado these days, with a voice caught somewhere between soprano and bass; all legs and arms and teenage awkwardness.

'I am fully aware that Damin Wolfblade is currently the anointed heir,' she informed Cyrus, turning her attention back to her son. 'However, he is barely thirteen. A lot can happen between now and his thirtieth birthday.'

Cyrus smiled in anticipation. 'Is there something you're not telling me, Mother?'

'What do you mean?'

'I mean, do you know of some . . . *accident* . . . likely to befall poor Damin?'

'Don't be absurd, Cyrus!' she snapped. 'And don't ever repeat such nonsense outside this room. Even a hint that I might be plotting something against the High Prince's heir would bring the entire family down.'

'But you are, aren't you?' he insisted, warming to the idea. 'I can never be High Prince while Damin lives. It follows, then, that if you're so certain I will be High Prince some day, you must have plans to remove the only obstacle standing in my way.'

'I could simply be waiting for fate to decide,' she shrugged.

'I know you better than that, Mother.'

'Then do as I say, Cyrus. Wear that damn coronet and ride in the carriage next to the High Prince when we leave the city this afternoon. The people of Greenharbour need to be reminded that you are a member of his family.'

'I'll be in the carriage with you and the High Prince because I'm the son of the High Arrion,' he pointed out. 'Nobody remembers some long distant relative of mine was a Wolfblade.'

'They will. When the time is right.'

Cyrus sighed and picked up the coronet, jamming it on his head with a scowl. 'Do I have to speak to him?'

'Who?'

'Lernen, of course! It's bad enough I have to ride in the damn carriage with him. Please don't tell me I have to make conversation with the old pervert as well.'

'It would be nice to give people the impression you're on speaking terms with the High Prince.'

'But what would we talk about, Mother? I certainly don't want to hear about what he gets up to in his private garden. Or risk him inviting me to join him in his bizarre little games.'

'Talk about racehorses. That should be fairly safe.'

'Will Princess Marla be riding with us, too?'

Alija shook her head and picked up the quill again. 'She's leaving for Krakandar tomorrow morning.'

'Is it true she's adopting Luciena Mariner?'

Alija's head jerked up in surprise. 'What?'

'Luciena Mariner. You know . . . that bastard old Jarvan Mariner sired on his mistress.'

'I know who she is, Cyrus. Where did you hear that?'

'I was talking to Xanda Taranger the other day in the barracks. He was on his way to deliver an invitation to

Luciena to meet with Princess Marla. The old man's mistress died about a month ago, he said . . . or hadn't you heard? Katira Keyne was her name, wasn't it? She was supposed to be the most beautiful *court'esa* that ever lived.'

'Why didn't Marla send *you*?' she asked. 'You outrank Xanda Taranger. He's been in the Guard barely a year and already she's singling him out?'

Cyrus seemed unconcerned. 'Keeping it all in the family, I guess. Anyway, I'm not a messenger boy. Do you suppose the daughter is as beautiful as her mother must have been?'

'I don't know,' Alija said, rising to her feet. She walked to the window and looked out, not really seeing the flat white rooftops of the city stretching before her.

What is Marla up to now? Is she just taking on another lost cause in a career littered with lost causes?

Marla Wolfblade was fond of lost causes, Alija had decided long ago. Why else would she continue to insist on aiding her useless brother so diligently all these years? Admittedly, her aid had probably helped Lernen keep his throne. Marla was thorough and conscientious, if not very imaginative, in Alija's opinion. On the few occasions Alija had been able to get close enough to touch Marla and read her thoughts, they were always bland and uninformative, her mind filled with trivial surface thoughts and rarely anything deeper or more dire than what she was planning to wear tomorrow. Still, this business with the Mariner girl was a little unsettling. 'Tell me *exactly* what Xanda said to you.'

Cyrus thought about it for a moment and then shrugged. 'Something along the lines of: "Princess Marla's asked me to visit Jarvan Mariner's daughter and invite her to the palace for lunch," I think.'

'That's a long way from saying she's planning to adopt the girl.'

'That was after he got back. And he didn't say it to me. I overheard him talking to the dwarf. He was complaining the girl seemed ungrateful, considering Marla was offering to give her a name. I can't really be certain. I didn't overhear that much and they were walking away from me at the time.'

'Why?'

'I was on my way to the barracks after escorting the princess back to her house from the palace, and they were headed for—'

'No! I mean why would Marla do this now? Why suddenly take an interest in the Mariner girl when she's ignored her all this time?'

'Katira Keyne is dead,' Cyrus reminded her. 'Marla can make contact with the daughter now without it being quite so scandalous, I suppose.'

'If Marla cared about scandal, she would never have married Jarvan Mariner in the first place. Or married that damned spice trader, Ruxton Tirstone, after Jarvan died. There has to be more to it.'

'Why?' Cyrus asked curiously.

She turned to stare at him. 'What do you mean, *why*?'

'Why must there be something more to it? Why do you always assume people are plotting against you, Mother?' He smiled suddenly. 'You should be careful. There are asylums full of people who think the rest of the world is plotting against them, you know.'

'You think this is funny?'

'I think you credit Marla Wolfblade with far more intelligence than she deserves, actually,' Cyrus countered. 'I've had to escort Her Royal Highness numerous times. You can't expect me to consider a woman who spends all day shopping for a single pair of shoes a serious threat, surely?'

'How many shops did she visit in search of her shoes?' Alija asked.

'Scores of them.'

'And how many shopkeepers did she speak to? Were they spies? Do you even know who her spies are? How many of those apparently innocent shopkeepers were actually contacts in her network?' She shook her head and sighed. 'You really must begin to think like a politician if you expect to take the throne some day, my dear.'

'It seems more like you expect me to develop an irrational fear of conspirators.'

'I wish you did fear them, Cyrus, whether you think it's irrational or not.'

'I'll try, Mother,' he promised. 'If only to keep you happy.'

She nodded in satisfaction. He was such a dutiful son. 'You *will* be High Prince one day, Cyrus. And it will be the proudest day of my life.'

'Then I suppose I shouldn't let you down this afternoon,' he announced, climbing to his feet. He straightened the coronet on his head and smiled at her. 'It's going to be as hot as a roasting pig out there this afternoon, riding through the streets in an open carriage.'

'Don't look to me for sympathy,' she warned with a sour smile. 'I'll be in that carriage right beside you, you know. Wearing a black woollen robe.'

'The things we do, eh?' Cyrus chuckled, crossing the room to kiss her cheek.

'The things we do for *Hythria*,' Alija corrected with a smile.

Cyrus laughed softly and turned for the door. Alija watched him leave, thinking no mother had ever been more fortunate in a son, while another part of her – the politician inside that never slept – wondered why Marla Wolfblade had suddenly decided to welcome Luciena Mariner into the fold, when she'd quite deliberately ignored the poor girl for the past eight years. And more importantly, why she'd left it until the day all the important people in the city were leaving Greenharbour.

Alija glanced out of the window again. It wasn't yet midday and the parade to farewell the High Prince from Greenharbour wasn't due to start until midafternoon. There was still time, she reflected, to see if she could discover what was going on. Marla Wolfblade suddenly deciding to welcome a baseborn commoner into the royal family was something that, as High Arrion, Alija couldn't let slip by unremarked.

Xanda thought the girl ungrateful, did he? Alija thought. *There might be an opportunity here.* Maybe a chance to get through the wall of protection surrounding the only obstacle to her son's ascension to the throne. Perhaps the forgotten daughter of Jarvan Mariner had good cause to despise the Wolfblades.

Perhaps enough cause to wish them harm.

And who would blame the child . . . abandoned and forgotten, publicly humiliated and ignored by the princess, when the whole city knew who she really was?

It might even be enough, Alija mused with a small, secretive smile, *to tempt Luciena Mariner into seeking revenge – revenge that could not, in any way, be traced back to the High Arrion of the Sorcerers' Collective.*

II

'Is it hot in Krakandar at this time of year?' Luciena asked.

Aleesha shrugged as she folded another of Luciena's formal gowns and laid it carefully in her trunk. 'How should I know? I've never been there.'

'I suppose I should take the cashmere shawl,' Luciena decided, standing in front of the shelves that lined one wall of the small room off the main bedroom where Aleesha stored her clothes. 'Just in case.'

'Why not take it all?' the slave grumbled.

Luciena turned to her in surprise. 'What's the matter with you?'

'Nothing.'

'Don't lie to me. You've been snapping at me all day, slamming things around, muttering under your breath . . . what's wrong?'

'I'm just a poor dumb slave, my lady,' Aleesha replied as she laid a blue and gold silk gown across the bed to fold it. Luciena's mother had bought that gown only weeks before she died. She'd never worn it. 'It's not *my* place to say.'

'I'm making it your place. Tell me!'

Aleesha stopped her folding and placed her hands on her hips, glaring at her mistress. 'Well, if you must know, I think you're a screaming bloody fool!'

'For agreeing to go to Krakandar with Princess Marla?'

'No,' the slave replied sarcastically, 'for deciding to eat eggs for breakfast this morning.'

'I have no choice,' Luciena sighed. 'You know that better than anyone.'

'You had a choice. You could have said no.'

'And what would happen to us if I did?' she asked. 'Princess Marla paid off our debts, Aleesha. If not for her intervention, I'd be fighting off that animal, Ameel Parkesh, by now. Or would you *rather* see me selling my body to a moneylender to spare you the effort of packing my trunks?'

'If you ask me, Marla Wolfblade bought *you* along with those damn debts,' the slave complained. 'Just because the bed has silk sheets and a feather mattress, Luciena, it doesn't make you any less a whore if you choose to lie on it and open your legs. Your mother should have taught you that.'

'For pity's sake, Aleesha! What did you expect me to do?'

'Anything but roll over without a fight and say: *Yes, your highness*,' Aleesha replied in a scathing falsetto voice. '*Of course I'll drop everything and follow you right across the country, put myself completely at your mercy, and let you dictate the rest of my life to me.*'

Luciena was wounded by Aleesha's scorn. 'You think I would've been better off taking my chances with Parkesh, do you? Or have you forgotten that *you* were the one who went racing off in a blind panic to fetch the Palace Guard because you thought I was in danger?'

'Don't flatter yourself,' the slave snorted, as she began folding the gown again. 'I just wanted an excuse to talk to that young officer again.' Suddenly Aleesha looked up and smiled mischievously. 'He was pretty cute, you know.'

'He's Princess Marla's nephew,' Luciena told her, shaking

114

her head at Aleesha's impertinence. There were going to be problems with her slave if she didn't learn to act a little more like a slave once they were travelling with the princess's entourage.

'That figures,' Aleesha shrugged. 'There's always *something* about the good-looking ones that makes them trouble. Is he the reason you agreed to go?'

'*What?*'

'I could sort of understand *that*,' the slave explained. 'I mean, I can't for the life of me imagine why you'd want to have anything to do with Princess Marla after cursing her every day of your life since your father died. But I can appreciate a bit of good old-fashioned lust. Is it the uniform, I wonder? Perhaps it's the sword? Or those tight leather trousers, eh? It's all those hours they spend in the saddle, you know, that gives them thighs like—'

'*Aleesha*! Stop it!' she ordered, raising her voice to emphasise her point. 'You've no idea what you're talking about!'

'Then explain it to me, my *lady*,' the slave responded just as loudly. 'Because the gods know, *I* can't think of any other logical reason why you'd go along with this!'

'I *have* explained it! Over and over again! Princess Marla paid off my debts!'

'You said the princess didn't want the money back.'

Luciena threw her hands up helplessly, not sure what else she could say to convince Aleesha she'd been left with no alternative. 'It's not that simple.'

'Yes, it *is* that simple,' the slave insisted. 'Let's get out of this while we still can. You hate these people and you don't belong with them.'

'I can't . . .'

The slave abandoned all pretence of packing and walked across the room to her mistress. With an encouraging smile, Aleesha took Luciena by the shoulders so she couldn't avoid facing her and added gently, 'Look, you don't have to pretend with me, pet. I remember your father telling you all those fanciful stories when you were small about how the princess was going to make you part of the family, how you'd have brothers and sisters and would live in a grand palace . . . And I remember how much you wanted it. But they were only stories, Luciena, and I know it hurt when you finally realised that . . . so don't give in now. We don't have to go to Krakandar. And for all you know, Princess Marla's just inviting you along so she can get you out of the city and have you killed.'

'Don't be ridiculous!' Luciena scoffed, pushing the slave away. 'If Princess Marla wanted me dead, she could have done it any time in the past eight years and nobody would have cared about it, with the possible exception of you and my mother.' Even as she uttered the words, she knew they lacked conviction. What had Marla told her? *You're not actually worth the price of an assassin.* 'Besides, she owns everything of mine already. Why would she need to have me killed?'

'That's a question I'm rather curious about myself.'

Luciena spun around at the unfamiliar voice and almost fainted with shock.

The High Arrion of the Sorcerers' Collective was standing in the doorway.

'My lady!' Aleesha gasped, falling to her knees.

Luciena was too stunned to speak. The High Arrion smiled and stepped a little further into the room. She was wearing a pale yellow sleeveless gown, rather than the traditional black robes of her office, but there was no mistaking the diamond pendant she wore, or her unconscious air of superiority. 'I'm sorry. I hope I didn't startle you. I did knock, but there doesn't seem to be anybody around to answer the front door.'

'Lady Alija!' Luciena said, finding her voice at last, curtseying as elegantly as she could manage.

'Ah, you know me!' the High Arrion declared with a smile. 'That's good. It'll save us going through all those tedious introductions. Do you have something cool to drink?' she added, looking at Aleesha.

'Of course, my lady,' the slave replied, scrambling to her feet. She hurried from the room, bowing several times on the way out.

Alija Eaglespike watched her leave and then turned to Luciena. 'You must forgive my rudeness, Luciena. You and your slave were having a rather heated discussion and I must admit I overheard quite a bit of it. In fact, it was your raised voices which alerted me to the fact that you were home.'

'I'm sorry, my lady.'

'You've nothing to apologise for, my dear.'

'Thank you ... I ... er ... I mean ... what are you doing here, my lady?'

'My gateman informs me you came to visit the Collective yesterday,' the High Arrion announced, looking around with interest. 'I came to find out why.'

'You didn't have to visit me personally, my lady.'

She smiled warmly. 'Well, when I heard you were considering an offer from Princess Marla, I thought I should give the matter my immediate attention. Is that what you wanted to see me about?'

'Um ... well, no, not really. It was about my cousin. In Fardohnya.'

Lady Alija raised an elegant brow in surprise. 'You have family in Fardohnya?'

'I think so.'

'You're not certain?'

'My father had a brother,' she explained nervously, totally unprepared to face the High Arrion with her request. 'They had a falling out long before I was born. My uncle followed his heart – and the wife my father didn't approve of – to

Fardohnya. He has three sons, according to his letter. And they have a number of their own children.'

Alija nodded as she strolled around the room, apparently engrossed in the painted murals on the walls. 'How lovely for you, my dear. What does that have to do with me?'

'One of my cousins has some sort of magical talent, according to my uncle.'

Alija looked at her in surprise. 'Does he now?'

'Well, I suppose . . . I don't really know.'

She smiled. 'And what were you hoping I'd do about it?'

'Well, I thought . . . or rather, my uncle thought . . . he should join the Sorcerers' Collective. I tried to make an appointment to see you because I was hoping, maybe . . .'

'What? That *I* would arrange it?'

'I've heard you're searching for gifted apprentices.'

'Not in Talabar,' the High Arrion replied wryly. 'Have you spoken of your magically gifted cousin to Princess Marla?'

'No, my lady.'

'What have you told your uncle?'

'Nothing, as yet, my lady. I mean, there's nothing to tell. And there's some doubt . . .'

'About what?'

Luciena shrugged, the preposterous notion of asking the High Arrion for help making her cringe with embarrassment as she spoke. *What was I thinking?* 'The timing of his letter is a little suspicious. Aleesha . . . my slave, thinks it's just an attempt by my uncle to extort money from me.'

'Your slave may well be right. And I'd like to help you, my dear, but any members of the Sorcerers' Collective foolish enough to set foot in Fardohnya are rotting in Hablet's dungeons. If you can get him to Greenharbour, I'd be happy to consider your cousin, but I can't do much more than that.'

In truth, Luciena would have been surprised at more. 'Thank you, my lady.'

'You're welcome, my dear,' Lady Alija replied, still studying the murals intently. 'And do take care in your dealings with her highness. I share some of your companion's concerns.'

Luciena looked at the High Arrion in surprise. 'My *lady?*'

'It seems remarkably out of character for the princess to suddenly decide to pay off your debts and welcome you into her family after all this time. Are you sure you've examined this offer closely?'

'It wasn't actually an offer, Lady Alija. It was a done deed before I could object.'

'Marla can be like that at times. Has she told you what she wants of you?'

'I'm not sure I understand . . .'

'Marla's generosity must come with some sort of obligation.'

Luciena shrugged. 'She expects me to marry someone of her choosing.'

'Did she say who?'

'No,' Luciena replied, shaking her head. 'Although she specifically told me not to set my cap at her nephew.'

'Who? Xanda Taranger?' Alija glanced over her shoulder with a smile. 'Not a bad bit of advice, really. He's a second son with few prospects of his own. She made no mention, then, of who she has in mind?'

'She said we'd discuss it after I'd met Damin.'

The High Arrion forgot about the murals and turned to stare at her. 'She's taking you to meet her son?'

Luciena nodded, wondering at Lady Alija's sudden interest. She was far more interested in that news, in fact, than the idea Luciena's cousin might be magically gifted. 'We're leaving for Krakandar tomorrow morning.' She waved her arm at the disorganised chaos lying around the room. 'Hence the packing.'

'That's quite a boon, Luciena,' Alija remarked with a raised brow. 'Princess Marla is very protective of her children. She doesn't usually allow strangers close to them. She fears assassins the way others fear spiders. It has something to do with a foiled attempt on Damin's life when he was a small child, I think.'

'She had little choice in my case,' Luciena informed the High Arrion. 'I have no intention of swearing allegiance to the Wolfblades without some idea of what I'm getting myself into.'

'Marla wants you to swear allegiance to her *son*?' The High Arrion's eyes sparkled in anticipation of her answer.

'She wants me to swear allegiance to her House. She said swearing allegiance to her son before he became High Prince would be considered treason.'

'And she'd be right,' Alija agreed.

'Is that why you really came here, my lady?' Luciena asked, a little worried. 'To see if I was plotting something against the High Prince?'

Alija laughed. 'My dear, at any given time, half the damned country is plotting something against the High Prince. No. I came here because I thought you'd requested an audience to seek my advice about Marla's offer.' Lady Alija took a step closer and smiled, reaching out to take both Luciena's hands in hers. 'But you seem to have made up your mind. There's just one little favour I'd like you to do for me, my dear. When you get to Krakandar.'

Luciena nodded silently, suddenly filled with a warm sense of well-being. Still holding her hands, Lady Alija closed her eyes. The warm feeling grew and Luciena began to feel so hot she feared she might faint. Strange thoughts that seemed to belong to someone else flitted through her mind. Her mother called out to her. She saw her father sailing out of the harbour on one of his ships, heading for some unknown destination. She saw Princess Marla beckoning her towards an abyss so black it ate all the light around it, sucking the warmth from the air and life from anything foolish enough to venture too close to its edge. The thoughts swirled through her head, making her dizzy, nauseous . . .

And then the strange feelings faded away and Luciena discovered she was lying on the floor of her bedroom, Aleesha kneeling over her with concern, calling out her name as if she'd been unconscious. The High Arrion was gone, as if she'd never been there at all, and a phrase was repeating itself, over and over, in Luciena's mind.

Welcome to the family, it said. *Welcome to the family . . . welcome to the family . . .*

12

The town of Acarnipoor in central Fardohnya boasted a population of nearly five thousand people. It was a sprawling settlement that wound along the banks of the Serpentine River, the village divided in two by the narrow, fast-flowing waterway. Several footbridges, and a more substantial bridge constructed of stone, joined the two sides of the town. As evening approached and the sunset tinted the white walls of the stuccoed houses pink, Rory climbed down from the back of the wagon where he'd been hiding since Vanipoor and looked up at the sky, hoping it wasn't going to rain.

The slowly moving wagon trundled over the stone bridge linking the two sides of the town, the driver unaware his passenger had disembarked. For that matter, the driver probably didn't even realise he'd had a passenger. Stretching his cramped limbs, Rory looked around with relief. Acarnipoor seemed large enough that he could mingle with the townsfolk for a time and not be noticed. He'd learned the hard way, these past few weeks, that small towns easily remembered a fair-haired boy who spoke Fardohnyan like a native but looked like a Hythrun. Particularly since there seemed to be notices nailed to just about every flat surface in Fardohnya these days, offering a reward for the boy rumoured to be a Hythrun spy. The boy rumoured to be a sorcerer. The boy wanted for murder.

Rory might have been safe, nobody might ever have connected him with the man on Victory Parade who got hit by an anvil, had it not been for an incident that happened a few days after he'd followed his cousin. Until then, despite an intensive investigation that disrupted the trade on Restinghouse Street for days, nobody thought anything of the fair-haired boy seen walking in the same direction as the victim and the whore he'd singled out for a bit of fun only minutes before his body was discovered with a dent in his skull matching the anvil on the ground beside him.

The problem started when somebody pointed the finger at Patria as the whore who'd accompanied the dead man into the lane. Early one morning, several days after the incident with the anvil, the family was woken by a loud pounding on the door to their small house. Grandpa Warak had stumbled over the sleeping bodies of Rory and his brothers and opened the door just as Rory sat up, rubbing his eyes and wondering what all the racket was about. The room was suddenly filled with soldiers, but they weren't the City Watch. These men wore the white and silver livery of King Hablet's Palace Guard.

'Arrest the Hythrun!' the officer ordered, as they tackled the old man to the ground. 'And find the girl!'

Other than to shove them out of the way, the soldiers ignored Rory and his brothers. His grandfather, however, was pushed down to the dirt floor of the hovel, a soldier's foot on his face, as his arms were twisted savagely behind him and bound with a piece of rope. A few moments later, he heard Patria scream as the soldiers dragged her from the lean-to out back and into the house.

Rory's head began to pound as the soldiers manhandled Patria into the room. It was his responsibility to do something, he knew. Even if he wasn't the cause of all this trouble, his father, Drendik, and his uncles, Abel and Gazil, had got a rare day's work last night on a lobster boat and had left before dawn to help clear the traps located on the other side of the harbour. With his grandfather under the boot heel of a Palace Guardsman – quite literally – the only one left to protect Patria and his brothers was Rory.

Scrambling to his feet, Rory hurriedly ordered his ten-year-old brother, Sinjay, to take the little ones and run to Ma Baker's house farther down the street. The soldiers weren't paying them any attention. If anything, they were just getting underfoot. Nobody stopped the younger children fleeing the house. They were too interested in Patria. And Rory's grandfather.

'So! A whore and her Hythrun lover, eh?' the soldier standing in front of Patria sneered, as two other soldiers struggled to hold on to her. Patria wasn't going anywhere without a fight.

'He's my grandfather, you idiot!' she snapped, and then spat at him to emphasise her point. A veteran of many spitting contests with her cousins, Patria's aim was impressive and a gob of spittle slid down the soldier's cheek. He wiped it away angrily and then backhanded Patria across the face for her trouble.

'Leave her alone!' Rory cried, aware how useless it was to rail against these men, but feeling he must. His temples were throbbing, his eyes watering with the pain building up in his head. 'She didn't do anything!'

'Not what we've been told,' the Guardsman with his boot on Warak Mariner's face replied. 'Seems your little friend here was the last one to see Horrak alive. Just before someone dropped an anvil on his head.'

'Like I could even *lift* an anvil!' Patria scoffed, still struggling against the men who held her.

'*Nobody* could lift that anvil,' the soldier holding down Rory's grandfather agreed. 'No normal man, at any rate.'

'We figured it had to have been moved by magic,' the officer Patria had spat on explained. 'And then what d'ya know? We find out poor old Horrak's last moments in this world were spent humping some cheap little whore who just happens to share her home with an old Hythrun posing as a fisherman. Seems pretty straightforward to me.'

The soldier standing over Warak bent down and dragged the old man to his feet. 'We all know the Sorcerers' Collective will do anything to get their filthy Hythrun tentacles back into Fardohnya.'

Patria looked at the Guardsmen in shock. 'You think my *grandfather* is a spy for the Sorcerers' Collective? You're mad!'

'Don't worry, Patria,' her grandfather advised with a resigned sigh. 'I knew they'd find me eventually. I couldn't keep hiding forever.' He turned to the officers. 'You might as well let the girl go. She knows nothing. It's all my doing.'

Rory felt as if his head was going to rupture.

Their minds had been made up before they'd even burst through the door, so the soldiers needed no further convincing that Warak Mariner was the sorcerer they'd been looking for. But they weren't going to let Patria go quite so easily. As they dragged his cousin towards the door, Rory cried out.

He'd only meant to object, he didn't even try to do anything else, but with his anguished cry, his headache suddenly vanished and things started flying around the room. The stools by the fireplace, the pot hanging over the coals, blankets, cutlery – anything in the room that wasn't nailed down was suddenly a missile. Rory had no control over his gift and no chance of directing the missiles. He just stood there as the maelstrom exploded around him and everyone ducked for cover.

It was obvious, even to the soldiers, who was responsible for the attack. Warak Mariner – the man they believed a sorcerer – was cowering on the floor, just like everyone else. Rory stood untouched in the middle of the chaos, his eyes wide and completely black, their whites consumed by the power he was inadvertently channelling. It lasted only a few moments, but it was enough. As soon as they could get clear, the soldiers fled the house.

And then it stopped, as suddenly as it had started.

Rory stared in confusion at what was left of his home. Patria and his grandfather slowly climbed to their feet, gazing at him warily.

'Rorin, lad?'

He looked at his grandfather blankly.

'Let it go, lad.'

Rory wasn't sure what his grandfather meant, but the feeling of invincibility he'd been imbued with was rapidly fading. He looked around the room, shaking his head. 'Did I do this?'

Warak nodded and gently took his grandson's shoulder, studying him closely. 'Aye, lad. You did.'

'Well, at least it got rid of the soldiers,' Patria said with a shrug. She didn't seem all that surprised. But then, she'd seen an anvil flying through a wall, so maybe a few household objects didn't impress her.

'It's a temporary respite,' their grandfather warned. 'They'll be back, and in greater numbers, as soon as they can gather reinforcements.'

'I'm sorry, Grandpa.'

'It's not your fault, Rorin. You can't help what you are.'

'What are we going to do?' Patria asked.

'Get your cousin out of the city,' Warak replied. 'Right now. Before they think to seal it.'

'They wouldn't seal the city just to stop Rory,' Patria began sceptically. And then she stopped and looked around at the devastation surrounding them. 'On second thoughts . . .'

'I'll take him to the city gate,' the old man said. 'You

find the rest of your cousins and make your way to over Widow Marlin's place. She'll hide you all until I get back.'

Rory stared at his grandfather. 'But I can't leave Talabar! What about Pa?'

'I'll explain it to your father when I get back. Right now, you have to get out of the city, Rorin.'

'But where will I go?'

'Hythria,' the old man replied heavily. 'The only safe place for you now, my lad, is Hythria.'

That had been nearly a month ago. By living on his wits and honouring the God of Thieves every chance he got, Rory had been able to stay out of the clutches of the soldiers, but it was getting harder by the day. At first, he'd kept ahead of the news that he was a wanted man, but now those damn posters were cropping up everywhere. The likeness was a poor one, but the description was accurate and his blond hair rare enough to cause comment. He was still a couple of hundred miles from Westbrook and the safety of the Hythrun border, but even then he wasn't sure what he was supposed to do. He had nothing more than the name of a distant cousin in Greenharbour, who might or might not be willing to aid him. He wasn't hopeful she would. His grandfather's letter asking for help had been ignored, or her answer had arrived after Rory left the city. There was nothing to indicate this Luciena – assuming he could find her – would be willing to lift a finger to help him.

Rory didn't have much choice, however, and thinking about it too much gave him a headache, which frightened him, because he was starting to associate those headaches with his uncontrollable magical talent. The last thing Rory needed now was to start hurling things around again. If he was going to do that, he might as well just go and sit in the town square with a target painted on his chest and wait for them to come for him.

With a sigh, Rory shouldered his pack and headed across the bridge as darkness closed in over the Jalanar Plains. If he didn't think about it, he wouldn't miss home too much. If he kept focused on the need to find a way to Westbrook, he could pretend he didn't miss his father, or his brothers, or his grandfather, or even Patria. And if he tried hard enough, sometimes he could even pretend he wasn't frightened.

As he reached the end of the bridge, Rory stopped suddenly. There was a poster stuck to the tall square pylon there. *Wanted for murder*, it proclaimed in large black letters that had smudged and run down the page in a recent rainstorm. Much of the rest of the poster was faded and unreadable, except for the word *sorcerer*.

That wasn't what caught Rory's attention, however.

What shocked him speechless was the little creature sitting on top of the pylon. It had large, liquid black eyes, grey wrinkled skin, and long drooping ears, and it was staring down at Rory as if it had been waiting for him to come along.

Rory stared up at the creature. He knew what it was. There were pictures of demons painted on the walls of every temple he'd ever been in. But he'd never imagined he'd see one in real life.

'It's rude to stare,' the demon told him. Its voice was surprisingly feminine and sounded rather peeved.

'Um . . . I . . . er . . .'

'A gifted wordsmith, I see.'

'*Wordsmith?*'

'Never mind,' the demon replied with a long-suffering sigh. 'You can't go into the town, boy, they're waiting for you. I'll show you another way around.'

'Who *are* you?'

'My name is Lady Elarnymire,' the demon informed him, drawing herself up proudly. 'Of the té Carn family. I was sent to keep an eye on you.'

'Keep an eye on me? By who?'

'By *whom*,' the demon corrected primly.

'Whatever. Did my grandfather have something to do with this?'

'Certainly not! I am an envoy of the Harshini, not some human fisherman.'

'The *Harshini*?'

'We'll get through this faster if we dispense with the echoes, my lad.'

'But—'

The demon jumped off the pylon and landed in the dirt at Rory's feet. 'Just follow me,' Lady Elarnymire instructed. 'And if you stop repeating every other word I say, I might even tell you who sent me.'

13

'Is it much further?' Luciena asked.

Marla opened her eyes. She had been dozing, lulled to sleep by the rhythmic rocking of the coach. She was tired from almost three weeks of forced inactivity, sitting in a coach each day as they travelled north towards Krakandar. It would be good to get home, just for the opportunity to stretch her legs.

'Another hour or two.'

'The last part of a journey always seems the longest,' her husband added, looking up from the book he was reading. He never slept in the coach, always seemed to be reading. It was a pose she had become accustomed to. Marla had never met anyone so well read as Ruxton Tirstone; it was certainly an unexpected boon in a commoner. But then, much about Marla's fourth husband had proved to be unexpected, not the least of which was his intelligence and his wry sense of humour. She had expected neither.

Ruxton Tirstone was a spice trader, an unremarkable-looking man of average height with the sort of nondescript features that never seemed to settle in one's memory on a first meeting. Ruxton was a self-made man, in his early forties, who owned the most comprehensive spy network on the continent. He had agents from Yarnarrow far north in Karien, in Fardohnya, even at the Citadel in Medalon. Marla had wanted access to that network and after Luciena's father, Jarvan Mariner, had died, she had set about finding a way to gain it.

She hadn't planned to marry again. Three husbands by the time she was twenty-three had seemed quite enough for one lifetime. But when Elezaar approached Ruxton Tirstone on Marla's behalf, the spice trader quickly realised he had something Marla wanted. He was newly widowed himself, with three children of his own whose futures he had to consider. He had a daughter, Rielle, he wanted to marry well and two sons, Rodja and Adham, who – even with his vast wealth – would never amount to anything other than merchants' sons without the patronage of someone with Marla Wolfblade's impeccable connections. The common-born spice trader had held out for a wedding with the High Prince's sister and, in the end, Marla had agreed. What he had was too valuable to allow it to fall into the hands of her enemies.

Strange, she reflected, *how the most calculated and cold-blooded marriage I've ever entered into has turned into the most amiable*. Laran Krakenshield had been a kind but distant husband. Her marriage to Nash Hawksword had been passionate and, for a short while, the happiest time of her life. But good things rarely last and her second marriage had ultimately proved the most bitter and painful experience of all. As for Jarvan Mariner – Marla's brief marriage to Luciena's father had barely left a mark on her.

But Ruxton was different. Confident and astute, he knew his value to Marla and was unafraid of her influence. He had wealth independent of hers and did not seem intimidated by the power she wielded. And he had benefited enormously from the deal. A royal endorsement for his spices was something one couldn't put a price on.

In keeping with their agreement, Marla had arranged

for Rielle to marry Darvad Vintner, the Lord of Dylan Pass and a cousin of the Warlord of Izcomdar. Even that had been extraordinarily easy to arrange. As if Kalianah herself had blessed the couple, they had met at the races in Krakandar last summer and been instantly smitten with each other. A few words in the right ears and the trader's daughter was soon promised to a Warlord's cousin, because she also happened to be the step-niece of the High Prince. Ruxton's sons, Rodja and Adham, would reap a similar benefit from their association with the Wolfblades. They were being raised in Krakandar, stepbrothers of the High Prince's heir and receiving the same education . . .

At least they would be, Marla thought with a frown, *if they hadn't so willingly helped Damin, Narvell and Kalan drive one tutor after another from the palace with their pranks.*

Still, she decided with a sigh of relative contentment, *it has proven a very good arrangement for everyone.* Ruxton Tirstone understood Marla's obsession with keeping Hythria safe, just as he understood her obsession with keeping Damin and the twins safe from harm. As a stable economy was as important to his endeavours as it was to his wife's, he aided her where he could, giving her unfettered access to the intelligence his spies gathered across the continent and beyond; intelligence from Karien, Fardohnya, Medalon and Hythria as well as the distant and vast southern continent, the secretive lands of the Denikans on the very edge of the Dregian Ocean. But most importantly, he supported Marla in whatever measures she took when it came to keeping their children safe. They had been married for five years now. Sometimes it felt like a lifetime. Other times as if it had happened only yesterday.

And every time I come home to Krakandar, my children have grown taller. Older. More distant.

'You'll see them soon,' Ruxton remarked, glancing across at Marla, as if he knew what she'd been thinking.

'They always seem to have grown so big,' Marla sighed, as the carriage rattled on past the lush lowlands of Krakandar. She could tell they were almost home. The deep peaty brown soil of the south had given way to the fertile red soil of the north. The cattle were a deep red-brown, with dopey white faces and haunches fat with juicy marbled beef, not the ferocious black and white behemoths they preferred in the southern provinces, with their stringy meat and their tasteless offal. There were sheep more often now, too, as they travelled north, sitting on the lush grass and watching the large retinue trundle by. Their by-products of meat, wool, leather and parchment were staples of Krakandar's prosperity, even more so since Mahkas had adopted the policy several years ago of encouraging breeding from ewes inclined to produce twin lambs.

There was just something about this place, Marla thought. The water here was clearer, the sky bluer and the grass greener. It was probably just her imagination, she realised; a subconscious need to believe that she had done the right thing to leave her children in Krakandar while she stayed in Greenharbour, covering for her brother's incompetence.

'I've missed out on so much of my children's formative years,' she remarked, still staring out of the carriage, 'leaving them in Krakandar to be raised by Mahkas and Bylinda.'

'And they're all still alive because of that decision,' Ruxton pointed out sympathetically. He put a finger between the pages to mark his place and closed the book he was reading. 'Don't keep beating yourself up over it, Marla.'

'Is the danger to the High Prince's heir so extreme that you need to stay parted from your children for so long each year, your highness?' Luciena asked curiously. Three weeks of close confinement in a carriage with Marla and Ruxton had not yet put the girl at ease with her new family.

She still insisted on referring to Marla and Ruxton as 'your highness' and 'Master Tirstone' and questioned them often on the smallest details about Krakandar.

'The first time they tried to kill him, Damin was only four,' Marla explained, without elaborating about who 'they' had been. She turned her attention back to the passengers in the carriage. 'I won't risk an attack succeeding.'

'My father once told me the worst thing about power was that it made people envious, and that once they envied you, avarice was the next dish on the menu.'

'Your father was a wise man,' Ruxton told Luciena. Then he smiled. 'Although for a man who got rich trading on the misfortune of his fellow sea captains, the sentiment was probably a bit tongue in cheek.'

Luciena straightened in her seat, visibly offended. 'My father was an honest man! He would never get rich trading on other people's misfortune.'

'He traded on their ignorance more than their misfortune, probably,' Ruxton told her. 'Your father acquired much of his shipping fleet by trading on the naivety of the Denikans. Jarvan Mariner's voyages across the Dregian Ocean were quite legendary, in fact. He was one of the few who ever made it to Denika and back and managed to show a profit.'

Marla frowned at Ruxton for repeating such nonsense. It was hard enough winning the girl over without Ruxton impugning her beloved father's memory. 'Ruxton is only telling you part of it, Luciena. But it's true your father acquired much of his shipping fleet by backing the promissory notes on other vessels and then calling them in when their owners couldn't pay after a particularly bad season. I don't know that I'd go so far as to call that trading on other people's misfortune. Or their ignorance. It's a fairly sound and common business practice.'

'You have the black heart of a true merchant prince,

Marla,' Ruxton observed with a wink in Luciena's direction. 'No wonder Hythria does so well under your guidance.'

'It's probably the only reason I put up with you,' she responded tartly.

'She really is very fond of me,' Ruxton explained to Luciena. 'Really.'

Luciena smiled warily, unsettled by their bantering. 'I'm sure her highness is very fond of you, Master Tirstone,' she agreed, glancing out of the window. 'Gracious! Is that the city?'

Marla leaned out of the window and looked in the direction they were heading. As they topped the rise, the high granite walls of Krakandar came into view in the distance. Even from this far away, the city was an impressive sight and she smiled with relief at the thought that they were almost home.

'Yes, Luciena, that is Krakandar.'

'It's huge.'

'You were expecting something smaller, perhaps? Or something more primitive?'

'I don't know really,' the girl replied, obviously not sure what she had expected. 'Will it take us long to get there?'

'Less than an hour now,' Marla predicted, settling back into her seat. 'If the lookouts have spotted us, I imagine they're in a panic right about now, getting ready for our arrival.'

Luciena turned to look at Marla. 'Do you always get a big welcome home, your highness?'

'Always,' Marla replied confidently.

14

'Where are the children?' Marla asked, as she ascended the palace steps.

Orleon, Krakandar's faithful chief steward, stood alone on the landing of Krakandar Palace. There wasn't so much as a one-man guard of honour waiting for them.

'I believe they are on an excursion down in the fens, your highness,' Orleon explained with a bow. 'Good afternoon, Master Tirstone. Welcome back to Krakandar.'

'Good afternoon, Orleon,' Ruxton replied cheerfully, less bothered than Marla that there was nobody there to greet them. 'You're looking well.'

'Thank you, sir. I'm feeling quite well, too.'

'Excellent! Has there been any correspondence sent on ahead for me?'

The old man nodded. 'A messenger came for you yesterday, sir. He's most anxious for your arrival.'

'The fens?' Marla demanded, glancing at Ruxton in annoyance. At that moment, Ruxton's messenger could be bringing them news that Fardohnya was invading and she wouldn't have cared. 'What, in the name of all the Primal Gods, are they doing in the fens?'

'Some sort of educational excursion, I believe, your highness.'

'Where is Mahkas?'

'Lord and Lady Damaran are in the city, visiting Lady Damaran's father, your highness. He's been unwell of late. I sent a messenger to advise them of your pending arrival as soon as your retinue was sighted on the highway. I'm sure they'll be back soon.'

'And they just went off into the city and let the children go down into the fens unescorted?' Marla demanded, horrified to think of the danger they might be in. 'Where is Almodavar?'

'Captain Almodavar is on a border patrol in Medalon, your highness. But you needn't fear. Captain Harlen escorted the children on their excursion. And I don't think they were planning anything too strenuous. Lady Kalan and Lady Leila went with the boys. I can have someone sent down to the fens to fetch them. It won't take—'

'Don't bother, Orleon,' Marla cut in with a scowl. 'I think I'll fetch them myself.' She turned to her husband. 'Care to accompany me while I find out what those demon-spawn you and I so optimistically refer to as our children are up to in the fens?'

Ruxton shook his head with a smile. 'They're all yours, my dear. I'm a city boy at heart. All those midges and bogs and creepy-crawly things . . . no, I think I'll stay behind, find out what news my messenger brings, and see if my daughter is still speaking to me. Feel free to tan the hides of those boys of mine if they've been causing trouble, though.'

'Never fear, I will,' she promised, before turning to Luciena. 'I'm sorry about this. Orleon will see you settled into the palace. I won't be long.'

'Could I come with you, your highness?'

Marla looked at her in surprise. 'It's quite a walk.'

'I don't mind,' Luciena shrugged. 'And in truth, after three weeks in that carriage I could do with the exercise.'

Marla shrugged. 'As you wish.' She turned to Orleon again. 'If Mahkas returns while I'm gone, tell him where I am. And please make sure Luciena's rooms are ready when we get back. She'll want a bath by then, I'm sure.'

'Of course, your highness,' Orleon said with a bow, and then he snapped his fingers and several guards hurried across from the guard post on the gate and fell in behind them to accompany the princess and her stepdaughter into the fens.

Krakandar was a walled city, built in three concentric circles, the last and most recent ring having been completed only two years ago. Mahkas had proposed the plan to increase the size of the city not long after he became regent, and the construction had boosted Krakandar's prosperity as well as its aesthetic appearance. The only problem they had encountered during the construction of the outer wall was the area around the underground springs that fed Krakandar and provided the city with its water.

While it was a strategically sound move to enclose the city's water supply within the city walls, the ground around the springs was marshy and boggy and a breeding ground for insects, as well as home to hundreds of thousands of birds who thrived on the abundant food supply. The engineers had proposed numerous solutions about what to do with the area, which began with draining the bog entirely, and ended with one rather elaborate scheme to build a series of elevated aqueducts to carry the water throughout the city. Both solutions would have resulted in the starvation of the water birds and other creatures who called the fens their home, something Marla suspected was such an insult to Voden, the God of Green Life, that it would result in Krakandar being laid to waste.

In the end, they had compromised. Enough of the fens were drained to allow a firm foundation for the enclosing wall. A less elaborate network of aqueducts had been constructed to keep the drained area dry and to channel the water into the city's public wells, and the remaining area had been left in its natural state. It teemed with birdlife and all manner of insects, otters and amphibious creatures. Marla had suggested a series of paths be built through the pools to allow the citizens of Krakandar access to the fens and declared the whole area a water park. She had even had a special brick path constructed down from the palace, so there was a private entrance allowing any guest of the palace access to the fens without going the long way around through the city.

It had all seemed a wonderful notion, until the children discovered how much fun you could have in a place like that. Since the first day she had taken the children down to view the newly completed pathways through the fens, Marla had fretted about one of them falling into and drowning in an unexpectedly deep pond, or being taken by some previously unidentified creature lurking in the depths of a murky pool.

The gate to the fens was open as Marla, Luciena and their small escort approached, flung wide as if someone had opened it in a hurry and not thought to close it. A little concerned, Marla picked up the pace and hurried into the cool depths of the overhanging willows that bordered the fens. She was suddenly feeling ill, as a foreboding premonition washed over her.

Her fears solidified into a sick certainty as she heard shouts in the distance. She broke into a run, leaving Luciena and her escort behind, certain it was Kalan's voice she could hear crying out in desperation. The leaf-carpeted path was silent under her feet as she picked up her skirts and hurried towards the cries of pain, the shouts . . .

Marla rounded a small curve in the path and skidded to a halt, stunned by what she found. The path skirted a muddy bog, veering away to the left. Standing on the edge of the path were the twins, Kalan and Narvell, the two Tirstone boys, Rodja and Adham, and Raek Harlen, the Raider captain assigned to watch over her children. None of them saw her; they were too busy shouting encouragement to another pair of boys involved in a fistfight, right in the middle of the muddy bog.

Panting heavily, Marla took in the scene with disbelief. Luciena and the guards caught up just as Raek turned and then bowed hastily when he realised it was the princess who stood behind him.

'Your highness!'

'Captain Harlen.'

'I ... er ... we weren't expecting you for another few days.'

'That is abundantly clear.'

Raek glanced a little guiltily over his shoulder at the boys in the bog. Filtered sunlight streaked the muddy quagmire with bands of light that made it hard to tell one from the other. 'They're in no danger, your highness.'

'Then would it be too much to ask, Captain Harlen, what those boys are doing?'

'Settling a few differences,' the Raider replied, as one muddied combatant threw a wild punch at the other. They were covered in mud from head to toe. Marla couldn't tell them apart.

'What are they fighting about?'

'It's complicated, your highness.'

The boy on the left retaliated with a blow that slid straight off his slimy opponent. Marla grimaced as he overbalanced and slipped, landing on the other boy, taking him down with him. They both fell into the mud, which made thick sucking noises as they struggled to regain their footing. It was as if the ground was hungry and didn't want to let go of this unexpected bounty.

'Try me, Raek. I'm sure I can handle it.'

The tall Raider smiled. 'I believe it started when young Leila refused to traipse through the bog to see the tadpole pool Kalan found here the other day.'

'I see,' Marla replied, glaring at her daughter.

Kalan had just noticed her mother had arrived. She smiled nervously and took a step closer to her twin. Marla could almost see the cogs of her mischievous little mind turning over as she desperately tried to come up with an excuse for being in the fens at all, a place she knew was off limits without the strictest supervision.

'In the ensuing discussion about the merits of various amphibious life forms,' Raek continued in the same bland voice, 'the boys decided there was an urgent need to collect a number of samples for scientific research.'

'*Scientific* research?'

'You have to give them points for being inventive, your highness.'

'It still doesn't explain why they're fighting.'

'When Leila complained about going into the fens, Damin called his cousin a sissy. She got upset. Starros felt it necessary to come to her defence.'

Interesting, Marla thought. 'And where is Leila now?'

'She ran back to the palace in tears, your highness. I believe it was that which prompted Starros to reprimand your son. Things just sort of . . . degenerated from there.'

'Who's winning?'

'Starros has the upper hand at present, your highness, although if the fight goes on much longer, Damin will surely triumph. Starros is quick, but Damin has more stamina.'

Marla threw up her hands and turned to Luciena. 'This wasn't the introduction to your stepbrothers that I had in mind.'

The girl was obviously trying hard not to smile. 'I imagine it wasn't.'

'Which one is he, Raek?'

'The one on the right, your highness.'

Marla shook her head and sighed heavily. 'And during all of this, you never felt the need to intervene, Captain?'

'My orders are to see the children remain safe, your highness, not to fight their fights or make their decisions for them.'

She shook her head at the folly of all men. 'That sounds like something Almodavar would say.'

'It was Captain Almodavar who gave me my orders, your highness.'

And a good order it was, too, Marla conceded reluctantly. With vigilant bodyguards watching his every move, it would be easy to simply fall into the trap of always guiding Damin along the right path. Easy and dangerous. Damin had to learn to think for himself. There was just something fundamentally skewed about a captain of Krakandar's Guard standing back while his two charges slugged it out over a trip into the fens that they shouldn't have been allowed to make in the first place.

'I think it's time to put a stop to it, Captain.'

'Starros won't be pleased,' Raek remarked. 'He doesn't often get the better of Damin.'

'I'm sure he'll learn to live with the disappointment.'

Raek nodded and put his index fingers into the corners of his mouth and let out a whistle that almost pierced Marla's eardrums with its intensity. She instinctively covered her ears, but at the sound the boys immediately halted their fighting and looked up at where Raek Harlen waited with Marla and Luciena.

'Enough!' Raek shouted to them. 'Get up here.'

The mud-encrusted boy on the left took a step backwards and slipped, landing on his backside. One of the Tirstone boys giggled at the sight, but stifled it quickly as Raek gave him a warning glare over his shoulder. The boy's equally filthy companion, with whom he had been trading blows only moments before, helped him up and together they waded through the sucking black mud to the edge, then clambered up the slight embankment until they were only a few feet from Marla. Both boys had bloodied noses mixed in with the mud, but their eyes were bright and they were panting heavily from the exertion.

The boy on the left grinned, a line of white teeth appearing in the black crack of his mouth. He took a step closer, his arms wide. 'Mother! You're back!'

Marla glared at him. 'Don't you come one step nearer, Damin. You're disgusting!'

'Your highness.' Starros greeted her with a surprisingly courtly bow, given he appeared to have been freshly spat out of the earth after being buried alive.

'Starros.'

'It's not what it looks like, Mother—' Damin began.

'Get back to the palace,' Marla ordered stiffly. 'Both of you. I expect you in the dining room in one hour, looking like civilised human beings.'

'Yes, ma'am,' Damin replied. He grinned a little wider, nudged Starros and the two of them took off at a run, back through the fens.

Marla shook her head as she watched them leave. 'He's incorrigible.'

'Aye,' Raek agreed.

Marla looked at him askance.

'But there's not a man in Krakandar who wouldn't die for him, your highness,' he added.

'Is that so?' She turned her attention to Kalan, Narvell and her stepsons. They were all looking more than a little shamefaced. 'Rodja, Adham. I suggest you follow Damin's example. Your father is waiting for you at the palace.'

The boys fled wordlessly in the direction Damin and Starros had gone. The twins made to follow but Marla

143

caught them by the collars of their shirts. 'As for you two . . .'

'It wasn't my fault, Mama!' Kalan protested, trying to wriggle free. 'Narvell made me do it!'

'But I'm the youngest!' Narvell objected, looking up at his mother with a plaintive smile. 'And Lirena says I'm easily led.' Marla felt her heart constrict for a moment. He was so like Nash, sometimes it actually hurt to look at him.

'I expect you both in the dining room in one hour also,' she informed them sternly. Then to Kalan she added, 'Dressed in your own clothes, young lady. Not your brother's castoffs.'

'Yes, Mama,' Kalan replied with entirely false submission. Marla let it pass and released the twins, who bolted in the direction their brothers had gone.

Marla turned to discover Luciena trying very hard not to smile as she waved away a cloud of midges. 'You find this amusing, Luciena?'

'No, your highness,' she said hurriedly. 'What will you do to them?'

'Kill them, probably,' Marla announced flatly.

The young woman raised a brow curiously. 'After all the trouble you've gone to, protecting your children's lives?'

'I said I wouldn't risk another attack against Damin succeeding, Luciena,' she reminded her new stepdaughter grumpily as she picked up her skirts and headed back along the path. 'I never said I wouldn't be willing to do the job myself.'

There wasn't really anything Luciena could say to that. The young woman fell into step beside Marla and, with their escort, they made their way back through the clouds of midges to the palace.

15

Mahkas Damaran, Regent of Krakandar, was mortified when he realised Princess Marla had returned to the palace while he was in the city visiting his father-in-law. He was even more upset to learn that the children had been caught playing down in the fens, and positively distressed when he learned that Damin and Starros had got into a fistfight.

He was even more horrified to discover that his own daughter had been the cause of the fight.

'What were you thinking?' he demanded of Leila, as she tried to explain things to her mother. He had found her hiding in Bylinda's bedroom, where she had fled when she realised how angry her father was after he had spoken to Princess Marla. He grabbed his daughter by the shoulder and spun her round to face him.

Leila's eyes filled with tears at his rough handling.

'You knew your aunt was due any day! Why did you follow the others down into the fens? Marla found the boys fighting in a bog! Over you!'

'It's not my fault!' she sobbed, frightened by his tone. 'I said I didn't want to go. Damin called me a sissy. I didn't know Starros was going to fight him.'

Bylinda looked almost as distressed as Leila did. She rose

to her feet and stepped a little closer to Leila. 'Mahkas, it's hardly her fault if—'

'Of course it's her fault!' he snapped at his wife. He turned back to Leila and shook her impatiently by the shoulders. 'You should have done what Damin asked, Leila, and then none of this would have happened.'

'But I hate it down in the fens! It's full of bugs and creepy-crawly things. And we're not supposed to go there anyway.'

'It doesn't matter,' Mahkas insisted. 'You'll be Damin's wife one day and you'll have to do everything he says then. You might as well get used to it now.'

'But I don't want to marry Damin!' she cried defiantly. 'I hate him!'

Mahkas shook her again, even harder. 'Don't say that! Don't even think it!'

'But it's true,' she sobbed. 'I don't want to marry him. And he doesn't want to marry me, either.'

'How could you possibly know that?'

'I asked him.'

Mahkas let her go with a shove, afraid he might really harm his daughter if he allowed his anger to get out of control. 'You *asked* him?'

Leila nodded, sniffing inelegantly as she backed away from him, not stopping until she bumped into her mother. Once she felt she had Bylinda's protection, the child stared up at her father rebelliously. 'Damin said he'd rather marry a Fardohnyan than marry me. So I told him I'd rather marry a snake.'

Mahkas was speechless. He looked at Bylinda in despair, certain this was somehow her fault. His wife shrugged as she pulled Leila a little closer. 'They're children, Mahkas. Damin's at that stage where all girls are annoying. And Leila's only eleven. All boys are disgusting when you're eleven.'

'I notice she doesn't seem to mind the bastard foster-ling,' he noted sourly. 'It's just her future High Prince and husband she seems to have a problem with.'

'Starros was just sticking up for her,' Bylinda pointed out calmly. 'He's like that with all the children. You know that. I've seen you compliment him on it. And Damin *can* be a little inconsiderate when he wants his own way and doesn't get it.'

'But don't you see what this *looks* like?' he demanded of his wife. 'Don't you understand how it undermines us? I've been pressing the idea of Damin and Leila's marriage since the night she was born. It's what we've always dreamed of. Our daughter – High Princess of Hythria! And you know it's the only way I'll ever truly be Krakandar's Warlord. Not *Regent* of Krakandar, but Warlord.' He forced a smile and looked down at his daughter. 'Isn't that want *you* want, sweetheart?' he asked, reaching out to caress her face. The child jerked back from his touch. *I shouldn't have yelled at her*, he thought despairingly. *Now she hates me, too.*

'Damin is not even thirteen, Mahkas,' Bylinda reminded him. 'There's no need to worry about this now. And no need to shout at Leila about it, either.'

'But I have to protect what's hers,' he insisted. 'Don't you see that?'

'It will be years before Marla allows Damin to marry, and his bride will be whoever offers Hythria the best alliance,' she warned. 'That may not be Leila.'

'Leila can give him Krakandar.'

'He owns Krakandar now, my love,' Bylinda reminded him gently. 'He doesn't need Leila to gain possession of something he already has.'

'You're missing the point. I almost have Marla convinced there is no more suitable consort in all of Hythria. And then she comes home to find Damin and Starros fighting over the girl? What must she *think*?'

'She's probably thinking that they're only children,' Bylinda answered reasonably. 'This doesn't alter anything, Mahkas. Leila isn't to blame and you're frightening her with your yelling. You're frightening *me*, too.'

Mahkas took a deep breath to calm his rage. Bylinda was probably right; there was nothing to worry about. Marla wouldn't let a childish argument stand in the way of a sound political decision. Damin was going to be High Prince some day and he needed a consort he could trust. Who better than his own cousin, raised with him from birth, educated with no other function in mind than being the wife of a High Prince? Marla understood that.

And when Damin was finally crowned High Prince, he would have to relinquish Krakandar. There was no more logical contender for the position of Warlord when that happened than the beloved uncle who had administered his province so effectively all these years . . .

'I'm sorry,' he conceded. 'It's just I've worked so hard for this.'

'I understand,' Bylinda said. She bent over, kissed Leila on the top of her head and told her to run along. Still wiping away her tears, Leila bolted from the room, glaring at her father as she fled. Instinctively Mahkas rubbed at the sore spot on his forearm, as he always did when he was stressed. The tiny scar that bothered him was so small he couldn't even recall how he came by it. Some minor nick in the training yards, no doubt. But it itched abominably, for no apparent reason, particularly when he was worried about something.

Bylinda placed her hand over his to stop him scratching at it. 'Leave it alone, Mahkas. You've rubbed it raw.'

'I've worked so hard,' he repeated, as much to himself as to his wife. 'I've been a good regent, haven't I? Krakandar has never been more prosperous. I love Damin like a son. The gods know, you're more a mother to him than his own mother has been. I just can't bear the thought of losing it all, Bylinda. Not now. Not after all this time.'

Before his wife could reassure him, a knock sounded at the door Leila had left open in her haste to escape her father's wrath. Orleon stood in the doorway, his expression giving away nothing. Mahkas wasn't sure how much he'd overheard, or if, indeed, he'd overheard anything at all.

'What?' he demanded of the chief steward.

'Princess Marla requests your presence, my lord.'

'Did she say why?'

'No, my lord.'

Bylinda smiled at him encouragingly. 'Go to her. I'll see you at dinner.'

Mahkas nodded, wondering if Bylinda's faith in him was simply blind love or a genuine belief in the righteousness of his cause. 'I'll see you at dinner,' he agreed, and then he turned and followed Orleon, still rubbing at the sore spot on his arm.

Marla was in the study Mahkas normally called his own, sitting behind his carved wooden desk, reading a small scroll, the type easily concealed and carried on the person of a courier. Marla's most recent husband, Ruxton Tirstone, stood behind her, reading over her shoulder.

They both looked up as he entered. Marla smiled briefly and pointed to the scroll. 'We're in the wrong business, Mahkas. We should be traders. You wouldn't believe the information Ruxton manages to get hold of in the guise of selling spices.'

'Really? How fortunate for us.'

Mahkas didn't like Ruxton Tirstone. He was far too sure of himself for a common-born merchant. With growing concern, Mahkas had watched Marla become more and more at ease in his company over the past five years. She respected the trader's opinion and listened to it more often than Mahkas thought prudent. His distrust of the spice trader was prompted by jealousy as much as dislike.

Marla didn't seem to notice his sarcasm, though. 'Look at this,' she chuckled, holding up a list of some kind. 'Would you like to know the goings-on in the Sisterhood? This is a complete list of Sisters of the Blade's postings throughout Medalon this year.' She glanced over her shoulder at Ruxton, shaking her head in amazement. 'How did you get this?'

'Ah, now that would be telling.'

'I don't see how the goings-on in the Sisterhood concern us in the slightest,' Mahkas remarked, a little annoyed that Ruxton was providing Marla with something so worthless and she didn't seem to know it. Didn't she understand the most valuable ally she had was her own brother-in-law, her son's regent, his own flesh and blood? Not some common-born trader with no breeding and just enough money to buy himself a bit of respectability. It was almost obscene.

'It pays to keep an eye on them,' Ruxton suggested. 'Particularly the ambitious ones. Trayla won't always be First Sister, you know.'

'And *you* know who the ambitious ones are, I suppose?' Mahkas asked with a vaguely condescending smile.

'I'd watch out for that one, for starters,' Ruxton said, pointing to a name on the list.

'Who?' Mahkas couldn't see the name and he was sorry now that he'd pursued the subject. All he needed was Ruxton showing off his knowledge of the inner workings of every other government on the continent to convince Marla that her husband was indispensable.

'Joyhinia Tenragan,' Marla read. 'Who is she?'

'Someone worth watching. Very smart. Very ambitious. And as ruthless as Hablet, by all accounts. She already has a son supposedly fathered by the Lord Defender. She'll be on the Quorum some day, you mark my words.'

'It says here she's been posted to Testra since last winter.'

150

This conversation was starting to exclude Mahkas completely. It was time to put an end to it. Time to prove that he had his own sources of intelligence, every bit as good as Ruxton's.

'Hablet of Fardohnya has another daughter,' he announced.

The spice trader nodded his confirmation of the news. 'He's sired half a dozen bastard sons on his *court'esa* now, and another three or four baseborn daughters,' he added, proving yet again that his intelligence was better than anybody else's in the country. 'This latest one takes the legitimate daughters to seven, I think.'

Smart-arse, Mahkas said silently. 'Hablet won't be happy with another daughter,' he noted, trying to keep the conversation going in the direction he wanted.

Marla smiled thinly. 'No. I don't imagine he will. Speaking of daughters, did you have a word with Leila about this afternoon's little fracas in the fens?'

Mahkas swallowed hard before answering. 'Marla, I'm sure she didn't mean to be the cause of so much trouble . . .'

'I'm sure of it, too, Mahkas,' the princess replied. 'I hope you made it clear to her that she's not to feel responsible for the infantile behaviour of her cousins. I don't want the child feeling guilty because Damin and Starros were looking for an excuse to let off a bit of steam.'

His relief was palpable. 'Of course. I knew that. I told her not to worry about it.'

'Too much idle time on their hands,' Ruxton laughed. 'That's the problem with those boys. Still, I suppose once Elezaar starts to whip them into shape, they'll have more to do with their time than fight each other.'

'What's the dwarf got to do with it?' Mahkas asked with concern. He loathed Marla's deformed little pet and resented every moment he was forced to allow the *court'esa* under his roof.

'He's taking on the role of tutor until Damin leaves for his fosterage at the end of summer,' Marla explained. 'In the meantime, Ruxton's going to see if he can find a suitable replacement. I wouldn't mind getting hold of a Medalonian tutor, actually. Their women are better educated than any other tutors – male or female – on the continent. Particularly in the areas of government and economics.'

Mahkas smiled condescendingly. 'Surely you'd not consider allowing your sons to be taught by a woman, Marla?'

The princess leaned back in her chair and studied him curiously for a moment without saying anything.

Immediately, Mahkas realised his mistake. 'Of course, I don't mean to imply that a woman couldn't . . . I mean, it's not that I think . . .'

Ruxton laughed at Mahkas's stammering efforts to extricate himself from his blunder. 'You're going to have to work a lot harder to get out of that one, I fear, brother-in-law.' He touched Marla's shoulder in a gesture of familiarity that Mahkas found more than a little disturbing. She looked up at him with a smile. 'I'll leave that with you,' he told her. 'There's a paragraph a bit further down detailing how much Hablet's spending on the Temple of Jelanna in Talabar that might interest you. Particularly as he's planning to import the marble to reface the temple.' Ruxton straightened up then and walked around the desk, bowing politely to Mahkas on his way out. 'I trust you'll excuse me, Mahkas. I need to spend some time with my own children or they'll start thinking I really have abandoned them. We'll see you at dinner, I hope?'

'Of course,' Mahkas replied.

We'll see you at dinner, I hope? he repeated sarcastically to himself. *This is my home. Who does this damn trader think he is?*

Mahkas turned his attention back to Marla as Ruxton

152

let himself out, closing the door behind him. 'I didn't mean to offend you, Marla.'

'I know you didn't. And I know you're not that fond of Elezaar. But he's a very good teacher. I can vouch for that myself. And he knows the children. They won't be able to cause mischief with him the way they have with everyone else.'

'Perhaps you should think about getting rid of Starros,' he suggested.

'Why?'

'Well, he's obviously the ringleader. He is the eldest, after all. Perhaps without his disruptive influence—'

'I would have thought the situation quite the opposite. My spies tell me it's Starros who often curbs the excesses of the others. Even Damin bows to his foster-brother's wisdom on occasion. That's not a gift to throw away lightly.'

'You have *spies* in the palace?' Mahkas asked with alarm.

Marla laughed. 'It's a figure of speech, silly. And don't worry about Starros. I have plans for him.'

'You do?'

'Don't looked so worried, Mahkas. I just want him to continue his education while Damin's away. I may have need of that boy some time in the future.'

'I see,' he said carefully, wondering if now was a good time to broach the subject again about Damin and Leila. Marla seemed in a surprisingly good mood, given the circumstances of her arrival. 'And what of the others? Do you have plans for them?'

'Well, Rielle is marrying young Darvad soon, and Ruxton expects his boys to follow him into the spice trade. Luciena and I will soon come to an agreement about her inheritance, and I'm rather hoping she and Xanda hit it off, because that will solve the problem of whom she should marry rather neatly. Travin is the heir to his father's estate in Walsark and is doing quite well, according to your last

153

letter. Narvell is the heir to Elasapine, so there's not much doubt about his future. As for Kalan, well, she's young yet. I haven't really decided what to do with her. No doubt there's a match out there that will suit us strategically, if nothing else.'

'And Leila?'

'Leila is your child, Mahkas. I wouldn't presume to plan a future for her.'

He nodded his agreement. 'Of course. You know, however, that I believe she and Damin . . .'

Marla sighed. 'Yes, Mahkas, I know. And as I've told you before, even a betrothal is years away for Damin. He turns thirteen in a few weeks. I have to get him through the next two years after that first, before he even gets access to a *court'esa*. I'm not going to commit either Damin or Leila to a marriage they may not want when they get older.'

'Leila adores Damin, Marla. She speaks of little else.'

Marla smiled sympathetically. 'Then let's see how they feel about each other when they're old enough to understand what marriage is all about, shall we?'

'As you wish.'

Marla rose to her feet and rolled up the scroll from Ruxton's messenger. 'It really is very rude of me to march in here and take over this way. Why don't you take your seat, Mahkas? I'm sure you have lots to tell me about what's been happening over the past year.'

She obviously didn't want to talk any further on the subject, so Mahkas had little choice but to bow to her wishes. He took the seat Marla offered him, thinking at least she hadn't said no to the marriage and while ever that situation remained, there was hope that he would one day become Warlord of Krakandar in his own right and no longer be the regent for anybody.

16

The family gathered for dinner that evening, as they always did on Marla's first night home. Dispensing with a formal arrangement in the dining hall, Orleon had arranged the tables in a much smaller horseshoe shape so that everyone could see each other. With the princess and her husband, her brother-in-law, sister-in-law, and the various children belonging to all of them, the diners numbered more than a dozen.

Marla had deliberately seated Damin next to Luciena and had warned him – quite openly in Luciena's hearing – to be on his best behaviour. The young prince smiled at Luciena when he arrived at the table. She wasn't sure if it was because he had heeded his mother's warning and decided to do his best to make his new stepsister feel at ease, or if it was simply in his nature to do so.

'So, you're the new one, eh?' Damin enquired cheerfully, as he took his seat. 'Welcome to the lunatic asylum.'

Luciena studied the boy curiously, trying to detect if he was genuine in his welcome or mocking her somehow. After a moment, she bowed her head politely. 'Thank you, your highness.'

'You don't have to call me that. Nobody else does.'

Luciena looked at him in surprise. 'Really?'

'Well, the slaves do,' he shrugged. 'And some of the townsfolk. But nobody around here does. Mother says I'll get enough of that when I'm older.'

That was the last thing Luciena expected to hear. She glanced across the table to where Marla was talking to Mahkas as she took her place, smiled nervously and took a sip from her wineglass. Damin was also served wine, although his was watered down, as was the wine served to all the children. He was a good-looking boy, big for his age, with fair hair and blue eyes, as if the gods had conspired to grant Hythria a prince who looked the part, even if he'd yet to prove he could act it.

'Have you met everyone yet?' Damin asked, looking around the table.

Warm candlelight reflected off the silverware, and the low hum of conversation filled the room with a soft buzz as everyone was seated. Luciena looked around, shaking her head. 'There's so many of them.'

'Then allow me to introduce them,' Damin offered, as the first course was served. He leaned back a little as a slave ladled the clear meaty soup into his bowl and then picked up his spoon and pointed it at the other arm of the table. 'The one with the blond hair and the black eye at the very end over there is Starros,' he explained, as Luciena began to sip her soup. 'He's my foster-brother. Been in the palace since he was five. We all know he's Almodavar's bastard, but he'll never admit to it.'

'Who's Almodavar?'

'The senior captain of Krakandar's Raiders.'

'Isn't Starros the one you were fighting in the fens this afternoon?'

'What gave it away?' Damin laughed. He also bore a magnificent shiner, even more impressive than the one he'd given Starros.

'Just a hunch,' Luciena replied with a smile, relaxing a

little with the wine, the tasty soup and the generally convivial atmosphere of the room. Despite her reservations, she felt herself warming to the young prince. There was little artifice about him and no hint of arrogance she could detect. On the other hand, this conversation now meant her total contact with Damin Wolfblade amounted to about ten minutes. Hardly time to take the boy's measure. She indicated the dark-haired young man sitting next to Starros. 'The one next to him is Travin Taranger, isn't he, Xanda's brother?'

'That's right. He and Xanda are my cousins. Their mother was my father's sister, Darilyn. She died before I was born.'

'And the young woman next to him?'

'Rielle Tirstone. She's Ruxton's eldest. If you want to make friends with her, you'd better do it quickly. Mother's arranged for her to marry Darvad Vintner from Dylan Pass, so she's leaving soon for Izcomdar. The chap sitting next to her is Travin's brother, Xanda, but you already know him.'

'I met him in Greenharbour,' Luciena confirmed, eyeing the dark-haired young man speculatively. She liked Xanda and was sure he'd gone out of his way to ensure she was comfortable on the journey here. Feeling her gaze on him, Xanda glanced up from the conversation he was having with Rielle and winked at Luciena, before returning his attention to whatever it was Damin's stepsister was telling him. Afraid she was blushing, Luciena quickly turned back to Damin. 'Xanda came to my rescue, actually. He was very chivalrous in my hour of need.'

Damin laughed. 'Good to hear he's doing something useful in Greenharbour besides drinking all the taverns dry. The girl on the other side of him is my cousin, Leila. She's Mahkas and Bylinda's daughter.'

'The cause of the fight?'

'News gets around this place pretty quick, doesn't it?' Damin remarked. He seemed a little put out that it was already common knowledge he'd been fighting Starros over Leila.

'Are you sorry you fought your foster-brother?'

'No,' the boy replied with a sudden grin. 'I was just hoping that we could come up with something more interesting to brawl over than a stupid girl. I don't know why Starros sticks up for her all the time. She really is a sissy, you know.'

Luciena glanced at him warily, but offered no comment.

Sensing her disapproval, Damin added a little defensively, 'She only ever wants to do boring, girly things.'

'Perhaps that's because she's a girl?' his new stepsister suggested.

'Kalan's a girl and she'll try anything we do.'

'That probably makes Kalan the exception, your highness, not Leila.'

'I suppose,' Damin shrugged. 'And really, you don't have to keep calling me "your highness", Luciena. It sounds a bit odd, actually, coming from a member of the family, as it were.'

'You'll have to get used to it some day.'

'But not today.'

She smiled. 'Very well . . . *Damin*. Not today.'

'Good. Now that's settled, let's get back to the introductions.' He pointed with his spoon to the small, slender woman on the head table, her dark hair arranged carefully, her clothes more formal than anyone else's in the room. 'Sitting next to Leila is my Aunt Bylinda, Uncle Mahkas's wife and, according to my mother, the most patient woman in all of Hythria, because she puts up with us. Next to her is Krakandar's regent, my uncle, Mahkas Damaran.'

'I met him earlier, too.'

'He's all right,' Damin informed her as they watched his uncle drink the last of his soup. 'We can usually get anything we want out of him.' Then he added in a lower voice, 'He gets a little crazy sometimes and you don't want to cross him, 'cause he's a sore loser. Fortunately, he picks on the Medalonians and not us when he's in a bad mood, but he's a good administrator. Mother says Krakandar didn't do nearly as well in the past, even under the governance of the Sorcerers' Collective.'

'Then he must be very good,' Luciena agreed, wondering what the young prince meant by *a sore loser*.

'Well, the next two at the table you know already – my mother and Ruxton Tirstone.' He leaned back a little so that Luciena had a clear view. 'On this side we have my half-sister, Kalan, sitting next to Ruxton, and the boy next to me is Narvell, her twin brother.' He nudged Narvell in the ribs. 'Say hello to Luciena, Narvell.'

'Hello to Luciena, Narvell,' his brother said through a mouthful of bread, winking at Luciena.

Damin elbowed him a little harder and grinned. 'Idiot.'

'The twins don't look much alike,' Luciena remarked.

'Don't let that fool you,' he warned. 'They're like opposite sides of the same coin. Hurt one and you'll have the other down on you like a falling building before you can blink. Kalan's smaller, but she's older than Narvell by twenty minutes. She never lets him forget it, either.' He leaned forward and pointed to the two boys sitting on Luciena's right. 'Those two reprobates on the other side of you are Ruxton's sons, my stepbrothers, Rodja and Adham Tirstone.'

On hearing their names, the boys looked up from their soup. The younger boy, Adham, who was sitting next to Luciena, grinned at her and added in a loud voice, 'Don't believe a word he tells you, Luciena. Damin's full of sh—'

'Adham!' Ruxton cut in loudly before his son could complete the sentence. 'This is a dinner table, not a back-street tavern.'

'Sorry, sir.' Adham winked at Luciena and finished off his soup with a loud slurp.

'So, there you have it,' Damin announced. 'The entire clan.'

'And you don't mind living here in Krakandar? Even though your parents live in Greenharbour?' she asked, rather overwhelmed by them all. Raised an only child in an almost entirely female household, she was finding this dinner a little more than she'd bargained for. They were all so boisterous. So *loud*.

'You say that like it's a bad thing,' Adham laughed.

'Don't you miss your mother, Damin? And what about you, Adham? Don't you miss your father when he's away?'

'Not really,' Adham said after thinking it over for a moment. 'Anyway, this place is heaps more fun than our old place in Greenharbour.'

'We'll have to show you the slaveways while you're here,' Damin offered. 'Then you'll see what we mean.'

'The *what*?'

'The slaveways. They're the tunnels that connect all the rooms in the palace. I think the one in your room comes out next to the bookcase in the sitting room.'

Luciena felt thoroughly bemused by the idea. 'I have a secret tunnel in my room?'

Before Damin could answer, his mother tapped the side of her glass with her knife to call them all to attention. She rose to her feet and raised her glass in a toast. Nobody looked surprised. This had the feeling of a ritual; something done the first night she came home every year, Luciena thought.

'To Hythria and the High Prince!'

'To Hythria and the High Prince!' they all echoed dutifully, rising to their feet and raising their glasses.

Luciena sipped her wine and glanced at Damin. He was quite the opposite of what she'd been expecting. He seemed no more dangerous than poor Mankel, the kitchen boy she'd had to sell before Princess Marla paid her debts.

160

Marla raised her glass once more, and her voice softened as she glanced around the table. 'To my family!'

'To family!' they responded, much more enthusiastically.

A few moments later, Mahkas Damaran raised his glass in the direction of the princess, bowing to her respectfully. 'Welcome home, Marla.'

Everybody cheered as Mahkas proposed his toast, the words obviously another family ritual. Luciena sipped her wine, still feeling a little lost in her new surroundings. As she resumed her seat, the reality – and the magnitude – of Princess Marla's offer to adopt her began to sink in. For the first time, it occurred to her that if she wanted it, she could become part of this family.

Just as I imagined when I was nine, sitting on my father's lap as he explained how things would be different now he was marrying the princess . . . how he wouldn't be able to live in our house any more, but that was all right because soon I'd have brothers and sisters and be a princess, because Papa is marrying the High Prince's own sister . . .

Luciena caught herself daydreaming and took another good swallow of wine. *I must be careful,* she reminded herself sternly, while in the back of her mind a disturbing echo bounced around her thoughts, taunting her, tantalising her, as if there was something she had forgotten to do. It whispered to her like a lover coaxing her out from behind a screen to reveal her nakedness in the cold light of day.

Welcome to the family, it whispered. *Welcome to the family . . . welcome to the family . . .*

17

When Luciena finally retired for the evening, exhausted both mentally and physically by the ordeal of her first day in Krakandar, it was to find Aleesha poking into every nook and cranny of the impressive suite, ooh-ing and aah-ing over each new little thing she discovered.

The room Orleon had allocated Luciena was vast. Located on the second floor, it was decorated with a carefully chosen mix of expensive Fardohnyan silks and Hythrun tapestries, while the furniture had clearly been influenced by Krakandar's proximity to Medalon. It was dark and heavy, and there were padded leather sofas either side of the marble-faced fireplace rather than the more traditional low table and scattered cushions she was used to. Even the existence of the fireplace reminded Luciena that she was far from home. Nobody in Greenharbour had a fireplace, unless they were pretentious beyond words or so poor they were living in a one-roomed apartment where the lack of space meant they were forced to cook in the same room where they lived and slept.

'This place has internal plumbing!' Aleesha announced as Luciena sagged against the door, the day finally done.

She treated the slave to a weary smile. 'This is supposedly

one of the greatest palaces in Hythria, Aleesha, and all you've noticed is the plumbing?'

'Wait until you see the size of the bath,' the slave predicted. 'Then you'll understand why I'm so impressed. How was dinner?'

'Only marginally less trying than lunch.'

'They seem nice people, though,' Aleesha suggested cautiously.

Luciena glared at her slave in irritation. 'What happened to *let's get out of this while we still can*?'

Aleesha shrugged. 'I've had time to rethink my position.'

'Rethink *your* position? What about: *You hate these people? You don't belong with them*? What was the other one? Oh, that's right! Princess Marla's just inviting me along to get me out of the city so she can have me killed, wasn't it?'

'I may have been a little hasty . . .'

'You've sold out, you traitor,' Luciena accused, pushing off the door and heading across the sitting room to the bedroom. 'You have no moral fibre at all, Aleesha. A few weeks ago, you would have cheerfully had me working my debts off by lying underneath Ameel Parkesh. One glimpse of a gold-plated stopcock and now you're telling me to throw my lot in with the Wolfblades.'

She walked past her treacherous slave and the large four-poster bed and opened the door to what she guessed must be the bathroom. She stopped dead and gasped. The bathroom was built on the same scale as the rest of the suite and covered with tiny blue-glazed tiles. Rather than the usual geometric pattern Luciena would have expected, she was astonished to discover the golden figure of a kraken worked in mosaics into the floor, its sinuous body winding around the base of the bathtub, its scales highlighted in emerald and gold tiles.

And it wasn't a bathtub so much as a small pool.

'See!' Aleesha declared. 'Now tell me *that* isn't worth a little compromise?'

Luciena turned back to stare at the slave. 'You're hopeless!'

'Elezaar says this is called the Blue Room,' Aleesha explained. 'He says it's reserved for only the most important visitors to Krakandar.'

'The Blue Room, eh?' Luciena remarked, walking back into the bedroom. The curtains on the bed were blue Fardohnyan silk, as was the matching coverlet and the pillows. The rugs were a complementary shade of blue, worked in a diagonal pattern, and hanging from the base of the brass candle-holders set into the walls were blue crystal teardrops. 'I bet someone was up all night thinking up *that* name. What else did Elezaar tell you?'

'Just general stuff, really. You know . . . where things are, what the routine is here. I'll be sleeping in slaves' quarters in the other wing. If you need anything, you just have to pull this cord here,' she informed her mistress, indicating a plaited blue and gold cord hanging near the bed. 'It rings a bell in my room and, if I use the slave-ways, I can be here in a few minutes.'

Luciena looked at Aleesha in surprise. 'They showed you the secret tunnels?'

'I don't think they're much of a secret. Everybody uses them. Even the children, according to Lirena. Orleon did give me a rough map, though. Apparently, it's not hard to get lost in them and I don't think he wants me bursting in on Princess Marla by accident, clutching an overflowing chamber pot.'

'I'd be rather put out, too,' Luciena agreed. 'Particularly as this place has internal plumbing and therefore no need for chamber pots. Overflowing or otherwise. Who's Lirena?'

'The children's nurse. She and Veruca were showing me around while you were at dinner.'

'And who is Veruca?'

'The other nurse,' Aleesha explained. 'Although I think she's retired now. She looked after Xanda and Travin when they were small.'

Luciena frowned at Aleesha's familiarity. 'That's Lord and Lieutenant Taranger to you, my girl. I must say, you seem to be getting along rather well with the rest of the household, considering you've been here less than a day. Are you sure it's me they want to adopt and not you?'

Aleesha shrugged. 'They're a lot more . . . I don't know . . . It's like . . . well, they're not as snobbish as I was expecting, I suppose. Except Orleon. And they all seem to get along. At least they do below stairs. If it wasn't for the slaves wearing collars, it'd be hard to tell the free servants from the indentured ones. And I couldn't believe how helpful they were. Elezaar said it's because Princess Marla brought you here. It's like she's given you her seal of approval, so her slaves are honour-bound to do the same to me.'

'I have Princess Marla's seal of approval, do I?' she asked, flopping onto the bed. She was exhausted and the feather mattress welcomed her like the arms of a long-lost lover. Luciena sighed with relief for a moment and then pushed herself onto her elbows and looked at Aleesha. 'That's very big of her, particularly as I've yet to give her mine.'

'Did you meet the young prince?' the slave asked, kneeling down to help Luciena off with her shoes.

'Who? Damin Wolfblade? I sat next to him at dinner.'

That seemed to impress Aleesha no end. 'What's he like?'

Luciena shrugged. 'Like any other twelve-year-old boy, I suppose.'

'So you'll be staying then?'

'You say that like I have a choice, Aleesha.'

The slave stood up, holding Luciena's shoes. She smiled hesitantly. 'I think . . . maybe . . . you should think about doing what the princess wants.'

'Do you now?'

'This place isn't so bad, you know, Luciena. And it's a damn sight better than living on the streets in Greenharbour.'

'Really? Three weeks ago you were accusing me of betraying everything I believed in for even thinking of coming here.'

'I hadn't seen this place three weeks ago.'

Luciena shook her head. 'I swear, Aleesha, I've never seen *anybody* seduced by a bathtub before. Suppose Princess Marla wants me to marry some filthy old brute who'll beat me every night before dinner?'

'Can I check out the plumbing in his palace before I answer that?'

Luciena laughed and hurled a pillow at the slave. 'Get out of here, you wicked wretch!'

'Don't you want my help getting ready for bed?'

'I'm sure I can manage.'

'You didn't want a bath?'

'I'll have it in the morning,' she said. 'You're far too eager to get in there and start sloshing around in my bathtub as it is. I'm going to make you wait a while. Consider it punishment for being so impudent.'

Aleesha looked disappointed. 'Are you sure you want me to go?'

'Yes! Now leave me!'

The slave put the shoes down by the door and glanced around the room uncertainly.

'Out!'

'Good night, Luciena.'

'Good night, Aleesha.'

Luciena flopped back onto the bed and closed her eyes. Somewhere in the other room, she heard a sliding panel move and then snick closed as Aleesha let herself into the slaveways. The bed seemed to embrace Luciena, drawing her down into pleasant slumber, even though she was still dressed, the candles still burned brightly and she hadn't even let down her hair.

I wonder if my Uncle Warak ever got my letter, she wondered, suffering a moment of guilt for not sparing her Fardohnyan cousin a thought since leaving Greenharbour. She had written back before she left the city, explaining she had no money, but now Luciena was beginning to worry that she'd done the wrong thing. *Perhaps I should have told them to wait a little longer*. If she accepted Marla Wolfblade's offer, she wouldn't need to send money to help her cousin. She could send a whole damn ship for him. *If I accept her offer . . . If I marry the man she chooses for me . . . If I'm willing to swear allegiance to the Wolfblades . . .* The thoughts faded into oblivion as sleep overtook her.

Welcome to the family . . .

It was the last thing Luciena remembered until she woke some indeterminate time later to find a stranger leaning over her in the darkness, his hand over her mouth to stop her screaming.

'Don't be frightened!' a voice hissed in the darkness. 'It's only me!'

Luciena struggled to sit up and, somewhat to her surprise, the intruder let her. She blinked owlishly, her heart pounding. '*Xanda?*'

He grinned at her, his teeth white against the gloom. 'Sorry about waking you like that. It's just I wasn't sure how you'd react to being startled and in this place it doesn't pay to cry out in the middle of the night. Not unless you want every Raider in Krakandar swarming into your room, looking for assassins under the bed.'

'Wha— what are you doing here?'

'We're all going out onto the roof,' he whispered. 'I thought you might like to join us.'

'We? Who is *we*?'

'Me, Travin, Damin, Starros, Rielle, the Tirstone boys . . . it's kind of a tradition around here. Did you want to come?'

She looked around the darkened room, wondering what time it was. 'It's the middle of the night, Xanda.'

'Well, there's no fun doing this in daylight.'

Luciena rubbed her eyes, forcing herself awake. 'Is insanity a family trait, or just something you seem to be afflicted with?'

'I think it's something in the water here,' he replied with a grin. 'You coming or not?'

She hesitated for a moment and then nodded, wondering if he was right about there being something in the water that made one crazy in this place. It would explain why Aleesha had suddenly turned into a raving Royalist. And, possibly, why she allowed Xanda to lead her into the sitting room. He pushed on a raised part of the panelling near the fireplace and the wall slid open to reveal a torchlit tunnel beyond.

'The infamous slaveways, I presume?'

'Scared?'

'Should I be?'

'Not unless you don't like confined spaces.'

Glancing along the passage, Luciena took a step forward, then abruptly stopped, 'Wait! I have to get my shoes.' She ran into the bedroom, felt about in the darkness for her shoes and then hurried back into the sitting room, hopping the last few steps on her left foot as she pulled the right shoe on.

Xanda waited for her to finish and then smiled. 'All set?'

She nodded and let him take her hand and lead her into the passage.

Despite the mental image she'd developed of dank passages carved from living rock draped with age-old cobwebs and dripping with condensation, the slaveways were obviously well used. And they didn't have far to go. Their destination proved to be another sliding door only a few hundred paces from her room.

This door, however, was locked. Xanda reached above the lintel, produced a heavy key which he used to unlock the door, and then replaced the key before standing aside to let her through.

'This is Damin's room,' he explained in answer to her questioning look. 'Nobody leaves the slaveways entrance to his room unlocked.'

'But the key's right there on the lintel,' she pointed out. 'Anybody could pick it up.'

'Only if you know it's there.'

She shrugged, thinking there must be some sort of logic in there somewhere, and followed Xanda through the doorway. This one led into a large dressing room. Xanda closed the door, made sure it had locked behind them, and then took Luciena through into the bedroom beyond, which seemed about the same size as her room. The tall windows either side of the dresser were open and it was to one of these that they went. Xanda climbed through and then turned to help Luciena.

Maybe this is their plan, a little voice in her head whispered. *They're going to lure you out here and then toss you off the roof.*

'It's all right,' Xanda assured her. 'I won't let you fall.'

Welcome to the family.

She hesitated for a moment and then offered him her hand.

Unlike the flat-roofed architecture common in both Hythria and Fardohnya, the Krakandar palace showed the influence of its northern neighbours. The roof was sloped and tiled, and three storeys up, the view, even by starlight, was spectacular. The city lay before them, dotted with pinpoints of warm yellow light, stretching away to the horizon so that it was hard to tell where the buildings stopped and the stars began. Behind them, the windows stretched up tall and symmetrical, topped by a series of smaller arched dormer windows above and another level of sloped red tiles.

The vast palace roof reminded Luciena of a mountain range carved by some god with a love of sharp angles.

Sitting on the tiles a few feet from where they had emerged were Damin Wolfblade, the fosterling Starros, both of the Tirstone boys and their sister Rielle. The younger children, Leila, Kalan and Narvell, were nowhere in sight. Neither was Xanda's brother, Travin.

Damin glanced over his shoulder and grinned. 'See, she's one of us now,' he told the others with a soft laugh.

'What does he mean?' Luciena asked Xanda warily as he held her hand and pulled her through the window. She inched her way forward until she was near the others and then sat down, feeling much safer once her backside was in contact with the tiles.

'Once you've been out here on the roof, you betray us at your peril,' Xanda explained, sitting down beside her.

When it was clear Luciena didn't understand, Starros added over his shoulder, 'What he means is that Almodavar would kill us all with his bare hands if he caught us out here.'

'That's comforting.'

Rielle smiled at Luciena's obvious confusion. 'It's a

Krakandar thing, Luciena,' she explained. 'I remember being just as flummoxed when I first arrived. The logic works like this: Almodavar hates snitches even more than reckless fools, so if you told anyone we've been out on the roof he'd kill you first for telling, and then kill the rest of us for being here.'

'Doesn't *anybody* know about you coming out here?'

'It used to be a lot harder when there was a guard in my room,' Damin admitted. 'But we got very good at blackmail. You'd be amazed at what a Krakandar Raider is willing to turn a blind eye to if you've got reason to report him to Almodavar.'

'And for even the slightest infraction,' Rielle chuckled. 'We're not the only ones frightened by the idea of incurring the wrath of Geri Almodavar.'

Luciena looked around at them. 'And you all think this is perfectly reasonable?'

'Don't you?' Damin chuckled.

'Truthfully? I think you're all quite mad. What if someone fell? We must be sixty feet off the ground here, probably more.'

'Nobody's fallen yet,' Adham assured her.

'*Yet* being the operative word,' Rodja pointed out. 'I'm with you, Luciena. This is utter insanity. I tell them that every time we come out here.'

'Then why do you do it?' Adham asked his brother curiously.

Rodja grinned. 'Because, secretly, I hope we *do* get caught out here. I want to see the look on Mahkas Damaran's face when he realises his precious heir to the Hythrun throne has been dangling off the palace roof.'

'Precious heir, eh?' Damin said. 'I'll remember that tomorrow morning in the training yards, Rodja Tirstone. When we're both armed.'

'You're on!' Rodja agreed. 'And you won't get to lay a

finger on me this time, your *highness*. I've been working on a new tactic.'

'It's called running away and hiding,' Adham announced loudly, which reduced the rest of them to fits of laughter.

'Keep it down!' another voice hissed loudly from the window. 'I can damn near hear you in the hall!'

Luciena turned to find Travin Taranger climbing through the window to join them. Under his left arm, he carried something that looked suspiciously like a wineskin.

Wonderful! she thought in alarm. *Let's sit on the palace roof, sixty feet off the ground, against the express orders of Krakandar's senior captain, and then add alcohol to the mix. What a brilliant idea!*

Travin walked across the sloped tiles as if he'd done it all his life, which was probably the case, Luciena decided. Travin and Xanda had been raised here in the palace and, like the toasts at dinner earlier this evening, this illicit gathering on the roof reeked of something so sacred it was almost a ritual in itself. Travin sat down on the other side of Luciena and offered her the wineskin.

'Ladies first?'

She accepted it warily. As she took her first gulp of the sweet berry wine, she wondered if perhaps she should have heeded Aleesha's advice in Greenharbour, because at that moment, fighting off Ameel Parkesh might have been marginally less dangerous than her current predicament.

It was the early hours of the morning before Xanda led Luciena back through the slaveways to her room. By then the wineskin was empty and she was more than a little drunk. Had it not been for Xanda's sure-footed aid, she was certain she would have plunged to her death when she tried to stand up and return to the palace through the open window in Damin's room. The others seemed unaffected by either the dizzying heights or the potent wine. Perhaps it was just that they had more experience with both.

They reached the entrance to her room and Xanda slid it open for her, then blocked the way with his arm. 'Will you be all right, Luciena?'

She nodded unsteadily. 'I'll be fine.'

'Sure you don't want me to help you into bed?'

Luciena stared at him in shock. She wasn't *that* drunk. 'I beg your pardon?'

He smiled. 'I thought you might need rescuing again.'

'I didn't actually ask you to rescue me the first time,' she reminded him, acutely aware of how close he was. 'That was my slave, remember?'

'You didn't exactly refuse my help, though.'

His lips were only inches from hers, his breath smelled of the sweet berry wine and Luciena's head was spinning. *Oh gods! He's going to kiss me!*

She couldn't understand why the thought panicked her as much as it did. Luciena wasn't an innocent. Her mother had made certain of that. Although she'd had to sell her *court'esa* along with the rest of her slaves, Luciena knew exactly what was going on here. *Just let him do it and then he'll go away*, she told herself. But another voice in her head chimed in, Princess Marla's. *'Don't get any ideas about my nephew.'*

Her fear of Marla Wolfblade's wrath proved enough to give her the strength to resist. At the last moment, Luciena turned her face away. Xanda hesitated uncertainly, obviously wondering what he'd done to offend her.

'I'm sorry, Xanda,' she told him softly, with genuine regret. 'It's just . . .'

'Let me guess. My aunt warned you away from me?' he asked with a faint smile.

'How did you know?'

'Because she warned me away from you, too.'

That almost shocked Luciena back into sobriety. 'You're kidding! What did she say?'

'I believe her exact words were: "I know she's young, rich and you think she's very pretty, Xanda, but we will find a suitable wife for you when the time comes. Don't presume to think your uncle or I will allow you to make such a decision for yourself."'

Xanda thinks I'm pretty?

'That's what she said to me. Almost word for word.'

'She might have been joking,' Xanda suggested, obviously not willing to give up without a fight.

'I've seen her joking face, Xanda. That wasn't it.'

Xanda sighed with resignation as he lifted a stray strand of dark hair from her face. 'Then I suppose this is good night?'

'I'm afraid so.'

'I'm not scared of my aunt, you know.'

'I am.'

He smiled ruefully. 'I'll see you in the morning?'

She nodded, suddenly not trusting herself to speak.

This time, when Xanda bent his head to kiss her, he didn't give her time to pull away. He pulled her close and kissed her until she was breathless and then fled without another word, leaving her alone in the torchlit slaveways, gasping.

It took a moment to get over the shock, but as soon as she was able to gather her wits, Luciena slammed the door in the panelling shut and hurried into the bedroom. She threw herself onto the bed, her head spinning, her heart thumping, her whole world suddenly turned on its ear. Desperately, she pulled one of the big fluffy pillows down over her head to drown out the cacophony of confusing emotions that swirled through her mind, wishing she had never left Greenharbour. Wishing she had never heard of the Wolfblades.

Wishing she'd invited Xanda to stay and to hell with Marla Wolfblade.

Welcome to the family.

Luciena fell asleep with that thought uppermost in her mind and didn't move again until the sound of Aleesha running her bath woke her the following morning.

18

The demon, Elarnymire, seemed to come and go as she pleased. Sometimes she waddled along beside Rory for hours. Other times, he didn't see her for days.

As a guardian, the demon left a great deal to be desired. Although she claimed to be watching over him, her help was sporadic and unreliable at best. She'd warned him it was too dangerous to enter Acarnipoor, but a week later let him spend a whole night shivering and miserable in the lee of a narrow cliff when a particularly savage storm hit just before sunset one evening and he couldn't find any other shelter. She'd appeared out of nowhere one morning and made him hide until a company of soldiers had ridden past, and then a few days later let him walk right into a whole company of guards from the Winter Palace in Qorinipor. He'd had to run for his life when one of them recognised him, and had been forced to hide in the long reeds on the edge of the lake for days, cold, wet and terrified. It was only after he finally emerged from his hiding place, faint with hunger and covered in insect bites, that the demon appeared again.

'I thought you said you were helping me?' Rory demanded of the creature when she popped up without warning on the road in front of him. He was dripping wet and shivering in the thin mountain air as the sun rapidly sank below the horizon, wondering where he was going to find food and shelter. He was used to being hungry, but born and bred in the humid warmth of Talabar, this lonely, frightening trek across Fardohnya to the dubious safety of Hythria was the first time in his life Rory had truly been cold.

'I said I was keeping an eye on you,' she corrected loftily. 'That's not the same thing.'

'You let me walk straight into those soldiers!'

'Don't be such a crybaby,' Elarnymire shrugged. 'You're alive, aren't you?'

'Who *sent* you?' he asked for the hundredth time, as the demon turned and began to waddle away from him down the road. 'You said you'd tell me!'

'I said I *might* tell you,' the demon replied.

'Was it my cousin?'

The demon shrugged without looking back. 'I don't know. Who's your cousin?'

'Her name is Luciena Mariner. She lives in Greenharbour.'

The demon stopped abruptly and turned to look at Rory in surprise. 'Your cousin is Luciena *Mariner*?'

'Yes!' he exclaimed excitedly, running to catch up. 'Do you know her?'

'Of course not, I was just asking, that's all.' The demon turned and walked on, leaving Rory white-knuckled with frustration. A few moments later, when she realised Rory wasn't following, Elarnymire stopped and turned to look at him. 'You coming, or are you just going to stand there dripping?'

'Why do you *do* that?' Rory was choking back tears, the fear, the cold, the gnawing hunger and the loneliness of his long journey finally catching up with him.

'Do what?' Elarnymire asked innocently.

'Torment me like that?' He wiped away a stray tear,

determined not to let the creature see him bawling like a baby.

'I'm a demon.'

'That's a terrible excuse.'

'Not where I come from.'

Rory wanted to scream at her. He wanted to cry. He wanted this to be over. He wanted to be home again with his father and his brothers and his grandpa. He'd been hungry all the time then, too, but at least he hadn't been alone.

The demon, perhaps sensing his distress, waddled back to him and reached up for his hand. She smiled, her liquid black eyes full of compassion. 'I really was sent to keep an eye on you, Rory, son of Drendik, but I can't tell you who sent me because you weren't even supposed to know I'm here. I've stopped you walking into the traps you had no hope of escaping, that's all. Anything you were likely to survive, I had to let happen.'

'But why won't you tell me who sent you?'

'Because it's a secret.'

It was like arguing with a post, Rory decided angrily. He snatched his hand from the demon's gentle grasp and crossed his arms defensively. 'All right then, keep your stupid secrets. Just tell me one thing. Are you supposed to let me starve to death?'

'Not if I can help it. Why do you ask?'

'I haven't eaten anything for three days.'

'Ah,' the demon said. 'Then I suppose we should find you something to eat.'

'Don't put yourself out on *my* account.'

Inexplicably, the demon laughed. 'I can't wait till we get to Westbrook and you meet . . . my friend.'

Rory stared at the demon. 'Is that where we're going? Westbrook?'

'If you're planning to get to Hythria on this road, my lad, there's no other place you *can* go.'

'And this person who sent you? He'll be waiting for us there?'

The demon was silent for a moment. She closed her eyes and then opened them and nodded. 'More likely we'll have to wait for him. As usual, he's running late.'

'So it's a man then, this person? Not a woman?' That was *something*. He'd not been able to get even that much out of the little demon before now.

'Yes, he's a man. Sort of. And that's all I'm going to tell you. If you keep questioning me, boy, I'll leave you to find your own food.'

Rory nodded and fell in beside the demon, his shivering abating a little as his clothes began to dry. Maybe he wasn't really alone. Elarnymire would help him find something to eat and apparently someone was coming to meet him in Westbrook. Maybe things were starting to look up for the first time since that anvil had burst through the tannery wall in Talabar.

When Rory finally reached Westbrook just over a week later, he stopped on the steep road and stared at the massive fortress with a deep sense of foreboding. The tall stone walls stood higher than he'd thought it possible to build and the twin castles flanked the road on either side like massive sentinels, ensuring nobody passed this way without the border guards knowing about it. It was really cold, too, this high in the mountains, and although it was officially summer, there were still patches of snow hiding in sheltered alcoves and nooks speckled across the slopes.

'Welcome to Westbrook.'

Rory looked down at the demon. He hadn't seen her for two days. 'Where have you been?'

'Around.'

'Am I supposed to meet your friend now?'

179

'In Westbrook?' the demon asked. 'Not yet. My friend is still a couple of weeks away.'

Rory looked down at the demon in despair. 'A couple of *weeks*? I can't hang around a place like Westbrook for a couple of weeks!'

'Why not?'

''Cause it's full of soldiers, for one thing,' he pointed out. 'And there's a price on my head. My description's been sent to every outpost in Fardohnya. And even if they don't recognise me on sight, where do I stay? What do I eat? I don't have any money. Even if I could hide in the stables or a loft somewhere, that place is too small not to notice someone thieving on a regular basis. Then I'll get caught, and thrown into gaol, and they'll realise who I am and I'm right back where I started.'

'Actually,' the demon mused, 'to be right back where you started, you'd have to return to Talabar.'

'You know what I mean.'

The demon was silent for a moment, and then she looked up at him curiously. 'What will happen if you're arrested?'

'I'll get thrown in gaol until they can send me back to Talabar so I can be hanged for murder.'

'And while you're in gaol, they'll feed you, yes? And you'll be out of the cold? With a roof over your head?'

Rory stared at the demon in shock. 'Are you crazy?'

'Think of it as free board and lodging. My . . . *friend* . . . can arrange your release when he gets here in a couple of weeks.'

'Suppose they don't throw me in gaol? Suppose they put me on the next wagon for Talabar and it leaves this afternoon?'

'I can arrange a delay, if the need arises. I'm here to help, remember?'

'I thought you were just supposed to keep an eye on me?'

'Don't argue semantics with me, boy.'

Rory shook his head, thinking this the most insane idea he'd ever heard. If the demon was wrong, far from saving his life, he might be marching willingly to his own hanging. The Plenipotentiary of Westbrook might decide to hold his trial immediately. By the time Elarnymire's mysterious friend arrived, Rory might be swinging from a gallows, his eyes picked clean by the ravens.

On the other hand, he had no way of hiding in Westbrook for more than a few days without being discovered, so maybe it wasn't such a crazy idea after all.

'Elarnymire, you said you only helped me out of the traps I couldn't escape, didn't you?'

'Yes.'

'So if you're telling me I can risk getting arrested here, that means I won't be hanged, doesn't it? That I'll escape?'

'Theoretically.'

'Theoretically?'

'I'm a demon, Rory, not a fortune-teller.'

The boy looked down at the demon and then back up the road to the forbidding twin castles of Westbrook, paralysed with indecision. If he listened to the demon he would definitely be arrested and possibly killed. If he didn't . . .

Well, that's just it, Rory realised. *The result is likely to be the same whether I surrender willingly or not.* The only difference, he mused, was that if he gave himself up he might avoid a beating when they caught him, which, Rory had observed, was the way soldiers tended to let you know you were under arrest. He sighed heavily, shivering as the cold wind tugged at his thin shirt. Even if it wasn't warm in the dungeons of Westbrook, at least he'd be out of the wind. And prison food was better than no food at all.

'If they kill me in there,' Rory informed the demon grumpily, 'I'm going to be really mad at you.'

'You won't be the only one,' the demon assured him.

Rory hesitated for a moment longer, and then, shaking

his head at the folly of what he was about to do, he set off towards Westbrook with a demon at his heels, mentally rehearsing what he was going to say to the guards on the gate when he surrendered.

19

Wrayan Lightfinger, the head of the Krakandar Thieves' Guild, received a summons to attend the palace some ten days after Princess Marla returned to the city.

The palace messenger arrived midmorning at his rooms on the third floor of the Pickpocket's Retreat and had to bang loudly on the door for quite some time before he woke. Wrayan didn't appreciate being disturbed when the sun was barely over the outer wall of the city. He didn't sleep often, but when he did, everyone in the Retreat knew he slept late. He was head of a guild that conducted most of its business in the hours of darkness. His working day began at sunset and finished at sunrise.

Wrayan forced his eyes open, threw back the covers, noted with interest that he was not alone, and staggered sleepily to the door, trying to recall the name of the girl in the bed. Fyora. He remembered now. She was a working *court'esa* who lived at the Pickpocket's Retreat. She'd been flirting with him for months. Last night, Wrayan recalled as he jerked the door open in annoyance, for no reason he could readily explain he'd decided to take her up on her offer.

'What?' he growled.

The young man who had been so rudely banging on

his door took a startled step backwards. He wore high polished boots and a green tunic embroidered with a kraken over his heart.

A palace lackey, then.

Quite naked and not the least bit shy about it, Wrayan glared at the lad.

'Are you Wrayan Lightfinger?' the lad asked, his brown eyes fixed firmly on Wrayan's face to avoid looking anywhere more embarrassing. He was blushing, Wrayan noted with amusement. And completely out of his depth down here in the Beggars' Quarter among all these thieves and whores.

'Who wants to know?'

'I have a message for you . . . him.'

'From who?'

'From *whom*,' the young messenger corrected, covering his nervousness with an air of superiority. 'Are you Wrayan Lightfinger or not?'

'Yes. I'm Wrayan Lightfinger.'

'Then I am pleased to announce that Her Royal Highness, the Princess Marla of Hythria, mother of the High Prince's heir, Lady of—'

'I know who she is, fool. Get to the point.'

The lad looked put out that he'd not been given a chance to complete the princess's impressive list of titles. 'As you wish, Master Lightfinger. Princess Marla requests that you attend her at the palace for lunch.'

'Does she now?'

'Am I able to tell Her Royal Highness that you accept her invitation?' It was clear the young man did not approve of the princess consorting with a known criminal. *The lower the servant the bigger the snob.* Brak was fond of that expression.

'I don't know. Are you?'

'What? I mean . . . well, yes . . . I'm able, it's just . . . I . . .

I mean, do you accept her invitation?' the lad stammered impatiently.

'Yes,' Wrayan informed him, just as impatiently. 'I accept. Was that all?'

'Yes.'

'Good.' Wrayan slammed the door shut before the young man could add anything further.

On the bed, Fyora was stirring, her dark hair spilling over the pillows. She was in her early twenties, still pretty, still relatively new to her profession. She had trained as a *court'esa* for a time, but didn't have that special 'something' that made her *court'esa* material. She'd been bought from the slave markets by Hary Fingle, the owner of the Pickpocket's Retreat, who had offered her the chance to buy back her freedom by working as a whore and a tavern wench for ten years. It didn't seem long when you were young and hopeful, Wrayan knew, but ten years as a working *court'esa* was a lifetime, and the chances were good that she'd be dead long before her tenure was over, given the dangerous life she led.

Still, if she'd had the brains to understand *that*, she would have been smart enough to make it as a *court'esa* and would currently be living in the lap of luxury, a pampered pet of some wealthy lord, not working the taverns of the Beggars' Quarter.

Wrayan was quite certain Fyora's attraction to him was prompted by who he was rather than by any real affection for him. He was a powerful figure in Krakandar's underworld. He might not be a nobleman, but in the Beggars' Quarter, he was the next best thing. The worst of it, Wrayan realised as he crossed the room, was that the owner of the Pickpocket's Retreat would probably bill him for her services, even though last night had technically been her night off and she was free to sleep with whomever she chose.

And Fyora had tried so hard to please him. He could

have asked anything of her and he suspected she would have willingly complied. Fyora might not be the brightest jewel in Krakandar's crown but she was smart enough to understand how much security she would gain as the mistress of the head of the Thieves' Guild and she was willing to do just about anything to get it.

But it wasn't going to happen. Not with Fyora. Not with any human woman. Brakandaran had warned him about this. She might be pretty and well trained, but Fyora was just another woman in a very long line of women who simply didn't measure up to Wrayan's impossible standards. The problem was his, not the women he took to his bed. He knew that. It just didn't make any difference.

Wrayan had slept with a Harshini princess. No mortal woman could compare to that experience, no matter how hard she tried. No other human alive could appreciate what it felt like.

Fyora stretched languidly and held out her arms to him. 'Come back to bed, lover.'

Wrayan shook his head and walked to the washstand instead. He splashed his face with the tepid water in the bowl and reached for the towel, wiping his face dry before he turned to look at her. Fortunately, he was in the habit of bathing and shaving before he slept, so he'd get away with not shaving again before he left.

'I can't, Fee. I have to go to the palace for lunch.'

Fyora glared at him and angrily threw back the covers. She climbed out of bed and began to hunt around for her clothes, obviously furious. Wrayan looked at her in astonishment. He didn't think he'd said anything to warrant such a reaction.

'Do you have some sort of problem with me having lunch?' he enquired with a puzzled look.

'I have a problem with being treated like a fool,' she snapped as she retrieved her shift from the floor.

Wrayan was quite wounded by the accusation. 'What did I say?'

'If you don't want me here any longer, you just have to say so, Wrayan Lightfinger. You don't have to lie to me.' She pulled the shift over her head and then dropped to her hands and knees, looking under the bed for her shoes.

'I didn't say anything about not wanting you.'

'Of course not,' Fyora retorted, looking up at him from her hands and knees. *'I'm having lunch at the palace,'* she mimicked sarcastically. 'You must think I'm even more stupid than most women you sleep with.'

'But I really *am* having lunch at the palace,' he protested.

'Lord Damaran needs your counsel, I suppose?' she asked, still hunting under the bed for her lost shoe. 'Or maybe it's Princess Marla who needs the advice of the great Wrayan Lightfinger. I heard she arrived back in the city last week.' Fyora had found one of her shoes and slipped it onto her foot.

'I've known the princess for a long time, Fee.'

She found the other shoe and hurled it at him, then angrily scrambled to her feet, limping to the door with one bare foot.

Wrayan had caught the flying shoe by reflex and was still trying to fathom her remarkable mood change, as Fyora jerked the door open and turned to him for one last parting shot. 'You're lying scum, Wrayan Lightfinger!'

Now that was just going too far.

Without warning, the doorknob slipped out of Fyora's hand and the frame rattled as the door slammed shut. She jumped away from it with a squeal of fright and turned to stare at him.

Then she screamed.

'Oh, for the gods' sake!' Wrayan cursed as he realised the small amount of magic he had drawn to slam the door was still enough to make his eyes darken. He crossed the room in three strides and pushed her up against the door with his hand over her mouth, stifling her screams. Wrayan wasn't sure what the rest of the residents of the Pickpocket's Retreat would make of the racket coming from his room. He was hoping, given the clientele who frequented the place, that most of the other guests would simply turn a deaf ear to the noise.

'Stop it!' he ordered impatiently, holding her against the door by force. Fyora's eyes were wide with fear. 'I'm not going to hurt you!'

After a moment, he felt her relax and he took his hand from her mouth. She stared at him in a wordless mixture of awe and terror. Wrayan let go of the power and knew his eyes were slowly returning to their normal colour. He cursed his own stupidity. Normally, he wasn't nearly so careless.

'I'm sorry,' he said, as gently as he could. He really liked Fyora. She didn't deserve to be tossed aside like a cast-off cloak. He decided to let her down as gently as he could. It was a wise decision for more than the obvious reason. Fyora worked here in the Pickpocket's Retreat, where Wrayan did much of his business and ate most of his meals. She had plenty of opportunity to get back at him if she decided he'd broken her heart. 'I didn't mean to frighten you like that. But I don't deserve to have you chucking things at me, either. I'm not trying to get rid of you. I really *do* have to attend the palace for lunch. I honour the God of Thieves, not Liars. And if you don't believe me, you can ask him yourself.'

'But how did you . . .'

'I used to be an apprentice at the Sorcerers' Collective.' He smiled, hoping to reassure her. She was looking at him as if he'd suddenly sprouted horns. 'Don't you listen to all the gossip about me?'

She searched his face, still trying to figure out if he was

telling the truth or perhaps preparing her for another round of torment. 'I . . . I thought it was just some story *you* spread about to make yourself sound mysterious.'

He smiled at her reassuringly. 'Well, now you know.'

'But your eyes . . . what *are* you, Wrayan?'

He smiled cryptically. 'Late, if I don't get dressed.'

He kissed her lightly and then let her go and turned to the chest at the foot of his bed, thinking this was an occasion for more formal attire than he usually wore. Princess Marla probably wouldn't care if he turned up wearing a sack, but Orleon was a stickler for rules of protocol. Still leaning against the door, Fyora watched him cautiously as he laid out his clothes.

'You really *are* going to the palace,' she said, when she saw the finery he dragged up from the bottom of the trunk.

'I thought we'd established that,' he remarked without looking at her. His boots were a little scuffed, but they would have to do. There was no time to get them polished to a parade-ground gleam. Lunch at the palace waited on no man. It would take him a good hour to get to the palace as it was, even if he rode, given the midday bustle of the city.

Fyora pushed off the door and came to sit on the bed beside him as he began to pull on his trousers. 'I'm sorry.'

'For what?'

'For doubting you.'

'You don't have to apologise,' he assured her. 'I suppose it is a little strange to think someone like me would get invited to the palace.'

'Do you really know the princess?'

'Yes.'

'Have you met her children?'

'Of course.'

'I've seen them. Just from a distance, mind you. At the races last spring. They were with Lord Damaran and Lord Bearbow in the stands.'

'I know. I saw them there, too.'

'He's a good-looking boy.'

'Who?'

'The High Prince's heir.'

'Damin?' Wrayan pulled on his shirt and stood up so he could tuck it in. 'I hadn't noticed.'

Her eyes narrowed suspiciously. 'What's he *really* like?' The question sounded more like a test than asking for his opinion.

Wrayan shrugged. 'He's smart enough, I suppose. And he can fight like a Raider. But then, anyone who's had Geri Almodavar teaching them how to fight since before they could walk ought to be good. He can be a bit precocious at times, but he seems to be a good lad at heart.'

Fyora shook her head in wonder. 'You really *do* know the royal family, don't you?'

He smiled. It took a while for things to sink in with Fyora sometimes. 'Yes, Fee. I really do know them.'

'Do you think . . .' she began hesitantly. 'Well, I mean, do you think there might come a time . . . you know . . . when you could introduce *me*?'

Wrayan had to forcibly stop himself from laughing aloud at the thought of presenting Fyora to Princess Marla. Fortunately, he was pulling on his boots, so Fyora didn't see the expression on his face. 'I don't think so, Fee.'

'Oh.' She sounded so disappointed, Wrayan almost felt sorry for her.

'Tell you what, though,' he offered, to ease her disappointment, as he stamped his feet into his riding boots. 'I know a Harshini lord who'd love to meet you.'

She sighed impatiently. 'The Harshini are all gone, Wrayan. Everyone knows that.'

'I know one that's still about,' he said, reaching for his jacket. It was dark blue, embroidered with silver knot-work on the cuffs, and the high collar was inlaid with velvet.

The only place he'd be seen dead wearing it was at the palace. Strutting about in such finery around the Beggars' Quarter was asking for trouble.

Fyora rolled her eyes at him sceptically. 'You really do think I'm stupid, don't you?'

'I'm serious! He pops in here every now and then to visit me. Who do you think taught me that trick with the door, Fee?'

She thought about that for a moment and then a slow smile crept over her face. 'A *real* Harshini lord?'

'He's a *real* Harshini lord. And I promise the next time he visits Krakandar, I'll arrange for you to meet him.'

She considered his offer for a time and then nodded. 'You *really* promise?'

'On my honour as a thief.'

His oath was good enough for her. She picked up her other shoe from the bed, stood up, reached up on her toes and kissed him soundly and then let herself out of the room, her broken heart apparently mended, her fears allayed, by the prospect of meeting a real Harshini lord.

'Brak is gonna kill me,' Wrayan muttered to himself as he watched her leave.

Still, it was highly unlikely that he'd ever have to keep that promise. It was five years since he'd seen Brakandaran the Halfbreed and he thought it might be another ten before the Halfbreed felt the need to wander through Krakandar again.

20

A groom hurried out to take Wrayan's horse as he dismounted in the broad paved plaza in front of Krakandar Palace. It was a warm day, although a little cloudy. A crisp breeze sent scudding shadows over the plaza, making the pennons on the palace roof snap loudly. Not surprisingly, Princess Marla's personal pennon stood out in the stiff breeze from the centre pole, indicating she was in residence. He'd only put one foot on the bottom step before Orleon appeared on the landing, as if by magic, with a faintly disapproving sneer.

'Master Lightfinger.'

'Orleon, my old friend!' Wrayan replied cheerfully. 'You're looking well.'

The chief steward frowned. 'As are you, Master Lightfinger. Business must be thriving in the seedy underworld of the criminal element.'

'Never been better,' Wrayan agreed, climbing the steps until he was face to face with the old man. 'Nice pendant, by the way,' he teased, eyeing the steward's heavy silver chain with its jewelled kraken pendant that was his proud badge of office. 'If you're ever in need of a little extra cash, come and see me. I could fence that for quite a bit.'

Orleon was not amused. The old man disapproved

mightily of Wrayan's friendship with Princess Marla, but was forced to tolerate it for her sake. 'I must inform you, sir, that on hearing you were invited to lunch today, I arranged a full inventory of the palace valuables. I'll know if anything goes missing.'

'I promise to be on my best behaviour then.'

'I'm serious, Master Lightfinger.'

'I know you are, Orleon. That's what makes you so much fun.'

'Wrayan!'

The thief turned in the direction of the shout before the chief steward could respond. Damin and Starros burst out of the palace doors and raced to the head of the steps to greet him. Wrayan was stunned by how much the boys had grown in the year since he'd seen them last, although nothing much else seemed changed about them.

'Hello, Damin. Starros.'

'Is he causing trouble already, Orleon?' Damin asked with a grin.

The old man muttered something rude under his breath and then bowed slightly in Damin's direction. 'Perhaps you and Starros would prefer to escort Master Lightfinger to lunch, your highness?'

'We'd be happy to,' the young prince replied.

'Then I will leave you in the care of the *children*, Master Lightfinger,' Orleon told him, and turned on his heel. He strode back into the palace, his back stiff.

'What did you say to make Orleon so mad?' Starros asked, falling in beside them as they followed the chief steward into the palace. Wrayan liked Starros. The fosterling had the quick wit of a truly intelligent mind and the sort of nature that seemed capable of handling any crisis. *Pity he's destined for a life in the Palace Guard*, Wrayan mused. *Starros would have made an excellent thief.*

'How do you know Orleon is mad at me?'

Starros smiled. 'He only ever calls Damin "your highness" when he's cranky about something.'

'I offered to pawn his pendant for him.'

Damin laughed delightedly. 'I wish you'd visit more often, Wrayan. If only for the effect you have on Orleon.'

'According to Orleon, I shouldn't be visiting at all,' Wrayan replied as they stepped into the cool dimness of the main foyer. 'How's your mother?'

'Same as always.' Damin shrugged as they crossed the polished granite tiles and headed up the grand staircase to the dining room on the second floor. 'She brought Luciena Mariner back with her this time. She's going to be officially adopted into the family.'

'Is she now?'

The news interested Wrayan greatly. He understood why the princess had married Ruxton Tirstone. Wrayan once joked to Marla that he would have married Ruxton himself to get access to the vast intelligence network the spice trader owned. But on many an occasion he'd wondered why Marla had married a man so far beneath her as Jarvan Mariner. And why she'd done nothing about his baseborn daughter all these years. Apparently, she'd simply been biding her time. The daughter would be a marriageable age by now, he guessed. As usual, Marla had her eye on the long-term future.

'I'm going to Izcomdar at the end of summer,' Damin announced, as they reached the head of the stairs and turned left along the carpeted hall. Tall paintings of generations of Krakenshield Warlords loomed over them as they walked, as if they were running a gauntlet haunted by the dead. Wrayan hated this hallway and was sure the painting hanging over the door to the library followed him with his eyes each time he came here.

'Is that where you're being fostered?' Wrayan asked, forcing himself to ignore the dead eyes of the portraits.

I should send someone in here to steal them. Then I wouldn't have to look at them whenever I come to visit. 'That's not so far away.'

It was common practice among the highborn to foster their children in another province between the ages of thirteen and eighteen, and Wrayan knew how politically fraught the decision about Damin's fosterage must have been for Princess Marla. He'd expected her to send him somewhere safe, among people she trusted, like Elasapine or Sunrise. Izcomdar, the province that bordered Krakandar to the south, seemed an odd choice.

'I know. Old Rogan's a bit of a bore, too. And nothing exciting ever happens there.'

'Damin was hoping they'd send him to Sunrise, so he could have a chance at killing some Fardohnyans,' Starros explained.

'I wish! The worst thing I'm likely to confront in Izcomdar is horse thieves.'

Wrayan smiled at the young prince's obvious disappointment. 'Maybe they'll be really scary horse thieves, Damin.'

'Fat chance,' the boy grumbled. Then he brightened and added, 'On the other hand, the *reason* he is plagued by horse thieves is that old Rogan breeds some of the best stock in Hythria. Did you know he has a strain of sorcerer-bred horses that's still as pure as it was when the Harshini were around?'

In the blink of an eye, the young prince's disappointment had turned to excitement. Damin was like that. He was the sort of person who managed to find something positive in any situation. Wrayan hoped the trait followed him in adulthood.

'What about you, Starros?' Wrayan asked. 'Now that Damin's heading off, does that mean you'll officially be joining the Raiders?'

'Princess Marla thinks I need more education. I'm staying in the palace for the time being.'

Which means she has you tagged for bigger and better things, my lad, than life as a simple Raider. It didn't really surprise him. Marla would never let an asset like Starros go to waste in the Palace Guard.

'Well, if you ever get bored, come pay me a visit. I'd be happy to show you the other side of life.'

Starros seemed amused. 'You mean if I ever get sick of living in the lap of luxury, having my every wish catered for, my own *court'esa*, and anything else I want provided for me?'

'I didn't say it was necessarily a *good* idea, Starros,' Wrayan laughed.

They reached the dining room doors, which two slaves opened for them as they approached. Princess Marla was already in the room; she was dressed in a simple green gown, standing near the window talking to an unfamiliar, dark-haired young woman whom Wrayan guessed must be Luciena Mariner.

The princess turned as they entered, her face breaking into a smile of genuine pleasure. 'Wrayan!'

'Your highness.'

He bowed low as she approached. Marla took both his hands in hers and examined him for a moment, then nodded with satisfaction. 'You're looking very well, Wrayan.'

'As are you, your highness,' he replied graciously. And she was looking well. Marla seemed to grow more beautiful every time he saw her.

'We didn't wake you with our thoughtless demand that you attend us for lunch, did we?'

'I don't mind missing a bit of sleep for you, your highness.' Wrayan had enough Harshini blood in him that he could go days without sleep and still function normally, but it was nice of her to ask.

The other children had noticed his arrival by now. Kalan came up beside her mother and smiled shyly at him. The little princess had a crush on Wrayan that he was quite flattered by – in fact, she was probably Wrayan's favourite among all the children.

'Orleon says the only reason you come here is because you're a thief and would never pass up a free meal.'

'He's got a point, Kalan,' Wrayan agreed with a laugh as Kalan's twin brother, Narvell, and the other children of the palace gathered around. As they clamoured for his attention, and Wrayan greeted them one by one, he glanced over their heads and caught Marla's eye, understanding immediately what she wanted of him.

Make sure they've not had their minds tampered with, she was telling him silently. *Do whatever you have to, Wrayan, but keep my children safe.*

'Well?'

Marla closed the door of her office and turned to look at Wrayan questioningly. Lunch had finished and, as usual, Marla had invited Wrayan to share a parting cup of wine in private. It was a rare privilege that irked Orleon no end, because many people the chief steward considered worthy of such an honour were denied. He couldn't understand why Marla never denied the thief.

Wrayan shook his head. 'They're all fine, your highness.'

'Are you certain?'

'Anybody able to tamper with the mind of someone in the palace would have to wield Harshini magic to do it. If nothing else, I'd feel *that* happening, no matter where I was in the city.'

'And the shield you placed on my mind? Is it still intact?'

'Yes,' he assured her, able to feel the delicate weave was

undisturbed, even from where he stood. It gave him a great deal of satisfaction to think he'd woven a shield over Marla's mind, and the minds of her children and her closet advisors, that his nemesis, Alija Eaglespike, couldn't even detect, let alone figure out how to penetrate.

'What about Luciena? Were you able to detect her thoughts?'

Wrayan shrugged. 'Only briefly. I didn't get enough time to examine her mind closely. I doubt she's planning to murder you all in your beds.'

'I'll arrange to have Luciena spend some time with you in private. If she's not an imminent threat, I suppose we can wait awhile. She's still very uncertain about us. I don't want to scare her off completely by announcing that I'm sending her off to the Thieves' Guild to have her mind probed.'

Wrayan smiled. 'Well, I don't think you've scared her too much. The most recurrent thought I picked up from her mind was "welcome to the family" so you must be doing something right.'

Marla nodded, obviously relieved. Then she smiled a little sheepishly. 'You know, both Elezaar and Corian Burl think I'm a fool for believing a word you say. They think you're nothing but a very clever confidence trickster.'

'If I was that, your highness, I'd be charging you more for my services than a free lunch once a year.'

Marla laughed softly and took a seat behind the desk of the book-lined room, indicating that Wrayan should take the seat opposite. She obviously wanted something else from him.

'Did you know that Tesha Zorell is thinking of retiring?' she asked, as she poured him a glass of honey-coloured wine with her own hand.

'No, I didn't. But I suppose it's not that unexpected. Who's taking her place?'

'I was hoping you'd have a suggestion.'

Wrayan shrugged a little uncomfortably, the goings-on in the Sorcerers' Collective something he thought he had left far behind him. 'It's been more than a decade since I was a member of the Sorcerers' Collective, your highness.'

'And there's not a single contender for the position of Lower Arrion who wouldn't have been there while you were the High Arrion's apprentice, Wrayan. I want to know who I can trust. More specifically, who Kagan trusted.'

'Nobody springs to mind as an outstanding candidate,' he said thoughtfully. 'Kagan always gave me the impression he universally despised everyone in the Collective. It's a bit hard to pin down who he might have thought well of. Particularly after all this time.'

'You'll give it some thought, though?' the princess asked. 'And tell me if you can think of a name?'

'The only name that springs to mind is Bruno Sanval.'

'Kagan trusted him?'

'He drank with him,' Wrayan clarified. 'Which was close enough to an endorsement for Kagan, I suppose. But I doubt he'd be interested in the job, your highness, even if you could somehow arrange to have him appointed. And you'd probably have to send an expedition into the very bowels of the Sorcerers' Collective library to find him. I don't think he's seen daylight for the past fifteen years.'

'Is he a librarian?'

'No. That would mean duties that take him away from what he really cares about.'

'Which is what?'

'The Harshini. He's obsessed by them. Kagan once claimed Bruno was trying to memorise everything about them in the library in case it burned down.' Wrayan smiled at the recollection. He hadn't spared Bruno a thought in years. 'He was particularly obsessed with the idea of locating Sanctuary.'

Marla raised an eyebrow, amused. 'Then I imagine he'd be rather interested in talking to you.'

'Probably.'

'Have you never been tempted to send him a note telling him you've been to Sanctuary? Just to put the man out of his misery?'

'No.'

The princess smiled in understanding. 'But you think he's the best man for the job?'

'I think Kagan despised him marginally less than the rest of his peers. But please, don't take my word for this. For all I know, he's a raving Patriot.'

'I'll look into it when I get back to Greenharbour.'

'You can't influence the appointment of the Lower Arrion, your highness,' he warned. 'You may have to just learn to live with the fact that Tesha's successor is going to be someone of Alija's choosing.'

Marla smiled coldly. 'I don't have to learn to live with anything of the kind, Wrayan. The Lower Arrion of the Sorcerers' Collective will be someone of *my* choosing, not Alija's.'

'Why keep playing these games with her, your highness? Why not just have her killed and be done with it?'

Marla didn't respond immediately. Nor did she seem shocked by the question. But then, nobody else in Hythria knew what Wrayan knew. The secret he shared with the princess was a bond forged eight years ago in Zegarnald's temple in Greenharbour the night Kagan Palenovar had died. That was the night Wrayan came out of more than five years of hiding to inform the princess that her husband, Nash Hawksword, and his lover, the Innate magician, Alija Eaglespike, were behind the plot to kill her son, Damin.

Not even Elezaar knew Nash Hawksword was dead because Marla had arranged it herself. Only Wrayan knew the truth – because he was the one who had organised Marla's first meeting with the Assassins' Guild.

'I'd do it myself, if you commanded me, your highness,' he offered.

'You're a thief, Wrayan, not an assassin.'

'For Alija, I'd consider a career change.'

Marla shook her head. 'I thank you for the offer. But I can't risk it. Things are quiet now. Alija thinks she has the upper hand. She's given up on her husband, Barnardo, taking the throne and has her eye on her eldest son, Cyrus, instead. He's not even twenty, so things will stay quiet for a time yet.'

'You've more patience than I, your highness.'

'I don't like surprises so I really have no other choice. If I know what's happening, I can control it. Hythria's stability is what allows me to maintain control. If Alija died unexpectedly, there would be chaos and I have no idea who would become High Arrion.'

'And if she dies under the slightest suspicion of foul play, even if they didn't suspect you, the Warlords would turn on each other, looking for the culprit, and we'd have a civil war,' Wrayan deduced, seeing her problem. He hated politics. Things were much simpler in the Thieves' Guild.

'It's better this way.' Marla sipped her wine and then smiled at him. 'But never fear, Alija's time will come. And if I can arrange it, I'll be more than happy to have you aid me in her downfall.'

'Just give me the time and place, your highness,' Wrayan said with unexpected ferocity. 'If you're going to take that bitch down, I want to be there.'

Marla smiled and raised her glass in his direction. 'To strange alliances, Wrayan.'

Wrayan picked up his cut-crystal glass, leaned forward and raised it to clink softly against hers.

'Strange alliances,' he said.

21

It was late afternoon before Wrayan got back to the Pickpocket's Retreat. As he rode through the crowded streets of the Beggars' Quarter he surveyed his own little kingdom and smiled, thinking he probably ruled as much of Krakandar as Mahkas Damaran.

He ruled the night, at least.

Since returning home eight years ago, with his reputation as a thief in Greenharbour preceding him, he'd been marked as the natural heir to the Thieves' Guild leadership. Four years later, when old Dasha Larenan died at the hands of his much younger wife, who was looking for the fortune she was sure the old man was hiding from her, there was barely a voice raised in protest about his successor. Wrayan's father, Calen Lightfinger, had been renowned as the best pickpocket in all of Krakandar while he was alive, and Wrayan had powerful friends that nobody in the Guild could match. Nor did they try. It wasn't even a merit thing. Wrayan knew he got the job because even professional thieves appreciated that you simply couldn't do better than a Sorcerers' Collective-educated burglar with the nickname 'Wrayan the Wraith' who enjoyed the protection of the High Prince's sister.

The stable boy from the Pickpocket's Retreat came out

to take his horse. Wrayan handed him the reins and a copper rivet for his trouble, and entered the inn through the back door, which led into the kitchens. The cooks were getting ready for the dinner crowd and barely noticed Wrayan as he threaded his way past the benches to the door that led into the taproom. A couple of the kitchen boys waved to him as he passed, and he waved back. He didn't linger in the stifling heat of the stoves. More than anything, he wanted to get out of his palace finery before too many people saw him dressed in such a fashion and started asking why.

As he entered the dimly lit taproom, he heard Fyora laughing before he saw her. She was sitting across the room by the unlit fireplace, on the knee of a tall, dark-haired stranger, clutching a foaming tankard of ale. Although he couldn't see the newcomer's face, Wrayan knew instantly, and without a shadow of a doubt, who it was.

'Found a new friend, have you, Fee?' he asked, coming up behind them.

Fyora looked over her shoulder, still laughing. When she realised who it was, she scrambled to her feet and hastily began to load up her tray, trying to give the impression she was simply there to clear the table, not sharing a drink with a potential client. 'Umm, Wrayan . . . I didn't . . . I mean, I wasn't . . .'

The dark-haired man burst out laughing, although it sounded a little forced, as if he was determined to have a good time regardless of what was happening around him. 'Don't tell me this is the boyfriend you were warning me about, Fee?'

The stranger had obviously been flirting with her long enough to learn her name. And Fyora was lapping it up. She only allowed people she really liked to call her Fee.

'*No*! I mean . . . sort of . . .'

'Party's over, Fee,' Wrayan informed her, sensing something strange in the newcomer. 'Go find somebody else to wait on.'

Looking mortified that she may have ruined her chances (with either Wrayan or the newcomer – he wasn't really sure), she fled the table in the direction of the kitchens.

'That was a bit harsh. We were just getting close, too.'

Wrayan shook his head, wondering if his idle promise to introduce Fyora to a real Harshini had been some sort of unconscious premonition. He took the stool opposite and studied the Halfbreed. He hadn't changed, nor had he aged a single day since Wrayan had seen him last, but there was something odd about him. An air of darkness, even despair, which seemed completely out of character.

'You're back.'

Brak took a swig from the tankard, then slammed it onto the table. 'You haven't lost your talent for stating the glaringly bloody obvious, I see.'

Wrayan stared at him curiously, wondering at the Halfbreed's sudden appearance. 'What are you doing here, Brak?'

'Can't I just drop by and visit an old friend?' Brak finished off his tankard and picked up the one Fyora had abandoned. 'I hear you're the head of the Thieves' Guild now. Congratulations. Dace must be beside himself with happiness.'

'Haven't spoken to him for a while. What about you?'

'The God of Thieves only talks to me when he wants something. Is Fee really your girlfriend?'

'She likes to think she is. Stop changing the subject. Why are you here?'

'What?' Brak asked, looking quite wounded. 'No pleasantries first? No "how are you, Brak?" No "what have you been up to all these years, Brak?" No, "how are the folks back home, Brak?"'

Wrayan smiled as he thought of Sanctuary. 'How *are* the folks back home, Brak?'

Brak's expression darkened and he hesitated before he answered. 'Same as always. Shanan misses you.'

'I miss her,' Wrayan replied, thinking it was Shananara té Ortyn's fault that he would never be satisfied with a human woman. 'What brings you to Krakandar?'

'I'm looking for someone.'

'Who?'

'Someone like you.'

Wrayan glanced over his shoulder to see who was within earshot before he answered. 'Like *me*?'

'Yeah, you know what I mean: big, pretty, dumb . . .'

'Very funny.'

Brak also looked around to see who might overhear them before he added, quite seriously, 'With ancestors that weren't all human.'

Wrayan leaned back on his stool and studied the Halfbreed warily. 'There's someone else with . . . my ancestry? How do you know?'

'The "folks back home" felt him touching the source. We thought it was you, at first, and then I realised it couldn't be.'

'Why not?'

'Because what we felt was coming from Fardohnya.'

'Then why are you here?' Wrayan asked. 'If this person is in Fardohnya, wouldn't you be better off *looking* for him in Fardohnya?'

'I thought you might like to come with me.'

Wrayan laughed aloud at the very idea. 'To Fardohnya? Are you mad? I can't leave Krakandar. I'm the head of the Thieves' Guild.'

'It'll get along without you for a few weeks, won't it?'

'That's not the point, Brak. I have responsibilities.'

The Halfbreed took a swallow from Fyora's tankard

and then looked at him closely. 'I need you on this, Wrayan.'

'You don't need anyone, Brak.'

'No, this time, I really do need you.'

'Why?'

'Because the only safe place for this . . . *person* is in the Sorcerers' Collective in Greenharbour. Once I find him, I need you to arrange that for me.'

'You can arrange it yourself.'

He shook his head. 'You expect me to walk up to the front door of the Sorcerers' Collective, announce that I'm the fabled Brakandaran the Halfbreed, that I've found a Fardohnyan with magical ability who I've kidnapped and brought illegally across the border?' He put his hand to his ear as if he was listening for something. 'I can already hear the Sisterhood gathering for the next purge up in Medalon.'

'Don't you think I'll get the same reaction if *I* walk up to the front door of the Sorcerers' Collective and announce that I'm the long-lost Wrayan Lightfinger and that I've found a Fardohnyan with magical ability that *I've* kidnapped and brought illegally across the border?'

'Ah, but you have connections in high places, Wrayan. I hear you and the High Prince's sister are very cosy.'

'What I have, Brak, is a burning desire to stay well clear of Alija Eaglespike and anything to do with the Sorcerers' Collective. I certainly don't want to hand her another magician so she can fry *his* brains when she decides he's too big a threat to her.'

'I couldn't agree more.'

'Then why ask me to help you?'

'Because at this point, the lad is probably going to die anyway. They've already worked out what he is.'

Wrayan shook his head suspiciously. 'You don't need my help to find him at all, do you? You know exactly where he is, and if you didn't you'd just send the demons to look for him.'

'His name is Rory,' Brak admitted. 'He's in a Fardohnyan dungeon just over the border in Westbrook. He was trying to get to Hythria when they caught him.'

'That's very tragic, Brak, but I'm not going anywhere.'

'He's only twelve.'

Wrayan sighed, 'What have you done, Brak?'

The Halfbreed looked at him with a puzzled expression. 'What do you mean?'

'Is this one of those "balance" things you're so fond of?'

'I have no idea what you're talking about.'

Wrayan lowered his voice a notch, certain Brak was lying to him. 'Don't you remember? After we killed those Kariens in the mountains outside Sanctuary? You took time out to save some little girl lost in the woods three days later because it restored the balance.'

'So?'

'So, I'm just wondering what you've done that requires you to break some twelve-year-old you've never met out of a Fardohnyan dungeon and find him a home in the Sorcerers' Collective?'

Brak shrugged. 'Let's just say this one's on credit.'

'Which means you'll probably have to do something really bad to make up for it,' Wrayan joked, wondering if he was simply imagining the dark veil of despair that shrouded Brak's aura. He hadn't seen the Halfbreed for years. Maybe Brak was always like this and he just didn't remember it. Wrayan glanced around the room again. It was filling slowly as people finished work for the day, but the taproom was large and they were still quite safe from eavesdroppers. 'Look, I'm not trying to be difficult about this, Brak. But really, even if I wanted to go with you, how would I explain a trip to Fardohnya?'

'I thought thieves and assassins knew no borders.'

208

Wrayan nodded in understanding as he realised what Brak wanted of him. 'I see. You want me to arrange a meeting with someone in one of the Thieves' Guilds in Fardohnya so you and I have an excuse to be in Westbrook. Why didn't you just come straight out and ask me that in the first place?'

'More fun this way. Will you do it?'

He sighed, wondering if he should go through the motions of objecting or just give in now to save time. In the end, he settled on the latter. 'It'll take some time to arrange. Will your boy last that long?'

'Elarnymire is keeping an eye on him for me.'

'You could just have the demons meld into a dragon, land you on the roof of Westbrook castle and break the lad out yourself in a spectacular blaze of magic, Brak.'

Brak patted Wrayan's hand patronisingly. 'Not real clear on the meaning of the phrase "staying hidden so everyone thinks the Harshini are extinct," are you, son?'

Wrayan smiled. 'I know. It'd be nice to think you could do something like that, though. And not have to worry about it.'

'The irony being that if the Harshini didn't need to stay hidden, I probably wouldn't need to break some poor child out of a dungeon for the crime of being able to wield magic. They're accusing him of murder, by the way. And being a Hythrun spy. King Hablet is firmly of the opinion that anybody with the slightest hint of magical ability is a Hythrun spy.'

'I'll have to write a few letters.'

'I'm not going anywhere.'

Wrayan rose from the table, wondering how much trouble this was going to cause. What Brak wanted of him was no small favour. 'Promise me you'll stay out of trouble while you're here.'

'I've had a lot more practice at keeping a low profile than you have, Wrayan. I can take care of myself.'

'I'll talk to you later then. I do have a job, you know. I have a few things to take care of first.'

'Excellent!' Brak declared, leaning back in his seat. 'In that case, would you mind sending the lovely Fyora back to me? Both my tankard and my lap are empty.'

Wrayan sighed. Some things about Brak never seemed to change. 'I'll send her back.'

Brak raised a questioning eyebrow. 'And you don't mind if she and I . . . ?'

'Knock yourself out.'

'You're a good lad, Wrayan.'

'I'm an idiot for letting you talk me into this,' he corrected.

'You don't really think that. Not deep down.'

'You're reading my mind now?' It wasn't a rhetorical question. Brak was more than capable of reading Wrayan's mind, although he was determinedly blocking any hint of his own thoughts from betraying him at the moment.

'I don't have to read your mind. I know you.'

And that was the problem, Wrayan knew, as he headed back through the taproom towards the stairs. Brak knew him well enough to know that if the Harshini had asked him to dance naked on a bed of burning coals, he would have done it. Not because he felt he belonged to the Harshini. Not because he believed in them, or even because there was something odd about Brak, some secret he was obviously hiding, although that fact alone intrigued Wrayan enough that he was almost willing to go along with the Halfbreed just to find out what it was.

Mostly, Wrayan admitted to himself as he climbed the stairs to his room, he would do this because helping Brakandaran the Halfbreed might mean a chance to see the Harshini princess, Shananara té Ortyn, one more time.

22

The problem of what to do with her future continued to plague Kalan Hawksword as summer wore on, exacerbated no end by the preparations for Rielle Tirstone's wedding, speculation about which husband Luciena would settle on (*that was easy*, Kalan thought, *she's been making moon eyes at Xanda from the day she arrived*) and Uncle Mahkas's unsubtle hints about Leila one day becoming Damin's bride. As the weather grew hotter and emotions in the palace grew more fraught over such earth-shattering things as wedding dresses and flower arrangements and attendants' hairdos, the only thing that seemed to lie in the future for the women of her family, Kalan decided miserably, was getting married.

Kalan didn't want to get married. It wasn't that she had any particular objection to the institution of marriage. It was just when you got married, you had to marry a boy, and kiss him and all that stuff. She wasn't so clear on what the other 'stuff' involved, but she knew that was what *court'esa* were for, and if you had a decent *court'esa* then why burden yourself with a husband? At ten, Kalan knew people were already starting to speculate about her future. Although she wouldn't marry until she was sixteen at least, there were plenty of likely contenders. And all of them were old. *Really* old. Some as old as twenty.

Her only escape, Kalan finally concluded, was to find something useful to do.

Kalan knew the way her mother thought. To escape marriage, she would have to think of something she could do that would convince her mother that she was more useful to Damin when he became High Prince if she remained unmarried. She spent a great deal of time thinking about the problem and finally decided that she needed help.

The help Kalan settled on was Elezaar.

Since Elezaar had assumed his new duties as their tutor, the palace children had settled into their daily lessons with a degree of fatalistic acceptance. There was nothing to be gained by tormenting the dwarf. He belonged to Princess Marla, so they couldn't threaten to have him sold off or dismissed, the way they had with other tutors. He had known most of the children since they were born and could tell in an instant if they were lying. He knew the palace almost as well as the children, so they couldn't even hide from him in the slaveways. And worst of all, he wasn't the least bit shy about reporting their progress (or lack of it) back to Princess Marla.

Despite this, the palace children were genuinely fond of the dwarf, so generally the lessons proceeded with little disruption. Even Damin managed to sit still for longer than his normal attention span, particularly if Elezaar was explaining his Rules of Gaining and Wielding Power.

It was after their lessons one hot afternoon, some six weeks after Princess Marla had returned to Krakandar, that Kalan decided to approach the dwarf and enlist his help. Elezaar had dismissed the children early today, partly because Darvad Vintner, Rielle's fiancé, had arrived for the wedding, along with Rogan Bearbow, the Warlord of Izcomdar, his daughter and son, Tejay and Rogan, and numerous other invited guests, and the whole palace was in an uproar getting ready for the ball scheduled the following evening to welcome them all to Krakandar.

The other reason they'd been dismissed early, Kalan secretly suspected, was because after Damin replied 'on the bottom' in answer to Elezaar's question about where the historic Treaty of Westbrook had been signed, they were all laughing so hard that even the dwarf realised he had no chance of getting any more sense out of them that day.

Elezaar was packing up the warboard when he realised that Kalan hadn't left with the others. The warboard was actually a large table into which had been built a miniature relief map of Krakandar Province and the surrounding terrain. This was where the boys learned tactics and strategy. Tiny armies of figurines painted in the colours of each of the Warlords, as well as the bordering nations of Fardohnya and Medalon, could be manoeuvred around the board, attacking or defending Krakandar, depending on which army the players commanded. Today, Damin, with Adham as his lieutenant, had been in command of a troop of Medalonian Defenders and had conquered Krakandar against Starros and Rodja's defending Raiders after a long and drawn-out struggle. The older girls had been excused because of the party and, by rights, Kalan should have been with them, but the dwarf knew Leila and Rielle were in their rooms trying on every dress they owned while they decided what to wear for tomorrow night's ball. Taking pity on her, Elezaar had let Kalan stay and help with moving the figurines around, rather than spend the morning with her stepsisters, choking with boredom.

The dwarf glanced at Kalan and then at the retreating figures of her brothers as the door to the nursery slammed shut behind them. 'Forget something?'

'Did you want a hand packing up, Elezaar?'

The dwarf smiled as he picked up the little figures and placed them, one by one, on the velvet-lined trays into which a slot was cut for each. 'What do you want, Kalan?'

'What makes you think I want something?'

'Children of royal blood never offer to help slaves tidy up unless there's something in it for them. It's one of those immutable laws of the universe I was telling you about the other day.'

Kalan frowned. If she was going to be an important person some day, she would have to learn to be much less transparent. Still, this way she didn't have to muck about finding a way to broach the subject delicately. 'What should I be when I grow up, Elezaar?'

The dwarf stopped what he was doing and looked at her curiously. He was standing on a stool so that he could reach the figurines in the centre of the table. 'A princess?' he suggested tentatively.

'I know *that*,' she snapped impatiently. 'But what am I going to *do*?'

'You'll have a household to run, I imagine. And it won't be a small one. You'll be sister to the High Prince when Damin inherits your uncle's throne. Whoever you marry will be a very important person.'

'But I don't want to *marry* a very important person,' she complained. 'I want to *be* a very important person.'

'What do you think you can do to alter your fate, Kalan?'

She shrugged. 'I don't know. That's why I'm asking you. Isn't your Second Rule of Gaining and Wielding Power to accept what you can't do anything about, and do something about the stuff you can?'

'Accept what you cannot change,' the dwarf corrected. 'And change that which is unacceptable.' He smiled and added, 'And be smart enough to know the difference.'

'Which is why I'm asking you, Elezaar. I want to find

something useful to do when I grow up. Getting married and being somebody's glorified housekeeper is unacceptable.'

Elezaar put the figurine he was holding into the tray and stepped down from the warboard.

'Come here, Kalan,' he beckoned, walking to the work-table by the window where she normally sat with the others during her lessons. The dwarf hoisted himself up onto one of the chairs and indicated she should join him. Kalan took the chair beside him, turning it to face him. Sitting down, they were almost the same height. Kalan's legs touched the floor, however, while Elezaar's didn't even reach halfway. 'Tell me what the problem is.'

'I don't want to be like Rielle. I want to do something important. Like Mama does.' She brightened as something suddenly occurred to her. 'Do you think I could *do* what Mama does?'

'What do you mean?'

'You know, I could rule Hythria while Damin has orgies and stuff.'

The dwarf looked as if he was about to choke on something. 'Kalan, do you know what an orgy is?'

She thought about it for a moment and then shrugged. 'It's some sort of party Uncle Lernen has a lot, isn't it?'

'Something like that,' Elezaar agreed with a strangled cough. 'But I doubt you'll be able to count on your brother ruling Hythria the same way your uncle does. Your mother has gone to rather a lot of trouble to ensure that doesn't happen.'

Kalan was getting exasperated with her limited options. 'Then what can I *do*? They don't let girls do anything useful. They won't let me be a Warlord, and that's not fair 'cause I was born first, so I should be the heir to Elasapine, not Narvell.'

'Not under the laws of primogeniture,' the dwarf explained.

'What does that mean?'

'It means succession through the male line. The only country I've ever heard of that doesn't practise it is Medalon. There, the succession is through the distaff line.'

'Well, that's not very fair. If people in Medalon can do it, why can't we?'

'Probably because along with their progressive notions about female succession in Medalon come a whole lot of other, rather less attractive ideas – like the Sisters of the Blade, and purges against anyone who believes in the Primal Gods. The Sisterhood was responsible for eradicating the Harshini, you know.'

'But they didn't really eradicate them. Wrayan says they're still around, just in hiding. He says he's met them.'

'Wrayan Lightfinger is a thief, Kalan,' Elezaar warned. 'Which means he's also a disciple of Jakerlon, the God of Liars, along with the God of Thieves. I know you like him. But he says a lot of things you probably shouldn't take at face value.'

'He's a magician, too.'

Elezaar rolled his one good eye sceptically. 'So he says.'

'But he is! He used to be the High Arrion's apprentice.'

'That doesn't mean he has any magical ability, Kalan.'

Now she was really confused. 'How can that be?'

'There haven't been any real magicians for over a century; nearly two centuries, in fact,' he explained. 'Once the Harshini were wiped out by the Sisterhood, the few that were left fled Hythria and Fardohnya and went into hiding—'

'Just like Wrayan says!' she interrupted triumphantly.

'Yes, just like Wrayan says,' Elezaar agreed patiently. 'But that was over a hundred and sixty years ago, Kalan. Even if they managed to find somewhere safe to hide, even if Sanctuary was a real place, and even as long-lived as they purportedly were, it's unlikely any of the Harshini have lasted this long. And that's why we don't have any magicians any more. Except for the odd Innate like Alija Eaglespike, who apparently really does have some ability, the rest of the Sorcerers' Collective are just people who study the texts of the Harshini, dreaming of what might have been, or people who think they can gain some sort of political influence. But without the Harshini, nobody really knows for certain how to make the magic work. All we have left are legends and people – like Wrayan Lightfinger – who like to make us think there's still a chance the Harshini are out there somewhere and will come back some day when the Sisterhood is no longer a threat.'

This was new territory for Kalan and she was fascinated by the possibilities. 'So the High Arrion before Alija? He wasn't a magician, either?'

'Kagan Palenovar? He couldn't light a candle without a flint and taper.'

'I see,' Kalan mused as a new, unexpected career direction opened up before her. 'How old does one have to be to become an apprentice sorcerer?'

This time, Elezaar didn't even try to hide his laughter. 'Forget it, Kalan. There is *no way* your mother would allow you to be apprenticed to the Sorcerers' Collective. Although . . .' The dwarf hesitated for a moment, a thoughtful expression on his ugly little face. Then he sighed and shook his head. 'No, it's not even worth considering. There is no chance your mother would permit it.'

'Why not? If I joined the Sorcerers' Collective, I could be High Arrion one day. That would help Damin when he's High Prince, wouldn't it?'

'It would be very useful,' the dwarf agreed. 'If you survived that long.'

'Why wouldn't I survive? Is the training terribly difficult?'

'It's not the training, it's the politics. There are factions in the Sorcerers' Collective who aren't very sympathetic to your uncle. The danger to you would be extreme.'

'I'm not scared of anything!'

'Your mother is, however.'

'But it's not fair! I want to do something important!'

He smiled at her, patting her hand comfortingly. 'And I'm sure your mother has something *very* important in mind for you,' he promised. 'I'm fairly certain it doesn't involve you becoming a sorcerer, though.'

Kalan snatched her hand away and jumped at to her feet. 'Don't patronise me, Elezaar. I might be a child, but I'm not stupid.'

The deformed little *court'esa* bowed his head. 'You're right, your highness,' he apologised. 'It was remiss of me to give you the impression that I thought you were so easily fooled.'

Elezaar had only ever called Kalan 'your highness' about three times in her whole life, so she figured his apology was genuine. It didn't help her much, though. She was still doomed to be somebody's wife, rather than *somebody*.

'What would I have to do to convince Mother I should join the Sorcerers' Collective?' she asked.

'Find yourself a *real* magician to watch over you,' he said with an apologetic smile. 'I can't think of any other way your mother would place you under the influence of someone like Alija Eaglespike.'

'Someone like Wrayan, you mean?'

'If you accept what he says about his ability, then yes. But I've never seen any proof of it.'

'Where do I find someone like Wrayan?'

The dwarf shrugged, obviously thinking such an impossible task would put an end to her foolish notion. 'Why don't you ask Wrayan?'

Kalan thought about that for a moment and then nodded decisively. 'Thank you, Elezaar. I think I will.'

Kalan was quite certain that, given sufficient warning, her mother would veto any notion of her daughter joining the Sorcerers' Collective unless it was a fait accompli. There was no way Kalan could send a message to Wrayan Lightfinger, however, without her mother finding out about it, so she was forced to find another way to contact him.

It was easy to sneak past Leila, sleeping soundly in her bed, into the dressing room and through the slaveways to Damin's room. Uncle Mahkas believed the entrance to Damin's room had been sealed, but several years ago, Damin and Starros had managed to have a copy made of the heavy key that opened the lock. That had been an exercise in strategy and tactics that would have impressed even Elezaar. They'd had to wait until Uncle Mahkas was away with Almodavar on a border patrol, get access to his office while he was gone, get the key out of the palace, copied and returned to the study, all without getting caught. Kalan was still astonished they'd got away with it.

Wrayan had helped them that time, too. He was the only person in the whole of Krakandar who had the sort of contacts who could copy a key on short notice without asking any questions. That was the best thing about Wrayan, Kalan thought. He probably knew what the children were up to – it was rumoured he could read minds, after all – but he didn't lecture them or tell them what they were doing was wrong. He just made the arrangements to get the key copied and warned the children never to attempt anything like it again without asking his help. The Beggars' Quarter was a dangerous place, he reminded them. Especially for sheltered, unsuspecting highborn children whose entire world was defined by the walls of a palace.

Kalan had to stand on her toes to reach the key, and then made certain the door had locked behind her. Even sneaking around the slaveways, Kalan had been so well indoctrinated about protecting her brothers, she would never have even thought of leaving the door unlocked. When she walked into the main room, she discovered it was empty, the candles flickering in the slight breeze coming from the open windows. Then she heard soft voices in the darkness and smiled.

She found the boys out on the palace roof, sitting on the sloped tiles watching the heat-lightning streak the sky to the south. They were all there: Starros, Damin, Rodja, Adham and, somewhat to her annoyance, her twin brother, Narvell. Kalan climbed through the window and inched her way forward on her bottom until she was perched between Damin and Starros.

'Hello,' she said brightly.

'What are you doing out here?' Narvell asked, sounding a little peeved. He was going through that stage, Lirena had explained to her, where it was more important to be 'one of the boys' than 'one of the twins'. 'You're not allowed out on the roof.'

'Neither are you,' she pointed out, wiggling her bottom a little to get comfortable.

'You know, if you fell from here, it'd kill you,' Damin said, leaning forward a little to look at the dizzying drop to the courtyard below.

'Then I won't fall,' she said simply. 'Leila says we could never get a message to Wrayan without getting caught.'

The boys looked at her in surprise.

'*What?*' Starros asked, speaking on behalf of all of them.

'I need to see Wrayan about something,' she explained.

'I told Leila you could help me, but she said you'd never be able to do it without getting caught.'

'We got Wrayan to help us with the lock,' Rodja reminded her.

'But Uncle Mahkas was away that time,' she said softly, aware that too much noise would bring the guards into Damin's room to investigate and they'd all be in serious trouble if they were caught out here on the roof. 'And Mama wasn't here, either. Leila says you'll never get away with it this time.'

'You never said anything of the kind to Leila, Kal,' Damin scoffed. 'She'd go running straight to Mahkas if she thought you were planning any such thing.'

Kalan frowned. The older they got, the less gullible her brothers seemed to be. Or maybe it was her? The boys didn't seem nearly so enchanted by their little sister as they once had. 'Could you do it, though? Get a message to Wrayan?'

'I'm quite sure we could,' Starros replied. 'The question is, Kalan, why would we?'

'I have to ask him something.'

'Write him a letter.'

'I can't risk it falling into the wrong hands.'

'*Into the wrong hands*,' Rodja echoed in an ominous tone. Then he laughed at her. 'You've been listening to my father's stories about his adventures with the spice caravans, haven't you?'

'I meant my mother, idiot!' she snapped, rolling her eyes. 'Not some Fardohnyan spy.'

'What do you want to ask Wrayan that you don't want Mother to know about, Kal?' Damin asked.

'You wouldn't understand.'

'Maybe not,' her older brother agreed. 'But there's no way we're going to help you get a message to him unless we know why.'

Starros and the other boys nodded their agreement.

Kalan frowned. She hated having to confide in them but knew Damin meant what he said. And it was worth the risk of ridicule. If they did agree to help her, the gods wouldn't stand in their way.

'It's complicated.'

'Try us,' Starros prompted with an encouraging smile.

'It's because I want to join the Sorcerers' Collective,' she said.

23

Of all the Krakandar siblings, Rielle Tirstone was the closest in age to Luciena, so they gravitated towards each other naturally. The spice trader's daughter was an outrageous flirt, but according to the gossip Aleesha had heard around the palace, that was all she did. She had her own *court'esa* – a handsome young man named Darian Coe – whom she was quite willing to share, but in general, it seemed her flirting was just a hobby; a way to pass the time until she married Darvad Vintner and started her new life as the mistress of Dylan Pass.

Her fiancé had arrived in Krakandar yesterday, along with his family, which included his uncle, Rogan Bearbow, the Warlord of Izcomdar, and a whole raft of relations from the province who were introduced to Luciena when they arrived and whose names she promptly forgot ten seconds after she met them all.

The only visitor who made an impact on her, really, was Tejay Bearbow. The Warlord of Izcomdar's only daughter was a year older than Luciena. Tall and solid, with thick blond hair that constantly threatened to escape the loose braid she impatiently fashioned to confine it, Tejay was handsome rather than beautiful, sturdy rather than lady-like, and was – so Aleesha had informed her mistress last night in a scandalised whisper – rumoured to be quite an outstanding swordswoman who could hold her own against most of the Raiders in her father's army.

The three girls had gathered in Rielle's room to discuss their wardrobe for this evening's ball, having narrowed down their selections from the day before to only a half-dozen garments each. Tejay was there under protest, she announced, as she flopped inelegantly onto the bed. Her father had decided she needed to look like a proper high-born lady at least once during her visit to Krakandar, and she supposed the ball was as good a time as any to pander to his unreasonable demands.

'The green or the red?' Rielle asked the other two girls as her slave held up the two garments in question. Luciena was sitting on the bed next to Tejay. In the past two days, Luciena was quite sure Rielle had made her slave parade the entire contents of her wardrobe for their approval.

'Depends whether you want to look like an old maid or a whore,' Tejay replied.

Rielle turned and studied the dresses thoughtfully. The green was a high-necked, wispy, floral silk creation. The red dress was an outrageous, crystal-beaded, Fardohnyan-inspired two-piece outfit that would flaunt as much as it concealed.

'I could live with whore,' Rielle said with a grin, taking the red dress from the slave and holding it against herself.

'What about your fiancé?' Luciena asked, a little shocked. She was the only one here whose mother had actually been a *court'esa*, yet she was astonished to discover how much more modest and reserved she was compared to these girls raised among Hythria's nobility.

'It doesn't hurt to let a man know you can be bought,' Tejay advised with a chuckle. 'You just need to make sure the price is high enough.'

Rielle laughed. 'And that if he's not willing to pay it,

somebody else is! One thing's for certain. With me dressed in the red, Darvad will never look at another *court'esa*. What do you think, Luciena?'

'Do you want my opinion on the dress?' she asked. 'Or on your rather skewed view of men and their *court'esa*?'

Tejay looked at her curiously. 'What do you mean *skewed*?'

'Nothing,' she said hastily, fearful she may have offended the other girls.

'Now, now!' Tejay scolded. 'You can't make a comment like that and refuse to elaborate. Explain or suffer the consequences!'

Luciena wasn't sure what the consequences might be, but Tejay didn't seem a person to be trifled with. She shrugged uncomfortably. 'I just meant . . . well . . . it's sort of not what you . . .' Luciena threw her hands up helplessly. 'It's too hard to explain.'

'Try anyway,' Tejay suggested. She glanced at Rielle for a moment and then turned to Luciena and added threateningly, 'Or do we have to find out the hard way if you're ticklish?'

Luciena smiled when she realised Tejay was teasing. 'Very well, then. If you're going to be like that, I'll see if I can explain it.' She tucked her feet under her on the bed before continuing. 'My mother was a *court'esa*, you see . . .'

'I heard she was something of a legend,' Tejay said, 'Wasn't she the greatest beauty in all of Greenharbour?'

'So they claimed,' Luciena agreed with a shrug. 'I never really noticed. She was always just Mother to me. But she used to tell me what it was like, being a *court'esa*. And why men prefer them to their wives.'

'Why is that?' Rielle asked, coming to sit on the bed beside Tejay.

'It's because *court'esa* are slaves,' Luciena explained, wondering how these girls could be so worldly, yet so ignorant, at the same time. 'Their sole purpose in life is to pander to their master. And it's more than just training. Their very survival depends on it. A wife, according to my mother, doesn't need to be nearly as accommodating. She has standing of her own, particularly if she's high-born. She has family, even children, who look up to her. Often she's responsible for running a large household and commands the respect of both her own friends and her husband's friends. More importantly, she *has* friends. If she's been indulged as a child, she's usually had her own *court'esa* whose sole purpose was to pander to *her* desires before she married, and often after. She's not equipped to give her husband the sort of adoration he secretly desires. And according to my mother, every man wants to be worshipped, whether he admits to it or not. So, when he finds himself married to a woman he barely knows, who's got no reason to worship him and every reason to doubt he's worth the trouble, he turns to his *court'esa*, because a slave has no choice but to worship her master or be sold off as unsatisfactory.'

'Your mother was something of a cynic, I suspect,' Rielle concluded. 'It won't be like that for me. Darvad loves me.'

'You've described *my* future rather succinctly, though,' Tejay sighed.

'You don't love your betrothed?' Rielle asked sadly. 'Even a little bit?'

'Love him?' Tejay scoffed. 'I can barely bring myself to *like* him.'

'I always liked his father,' Rielle said, looking a little puzzled by Tejay's attitude. 'Chaine Lionsclaw is one of Princess Marla's most trusted allies. They've come to Krakandar a number of times. I know he's a little sensitive about his father being baseborn – and his own common-born start in life – but Terin never struck me as being *that* bad.'

'Who's Terin?' Luciena asked, a little confused. These people all knew each other intimately. She was still trying to get the *children* in Krakandar straight in her mind, let alone figure out who might be who in the vast network of family and friends the Wolfblades had gathered around themselves.

'Chaine Lionsclaw's son,' Tejay told her. 'He's the Warlord of Sunrise Province. Chaine was the previous Warlord's unacknowledged bastard and he didn't get control of the province – or the title that went with it – until a couple of years after Glenadal Ravenspear died. Terin was eight or nine before he could call himself highborn.' Tejay rolled her eyes. 'He has a chip on his shoulder the size of the Greenharbour Seeing Stone about it, too.'

'Can't you refuse to marry him?'

'Are you going to refuse the husband Princess Marla offers *you*?' Tejay asked pointedly.

Luciena shrugged. 'I don't really have a choice.'

'None of us has a choice, Luciena. The best I've been able to do is delay the inevitable for a while.' Suddenly her gloomy expression vanished and she smiled brightly. 'But now, thanks to your precious stepbrother, I've been able to delay the wedding for another whole year, maybe longer if I'm lucky! I love that boy already!'

'Do you mean Damin?' Rielle asked.

Tejay nodded. 'Princess Marla spoke to my father last night and asked him if he would take on Damin's fosterage. I was able to convince dear papa that he'll need me at home, at least for the first year, until Damin settles in.'

'Won't your fiancé be upset with the delay?' Luciena asked.

'Do I look like *I* care? Anyway, as Rielle said, the Lionsclaws are close allies of Princess Marla. Chaine won't object to the delay if it's because of Damin and I really don't give a wooden rivet about what Terin thinks.' The

227

Warlord's daughter studied Luciena curiously for a moment. 'Have you been told yet who Princess Marla expects you to marry?'

Luciena shook her head. 'I haven't officially agreed to the adoption yet.'

Tejay smiled indulgently. 'Do you honestly think you're being given a choice?'

'That's what Princess Marla agreed to.'

'Try refusing the offer, Luciena,' Tejay suggested. 'I think you might find you don't have quite as much choice as you imagine.'

'I won't let her bully me.'

'Marla doesn't bully anybody,' Rielle warned. 'She's far too subtle for that. She just tells you one thing, knowing full well you'll probably go and do the exact opposite, and just when you're patting yourself on the back, thinking you've finally managed to get one over on the great Marla Wolfblade, you discover you've done exactly what she wanted all along.' The dark-haired girl laughed. 'It's what she did to me.'

'What do you mean?'

'She warned Rielle away from my cousin, Darvad,' Tejay informed Luciena, apparently just as amused by the whole thing as Rielle. 'It was at the Krakandar races, last year, wasn't it?'

Rielle nodded. 'She took me aside before the races and told me that Darvad Vintner was riding for Izcomdar this year and that he was the Warlord's nephew, and that she expected me to behave myself in a manner befitting a trader's daughter. Then she lectured me about how even though he was young, and rich, and good-looking, I wasn't to get any ideas about him, because Lord Bearbow would never countenance a common-born wife for any nephew of his.'

Luciena frowned, thinking Rielle's tale had a horribly familiar ring about it. 'What did you do?'

'I was furious, naturally,' Rielle laughed. 'So I marched straight down to the stables and threw myself in front of Darvad Vintner's horse.'

'You didn't!'

'She did, too!' Tejay assured her. 'You should have seen the look on poor Darvad's face. He thought he'd killed her. And Rielle! What an actress! I swear, by the time he got her back to the stables, she had him ready to throw himself on his sword for her. And it was only twenty feet away! I tell you, Luciena, if you ever need lessons in how to seduce a man, forget asking a *court'esa*. Just speak to this girl here. *Nobody* swoons as well as Rielle Tirstone, and I've seen some good ones in my time.'

Rielle laughed at the compliment. 'Why, thank you, Tejay.'

'Did he really fall for you so quickly?'

'Of course not! Tejay's exaggerating. It took five, maybe ten minutes longer than that! Anyway,' she continued, climbing off the bed and holding the red dress out for another look. 'To cut a long story short, Darvad and I sneaked around behind everyone's backs for the whole two weeks of the races, thinking we were being terribly clever and that our affair was the best-kept secret in the province. By the time Lord Bearbow was due to return to Natalandar, Darvad and I were so desperately in love that we confronted him and my father. Darvad threatened to throw away his entire inheritance or kill himself, if necessary, unless they allowed us to marry.'

'What did they do?'

'There's no need to kill yourself, lad!' Tejay declared in a gruff, masculine voice, which Luciena guessed was a fair imitation of her father. 'You can marry the wench if you want. We signed the agreement last summer.'

'Last *summer*?'

'That's right. Princess Marla had arranged the whole

thing the year before with Lord Bearbow. I'm not sure whose idea it was to keep Darvad and me in the dark about it, though. I suspect it was my father, actually. He's a bit of a romantic at heart, while I don't think Princess Marla even knows what it *feels* like to really be in love.'

'Don't you *mind* being manipulated like that?' Luciena asked, a little disturbed to think she was being controlled in a similar fashion. 'Even a little bit?'

'Not really,' Rielle shrugged, as she held the dress against her body and examined herself critically in the mirror.

'Sometimes it's better not knowing the future,' Tejay advised. 'I was informed I was going to marry Terin Lionsclaw when I was twelve and I've despised him ever since, on principle. I often wonder what would have happened if I'd not been told anything and he'd just come along one day and swept me off my feet.'

Luciena frowned, remembering Marla's warning about Xanda Taranger. And the princess had given her nephew the same warning. *Is it all just part of the game? Did Xanda kiss me because he likes me, or because he thinks he can't have me?*

'Do you really think I should wear the red?' Rielle asked, oblivious to Luciena's inner turmoil.

'You might as well,' Tejay suggested. 'What about you, Luciena?'

'What?'

'What are you wearing?'

'Um . . . the blue and gold dress, I thought,' she replied, forcing her thoughts away from the puzzle that was Xanda Taranger and back to the subject at hand. Aleesha had laid the gown out across the back of a chair. 'It's new.'

Tejay studied it for a moment and then looked at Luciena. 'You're going to need something around your neck,' she advised. 'Something gold, to pick out the high-lights in the dress.'

'I sold all my jewellery before I came to Krakandar.'

'Then we should go shopping,' Rielle declared delightedly. 'There's bound to be something in the markets that will do. And I could look for some ruby earrings, to go with my dress, at the same time.'

'If it means getting out of the palace for a while, I'm all for a shopping expedition,' Tejay agreed, pushing off the bed. 'What do you say, Luciena? Shall we go into the city, beggar our fathers and enrich the merchant classes of Krakandar for a bit of light entertainment?'

Luciena nodded, a little uncertainly. 'Why not?'

Tejay grinned and rubbed her hands together. 'Then let's go shopping.'

24

Having extracted a promise from her brothers to help her visit Wrayan Lightfinger, Kalan's next problem was trying to find a legitimate excuse to leave the palace. She had spent a good deal of the night wide awake in the darkness, silently beseeching Jakerlon, the God of Liars, to provide her with a plausible excuse.

Jakerlon must have heard her prayers. Not long after lunch, Kalan overheard Rielle, Luciena and Tejay Bearbow announce they were going shopping in the markets. The young princess quickly invited herself along and somehow managed to convince the older girls that Damin, Rodja, Adham, Narvell and Starros had nothing better to do – and wanted nothing more – than to accompany them into the city.

It was such a glorious day, and the markets weren't that far from the palace, so the girls had decided to walk. Unfortunately, Damin wasn't allowed anywhere outside the palace without a substantial bodyguard so it took much longer than normal to get organised, and the older girls were tapping their feet with impatience by the time Captain Harlen announced they were ready to leave. Finally, some two hours after the young ladies of the palace had declared their intention to go shopping, Kalan, surrounded by tall

Raiders, her older sisters, Tejay Bearbow and her brothers, set off into the city, each step taking her closer to – she was quite certain – her new destiny.

The presence in the markets of the children from the palace caused a stir, particularly when the citizens of Krakandar realised one of the group was their young prince, but it settled down after a while and they were left to shop in peace. The three older girls appeared determined to try on every single piece of jewellery they saw, and then discuss the comparative merits of each item, before moving on, declaring it the wrong colour, the wrong shade, the wrong size or just simply *wrong*.

Before long, the guards were bored and the crowd of spectators faded away. To keep up the illusion that she wanted to shop with the bigger girls, Kalan paid five copper rivets – all the money she had on her – for a small amethyst drop on a copper wire. As they moved to the next stall, Kalan glanced at her brothers. Adham winked at her and began to wander across the way towards a stall stacked with cages filled with chickens. An alert guard accompanied Damin and Narvell, who deliberately walked in the opposite direction, as Starros and Rodja surreptitiously made their way around the other side of the cages. Nobody paid much attention to what they were up to. Kalan waited for their cue, poised and ready to slip away, as soon as her brothers gave the signal.

'Here!' Tejay was telling Rielle as Kalan turned to see what they were doing. They had stopped at a stall under a brightly coloured awning to examine the various goods the merchant had on offer. This one seemed to be selling mostly copper pots and kitchenware, but also had a small tray of copper wire bracelets and necklets near the back of his table. 'This is what you need, Rielle! A Fardohnyan bride's blade!'

'What's that?' Kalan asked, feigning interest in what the older girls were doing.

'According to legend, in ancient times Fardohnyan brides carried a sword on their wedding day,' Rielle explained. 'I'm not sure why.'

'I am,' Tejay laughed. 'Have you ever *seen* a Fardohnyan?'

'Can I see it?' Kalan asked, temporarily distracted by the little gold blade and its jewelled sheath. It was very pretty.

'Careful, Kal,' Rielle warned. 'It's sharp.'

Kalan examined the dagger closely, impressed by the workmanship.

'How much is it?' Tejay asked the stallkeeper.

'Seventy-five gold rivets,' he announced.

Tejay took the blade from Kalan's hand and put it back on the table. 'Come on, ladies. We don't deal with extortionists.'

'But, my lady!' the merchant cried. 'I traded my firstborn son for that knife!'

'You were robbed,' Tejay informed him unsympathetically. 'I wouldn't give you more than thirty for it. And that would be charity.'

'For sixty-five, I might be persuaded my loss was not in vain,' the man wailed plaintively.

Kalan bit back her smile as the merchant traded insults with Tejay. She was extraordinarily good at haggling, and the merchant seemed to appreciate her skill. In fact, they both appeared to be having a high old time. After a few more outrageous claims by the merchant and equally outrageous responses from the Warlord's daughter, they eventually agreed on a price of forty-five gold rivets, which Tejay parted with reluctantly, still complaining she was being robbed. The merchant wrapped the blade in a swatch of pale silk and presented it to Tejay with a small bow.

'Rarely have I enjoyed a transaction so much, my lady.'

'You should visit the markets in Natalandar some day, sir. I'm sure you'd find the experience quite invigorating.' She accepted the knife and handed it to Luciena. 'Here. This is for you. In case it turns out Marla has promised you to a Fardohnyan.'

Luciena looked stunned by the gift. 'But I couldn't . . .'

'Take it, Luciena,' Rielle advised with a laugh. 'She's probably only giving it to you so she can borrow it back when she marries Terin.'

Luciena smiled. 'Then I'll gladly loan it to you on your wedding day, my lady.'

'I was hoping you'd say that,' Tejay said. Then she placed her hand on Luciena's shoulder and smiled. 'Welcome to the family, Luciena.'

If Luciena offered Tejay a reply, Kalan never knew because at that moment a stack of chicken cages behind them toppled to the ground with an almighty crash.

Amid the screams of the shocked people in the crowded markets, the shouts of their guards, the squawking of the startled chickens and the cries of the angry stallholders, Narvell shoved her between two of the stalls and someone grabbed her arm, pulling her away. Before she knew what was happening, Kalan was running through the markets towards the Beggars' Quarter, free of any sort of armed guard for the first time in her life.

About an hour later, Kalan found herself standing outside the Pickpocket's Retreat, flanked by Damin and Starros. Rodja and Adham had stayed in the markets to make certain their diversion kept the guards occupied long enough to let them get away cleanly. Kalan looked around nervously. Just up the street, a ragged, blind beggar rattled a wooden box at passersby, and on the corner, a couple of rough-looking louts leaned against the wall, eyeing the strangers warily.

Several blocks away in the vast Krakandar markets, there

was probably a riot going on, as the guards responsible for the protection of the royal children realised they'd just lost three of them.

'We don't have much time,' Starros warned, gently pushing Kalan ahead of him towards the cool, dim interior of the taproom. She hesitated on the threshold. Kalan had never been in a tavern before. The smell overwhelmed her as much as the decor. It reeked of stale beer, old food and mouldy straw. It was still fairly early in the afternoon, so there were few customers and fortunately none of them paid any attention to the three newcomers. Unconsciously, Kalan reached for Damin's hand and felt it close over hers comfortingly.

'Now what?' she whispered nervously.

'We ask for Wrayan, I suppose,' Starros suggested.

'Are you sure this is the right place?' Kalan was worried about that. The Wrayan she remembered always appeared far more sophisticated than this dingy establishment seemed to imply.

'Only one way to find out,' Damin shrugged. He raised his hand and snapped his fingers in the direction of the nearest servant. 'You there! Wench! Come here!'

Kalan cringed at Damin's tone, as the young woman he had hailed looked up in surprise from the table she was wiping. She tossed her dishrag down and sauntered across to the door, eyeing them up and down suspiciously. As she drew closer, Kalan decided the girl was actually quite pretty in a rough, peasant sort of way. She had dark hair and eyes darkened with kohl and her lips had been reddened with berry paste. Around her neck, she wore a leather slave collar, tooled with a geometric design in a vain attempt to make it look decorative.

'Who are you calling *wench*, little boy?' she asked. She seemed amused by them, not intimidated.

Damin held his ground admirably in the face of her

mocking smile. 'Please inform Wrayan Lightfinger we are here to see him.'

The woman studied the three children for a moment and then laughed. 'You're here for Wrayan?'

'Is he here?' Starros asked.

'Who wants to know?'

Kalan looked up at the boys and frowned. This was all wrong. In her imagination, Wrayan had been waiting for them on the threshold of a rather nice inn where the tables were covered with snowy white cloths and high tea was served in a delicate Walsark porcelain tea service. She'd never dreamed they'd have to deal with some insolent tavern *court'esa* who obviously thought they were a joke.

'We're friends of his,' Kalan said hurriedly, before Damin got all wounded and announced who he was to all and sundry. 'What's your name?'

The *court'esa* bent over and studied Kalan in the dim light. 'By the gods! You're just a little girl. My name's Fee. And what's a pretty little thing like you want with a rogue like Wrayan Lightfinger?'

Kalan hesitated and stared at the *court'esa* in surprise. Nobody had ever called her a pretty little thing before. 'Is he here?'

'No, sweetie, he's gone,' she said, still studying Kalan closely.

'Gone where?' Damin demanded impatiently.

Fee looked up at him with a frown. '*Gone where* is none of your business, my lad. The likes of Wrayan Lightfinger don't have to answer to . . .' Fee's voice trailed off and she stared at Damin for a long moment, and then back at Kalan, and then she paled and added in a breathy whisper filled with awe, 'Oh, by the gods . . .'

Now we're for it, Kalan thought. *She's recognised us.*

As usual, it was Starros who thought fastest. He slipped

his arm through Fee's before she could drop into a curtsey. 'Please, not here!'

Fee looked at Starros in shock. 'You're the other one. Almodavar's bastard.'

Kalan smiled. She had thought only people living in the palace knew about Starros. Apparently, the whole city knew.

'Is Wrayan here or not?' Starros asked in a low voice, looking around to see if anyone was paying attention to them. 'We really need to see him.'

Fee shook her head and then jerked it in the direction of the table she'd been wiping down. 'Over there. People will start to wonder if we stay here blocking the door.' The *court'esa* led the way and a moment later they were seated in the booth, with Kalan next to Damin and Fee next to the dusty window beside Starros.

'Where is he?' Damin asked impatiently.

'Fardohnya, your highness,' Fee told him, apparently in awe of whom she was addressing. Kalan rolled her eyes. *Fancy anyone being in awe of Damin!*

'Please don't call me that,' he begged. 'What's he doing in Fardohnya?'

The wench shrugged. 'Meeting someone from the Guild over there, I suppose.' She smiled, probably realising how bad it sounded. 'You know what they say: *thieves and assassins know no borders.* He and Brak left about a month ago.'

'Brak?' Starros asked. 'Who is he?'

'A friend of Wrayan's.' Fee looked at the three of them and shook her head. 'I'm not sure I should be telling you this.'

'Don't worry,' Damin assured her with a scowl. 'When I have him arrested for treason on his return, I'll make sure your name isn't mentioned.'

'*Damin!*' Kalan objected. The poor *court'esa* looked as

if she was about to faint. 'Don't pay any attention to him, Fee. He's joking.'

'Wrayan is completely loyal to Hythria, your highness,' Fee hurried to assure the young prince. 'You must believe that! If he's gone to Fardohnya, I'm sure it's nothing dishonest.'

Starros smiled as he glanced around the room. 'He's the head of the Thieves' Guild, Fee. I'm not sure dishonest is the word you want there. We need to go, Damin. Now.'

Kalan's brother nodded and turned to his sister. 'Sorry, Kal.'

'Can I leave him a message?'

Damin glanced at the wench. 'Can we trust you to give Wrayan a message when he gets back?'

'Of course!'

'Then tell him Kalan Hawksword came to see him,' she volunteered, before Damin could leave a message on her behalf. 'And that I need him to come to the palace. As soon as he gets back.'

'I'll tell him.'

Kalan smiled at the nervous young woman, wishing she had something with which to pay her. Damin didn't seem to care. He prodded Kalan, none too gently, so she slid across the bench, pulling the hood of her undistinguished cloak a little further forward. Starros was already heading for the door. They had very little time to get back to the markets, Kalan knew, before word reached the palace that they were missing and Uncle Mahkas decided to seal the city until they were found.

'Thanks for your help,' Kalan said over her shoulder as Damin took her hand and pulled her towards the street. She stopped abruptly, shook free of Damin and ran back to the table. Reaching up behind her neck, Kalan undid the clasp of the copper necklace she'd bought earlier. 'This is for you.'

'I couldn't!' Fee gasped in awe.

'Take it!' Damin commanded. 'We have to go, Kal!'

'Thank you!' Kalan called over her shoulder as Damin hurried her to the door.

Her last sight of the tavern wench was of her sitting at the table, holding the necklace Kalan had given her, with tears in her eyes.

'Why did she cry?' Kalan asked as they slipped through the crowds back towards the markets.

'Who?' Damin asked as he dragged her along.

'That girl in the tavern. Fee. She cried when I gave her that necklace.'

'Slaves don't expect gifts from people like you,' Starros explained, stopping and holding an arm out to halt the other two. 'Or payment.' He glanced down at her and smiled, ruffling her hair fondly. 'That was a nice thing you did for her, Kalan.'

Starros turned his attention back to their route, cautiously glancing along the next street before allowing the other two to proceed. They stopped like that at every street corner until they were almost back at the markets. It took more than two hours. As they neared the city's inner wall, they could hear the commotion going on as the Raiders searched the crowded marketplace for their lost charges.

'When we get back to the first row of stalls, we should split up.'

'I could cry and pretend I was lost,' Kalan volunteered.

'Or you could tell us where you've been.'

The three of them spun around to find Geri Almodavar, Raek Harlen and several dozen Palace Guards filling the street behind them.

Kalan's heart sank. *Now we're really in trouble.* Damin, however, appeared ready to bluff his way out of it. He stepped forward boldly.

'There! You see, Starros!' he declared, grinning at the soldiers rapidly surrounding them. 'I told you it wasn't possible to give a Krakandar Raider the slip for more than an hour to two. Thank you, Captains. I just won a wager thanks to your efficiency. Sorry for giving you a fright, but you can dismiss the search parties now. I trust they enjoyed the exercise as much as we did.'

Almodavar smiled thinly. 'Nice try, Damin.'

'You *didn't* enjoy it?'

Almodavar glanced over his shoulder at his men. The Krakandar Raiders were efficient. There was barely a person left in the street not wearing palace livery by now. The captain smiled coldly. 'We had a wonderful time searching several acres of market stalls, looking for you three, didn't we, lads?'

'Highlight of my whole week,' Raek Harlen agreed, coming to stand beside Almodavar, his hand resting on the hilt of his sword.

Kalan frowned. It was never a good sign when Krakandar's captains stood shoulder to shoulder scowling like that, even when they were supposedly on your side.

Damin must have come to the same conclusion. He glanced at Kalan and Starros with a rueful smile, then turned back to face the guards. 'I guess this means another forty laps of the training yards?'

Almodavar glanced at Raek before he replied. 'Forty laps? You should be so lucky, my boy. More like four hundred.'

'Assuming, of course,' Raek Harlen added, with a degree of malicious glee that made Kalan cringe, 'you three survive explaining where you've been to your mother.'

25

Even surrounded by the towering Sunrise Mountains, Winternest dominated the landscape as Wrayan and Brak approached, its massive walls rising out of the mountain-side and looking just as eternal. The castle guarded one of only two navigable passes across the Sunrise Mountains between Fardohnya and Hythria. This one was known as the Widowmaker Pass. The other pass was much farther south, near Highcastle.

Against the majestic backdrop of the snow-capped mountains that flanked the fortress, it seemed as if the building had grown from the very rock of the mountain itself, rather than been constructed by mere mortals. *Not surprising*, Wrayan mused as they rode up the steep highway leading to the massive keep at a laboured walk, because it hadn't actually been built by mere mortals. It had been built by the Harshini, its tall spires and elegant lines achingly reminiscent of Sanctuary.

The keep served as a garrison, customs house, inn and fortress and catered for much of the traffic that moved between Hythria and Fardohnya. As they drew closer, Wrayan realised Winternest was actually two castles in one, built either side of the road leading through the pass into Fardohnya, joined by an arched and heavily fortified bridge high above the road that linked the northern wing to the southern wing. By the amount of traffic heading through the southern gates, he guessed that was where most of the commerce of the border post was carried out. The other side was probably the private domain of Sunrise's Warlord, when he was in residence.

The road was paved now, right up to the keep and all the way through the pass to Westbrook on the Fardohnyan side of the border. Sunrise's Warlord, Chaine Lionsclaw, fulfilling an agreement Damin's father made years ago with Hablet of Fardohnya, had paved the narrow pass through the mountains in a massive construction project which had taken the better part of seven years to complete and had proved a test of engineering skills far beyond that initially anticipated. The pass had been awkwardly narrow in places, causing traffic jams that contributed much to its reputation for being a maker of widows. Fardohnyan engineers had come up with a solution in the end, figuring out a way to harness the explosive powders used in fireworks and using them to blast through solid rock. The result was a much wider pass that could be kept clear of snow all winter, no more traffic jams and, subsequently, far fewer widows.

The recipe for the explosive powder, however, was a jealously guarded secret, for which there was a king's ransom on offer to anybody able to discover it. In the past, Wrayan had toyed with the idea of using the considerable resources available to him through the Thieves' Guild to discover the secret, but as the mill where the powder was made was closely guarded, and Hablet had either executed or cut out the tongue of anybody who even thought they knew the process, he'd decided the risk just wasn't worth the reward. But he hadn't abandoned the idea altogether, and it was on this flimsy pretext that he'd arranged to meet with a man from the Fardohnyan

Thieves' Guild to discuss the possibility of purchasing the secret of the explosives.

There was almost no chance the man would help Wrayan in his quest, but that wasn't really the point. Wrayan needed an excuse to be in Westbrook and the meeting gave him one. The rest was up to Brak.

That there was something seriously amiss with the Halfbreed had become more and more evident the longer Wrayan was in his company. On the surface, he seemed the same old Brak. He caroused with whores every chance he got, drank more than most men could stand without it having a noticeable effect on him, and joked about everything and everybody who crossed his path. But there was a brittle edge to his humour, a dark side to his revels. He acted like a man trying to drown his pain, not a man looking for entertainment.

There were other hints, too, Wrayan noticed. Strangely, there was no sign of any demons around the Halfbreed. Wrayan knew Brak discouraged the demons from following him about in the human world, but he also knew that a few of them – Eyan and Elebran in particular – worshipped the very ground Brak walked on and spent every moment they could dogging his heels. But there had been no sign of the little demons during the four weeks it took the two travellers to reach Winternest. Brak hadn't mentioned them, either.

At first, Wrayan didn't think much of it. Brak was over seven hundred years old. He had secrets enough for a dozen lifetimes. But as the weeks progressed, Wrayan's sense that Brak's pain went far beyond simple remorse grew stronger. He wondered if his inclusion on this fool's errand was merely a ruse to give the Halfbreed an excuse to share his burden. He would allow no mental communication between them: a sure sign there was something going on in Brak's head that he had no wish to share. He'd deliberately thrown himself recklessly into a brawl at a tavern in Zadenka, on the border between Krakandar and Elasapine, and then picked another fight with a wagon driver on their way through the city of Byamor. On both occasions, Brak had provoked his opponents and picked men bigger and more belligerent than he was, as if he sought a beating. And he fought like a man seeking oblivion.

But Brak remained silent about whatever tormented him, and Wrayan was wary about asking, certain that if Brak wanted to talk about it, he would do it in his own good time. As they approached the border fortress, however, he felt compelled to say something. Brak may have some dark load weighing on his soul, but Wrayan couldn't afford to have him unburden his pain in a place like Winternest.

'Let me do the talking when we get inside,' Wrayan suggested, as they urged their horses up the cobbled road. The air was much thinner up here and although there was little trace of snow by the roadside, there were still sheltered pockets of white scattered across the mountain in the shadows of the thickly forested slopes, and their breath frosted as they spoke.

'Why? Don't you think I know how to talk to a customs official?' It was the first thing Brak had said for hours, another reason for Wrayan's concern. Brak was not normally so taciturn.

'I think, in light of your present mood, it might be better if you left it to me.'

Brak glanced at Wrayan. 'In my present *mood*?'

'You have been a bit irritable lately.'

'You've got more balls than a pawnbroker's sign, Wrayan,' the Halfbreed told him with a shake of his head. 'I'm not in any damn mood.'

'I see,' Wrayan mused. 'That fistfight in Byamor was just you letting off steam then, was it? And the one in Zadenka? And then there was that poor woman in the markets in that village we passed through this morning, who you turned into a quivering mass of tears because you didn't like the look of her apples . . .'

Brak turned his attention back to the road. 'That doesn't mean I'm in a *mood*, Wrayan.'

'Even so, I still think you should let me do the talking,' Wrayan insisted. 'Whether you're in a mood or not.'

'Fine,' Brak shrugged. 'You do the talking.' The Halfbreed fell silent after that and didn't say another word until they were riding through the gates of Winternest.

As it turned out, they had little trouble with the customs men. Wrayan was Hythrun, after all, and carrying no goods for trade, and although Brak's father had been a Medalonian, he spoke Hythrun like a native and knew how to blend in, so nobody paid him much attention. The customs man waved them through with barely a second glance, although he did advise them to join one of the caravans travelling to Fardohnya for safety.

Widening the pass had made travel between the two countries easier, but it had also opened up the route to bandits, who found the numerous abandoned campsites and the web of tracks that linked them to the pass and to each other, left by the workers employed to build the pass, the perfect environment for highway robbery. The bandits attacked swiftly, savagely and without warning, disappearing back into the mountains as quickly as they came. It was rumoured, the customs man added in a conspiratorial tone, that they weren't really bandits at all. The popular belief around Winternest was that the bandits were Fardohnyan soldiers in disguise, robbing and pillaging every Hythrun caravan they could lay their hands on for the enrichment of their king. Wrayan didn't discount the rumour. It sounded like something Hablet would do.

'There's a particularly savage gang known as Chyler's Children working the Fardohnyan end of the pass at the moment,' the customs man added, when Wrayan seemed unimpressed by his warnings. 'They're very dangerous at this time of year.'

'We'll watch out for them,' Wrayan promised.

'Two men riding alone is an almost irresistible temptation.'

'Truly, we can take care of ourselves,' Wrayan insisted, thinking no band of thieves and robbers stood much of a chance against two sorcerers with no inhibitions about using their powers to defend themselves.

'You could ride with one of the caravans,' the customs man suggested. 'They never knock back an extra blade to watch over their cargo.'

Wrayan politely declined the offer of an introduction to one of the Hythrun caravan drivers, wondering if the man got some sort of kickback for arranging extra security. Instead, he and Brak mounted up again and, just before midday, rode under the bridge connecting the two castles of Winternest and headed into the Widowmaker Pass.

26

One thing Marla had recently learned about loyalty was that it had a downside. It was all well and good to be able to trust your life to someone, but when it came to interrogating six children who were all prepared to take the fall for their comrades, it was the most frustrating quality she had ever encountered. By the time she was finished questioning them, Marla had six completely different versions of what had happened in the markets and the culprit was Starros, Damin, Rodja, Adham, Narvell or Kalan, depending on which one of them she was speaking to at the time.

Hours of interrogation and she was no nearer the truth than when she started, although her heart had slowed to a more normal rate and she could breathe again – something she'd been incapable of when the first message arrived at the palace informing her that Damin and the other children were missing.

'Any luck finding out what really happened today?' Rogan Bearbow enquired, entering Mahkas's office a few moments after Marla had banished Damin from her presence in disgust with the warning that she didn't want to speak to him again until he was prepared to tell her the truth. The Warlord was dressed for the ball, in a severe black outfit that drew attention to his powerful body. Along with all the other reasons Marla wanted to strangle her children at the moment, she was furious at her sons for pulling this prank while Rogan Bearbow was here to witness it.

'I don't know where I've gone wrong with Damin,' she said, forcing a laugh she didn't feel. 'He's not normally so . . . reckless.'

In reality, Marla had sent Damin to his room to avoid the temptation of strangling him with her bare hands herself. *Doesn't he know the danger?* she asked herself, over and over. *Haven't I impressed upon him yet how easy it would be for an assassin to slip a blade between his ribs in a crowded market? Why does he delight in tormenting me like this?*

The Warlord nodded sympathetically. 'It's dreadful, isn't it? All that hard work, the tutors, the training . . . and all you've got for your trouble is a very resourceful boy, smart enough to give Krakandar's finest warriors the slip. A boy who's so loyal to his friends that he'd rather be punished himself than let the others take the blame for something he was involved in. I can see why you're so upset with your miserable failure.'

Relieved beyond words that Rogan viewed things so favourably, Marla allowed the briefest of smiles to flicker across her face. 'You're very kind, my lord. Unfortunately, I'm not ready to look upon this little escapade quite so generously, just yet.'

'In your place, nor would I,' Rogan replied. 'But I do think this episode displays more of Damin's character than you realise, your highness. And it's not all bad.'

'I appreciate your advice, my lord. I'll see you at the ball?'

'I was just on my way there now,' he informed her. 'And don't think you're the only one worried about what their children are up to. I live in mortal terror of what that daughter of mine has decided to wear to the ball this evening.'

Marla smiled sympathetically. 'I think you fear unnecessarily. Tejay spent much of the day with Rielle and Luciena discussing ball gowns, I believe. If she sought their advice, you can safely assume she won't be wearing chain mail.'

'One can only hope,' Rogan agreed with a smile. 'Don't let the distractions of a childish prank deprive us of your company for too long, your highness.'

'I'll be there as soon as I can,' she promised.

After Rogan left, Marla paced the room for a time, trying to think of a way to deal with her errant children. She was still pacing when Elezaar came looking for her a little while later, and no closer to solving her dilemma.

'They're asking after you in the ballroom,' he informed his mistress as he closed the door to Mahkas's study behind him. 'Mahkas is trying to cover for you, but your absence is very noticeable.'

'I'll be along soon.'

'You could put off dealing with the children until morning, couldn't you?'

'And give them even more time to corroborate each other's stories?'

'So which of them is lying?'

'If only I knew. According to Damin, it was his idea they give their guards the slip and see how far into the Beggars' Quarter they got before they were caught.'

'And Kalan and Starros just tagged along for the adventure, eh?'

Marla walked to the window, crossing her arms as if suddenly chilled. 'A very plausible tale if I believed for one moment that Starros would "just tag along" with Damin on such a flimsy pretext, or that any of the boys would endanger Kalan to do something so monumentally stupid.' She turned to Elezaar thoughtfully. 'Perhaps I should speak to her again. I suspect Kalan is the weakest link in this chain of deception. Maybe she'll crumble where the boys won't.'

'I'd not be too sure of that, your highness,' the dwarf mused, climbing into the chair opposite her desk.

'Do you know something about this escapade that I don't?'

'Perhaps.'

'*Well . . . ?*' she prompted impatiently.

'Kalan was asking me about joining the Sorcerers' Collective the other day.'

Marla stared at him. 'She *what?*'

'Kalan is trying to decide what she wants to be when she grows up. She came to me for advice and the conversation got around to the Sorcerers' Collective, and one thing led to another . . .'

'You actually *encouraged* my daughter to think I'd let her join the Sorcerers' Collective?' Marla gasped.

'No! Not at all!' Elezaar assured her hastily. 'Quite the opposite. I pointed out that there was almost no chance you would agree to such a thing.'

'*Almost* no chance?' Marla repeated.

'I didn't want to disappoint the child, your highness.'

Marla sighed. 'What did you tell her, Elezaar?'

'I . . . well, I sort of implied that you *might* let her join the Sorcerers' Collective if she had someone with magical ability to watch over her.'

'Someone with magical ability?' she echoed incredulously. Then understanding dawned on her and she threw her hands up. 'Of course! Wrayan Lightfinger. She was trying to get to the Beggars' Quarter to see Wrayan.'

'Possibly.'

'You think she was trying to do something else?'

'The children were missing for over three hours, your highness. You might want to consider the possibility that they were successful in their mission to meet with Wrayan and that's what they're hiding from you.'

I'll kill them myself, Marla decided. *I'll poison them at dinner tomorrow. Or maybe while they're bathing tonight. I'll just go in and drown the lot of them. End of problem.*

'What did I ever do to deserve this?' she asked aloud.

Elezaar smiled. 'Perhaps a word to Master Lightfinger will clear the whole thing up?'

Marla nodded. 'Have a message sent to him. Tell him I require his presence at the palace at his earliest convenience.' Wrayan would know she meant *now*.

'And what are you going to do to the children?'

She shrugged. 'I'm sure Almodavar can come up with something suitably punitive for the boys. As for Kalan . . . well, if my daughter wants to join the Sorcerers' Collective then I have a bigger problem than a few missing children to worry about, Elezaar. A much bigger problem.'

News arrived back at the palace a couple of hours later that Wrayan Lightfinger was unable to attend the princess because he was no longer in the city. According to the messenger Elezaar had sent to the Pickpocket's Retreat, Wrayan had been gone for over three weeks and wasn't expected back for a few more yet.

Puzzled, but a little relieved that Kalan had not made contact with him, Marla made her excuses and left the ball, having decided to speak to her daughter directly. This insane notion about joining the Sorcerers' Collective had to be nipped in the bud and the sooner it was done, the better.

Banned from the party and confined to her room as punishment, Kalan rose to her feet hurriedly when her mother entered.

'If you've come to ask me to change my story, I won't,' Kalan declared belligerently as soon as Marla closed the door.

'Even if you're lying?'

'But I'm not lying!' she protested. 'What I said happened

252

is the truth. I decided to see if I could give the guards the slip. Narvell and the Tirstone boys helped me by creating a diversion and Starros and Damin came after me to make sure I was all right. It's all my fault.'

Marla smiled and took a seat on one of the chairs by the unlit fireplace. 'So your brothers are liars then?'

'Of course not!'

'Yet all of them claim to be the instigator of this affair. You can't all be telling the truth, which means at least five of you are lying. If I'm to believe my daughter, I must see your brothers are punished, not only for their prank, but for their dishonesty as well.'

Kalan frowned and took the seat opposite her mother. 'Can't you just . . . let it go?'

'Not until I know the truth.'

Marla waited while Kalan thought on that for a moment, wondering when she had grown so tall. She wasn't as porcelain pretty as her cousin Leila, and would certainly never be the temptress Rielle was, but Kalan had a feeling of depth about her, a strength of character that belied her meagre ten years.

'I believe,' Marla added, when Kalan continued to maintain a stony silence, 'that it may have something to do with your wish to join the Sorcerers' Collective.'

Kalan stared at her mother in surprise. 'How did you . . . ? Of course, Elezaar told you, didn't he?'

'Elezaar is, first and foremost, *my* slave, Kalan. You should remember that before confiding in him.'

'Well, I won't be making *that* mistake again!' the child declared, crossing her arms defensively.

'Did you want to talk to me about it?'

'About what?'

'About joining the Sorcerers' Collective.'

'Why? You're just going to say no.'

'And do you understand *why* I'm going to say no?'

253

'Because of politics,' Kalan replied, in a bored voice. 'Everything is about politics. Everything I learn is about politics. Everything I *do* for the rest of my life will be about politics. You'll marry me off to some disgusting old man I've never laid eyes on before because of politics. Politics, politics, *politics*!'

'If you hate politics so much, I would think you'd be grateful I'm going to deny you the Sorcerers' Collective. There's no greater hive of political manipulators in all of Hythria.'

Kalan glared at her. 'All I am to you is the spare daughter you can use to make some great alliance to secure Damin's throne some day.'

Marla was cut to the quick to think Kalan thought so little of her. 'That's not true, Kalan!'

'Then what's your plan for me, Mother?' she demanded. 'What am I being groomed for?' When Marla couldn't answer immediately, Kalan nodded with satisfaction, as if her point was proved. 'See. You're not interested in what I can do – only who I can do it *to*. Well, make sure you get me a good *court'esa* when the time comes, Mother. I'm going to need to know that sort of stuff when I marry some grubby old creep you've picked out for me to seal your great alliance for you.'

Marla rose to her feet, hurt beyond words by Kalan's scathing tone. She couldn't believe her own daughter thought her so calculating, so cold. What was it Luciena had said? *There are rumours about your ruthlessness.* 'I'll speak to you again, young lady, when you've a more civil tongue in your head.'

'Don't you mean a more complimentary one?'

Marla didn't dignify the child's accusations with a reply. She turned on her heel and strode from the room, hurt most by the realisation that there was more than a modicum of truth in Kalan's words.

But as she opened the door and stepped into the hall, Kalan's accusation was abruptly forgotten. The sound of something breaking and a loud shout came from the room next door. Damin's room.

Instantly alert, the guards on duty outside the room drew their weapons as they turned and burst through the door in response to Damin's shouted cry for help. Her heart in her mouth, Marla rushed in behind them.

The sight that confronted Marla in her son's room left her speechless.

Damin was standing over Luciena Mariner, who lay facedown on the rug, held firmly there by Damin's boot, which rested, none too gently, across the back of her neck, pushing her face into the floor. With his right hand, he held her right wrist, twisted upward at a painful angle, and in his left was a small blade with a golden hilt. Its jewelled scabbard lay on the floor near Luciena's face. On her jaw was a rapidly purpling bruise where she'd obviously been hit and her nose dripped blood onto the priceless Fardohnyan silk rug, creating a slowly spreading stain beneath her.

Tears of pain spilled silently down the young woman's cheeks and her expression was one of abject terror. The moment of horrified silence that followed was broken only by Luciena's whimpering sobs and the odd counterpoint of the orchestra playing a bright tune in the ballroom downstairs.

The princess stared at Luciena, aghast, and then looked at her son. He didn't look like a child. He was breathing heavily, no doubt from the exertion of overpowering Luciena. His eyes burned brightly, almost savagely. For a brief moment, Marla felt she'd been given a glimpse of the future and saw the man Damin would one day become – and it was a dangerous one.

'What's going on in here?' she demanded, when she

finally found her voice, her mind unable to think of any reason why Damin would attack Luciena so brutally.

'I was hoping someone would be able to tell *me*,' Damin replied, letting Luciena's arm go with a shove and stepping back from her. Free of Damin's boot, Luciena struggled to sit up, looking around in blank, incomprehensible fright. He still held the small knife. Fortunately, Marla couldn't see anything that looked like a stab wound on either Luciena or her son.

'Damin!' she demanded impatiently, in no mood for any more of his pranks this night.

Her son stared down at Luciena and then spoke to the guards. 'You might want to restrain her before she tries anything else.'

'Restrain her?' Marla demanded, waving the guards back. 'Damin? What happened?'

'What happened?' he repeated incredulously, suddenly a child again. 'I'll tell you what happened, Mama. This wonderful new stepsister you brought us . . . well, she just tried to kill me.'

27

Marla Wolfblade knew only one way to deal with a crisis and that was by falling into a regimen of ruthless practicality. Mahkas knew this from experience, and as he hurried along the hall in response to the brief note Elezaar had just delivered to him in the ballroom, he was terrified by what he might find.

Because someone had just attacked Damin, right here in the palace.

And when she was afraid for her children, Marla was liable to do anything.

As he strode along the hall, leaving the dwarf panting in his wake, Mahkas ran through a mental inventory of the steps he'd taken to protect Damin. He rehearsed his excuses, silently justifying everything he'd done over the past thirteen years to keep his nephew safe.

The note in his hand was screwed into a tight ball, his knuckles white with fear. Unconsciously he rubbed at the small scar under the sleeve of his formal embroidered coat with the crumpled paper, not even aware he was scratching at it again. In the background, the orchestra struck up another tune, a folk dance Mahkas remembered learning when he was a child. The distant music evoked a rush of memories he didn't have the time or the courage to deal with . . . *Darilyn laughing at him because he couldn't remember the steps . . . Laran counting aloud as their mother, Jeryma, led him through the dance . . . and years later, in Cabradell Palace . . . Riika, barely ten years old, laughing delightedly as she mastered the same dance with her big brother, Mahkas, while Glenadal smiled indulgently as he looked on . . .*

Concentrate! Mahkas ordered himself impatiently. Now wasn't the time for reminiscing. Particularly about Riika. Now was the time for deciding how he was going to deal with Marla.

Will she blame me? he wondered anxiously.

It's not my fault. Almodavar's responsible for security in the palace. If someone got to Damin, then, plainly, it's his fault. I have done everything humanly possible to protect my nephew, short of locking him in a padded cell. Yet it hadn't been enough. Somehow, an assassin had slipped through the cracks and tried to kill the High Prince's heir.

What if she decides to replace me as regent?

Mahkas's fear was a valid one. If Marla decided Mahkas had failed in his duty as Damin's protector, there was nothing to stop her going to Lernen and demanding the Regent of Krakandar be replaced. She might even try to supplant him with that self-serving, overly smart, far-too-full-of-his-own-importance husband of hers, Ruxton Tirstone.

That makes sense, Mahkas concluded anxiously. *It would be just like that glorified shopkeeper to think he could wheedle his way into his stepson's regency. All that nonsense about the wonderful intelligence he provides, the help he gives her. All those smug looks, the subtle touches, the secret smiles . . . all of it designed for no other purpose than to let me know that Marla turns to him for advice more often than not these days, rather than me.*

Come to think of it, Ruxton may even have been responsible for the attack on Damin, Mahkas reasoned, warming to the notion of a betrayal from within the family. *How else would a spice trader ever manage to get promoted to Regent of Krakandar without something dramatic happening? Something designed specifically to discredit the incumbent regent?*

The more he thought about it, the more logical his assumptions seemed. *I never liked that snide little bastard . . .*

Mahkas reached the door to his study and took a deep breath. He understood what was happening now. Marla wouldn't like what he had to tell her about her husband, but it made perfectly good sense and he was sure he could convince his sister-in-law of her foolishness in trusting someone so far beneath her.

Bracing himself for the confrontation, Mahkas took another deep breath before he opened the door and stepped inside.

Almodavar was already there, along with Raek Harlen, two other bodyguards flanking the entrance and Damin, who was sitting on the edge of the desk swinging his legs back and forth, as he listened to his mother discussing the attack with the two officers. The boy seemed unharmed, which was a relief.

'Sorry to drag you away from the ball, Mahkas,' Marla remarked, looking up as he closed the door behind him. 'But we've had an incident I thought you should be apprised of.'

Mahkas nodded, a little surprised to find Ruxton wasn't here. 'Your note said there'd been an attempt on Damin's life.'

'There was,' Marla confirmed.

'I want the city sealed,' Mahkas ordered, turning to the Raiders. 'And the palace guard doubled. Call up every man, even those off duty.'

Neither Almodavar nor Harlen moved to respond to his

order. Mahkas could feel his palms sweating as the panic threatened to unman him. *Oh gods, has she replaced me already? Is that why I'm here? To be told I'm no longer Krakandar's regent?*

'Belay that,' Marla countermanded, although neither officer had shown any inclination to do as he'd ordered.

'But Marla—'

'Unless you fancy Luciena has an army gathering just over the border to invade us, Mahkas, I'd really rather not draw attention to our domestic problems while Rogan Bearbow and half the noble families in the north are kicking their heels up in the ballroom.'

'Luciena?' he asked in confusion. 'Luciena *Mariner*?'

'That's who tried to kill me,' Damin announced. He didn't seem unduly upset or in the slightest bit injured. But then, the boy had taken down Geri Almodavar in the dark. A slip of a girl like Luciena would have presented no problem at all.

'Is that true?'

Before Marla could answer, the door opened behind Mahkas and the dwarf waddled in. 'I want you to find Xanda,' Marla ordered the Fool, ignoring Mahkas in favour of her pet. 'Tell him I want him to bring Luciena's slave to me.'

'Shall I tell him why?'

'Only if you can do it quietly.'

'As you wish, your highness.' The dwarf bowed and closed the door on his way out.

Marla then turned to Mahkas and deigned to answer his question. 'I'm afraid it is,' she confirmed.

'But . . . *why*?'

'That's something we'd all like to know,' Almodavar replied.

'Didn't someone think to ask her? Or is she . . . ?' He glanced at Damin with concern, recalling how Almodavar had given the lad forty laps of the training yard for failing to follow through that night the captain had sought to test his ability. Surely, Damin hadn't killed the girl?

Dear gods, he's not yet thirteen . . .

But the boy grinned, rather flattered it seemed by his uncle's uncertainty. 'Do you really think I killed her, Uncle Mahkas?' He turned to Almodavar. 'See, *he* thinks I can do it.'

'Aye,' the captain agreed. 'But I've yet to see you do much more than brag about it, lad. You *should* have killed her. The same way you should have killed me.'

'I appreciate the sentiment, Almodavar,' Marla said. 'But in this case, I'm rather relieved he *didn't* kill Luciena. Like Mahkas, I would very much like to know *why* she attempted to kill Damin and, more importantly, if she was acting alone or if this is part of a much larger conspiracy. None of which would be possible if he'd ended her life.'

'And I didn't make the same mistake as last time,' Damin assured them, directing his comment mainly at Almodavar. Mahkas suspected Damin could feel another forty laps coming on and was anxious to avoid them. 'You told me I had to kill my attacker because that was the only way to make *certain* they were disabled. Well, I made certain Luciena was disabled. I just did it by putting my foot on her neck until help arrived, instead of killing her.'

Laran would have done something like that, Mahkas thought. *He doesn't look much like his father, but Damin Wolfblade has a lot of Laran Krakenshield in him.*

Mahkas wasn't sure if that was a good thing or a bad thing.

'I think we should be applauding Damin's clear thinking, not chastising him for it,' Mahkas told the captain, quite deliberately siding with his nephew. He made a point of letting Damin see he was on his side, every chance he got. 'But . . . *Luciena* tried to kill him?

Why, it's almost too fantastic to credit! I had a few misgivings about your decision to adopt the girl, Marla, but she seemed to be fitting in so well. Did she say nothing, even during the attack?'

'Not much,' Damin told him. 'She just came in through the slaveways waving that stupid little knife around with this weird look on her face. Even when I asked her straight out what she thought she was trying to do, she didn't answer me. It was like she couldn't even hear me talking.' Damin glanced over his shoulder at his mother and added with some concern, 'I know you told me it's wrong to hit a woman, Mama, and I tried to warn her before I laid a hand on her. Truly, I did. She just wouldn't stop coming at me. And she did have a knife.'

'I know, Damin,' Marla assured him. 'You're not in trouble. Not about *that*, anyway.'

'How did Luciena get through the slaveways?' Mahkas demanded of the Raiders. 'The door to Damin's room is supposed to be sealed.'

'It was locked when we checked it,' Raek Harlen confirmed. 'We don't know how she got through it.'

'Do *you* have any idea, Damin?' Marla asked.

The boy shook his head. 'No, Mama.'

He's lying, Mahkas thought, although he couldn't imagine why. 'Has she said nothing since?'

'She's not said a word, my lord,' Almodavar confirmed. 'We've got her down in the cells at present, but you'll not get much sense out of her. It's like she's battle shocked.'

Marla frowned. 'What do you mean?'

'You see it in battle sometimes, particularly among young soldiers confronted with their first kill. They go into a kind of daze. It's as if the rest of their body shuts down while their mind tries to deal with what they've seen or done.'

'And do they recover?'

'Most of them.'

'And you think Luciena is in some sort of battle shock?'

'I don't know, your highness. I'm just saying that's what it looks like.'

'And how long does this recovery usually take?'

'Hours,' Almodavar shrugged. 'Days. Sometimes weeks.'

'And sometimes not at all, I suppose.' Marla shook her head, clearly puzzled by the entire incident. 'It makes no sense. As you say, Mahkas, she seemed to be fitting in so well.' Marla leaned back in her chair – Mahkas's chair – and looked at her son thoughtfully. 'Have you had any trouble since she arrived, Damin? Before tonight?'

He shrugged and looked over his shoulder at his mother again. 'No. I mean, it's not like she's my best friend or anything, but she's always seemed nice enough. Maybe she said something to Rielle or Tejay.'

'What have Rielle Tirstone or Tejay Bearbow got to do with it?' Mahkas asked.

'The boys and I went down to the markets with them earlier today. And Kalan, too. Kal was talking to them just before . . .' Damin hesitated and then smiled sheepishly. 'Just before that other . . . incident.'

'And don't think I've forgotten about that,' his mother reminded him.

'I think we need to interrogate the girl,' Mahkas announced. 'Torture her if necessary.'

'I find torture is rarely necessary, Mahkas,' Marla informed him, clearly displeased by his suggestion.

'I just meant—'

'Yes, I know what you meant.'

Before Mahkas could defend his statement, the door opened again. This time it was his nephew, Xanda Taranger, who entered the office, followed closely by the slave Luciena had brought to Krakandar. The plump blonde's eyes were swollen and red-rimmed. She had obviously been crying.

'Your highness,' Xanda said, bowing to his aunt quite formally. A few months in Greenharbour had taught Mahkas's nephew some court manners, it seemed.

Marla bowed her head in acknowledgement of the greeting and turned her attention to the slave. 'Your name is Aleesha, isn't it?'

'Yes, your highness.'

'Do you know what's happened here tonight?'

She nodded, tears filling her eyes.

'Would you care to enlighten us as to why?'

'Your highness?'

'I'm assuming you know when your mistress joined the Patriot Faction.'

'I . . . I don't understand . . .'

'Your mistress attempted to kill the heir to the throne of Hythria this evening, Aleesha,' Marla pointed out. 'Unless she was acting out of some misguided notion of vengeance at the way she's been mistreated, I can only assume the attack was politically motivated. I am offering you the opportunity to provide us with the information we require, to save your mistress.'

'Save her?' Aleesha looked warily at the unsympathetic faces surrounding her. 'Save her from what?'

'Lord Damaran was just asking for permission to torture the information from your mistress, and Captain Almodavar has been chastising Prince Damin for not killing her. If you wish to save your mistress from those who feel high treason and attempted murder should not be punished by anything less than hanging, I suggest you tell us what you know.'

The slave shook her head as the tears spilled down her cheeks. 'I know nothing, your highness. Truly. There must be some mistake. Luciena would never do anything like this.'

'Who are her accomplices?' Marla insisted. 'Her friends?'

'There's nobody—'

'Her mother's friends, then?' the princess demanded. 'She was a well-known *court'esa*. Who were *her* customers, her regular clients? Was this plot hatched in Katira Keyne's bed and left to her daughter to follow through when the opportunity arose?'

'No!' Aleesha sobbed, becoming more distressed by the minute. 'No! No! *No*! You have it all wrong! Katira retired when she had Luciena. She never entertained another man after she became Jarvan Mariner's mistress. He insisted on it. There were no clients, your highness. There is no plot!'

'Maybe it was the debts,' Xanda suggested.

Mahkas turned to look at him. The young man seemed almost as upset as the slave. 'What debts?'

'Luciena was in dire debt after her mother died. Maybe Elezaar didn't find them all. Maybe there's another debt we didn't know about? One where the payment was going to be settled in return for Damin's life?'

'I hope it was a big one,' Damin remarked brightly. 'I'd hate to think my life was traded for the few rivets left owing on the cobbler's account.'

Mahkas sighed inwardly. The boy really should learn to take things more seriously.

'Damin!' Marla snapped at him in irritation, apparently of the same opinion. 'Be quiet!'

'Please, your highness,' Aleesha begged, sniffling back a fresh round of tears, 'I don't know why this happened. All I know is that my mistress would never try to kill anyone, and especially not a little boy.'

'I'm not a little boy!' Damin objected to nobody in particular.

'Damin, shut up or leave the room!' his mother barked angrily.

Aleesha fell to her knees, as if her subservient pose gave

weight to her words. 'Please, your highness. If this really happened, then something is dreadfully wrong. Luciena's not plotting with anyone! And even if she wanted to, who would plot with her? Until you offered to adopt her, Princess Marla, my mistress was the penniless, baseborn daughter of a *court'esa*. Even if someone knew you were planning to invite her here to Krakandar, there was no time between when you made the offer and when we left Greenharbour for her to plot anything with anybody.'

'She spoke with Ameel Parkesh,' Xanda reminded the slave.

'And you were there, Lieutenant!' the slave retorted impatiently. 'And you saw what he wanted of Luciena. You were the one who sent him packing! The only other person we saw before we left Greenharbour was the High Arrion and you're not going to accuse *her* of plotting against the High Prince's heir, are you?'

A deathly silence descended over the room. Marla visibly paled.

'Your mistress visited Alija Eaglespike before you left Greenharbour?' she asked in a voice devoid of all emotion.

'The day before we departed,' the slave confirmed. 'And it wasn't Luciena who went to visit her. It was the other way around. In fact, when Luciena tried to get in to see her the first time . . .' The slave hesitated, realising how damning her statement seemed.

'What did the High Arrion want with your mistress?' Mahkas demanded.

'I don't know, Lord Damaran. Lady Alija sent me to fetch drinks. They probably spoke about Luciena's cousin in Fardohnya.'

'So your mistress is in league with the Fardohnyans then,' Almodavar concluded. 'And they're the ones behind this attack.'

'No!' Aleesha cried. 'She's not in league with anyone.

266

I don't *know* what they spoke about. All I know is that when I returned with the drinks, Lady Alija was gone and Luciena was lying on the floor in a dead faint.'

Marla's expression hardened. 'Captain Almodavar,' she said, without taking her eyes from the slave. Her voice chilled Mahkas to the core. Even Damin turned and looked at her askance, seeing a side of his mother he'd not seen before.

'Yes, your highness?'

'I want you to go down to the cells and kill Luciena Mariner.'

There was another moment of thick silence before Almodavar responded. 'Your *highness*?'

'I want you to kill her, Captain. I don't care how. I just want her dead.'

The merciless order left even Mahkas gasping. 'But shouldn't we investigate—'

'Her mind has been tampered with,' Marla informed them. 'She is a threat while ever she continues to draw breath. I want her dead.'

'You can't!' Xanda objected.

Marla turned her icy stare on her nephew. 'I can.'

'Then you mustn't!' he corrected. 'If Luciena's mind has been tampered with – if the High Arrion has done it – you can't just kill her out of hand.'

'You don't seem to understand, Xanda,' Marla replied. 'She is a puppet and somebody else is pulling the strings. It might be the Fardohnyans or it might be the Patriots. I don't really care. I will not leave a threat like that alive and anywhere near my children.'

'I do understand,' he argued. 'Better than you think. And that's my point. If her mind *has* been tampered with, you need to know why. And more importantly, why *now*? What's changed in Hythria's political climate recently? Why choose now to remove Lernen's heir? Was this planned long ago or just an opportunistic attack? There's more going on here than just a girl we thought we could trust suddenly turning into an assassin. Aunt Marla, and you'd be a fool to ignore it.'

He's smarter than he looks, Mahkas decided, having never given Xanda much credit in the past for his intellectual capacity. Then again, Mahkas thought dryly, maybe he wasn't so clever, after all. *A smart man would think twice before accusing Marla Wolfblade to her face of being a fool.*

'And how do you suggest I do that, Xanda?'

'Wrayan Lightfinger.'

'But Wrayan's gone to Fardohnya,' Damin announced.

They all stared at him.

'Or so I've heard,' he added hastily, when he realised what he'd just revealed.

'We'll discuss *how* you know that later, young man,' Marla warned her son with an ominous glower, and then she turned her attention back to her nephew. 'But Damin is right, Xanda. Wrayan's not here. Do you propose I leave Luciena free to wreak what havoc she wishes until the head of the Thieves' Guild chooses to grace us with his presence again at some indeterminate time in the future?'

'Of course not, Aunt Marla. Keep Luciena confined, by all means. But don't kill her out of hand. Not yet. Not without giving Wrayan a chance to probe her mind and find out what's really going on.'

The princess thought about it for a moment and then nodded reluctantly. 'Very well, she lives – either until Wrayan gets back or I leave for Greenharbour at the end of summer.'

'And if Wrayan Lightfinger determines that her mind *hasn't* been tampered with?' Mahkas asked, privately sceptical about the thief's ability to wield any sort of magic, but wise enough not to challenge Marla on the issue.

'Then she dies.'

Relieved beyond words to learn someone else was to be held accountable for this disaster, Mahkas nodded slowly in agreement.

He didn't doubt for a moment that Marla meant every word of her promise to kill Luciena Mariner. And he wondered if he was the only one in the room who understood that the princess hadn't actually called off the execution. She'd merely delayed it for a while.

28

Brak rode in silence for the first few miles of the steep pass, impressed by the work that had gone into making a narrow slice between two peaks into a navigable road. Familiar with the building techniques of the Harshini, who had the benefit of magic to aid them in their work, he was used to seeing construction on a grand scale. What made this impressive was that it had been done with nothing more than human ingenuity and sweat. There had been no magical assistance in the Widowmaker to widen the road or transport the granite high into the mountains; no sorcerers to search for weaknesses in the rock, or instinctively feel for the easiest path, or the best place to lay foundations. They'd done it the hard way, using mathematics, engineering, a little bit of inspired guesswork and a huge force of slave labour. The mountain had been blasted away in places, the exposed rock face sharp and raw like a gaping wound on the flesh of the mountain. The walls had been reinforced in places, too, and the road snaked through it, paved in red granite from Krakandar that looked strangely out of place among the black rocks of the Sunrise Mountains.

Maybe the one good thing to come out of the Harshini exile, Brak decided, *was that it gave humans a chance to discover what they were capable of when forced to rely on their own resources.*

Wrayan rode beside him in silence, for which Brak was extremely grateful. He had no wish to talk. No wish to do much of anything. His world was defined only by his desire to see this Fardohnyan child he had never met delivered into safe hands. He needed to make some small amends for his crime; he needed to attempt some noble deed to atone. After that, Brak had no plans. He had nothing. His future was as empty as his soul.

Brak was counting the days until summer ended and Korandellen hid Sanctuary out of time once more. The ache would fade then, for a time. It wasn't as strong when the settlement was hidden, although it never truly left him. Brak needed the pain to go away. He needed memories of Sanctuary and the Harshini to fade into a distant blur.

At the same time, he savoured the torment. It was a cruel punishment, but a punishment he felt he deserved.

There is no going back, Brak told himself harshly. He deserved to suffer and all of the torments of the Seven Hells of Men probably couldn't penalise him enough for what he'd done. *I can never go back. Never go home. Never.*

And he figured he wouldn't need to. Once he and Wrayan had found this child locked in the dungeons of Westbrook, Brak would help Wrayan release him and then cover their escape. He would make sure they got away cleanly.

That was the reason Brak had invited Wrayan along on this journey. He needed to see this child got back to Hythria in one piece. He needed the boy to be placed somewhere he had a chance of growing up. Wrayan would see to it. He was a confidant of the High Prince of Hythria's sister, after all, and undoubtedly still had contacts in the Sorcerers' Collective. Wrayan would see the boy was safe.

'Can you hear that?'

Brak glanced at Wrayan. He could hear nothing at all but the sound of his own misery. 'Hear what?'

Wrayan cocked his head. 'Sounds like fighting.'

Instinctively, Brak's hand moved to the hilt of the serviceable Defender blade he carried. Now that Wrayan had brought it to his attention, he could hear it over the faint rush of a waterfall – the metallic scraping of blade against blade and the panicked shouts of men under attack. He listened carefully, not sure if the sounds were coming from ahead or behind them. The walls of the Widowmaker did strange things with echoes.

'It's ahead of us, I think,' Wrayan said.

Brak gathered up his reins, pleased by the thought of facing some action. It didn't hurt nearly as much when he was fighting. The need to stay focused on survival swamped the guilt and the pain for a time. His horse, sensing the change in his rider's demeanour, reared in anticipation.

'Probably a caravan under attack.' Brak grinned humourlessly, drawing his sword with a dramatic flourish. 'Let's go do our good deed for the day.'

Wrayan grabbed him by the arm before he could move. '*You* might fancy the idea of being a dead hero, Brak, but I'm rather fond of seeing the day out, thank you.'

'You just want to sit here and do nothing?'

'There're only two of us. Exactly how much difference is that going to make to a caravan under attack from bandits who are probably very well trained Fardohnyan soldiers in disguise?'

'You have no idea how much difference one man can make, Wrayan,' Brak snapped, shaking free of Wrayan's restraining hand. 'Come with me or not,' he added, more harshly than he'd intended. He kicked his horse forward into a gallop without waiting to see if Wrayan was following. 'I really don't care.'

*　*　*

The road curved ahead, following the natural contours of the pass. Here there had been no need to blast through rock to open up the road. It was almost wide enough to let another caravan pass. The forested slopes reached all the way to the edge of the road and, on the left, a small spring high above fed a narrow waterfall that poured down the face of the mountain in a constant tumble of white water. As he rounded the bend, Brak heard the sound of a horse following him, which meant Wrayan had decided to join his hopeless quest after all.

Just beyond the next bend in the road, he found them.

It was only a small caravan – no doubt the reason it was attacked – three canvas-covered, ox-drawn wagons caught between a felled tree the bandits had used to block the pass ahead and the swarm of men attacking from behind. The dozen or so Fardohnyan bandits were dressed in a motley collection of dark civilian clothing, which made it hard to tell them from the defenders. Those, he guessed, were the terrified-looking men standing with their backs to the wagons, holding off their assailants awkwardly. Most of the caravan guards seemed to be dead already; only the merchants were left to defend their property.

Brak urged his horse forward, careless of any lookouts that might be posted above, half-hoping for the solid thunk of an arrow in his back to end this downward spiral into self-destruction into which he could feel himself plunging. He couldn't go on like this. Although not immortal in the truest sense of the word, Brak's life span was that of a Harshini. He had lived more than seven hundred years now and, barring accidents, would likely live a thousand or two more. He couldn't carry the burden of his guilt for that long. He could barely lift it now.

With a glance, Brak took in the situation and then ploughed into the mêlée. He took out the first three bandits before they even realised someone was attacking them from behind. As soon as they became aware of the threat, however, the outlaws turned on him. Brak fought the next man off with ease – one can become quite expert with a blade after seven hundred years of practice – and then he turned to face his next attacker.

This man seemed a little more cautious. Brak had already taken out four of his companions. The Fardohnyan obviously judged this new opponent worthy of respect. He was swarthy and brown-eyed, but not fearful. Brak dismounted, not taking his eyes from the man, and pushed the horse clear as the bandit lunged for him. His first few strokes were careful, as if he was testing Brak's skill. Or his resolve. He moved sideways, forcing Brak to move with him, to keep him in sight. Then the bandit feinted, forcing Brak to move again until the bandit's back was to the wagons.

Clever, Brak thought, realising he now had his back to the rest of the bandits and no way of seeing one of them come up behind him. *Is this how it's going to end?*

Was it really going to be this easy?

A sudden cry behind him caught Brak's attention. He glanced over his shoulder to discover another man, his curved scimitar raised to strike in a blow that would have cleaved his skull in two had it connected. But the blow never fell. The man seemed frozen for a moment in time, and then he toppled forward, a small throwing knife embedded to the hilt in his neck.

Wrayan, Brak thought, looking around for the thief.

He couldn't see him, but he could feel the faintest prickle of magic against his skin, which meant Wrayan had had the presence of mind to draw a glamour around himself before he plunged into battle, and was effectively invisible. As he turned back to face the other bandit, he saw that man fall, too. The bandit had a shocked look on his grubby, stubbled face as he studied the six inches of metal unexpectedly protruding from his ribs. He slipped off the blade as he fell forward and suddenly Wrayan appeared behind him, as if from thin air, his dark eyes fading to their normal colour as he dropped the glamour and pulled his sword free.

'Are you *trying* to get yourself killed?' he snapped at Brak. 'Duck!'

Brak ducked as Wrayan swung his blade in a wide, inelegant arc above the Halfbreed's crouching form, almost taking another bandit's arm off at the shoulder. The man screamed and dropped his sword, then turned and fled back towards the forested slopes of the mountain pass. His departure seemed to give the merchants heart and they attacked the remaining thieves with renewed ferocity. Within a few moments, the rest of the Fardohnyans decided this caravan was now a lost cause and they followed their wounded companion back into the forest, leaving their dead comrades behind.

Brak glanced around at the dead guards and the dying bandits as he wiped his blade on the shirt of the nearest corpse and then sheathed it. He looked over at Wrayan. The young man wasn't a killer at heart, Brak knew, for all that he could wield a competent blade when the need arose. But neither was he squeamish. One didn't hold down a position like head of a Thieves' Guild for long if one couldn't deal out a bit of rough justice when the need arose.

'I guess they don't call this place the Widowmaker for nothing, eh?'

Wrayan didn't answer him. The thief simply sheathed his own sword and went to see what he could do to help the merchants.

By the time they'd helped load the bodies of the dead guards and the Fardohnyan bandits into the last wagon and pushed the felled tree off the road, it was almost sunset. Brak had thought it more logical to leave the corpses behind, but the caravan owner, a tubby little Hythrun named Kelesan Hull, insisted they take the bodies with them. He wanted to present the Plenipotentiary of Westbrook, the garrison commander of the Fardohnyan fort, with evidence of the attack and demand compensation. To do that, he needed proof.

'Eight dead guards and six dead bandits make for some fairly solid evidence,' Wrayan explained when Brak asked why they were loading the dead men onto the wagon. He would have taken his own men and left the bandits for their friends to retrieve later.

Brak had barely spoken to the merchants since he and Wrayan had rescued them, letting Wrayan do most of the talking. He was in no mood to socialise anyway. Brak wasn't upset about the men he'd killed. He was sorry that he wasn't one of them.

'Master Hull has invited us to join his caravan for the rest of the trip through the pass.'

Brak shook his head and glanced over at the hopeful merchant, who was wringing his hands as they tied the last wagon down and looking west towards the setting sun, no doubt wondering which was worse – travelling in darkness or spending a night in the pass with more of Chyler's Children in the vicinity.

'He wants *us* to protect his cargo from thieves?' Brak smiled humourlessly. 'You didn't mention you were head of the Krakandar Thieves' Guild, I'm guessing.'

'The subject didn't actually come up.'

'Does he think two men will do where eight failed?'

The thief shrugged. 'It's not likely they'll be attacked again before we reach Westbrook.'

'Then they hardly need us, do they?'

Wrayan looked at him with a frown. 'You were the one who wanted to rescue them in the first place, Brak.'

'I wasn't looking for a job opportunity out of it.'

'Which begs the question of what you *were* hoping to achieve, ploughing into that fight like you have a death wish.' Wrayan's eyes narrowed suspiciously. 'Do you want to tell me what's really going on?'

There's always a downside with the smart ones, Brak thought. *I should pick more stupid friends. Things would be a lot less complicated.*

'There's nothing going on, Wrayan. I just felt like a bit of exercise.'

'*Exercise?* the thief repeated incredulously. 'You killed four men. And you could have got us *both* killed!'

'Don't exaggerate. Anyway, you cheated. You used magic.'

Wrayan opened his mouth to protest and then suddenly closed it again, as if there was simply no point in arguing about it. With a snort of frustration, the thief threw his hands up, turned on his heel, and went to explain to Kelesan Hull that he and his companion were not available as guards for the remainder of their journey through the Widowmaker Pass into Fardohnya.

29

The pain in Luciena's head was unbearable. It had started, she recalled dimly, down in the markets. They'd been looking at that Fardohnyan bride's blade. She remembered Tejay Bearbow haggling with the merchant. She remembered Tejay making her a gift of the delicate little dagger.

And she remembered Tejay saying, 'Welcome to the family.'

After that, Luciena didn't remember very much at all . . . not until hours later when she discovered she was in Damin Wolfblade's room, just after he hit her on the jaw, knocked her down, almost wrenched her arm from its socket and then stood on her neck while he accused her of trying to kill him.

What had happened in the intervening hours was a complete mystery.

Luciena put her pounding head in her hands, recalling the look on Princess Marla's face as the guards had hauled Luciena to her feet. It was her contempt that ate at Luciena more than anything.

'So, this is how you repay my generosity?' the princess had said to her. If Marla had been the God of Storms, her voice alone would have brought on an Ice Age.

Luciena tried to shake her head; she tried to deny she'd done anything wrong. But the pain was unbearable and there were no words available to her. For some reason, she couldn't speak, even though she'd desperately wanted to protest her innocence. And even if she'd found her voice, what was she supposed to say? She didn't remember any of it. She'd certainly never set out to harm Damin Wolfblade and had no recollection of sneaking through the slaveways and using the hidden key to his room. The guards outside Damin's door hadn't granted her entry so, short of her scaling the outside wall of the palace – unlikely – even Luciena admitted there was no other way she could have got in there.

But why? she asked herself, over and over. *Why would I do something like that?*

There was no logical reason for any of this. Luciena had no gripe against Damin. Since coming to Krakandar she'd even begun to soften towards Marla, understanding a little of the pressures that dictated the princess's actions. The children of Marla's extended family had welcomed her with remarkably little fuss. Even Lord Damaran, although clearly dubious about Luciena's pedigree, had treated her with distant cordiality.

It's what I always wanted. Why would I throw it all away?

Locked in the hot, close confines of her bare prison, Luciena had had all night and much of the day to ponder that thought. In the cells behind the Raider's barracks – thankfully they didn't have dungeons here – she'd done little else but wonder how this could have happened to her.

In a way, the thoughts were a welcome distraction. Trying to figure out why she'd attacked Damin meant she didn't have to think about her future. *Not that I have a future.* Luciena was under no illusions about the inevitable fate of anybody foolish enough to assault the High Prince's heir.

Breakfast was served in her cell the following morning and she sat on the edge of the straw pallet in her ruined ballgown and ate the slops mechanically. She didn't taste a bite, but wasn't sure if that was the result of her misery or simply the tastelessness of the gluey gruel that passed for food here. They gave her a jug of tepid water and a bucket to use as a toilet and then left her alone to ponder her fate, hour after torturous hour, the silence and the isolation more frightening than being yelled at. It was as if they'd thrown her in here and forgotten all about her.

Maybe that's my punishment. 'Lock her up and throw away the key.'

Would Marla Wolfblade be content with that? *Probably not. She's more your blood-for-blood sort of woman.* She was practical, too. For the fool who dared threaten one of her precious babies, death was far cheaper than long-term incarceration.

It was almost sunset, and the pain had abated a little, when the lock on the door rattled, making Luciena jump to her feet, filled with a fear that was nauseating in its intensity. Suddenly, being ignored seemed so much better than being forced to confront the possibility they had come to carry out her execution.

The door opened. Luciena almost fainted with relief to discover it was Xanda Taranger. Then she noticed the look on his face and wondered if, perhaps, execution wouldn't have been easier to deal with.

He studied her for a long moment before he spoke. Luciena imagined the picture she must present. Her beautiful blue and gold gown was a ruin. The skirt was crumpled, the bodice stained by unsightly damp marks under her arms and across the small of her back. The smell of her unwashed body seemed to fill the small, airless cell. Her dark hair was in disarray and they'd taken her shoes and jewellery from her when she was thrown in here to await judgment.

When Xanda finally spoke, his voice was icy. 'Are you feeling better?'

Does Marla give the whole family lessons in speaking like that? she wondered irreverently. Fear was making her foolish, almost hysterical. The idiocy of the thought made her want to giggle, a fatal impulse she forced herself not to give in to. Instead, she nodded, not trusting herself to speak – or even certain she was able.

'Captain Almodavar claims you're in some sort of shock.'

Luciena nodded again, warily. Not long ago, Xanda had wanted to kiss her. He looked at her now as if he wished they'd never met. It surprised Luciena to discover how much that hurt.

'I . . . I don't know . . .' she managed to stammer, her urge to giggle forgotten as tears blurred her vision.

Xanda looked down at his boots.

'What's going to happen . . . to me?'

'Nothing for the moment,' he informed her with all the emotion of a slave delivering a report on the state of the livestock. 'I think . . . I mean, there's a suggestion someone tampered with your mind. You won't be executed until we know for sure.'

'But I *will* be executed,' she said, finding it easier to reach for the words she wanted each time she spoke. The veil of her torpor was wearing away, abraded by fear.

For the first time, Xanda showed some sort of emotion when he looked at her, and it seemed to be despair rather than the anger she anticipated. 'What did you *expect*, Luciena? You attacked the heir to the Hythrun throne! You tried to kill him!'

'But I don't *remember*!' she cried, wiping away her tears impatiently so she could see him more clearly. 'I don't remember anything!'

He shook his head in disbelief. 'Gods, even if I could bring myself to believe your mind wasn't your own, he's only a child! Didn't some part of you understand what you were doing?'

'I don't *know* what I was thinking, Xanda! The first coherent memory I have after the markets yesterday was Damin belting me in the jaw, just before he tried to rip my arm off.' She wanted to add that he might only be a child, but Xanda's precious little heir to the Hythrun throne had a fist like a sledgehammer and she had the bruises to prove it. But apparently nobody cared about her injuries.

Surprisingly, Xanda's demeanour softened a little. He took a step closer and grimaced as he examined her bruised jaw. 'It looks pretty painful.'

'I'll live. At least until they hang me.'

He reached out and touched her injured face with unexpected gentleness. Luciena wasn't sure how it happened, but the next thing she knew Xanda was holding her in his arms while she sobbed against his shoulder. She clung to him desperately, the horror of her predicament finally getting the better of her. Xanda let her cry, saying nothing, seemingly content to just hold her close and comfort her.

After a while, the tears abated and she sniffed and leaned back in his embrace. 'Won't you get accused of being a traitor, coming here to visit me?'

Xanda shook his head. 'I'd have come anyway. I sort of feel responsible for this. I was the one who convinced you to visit Aunt Marla. If I hadn't done that, she wouldn't have invited you here. And if she hadn't invited you to Krakandar, Alija probably wouldn't have tampered with your mind—'

'Alija?' she asked in shock. 'You mean Alija *Eaglespike*? The High Arrion?'

Xanda nodded. 'I'm hoping she's the one who made you do this. Otherwise you'll be hanged as a Fardohnyan spy. We won't know for certain until Wrayan gets back, though.'

Now she was really confused. 'Wrayan? The man from the Thieves' Guild who came to lunch that day? The chap Kalan has a crush on?'

Xanda smiled faintly. 'That's the one.'

'What's he got to do with anything?'

'Wrayan's a sorcerer,' Xanda told her. 'He'll be able to tell us what happened to you.'

'And what happens if this Wrayan of yours decides my mind *hasn't* been tampered with?'

Xanda hesitated before he replied. 'Then the only conclusion we can draw is that you knew exactly what you were doing. That you're a Patriot assassin. Or working for the Fardohnyans.'

She stepped out of his arms, shaking her head. 'But that's impossible! I don't even know any Fardohnyans.'

'That's not what your slave claims.'

Luciena sighed and threw up her hands. 'My father had a brother . . . they fought when they were young men and hadn't spoken to each other for over thirty years when my father died.'

'Then why were you trying to see the High Arrion?'

'I got a letter . . . it came out of the blue. I'd never even heard from my uncle before. He claimed his grandson was magically gifted. Aleesha thought he was just trying to extort money out of me.'

Xanda smiled sympathetically. 'You don't have to make up stories about stray magicians to convince me you're innocent, Luciena.'

'I'm not making *anything* up,' she protested. 'My cousin is an Innate, or something like that – I've never met him, actually, so I can't say for sure.'

'And you believed this letter?'

Luciena shrugged, resenting Xanda's tone. She wasn't

nearly as gullible as he believed. 'For all I know, it's true. I know my father used to joke all the time that we had a Harshini ancestor. When Warak Mariner wrote wanting me to arrange passage for his grandson to Hythria so he could join the Sorcerers' Collective as an apprentice, it didn't seem that outrageous to me.'

'So you get a letter from a complete stranger in Fardohnya and you immediately race off to see the High Arrion? To do what? Enrol your cousin in the Sorcerers' Collective?'

'What else was I supposed to do? If you recall, I was flat broke by then so I couldn't have sent him money, even if I'd wanted to. I thought . . . if Rory really was gifted, then maybe Lady Alija . . .' Her voice trailed off as she searched his face, hoping for some sign that he believed her. 'Why are you interrogating me like this? I swear on my mother's grave, I'm not making this up, Xanda. I'm a loyal Hythrun. I didn't come to Krakandar to harm your cousin. Or anybody else, for that matter.'

Xanda nodded again and then, after a long moment, he smiled cautiously, taking her hands in his. 'Actually, I don't believe you did, either.'

'But it's not up to you, is it?'

'No.'

'Should I speak to Princess Marla? Tell her—'

'That's probably not a good idea right now.'

Thinking of the rage Marla Wolfblade must be in, Luciena had the feeling Xanda's words might be something of an understatement. She sighed heavily, consoling herself with the thought that at least they weren't planning to drag her out into the courtyard and summarily execute her. 'How long do I have to stay locked up in these cells?'

'Until Wrayan gets back.'

She could feel the despair starting to overwhelm her again. 'Will you visit me, every once in a while?'

'Do you want me to?'

Luciena nodded. 'Yes.'

'Then I'll come.'

Despite the hope that simple promise gave her, the silence quickly grew thick between them, taut and filled with unspoken emotions that neither of them was sure about or willing to examine too closely. When she could bear it no longer, Luciena shrugged, certain the only thing she *could* say to him was the truth. 'I'm innocent, Xanda. You'll see.'

Xanda let go of her hands, nodding guardedly. She wasn't sure if he was agreeing that she was innocent, or that he'd see soon enough, one way or the other. He moved back towards the door and knocked on it. The guard waiting outside unlocked it and waited for Xanda to step outside.

'I'll try to come again tomorrow,' he promised.

The thought that at least one person might still be on her side bolstered Luciena's fading courage. 'I'll try to squeeze you into my busy schedule.'

Xanda smiled at her weak attempt at humour. 'I'd appreciate that.'

'Thank you.'

'For getting you into this mess?' he asked heavily.

'For believing in me.'

He didn't reply to that; perhaps just as uncertain about his feelings as she was. In the end, after hesitating for a moment, he simply turned and left the cell. The guard closed the door behind him and locked it and Xanda's fading footsteps in the corridor outside were the last thing Luciena heard for a long, long time.

30

The man from the Fardohnyan Thieves' Guild was waiting for them when they arrived at Westbrook, just as the gates were closing for the evening. A rather less impressive version of Winternest, Westbrook was built to a similar scale, although it lacked the elegant lines provided by a bridge over the road linking the two arms of the keep. Brak recalled that the current buildings had replaced a ramshackle fort, constructed mostly of wood – a dilapidated series of dangerously unstable structures, that had been unroofed, without fail, almost every winter, surrounded by a flimsy wooden palisade that wouldn't have stopped a concerted attack by a gang of hungry children.

Now it's a solid, damn-near-impregnable fortress, Brak thought, trying to remember the first time he had come through here. It must have been more than six hundred years ago, he realised with mild surprise, back when it was still under construction. *No wonder it's starting to look old.*

Brak and Wrayan rode into the vast bailey of the northern keep behind a long Hythrun caravan they had caught up with in the last half mile of the pass. The lead wagon was loaded with barrels of ale and several large clay jars of mead, the next three were stacked with bales of wool and the remaining half dozen were wagonloads of raw quartz from the mines near Byamor in Elasapine. Wagonloads of raw quartz were much less tempting to bandits. Despite the gold locked inside the rocks, they weighed too much for too little return to a criminal, so the ore caravans were usually allowed to pass though the Widowmaker unmolested. Still, it was heavily guarded and the caravan owner visibly relaxed as the first gate boomed shut in the darkness.

'Wrayan Lightfinger?'

Brak dismounted and turned to look at the man who had spoken Wrayan's name. He was a slender fellow of average height with pale, piercing grey eyes that didn't seem to belong in his swarthy face. He was holding a torch in his left hand, which spluttered and flared, making it impossible to read his expression. Next to him was a lad of about ten, who looked more like a stable boy than a thief.

Wrayan peered at him in the gloom, too, and then nodded. 'Danyon Caron?'

The Fardohnyan thief offered Wrayan his handshake, glancing over Wrayan's shoulder at Brak. 'Who's your friend?'

'This is Brak Andaran.'

'From the Guild?' Danyon asked suspiciously.

'I can vouch for him,' Wrayan said.

The Fardohnyan thief nodded. 'The boy will see to your horses,' he told them, as the lad stepped forward. 'For a price.'

Wrayan fished a few copper coins from the pouch at his belt and handed them to the boy. The lad looked at them critically for a moment and then silently held out his hand for more. With a shake of his head, Wrayan handed over more coins. This time the child seemed satisfied. He pocketed the copper rivets and took the reins of both horses, leading them away to the stables on the left.

'Seems robbery isn't restricted to the Thieves' Guild around here,' Wrayan remarked.

The Fardohnyan thief shrugged. 'Boy has to make a living. You almost didn't make it before the fortress closed,' he added as the second massive metal-reinforced gate was ponderously pushed shut for the night.

'We were delayed,' Wrayan told his contact, as they walked up the steps towards the keep's main hall with Brak trailing them. 'Trouble with bandits in the pass.'

'Getting so you can't make a decent living these days, without some thief attacking you,' Danyon agreed with a smile. There was music coming from the hall and the sound of many voices. Everybody staying in the keep tonight would be gathered in the hall, Brak knew, the ritual here having altered little in the hundreds of years the fortress had stood.

'Were they yours?' Brak asked curiously.

'All thieves worship Dacendaran, Master Andaran.'

'That's not what I asked.'

Danyon smiled cryptically but didn't offer any other answer. He turned to Wrayan instead. 'Good thing you got here when you did. I'd just about given up on you. I've been here for three days and this isn't my favourite place in Fardohnya, you know. If you didn't get here tonight I was going to head back to Qorinipor in the morning.'

'Thanks for waiting,' Wrayan replied. 'Is there somewhere we can talk in private? Do you have a room here?'

The Fardohnyan shrugged. 'Nobody has a room here, Wrayan, unless you're very good friends with the Plenipotentiary of Westbrook. Everyone bunks down in the main hall at night. But don't worry about being overheard. You can't hear yourself think in there when it's busy. Unless someone is reading our minds, we'll be secure enough.'

That comment got a faint smile from Wrayan, who glanced back at Brak. He shrugged. 'You go on ahead. I think I might check on the lad with the horses. That beast of mine can be a bit of a bastard,' he warned, then added with a pointed look at Wrayan, 'when he's in a *mood*.'

Wrayan didn't rise to the bait. 'I'll see you later then.'

Brak watched Wrayan and Danyon Caron disappear into the hall, and then turned for the stables. The lad was doing a competent job, although the stables were quite crowded and the horses were forced to share a stall. Fortunately, Wrayan's mount was a mare and Brak's a gelding. After the better part of a month on the road together, the two horses were familiar with each other's company. The stable boy stared at Brak suspiciously when he arrived, but his wounded feelings were quickly soothed by the application of more copper rivets. Brak asked him to re-saddle the horses after they were fed and rubbed down. The boy demanded even more money – which Brak parted with reluctantly – and then went back to brushing down Wrayan's mare.

That minor but important detail taken care of, Brak left the stables and headed across the deserted bailey. Even though it was summer, the nights were cold at this altitude, but the wind had dropped and the sky was a dark blue carpet sprinkled with precious stones. Only the faint sounds of music and raised voices from the hall disturbed the night, the creaking leather armour of the guards on the wall-walk above, and the occasional drunk staggering out of the hall to take a leak in the shadows. The Hythrun caravan with its load of ore was parked near the stables, the guard sitting on the lead wagon nodding off to sleep on his watch. He didn't even stir as Brak slipped past him. In the deep shadows between two of the outbuildings, Brak stopped and glanced around to ensure he was unobserved, and then he closed his eyes and sent out a silent call.

Elarnymire!

The little demon popped into existence in front of Brak almost before he completed the thought. She blinked at him with her huge, liquid black eyes, her ears drooping, a disapproving frown on her wrinkled little face.

'Well,' the demon announced. 'You took your sweet, precious time getting here.'

He squatted down until he was face to face with the little demon. 'I had to fetch Wrayan,' he replied in a whisper, glancing through the darkness of the laneway to the bailey beyond. There was no sign of anybody, and Elarnymire would probably vanish the moment someone approached, but he'd still have to explain what he was doing lurking in a laneway, talking to himself, if he was discovered.

'What use is Wrayan Lightfinger, Brakandaran? Admittedly, the lad can wield a little magic, but he has so little Harshini in him we can't even tell which clan he belongs to,' Elarnymire reminded him. 'No more than the child they hold in the dungeons here.'

'Which is precisely why I need him,' Brak explained. 'Even if I *could* go back to Sanctuary, my lady, this child doesn't belong among the Harshini. He's human. Wrayan will see him safe. Is he all right?'

'They're not feeding him very well,' Elarnymire informed him. 'But he's not starved yet. And they put him in with the women rather than the men. He's been getting a little impatient. Did you want me to tell him rescue is at hand?'

'No, I'll find him.' Brak looked at her curiously. 'Was it your doing, to keep him with the women here?'

The demon shook her head. 'You told me not to interfere.'

Brak smiled thinly. 'And you always do *exactly* what I ask.'

Elarnymire shrugged. 'Truly, it wasn't my doing. He's a child and several of the women incarcerated here have children with them, too. I suppose they thought that's where he belonged.'

Brak was relieved to hear it. The fate of a twelve-year-old boy in a dungeon full of hardened criminals was not likely to be pleasant. 'I'll go and get him now then.'

'Why now?'

'Why not?'

'They've closed the gates.'

'They'll open again soon,' Brak predicted confidently.

Elarnymire didn't seem very happy, but she nodded in agreement. 'And when this is done? What then?'

'What do you mean?'

The demon looked up at him with a harsh, unblinking stare. 'Are you coming home, Brakandaran?'

Brak didn't answer immediately. When he did, all the anguish of his terrible deed felt concentrated into a painful lump stuck somewhere in the pit of his belly. 'I have no home any more, Elarnymire.'

The demon placed her long bony hand over his. 'Only you believe that, Brakandaran. The Harshini will welcome you in Sanctuary. Korandellen and Shananara *want* you to go back. Even the Gatekeeper asks after you.'

'I can never go back, Elarnymire. You know that.' He shook off her hand and stood up, leaning against the cold stones of the outbuilding. 'Koran and Shanan know it, too.'

'And this is how you intend to repay the Harshini for all they've done for you?' she asked, looking up at him crossly, 'By turning your back on them?'

291

'You saw what I did, Elarnymire,' he said, almost pleading for her understanding. 'Turning my back on the Harshini is the biggest favour I can do them.'

'They don't think so.'

'That's because they're not capable of thinking anything else!' he hissed angrily, wishing the demon would just let it drop. There was no discussion to be entered into; no chance of him changing his mind. He had a job to do; a small chance to redress some of the balance, and then . . . well, he had no plans beyond that. Merely hope for a painless oblivion. Brak sighed ruefully, wishing he could control his temper a little better. 'I'm sorry, my lady. I don't mean to snap at you. I thank you for watching over the child. I'll take care of him now.'

'Do you know where to find him?'

A brief, sour smile flickered over Brak's face. 'I know where the dungeons in Westbrook are, my lady. I've been a guest in them more than once.'

'Did you want me to give the king a message when I get back to Sanctuary?'

Brak hesitated and then shrugged. 'I don't know, Elarnymire. How many times can I say I'm sorry before he's sick of hearing it?'

'Once was enough for Korandellen.'

'Then tell him . . . tell him if he ever really needs me, I'll be there for him. But other than that . . . I think it's better this way.'

Elarnymire nodded solemnly. 'As you wish.'

'My lady,' he added quickly, sensing the demon was about to vanish.

'Yes?'

'Don't come looking for me. Or let the others waste time trying to find me. Please.'

The demon hesitated for a moment and then nodded again. 'You can't deny *what* you are, Brak, any more than you can deny *who* you are. But I will pass on your message. And I will tell my brethren you wish to be left alone. I cannot speak for the gods, though. They may not be so easy to discourage. You're a particular favourite of Kalianah, as I recall.'

'Don't worry about the gods. They have a very short attention span. Thank you.'

'You have no need to thank me, Brakandaran,' the demon said. 'If anything, I am doing you a disservice by pandering to your irrational request.'

'I'm grateful, my lady, nonetheless,' Brak said, with a slight bow.

The demon seemed unconvinced. 'Death will not make the pain go away, Brakandaran. That is not his function.'

Without waiting for him to respond, Elarnymire vanished from sight, leaving Brak a little disturbed by how easily the demon could see through him; and the uncomfortable feeling that she was probably right about Death not being sufficient to put an end to his torment.

There's no time to worry about it now, Brak decided, pushing away his pain to make room for much more practical concerns. To reach the dungeons, he had to go back through the main hall. He glanced around the yard before he emerged from the shadows of the laneway, hesitating as a figure came out of the main building. He was a tall man, with long well-groomed hair, and wore a large chain and medallion around his neck.

The Plenipotentiary of Westbrook himself, Brak thought, wondering about the name of the man who held the job these days. The title was an archaic one that dated back to the early days of the new nation of Hythria. That must have been over a thousand years ago now, Brak realised.

Brak waited for a moment as the Plenipotentiary stopped on the top step to take a deep breath of the crisp evening air, then watched him walk across the bailey to a doorway in one of the other buildings to the right of the hall – probably where his quarters were housed. Once the door was closed, the torchlit bailey was deserted again, except for the dozing caravan guard. Brak crossed the cobbled yard. His eyes darkening as he wrapped a glamour around himself so he wouldn't be seen, he entered the main hall of Westbrook.

31

Wrayan looked up as Brak entered the hall, obviously searching for him. He was in the far corner on the right, sitting opposite Danyon Caron, nursing a metal tankard. The Fardohnyan Guild thief was laughing – probably over the amount Wrayan was offering for the secret of the explosive powder Fardohnya guarded so closely. Wrayan must have felt the prickle of magic Brak called up when he pulled the glamour around himself, but his eyes slid over Brak as if he wasn't there.

Brak strode the length of the vast hall, sidestepping several drunken caravan guards who were trying to molest the girls serving drinks. He gave one of the young women a surreptitious hand, fending off her tormenter with an unseen kick to the man's groin that dropped the would-be groper like a sack of barley, sent his friends into gales of laughter at what they thought was his clumsiness, and left the fool writhing on the floor clutching his bruised manhood with tears streaming down his face. The dark-haired wench Brak had saved from the drunkard's unwelcome attentions continued to move between the crowded tables, handing out foaming tankards of ale, oblivious to the favour done by her unseen benefactor.

There were a number of families in the hall, clustered

together nervously as they tried to stake a claim near one of the fires before everyone settled down for the night, and a few cheerful souls anxious to dance to the band of musicians playing in the corner. Closest to the doors that led down into the dungeons were a number of off-duty troops of the garrison. Brak slipped past them with the same ease he had everyone else in the hall. They weren't watching the door to the lower levels, in any case. Most of the soldiers were still laughing over the drunken caravan guard writhing in agony on the floor a few tables away.

The noise of the hall faded as the thick door closed behind Brak to reveal a narrow, torchlit staircase. Dropping the glamour, but keeping hold of his power, he headed down the stairs, no longer attempting to conceal his approach. When he arrived at the bottom, he found a large room filled with tables and bench seats that were lit with oil-filled torches set into brackets along the walls every ten feet or so. Remarkably, they appeared to be the original torches crafted by the Harshini, their delicate iron scrollwork at odds with the rank depression of this place.

Towards the back of the hall, two broad, dark corridors led into the darkness and the dungeons beyond. They weren't meant to be dungeons, Brak knew. The Harshini had designed this place as dry-goods storage and wine cellars for the keep. No sooner had they finished the keep and presented it to its new owners, however, the wooden interior walls with their beautifully painted murals had come down and been replaced by iron bars.

There were about a dozen men dicing around the table nearest the fireplace, opposite the entrance to the dungeons, dressed in the grey and blue livery of Fardohnya's regular army. Unlike the Hythrun High Prince, the Fardohnyan king allowed none of his subjects to raise their own armies. Hablet's soldiers came from all over Fardohnya, pressed into service either as payment of their liege lord's taxes or as punishment for any crime that didn't warrant a lashing, death or slavery, which were the only real options under the Fardohnyan penal system. The officer class was mainly drawn from the sons of the nobility, but there was a sizable number of mercenaries and plenty of volunteers who sought a military life to avoid the drudgery of the farm or their father's trade. They probably weren't the worst army in the world (Brak privately awarded *that* honour to the Kariens and their feudal rabble up north) but Hablet's army lacked the sharp discipline of the Medalonian Defenders, or the relentless dedication to honouring Zegarnald, the God of War, for which the Hythrun Raiders were so famous.

One of the soldiers looked up as Brak appeared at the foot of the stairs. He stared blankly at this unexpected visitor for a moment, not really seeing his totally black eyes, and then his head fell forward and hit the table with a soft thud, followed by the heads of his companions. Brak smiled humourlessly. The guards were fast asleep and would probably stay that way right up until somebody from upstairs came down and woke them up to enquire if they were aware all their prisoners had escaped.

Helping himself to the large ring of keys on the belt of the man sleeping at the head of the table, Brak whistled tunelessly as he entered the first corridor. This was where the men were incarcerated. He did wonder, for a fleeting moment, about the calibre of criminals he was letting loose, and then pushed the thought away. The law in Fardohnya was applied very much by the rule of wealth – meaning the wealthier you were, the less likely you were to be charged with a crime. Despite what these men were being held for, their biggest crime was being too poor to buy off the local magistrate (in Westbrook's case that meant the Plenipotentiary) or any of the other officials who expected a gratuity in order to ensure justice was done.

Taking a torch down from the wall to light his way, Brak unlocked each cell as he came to it and threw the door open wide. He made no other announcement of his intention to free the prisoners. Until the convicts in the women's cells were also free, he didn't want a mass exodus anyway. Some of the prisoners were asleep; others stared at him as if they were still dreaming. Brak unlocked the last of the dungeons and then walked back towards the guardroom and the other corridors accompanied by the hushed and disbelieving whispers of the male prisoners as they realised their cells were open.

He did the same thing when he came to the women's cells, except this time as he opened each door he asked in a loud whisper, 'Is there a boy called Rory in here?'

In the third cell he opened he got a reply. A woman pushed forward and grabbed his arm as he was turning to open the next cell.

'Who wants to know?' she demanded of him.

Brak studied her in the flickering light of the torch. She was about thirty-five, he guessed, maybe a little older, and not unattractive. Her hair was hidden under a knotted scarf, her eyes were dark and she was dressed in men's trousers and a sheepskin coat. Brak got the feeling, just from the fearless way she confronted him, that this was a woman who could take care of herself. She certainly wasn't a working *court'esa* arrested for not paying her dues. He wondered briefly what she'd done to find herself in the dungeons of Westbrook.

'Do you know where he is?' Brak asked, raising the torch a little higher to look around the cell. The other women were huddled under their blankets, as if they didn't really believe they were being rescued. He could see no sign of a child.

'You didn't answer my question,' the woman accused.

'Nor you mine,' he pointed out in reply.

The woman's eyes narrowed cannily. 'You have a plan for getting him out of here, I suppose?'

'Yes.'

'Take me with you then, and I'll tell you where he is.'

Brak hesitated, wondering if he should accept the help of this woman. Or indeed, if he even needed her help. The lad had to be here somewhere.

The woman stared at him, waiting for his answer.

'Where is he?' Brak asked, deciding it wasn't worth arguing about.

'They took him out of here earlier this evening.'

'To where?'

'There's an important fellow here from one of the Guilds in Qorinipor,' she explained. 'He likes little boys and the Plenipotentiary of Westbrook likes to keep his options open, if you know what I mean.'

Brak cursed softly. It would be coincidence beyond belief to imagine there was another high-ranking member of any Guild currently visiting Westbrook this evening. His task had just become vastly more complicated. He might have to extract the child from under the nose of Wrayan's contact in the Thieves' Guild.

Wrayan wasn't going to be very pleased about that, he guessed.

The newly released prisoners pushed past him, heading for the door, ready to stage a mass breakout. There was little time before they surged out of the dungeons and all hell broke loose upstairs.

'What's your name?'

'Chyler Kantel,' the woman replied.

The name seemed vaguely familiar to Brak, but he didn't have time to wonder where he'd heard it before. He tossed the keys to her. 'Let the others out.'

Chyler caught the keys easily and hurried along the corridor to let the other women free.

Brak sagged against the bars of the now-deserted cell, still cursing. The boy hadn't been in the hall with Danyon, so he probably had him stashed in a room somewhere, despite what he'd said earlier about there being no private rooms in Westbrook unless you were a friend of the Plenipotentiary.

Brak recalled the man walking across the bailey to his quarters on the other side of the keep. If the Plenipotentiary of Westbrook was trying to curry favour with the Thieves' Guild, he might well have offered Danyon the use of a room in his own quarters to amuse himself with the boy.

He was going to have to involve Wrayan directly now, Brak realised. The problem was, even if he had the time before the newly released prisoners surged up the stairs to the main hall, there was no way to let the Hythrun thief know what was going on without getting him away from Danyon Caron first.

Not unless Brak was willing to open his mind and speak to Wrayan mentally.

After all the trouble he'd taken to conceal his thoughts from Wrayan, it seemed like failure to allow the young man access to his mind now.

Wrayan could use only a fraction of the magic Brak could call on, but if he had a talent at all, it was for telepathy. The moment he made mental contact with Wrayan, his terrible secret would be a secret no longer.

'They're all out,' Chyler informed him, tossing the keys down the drain in the centre of the cell. They clattered against the stone for a few moments and then landed with a splash at the bottom of the sewer. Chyler smiled. 'It's going to take them a little while to get these cells locked again.'

'Where would they have taken the boy?'

'Maskaar's quarters, probably.'

'Who?'

'Pasha Maskaar,' she told him. 'Our esteemed Plenipotentiary of Westbrook.'

'Tall chap? Slicked-back hair, and—'

'Thinks his shit doesn't stink?' Chyler finished for him with a sour grin. 'That's him. Met him, have you?'

'I saw him earlier this evening. Would he harm the boy?'

'Not personally. Boys aren't his particular inclination.'

'Do you know where to find his quarters?'

She rolled her eyes. 'Every woman in Westbrook knows where Pasha Maskaar's quarters are . . . what's your name, by the way?'

'Brak.'

'Like the Halfbreed in the legends?' she asked, amused by the notion. 'Your parents must have had a sense of humour.'

The released prisoners had stopped milling about aimlessly and were starting to move towards the stairs.

'We'd better stick with the mob,' he suggested, glancing over his shoulder. He debated reaching for Wrayan's mind again, but the idea of exposing his own vulnerabilities was still too painful to contemplate. He glanced at Chyler, thinking she was probably his next best bet. 'Can you take a message to someone for me? Up in the hall?'

'I thought you wanted to find Rory?' she reminded him as they followed the edge of the crowd. There were probably more than fifty prisoners pushing their way upward. There was going to be a riot when they burst out that door at the top of the stairs.

'I do,' Brak agreed. 'But I can find the Plenipotentiary's quarters on my own. If you want to get out of Westbrook in one piece, however, I need to get a message to my . . . accomplice.'

'And what does your *accomplice* look like?'

'He's Hythrun. Tall, dark hair . . .' Brak smiled briefly as they started up the stairs. 'And you'll probably think he's good-looking. He's thirtyish, but looks younger. He's sitting at the far end of the hall on the left going out. He's drinking with a Fardohnyan named Danyon Caron.'

'Danyon's *here*?' Chyler asked in surprise. 'Well, that solves the mystery about who Maskaar wanted poor Rory for.'

'You know him?' Brak asked curiously.

Chyler smiled. 'You don't think I wound up in the dungeons of Westbrook because of my wide circle of friends at the Winter Palace, do you? What's the message?'

Before he replied, Brak grabbed her arm and held her back for a moment, letting the surge of prisoners move ahead of them. He waited until the curve of the stairs took the last of the stragglers out of sight and then turned to Chyler. 'His name is Wrayan Lightfinger. I need you to tell him to meet me at the gate. There'll be horses waiting for him. I'll be there with the boy. Tell him he doesn't have long.'

'What about me? You promised you'd help me get out of here.'

'You can leave with him.'

She stared at him with a shrewd look. 'What about you then?'

'I'll make sure you get away.'

'That's very noble and self-sacrificing of you,' she remarked.

'I'm a very noble and self-sacrificing sort of fellow.'

Chyler studied him closely, as if she was trying to read his real intentions, and then shrugged. 'Cross me and you'll be sorry,' she warned.

'Just deliver the message.'

The woman nodded and followed the others up the stairs, taking them two at a time. Brak waited until she was out of sight before he pulled the glamour around himself again and followed her up to the main hall and the riot he had let loose along with the prisoners of Westbrook.

32

Wrayan's first hint that something was amiss with Brak's plan wasn't the sudden shouts as the fifty-odd prisoners previously incarcerated in Westbrook's dungeons burst out of a door at the other end of the hall. He'd been expecting that. It was the unexpected arrival of Brak's messenger.

The prisoners had surged forward and were halfway down the hall before the soldiers drinking near the door even thought to react. The crowd wasn't unsympathetic to the plight of the escapees, either. Some may have been friends or family members of those held prisoner here. The soldiers quickly found their way severely hampered by the mob.

Danyon looked over his shoulder at the sudden shouts and the tables being pushed over, a puzzled look on his face. 'What the hell . . . ?'

'I think all your prisoners just got loose,' Wrayan remarked blandly.

'They're not my prisoners,' Danyon pointed out, turning his back on the chaos and picking up his ale. He took a good mouthful before wiping away the foamy moustache it left on his upper lip and grinned. 'Not my problem.'

Wrayan smiled, thinking he'd probably react the same

way if he was to find himself witness to a mass breakout in Krakandar. He looked around for Brak. Somewhere in this mêlée, the Halfbreed should be pushing through with the boy. Then – if everything went according to plan – it was out into the bailey where their freshly saddled horses should be waiting, through the gate (which Brak had assured Wrayan would be open) and into the Widowmaker Pass and safety across the border. He'd felt Brak drawing on his magic, could feel it faintly still, but could see no sign of the Halfbreed. The guards were clambering over tables, pushing everybody out of the way in their haste to apprehend the prisoners, some of whom had managed to acquire weapons by now. A few of them had turned to fight the oncoming soldiers, but the majority were simply trying to make it outside to the illusion of freedom.

'Idiots,' Danyon remarked. 'How far do they think they're going to get with the gate closed?'

'A lot further than you, Danyon Caron.'

Both Wrayan and Danyon were startled by the sudden appearance of a woman behind the Fardohnyan thief. She was short but compact and quite handsome, despite the grime on her face. With one smooth movement, she had Danyon's dagger out of its scabbard at his belt and rammed it into the thief's back with a sharp, upward thrust. Danyon fell forward onto the table heavily.

Wrayan jumped backwards, knocking the bench over in his haste. He stared at the woman in shock. 'You *killed* him!'

'Are you the Hythrun?'

The shouts and cries of the escaping prisoners meant they were effectively isolated in a small pocket of silence. '*What?*'

'Is your name Lightfinger?'

'Yes.'

'Then you're the one I want.' The woman leaned over

Danyon's dead body, smiling. 'I warned you never to come here again, you slimy little prick.'

'You killed him!' Wrayan repeated incredulously.

'Not often enough,' she replied, jerking the dagger free.

Wrayan had no idea why he'd just witnessed a murder, and it wasn't the careless ease with which this woman had killed Danyon that shocked him. He lived on the darker side of human society and knew how cheap life was among thieves and whores. For that reason, there were rules governing meetings such as this and a guarantee of safety was foremost among them. What chilled him to the core was the realisation that if Danyon Caron had let it be known in Qorinipor that he was coming to Westbrook to meet with Wrayan Lightfinger of Krakandar, that made Wrayan the most likely suspect in Danyon's murder. Finding himself accused of killing the head of a guild of another city was something Wrayan could well do without.

'I've got a message for you from someone called Brak.'

The name pierced through the shock enough to get Wrayan's attention. '*What?*'

'Your friend, Brak. He said to meet him outside. He has horses waiting for us.'

'Us?' Wrayan repeated blankly.

'I'm coming with you.'

'You just killed the head of the Qorinipor Thieves' Guild.'

'Pretty good reason for not hanging about here then, don't you think?'

Wrayan couldn't argue with that. The need to get out of the hall, out of Westbrook, was suddenly his most urgent priority, with or without Brak's lost Fardohnyan child. He looked towards the door. The bulk of the soldiers were pursuing the escapees into the yard, and everyone else was racing outside to watch the fun and games. Without waiting to see if the woman was following, Wrayan headed for the door at a run.

The bailey was in chaos when they finally managed to push their way outside. Not only had extra guards been called up, but the gate was half-open and one very angry and loud Kelesan Hull was standing there, arguing with the officer on duty about whether or not he should be allowed to come in. The prisoners, realising the gate was unsecured, had surged towards it while the soldiers tried to get it closed again, but Kelesan's wagon was blocking the gate and he was refusing to budge, so there was little hope of them getting it shut in time.

Wrayan hesitated on the top step, taking in the scene with a glance.

'They'll never get it closed again,' the woman chuckled, coming up beside him. She seemed singularly unperturbed by the fact that she had just committed cold-blooded murder.

'And we'll never get through it,' Wrayan pointed out, frowning at the crush of people heading for the gate. 'Where's Brak?'

The woman spotted him first. 'There!'

Brak was running towards the stables from one of the buildings off to the left. Over his shoulder was a limp, ragged bundle. They ran down the steps and pushed their way across the yard, catching up with him as the stable boy brought out their horses.

'Mount up and take him,' Brak ordered as soon as he spied Wrayan.

Wrayan snatched the reins from the stable boy and swung into the saddle. He barely had his feet in the stirrups before Brak was handing the limp child up to him. 'He's been drugged,' Brak explained.

'All part of the evening's entertainment,' the woman remarked sourly, climbing into the saddle of Brak's gelding. 'We're never going to get through that gate, Brak.'

'No need. There's another way out.'

'How do you know?' Wrayan asked, adjusting his grip on the boy for fear of losing him. He wasn't too thrilled about the woman joining him in their desperate escape, either.

'I was here when the Harshini built this place, Wrayan. Follow me.'

Brak led them away from the stables and further from the gate and the riot, the noise fading a little as they rounded a corner and rode down a lane between two of the outbuildings on the eastern wall, which finished in a dead end.

'Oh! A dead end!' his new companion remarked, when she saw they were trapped. 'This plan just gets better and better, doesn't it?'

'Have a little faith,' Brak said, and then turned to face the wall. Wrayan felt the Halfbreed drawing on his magic and suddenly the wall faded to reveal a postern gate tall enough for them to ride through. The woman stared at it with the same sort of stunned surprise that Wrayan imagined he must have showed when she so coldly rammed a knife into Danyon Caron's back.

Wrayan shook his head in wonder. 'They built a secret gate.'

'The Harshini might be naive, Wrayan, but they're not stupid.' Brak opened the gate, which apparently wasn't even locked. 'Now get out of here. And don't stop at Winternest.' Brak reached into his vest and pulled out something, which he handed to Wrayan. It was a cube of transparent material showing a dragon clutching the world in its claws, attached to a fine gold chain.

'What's this?'

'If things get desperate,' Brak told him, glancing back down the lane to ensure they were still unobserved, 'and I do mean desperate, Wrayan, call them. Someone will come.'

Wrayan looked at the pendant in shock. 'But they can't leave—'

'They can leave Sanctuary any time they want, Wrayan. They just choose not to. Now go!'

'But . . . what are *you* going to do?'

'I have to stay here and close this gate behind you.'

'Can't you do that from the other side?'

'No. Now leave! You don't have much time. Take care of the boy and don't get yourself killed any time soon, all right?'

Wrayan had a dreadful feeling that Brak was saying goodbye, but before he could reply, shouts at the end of the lane made him look around. Soldiers were charging down between the outbuildings, waving torches and swords with equal menace.

'Go!' Brak cried, slapping the rump of Wrayan's mare. The horse surged forward through the hidden gate, followed a moment later by the Fardohnyan woman on Brak's gelding. No sooner were they through the gate than it vanished and the wall behind them changed back to the appearance of solid rock.

Brak's horse reared. The woman fought to control it as Wrayan stared at the wall, the shouts and cries of the guards on the other side leaving no doubt about Brak's fate. He wouldn't have had time to close the gate and draw a glamour around himself to hide from the oncoming soldiers.

'We need to get out of here!' the woman reminded Wrayan urgently.

He was still staring at the wall, his eyes misted with tears.

'Hey! Lightfinger! Can you hear me?'

Wrayan forced back his shock and grief to look at his new travelling companion. The child in his arms showed no sign of regaining consciousness. 'I hear you.'

'Then let's ride, my friend,' she advised, 'because it's not going to be long before they decide that secret gate your friend conjured up for us might not have been a figment of their limited but collective imaginations.'

'But Brak—'

'He's probably dead.'

Wrayan glared at her, wishing this woman, whoever she was, would not deal with death quite so casually. Her expression softened a little when she saw his grief and she smiled. 'He said he was here when they built this place. I suppose that's how he knew about that gate.'

Wrayan nodded mutely, still trying to deal with the notion that Brak might be dead.

'That would make him what? Over six . . . maybe even seven hundred years old?'

Wrayan nodded again, but remained silent.

'He knew how to open it, too.' The woman gathered up her reins and shook her head in wonder. 'By the gods . . . he really was the Halfbreed, wasn't he?'

'Yes,' Wrayan replied, pulling the unconscious child a little closer to him. 'He really was.' *And someone*, he thought, numbed by the very idea, *is going to have to tell the Harshini that Lord Brakandaran té Carn is dead.*

But that was something he could deal with later. First, he had to get out of Fardohnya in one piece. In light of the company in which he suddenly found himself, that might prove more difficult that he'd anticipated. He stared at the woman, wondering what he'd done to deserve being burdened with such a dangerous liability.

'Do you have a name?' he asked, turning for the Widowmaker Pass.

'Kantel,' the woman replied, kicking Brak's mount into a canter with the awkward seat of one unfamiliar with horses. 'My name is Chyler Kantel.'

33

Wrayan rode through the Widowmaker Pass almost without stopping, anxious to put as much distance between himself and Fardohnya as possible before dawn. He wanted to get past Winternest, too, before the Hythrun fortress came awake.

Chyler Kantel deserted him even before they were over the border. As soon as they reached the first of the bandit trails in the pass, she hauled Brak's horse to a stop and dismounted. Wrayan turned to find out what she was doing. *Perhaps she needed to relieve herself,* he thought. She shouldn't need a rest. They hadn't been on the road long enough for that.

'This is where you and I part company, Wrayan Lightfinger,' she announced, handing him the reins of the gelding.

Wrayan glanced at the trail winding up the steep slope into the forest and nodded in understanding. She was a bandit, an accomplished killer, and a Fardohnyan at that. There was no reason for her to go to Hythria. And then it came to him. 'Chyler's Children,' the customs man had called the Fardohnyan bandits.

'Back to work, eh?'

She shrugged. 'I'm a follower of Dacendaran. I prefer to think of it as a divine calling more than a career.'

He accepted the reins of the other horse, wondering if he could risk putting the child on it, but the boy was still unconscious. 'You know, in Hythria they believe you're in the pay of the Fardohnyan king.'

'Hablet doesn't pay for anything,' Chyler scoffed.

'So it's just chance that you target the Hythrun caravans and leave the Fardohnyan merchants alone?'

She smiled. 'One can be a thief *and* a patriot, you know. The two aren't mutually exclusive.'

'Will you answer one more question before you go?'

'You want to know why I killed Danyon Caron?'

'Yes.'

Chyler pointed at the ragged, limp bundle Wrayan was holding. 'That boy you have there? He almost met the same fate this evening as my nephew did a year ago.'

Wrayan's expression must have been sufficiently confused that she felt the need to explain further.

'Most of my people have families in the area, Master Lightfinger, either living at the fort or working as trappers and loggers in the mountains around here. Danyon Caron paid a visit to the village where my sister lives a bit over a year ago. He was just passing through. But one night was all it took. Poor Odie . . . he's not spoken a word since that night. He just stares into the distance, wasting away before our very eyes.' Chyler's expression hardened. This was not a woman to be crossed lightly. 'Anyway, I passed through the village a couple of weeks later and my sister told me what had happened and who'd done it. I'm not stupid enough to try to take down a Guild man as highly placed as Danyon Caron – not on his turf, at any rate – so I sent him a message. I warned that sleazy little bastard that if he ever came near Westbrook again – my turf – I'd have him for what he did to my nephew.'

'How is it that you wound up in the dungeons?'

'He had a meeting with some big note from one of the

Hythrun Guilds. The Wraith, his name was, so I hear. Apparently, he insisted they meet at Westbrook. Danyon knew I'd kill him the first chance I got, so he lured me into the fortress on the pretext of shifting some stolen goods. I should have known just from the price they were offering for the stuff that it was a trap. I was arrested the day he got here.' Chyler studied Wrayan for a moment in the starlight and then swore softly. 'I'll be damned! I suppose you're the big note from Hythria?'

'Not a title I'd usually grant myself.'

'Wrayan the Wraith, eh? I've heard about you.'

'Have you now?'

'I heard you single-handedly lifted the entire contents of the Sorcerers' Collective museum in Greenharbour a few years ago.'

'That's a gross exaggeration.'

She seemed amused. 'In my experience, most claims to fame usually are. But thanks, anyway.'

'For what?'

'Your visit to Westbrook gave me a chance to even the score with that prick, Caron. And the best part is – nobody will even know it was me who did it.'

'No,' Wrayan agreed. 'They'll probably blame it on the "big note" from Hythria that Danyon Caron came to Westbrook to meet.'

That seemed to amuse Chyler Kantel rather than worry her. 'Good thing you're headed home then, eh? Not planning to come back this way any time soon, I hope?'

'I'm not likely to now that I'm probably wanted by the Qorinipor Guild for murder.'

'I'm sure you'll be able to clear up any misunderstanding in the Guild. You being a "big note" and all.' She reached up and patted Rory's shoulder in farewell. 'What'll happen to him now?'

'He'll be safe with me.'

'They thought he was a sorcerer, you know. Claimed he killed a man in Talabar. He's a brave kid – surrendered himself so he wouldn't freeze to death in the mountains. That takes real guts when you're wanted for murder. You could tell he was scared, but he was convinced help was on the way.' Chyler smiled. 'The Halfbreed coming for him is proof enough he's what they claimed, I suppose. You one of them, too?'

Wrayan shrugged, not exactly sure what *one of them* was supposed to mean. He guessed she meant someone with magical talent. 'Sort of.'

'You'll see him safe then. In Hythria somewhere? Somewhere they won't find him?'

'Yes.'

She hesitated a moment longer, then turned suddenly and took the steep path into the forest without looking back.

And that was the last Wrayan saw of Chyler Kantel.

He stopped several hours past sunrise in a small copse of trees by the roadside some twenty miles south of Winternest. The horses were exhausted and Wrayan's arms felt as if they were made of lead after carrying the weight of Rory all night while towing Brak's horse behind them. He lowered the boy to the ground and groaned as his stiff muscles protested their sudden release. Wrayan let the horses drink their fill while he checked on the boy. He was becoming increasingly concerned that the child was showing no signs of life yet. And all he could do about it was worry. He had no idea what he'd been drugged with and no healing talent to do anything about it anyway, even if he'd known. The child was thin and, surprisingly, as fair-haired as any Hythrun child. His skin was pallid, his lips pale and tinged blue, but whether from the cold or some side effect of the drug he'd been given, Wrayan had no way of telling. But the child's breathing seemed even enough and the pulse at his neck was strong and steady.

Wearily, Wrayan sat on the damp grass beside the boy and let the events of the past few hours wash over him. He was drained from trying to imagine a scenario in which Brak had survived. He was numb at the thought that a man who had lived so long and through so much, a legend who meant so much to the Harshini, could be so easily pushed into the arms of Death.

Wrayan reached inside his shirt for the pendant Brak had given him and studied it for a moment, wondering how it worked. He could feel the magic locked in the little crystal cube, but wasn't sure what he was supposed to do with it. Perhaps this was a device to amplify one's telepathic abilities? Wrayan was a competent enough telepath, but he didn't have the power to reach Sanctuary. The furthest he'd ever tried to reach was just over a hundred miles. The hidden Harshini settlement in the Sanctuary Mountains must be over a thousand miles from here.

And even if he could reach out and touch the minds of the Harshini, who would he call? And what would he say?

Slipping the little cube back into his shirt with a weary sigh, Wrayan lay back on the grass next to his unconscious charge and closed his eyes. He would rest for a moment, he decided, and figure out what to do about Rory, about Brak, about the trouble he had coming with the Thieves' Guild, and everything else, when he'd had a few minutes to relax . . .

Which was Wrayan's last coherent thought until he woke up to discover it was dark again and Shananara té Ortyn was kissing him.

'Are you *mad*?'

Shananara sat back on her heels and looked at Wrayan

with a puzzled expression. 'I thought you'd be glad to see me, Wrayan. Was I wrong?'

Wrayan struggled to sit up, his mind still having trouble grasping the notion that Shananara was actually here in front of him on the side of the road, a thousand miles from the safety of Sanctuary. There was a small fire going and the smell of something delicious cooking over it. She had obviously been through his pack and found his gear.

Desire warred with common sense as he stared at her. 'What . . . what are you doing here?'

'You called me.'

'No, I didn't.'

The Harshini princess reached into his shirt and pulled out the little crystal cube on the chain around his neck. 'Yes, you did, my love. I gave this to Brak, by the way. Is he around?'

That was one question Wrayan was nowhere near prepared to answer. 'How did you get here?' he asked instead, looking around for some sort of transport. She was wearing Dragon Rider's leathers, her statuesque body outlined in distracting detail, but there was no sign of any animals other than the two horses he'd brought with him.

'By dragon, of course!' she laughed. 'I let the meld go when I got here. I wasn't sure what the locals would think about a dragon sitting by the side of the road. Dranymire and the other demons are around here, somewhere. They'll come back when I need them.'

'Your highness . . . Shananara . . . have you *any* idea how dangerous it is for you here?' he gasped. The road was deserted, fortunately, but there was no telling who was out there. No telling who had seen a dragon flying over the mountains, either.

'This is Hythria, Wrayan. It's probably the safest place for a Harshini outside of Sanctuary. That's why Brak wanted you to take this child back with you, wasn't it?'

Wrayan nodded, rather alarmed to think the child was still out cold. Rory lay peacefully on his side, his skin and lips a much healthier colour than when Wrayan had dozed off.

'He's sleeping now,' Shananara assured him, noticing the direction of his gaze. 'There is no more poison in his blood.'

'Did you do that?'

She nodded. 'It's a good thing you are doing for this child, Wrayan.'

'Brak wanted me to take him to the Sorcerers' Collective.' He found it hard not to choke on Brak's name.

'That's probably the best place for him.'

Wrayan frowned. 'You might not say that if you knew the current High Arrion, your highness.'

The princess shrugged, her inhuman black-on-black eyes reflecting no fear or concern about the danger to Rory. 'High Arrions come and go, Wrayan. This one is no better or worse than many others who have held the job.'

'But when she discovers the child has talent—'

'She will try to manipulate it,' Shanan finished for him. 'And the child.'

'That won't be good,' Wrayan pointed out. 'For anybody.'

'Then we shall teach young Master Rory to protect himself before we let him loose among the wolves, eh?'

'Nice theory, but it would take a lifetime to teach him what he'd have to know to fight off someone like Alija Eaglespike,' Wrayan said. He spoke from bitter experience.

'But only a few moments to teach him what he *needs* to know,' Shananara replied with a smile.

'I don't understand.'

'He's still young enough to teach him the Harshini way,' the princess explained. 'It's only when you get older that it gets difficult. Odd, though, that he's displayed his ability so young. Still, maybe it's a good thing. You were about the same age when you discovered your ability, weren't you?'

'A year or two older, I think,' Wrayan said, rather confused. 'Why is it easier to teach him now rather than when he's older?'

'Well, for one thing, I can pass the information on directly through a mind link. He's still young enough to learn that way without it harming him. The older you part-humans get, the more the mind instinctively resists the intrusion, which is why we couldn't teach you the same way when you came to us at Sanctuary.' She reached out and touched Wrayan's face, her caress setting fire to his skin. 'Of course, you would have picked up a few pointers when we shared a mental bond while we made love.'

Wrayan pushed her hand, and that very distracting memory, away. Shananara was desire heaped upon lust and it was all he could do to resist her. He didn't need that particular reminder right now, and Brak's scathing reprimand the morning after his one incredible night with Shananara still stung when he thought about it.

'Tell me why it's a good thing he's discovered his talent so young,' he asked, trying to sound businesslike.

'The mind is a strange place, Wrayan,' Shananara said, sitting back on her heels again, not fooled for a moment by his apparent disregard for her touch. Fortunately, neither did she press the matter. Instead, she set out to explain the problem as if lecturing a class of apprentices. 'It has ways of protecting itself, particularly the human mind, which seems a little more . . . shall we say . . . *fragile* than most. When it comes to those of you with the ability to tap into the source, the mind instinctively seems to know the danger. Hence, the stronger the power, the later the child becomes aware of it. And the more painful the awakening. Brak was in his late teens before he could do so much as light a candle. Pure Harshini sometimes can't reach their full potential until they're in their early twenties.'

'So you're saying Rory's not very powerful then?'

318

'Probably not as strong as you,' Shananara agreed, 'but he'll have much better control of it than you do. Training *can* win out over raw talent, you know.'

'Which is why you're not worried about Alija,' Wrayan concluded with relief. He'd been fretting about putting this child in her power ever since Brak first suggested it. 'How long will it take?'

'It's already done, my love,' she informed him smugly. 'Why do you think the child sleeps so heavily?'

'You mean he's just going to wake up and discover he's a Harshini sorcerer?'

Shanan laughed softly. 'He may need your guidance a little to begin with, but he'll find his own way soon enough.'

Wrayan nodded, thinking he shouldn't stall telling her about Brak. He just didn't know how to broach the subject. Nor should he delay it much longer, regardless of how painful a duty it might be. Every moment she spent away from Sanctuary placed not only Shananara, but all the Harshini, in danger.

'Shanan, there's something I have to tell you . . . about Brak.'

Oddly, Shananara didn't smile the way she did with everything else. 'What's he done this time?'

'He's . . .' Wrayan could barely get the words out. 'I'm so sorry, Shanan . . . but he's . . . he's dead.'

The Harshini shook her head. 'No. Brak's not dead, Wrayan.'

'But . . .'

She took his hand in hers and squeezed it comfortingly. 'Brak isn't dead, my love, as much as he would wish to be. Death isn't ready for him yet.'

'What do you mean, *as much as he would wish to be*?' he asked, pulling his hands away from her distracting touch.

'Brak did something he's having trouble dealing with, that's all.'

319

'A death wish is a bit more than "having trouble", your highness. What did he do that was so terrible?'

'He didn't tell you?'

'I wouldn't be asking if he had.'

Shanan sighed and looked down, brushing an imaginary speck from her spotless dragon leathers before she spoke. The firelight reflected off her golden skin, making her features melancholy. 'Lorandranek disappeared before the Feast of Kalianah this spring. He was gone for months. Korandellen was worried about our uncle. He's been . . . restless of late.'

'The king was always restless, as I recall,' Wrayan said. Lorandranek had never been happy cooped up in Sanctuary, but as the strongest of the strong, it fell to him to hold Sanctuary out of time to save it from accidental discovery by the forces who wished to see his race eradicated.

'This was different. He handed over the burden of the time spell to my brother and left Sanctuary even while it was still out of time to go roaming the mountains, something he'd never done before. He was distracted, moody—'

'I didn't think Harshini were capable of being moody,' Wrayan interrupted.

'Neither did we,' she agreed with another heavy sigh, before resuming her tale. 'Anyway, we hadn't seen him for a while and we were worried about him, so Korandellen sent Brak into the mountains to bring him home.'

Wrayan hadn't thought the Harshini capable of worry, either. 'What happened?' he prompted gently, when Shananara seemed reluctant to go on.

'Brak found him. Eventually. He was living in a cave with a young human woman. He was trying to . . .' She threw her hands up with a helpless smile. 'I can't even say it.'

'Say what?'

Shananara took a deep breath before she spoke. 'Brak

took a life to save a life, Wrayan,' she managed to get out with obvious difficulty. 'That's the closest I can come to describing it.'

'You mean he killed someone to save Lorandranck?'

She shook her head, unable to articulate the words. Wrayan looked at her in shock, finding himself almost as incapable as the Harshini of speaking the alternative aloud.

'Dear gods!' he murmured, shaking his head in denial as the princess patiently waited for him to work out himself what had really happened. 'You can't mean he killed . . . ?'

The princess shrugged helplessly. 'My uncle was driven insane by something we don't understand, Wrayan. His last words were of something the gods had asked of him; of it being too great a burden. We have no idea of what he was speaking. All we know is that Lorandranek, King of the Harshini, was driven to an act of violence our race is incapable of and Brakandaran was forced to end his life to save the life of an innocent. I know no more than that. All our attempts to have Brak return to us have failed. He has shut us out. We have forgiven him, but he will never forgive himself. He now hopes that Death will grant him the same oblivion my uncle sought, but it cannot be so. Death is a Primal God as much as Kalianah or Dacendaran and he has his own agenda. He will not allow Brak into his realm. Not yet.'

Dear gods, what must have happened to make Brak do such a thing? Wrayan put his head in his hands, trying to come to terms with everything Shananara had told him. He was almost sorry he'd asked, but it explained so much about Brak's strange behaviour on the way to Fardohnya. *He'd killed his king. Not just his king; Lorandranek was his friend, too. He must have been going out of his mind.*

'I heard him fall, Shanan.'

'Perhaps,' she agreed, 'but he is not dead. I can promise you that much.'

Wrayan allowed himself a small smile.

'What?' Shanan asked curiously. She wasn't capable of the same range of emotions as a human. It was all part of the Harshini inhibition against violence. All those emotions that drove one to extremes, like hatred or jealousy, revenge, grief or anger, were denied them. Shananara knew Brak had killed Lorandranek, but she was no more able to hate or despise him for it than Wrayan was able to understand how she felt.

'I was just thinking,' he said, smiling wider for Shananara's sake. His own grief over Lorandranek's death or Brak's part in it would be inexplicable to her. 'Only Brak would manage to annoy Death sufficiently that he'd deny him entry into his realm.'

Shananara smiled. 'He never was renowned for his respect for the gods.'

'Will the Harshini be all right?'

She nodded. 'When I go back, Korandellen will hide us again. This time, I fear, we must stay there. There is something afoot, some game the gods are playing, and until we learn what it is, Koran thinks it safer if we stay out of time.'

The relief he felt knowing the Harshini would be safe was tinged with the bittersweet realisation that he would probably never see Shananara again.

'We have tonight, though,' she said, as if she had just realised the same thing. 'Before I have to go back.'

Wrayan was kissing Shananara before she finished speaking. He'd lived for this moment; waited for it for more than twelve years. But even as she slid her arms around his neck and he lay back against the stony ground, a traitorous thought wormed its way into his consciousness, spoiling the moment. Was this what had driven Lorandranek to an unthinkable act of violence? Was the Harshini king's fear of creating a demon child sufficient to overcome his deeply

322

ingrained aversion to bloodshed? It was a timely reminder of the consequences of giving in to desire.

With more moral strength than he'd thought he owned, Wrayan broke off the kiss and pushed the woman of his dreams away, shaking his head, a part of him unable to believe that he was voluntarily passing up an opportunity like this. 'Brak threatened to kill me if I ever slept with you again.'

'Then we shan't sleep,' she suggested seductively.

'He meant it, Shanan,' Wrayan warned. 'And he had good reason. I don't want to be responsible for bringing a demon child into the world. Do you?'

She shook her head reluctantly and rose gracefully to her feet. 'I should never have told you Brakandaran still lives. Then you would not fear his censure.' She held out her hand to him and helped him up, drawing him closer as he stood. 'I will treasure the short time we did have together, though, my love. It will sustain me through the long nights ahead.'

This close to Shananara, Wrayan could barely breathe. He could feel her hot breath on his face and the outline of her inhumanly perfect body again his own. 'Sustain you? It's *ruined* me.'

'I didn't mean to spoil you for any other woman,' she breathed softly, brushing the hair off his face with a finger that felt charged with lightning. 'I'm sorry.'

'Just let me go, Shanan. *Please.*'

She nodded and stepped back from him. 'I can see I am being cruel by lingering here. And I really should get back. Will you and the child be all right now?'

Wrayan nodded, unable to speak for fear he would open his mouth not to say good-bye, but to beg her to stay.

As if she knew what he was thinking, she smiled at him and then turned towards the road. Already, at her silent command, the demons had begun to materialise out of thin air. There were hundreds of the little grey demons; the oldest and most numerous belonged to the royal family. He watched in silent awe as they blurred into the meld. A few moments later, a magnificent golden dragon, the size of a two-storey building, took shape before him. When the meld was finished, Shananara stepped forward and scratched the bony ridge over the dragon's eyes fondly, then turned to look at Wrayan.

'Goodbye, Wrayan.'

'Goodbye, Shananara.'

'Wait!' He hurried after her, slipping the chain of the tiny crystal cube Brak had given him over his head. Oddly, it felt like a polished cube of crystal now – it no longer felt magical. Only a lump of stone.

Shananara stopped and turned to look at him. He held it out to her. 'You should take this. It was Brak's.'

'It still is,' she assured him with a smile.

'If he's still alive . . . you'll see him again before I will.'

The Harshini princess smiled wistfully. 'I don't know when Brak will return to Sanctuary, Wrayan. You keep it. I'm sure he won't mind. And you never know. You may get a chance to return it.'

He glanced down at the little crystal cube with its etched dragon embedded in the centre and shook his head. 'It's too tempting.'

'What's too tempting?'

'This,' he replied, holding the chain up for her to see. 'I know you have to hide, Shananara, and I know you probably won't emerge again in my lifetime . . . but . . . please . . . don't leave me with a way to call you back and expect me not to use it some day. I don't think I'm that strong.'

She stepped a little closer and reached out for his face, her smile so bittersweet he wanted to drown in it. 'I think that's the nicest thing a human boy has ever said to me.'

He closed his eyes, feeling her soft hand on his face, aware he would never feel it again. The mere thought made him want to die of longing. 'I'm not trying to be nice, your highness. I'm trying to be honest.'

'An honest thief,' she chuckled, dropping her hand and stepping away from him. 'But you needn't fear the temptation to call me out of hiding, my love. A *couremor* can only be loaned to another the once, before the maker must infuse it again with their magic.'

'A *what*?'

'This little trinket Brak left you is a *couremor*,' she explained. 'Roughly translated into Hythrun, it means a link between lovers, or a lover's link. We used to make them, long ago, back when it wasn't all that uncommon for humans and Harshini to be . . . intimate. A Harshini would infuse it with magic and leave it with their human lover so they could call him or her in time of need. Or longing. It only works once though, partly because it's not that easy to store magic in an inanimate object, and partly because it was safer that way. We don't make them any more. There isn't much point, these days.'

Wrayan was still more than a little confused. 'But if Brak infused it with magic, how come it called you?'

'It calls to the one you love, Wrayan.'

He looked away, unable to meet her eye. The pain was torment. She knew he loved her, but deep down she didn't really understand what it meant to him. That was why they called it Kalianah's curse. The Harshini had no real comprehension of human love.

'What if Rorin had used it?' he asked, hoping a change of subject would make the ache go away.

'It would have summoned Brak.'

'I'm glad it was you who came,' he said with a smile. 'I'm not sure what I would have done if I'd opened my eyes to find Brak kissing me awake.'

She laughed and kissed his cheek once more and then turned to the waiting demon meld. The princess climbed onto the dragon and as soon as she was settled, it beat its massive wings, almost blinding Wrayan with the dust kicked up by the downdraft. He stepped back and watched as Dranymire lifted into the sky and disappeared against the star-scattered night.

He heard a noise behind him and turned to find Rory had finally woken. He was sitting by the fire, rubbing his eyes, and looking around in confusion.

'Hello.'

'Who are you?'

'My name is Wrayan Lightfinger.'

'Where am I?'

'Hythria.'

Rory squinted at him in the darkness. 'You were in my dream.'

'What dream?'

'The one with the pretty lady. And the dragon.'

Wrayan walked back to the small clearing from the road and sat himself down beside the child with a friendly smile. 'You and I need to have a very long talk about a few things, my lad.'

'Am I in trouble?'

'Only if someone else besides you and me saw that dragon just now,' he said.

34

Despite the distraction of the attempt on Damin's life, the wedding between Rielle Tirstone and Darvad Vintner went off without a hitch on a perfect summer's day, a little over a week after the attack. In the grand tradition of all Hythrun weddings, particularly for those of noble birth, three days later the party was still going on.

Marla surveyed the ballroom with satisfaction, leaning back in her seat, thinking that, at last, something had gone according to plan. Not that she would have allowed anything short of the death of the bride or groom to prevent this wedding taking place. The alliance with the Bearbows of Izcomdar, Alija's own kinsmen, was far too important to Marla for her to allow anything as mundane as an assassination attempt on one of her children to interfere with it.

Damin was all set to spend his fosterage with Rogan, who had been both delighted and honoured to discover he had been chosen as mentor for Hythria's heir. Rielle had confided to Marla a few days ago that Rogan's daughter was just as pleased with the arrangement, as the fosterage gave her an excuse to further delay her own wedding to Terin Lionsclaw. Knowing what a headstrong and forthright young woman Tejay was, Marla suspected Terin would be just as delighted with the delay. The couple was rumoured to despise each other and when they finally got around to getting married, it was destined to be a tempestuous and stormy relationship.

'Good lord! You look like you're at a funeral, Marla, not a wedding,' Ruxton remarked as he took his seat beside her. He was flushed and breathing hard; no doubt from the energetic dance he'd just partnered his newlywed daughter through. The music had changed and Rielle was dancing with Darvad again, Marla noticed, now her father had retired from the dance floor.

'I was just thinking about . . . things, that's all,' she replied, looking down over the reception tiredly. This was the third – and thankfully, the last – day of the wedding celebrations and the festivities were in full swing. Marla was looking forward to it all being over and things returning to some semblance of normality.

'Try to smile anyway,' Ruxton suggested. 'You'll scare the bride, otherwise.'

Marla looked down at her stepdaughter who, hand in hand with her new husband, was skipping through a long archway made of the raised arms of the other dancers. She smiled as she watched them and then turned to her husband. 'I don't think anything could dent Rielle's happiness at the moment.'

'Probably not,' he agreed. 'Thank you.'

'For what?' she asked. 'This was part of our deal, Ruxton. You give me access to your intelligence network and I'll arrange highborn marriages for your three children. You don't have to thank me for keeping up my end of the bargain.'

'I wasn't. You promised me a nobleman for my daughter and that's what you gave me. But you were under no obligation to find her a decent man, or to ensure the union was a happy one. I appreciate the effort you put in, trying to give her some chance at happiness.' He leaned forward to pick up his wineglass. 'I think underneath that cold and ruthless exterior, Marla Wolfblade, you're a big old softie.'

'Well, don't let it get around,' she warned. And then she looked at him curiously. 'Do you really think I'm ruthless, Ruxton?'

He smiled warily. 'This reeks of a trick question. Do you *want* to be ruthless?'

'To be honest, I never really thought about it. It's just you're the second person who's accused me of it.'

'Who was the other poor sod, and was I invited to his funeral?'

Marla smiled. 'Not yet.'

'Not *yet*?'

'It was Luciena.'

'Ah!' Ruxton said, taking a sip of wine.

'I wish you wouldn't do that.'

'Do what?'

'Say "ah!" like that. I know you're burning to say something else, but you never do. It irritates me.'

'What you do with Luciena Mariner is none of my concern,' Ruxton reminded her with a shrug. 'That was also part of our agreement, remember? You don't enquire too closely into my affairs and I'll stay out of yours.'

'But you have an opinion,' she accused.

'Which I'm quite content to keep to myself.'

'What if I want to know what it is?'

'Then I'll tell you. If you insist. Just don't get mad at me if you don't like it.'

'Then I *insist* that you tell me,' she demanded. And then she smiled and added, 'And I'll get as mad as I want to, thank you. I'm the princess in this family.'

'Then far be it for a poor trader to deny you,' he laughed. Ruxton held out his wineglass for a refill to one of the slaves standing back from the head table waiting to serve them, before he added in a slightly lower voice, 'Seriously, though, in your shoes, the first question I'd like answered before I did anything is this: did Alija really tamper with Luciena's mind?'

Marla shrugged. She didn't know for certain and had no way of confirming her suspicions one way or the other. There was still no sign of Wrayan Lightfinger. The reason for his visit to Fardohnya, along with his expected date of return, remained irritatingly vague.

'Let's assume for the moment that she did. What then?'

'Then I'd be asking what young Xanda was asking the night the attack happened. Why now? What's changed recently that would make Alija attack Damin at this point in time, not a year ago, or a year *from* now?'

'Nothing's changed,' Marla shrugged.

'Nothing except your decision to adopt Luciena.'

She looked at her husband thoughtfully. 'Are you saying her fanciful tale of some long-lost uncle in Fardohnya seeking help for her magically gifted cousin is true and this was just an opportunistic attack?'

'I don't know,' Ruxton admitted. 'All I know is that Mahkas lets nobody near the palace – or Damin – who can't prove they come from at least three generations of Royalists. I'd be surprised if the Assassins' Guild was willing to take on a contract to eliminate the High Prince's heir. They don't like getting involved in political assassinations that might bring them unwanted attention. It rather limits the options for anyone looking for a way to get close to Damin.'

'Until I brought Luciena here.'

Ruxton nodded. 'So put yourself in Alija's shoes for a moment. Let's suppose Luciena's not a Fardohnyan spy. Suppose she really did get a letter asking for money from her long-lost uncle. Xanda believes her.'

'Xanda is hardly what I'd call an objective witness, Ruxton.'

'Granted. But it would explain why Luciena tried to see Alija before we left Greenharbour.'

'But not why Alija visited her.'

Ruxton shrugged. 'Alija probably heard about the adoption – rumour travels faster than heat in Greenharbour – and took a punt. She primes Luciena as an assassin and then sits back and waits for nature to take its course, knowing full well the first thing we'll do after the attack is discover Luciena has family connections in Fardohnya, believe she's a spy and assume that's why she killed Damin.'

'I can assure you, nature *will* take its course,' Marla promised. 'For Luciena, at least. All the way to the gallows.'

'At which point Alija will realise she's failed and she'll have to start all over again, looking for another angle of attack,' Ruxton pointed out.

The music changed and the dancers pushed and shoved into lines for the Novera, which was suddenly popular again, after being almost forgotten for the past five years or so. Rogan Bearbow was dancing with Kalan, while his daughter partnered Damin. Starros was with Leila and Narvell was caught in the grip of some elderly cousin of Darvad's who almost smothered the child with her bulk. Marla smiled and then hesitated as the music started up, suddenly overwhelmed by memories of the first time she had danced the Novera in Greenharbour. With Nash . . .

Pushing the unwanted images aside, she studied her current husband curiously. 'Surely you're not suggesting I do nothing about this attack on my son?'

'Not at all,' he said. 'I just think that if you hang Luciena, you're sending a very loud message to Alija telling her the attack failed and she'd better start looking for another way to harm him.'

Marla smiled grimly. 'Then this is a *good* thing.'

'If you say so.'

Marla glared at Ruxton. 'What's *that* supposed to mean?'

'Nothing, really. Just a thought . . .'

'Ruxton!'

He shrugged and sipped his wine, quite deliberately taking his time before he answered. 'I was just thinking . . . if Alija thinks she's primed Luciena to attack Damin when the time is right, she'll probably do nothing more to harm him until she's convinced the plan has failed. If you don't hang the girl, if you carry on as if nothing happened, for all Alija knows, Luciena is still biding her time, just waiting for the right opportunity.'

'You're suggesting I just pretend none of this happened!' she gasped.

'You're going to have me beheaded now, aren't you?' he said with a rueful sigh. 'I knew I should have kept my big mouth shut.'

'But the whole notion is . . .' Marla stopped and thought about it for a moment. Ruxton might have a valid point. If Alija believed she had an assassin close to Damin just waiting for the opportune moment, she'd have no need to recruit any other assassins until she was convinced Luciena had let her down. That might take months. Even years. 'Actually, Ruxton, it's inspired.'

'So this means you're not going to behead me?'

'Not at the moment. Do you really think she'll do nothing?'

'Who, Alija? Possibly. Of course, the catch in this brilliant exercise in double thinking is the question I posed originally. Did the High Arrion really tamper with Luciena's mind, or did you just inadvertently bring a Patriot Faction viper or a Fardohnyan spy into the nest without realising it?'

'That's the crucial question, isn't it?' Marla agreed, and then she looked across the hall and groaned, Alija and Luciena momentarily forgotten. 'Oh gods, not again!'

Ruxton followed her gaze and shook his head when he saw what was happening. Mahkas had interrupted the

Novera and rearranged the couples so that Damin was dancing with Leila and Starros was now partnered with Tejay Bearbow.

'You really should do something about your brother-in-law,' Ruxton remarked.

Marla nodded, aware that Ruxton was right, but not sure how to handle the situation. Now that Damin was due to leave for his fosterage, Mahkas was getting nervous about the lack of a formal betrothal agreement between his daughter and Marla's son.

'I don't know why he keeps on like this,' Marla sighed. 'I've never actually said they were getting married.'

'But you haven't said no, either.'

'Still . . . it's not as if it's urgent, even if I *had* agreed to it. Damin's not even thirteen for another week.'

'Mahkas is just afraid Damin will fall in love with some other Warlord's daughter while he's away,' Ruxton said.

Marla smiled. 'Damin could fall in love with the Goddess Kalianah herself, for all I care, Ruxton. He still won't be allowed to marry anybody who can't support his throne.'

And that was the problem. Marla liked Leila well enough, but she had nothing to recommend her politically. There was nothing to be gained, no treaty to be assured, no territory or wealth to be secured, by marrying Damin to his cousin. The only one who would really benefit from such a union would be Mahkas Damaran, a fact Elezaar delighted in pointing out every time Mahkas raised the subject.

She watched the children dancing together. It was clear, even from across the room, that the cousins were not thrilled with Mahkas's interference. As Mahkas left the dance floor, looking very pleased with himself, Bylinda took him aside and whispered something to her husband. She didn't look any happier about Mahkas's meddling than the children did.

'You should put him out of his misery,' Ruxton said. 'It's embarrassing.'

'I know,' Marla agreed. She glanced down at her glass and noticed it was empty. She needed to be careful. Marla never drank to excess, yet she hadn't even felt that last glass going down. Across the hall, the people standing around Mahkas and Bylinda looked away politely, pretending they didn't notice the whispered altercation going on between the Regent of Krakandar and his wife. 'But even if I thought Damin marrying his cousin was a good idea, I wouldn't agree to a betrothal now.'

'You want to keep your options open,' Ruxton concluded.

She nodded. 'I want every nobleman in Hythria with a daughter of marriageable age to think he might have a chance of an alliance with the future High Prince,' she said. 'I'm certainly not going to spoil it by betrothing Damin to his cousin at the age of thirteen and ruining hopes of any other union.' It was getting increasingly difficult to explain this to Mahkas, who was becoming more and more suspicious that Marla simply didn't want the marriage to go ahead at all. 'I'm actually looking forward to returning to Greenharbour this year. It's much easier to ignore Mahkas's unsubtle hints when they're in a letter.'

'Well, it won't be long now,' Ruxton reminded her. 'Another few weeks and we'll have to start thinking about setting a departure date.'

'Which also means I'm running out of time to fix my other problem,' Marla said, holding her own glass out for a refill as a barefoot slave approached.

'What other problem?'

'Kalan,' Marla told him with a frown, taking a sip of the sweet, potent wine. 'I still haven't got the faintest idea what I'm going to do about Kalan.'

35

Wrayan Lightfinger took his time returning to Krakandar, mostly to give his young companion a chance to come to grips with his new circumstances. The young Fardohnyan boy had fallen asleep a fugitive and woken up a fully trained Harshini sorcerer.

That was rather a lot to ask of a twelve-year-old.

He was looking forward to getting home, though. Wrayan had left his chief lieutenant, a thief named Luc North, in charge during his absence. A talented forger, the man was trustworthy, careful but unimaginative. He also lacked ambition, which made him a fairly reliable stand-in – there was nothing more dangerous than an ambitious underling given a taste of power when the boss was away. But if anything out of the ordinary had happened while Wrayan was gone, Luc probably wouldn't know how to deal with it. Wrayan could be returning to a Guild that was running like clockwork or one that had fallen into complete chaos. He had no way of telling until he reached the city.

Although he was impressed by Wrayan's position as head of the Krakandar Thieves' Guild, Rory seemed much more taken with the notion that Wrayan was on speaking terms with the ruling family of Krakandar. The lad spent quite a bit of time questioning him about the Wolfblades, and how he came to know them. Wrayan wasn't sure why the child was so interested, but he found himself telling far more than he intended. When he related the story about his magical battle with Alija Eaglespike and how he'd come to meet Brakandaran and the Harshini, Rory was fascinated. As the boy was destined for the Sorcerers' Collective, Wrayan felt obliged to warn Rory about the High Arrion, but he seemed unconcerned. Along with using his magical talent, Shananara had shown Rory how to disguise it. The child was disturbingly confident that Alija would never discover his true ability unless he chose to reveal it to her.

Once again, Wrayan was forced to reassess his opinion of the Harshini. It was easy to think of them as naive and childlike. That Shananara had thought to endow Rory with such a skill hinted at a degree of cunning of which he had never really thought the Harshini capable.

Rory's talent, as it turned out, was for manipulating objects. He could move things just by thinking about it, from quite large objects – like the anvil he'd accidentally thrown through a wall in Talabar, killing his cousin's client – to the minute, such as flesh and blood, which meant he had some considerable talent as a healer. He informed Wrayan of this with an air of wonder one morning, as they rode towards Byamor, still coming to terms with the notion that his previously uncontrollable ability was now his to command.

Wrayan had smiled at the look of wonder on the child's face. He'd be just as enchanted to wake up one morning and discover he could wield his magic so skillfully, he thought. Unfortunately, Wrayan was introduced to the Harshini when he was much older than Rory, so his education had been far more painstaking and, apparently, not nearly as much fun.

* * *

'What will happen when we get to Krakandar?' Rory asked.

They had taken shelter this rainy evening in an abandoned farmhouse several miles north of the Elasapine border. They'd been on the road for about three weeks now and had crossed into Krakandar Province the day before. The weather, which had until now been quite pleasant, had deteriorated rapidly in the past day, and they'd finally decided to wait out the rain when it began to drop hailstones the size of marbles on their unprotected heads. The hail had stopped about an hour before, with the light rapidly fading, but the rain still pelted down and Wrayan thought it unlikely they'd get much further today.

He turned to study Rory, wondering if he should tell him the truth or spin some story that would make him feel more secure. He settled on the truth. The boy was remarkably accepting of his strange plight, a fact that made Wrayan wonder, if along with filling his head with knowledge, Shananara had done something to dampen the child's emotional turmoil at the same time. In the past few months, Rory had accidentally killed a man, been torn from his home, pursued across hundreds of miles of Fardohnya, arrested as a Hythrun spy, drugged, kidnapped, sprung from a Fardohnyan jail and finally confronted with the lost race of the Harshini, yet he acted as if these were perfectly normal, everyday events. There had to be some magic involved. Wrayan couldn't detect that his mind had been tampered with, but that didn't mean it hadn't, of course. Just as Alija couldn't see Wrayan's hand in the mind shields that protected Marla and her family, Shananara's skill was so far above Wrayan's ability that she could have done any number of things to the child and he wouldn't have been able to detect it.

'I'll take you to meet Princess Marla,' Wrayan told him,

shifting his saddle so he could use it as a pillow. 'If you're going to join the Sorcerers' Collective, you'll need her patronage.'

'Why do I have to join the Sorcerers' Collective?' Rory was squatting beside the fireplace, eating the remains of the stew Wrayan had prepared for their dinner directly from the pot. It was his third helping. There didn't seem to be enough food in Hythria to fill the child up.

'Because you're a sorcerer?' Wrayan suggested, shaking out his blanket.

'I know *that*. I mean, what's the point, though? Isn't the idea of joining the Sorcerers' Collective to learn how to wield magic?'

'You'd think so.'

'But I already know more than anyone in the Sorcerers' Collective could teach me,' Rory pointed out through a mouthful of stew. 'What else is there to learn?'

Wrayan smiled. 'I'm sure there's something Shananara forgot to tell you.'

'They probably won't let me in,' the boy shrugged.

'Why not?'

'I'm Fardohnyan.'

'That shouldn't matter. There was a time when people from all over the world studied in Greenharbour.' He glanced at the boy's fair hair and blue eyes as he sat on the floor. 'Besides, you don't look it.'

'My grandfather was Hythrun,' Rory explained. 'He always called me Rorin. That's my Hythrun name, he used to tell me. He said it meant "one whose future would unfold in unexpected directions."'

'He got that much right,' Wrayan chuckled, pulling the blanket over himself. 'And he taught you well. You speak Hythrun like a native.'

'My grandpa was a sailor. He lived in Talabar most of his grown-up life, but he had the *worst* accent,' Rory said, smiling in remembrance. 'It was just easier to talk to him in Hythrun. At least that way you had some hope of understanding him.'

'Lucky for us you did. Do you think you could pass for a Hythrun?'

'I suppose. Why?'

'Fewer questions, for one thing. We can say you come from Krakandar, which would explain why Princess Marla is sponsoring your application to the Collective. If we give you a Hythrun surname, nobody need ever know you came from Talabar.'

'Do you think I'll be able to find my cousin when I get to Greenharbour?'

Wrayan settled his back against the wall of the farmhouse, and stretched his legs out and closed his eyes. 'I wouldn't get too excited about it, lad. Greenharbour's a pretty big city. Do you know his name?'

'*Her* name,' Rory corrected. 'It's Luciena Mariner. My father and her father were brothers.'

Wrayan opened his eyes and stared at the boy. 'You are Luciena Mariner's *cousin*?'

Rory nodded warily. 'Is this a bad thing?'

'Not really,' Wrayan replied with a sigh, as a whole swathe of remarkable coincidences suddenly became clear. 'It just explains a few things Brak never bothered to mention.'

'Do you think we'll ever see him again?'

'Who? Brak?' Wrayan shrugged. 'I couldn't say. He has a habit of turning up when you least expect him. Are you *really* Luciena's cousin?'

'You keep saying that like you know her.'

'I've met her,' Wrayan said. *The same day Brak turned up without warning, after a five-year absence.* 'She's in Krakandar with Princess Marla,' he added, shaking his head, wishing, for once, Brak wasn't so damned fond of being cryptic. *Why couldn't he just come straight out and say: Wrayan, there's a child in trouble and I need you to help me rescue him, oh, and by the way, that girl you met today in the palace? You might want to introduce the two of them when you get him home. He's her cousin.*

'Does that mean my grandpa was right? I really am related to the Hythrun royal family?'

Wrayan smiled. Now he understood Rory's fascination with the Wolfblades. 'I suppose, if you're really Luciena's cousin, then you are. In a roundabout sort of way.'

'Do you think I'll get to meet Luciena when we get to Krakandar?'

Wrayan closed his eyes again. 'Yes, Rory, you'll get to meet her.'

'What's she like?'

'I don't know her well enough to say.'

'Do you think she'll like me?'

Wrayan opened one eye and glared balefully at the boy. 'If you don't shut up and let me get some sleep, Rory, I'll throttle you and you'll never find out.'

Rory didn't seem to take his threat very seriously. 'It's kind of a funny coincidence, isn't it? You knowing my cousin?'

Coincidence, my arse, Wrayan replied silently. But aloud he said, 'You wouldn't read about it.'

'Do you think the Harshini had something to do with it?' When the boy received no reply, he hesitated for a moment. 'Wrayan?'

Feigning sleep, the thief pretended not to hear Rory's question about the Harshini and the remarkable coincidence that had sent Wrayan into Fardohnya with Brak to find him. After a while he heard Rory settling down on the other side of the fire, and not long after that the slow, even breathing that indicated the child was asleep.

But he lay awake listening to the rain for a long time,

thinking about Rory's question. *Do you think the Harshini had something to do with it?* the child had asked.

You can count on it, Wrayan replied silently, only now beginning to realise just how expertly he'd been manipulated into doing what the Harshini wanted. *You can count on it.*

36

Luciena lost count of the days she spent locked in the cells waiting for something to happen. Waiting for some hint about her eventual fate; some announcement or decree about whether she lived or died. Sometimes it felt like she'd been here for a lifetime; other times, it seemed like only yesterday that she was sprawled across the silk coverlet on Rielle's bed, helping her new stepsister decide what to wear to the ball, while she and Tejay wondered about their future husbands.

It was hot and airless in the cells. Luciena had long since shed her ruined ballgown in favour of a simple linen undershift that, while hardly elegant, at least made her confinement bearable. Once a day she was allowed out into the yard to stretch her legs, while slaves changed the bucket and cleaned the cell.

She got to know the names of her jailers after a while; she had been incarcerated long enough to learn the names of their wives and even some of their children, too. She knew the fat corporal on the night shift had been banned from taking part in raids over the Medalon border until he lost some weight because his horse couldn't carry his bulk over the dangerous Bardarlen Gorge, and that the young lad who delivered her food each morning was hoping to be promoted to corporal on the Feast of Zegarnald when all the mercenaries' contracts came up for renewal. She learned that Arkin, the dark-haired Raider in charge of the afternoon detail, had lost his arm to gangrene following a poorly treated arrow wound, and that Corporal Nyar's limp was due to a badly fractured ankle that had never healed properly.

Xanda visited her every day. They had settled into an uneasy friendship, full of strange, unspoken promises and silent assurances that Luciena often thought she might be imagining. His visits were filled with long, uncomfortable silences that sufficed for all the things they were too afraid to speak aloud. They were both acutely aware that, at any moment, Luciena might be declared a traitor and hanged for her crime. She might – just as probably – be acquitted, if Princess Marla determined the attack had not been her fault and she did not represent a continuing danger to Damin or anyone else in the family.

But time is running out, Luciena thought, standing on her toes to see if she could determine the position of the sun through the small barred window. It was hard to keep track of the time here, and she was beginning to suspect that Xanda was late, which could mean he wasn't coming today.

The patch of blue she could see through the window told her nothing. With a sigh, Luciena turned and leaned against the wall, the undressed granite rough but cool through the thin linen of her shift. *Summer is almost over,* she realised. *And when it is, I'm done for. Marla's not going to leave me to rot here while she returns to Greenharbour.*

Proved innocent, or dead. They were Luciena's only options.

The lock on the door rattled. Luciena smiled with relief and stood a little straighter, glad that Xanda had finally arrived. She wanted to ask him if Princess Marla had set her departure date yet. If there'd been any news at all, actually, about her fate.

But when the door opened, it wasn't Xanda who stepped into her cell. It was Captain Almodavar. She stared at him, feeling her knees go weak.

This is it, she concluded with despair. *They've come for me.*

'Miss Mariner.'

Oh, Xanda! Wouldn't they even let you say good-bye?

'Captain.'

'Would you come with me, please?'

Luciena was surprised by how politely the captain addressed her. And a little annoyed by it. Did he think she was going to let him lead her quietly to her own execution?

'No.'

Almodavar stared at her in surprise. *'Pardon?'*

'If you want to hang me, Captain, I'm afraid you're going to have to drag me out of here. Kicking and screaming.'

'Gladly, Miss Mariner,' he said. The faintest glimmer of a smile flickered across the captain's battle-weary face. 'But as I came to escort you to the palace and not the gallows, I was hoping you'd be a little more cooperative.'

'Princess Marla wants to see me?' Not once had Marla made any attempt to speak with Luciena the whole time she'd been incarcerated. 'Why?'

'I'm not in the habit of interrogating her highness about her business.'

Luciena squared her shoulders with determination, relieved that, one way or another, her ordeal would soon be over. 'Then take me to her,' she said. 'And let's be done with this.'

Marla was waiting for Luciena in the solar. It seemed an odd place to meet. There were no guards inside, either, although Luciena didn't doubt Almodavar was merely a shout away. She wasn't sure if the absence of guards meant she was no longer in imminent danger of being hanged, or if it simply meant Marla wasn't afraid of her.

The princess was standing by the glass wall that looked out over the gardens, wearing a dark green robe that complemented her perfectly groomed blonde hair. As usual, she looked in complete command of her surroundings. It was rather disheartening, however, when Marla turned to face her. The look on the princess's face did not augur well for Luciena's future.

Luciena curtseyed with all the dignity she could manage in her grubby undershift. 'Your highness.'

'Luciena.'

'Captain Almodavar said you wanted to see me.'

'I'm leaving in a few days,' the princess announced. 'To escort Damin to Natalandar for his fosterage on my way back to Greenharbour. You remember Damin, don't you, Luciena? The boy you tried to kill?'

'Your highness—'

'I don't know what disgusts me more,' Princess Marla continued, as if Luciena hadn't spoken, 'your brazen gall, or the way you insinuated yourself into my family for the sole purpose of killing my son.'

'*You* invited *me* into your family, your highness,' Luciena felt compelled to remind the princess. 'I didn't insinuate myself into anything.'

'And that excuses your actions, I suppose? Because it's *my* fault?' Marla looked at her curiously. 'We never even met until a few months ago. How could you despise me so deeply you would willingly aid Hythria's enemies?'

'I'm not a spy.'

'Then you're a Patriot.'

'I'm not a Patriot, either.'

Marla seemed quite surprised by her denials. 'Then you were motivated by simple hate. What did the Wolfblades ever do to you?'

'You promised me a family,' Luciena accused, figuring she couldn't get into any worse trouble than she was already in, so she might as well have her say. 'I remember when my father came home and told us he was going to marry you. I might have only been nine, but I still remember. He was so happy. Not for himself, but for me. He was a commoner and I was his only child, and baseborn at that. This marriage was for me, he said. Princess Marla was supposed to make it all wonderful for us. Instead of a slave's brat, I was going to be a princess. I'd have brothers and sisters and—' She stopped abruptly, realising the only thing she was doing was exposing her own pain. Marla appeared unmoved. 'It turned out to be a lie, didn't it? There was no invitation to the palace. I remained an outcast until it suited your purposes to bring me into the fold once my slave-born mother was dead and you didn't have to confront the idea that your stepdaughter was the get of a commoner and a *court'esa*.'

Marla shook her head. 'The fairy-tale family you so hungered for came at a cost your father wasn't willing to pay, Luciena. It was at his request that I left you with your mother after we married.'

'Easy to say now, when he's not here to disagree with you.'

Marla walked a little closer to her. 'I don't have to explain myself to you, Luciena. Or justify anything I've done. What I must do, however, is make a decision about what to do with you, and right now you're making it very easy for me.'

'Let me guess. You're going to have me killed? What a shock! I'm surprised you've waited this long.'

'You've Xanda Taranger to thank for the delay. I was all for killing you the night you attacked Damin.'

'Why didn't you?'

Marla smiled faintly, the first time Luciena had seen even a hint of softening in the princess. 'Because I'm very fond of my nephew and he's convinced you're innocent. I'd hate to give him cause to feel about me the way you do.'

'That can't be the only reason.'

'It's not,' Marla agreed. 'But it's the only one that matters at the moment.'

Luciena stared at the princess in confusion. 'I don't understand.'

'I'm giving you one last chance, Luciena, to prove your tale is the truth. Convince me, and I will let you live. Fail to convince me, and you won't be going back to your cell, I can promise you that.'

'Xanda said you were waiting until Wrayan Lightfinger returned. He can prove I'm innocent.'

'Unfortunately for you, Wrayan isn't here and I don't have time to wait for him any longer. So convince me, or tell me what you'd like engraved on your headstone. I'm fine with it, either way.'

Luciena stared at Marla, wishing she could tell if the princess was bluffing. 'I don't know how to prove my innocence, your highness.'

'What of this letter from your uncle you claim to have? The one who was trying to extort you? Can you produce that?'

'I left it in Greenharbour.'

'Can anyone confirm your story?'

'My slave, Aleesha—'

'Your slave hardly counts as a reliable witness. Isn't there somebody else?'

'The High Arrion—'

'Is the last person you should use as a character witness in my house. Did you discuss the matter with Farlian Kell?'

'No.'

'With *any*body?'

'No.'

'You're not doing much to help yourself, Luciena.'

'If I'd known I was going to be accused of treason and attempted murder, your highness, I would have been a bit more careful to establish my alibi before I left Greenharbour.'

The princess frowned at her tone. 'Your attitude isn't helping you, either.'

'I'm sorry, your highness, if I'm not showing you the correct amount of respect while you pass a death sentence on me!'

The thought occurred to Luciena, even as she uttered the words, that she was probably passing a death sentence on herself by being so insolent. But she couldn't help it. This was so unfair. All her dreams had been so close to coming true. Everything had been on the cusp of being so perfect. And then, for reasons she couldn't understand, or even remember, it had been snatched from her grasp and the only one she had to rail at was Princess Marla.

The princess seemed disappointed by her outburst. 'Very well, Luciena, if that's how you feel, then you leave me no alternative. I know you won't believe me, but I'm genuinely sorry it's going to end like this. You had a great deal of potential.' Marla turned towards the door. 'Captain!'

Luciena stared at the princess, horrified to realise she meant to put an end to this immediately. Almodavar stepped into the solar, his expression grim. 'Your highness?'

'Miss Mariner is not in the mood to cooperate. You may proceed with her execution as soon as you're ready.'

'You're bluffing,' Luciena accused, certain she must be dreaming. 'You won't hang me here in Krakandar. Not where your children can witness it.'

Marla smiled grimly. 'If you think I'd shy away from teaching my children a salient lesson about the best way to treat traitors, Luciena, then you don't know me at all.'

Almodavar took a step towards her and the true depth of Luciena's dire predicament began to sink in. *They're going to kill me*, she realised, suddenly feeling ill as she backed away from him. *They're really going to kill me.* She shook her head, trying to deny the awful truth.

Well, I'm not going without a fight, she decided. *Kicking and screaming. All the way . . .*

Almodavar's hand was resting on the hilt of his sword as he neared her. 'Miss Mariner—'

Suddenly, the door flew open and Xanda burst into the room. 'Wait!'

Luciena wanted to cry. Her first thought was that he'd come to save her, but he didn't even look at her. *By all the Primal Gods, not even Xanda wants to save me.* Luciena looked down at her hands. She was shaking uncontrollably and the room was starting to spin.

Marla turned to her nephew, clearly not pleased by the interruption. 'I asked not to be disturbed, Xanda.'

'But—'

'Not now, Xanda.'

'But, Aunt Marla, before you—'

'Xanda!'

'Wrayan Lightfinger's here!' Xanda announced, refusing to be silenced. 'And I know he's supposed to be a great magician, but I doubt he's all that good at communing with the dead, so perhaps we should get him to speak to Luciena *before* you hang her?'

If Princess Marla said anything in reply to Xanda's announcement, Luciena never heard it. The room was doing cartwheels in front of her eyes.

Xanda's suggestion that Princess Marla delay her hanging until she'd spoken to Wrayan Lightfinger was the last thing she remembered before she fainted.

37

'Luciena?' a voice whispered. 'Can you hear me?'

Luciena's eyes fluttered open. Xanda was leaning over her. She smiled wanly. 'I had this strange dream,' she told him sleepily. 'I was in the solar and Princess Marla ordered Almodavar to take me away and then you burst in and said Wrayan Lightfinger was back . . .' She blinked again and looked around the room . . . everything was blue. It wasn't her cell. In fact, it looked suspiciously like her old room in the palace.

Anxiously, she struggled to sit up, but a firm hand pushed her back down. 'Steady on there, old girl,' an unfamiliar voice warned. 'You might want to wait a bit before you do anything too strenuous.'

Luciena turned her head to look at the man who had spoken and then back at Xanda, suddenly filled with apprehension. 'It wasn't a dream, was it?'

He shook his head.

'My head hurts.'

'Sorry about that.' The stranger looked down on her with a smile. To her intense relief, it was Wrayan Lightfinger. She didn't know how long she'd been here, how long she'd been unconscious. Luciena certainly had no idea how she came to be back in her old room. These blank spots in her memory were developing into a disturbing trend. 'Did you . . . I mean, were you able to tell . . . ?'

'Oh, yes!' Wrayan agreed. 'But you should be fine now. Alija's heavy-handed attempt at coercion is no real match for a bit of Harshini-trained finesse. The headache should go away eventually. In an hour or so.'

'So the High Arrion definitely did something to me?' she asked. It was rather aggravating, this notion that other people could rifle through her thoughts at will while she knew nothing about it. 'Does this mean you're satisfied I'm not a dangerous Patriot or a Fardohnyan spy burning with the need to bring the Wolfblades down?'

Xanda sat on the bed beside her, taking her hand in his. 'It helped that Wrayan arrived back in Krakandar with your magically gifted cousin in tow,' he told her with a smile. He seemed concerned, but it was hard to tell. 'With proof that the letter from your uncle actually existed, I think we can safely assume you really aren't a Fardohnyan spy. And now Wrayan's been able to verify that your mind was tampered with, it shouldn't be too hard to persuade Marla you're not a dangerous criminal.'

'But why would Lady Alija do something like that to me?'

'Do you recall what happened when she came to see you in Greenharbour?' Wrayan asked.

Luciena frowned. Her headache made it hard to remember. 'We were talking about coming to Krakandar . . . she was asking what Princess Marla wanted of me . . . then she took my hands . . .' She shrugged helplessly. 'The next thing I recall is Aleesha was standing over me, telling me I'd fainted.'

'Welcome to the family,' Wrayan said.

She frowned and then nodded as the memory came to her. 'Yes, I kept thinking that. It was like a tune that gets stuck in your head and won't go away.'

'It was the uppermost thought in your mind,' Wrayan

corrected. 'Actually, now I come to think of it, it was the *only* thought in your mind. I should have realised what was going on the first time.'

'You've done this to me before?'

Wrayan nodded. 'The day we first met. I just brushed over your thoughts that day at lunch. The phrase kept repeating itself, over and over, but I thought it was just you – you know, as if you told yourself the same thing often enough, eventually you'd come to believe it? It must have been the trigger.'

Xanda looked up at Wrayan with a frown. 'Are you saying that all it needed was for somebody to say those words to her?'

Wrayan nodded. 'And she'd turn into an assassin.'

'Why didn't you see it before?'

The thief shrugged apologetically. 'I wasn't looking for it. There was no reason to think Luciena had ever met Alija, and she's an Innate so she can't impose her will on anybody unless she can touch them. Anyway, I'd arranged with Princess Marla to come back a few days later, to take a closer look at Luciena's mind and then shield it. I would have picked up the interference then.'

'So Alija filled Luciena with the desire to kill Damin and then pointed her at him like a loaded crossbow. All it needed to set her off was for someone to spare the girl a few kind words.'

Wrayan nodded. 'Do you remember anything else, Luciena?'

'No.' She shook her head, despite the pain. It all seemed too incredulous to be real. Then she sat bolt upright. 'Hang on, did you say you had my magically gifted cousin in tow? Rory? You found him?'

'It's a long story,' Wrayan said, 'and right now, I have to report to the princess.'

'Where is he?'

'Having the time of his life in the day nursery getting acquainted with his royal Hythrun cousins-by-marriage,' the thief told her with a grin. 'You can see him in a little while. Will you be all right with Xanda until I get back?'

Luciena turned her gaze on the young man. She wished she could tell what he was thinking. 'I'll be fine.'

Wrayan nodded. 'Then I'd better speak to Marla. Don't let her get up for a while yet,' he added to Xanda, before heading for the door.

With a sick feeling in the pit of her stomach, Luciena watched the thief – or was it the sorcerer? She wasn't really sure on that point – leave the room.

'What do you think she'll do?' she asked Xanda anxiously.

'I don't know,' he admitted, squeezing her hand with an encouraging smile. 'But Wrayan says you're no danger to anybody now, so that's a good thing. And Aunt Marla listens to him, so you have a chance. Although, I understand she's rather peeved with him for staying away for so long, so she might not be as amenable to his suggestions as she usually is.'

Luciena sighed, wishing the pain would go away. Even the candles in the room were hurting her eyes. 'I didn't think I *was* a danger, Xanda. Not to anybody. Even before I apparently tried to stab your cousin.'

Xanda smiled faintly. 'Don't worry too much about Damin. He can handle himself.'

'I know,' Luciena agreed with feeling. 'I had the bruises and the arm he just about wrenched out of its socket to prove it.'

His smile faded. 'I wish I could tell you what was going to happen to you, Luciena. Aunt Marla might decide you're not worth the risk, or she might believe Wrayan and do what Ruxton is suggesting . . . I really don't know.'

She lay back against the soft pillows. The silk sheets and satin coverlet seemed strange after weeks of a straw-filled pallet and no pillow at all. But she felt dirty. Luciena wasn't sure if she'd tried to kill Damin Wolfblade on purpose, but she was fairly certain that right at this moment, she'd cheerfully kill the whole Wolfblade clan if it meant getting a bath. Then something Xanda had said struck an odd note in her mind and she looked at him curiously. 'What did Ruxton suggest?'

'Something about acting as if nothing's happened so Alija will think you're still waiting for your chance at Damin.'

'That sounds . . . precarious.'

'I don't know the details. I just heard them discussing it in passing.'

She closed her eyes for a moment and then opened them and looked around in alarm as something else occurred to her. She struggled to sit up again, although it made her quite light-headed. 'Where's Aleesha? What happened to my slave?'

'She's fine. She was reassigned to the laundry while you were . . . away.'

'So poor Aleesha was punished for my crime, too?'

Xanda pushed her back against the pillows, gently but firmly. 'It was just a precaution, Luciena. She might have been your accomplice.'

'Assuming I was actually *plotting* something.' Luciena sighed, wishing things had gone differently between them. Xanda had remained her one true friend through all of this. She studied his face in the candlelight, wondering what might have happened if she'd met him some other way. If his aunt wasn't the High Prince's sister. *If I hadn't tried to kill his cousin.*

'Do you think I'm a traitor, Xanda Taranger?'

'No.'

'Will you tell your aunt that?'

'I already have. On several occasions.'

'It didn't get me out of jail.'

'It stopped you from getting hanged, though,' he pointed out with a smile. He was still leaning over her, still holding her down.

Don't get any ideas about my nephew, she heard Marla say, the thought echoing somewhere through her aching head. Then another voice emerged through the throbbing pain. *She just tells you one thing*, Rielle Tirstone's voice said, *knowing full well you'll probably go and do the exact opposite.*

The hell with you, Marla Wolfblade.

Convinced she had nothing left to lose, Luciena slid her arms around Xanda's neck and pulled him down to her. She kissed him, hungrily, desperately, and with little thought to the consequences. She didn't care. Not any more. Neither did Xanda, if the way he kissed her back was anything to judge by. He kissed her like there was no tomorrow, which made her want to cry, because for Luciena, there probably wasn't.

But if she was going to die, she was determined to have one moment of happiness before they took her away. *They always give the condemned one last wish, don't they?*

'Well, I see you two aren't wasting any time.'

Xanda leapt off her in surprise as Luciena pushed herself up on her elbows to find Princess Marla and Wrayan Lightfinger standing at the foot of the bed. Her head was pounding and she could barely hear herself think for the rushing of blood through her ears. She cringed inwardly, waiting for Marla to explode with fury. By the look on Xanda's face, he was expecting the same thing.

But Marla didn't get angry. She didn't even seem annoyed.

'Please,' she said coolly. 'Don't let us interrupt you.'

'Aunt Marla,' Xanda began nervously. 'It's not what it looked like . . . we weren't . . . I can explain . . .'

'I'm *court'esa* trained, Xanda, and have given birth to

three children. I don't actually need an explanation.' She turned her regal gaze on Luciena, frowning at her grubby shift. 'You and I have a great deal to sort out, young lady. But I imagine you'll want to bathe before we talk. I'll have Orleon reassign your slave so she can assist you, shall I? Or perhaps,' she added with a hint of amusement, 'you'd rather have Xanda wash your back.'

With that, the princess turned on her heel and left the room, Wrayan following in her wake. Luciena stared after her and then looked at Xanda, who appeared thoroughly bemused. And then she heard Rielle's distant voice in her head again.

Just when you think you've finally managed to get one over on Marla Wolfblade, she could hear the young woman saying, *you discover you've done exactly what she wanted all along.*

38

Another summer almost done, Elezaar mused as he approached Marla's private sitting room in a strangely reflective mood. *Another year gone. Another year in which Alija Eaglespike has not paid for her crimes.*

Marla turned from the window as he opened the door. Her trunks were stacked in the corner waiting to be collected; the shelves were bare and only her small writing case remained unpacked.

'She's on her way,' he announced, waddling into the room, closing the door behind him.

Taking a deep breath, the princess faced the door and braced herself for the inevitable confrontation with her daughter. Kalan had grown increasingly remote since the day she and her brothers had given their guards the slip in the marketplace. In fact, Kalan had barely had a civil word for her mother. Over the past few weeks, Elezaar had observed, their relationship had deteriorated to the point where mother and daughter were barely speaking.

The painful thing for Marla, the dwarf knew, was that she understood her daughter's dilemma. She remembered what it felt like to be negotiated over like a piece of prime beef because of whose sister she was. At ten, Kalan could already see the writing on the wall. Despite her sharp mind (or perhaps because of it), she knew she was doomed to the future Marla had avoided by the bare skin of her teeth and there was nothing her mother could do to save her from it.

The real tragedy, however, in Elezaar's mind, was that Kalan's suggestion she should join the Sorcerers' Collective was a brilliant idea. So brilliant, in fact, Elezaar wondered why he'd never thought of suggesting such a thing himself. To have someone in such a position of power some day; a member of the family.

Someone who could challenge Alija.

The idea was so seductive, Elezaar found himself running various scenarios through his mind, trying to come up with a way to achieve it. It wasn't easy. Marla already had Wrayan setting mind blocks on herself and her children to protect them. She'd relaxed her guard for a mere moment with the Mariner girl, and the next thing they knew, Luciena was attacking Damin. It had taken some very clever talking on Elezaar's part before the princess could even bring herself to contemplate the notion of placing Kalan, or any other member of the family in such danger, regardless of any eventual benefit.

Not everything his mistress had set in motion was proving so trying, though. Starros was dealing well with the extra lessons Elezaar had set for him, reinforcing his opinion the boy would make an excellent seneschal some day. Ruxton had found a new tutor for the children, a former *court'esa* once belonging to the late Lady Jeryma at some time in the distant past. He was an old man now but reputedly had a mind as sharp as that of his charges and would brook no nonsense from them. The man was due to arrive in the next few days to take over the burden of the remaining children's lessons. Elezaar was mightily relieved. He had feared all summer long that he would be left behind when Marla returned to Greenharbour.

Rielle and Darvad had left the city, escorted back to Izcomdar by Rogan Bearbow and his entourage. Damin would follow in a few days, leaving Krakandar with Marla and Ruxton. They would return to the capital via Rogan's stronghold at Natalandar, see Damin safely settled in his fosterage, and then continue south, arriving in Greenharbour just before the Feast of Zegarnald in the autumn.

But that still left the problem of what to do with Kalan . . .

A knock on the door distracted Elezaar. Marla called permission to enter. Kalan stepped into the study wearing her accustomed scowl. He had seen little else in the way of expression on Marla's daughter's face over the past two months.

'Mother,' Kalan said, stopping before the princess with a barely respectful curtsey. She ignored Elezaar.

'Kalan.'

'Your *slave* said you wanted to see me.' That was her way of letting Elezaar know she still hadn't forgiven him for telling her mother about their discussion.

Marla ignored her daughter's scathing tone. 'I have come to a decision about your future, Kalan. As I'm leaving tomorrow, I thought you might like to know what it is.'

The girl straightened her shoulders defiantly. 'I will kill myself before I marry some sleazy old man just to seal a stupid treaty!'

Elezaar bit back a smile. She was a feisty little thing, this daughter of Marla's.

'Actually, I was hoping you'd come back to Greenharbour with me.'

Kalan stared at her mother suspiciously. 'Why?'

'Wrayan tells me the process of acceptance into the Sorcerers' Collective is quite laborious under normal circumstances. It will be much easier if you're in the city while we go through the formalities.'

Kalan's head jerked up. '*Wrayan* said that?'

'I can't imagine why anybody would *want* to join the Sorcerers' Collective, mind you,' Wrayan said behind her, appearing out of thin air.

His sudden appearance made even Elezaar jump and he'd known all along that Wrayan was there. He just hadn't seen him pull that rather impressive disappearing act.

Her scowl forgotten, Kalan squealed with glee and threw herself at the thief. 'Wrayan! You're back!'

Wrayan hugged the child briefly and then pushed her away, aware that Marla thought her daughter's crush on him was a little misplaced.

'Yes, he's back,' Marla said. 'And you just walked straight past him, Kalan, without even knowing he was there. Do you understand that?'

'But Wrayan's a sorcerer! He did something so I couldn't see him.'

'This is precisely the point I have been trying to make for the past two months. Alija Eaglespike is also a magician,' Marla warned. 'And you are not. You would have no defence against her. You *must* understand that, and I'm going to need to be convinced that you are fully aware of the danger before I let you anywhere near the Sorcerers' Collective.'

'But that's not . . .' She hesitated and looked at her mother. 'What do you mean, *before you let me anywhere near the Sorcerers' Collective*? You're going to let me *join*?'

'I'm thinking about it.'

Kalan stared at them in confusion. 'What changed your mind? You said you'd never agree.'

'The arrival of Luciena's cousin has changed matters somewhat.'

'You mean Rory?'

'He'll be joining the Sorcerers' Collective when you get to Greenharbour,' Wrayan explained. 'With someone in the Sorcerers' Collective your mother can trust – and, more importantly, someone Alija can't influence – the danger to you might be a little more . . . manageable.'

'So he wasn't pulling my leg then?' she asked Wrayan. 'He really can wield proper magic?'

Wrayan smiled. 'Yes, he can wield *proper* magic.'

'Wow,' the girl replied, suitably impressed.

Marla wasn't nearly so enthusiastic as her daughter. 'Don't get too excited, Kalan. Despite both Elezaar and Wrayan championing your cause, I'm far from convinced this is a good idea. There are certain negotiations that have to take place before you're accepted into the Sorcerers' Collective, too,' her mother explained. 'I imagine, at the very least, it's going to cost me a new temple in the grounds of the Sorcerers' Palace.

'On the bright side, along with my patronage – and the fact that you are the High Prince's niece – comes the ability to dictate a few conditions about your apprenticeship. I plan to ask Bruno Sanval to take on Rorin's apprentice-ship, which should keep him out of Alija's way. But if I allow you to follow him – and it's a very big *if* – it will be on the express condition that you and Rorin are never separated.'

'Why not?'

'Rorin can maintain a link with you that will tell him if something happens to you,' Wrayan explained. 'Don't ask me how – it's a magical thing and you wouldn't under-stand.'

'*Really?*' Kalan gasped. She looked set to burst some-thing vital. 'Do you really mean this, Mama?'

Marla held up her hand to dampen her daughter's enthu-siasm. 'Understand, Kalan, once I've done this, you're on your own. If you fail, young lady, you won't have to worry about what Alija might do to you, because I will send you back here to Krakandar and marry you off to the scabbiest, most disgusting old man I can find, just so you can prove your continuing loyalty to your family.'

Kalan grinned broadly, the first genuine sign of happiness Elezaar had seen in the girl for months. 'I won't fail, Mama. I'll be High Arrion some day. Just watch me.'

Marla glanced at Wrayan with a shake of her head, obviously wondering what she had unleashed.

'May the gods help the Sorcerers' Collective the day *that* happens,' Wrayan chuckled.

'May the gods help us all, Wrayan,' Marla replied, rolling her eyes. 'I have a bad feeling we're going to need it. Elezaar, would you have some tea brought in?'

'Of course, my lady.'

'If you're being so nice to Luciena's cousin, does that mean you're not going to hang her as a spy, after all?' Kalan said, looking at her mother curiously.

Elezaar hesitated on the threshold, wondering how Marla would reply.

The princess shook her head. 'As it turns out, Luciena was an innocent pawn in a game she didn't even know she was playing. And you should never forget what happened to her, Kalan. If you drop your guard for a moment in Greenharbour, the same thing could easily happen to you.'

Elezaar didn't hear the rest of the conversation. He smiled to himself and let the door shut behind him, thinking that of all the delicious punishments he could have unleashed on Alija Eaglespike, the most harrowing might yet prove to be Kalan Hawksword.

'Elezaar!'

The dwarf turned, a little surprised to find Ruxton Tirstone hailing him. 'Are you looking for the princess, sir? She's in her sitting room with Master Lightfinger and Kalan.'

Ruxton rolled his eyes. 'There's a plan afoot I'll bet I

want no part of. However, I wasn't looking for Marla. I was looking for you.'

'Did you want something, sir?'

'It's more about what I can do for you, actually.' The trader glanced up the hall, taking Elezaar by the elbow gently. He moved away from the door to ensure they were alone before he continued. 'Do you remember telling me about your brother?'

Elezaar frowned, wishing he had never mentioned the subject. But he'd always enjoyed a cordial relationship with Marla's fourth husband. They had shared many a cup of ale in the kitchens late at night when the rest of the household was asleep. Although he'd never been a slave, Ruxton had a lot more in common with Elezaar, in fact, than with his royal wife. It was during one of those late-night ales that, in a rare burst of inexplicable sentimentality, Elezaar had told Ruxton about Crysander.

'My brother is dead, Master Tirstone.'

'Perhaps,' the spice trader agreed cautiously.

Elezaar's eyes narrowed. 'What does that mean?'

'Just that I've heard a rumour or two. Nothing substantial, mind you. But it might be worth investigating. If you wanted me to look into it, that is?'

For a moment, the hall of Krakandar Palace faded, replaced by the stark black-and-white tiles of Ronan Dell's house. *The captain's blade – Alija Eaglespike's captain – plunging into Crys without warning . . . the man driving his dagger up under Crys's rib cage and into his heart . . . Crys falling . . . the creak of leather as the captain bends over to check Crys is really dead . . .*

Elezaar shook his head to clear the haunting nightmare. 'My brother is dead, Master Tirstone. I thank you for your concern, but I'd appreciate it if you'd just let the matter drop. And that you mention it to nobody.'

'As you wish,' Ruxton replied. 'I just thought—'

'Only pain lies down the road of false hope,' Elezaar shrugged. 'Crysander is dead and I am taking steps to ensure the person responsible will pay.'

'Are you certain you don't want my help?'

'Certain, Master Tirstone.'

The trader shrugged, as if he couldn't figure out Elezaar's reasoning, and turned back in the direction he'd come.

Elezaar continued towards the stairs to get Marla's tea, thinking Ruxton just didn't understand. Revenge would be a long time coming for Elezaar. The dwarf didn't mind that Alija would probably never know he had engineered her downfall. All Elezaar cared about was that the seeds for Alija Eaglespike's destruction had finally been sown in fertile ground and that – albeit, quite a few years from now – he would live to witness the bitter but oh-so-satisfying harvest.

PART 2

THE PAIN OF TRUTH;
THE COMFORT OF
LIES

39

A loud cheer went up as the horses crossed the finish line, another stallion from the stables of the High Prince taking the honours, a fact that irked Alija Eaglespike no end. Not being renowned for their horseflesh, Dregian Province had no horses running in the races today, but it would have been nice to think someone other than Izcomdar Province and the High Prince's own stables had a chance at the prize money. She fanned herself impatiently with a copy of the racing program, silently cursing the dust, the muggy Greenharbour winter that never really cooled down, the unwashed crowds and the High Prince's good fortune. It irritated her beyond belief to realise Lernen Wolfblade's success at the races was directly attributable to a gift of four sorcerer-bred horses from her own cousin, Rogan Bearbow, to Lernen's air-headed nephew, Damin Wolfblade, when the young man finished his fosterage in Izcomdar six years ago.

Alija glanced down the grandstand to the High Prince's private box and frowned as she studied the heir to Hythria. Although as High Arrion she was welcome to sit with the High Prince, Alija preferred the Eaglespike enclosure, situated above and behind the royal box, the perfect vantage point from which to study the occupants below.

Damin Wolfblade sat on a low couch beside his uncle,

laughing about something – probably their remarkable good fortune at the races today. Next to Damin sat Adham Tirstone, and beside him a young woman Alija didn't know, who seemed rather jaded and bored with the whole thing. The High Arrion paid little attention to the girl. She wore a jewelled collar, indicating she was a *court'esa*. A slave, then, probably belonging to either Adham or Damin. She certainly wasn't there to entertain the High Prince. Dismissing the slave as insignificant, Alija turned her attention back to Damin Wolfblade.

Marla's son was twenty-four now, having survived all attempts to assassinate him thus far. Not for the first time, as Alija studied the young man, she wished Damin had been more of a Wolfblade and less his father's son. Laran Krakenshield, although not a handsome man, had been a tall and imposing figure. Simply because of his stature, the young prince gave people the impression he was far more notable than he really deserved.

As if he knew she was thinking of him, the young prince looked up. Their eyes met for a moment. Damin smiled cheerily, waved, and then returned his attention to whatever his stepbrother, Adham Tirstone, was telling him. Alija cursed softly under her breath, wondering what it would take to be rid of him.

It was twelve years since the last time Alija had unsuccessfully tried to eliminate the heir to Hythria's throne. Twelve years of watching and waiting. Twelve long years in which Marla's daughter, Kalan, had graduated from her apprenticeship to become a full member of the Sorcerers' Collective. Twelve long years since Luciena – now formally adopted by Marla – had taken over her father's shipping empire and married Marla's nephew, Xanda Taranger, giving him three children along the way; all without a hint of suspicion that Alija had ever been inside her mind or that Luciena posed any sort of threat to Damin. It was twelve long years since Damin Wolfblade was sent to Rogan Bearbow to begin his fosterage, too. In that time, Alija's eldest son had married and already produced a daughter, while Marla had continued to prop up her brother's precarious position by acting as his aide.

Besides his frustrating insistence on refusing to die whenever she tried to arrange it, Damin Wolfblade was an irritation to Alija for a number of other reasons. His natural charm was one of them – and probably more danger to her plans than any inherent streak of political ruthlessness or leadership ability the young man might possess. People automatically liked the High Prince's heir, just because he was young and fair and always seemed to be laughing.

Fortunately, not everyone was taken in by a winning smile. It was clear to all who'd met him that Damin Wolfblade took nothing seriously, a fact that even Marla had complained about on occasion. Privately delighted by this obvious flaw in the young man's character, the High Arrion had advised the princess to put aside her concerns and let nature take its course. 'He'll grow out of it,' she assured Marla frequently, hoping he never did. Of one thing Alija was certain: when it came to a showdown – and it would, because Cyrus Eaglespike, not Damin Wolfblade, was destined to rule Hythria – her eldest son's serious and thoughtful nature would make him a far more attractive candidate for High Prince. That had been her mistake with Barnardo, she willingly acknowledged now. There was no point offering to remove one fool just to replace him with another.

The people want someone they can look up to, not the frivolous charm of an inexperienced, albeit handsome, young man with no sense of responsibility whatsoever.

Alija watched Damin chatting with his uncle and his stepbrother, wondering what the young prince and his sick old uncle had in common. Damin was here in Greenharbour to learn, supposedly, but if he was learning statecraft, he certainly wasn't learning it from his uncle and he certainly wasn't doing it at the palace. According to Alija's spies, when Damin wasn't training with the Palace Guard, or at the horse races, or partying with his close-knit circle of friends, he was holed up in Marla's townhouse learning the gods-alone-knew-what under the tutelage of that damned dwarf.

Damin had inherited much of his mother's blond good looks along with his father's breadth of shoulder, which made him a popular figure with the young women of Greenharbour, although he'd been careful to avoid scandal with any woman of his own class. He paid frequent visits to Zegarnald's temple, made a point of training regularly, and could hold his own with the best of them; a fact which did not surprise Alija in the slightest, given the training Damin had received as a boy. He undertook minor royal duties with good-natured forbearance, had kept his nose out of anything controversial – once again, that was probably Marla's doing – and was generally considered quite harmless when it came to anything political. Although he obviously enjoyed a cordial relationship with the High Prince, he rarely ventured near the palace and had never – as far as Alija knew – taken part in one of Lernen's orgies in the roof garden on the west wing. The only good thing that said about Damin Wolfblade was that he didn't share his uncle's perversions. He probably had a whole new set of his own.

'More wine, my lady?'

Alija glanced up at the slave and nodded, holding out her cup for a refill as Damin Wolfblade rose to his feet below her to greet some new arrivals to the royal box. Lernen remained seated, but turned on his couch to greet the newcomers. Luciena and her husband, Xanda Taranger. Alija could feel her ire rising. Aware that in such a public

370

place, people were probably watching her with the same amount of interest that she was watching the royal box, she let no emotion show as the couple took their seats behind the High Prince.

Alija's attempt to use Luciena Mariner as an assassin when Damin was still a child had proved a complete failure. Either the coercion had worn off before Luciena reached Krakandar, or nobody had ever uttered the trigger phrase in her presence. *Unlikely*, Alija thought, watching the ease with which the once penniless *court'esa's* daughter seemed to mingle with her betters. A respected businesswoman, married to a Taranger and adopted sister to the next High Prince, Luciena had led a charmed life these past twelve years. She'd given birth to three healthy children, ran a trading empire most men would have given a limb to command, and was treated as a member of the High Prince's inner circle.

The failure of Alija's plan to use Luciena as an assassin still grated, mostly because she had no idea how it could have failed. She would have understood if Luciena had been caught and subsequently executed for attempting to kill Damin – that had always been a risk of the plan. But the whole damned Wolfblade clan carried on as if nothing had happened at all. And maybe *that* was the explanation. There was no way Marla would have allowed the girl to live if she perceived her as a danger. That Luciena remained alive was proof she had never presented any sort of threat to the family.

Alija just couldn't understand how the coercion had failed. To compound the problem, it was almost two years after she'd first met the girl and placed the notion in her head to assassinate Damin before Alija was able to get close enough to Luciena again to touch her (and therefore, her mind) to find out what had gone wrong. Not surprisingly, by then no trace of Alija's handiwork remained. Luciena's mind was filled only with shallow thoughts, mostly focused on her husband and the impending birth of her first child. The contact had been quick – a mere brush as they passed in the hall – which meant Alija had little time for an in-depth analysis, so to this day she had never discovered a satisfactory answer to the puzzle.

If she'd thought it was hard getting to Damin while he was in the custody of Mahkas Damaran in Krakandar, it was damn near impossible in Rogan Bearbow's stronghold at Natalandar. Even though Rogan was her cousin, he took his responsibility for Damin's safety so seriously, Alija was certain he would have put one of his own children to death if he thought they were a threat to the young prince.

So Damin had done his fosterage in Izcomdar and at the age of eighteen had come to Greenharbour, presumably to begin learning what was expected of him when he eventually assumed the role of High Prince. He was careful who he slept with, restricting his pleasures of the flesh to those *court'esa* owned by Marla's household. Alija attributed that to Marla's common sense rather than her son's. (The Lady of Eaglespike was just as adamant that her own sons, Cyrus and Serrin, not expose themselves either to assassination or some unspeakable disease by consorting with brothel-owned *court'esa*.) The young prince never ventured out of doors alone and certainly not without a phalanx of dedicated bodyguards all apparently willing to throw their lives away in defence of Hythria's heir.

There were days when, confronted by the difficulties of disposing of someone so well protected, Alija wondered if she should even bother killing him. The more she saw of Damin Wolfblade, the more she was convinced that Cyrus would eventually take the throne, even if Damin were still alive. Alija knew the Warlords were sick of being ruled by wastrels and, in his six years in the city, Damin Wolfblade had proved to be little else.

That was how she consoled herself, at least. The truth was, Alija had not had another opportunity in twelve years – until today – to rid the world of Lernen's heir.

'Tarkyn Lye is here, my lady,' Tressa announced behind her.

Alija waved him forward, not taking her eyes off the royal box below.

'Well?' she asked.

'Everything is set, my lady.'

'Are you certain?'

'Yes, my lady.'

'And there is no way this can be traced back to me?'

'I made certain nobody saw my face.'

She turned and smiled at him briefly, even though he couldn't see it. Tarkyn would sense her approval. He always did. 'If this works, Tarkyn, I'll see you are handsomely rewarded.'

'I ask for nothing more than the chance to remain in your service, my lady.'

'And the odd pocket full of gold, too, as I recall.'

He shrugged and smiled ingenuously. 'One of the many perks of remaining in your service, my lady.'

'And you're absolutely certain this can't be traced back to anybody connected to me or Dregian Province?'

'The man is Denikan, my lady. He barely speaks enough Hythrun to understand what was required of him. Even if he knew who hired him, he couldn't tell anyone. And let's face it, it's a good chance he'll be dead long before anyone gets around to questioning him, either from the bodyguards or his . . . condition.'

'You didn't allow him to touch you, I hope?'

'Of course not, my lady.'

Alija nodded and turned back to watching the track. The horses were lining up for the next race, a three-mile marathon that would test the mettle of every horse and rider taking part. With a satisfied smile, Alija snapped her fingers. Tressa hurried forward to do her bidding.

'My lady?'

'Go down to the royal box for me, Tressa. Tell the High Prince I'll wager a hundred gold rivets on Lance of the Wind coming in ahead of that useless nag of his, King's Ransom.'

The slave bowed and hurried away to deliver the message. 'You're bound to lose,' Tarkyn warned. 'King's Ransom hasn't lost a race all season.'

'I can't lose, Tarkyn,' she replied. Down in the royal box, Lernen got the message and turned to wave to Alija to acknowledge the wager. She smiled at him with satisfaction. 'Not today.'

'I hope you're right, my lady.'

Alija nodded. 'You'll know I'm right, Tarkyn, when you hear the bells tolling throughout the city a few days from now, announcing that the High Prince's heir is dead.'

40

It was well past midnight by the time Damin Wolfblade and his friends left the Lurching Sailor and made their way drunkenly out into the street. It was a clear night and all of them had done well at the races so they had much to celebrate.

As they emerged from the tavern, Xanda Taranger had his arm around Adham Tirstone. Watching them stagger through the door ahead of him, Damin couldn't say for certain who was holding up whom. They were, however, singing a loud and rather crude ditty about a crabby old whore called Davyna, forced to resort to some rather extreme measures to find customers. As the song progressed, the poor old whore's efforts grew more and more obscene until even Damin winced to hear about it. Admittedly, it might have had something to do with the fact that, between them, Xanda and Adham couldn't carry a tune in a water bucket, but he was sure someone would eventually complain. No sooner had the thought occurred to Damin than a screeching voice yelled at them to shut up; it came from the upper storey of the house across the street from the Lurching Sailor. Across the way, another couple of revellers, a *court'esa* on each arm, wove their way unsteadily down the street. Leaning against one of the pillars holding up the tavern's awning was a Denikan sailor who looked rather the worse for wear. Other than that, the street was deserted.

'Nobody in this city appreciates fine music,' Adham complained loudly, stopping unsteadily in the middle of the street to make an obscene gesture with his finger in the general direction of the owner of the screeching voice.

'Actually, I think you'll find they appreciate it very well,' Damin laughed as he stepped down onto the street. 'Which is why they're yelling at you to stop.'

'Well, that's a fine state of affairs!' Adham snorted indignantly. 'What do we do now?'

'We could go back to my house,' Xanda offered with a crooked smile, clinging to Adham to maintain his balance. 'Luciena likes music.'

'I'm not *that* drunk,' Adham announced, pushing Xanda away so he could attempt to stand on his own two feet. 'She's gonna kill you for staying out so late as it is . . . not my job to add to the body count.'

Xanda shook his head, struggling to maintain his balance. 'She won't kill me. She loves me.'

'When you're sober.' Damin was drunk, too, but not quite as far gone as his cousin. He turned to the other two men who had accompanied them out of the tavern. Big men who were conspicuously armed, both were sober and neither was smiling. They weren't friends. These men were handpicked bodyguards. 'Goren, go find a litter to see Lord Taranger home, would you?'

The man on the left nodded and turned back into the tavern. If the Lurching Sailor didn't have a litter of its own, the owner would know where to get one at this time of night.

Xanda looked at Damin, quite forlorn. 'You're sending me *home*?'

'I'm keeping my promise to Luciena.'

'What did you promise her?' Adham asked. Not having

376

a wife to concern him, he obviously thought Xanda's predicament quite amusing.

'That Xanda'd be home before dawn.'

'What possessed you to promise her that, you fool?' Xanda gasped in horror.

'She did promise not to disembowel me in return for this one small favour.'

'See!' Adham declared smugly. 'This is what you get for having a wife, Xanda. Damin and I don't have to be home before dawn.'

Xanda shook his head. 'Damin, Damin, Damin. You're going to have to stop listening to Luciena when she says things like that. You know she doesn't mean it.'

'She tried to kill me once before,' he pointed out reasonably.

'A mere youthful indiscretion and, anyway, she failed miserably, as I recall. Or have six years in Greenharbour made you lose your edge so badly that a girl could take you down these days?'

Damin grinned at the idea. 'Wanna find out?'

Before Xanda could respond to Damin's challenge, Goren emerged from the tavern. 'The owner's litter is out on a job, my lord, but he says we'll find one easily enough over on Moss Street.' It wasn't an oversight on Goren's part that he addressed Damin as 'my lord' and not 'your highness'. There was no need to draw undue attention to Damin's identity when they were simply out on the town having a bit of fun.

Adham nodded in agreement. 'They line up outside Madam Leska's waiting for her customers. No doubt the litter bearers think anyone who can afford one of her *court'esa* can afford a ride home afterwards.'

'I heard they lined up outside Madam Leska's because after her *court'esa* are done with you, a man isn't *capable* of walking anywhere,' Damin laughed. He put an arm around his cousin and the other around his stepbrother and steered them in the direction of Moss Street. 'Still, I would like to be a fly on the wall when Xanda tries to explain to Luciena why he arrived home in a litter hired from Madam Leska's.'

Weaving down the street drunkenly, Xanda frowned at his cousin. 'You really are an evil little bastard, aren't you, Damin Wolfblade? The gods help us all when you're ruling the whole damned country.'

'Well, I am planning complete world domination, you know,' Damin informed them cheerily. 'I thought I'd invade Fardohnya the first week and then wipe out Medalon on my way north to obliterate the Kariens a couple of weeks after that. Then we might take a short break while we plan our conquest of nations across the southern oceans.'

'Could be fun,' Adham agreed. 'Do we *have* to rape and pillage all the way, though?'

'I suspect we do. I don't think I can really call myself an evil tyrant if I don't at least make the effort. Why?' he asked his stepbrother curiously. 'Do you particularly *want* to rape and pillage?'

'Well, I'm sure it'd be fun the first few villages we passed through, but it must get rather tiring after a while. I'm not sure I'd have the stamina to see me all the way to Karien. And Xanda would have to ask Luciena first, before he could rape and pillage anybody.'

'You're assuming I even want to have anything to do with your diabolical scheme,' Xanda said, sounding a little miffed that Adham thought he might have to ask his wife's permission.

'Don't you *want* to be my evil minion?' Damin asked, wounded that his cousin might even consider refusing. 'It'll be great fun! I'll even promise not to kill you out of hand unless I'm really feeling out of sorts.'

378

'A minion can't ask for much more than that,' Adham declared with a loud hiccough.

Xanda thought about it for a moment and then nodded unsteadily. 'Promise to stop promising my wife you'll have me home before dawn and we might be able to do business, your royal evil-tyrant-ship.'

Damin agreed with a laugh and, with Goren leading the way and the second bodyguard, Clem, following behind them, the drunken young men turned into Fisherman's Lane, which would take them through to Moss Street.

'Of course, if you let Xanda be a minion, you'll have to make Travin one, too,' Adham warned Damin as they traversed the dark lane. 'And probably Kalan, 'cause she's such a bossy little thing, she'll never let you rule the world unless you cut her in for a piece of the action. Rorin might come in handy, too, being a sorcerer and all.'

'And Rodja can be your bookkeeper,' Xanda suggested. 'All evil empires need someone to keep the books. I mean, how do you know what spoils you've collected if you haven't got someone like Rodja to count it all for you?'

'And don't forget Starros,' Damin reminded them, getting right into the spirit of things. 'He'll have to be my chamberlain. Do you think he'll get upset if I tell him I want a eunuch for the job?'

They reached the end of Fisherman's Lane. Across the street, a line of litter bearers waited patiently for the patrons of Madam Leska's to conclude their business. He turned at the sound of someone falling. Behind them, the drunken Denikan had followed them but had slipped and lay facedown in the lane. Dismissing the foreigner as inconsequential, he turned his attention back to Madam Leska's, which seemed to have the total attention of his stepbrother and his cousin. A line of flaming torches lit the path leading to the rather grand foyer some thirty feet from the edge of the road and they could hear the music and laughter from across the street.

'Maybe,' Adham suggested thoughtfully, 'we should take a quick look inside?'

'Or maybe not, my lords,' Goren informed them, glancing back over his shoulder at his three charges.

Adham glared at the big man impatiently. 'When Princess Marla hired you, Goren, did she advertise for a bodyguard or a killjoy?'

'A babysitter,' Goren replied bluntly. 'Stay here. I'll organise some litters.'

'We only need one for Xanda,' Damin pointed out.

'The others are for you and Master Tirstone, my lord. It's time you were getting home, too.'

'Ha!' Xanda barked triumphantly. 'I might have a wife waiting to kill me when I get home, but at least I'm not still answerable to my *mother*.'

Adham burst out laughing at that. Damin wasn't nearly so amused. Even drunk, he was painfully aware of the truth in Xanda's words.

'I'll have you know—' he began, but he didn't get a chance to finish the sentence. The drunken Denikan had picked himself up and staggered into their midst.

'Whoa there!' Clem said, grabbing the sailor before he could lay a hand on the prince. 'Go sleep it off somewhere else, eh?' He shoved the man clear, but the Denikan seemed oddly determined to approach them.

'You prince?' he asked in broken Hythrun, refusing to be put off.

He sounded desperate, rather than drunk, Damin thought.

'You prince? You help?'

'I told you already,' Clem insisted, 'there's nobody here for you, my lad. Back to your ship now. Move along.'

'You prince?' the Denikan insisted, pushing past Clem

desperately as he tried to approach Damin. He coughed painfully, his spittle flecked with blood. 'You help! They say you help!'

'He knows who you are,' Xanda remarked in a voice that suddenly sounded remarkably sober.

Adham nodded his agreement. 'He followed us from the Lurching Sailor.'

'You Prince Damin!' the Denikan cried, loud enough to attract the attention of the litter bearers outside Madam Leska's. 'You help!'

'Shut him up, Clem,' Xanda ordered, looking around in concern, but the bodyguard didn't need to be told. He already had his hand over the sailor's mouth to keep him quiet. The Denikan struggled weakly against Clem's hold, but either he lacked the strength to fight off the big body-guard or he wasn't very serious about it.

Damin stepped a little closer and studied the young man curiously. He was, like every Denikan Damin had ever seen, handsome, dark-skinned and muscular, his long dark hair arranged in an intricate series of thin braids threaded with beads. He wore an open vest and his skin appeared bruised beneath it, as if he'd been beaten, quite savagely. Damin indicated that Clem should let him speak. 'What do you want with me?'

'You prince? You help?'

He took an involuntary step backward. The man's breath was foul, but it was the stench of sickness, not sour ale.

'He keeps saying that,' Adham remarked. 'It's like they're the only Hythrun words he knows.'

'Do you speak Denikan?'

The young trader shook his head. 'Not even a little bit. What about you, Xanda?'

'I know the words for *how much* and *get your hands off my wife,*' Xanda joked. Then his smile faded. 'Some sailor knowing a few words of Hythrun doesn't explain how he knows who you are, Damin.'

The Denikan said something in his own language; a rush of words that meant nothing to them. The outburst appeared to exhaust the young man and he sagged, semi-conscious, in Clem's grasp.

'He's burning up,' the bodyguard remarked with a frown.

Damin looked at the sailor with concern, reaching out to check his fever just as Goren arrived back with the litters he'd arranged to take them home.

'No!' he shouted, slapping Damin's hand away. 'Don't touch him!'

'What's wrong?'

'Look at him,' Goren ordered.

'He's covered in bruises,' Adham pointed out, a little puzzled.

'They're not bruises,' Goren warned. 'He's bleeding into his skin. Did he touch you at all, my lord? Any of you?'

Damin shook his head, wishing it was clearer. 'He was asking for me, but Clem stopped him before he got too close. Do you know what's wrong with him?'

'Not for certain,' the big man replied. 'But I can make a pretty good guess.' He turned his attention to Clem, who was still holding the young Denikan sailor. He had a grim, almost resigned look on his face. The two bodyguards stared at each other for a moment before Clem lowered the Denikan to the ground. Goren turned to face Damin and the others. 'I want you to get in those litters and go home, my lords,' he ordered. 'Now. No argument. No complaints.' There was something in the voice of the big, normally taci-turn man that warned them this was no longer a laughing matter.

'You'll take care of the Denikan?' Damin asked, brushing aside Adham's puzzled demand for an explanation.

'For all the good it will do,' Clem warned, looking up

at the prince. He was squatting over the sailor, who appeared to have lapsed into unconsciousness. 'He'll be dead soon.'

'And what about you, Clem?' Damin asked, acutely aware that he was the one who had put himself between his prince and the danger this foreigner represented.

'I'll take care of Clem,' Goren promised. 'But he can't go back to the palace.'

'Damin? What's going on?'

'Nothing, Adham. Take the litter and go home. You too, Xanda.'

There was no trace of frivolity in the young prince's voice. The others looked at him strangely, unused to seeing him so grave, and then did as he bid, turning for the litters with no further argument. As soon as they were on their way, Damin turned back to Goren.

'You need to get out of here, too, your highness.'

'I know,' Damin agreed. Then he asked the question he'd been too afraid to voice while his stepbrother and cousin were nearby. 'It's plague, isn't it?'

Goren nodded, glancing down at Clem with a frown. Clem knew it, too, and that he was probably going to be its next victim. Across the street, the music and the laughter coming from Madam Leska's continued unabated, oblivious to the danger on its very doorstep.

'Do you think he's been in contact with many people?'

'Hard to say,' Goren shrugged. 'He's almost dead. He could have been wandering around the city infecting people for days.'

'He was asking for me by name.'

'Which means someone else in Greenharbour knew what was wrong with him and probably cut him loose,' Goren suggested. 'And then sent him after you.'

Damin shook his head. 'Nobody could want me dead so badly they'd risk infecting the whole city with plague, surely?'

Goren shrugged. 'It's my job to keep you alive, your highness, not second-guess your assassins. Now get in that litter, go home, wake your mother and tell her what's happened. And then start packing.'

'Packing?'

'If the city is struck down by plague,' Goren warned, 'you'll be on the first coach back to Krakandar. You mark my words.'

Damin stared down at the half-dead sailor for a moment, feeling the weight of his position as Hythria's heir pressing on his shoulders. It simply wasn't fair that such pain and devastation should be let loose, all for the simple purpose of killing one man.

'This is going to get bad, isn't it, Goren?'

'Yes,' the big man agreed heavily. 'It's going to get very bad, your highness. Very bad, indeed.'

41

The King of Fardohnya had much to be grateful for, he knew, but it didn't really help much to count his blessings. Eleven legitimate children and that many again born of his numerous *court'esa* was proof, surely, that Jelanna, the Goddess of Fertility, was smiling on him.

By the gods, I've spent enough money on her damn temples, Hablet reminded himself, as he stepped into the harem garden. *I ought to be her favourite.*

But if he was Jelanna's favourite, the goddess had a strange way of showing it – she had blessed him with eleven legitimate children. And not one of them was a son.

Sometimes, on the rare occasions he was feeling reflective, Hablet wondered if this was punishment for killing Riika Ravenspear all those years ago. Although her death was patently Lecter Turon's fault, Hablet's cursed ability to produce nothing but legitimate daughters (in another cruel twist of fate, he had no trouble producing bastard sons) could be easily traced back to that fateful day, almost a quarter of a century ago. He had stood in the hall of his Winter Palace at Qorinipor in southern Fardohnya, in the shadow of the Sunrise Mountains, and let Laran Krakenshield extort three and a half million gold rivets from him, just because Hablet was feeling bad after his chamberlain had inadvertently killed the Warlord of Krakandar's sister.

That entire regrettable episode was, in Hablet's mind, a disaster from start to finish. Lecter's plan to kidnap the newlywed Marla Wolfblade was a fiasco. First, they'd kidnapped the wrong girl. Then they'd killed her before realising she was the sister of the richest and, arguably, most powerful man in Hythria. And then, like a fool, he'd listened to Lecter again and agreed to take Princess Shanita of Lanipoor as his wife, distracted by the notion of all that money (and his brand-new coach) being carried across the border into Hythria.

Hablet's first official marriage had proved almost as calamitous as his dealings with the Warlord of Krakandar. When the Prince of Lanipoor was bribing Lecter Turon and listing his daughter's numerous virtues, he'd neglected to mention that along with her excellent childbearing hips and outstanding beauty she was a spiteful, vindictive and murderously jealous little bitch. A shrieking harpy in the flesh. Even the praise of her much-vaunted hips had been misleading. After six years and a series of disappointing miscarriages, Princess Shanita had finally given birth to the first of his many daughters within days of Hablet's Hythrun *court'esa*, Welenara, producing his firstborn – albeit illegitimate – son.

Furious her achievement had been overshadowed by a slave – and a foreign slave at that – when the child was only days old, Shanita arranged to have both the *court'esa* and her newborn poisoned. Fortunately for Welenara and her son, the princess had few friends in the harem. One of Hablet's other wives learned of the plot and betrayed her, no doubt hoping to replace the Lanipoorian princess as his senior wife. Hablet had beheaded Her Serene Highness, the Princess Shanita of Lanipoor, when her daughter was a mere two months old and anybody who did not wish to share the late princess's fate had wisely made no mention of Hablet's first wife in the hearing of Fardohnya's king since that day.

Her legacy, however, was still causing him grief. It was in search of Shanita's only child that Hablet had come to the harem gardens this morning.

Following the sound of shouts and laughter, he rounded a bend in the gravelled path and discovered a number of his children – both legitimate and baseborn – engaged in a boisterous game of rope ball on the lawns surrounding a Harshini-style pavilion. In the shade of the white circular podium, with its delicate wrought-iron arches that looked as if they'd been crafted out of spun-sugar, a number of his wives, three of his currently favoured *court'esa* and several slaves responsible for the care of his many children watched over the game, smiling indulgently. The women sipped chilled fruit juices and watered wine and gossiped about those other wives and *court'esa* whose absence made them the only reasonable topic of conversation.

Hablet stopped and watched the game for a moment. It was called rope ball because each of the players held a short piece of red or blue coloured rope behind their backs, to prevent them touching the ball with their hands. To drop the rope was instant disqualification and a point to the opposing team. The ball was an inflated pig's bladder and, with their hands restrained, the only way to move the ball into the goalposts at either end of the lawn was to kick it. This resulted in a great deal of hilarity, much falling over and some none-too-gentle pushing and shoving as the players attempted to gain control of the ball.

He spied his eldest child in the mêlée, playing for the red side. She wasn't the tallest player or the most skilled, but she was invariably voted captain of their impromptu teams, a disturbing tendency that told Hablet more about his daughter than she probably realised.

The game stopped when Hablet stepped out of the shadows of the flowering hibiscus shrubs on the edge of the lawn. Dropping their coloured ropes, the younger children ran to him when they spied their father, gleefully ignorant of his mood. The elder girls and several of his baseborn sons held back a little, having learned to be cautious of him. That amused Hablet for some reason. He wasn't sure why. Maybe he just liked the notion that his children could fear him as much as they professed to love him.

'Adrina!' he called over the heads of her younger siblings after he'd greeted them each by name.

She looked up when he called her, revealing her best feature, which was eyes the colour of polished emeralds. They were the eyes of a temptress. Bedroom eyes, Lecter Turon called them, although he didn't mean it as a compliment.

Adrina favoured her mother in looks, which Hablet found rather disturbing. She had a luscious head of wavy, dark hair and a body that would undoubtedly blossom into sinful voluptuousness when she was older. At eighteen, she had yet to outgrow completely the coltishness of youth, but what she lacked in natural beauty or grace, Adrina more than made up for in wit and intelligence.

And that was what made her so damned dangerous.

'Father?' she replied with no hint of fear. She was flanked by her two closest siblings, Hablet's baseborn sons, Tristan and Gaffen.

Tristan was the same age as Adrina. He was Welenara's son, the one Shanita had tried to poison, and tall, fair, blue-eyed and far too popular for the bastard son of a king with no heir. Lecter was already advising the king to throw him in the army and send him south to the Sunrise Mountains. Out of sight and out of mind, Lecter kept saying. And it wasn't a bad idea. At worst, the boy might kill a few Hythrun. At best, Tristan would be killed himself in the upcoming battle, and the problem of what to do with him would be solved. But Hablet couldn't bring himself to do it. It would break Welenara's heart and, besides, Hablet genuinely *liked* Tristan. Until he had a legitimate son, he really didn't want to see the boy killed, even in the noble pursuit of Hythrun blood.

Gaffen, on the other hand, was much less of a problem. His mother had been a *court'esa*, too. He was also fair-haired (Hablet had a particular weakness for blondes), big and solid and probably the most dependable of his base-born children. His only ambition was to join the navy as soon as he was old enough and travel the world. His only fault, as far as Hablet knew, was how easily enticed into mischief he was by his half-brother and half-sister. They formed a triumvirate of trouble that Lecter often advised him he would be wise to break up. The closeness of his three eldest children might cost him his throne some day, if he wasn't careful.

Or so his chamberlain was fond of telling him.

'Walk with me, petal,' the king commanded. 'I want to talk to you.'

Adrina stepped forward, smiling. She had to know what he wished to discuss with her, yet she appeared unbothered by it. Falling into step beside him, his daughter slipped her arm through his and led him away from the pavilion and the eager, straining ears of her numerous stepmothers.

'What did you want to talk to me about, Daddy?'

'Don't you *Daddy* me, young lady,' he scowled, as they stepped onto the gravelled path. 'You know damned well what I want to talk about.'

'Balkar of Taranipor, I suppose,' she replied with a sigh.

'I was expecting to announce your engagement this morning, Adrina.'

She laughed. 'Don't be absurd, father! I wouldn't marry that fool if he was the last man in Fardohnya.'

'At the rate you're turning them down, my petal,' the king pointed out peevishly, 'you may very well end *up* marrying the last man in Fardohnya. When I said you could choose a suitable consort, I didn't mean you could take your pick of every eligible bachelor in the country.'

'If only you'd *offer* me every eligible bachelor in the country,' she shot back. 'Instead of just the poor, idiot, backwater ones.'

'How can you tell? You've rejected every man I've offered!' he accused. 'Half of them before you even laid eyes on them.'

'Bring me a man with wealth, power and ambition, Daddy,' she suggested with a mischievous grin. 'Just watch how fast I agree to marry him then.'

Wealth, power and ambition. Hablet shuddered at the mere notion of Adrina married to a man like that.

'You can't just keep rejecting suitors, Adrina. People are starting to talk; you're getting a reputation for being a shrew.'

'Good. Maybe then the weak-spined ones will stay away.'

'Do you want to be an old maid?'

'If the alternative means taking a husband like Balkar of Taranipor, then I don't mind at all.'

He shook his head in despair. 'What am I supposed to do now? You offended the entire Taranipor family.'

'You probably care less about that than I do,' she laughed.

'Won't you reconsider? He's quite well off, you know.'

'I know slaves who are richer,' she declared. 'Your chamberlain among them.'

Hablet sighed. 'Lecter only has your best interests at heart, petal.'

'And I'm the demon child,' she scoffed.

Hablet looked down at her and shook his head. 'You cost him a great deal, you know. The bribe he accepted to promote Balkar as a suitor was substantial. Now he'll have to return it.'

'I'm heartbroken,' Adrina replied, clearly delighted by the prospect.

Hablet smiled. As a spectator sport, very little rivalled watching the sly eunuch and his equally devious daughter trying to outsmart each other. The animosity between them was legendary and, by comparison, most of the other political shenanigans that went on at court were mere skirmishes. If he was honest with himself, he knew that for fear of being robbed of his main source of entertainment, Hablet let Adrina get away with just about anything. He let her reject husbands; he let her aggravate Lecter Turon; let her dictate far more about her own fate than was proper for a well-bred Fardohnyan lady. It drove Lecter Turon mad. And that seemed only fair, too, because if the king *had* been cursed by Jelanna after Lecter killed Riika Ravenspear, then it wasn't mischief he was creating, so much as justice.

But even if it wasn't justice, it was fun. The look on Lecter's face whenever Adrina turned away another suitor was priceless.

Sadly, when they finally found her a husband, Adrina would have to leave the palace and the games would be over. Hablet would be lucky if he saw her again. *Which*, Hablet had to admit, *is why I indulge Adrina as much as I do.* By Hablet's estimation, his chamberlain had taken close to a quarter of a million in bribes on this one matter alone since Adrina had turned sixteen. And he'd had to give the vast majority of it back, because bribes of that significance were usually dependent on a successful outcome.

Hablet had no objection in principle to his chamberlain using his position to enrich himself. But it was useful to remind Lecter Turon occasionally that he was a slave and that nobody was invincible – or indispensable. The eunuch was clever, conniving and manipulative (which was why Hablet kept him around). A man like that could be just as much a liability as an asset. Adrina kept him in check by being just as clever, conniving and manipulative. It was why he kept Adrina around, too.

And for that reason, he walked arm in arm with his daughter along the gravelled paths of the harem gardens in the warm winter sunlight, scolding her rather than punishing her.

Adrina had her uses, after all.

'What am I going to do with you?' he moaned.

'Let me marry someone of my own choosing.'

'All seven hells will freeze over before that happens, petal.'

'Then give me something useful to do.'

'Like what?'

She shrugged. 'I don't know. Some official position at court, maybe?'

'But you're a woman.'

'What's that got to do with it?'

He thought about it for a moment and then nodded, as one useful task came to him. 'Very well. If you promise to behave yourself, you may be my hostess occasionally for dinner when my guests arrive later in the week.'

'What's so special about them that you need a hostess?' she asked.

'They are from Hythria.'

'Anyone I know?'

Hablet frowned. 'I would hope you don't socialise with *any* Hythrun, Adrina.'

'You've let me out of the palace about four times in my whole life, Father. Exactly when was I supposed to make the acquaintance of any soul not in your employ?'

'True enough,' he conceded. Interesting how she had dropped the *Daddy*, now she realised she was no longer in trouble. 'But I confine you for your own protection, petal, you understand that, don't you? There is plague out there. Hythria is rampant with it.'

'That's just this year's excuse, father. Hythria hasn't been rampant with plague for the past eighteen years, just the past few months.'

'I'm not concerned about the past eighteen years, Adrina. Only that I keep Fardohnya safe now.'

'That's why you're massing troops near Qorinipor and Tambay's Seat, I suppose?' she asked with a raised brow. 'To keep Fardohnya *safe*?'

'Naturally. And by the way, how do you know about that?'

She smiled innocently. 'So who are your guests?'

'Xanda and Luciena Taranger.'

Adrina was silent for a moment and then nodded. 'Luciena Taranger. Adopted daughter of Marla Wolfblade, which makes her the adopted niece of Hythria's High Prince, the legendary pervert, Lernen Wolfblade. Her father was a commoner – Jarvan Mariner, Princess Marla's third husband. When Marla adopted her at the age of seventeen, she became the owner of near half the trading ships currently sailing out of Greenharbour, and rather a lot of those sailing from Fardohnyan ports, too. About the same time she was adopted, she married Xanda Taranger, who is, if I remember correctly, the nephew of the late Laran Krakenshield, which makes him a cousin to Damin Wolfblade, the heir to the Hythrun throne. It was a commonly held belief at the time that Luciena's adoption was contingent on her marriage to Marla's nephew. What are they doing here in Talabar?'

Hablet frowned. *This is why she's dangerous*, he thought. The events she described happened nigh on twelve years ago. She was six years old at the time. His next eldest legitimate daughter, Cassandra, probably couldn't even name all her own siblings. 'They're supposedly coming to Talabar to expand their operation in Fardohnya. Should I enquire more closely about how you know all this about the Wolfblades?'

'I live to learn, Father,' she replied with a dramatic sigh.

'Trapped here in the harem and denied a life with any meaning at all, the only joys I have are my music and my studies.'

'What a load of horse shit!' the king snorted, scratching at his beard. 'You can't play a note on that damned harp I bought you.'

'But it did come with a very nice music teacher,' she reminded him with a languid smile. 'I got plenty of use out of *him*.'

'So Lecter informs me,' the king grumbled. 'We have *court'esa* for that sort of thing, Adrina. You've no need to take lovers.'

'It's not about need, Father,' she reminded him. 'It's about want. Isn't that what you believe? Take what you want?'

'I didn't mean for you to follow my advice quite so literally, girl.'

She looked up at him with those wicked bedroom eyes and smiled. 'But you love me for it anyway, don't you, Daddy?'

'There may come a time when I don't,' he warned, annoyed that she thought he would fall for such blatant flattery. He wondered if Lecter was right, after all. Maybe he should insist she marry that fool from Taranipor. Maybe the safest thing to do was to banish Adrina from Talabar and send her somewhere she could do him no damage.

'I suppose, come that day, we'll find out who the clever one really is,' she laughed, squeezing his arm affectionately.

As he looked into those remarkable emerald eyes, Hablet suddenly understood something about his eldest daughter. Adrina wasn't afraid of him.

And that made Hablet just a tiny bit afraid of Adrina.

42

Starros pushed his way through the crowded streets of Krakandar's Beggars' Quarter, wondering at the preparations for the Feast of Kaelarn. The streets were festooned with blue bunting and there were buckets of water outside almost every door as an offering. It was a bit of a joke, really. They were miles from the ocean here in Krakandar City, the nearest seaport being Port Sha'rin to the west, in the Gulf of Fardohnya, several hundred miles away. Still, the God of the Oceans was a powerful god, he supposed, and it probably didn't pay to antagonise him.

There was a street parade planned for later in the day and then the ball tonight at the palace, followed by fireworks and probably impromptu parties in every other street in the city as the night wore on. Krakandar's cattle raiders had liberated a goodly number of prime Medalonian beef cattle for the feast and everyone was looking forward to a night of gluttony and drunken revelry. Starros glanced up at the sky and picked up his pace as he realised he didn't have long. He had to get back to the palace before the guard of honour arrived and the start of the parade – although, unlike everyone else in Krakandar, that was what he was least looking forward to.

He turned into the next street and spied his destination.

The Pickpocket's Retreat was a large establishment and quite well off, given its location in the Beggars' Quarter. The paltry exterior belied its comfortable interior, however. Starros had seen enough of the inner rooms to know the outer façade and taproom was more for show than anything else. This was the Beggars' Quarter, after all, and it didn't pay to flaunt one's wealth too loudly in these streets.

He pushed open the door and looked around, spying Wrayan Lightfinger at a table in the corner by the window, talking to his chief lieutenant, Luc North. The two men seemed deep in conversation about something quite serious and, for a moment, Starros debated the wisdom of disturbing them. He knew Wrayan well enough to know he was better off remaining ignorant about his business. While he was wondering about it, the thief glanced up, smiled when he saw Starros, and beckoned him over.

'Well, if it isn't the future chief steward of Krakandar Palace,' Wrayan said with a grin. 'Bring our esteemed guest a drink, Fee!'

'I'm not disturbing you, am I?'

'We're finished,' Luc told him, rising to his feet. 'I'll come by later and tell you how it went,' he added to Wrayan. Then he smiled at Starros. 'Nice to see you again, Starros.'

'You too, Luc,' Starros replied.

The man tipped his hat and turned for the door. Starros watched him leave curiously, and then turned back to Wrayan. 'I didn't interrupt something important, did I?'

'It's nothing Luc can't handle,' Wrayan shrugged. 'Just a territorial dispute. It won't get really nasty unless the . . . miscreant . . . fails to heed the Guild's warning.'

'What do you define as "really nasty"?'

Wrayan smiled. 'You're better off not knowing, my friend. How's life up at the palace treating you? Been promoted yet?'

Starros slid onto the bench seat opposite Wrayan that Luc had just vacated, shaking his head. 'It'll never happen.'

'What will never happen?'

'Me ever becoming chief steward of anything. Orleon's going to live forever.'

Wrayan laughed as Fyora hurried over to the booth and placed a tankard of fresh ale in front of Starros. She smiled at him, but Wrayan sent her away. 'Gods, Fee, he's just walked in the door. Give the poor man time to have at least one drink before you try to jump him.'

'I wasn't jumping anyone, Wrayan Lightfinger,' she snorted indignantly. 'I was merely taking care of our most distinguished patron. Can I get you anything else, my lord?'

Starros smiled. 'Thanks Fee, I'm fine. And truly, you don't have to call me that. I keep telling you. I'm no more highborn than you are.'

'But you're a *gentleman*, Starros,' she told him while glaring pointedly at Wrayan. 'Some people just don't know what that means.' Fee flounced off in the direction of the kitchens, her head high, as if that alone would give her class.

'You two have a falling out?'

'No more than usual,' Wrayan shrugged. 'Although it might have something to do with a *court'esa* who's been visiting my rooms of late that Fee doesn't really approve of.'

'What's wrong with her?'

'She has a pulse.'

Starros laughed. 'She's jealous?'

'I can't imagine why. Fee gave up on me a long time ago. These days, the lovely Fyora has her heart set on becoming mistress of this establishment.'

'Shouldn't she have worked off her bond by now?' Starros asked curiously, thinking Fyora had been at the Pickpocket's Retreat for as long as he could remember. It was twelve years since the first time he had sneaked down here with Damin and Kalan.

Wrayan nodded. 'She did. Years ago. I think she hangs

around here because it's all she knows. Either that, or she's waiting for old Fingle to marry her.'

Hary Fingle was the owner of the Pickpocket's Retreat. He was the man who had originally purchased Fyora for the tavern and, just as she showed no inclination to leave, even though she was nominally free, he showed no inclination to be rid of her.

'Is Fingle likely to marry her?'

'He might,' Wrayan shrugged. 'He certainly couldn't run this place without her. I suppose the day that occurs to him, he'll propose.'

'How come you never married, Wrayan?'

The thief looked at him with a disapproving frown. 'Did you really come all the way down here from the palace just so I could slap you?'

'No,' Starros laughed. 'I actually came with a message. You're invited to lunch tomorrow.'

'I'll bet Mahkas doesn't know about it.'

'I do believe Lord Damaran is leaving for Walsark first thing in the morning,' Starros remarked. 'So it'll just be me and Leila, Damin and Kalan.'

'Where are the rest of them?'

'Narvell's still in Elasapine,' he explained, holding up his hand to mark off the various members of the family as he accounted for them. 'Old Charel Hawksword's finding it harder and harder to get about these days, and he likes to keep his heir close by his side. Last I heard,' he continued, counting off another finger, 'Adham was in Medalon somewhere, looking for warehouse space to store the spices Ruxton can't unload because of the restrictions on trade that Karien and Fardohnya have imposed since the plague hit. And Rodja's stuck in Greenharbour with Princess Marla and Ruxton.'

'Nasty thing, the plague,' Wrayan agreed.

They'd been lucky here in Krakandar, Starros knew. The

relative isolation of the northern city protected them from the disease. There were reports that as many as a third of the population of Greenharbour had been struck down by it and, for the first time in living memory, the Fardohnyans had voluntarily closed the passes at both Highcastle and Westbrook to prevent the spread of the disease across the border. It was the reason Damin was coming home for the Feast of Kaelarn and not staying in Greenharbour, where tradition demanded the High Prince's heir should remain until the Summer Retreat. But the risk was too great, so Damin was returning to Krakandar and the whole city was in an uproar because of it. With other provinces he'd been required to visit, this was the first time their prince had been home in more than four years.

'Xanda and Luciena are on their way to Talabar, I heard, to do some deal with the shipbuilders there,' Starros continued, counting off another finger. 'They're planning to stay in Fardohnya with their children until it's safe to return, I think. Rielle and Darvad won't move out of Dylan Pass for the same reason. And poor Travin's up at Walsark, running around like a headless chicken trying to get everything in order before Mahkas arrives, which is kind of funny because Mahkas made the arrangements to visit Walsark before he learned that Damin was coming home, and now he's kicking himself that he has to leave the day after Damin gets here. Sort of gets in the way of his plans for Leila, I think.'

'If he's only going to Walsark, he won't be gone that long, surely?'

'Only a few days,' Starros agreed. 'But he's still not happy about it.'

Wrayan looked at him with a raised brow. 'How is the lovely Leila, by the way?'

'She's fine.'

'*Just* fine?'

Starros shrugged and looked out the window. There were a lot of people on the street and, curiously, they all seemed to be heading in the same direction. 'There's nothing to talk about, Wrayan.'

'I suppose not. Is Damin home yet?'

Starros shook his head and turned his attention back to Wrayan. 'Almodavar rode out this morning with a guard of honour to meet them. We're expecting him and Kalan just before midday.' He smiled sourly. 'You don't think Mahkas is putting on a street parade this afternoon just for the God of the Oceans, do you?'

'Let me guess. He's arranged something really tasteless and embarrassing to remind everyone his daughter is going to marry Hythria's next High Prince, yes?'

Starros nodded. 'Leila's already threatening to fake her own death to get out of it. I don't think Damin's going to be terribly thrilled about it, either. He hates all the pomp and ceremony associated with being Lernen's heir and I'm sure he's secretly delighted Greenharbour's been struck with the plague, just so he can get out of the city for a while. The first thing he's going to want to do when he gets home is go raiding over the border, not be put on show by Mahkas like some battle trophy.'

'This wouldn't be happening if Princess Marla was here,' the thief suggested, his smile fading. 'In fact, I think she'd be furious.'

'It's not that I haven't been tempted to write to her about it, but—'

'But you're afraid she'll think you're motivated by personal rather than political concerns?' Wrayan asked sympathetically.

'That's the problem, Wrayan, I *am* motivated by personal rather than political concerns,' he admitted. 'There's just no way to make Mahkas see that Princess Marla is never going to allow Leila to marry Damin.'

'Maybe Damin can make him see reason?'

'I wouldn't wager the family fortune on it. If Marla's told him not to rock the boat, Damin may simply do what the princess has done for the past twenty-three years and just dodge the issue every time Mahkas mentions it.'

'What about Lady Bylinda?'

'She's had no more luck than anyone else convincing her husband he's dreaming. I think she's on Leila's side, but she would never go against Mahkas. Not for any reason.'

Wrayan seemed to sense how much the whole messy situation was bothering Starros, so he forced a smile and changed the subject. 'You say Kalan is with Damin? Does that mean Rorin is coming back, too?'

'I assume so. To be honest, I never thought to ask.'

'It'll be good to see both of them again.'

Starros took a sip of his ale and then smiled suddenly. 'You know Kalan still has the biggest crush on you.'

'I'm sure she's well and truly over it by now, Starros.'

'Don't count on it,' he laughed and added curiously, 'Then again, maybe she and Rorin are . . . you know . . . more than friends now? I mean, they're awfully close.'

'I try not to think about it.'

'Why?'

'In my mind, Kalan is still ten years old, Starros. I can't deal with the idea she's all grown up and a damned sorcerer to boot. Makes me far too aware of how old I'm getting.'

'She's had her own *court'esa* for more than six years, Wrayan. You don't think that small but significant milestone indicated she was no longer a little girl?'

'I try very hard not to think about that, too.'

'It makes sense, though,' Starros mused. 'If I was in Kalan's position, I'd probably want to sleep with Rorin.'

'Be certain to mention that to him when he gets home. I'm sure Rorin will be delighted to learn you fancy him.'

Starros laughed. 'You know what I mean. Given the

nature of the Sorcerers' Collective and the fact that they can't afford to trust anybody but each other, it just makes sense for Kalan and Rorin to be—'

'Sense hasn't got anything to do with love,' Wrayan cut in. 'Don't ever make that mistake.'

'That's true enough,' he agreed, taking another mouthful of ale. 'Are you sure you're just not jealous of the fact that she actually graduated from the Collective, Wrayan, and you never did? Weren't you the oldest apprentice that ever lived, or something?'

'They haven't taught you much about tact and diplomacy up on the hill, have they?' Wrayan remarked with a frown. 'No wonder Orleon plans to live forever.'

Starros finished his ale and smiled apologetically. 'I'm sorry. I'm probably going to be the oldest *assistant* chief steward that ever lived, so I shouldn't mock your seedy past.'

'Mock away,' Wrayan shrugged. 'It was that long ago now, it feels like it happened to someone else. Mind you, if you ever decide you don't want to be the oldest assistant chief steward that ever lived, you could always come down here and work for me. We can always do with another bright mind.'

'Become a thief?' Starros laughed.

'Don't knock it 'til you've tried it,' Wrayan suggested. 'Anyway, what's wrong with it? Honouring the God of Thieves is a noble pastime.'

'Well, for one thing, it's against the law.'

'Actually, it's not.'

'Not a surprising position to take,' Starros remarked, 'given you're head of the Thieves' Guild.'

'It's not a *position*, Starros, it's a fact.'

'What are you talking about?'

'We honour all the gods equally in Hythria – well, in theory, at least. To pass a law making it illegal to honour one of the gods is actually quite sacrilegious. We steal cattle off the Medalonians all the time, and nobody considers that a crime.'

'The Medalonians think it is.'

'Yes, but they're all atheists, so their opinion doesn't count.'

'Fair enough. But I still don't understand what you mean about thievery not being illegal.'

Wrayan shook his head in wonder. 'What do they teach you up at that palace, boy? Check the statutes. The Harshini wrote most of our laws, remember, so the overriding premise is the principle of "do no harm". Our laws prohibit harming our fellow citizens, but the crimes themselves are not actually specified. Theft is honouring Dacendaran. Even murder is honouring Zegarnald if it's managed in such a way that only your foreign enemies suffer for it.'

Starros considered that for a moment and then nodded in understanding. 'So we can steal all the Medalonian cattle we want to honour Dacendaran, because it's not harming anybody in Hythria, but if I was to steal your life savings, I'd be doing a Hythrun harm, therefore it's against the law.'

Wrayan smiled. 'Actually, if you were to steal my life savings, I'd probably have you kneecapped, old son, but you've got the idea.'

'And that's what you do all day, I suppose? Find ways to honour Dacendaran by doing no harm?'

'It's more like keeping the harm to a minimum,' Wrayan corrected. 'And mostly it's at night, but basically, yes, because of a foolish oath I made in my youth, I am really nothing more than the high priest of a cult dedicated to the God of Thieves.'

'What foolish oath?'

'It's a long story,' Wrayan shrugged. 'Maybe I'll tell you about it sometime. Just believe me when I say you should never make a pact with any god unless you've read the fine print.'

Starros smiled disbelievingly. 'You mean you've actually spoken to the God of Thieves?'

'More times than I care to recall.'

'You don't act like someone who's had a religious encounter with a god.'

'Which just goes to show how little you know about the gods.'

Starros wasn't sure if he should believe Wrayan or not. And he didn't have time to find out if Wrayan was telling the truth, in any case. It was almost noon. Damin and Kalan would be here soon and Starros was expected to be at the palace to meet them when they arrived.

He rose to his feet as the sound of a horn blew out over the city, a call picked up by more horns further inside the walls. A moment or two after that, another working *court'esa* slammed through the doors of the tavern and hurried to the bar to speak with Fyora, who was daydreaming behind the counter as she idly dried a tray of tankards.

'Thanks for the drink, but I really need to be getting back.'

'You're welcome. Tell the others I said hello. And that I'll definitely be there for lunch tomorrow.'

'I will.'

'He's here!' Fee suddenly squealed excitedly. 'He's back!'

They both looked over at the bar where Fyora was untying her apron, her chores abandoned. She hurried over to the table with her friend in her wake. The other *court'esa* seemed as excited as Fee. 'He's here!'

'*Who's* here?' Wrayan asked.

'Damin Wolfblade,' Starros sighed, guessing that was what the horns were all about. Who else would engender such high emotions in the citizens of Krakandar? He glanced out of the dusty window and noticed that the crowd pushing through the side streets to Krakandar's main thoroughfare had grown considerably, even in the short time he'd been talking to Wrayan.

Wrayan shook his head. 'You know it can't be good for the boy, all this adulation.'

'I wouldn't worry too much,' Starros assured him. 'I don't think Damin takes it too seriously.'

'Starros,' Fee ventured cautiously, slipping her arm through his with a coy little smile. 'Are you going out to meet him?'

'Actually, I'm supposed to meet him at the palace.'

'But you could do it here in the Beggars' Quarter, couldn't you?' she suggested hopefully. 'I mean, it's on the *way* to the palace, after all . . .'

'Just ask him straight out, Fee,' Wrayan advised. 'He doesn't bite.'

Starros smiled at the *court'esa*. He hadn't forgotten the favour they owed her. Fyora had kept their confidence all these years and never betrayed the fact that he, Damin and Kalan had made it all the way to the Pickpocket's Retreat that day they slipped away from their guards in the marketplace. She still wore the cheap little copper and amethyst trinket Kalan had given her for passing their message on to Wrayan. It was probably her most prized possession. 'You want to come with me and say hello to Damin?'

'Would that be too big a favour to ask, my lord?'

'Not if you promise to stop calling me that.'

She clapped her hands in glee. 'Can my friend, Meris, come, too?'

Starros shrugged. 'Why not?'

Fyora squealed with delight and wrapped Starros in a crushing bear hug before turning to her equally delighted friend and hugging her, too.

'You really shouldn't encourage them,' Wrayan warned. 'Or Damin, either, for that matter.'

'It won't hurt him to say hello to a few of the ordinary folk.'

'It might if they start treating him like a god.'

Starros knew what Wrayan was getting at and resented the implication. He shook his head in denial. 'Damin is nothing like his uncle, Wrayan.'

'I know that,' the thief replied. 'But it's not me Damin's going to have to convince of that if he expects to be High Prince some day. It's the other Warlords.'

Wrayan was right, even if Starros didn't like to be reminded of it. But there was no chance of any further discussion on the matter. Fyora and her friend had their promise of an introduction to the Prince of Krakandar and Starros wasn't going to be allowed to think of anything else until that happened. He raised his hand in farewell to Wrayan as the women dragged him towards the door. As they stepped through onto the street, he shrugged and gave in to the inevitable.

'Well, ladies,' he said, taking each of the *court'esa* by the arm and heading in the direction of the rest of the mob rushing out to catch a glimpse of their beloved prince. 'Let's go welcome the mighty Damin Wolfblade home.'

43

Despite the fact that Damin Wolfblade had grown up with the knowledge that he would some day be High Prince of Hythria – knowing that he was different because of a simple accident of birth – he could never quite understand the fascination his very existence seemed to hold for others.

That people were interested in the most minute and intimate details of his life seemed quite bizarre. That they frequently expected him to be nothing more than a younger, more malleable version of his uncle irritated the hell out of him.

It hadn't always been like this. Surrounded by his siblings and his cousins as a child in Krakandar Palace, he'd been treated no differently than any other member of the family, kept firmly grounded by Almodavar's contempt for anything even remotely smelling of arrogance. Damin didn't really appreciate his position until he left Krakandar and arrived in Rogan Bearbow's stronghold at Natalandar to begin his fosterage. People seemed to assume one of two things about him outside the close circle of his family – that he was somehow endowed with some sort of divine aura because of his princely status and required special treatment, or that he was a spoiled, useless wastrel in the making.

Damin rather resented his uncle for that legacy. He'd spent enough time in Greenharbour to have no illusions about the type of man his uncle was, and knew the hardest job ahead of him, if he lived long enough to become High Prince – Damin had no illusions about the likelihood of assassination, either – would be to persuade the Warlords of Hythria that he was capable of more than organising an orgy in the roof garden on the west wing of the Greenharbour Palace.

'Gods, Damin, I thought you'd be happy to be home,' Kalan remarked, riding up beside him. 'You look like you're on your way to your own funeral.'

She was wearing a riding habit rather than her formal sorcerer's robes, for which he was grateful. Damin could never quite get his head around the notion that his little sister was a full member of the Sorcerers' Collective now. It just didn't seem possible that the bossy little tomboy he'd left behind when he went to Izcomdar was now so mature, so grown up . . . so wise.

He smiled then, and realised he'd been letting his thoughts reflect on his face. Elezaar was always telling him off for that.

'Sorry, Kal. Just daydreaming. What do you suppose the chances are of us sneaking into the city?'

Kalan glanced around at the two hundred soldiers Almodavar had had waiting for them at the Walsark crossroads this morning and smiled. Between Almodavar's Guard of Honour, the thirty or so Greenharbour Palace Guards Damin had brought from the capital, the ten Collective guards that had travelled with Kalan and Rorin before they met up with Damin in Grosburn, their various servants, slaves, spare horses and luggage wagons, it was a considerable entourage gathered behind them.

She laughed. 'I wouldn't hold my breath if I were you.'

Although still winter, it was unseasonably warm and

Damin rode in only a linen shirt and trousers, having shed his jacket some miles back. He sighed and turned in the saddle to speak to Almodavar, who rode next to Rorin, just behind them. 'Whose idea was this damn honour guard anyway, Almodavar? Yours or my uncle's?'

'What do you think, lad?' Almodavar asked.

'My uncle's idea then,' Damin concluded, turning back to face the road ahead. 'I might have known.'

'I'd be more likely to give you forty laps of the training yard,' Almodavar called after him. 'You look like you've been enjoying too much of the high life in Greenharbour.'

Damin turned in the saddle again and grinned at the captain. 'Are you saying I'm not up to a good fight any more, Almodavar?'

'You're more past it than I am, lad, and I'm twice your age,' the older man accused, riding up beside him.

Damin turned to face him now that they were riding side by side. 'I could take you down by the time I was twelve, you old renegade,' he boasted.

'Aye, but I had you in the training yards every day back then. When was the last time you wielded a blade in anger?'

'Last night at dinner,' Kalan answered for her brother with a grin.

Damin gave his sister a wounded look, thinking that she, of all people, might come to his defence. He turned to Almodavar, determined to defend his honour. 'I can see we're going to have to settle this one way or the other, Captain. I'll meet you in the training yards at dawn tomorrow, shall I? Then we'll see who's past it.'

'Dawn, eh?' Almodavar remarked thoughtfully. 'Sure you remember how to get up that early, your highness?'

'Do you think anyone will notice if I have Krakandar's most senior captain put to death for disrespect?' Damin asked his sister curiously.

'Somebody might,' she chuckled. 'Besides, it would be rather a pity to execute him today. Almodavar looks very dashing in his full ceremonial armour.'

Damin turned to study the captain for a moment and then nodded in agreement. 'Well, that settles it. Can't execute someone who looks dashing in their full ceremonial armour now, can we?'

Almodavar shook his head and sighed heavily. 'You'd think after all the effort they expended on you, Damin, you'd have learned how to behave like a prince by now.'

Damin's good humour waned a little at the reminder. 'Oh, never fear about that, old friend. I'm very good at behaving like a prince. Ask any of those fools in Greenharbour I have to deal with on a regular basis. The problem lies in the definition of princely virtues, I fear. Or, in the case of our esteemed High Prince, the complete lack of them.'

'Well, it's good to have you home again, in any case,' Almodavar said with a genuine smile. 'For a while, at least.'

'It's nice to think that wretched plague is good for something,' Kalan agreed, and then she frowned. 'Do you think Mother and the others will be safe?'

'I'm sure the princess would have left Greenharbour by now if she feared for herself, Kalan,' Almodavar said. 'Or the rest of your family.'

'She feared enough for Damin to send him away. And she won't let me or Rorin return to the city.'

'They're not letting anybody into the city, I hear. And Damin is a special case,' the captain reminded her. 'Nobody in their right mind allows both the High Prince and his heir to remain in the same city when there's plague about.'

Damin nodded his agreement. He understood the reasons behind the decision to send him to Krakandar. What surprised him more was how long Marla had been willing to wait before she sent him home.

* * *

With the high red walls of Krakandar looming taller as they neared them, Damin felt a sudden warm rush of affection for his home that shocked him with its intensity. Although he'd not lived here since he was thirteen, there was no other place that made Damin feel the same way. He'd been welcomed like a member of the family at Rogan's stronghold at Natalandar. He had enormous respect for Lord Bearbow and thought of the Warlord's daughter, Tejay, and his son, Rogan, with the same affection he did his own siblings. But it wasn't the same, and now that he spent most of his time in Greenharbour, he felt even less at home. What he had really wanted to do when he finished his fosterage – and what he knew his mother and the High Prince would never permit – was to spend a few years with the Raiders in Krakandar, stealing cattle from the Medalonians over the border. *Now* that *would really have been fun.*

Krakandar sprawled across the surrounding slopes, radiating out from the central ring with the geometric precision of a planned city. Its population numbered more than twenty-five thousand, according to Mahkas's latest census. Krakandar had a solid strength about it that had always made Damin feel secure. He was surprised at how much he had missed that feeling. As they neared the city, it was as if the muscles in his back, living in constant anticipation of a blade or an arrow, suddenly unclenched and, for the first time in six years, Damin felt as if he could afford to relax.

As they rode under the massive portcullis, Damin glanced up and waved to the Raiders standing high above the gate on the wall-walk. He was greeted with a whoop of delight and suddenly a horn blew, announcing his arrival to the guards on the inner walls. A few moments later, another horn picked up the call and then a third sounded from the innermost wall of the city, blowing in long, clear notes on the still air.

Getting through the first ring wasn't that difficult. Word

411

was still being spread through the city that their prince was home. This was the industrial centre of Krakandar and most of the people were still at work. No matter how much a man wanted to catch a glimpse of his prince, a large loom didn't stop quickly, a forge had to be kept hot and one couldn't just drop one's tools to go sightseeing. Quite a few did, however, but it wasn't a large crowd so Damin allowed himself the small hope that the rest of the city would react to his return in the same manner. He didn't mind a few people lining the street to wave as he rode past. It was the chanting mobs that really got to him, and after the scare in Greenharbour with that plague-infected Denikan sailor, he knew how vulnerable he was to the most unlikely dangers.

His hope of an anonymous arrival lasted right up until they rode through the second portcullis and into the Beggars' Quarter. The street was packed with people, the buildings decorated with blue bunting, which Damin fervently hoped hadn't been put up for his arrival.

Almodavar saw the direction of his gaze and smiled. 'It's the Feast of Kaelarn, Damin,' the captain reminded him. 'Your uncle has a street parade planned for later today.'

'He does?'

'I believe you are to be the centrepiece,' Almodavar informed him, and then almost as an afterthought, he added, 'Along with your cousin, Lady Leila.'

Damin turned to Almodavar, all trace of his good humour drowned out by the news. 'Please tell me you're kidding, Captain.'

'I fear not, your highness.'

Damin swore softly. He'd been hoping Mahkas had forgotten all about his long-held dream of marrying his only daughter to Damin. 'I'll speak to Lord Damaran about it.'

'I'm sure Lady Leila would be most grateful for that,'

Almodavar told him, confirming his suspicions that his cousin no more wanted to marry him than he wanted to marry her. She was already twenty-three, and Mahkas had reportedly knocked back countless offers for her hand, sending ever more insistent letters to Marla every few months, begging for the engagement to be made formal. It suited Marla to neither confirm nor deny the general belief that Damin would marry his cousin, however, so she did nothing to disabuse Mahkas of the notion.

There was little chance to talk after that, as they pushed their way through the city. Almodavar fell back, letting Damin take the lead behind the outriders carrying the Krakenshield and Wolfblade banners. The prince waved to the people as he passed, astonished at how many of them seemed genuinely pleased to have him home. He wondered, sometimes, how they all knew who he was. He hadn't even been to Krakandar for four years. He could be anybody, yet they were clapping and cheering his passing, as if they were all close, personal friends.

And then he spied a familiar face in the crowd to his right, the face of a man who really was a close, personal friend. With a delighted shout, he brought the entire entourage to a stop as the young man stepped out of the crush of people and onto the street. One of the guards attempted to stop him, until he saw who it was, and then stepped his horse back to let him pass.

'Starros!'

'Gods, they let just anybody ride through those gates these days,' his foster-brother said with a grin, catching hold of Damin's bridle. His mount was jittery, with the crowd pressing in on them, and Starros probably didn't fancy being trampled. He waved to Kalan with a smile. 'Welcome home, Kalan.'

'Did you come all this way to meet us?'

'Of course not! I happened to be in the neighbourhood,

that's all. Which reminds me. Can you do me a quick favour?'

'Anything!'

Starros turned and beckoned to someone in the crowd. A moment later, two working *court'esa* stepped onto the street and pushed past the guards to huddle close to Starros.

'Your highness, this is Fyora. Do you remember her from the Pickpocket's Retreat?'

'How could I ever forget,' Damin replied gallantly, with a low bow in the saddle. 'In fact, I've been meaning to reward you with a peerage for not ratting on us that day, my lady. You saved me from a great many more laps of the training yard than you will ever know.'

He reached down and took her hand, kissing her palm in the traditional manner. Fee was too overwhelmed to speak and looked ready to faint with happiness. Her friend was almost as ready to swoon. 'And who is this lovely lady, Fee?'

'This is Meris, Fee's friend,' Starros volunteered. 'I promised her she could meet you as well.'

'Then I'm delighted to make your acquaintance, Miss Meris.' He kissed her palm as well, just for good measure. It never hurt to have the lower classes on your side. Elezaar was always telling him that, too.

The *court'esa* beamed at him and dropped into an awkward curtsey as Almodavar pushed his way forward, not at all happy about the interruption to their progress. 'Damin, we have to keep moving.'

'I know, I know. Moving targets are harder to hit.' He turned to Starros and the *court'esa* with an apologetic smile. 'Sorry ladies, but we have to push on. What about you, Starros?'

'Well, if I run all the way there,' Starros told him with a groan, 'I should get back to the palace just in time to greet you with the rest of the welcoming committee.'

414

'Don't be stupid. Ride with us. You can fill me in on the way about this ridiculous plan Mahkas has for the parade this afternoon.' He snapped his fingers at the nearest mounted guard. 'Iyan! Let Starros have your horse. You can ride one of the spares at the back.'

The Raider dismounted without argument and led his horse over to Starros, who offered the man a thankful nod and swung into the saddle. He fell in beside Damin and they moved off again, Damin waving to the crowd as they rode.

'So, what did you get in return for introducing me to a couple of working *court'esa*?' he asked with a wink and a wave to a particularly pretty girl calling his name from the balcony of one of the many brothels in this end of town.

'Nothing,' Starros shrugged.

'*Nothing?* Damin echoed in disbelief. 'Old Orleon's not teaching you anything terribly useful, is he?'

'It was a favour to Fee, Damin. The gods know, we owed her one. If she'd told on us that day . . . your mother would have killed me, had you lashed, and had Kalan bricked up in her room.'

'That's true. You're looking well, I have to say.'

'So are you.'

Damin laughed. 'According to Almodavar I'm the victim of too much high living in Greenharbour. He's going to sort me out in the morning, so he claims.'

'At dawn,' Almodavar reminded him loudly, calling out to be heard over the noise of the crowd. 'You'll probably need to wake him, Starros.'

'I'll see he's there on time,' Starros called back to the captain, and then his smile faded a little and he dropped his voice so that only Damin could hear him. 'So Almodavar told you about the float, did he?'

'He said something about it.'

'It's a thirty-foot-high moving platform covered in blue

415

silk to represent the ocean. It has a bower on top for you and Leila. You're going to be dressed as Kaelarn. I think Leila is supposed to represent the goddess, Kalianah.'

Damin continued to smile and wave, his outward demeanour at complete odds with the anger he could feel building inside him at his uncle's presumptuousness. 'And he seriously thinks I'm going to agree to this?'

'You know Mahkas, Damin. He's had his heart set on you marrying Leila for so long, he's convinced himself it's real.'

'And what does Leila think of it, do you suppose?'

'She doesn't want any part of it. Or you,' Starros added, grinning suddenly. 'She still hasn't forgiven you for calling her a sissy, you know.'

'Well, she was being a sissy.'

'Yes, but that doesn't mean you should have called her one.'

Damin shook his head, thinking some things in Krakandar hadn't changed at all. 'You still defend her over every little thing, don't you?'

'Someone has to.'

Damin looked at his foster-brother curiously, wondering at his tone. 'Do you want to tell me what's really going on, Starros?'

He nodded and pointed at the gateway of the inner ring and the palace only a few hundred feet ahead of them through the forest of people. 'I will, Damin. But not here and not now. It's neither the time nor the place.'

Starros is right about that much, Damin thought, as they pushed their way forward, although the way he spoke sounded a little more ominous than Damin thought the occasion warranted. *Mahkas can be a bit pigheaded, but surely there's nothing happening here in Krakandar that warrants such a dire tone?*

Well, he would find out soon enough, he figured,

although it took another half an hour to make it to the gate. Then suddenly they were through and the crowd fell back as they rode into the vast inner courtyard of Krakandar Palace, where the rest of the family were waiting to greet him.

44

Mahkas Damaran had listened to the horns announcing the arrival of his nephew with the sense of anticipation common to all men who believe their fondest dreams are about to come true. He hurried to gather the welcoming delegation and move them out onto the top of the broad palace steps to await Damin's arrival, rubbing at the sore spot on his arm, as he always did in times of heightened stress. He was determined to make absolutely certain Damin knew how glad they were to have him back home.

This was the first time since the young prince had left for his fosterage with Rogan Bearbow in Izcomdar, when he was thirteen, that Damin had returned home without Princess Marla and certainly the only time he'd come home for an extended visit. His other visits had been too short or too busy to give the young people any sort of chance to get close to each other.

Damin's most worrying visit, Mahkas remembered, idly rubbing at his arm, had been eight years ago, the year Damin turned sixteen. Marla had purchased a *court'esa* for her son in Greenharbour and brought the young woman to Krakandar for the Summer Retreat. Reyna, her name was, Mahkas recalled. She was, not surprisingly, a stunning young woman. Marla had paid a record price for her. It was the talk of Greenharbour for months. (A few people even accused her of artificially inflating the price of slaves, simply so her husband could realise a profit on a shipment of slaves he had brought in from Fardohnya around about the same time.) Damin, understandably enough, had been completely besotted by his new *court'esa* and had eyes for nothing and nobody else the whole time he was home. By the time he returned to Rogan in Izcomdar, he had barely spoken two words to Leila all summer long. Furious his nephew was so easily distracted, Mahkas had promised to send Reyna to Natalandar along with Damin's luggage, which was due to follow him a few days after he left Krakandar. But rather than tell Reyna to get packed, the day after Damin left with Marla and Ruxton, Mahkas arranged to have her bunk searched, where his men found several pieces of Bylinda's jewellery hidden under her pillow. Ignoring Reyna's loud protestations of innocence, Mahkas had the girl whipped until she was scarred for life, and then sold off as a fruit-picking slave to a vine-yard just over the border in Elasapine. He sent a letter to Marla, explaining that the girl had been a thief and had been punished accordingly and that had been the end of it.

Damin, interestingly enough, had never asked to own another *court'esa* until he moved to Greenharbour, contenting himself with those slaves belonging to Rogan's household.

This unexpected visit was fate, Mahkas knew. There would be time now for things to develop as they should. Time for Damin and Leila to fall in love. The plague in Greenharbour and all the terrible deaths that came with it were the gods' way of putting Damin where he needed to be, to allow all of Mahkas's dreams to be fulfilled.

Everyone had their assigned places in the welcoming party, organised strictly by rank. His wife and daughter stood with Mahkas at the head of the steps. Bylinda was looking a little pale, but Leila stood by his side, tall and beautiful in the bright spring sunlight, dressed in a gorgeous lavender gown he'd bought her especially from Fardohnya, looking every inch the fit consort for a High Prince, which Mahkas was quite sure Damin would acknowledge the moment he laid eyes on his cousin again.

Mahkas tried to understand Marla's reluctance to formally announce the betrothal. It was a commonly held belief that a man shouldn't marry before he was twenty-five or thirty, although she'd been quick enough to allow Xanda to marry Luciena at seventeen, when there was a shipping fortune at stake, he recalled a little sourly. In principle, Mahkas agreed with the notion of a man sowing a few wild oats before he settled down. The trouble was, Leila wasn't getting any younger. Damin was only twenty-four and if he waited until he was thirty to take a bride, Leila would be almost twenty-nine by then and well into the danger years for childbearing.

If that happened, Mahkas's biggest fear was that Marla might decide to look for a younger bride for her precious Wolfblade line – a girl still in her late teens or early twenties, who might more safely bear a number of healthy children. It was a valid fear, Mahkas knew. Bylinda had only ever been able to carry one healthy child to term (and a daughter at that). With her mother's poor history, Marla might look at Leila and be justifiably concerned that the daughter would suffer the same problems as the mother. The very thought of it made the regent fidget nervously and rub at his forearm. Out of habit, Bylinda slapped his hand away almost unconsciously, as she always did when she saw him worrying at it, so to distract himself he turned to make sure everybody was in their place.

Behind the Regent of Krakandar and his family were arrayed a score of other palace functionaries and behind them the servants and slaves Mahkas had deemed worthy of the honour of greeting his nephew. Old Lirena was there, leaning heavily on her cane, the slave who had nursed Damin and his siblings when they were babies, along with a number of other palace staff who had known Damin since he was born. It was important, Mahkas knew, for Damin to have that sense of homecoming only this place could provide. He knew the value of a man having a place he could truly call his home. As he surveyed the crowd of well-wishers, Mahkas frowned. Starros was missing, he noticed. Orleon stood alone, with no sign of his young assistant.

'Is Starros unwell?' Mahkas enquired of his wife, puzzled by the young man's absence. Despite his baseborn status, Starros had counted himself one of Damin's closest friends in childhood. He couldn't imagine any circumstance short of unconsciousness that would have kept him away from this event.

'I don't think so,' Bylinda replied, just as puzzled by his absence.

'He had some business in the city,' Leila told them. 'I'm sure he'll be back soon. Starros wouldn't miss this day for anything.'

Mahkas nodded. 'I know. Which reminds me, Leila, of something I've been meaning to mention for a few days now, but with all the fuss of Damin's arrival, it kept slipping my mind.'

'What's that, Papa?'

'Now that Damin is home, it might pay to be a little more . . . *circumspect* in your dealings with Starros.'

Leila stared at him in shock. '*What?*'

'Now, now, don't get upset. I know Starros is a friend. But you're not children in the nursery any longer, Leila. You need to start keeping company with friends of your own class. Starros is a bastard fosterling promoted to assistant chief steward. I don't want your fiancé to think there is anything untoward in your dealings with the servants.'

'Damin is *not* my fiancé, Papa,' Leila insisted in a low, irritated voice, aware that their conversation might easily be overheard. 'And Starros isn't just a servant.'

Mahkas was starting to get truly annoyed by his daughter's constant refusal to acknowledge the truth of her situation. 'Just because it hasn't been formally announced doesn't mean your betrothal to Damin is not going to happen, Leila. And the sooner you start to acknowledge the truth about Starros's station in life, the better.' Before Leila could argue the point with him, he took her hand and squeezed it with an encouraging smile. 'Now, don't be mad at me. Smile for your papa, eh? Anybody would think you're not happy to welcome Damin home.'

Leila refused to answer, but she did manage a thin smile, which relieved Mahkas a great deal. She was just being waspish, he told himself. Maybe it was her moon-time. Women were notoriously fickle and moody at times like that. There was no more time to worry about it, however. Another horn sounded and finally the guard of honour pushed their way through the crowd outside the wall and rode under the large arched gateway into the courtyard.

Two outriders carrying the banners bearing the wolf's-head escutcheon of the Wolfblade House and the rampant kraken of Krakandar led the parade into the inner court-yard, followed by another two men on horseback. Behind them rode the captain of the guard, Almodavar, and with him a young man and woman whom Mahkas guessed were Kalan and her companion, Rorin. Not seeing Damin imme-diately, he looked again at the two riders at the head of the column and frowned. The one on the left, Mahkas suddenly realised with concern, was his nephew, Damin Wolfblade, dressed in a simple shirt and trousers, far too casual for such an important entrance into the city. *What is he thinking?*

And then Mahkas's blood ran cold as he realised the man riding next to Damin, in the position of honour at the prince's right hand – in the most appalling breach of protocol Mahkas could ever recall – was his assistant chief steward, the bastard fosterling, Starros.

Mahkas and Bylinda stepped forward to greet him, as Damin dismounted at the foot of the steps. The prince took them two at a time, halting just below the landing where they waited, and bowed respectfully to his uncle.

'Welcome home, Damin!' Mahkas announced loudly, stepping forward to embrace his nephew and forcing a smile he certainly didn't feel. 'You've been sorely missed here in your true home.'

Damin seemed genuinely delighted to be back. 'I've sorely missed it, too, Uncle. Hello, Aunt Bylinda.'

Bylinda curtseyed politely and offered Damin her hand. 'It's good to see you again, Damin.'

Damin kissed her palm and smiled warmly. 'It's always a pleasure to see my favourite aunt, my lady. You're truly the only reason I wanted to come home.'

Bylinda blushed at Damin's flattery, not immune to his charm even though she'd helped raise the boy. Mahkas turned to discover Leila, against his explicit instructions, had not rushed forward to greet her cousin. She hung back as if is she wanted no part of the celebrations. 'Leila, don't be shy. Come! Welcome Damin home!'

With some reluctance, Leila stepped forward, but she didn't try to embrace Damin. She coolly offered him her hand. Mahkas could have slapped her for being so intransigent, but Damin didn't seem to mind. He accepted her hand and kissed her palm with the same grace he had her mother's hand and smiled at her.

'You look thrilled to see me, cousin.'

There was a touch of irony in Damin's tone that Mahkas thought rather concerning.

'You have no idea, Damin,' she replied unsmilingly.

'We'll talk soon,' he promised, and then kissed her palm again. 'In private.'

Leila smiled at her cousin then, and slipped her arm through his as Damin stepped up to the landing. Vastly relieved by this obvious sign of affection by his daughter, Mahkas turned to greet his niece and her companion from the Sorcerers' Collective.

Kalan was polite enough when she greeted him and introduced him to Rorin, as the rest of the welcoming delegation formed two lines leading to the palace doors. Mahkas had always thought Kalan a bad influence on Leila and had been rather relieved when Marla had taken her from the palace to be apprenticed to the Collective, along with Rorin Mariner, this cousin of Luciena's who seemed to have appeared from nowhere and been adopted into the family with no explanation at all. On the landing, Damin, with Leila still holding his arm, was working his way down the lines, greeting each person by name.

And then he stopped abruptly and turned to Mahkas. 'Oh, while I think of it – Starros tells me you had something planned for the parade this afternoon, Uncle.'

'That's right,' Mahkas said, wondering what had been said. If Starros had spoiled his surprise in any way, Mahkas silently promised himself he would kill the too-smart-for-his-own-good little bastard with his bare hands.

'And he tells me I'm supposed to be the main attraction.'

'We must honour Kaelarn, Damin, and I thought—'

Damin laughed. 'We're miles from the ocean, Uncle. I'm quite sure Kaelarn's wrath won't reach us here if I don't take part in your little parade. It's been a long ride from the crossroads this morning and I've already greeted half the city in person. You won't mind if I settle for watching the parade from the wall-walk over the gate, will you?'

Damin turned back to greeting the servants without waiting for Mahkas to answer. The look Leila gave her father was quietly triumphant.

Furious, Mahkas grabbed Starros by the arm as he made to follow them and pulled him aside. 'What do you think you're doing?' he hissed.

Starros looked at him with a puzzled expression. 'I wasn't aware that I was doing anything.'

'You ride in here at the right hand of Krakandar's prince, acting as if you deserve some special consideration. You ruin my parade. Who do you think you are?'

'Damin asked me to ride with him, my lord. We're friends.'

'Then perhaps my nephew needs to rethink who his friends are,' Mahkas told him in a low, angry voice, conscious that people were wondering what he was saying to the young man. 'Now get back to Orleon, boy. And I don't want to see you again unless you're serving your betters, not trying to pretend you're one of them.'

Mahkas let Starros go with a shove and hurried to catch up with his nephew and his daughter, thinking that as soon as he had Damin and Leila safely married, it might be time to start thinking of a way to remove Starros from the palace completely.

45

From the moment they arrived in Talabar, Luciena knew something was amiss.

It was more than the unexpected and unasked-for escort of Fardohnyan troops waiting for them on the wharves when they docked. It was more than the uneasy cooperation of the stevedores who helped tie up the ship, or the sly glances of the merchants who stared suspiciously at their Hythrun vessel from the decks of their own magnificent Fardohnyan ships. It was a gut feeling Luciena had come to trust; a feeling she couldn't explain, but knew – beyond doubt – that she should listen to.

Xanda, normally the most optimistic of men, was down on the wharf talking to the soldiers. Even from here, Luciena could see the worried expression her husband wore as he listened to the captain of the Fardohnyan guard. Watching from the deck of the trader she had commandeered for the voyage to Talabar, Luciena didn't need to be a mind reader to know what bothered her husband.

There was more than just Xanda or Luciena in danger here.

Believing they would be safer on the open sea than trapped in a plague-ridden city, Luciena had made the difficult decision to bring their three children with them on this journey, the eldest of whom, Emilie, was only ten years old. Their two sons, Jarvan and Geris, were eight and six. The children were still belowdecks, anxiously awaiting permission to go ashore. Chewing nervously on her bottom lip as she watched Xanda talking to the Fardohnyan captain, Luciena fought down the urge to order Captain Grayden to untie the ship and push off while they still had a chance of getting her children away from this place.

She was on the verge of issuing the order when Xanda turned and headed back up the gangway of the ship, nimbly jumping to the deck when he reached the top of the treacherous plank. For a man born and bred in landlocked Krakandar, he had taken to the sea like a fish suddenly reintroduced to water after a lengthy absence. Luciena had never seen him seasick, unsteady on his feet or even nervous during a storm. It grieved her a little sometimes to think that he was such a natural seaman, while the daughter of the legendary Jarvan Mariner had proved to be a fair-weather sailor, at best.

'What did he say?' she demanded of her husband as Captain Grayden met them at the head of the gangway.

'He welcomed us to Talabar,' Xanda informed her. 'Very polite about it, he was.'

'And?' the captain prompted.

'And it seems that every accommodation house in the city is suddenly and unaccountably full.'

Luciena glanced down at the waiting troop before looking at Xanda with a puzzled expression. 'So . . . what? Are they saying we have to stay on board the ship?'

'No,' Xanda replied. 'Apparently, in an act of extreme generosity, the king has made rooms available for us in the Summer Palace.'

Captain Grayden shook his head, clearly unhappy with the idea of them putting themselves directly under the power of Fardohnya's notoriously unreliable king. 'I say we pull up anchor and leave while we still can, my lady.'

'And go where?' Luciena asked, just as concerned, particularly for her children. 'We can't go home while the plague still ravages Greenharbour.'

'What about Medalon?' Xanda suggested. 'We could sail upriver to Bordertown and wait out the plague there.'

'Not with the draught of this ship,' Grayden advised. 'The Glass River's not that deep.'

Luciena looked out over the city of Talabar, torn with indecision. The morning was typical of Talabar – a flawless sky resting on a calm, sapphire sea. Curving around the harbour and built from the pale pink stone of the neighbouring cliffs, the city glowed softly in the late winter sunshine. On the left, at the end of the wharf district, a series of carved stone steps led up to the paved road that circled the harbour. Flat-roofed villas belonging to the wealthy and the powerful were perched at random intervals across the distant terraced hills surrounding the bay. The city itself was interspersed with countless palm-shaded emerald parks and the tall edifices of the many temples that dotted it, the numerous spires aiming for the sky, as if each one was a finger pointing to the clouds – the home of the Primal Gods – trying to reach out and touch the divine realm to see if it was real.

Talabar was a deceptively beautiful city, Luciena thought. It appeared warm and friendly. On the flat roofs of the houses closest to the docks, a few people had even gathered to watch, probably wondering why there was a contingent of the King's Guard waiting to meet a Hythrun ship. Further along, near the warehouses on their right, the wharves were crowded with cargo ships, irate-looking merchants and barechested, sweaty stevedores shouting at each other as they unloaded their wares.

She looked at Xanda and knew what he was thinking. Had it just been the two of them, he wouldn't have hesitated to accept the King of Fardohnya's highly suspicious offer, content they could handle him and his untrustworthy hospitality. But with the children here . . . they could all too easily become pawns in a game that might turn deadly at any moment.

'What do you think?'

'I'm all for pulling up anchor and getting the hell out of here while we still can,' Xanda admitted, 'but as you said, where do we go?'

'With the supplies and water we have left on board,' Grayden informed them, 'we'd be lucky to make it to the Isle of Slarn.'

Luciena shook her head at the impossible decision. 'I think, that if it came to a choice between returning home to face the plague in Greenharbour or the colony of Malik's Curse sufferers on Slarn, I'd rather face the plague.'

Xanda nodded in agreement. And then he smiled thinly. Luciena assumed he was trying to be encouraging. 'The offer may be genuine, you know.'

Even Grayden nodded his agreement. 'Your husband speaks the truth, my lady. I doubt Hablet of Fardohnya would be foolish enough to harm the niece and nephews of Hythria's High Prince.'

She nodded reluctantly. 'I suppose we don't really have much choice.'

That was as close to saying yes to Hablet's offer that she could bring herself to articulate. Xanda didn't object to her decision, which meant he also acknowledged they had little choice in the matter. 'I'll go down and inform the captain that we'll be happy to accept his offer to escort us to the palace then.' He turned and headed for the gangway. Then he hesitated at the rail and suddenly laughed.

Luciena looked at him curiously. 'What?'

'I was just thinking, Hablet would have found out we were arriving today from your shipping agent, wouldn't he?'

'Probably,' she agreed, not getting the joke at all.

'But you only told your agent our approximate arrival time and the reason for our visit, not who was on board, right?'

'Of course.'

'So Hablet probably doesn't know we have the children with us.'

'I suppose not. But I still don't see what's so funny.'

'I was just wondering . . . how long do you think it's going to take Jarvan and Geris to totally destroy the Summer Palace?'

Even Luciena couldn't help smiling at the thought of her two rowdy sons running amok through Hablet's palace. 'Given their past history, I'd say no more than an hour. Two at the most.'

He leaned forward and kissed her cheek. 'See? Already things are looking better. If Hablet is up to something, he may soon find himself reassessing his plans when he realises he's invited the two most fervent disciples of the God of Total Chaos to stay in his palace.'

Luciena shook her head, wishing she had Xanda's ability to joke about the direst situations. It was a trait he shared with his brother, Travin, and his cousin, Damin, who was even more adept at making light of everything. In fact, the more life-and-death the circumstances, the more the cousins seemed to want to find some sort of black humour in it. She wasn't sure if it was a family characteristic or just a foolish male tendency. 'That's supposed to make me feel better, I suppose?'

'The idea warms the very cockles of *my* heart.'

She scowled at him. 'Tell me again why I married you, Xanda Taranger?'

'It was that or be hanged, as I recall.'

'I knew I couldn't have done it willingly.'

He must have noticed the concern on her face. After twelve years together, there wasn't much she could hide

430

from him. 'Cheer up, Luci,' he ordered as he climbed onto the gangway. 'Worse things have happened to us.'

Not lately, Luciena thought as she watched Xanda walk the narrow, bouncing plank as if it was a solid walkway half a mile wide. When he reached the dock, she leaned over the rail and called out to him. 'Xanda!'

He turned to look up at her. 'Yes?'

'There's no such thing as a God of Total Chaos.'

'Tell that to your sons,' he called back with a smile, and then he turned and walked the short distance to where the Fardohnyan captain was waiting, to inform him that he, his wife and their three children would be pleased to accept the King of Fardohnya's hospitality.

46

It was close to midnight before the ball to welcome Damin home concluded and another hour or more after that before Starros was able to seek his bed. He was exhausted and worried, for Leila's sake more than his own. Damin's casual dismissal of Mahkas's plans for the parade that afternoon had infuriated the regent and although he had fixated on Starros as the author of all his woes, Mahkas obviously suspected his daughter was deliberately undermining his plans for her future and seemed dangerously angry with her, too.

The evening had been very unpleasant for Starros, watching Mahkas do everything he could to force Damin and Leila together and being helpless to prevent it. The only bright spot in the whole sorry spectacle was the knowledge that Mahkas was leaving for Walsark in the morning and would be gone for several days, leaving them in relative peace.

Leila had suffered through the ball, stiff with embarrassment. Even Lady Bylinda looked as if she was cringing on occasion. The only one, in fact, who seemed oblivious to Mahkas's unsubtle hints was Damin. Six years of playing politics in Greenharbour had obviously taught the young prince a few things. He deftly kept the conversation away from anything remotely matrimonial, and whenever Mahkas tried to point out Leila's beauty, or grace, or accomplishments – like an auctioneer listing the assets of a particularly fine racehorse – Damin would counter with some anecdote about Leila from their childhood which shattered the illusion Mahkas was trying so hard to create.

Damin Wolfblade was a far better politician, Starros realised this evening, than anybody suspected.

Knowing the education Damin had received as a boy – and having been the beneficiary of much the same education himself – Starros knew what Damin had been exposed to. But he'd never seemed to pay that much attention to it when they were children. In fact, he would have bet money on Damin not having learned much at all. Perhaps it was the practical lessons he was learning in Greenharbour that had honed his awareness. Or perhaps Marla's sharp political instincts were just that – some inexplicable hereditary trait passed from mother to son.

If that was the case, Starros hoped Damin had the wit to conceal his ability until he was forced to reveal it.

The Warlords of Hythria want a High Prince they can look up to as a noble figurehead, not one who might actually be strong enough to rule them, he thought, tossing his shirt across the high-backed chair in the corner of his room.

Starros had just finished wearily pulling off his boots when he heard the sound of a door closing in the small dressing room adjacent to his bedroom. He immediately forgot all about Damin and whether or not he might make a good High Prince, or what the Warlords would make of him. The door inside the tiny dressing room clicked shut and a moment later Leila emerged from the slaveways, dressed in a nightgown, her long fair hair hanging loose around her face, rippled from being braided so tightly all day. She crossed the small bedroom in three steps and wordlessly stepped into his arms. He held her close; a moment of sheer bliss for both of them when neither said a word, so neither of them was able to shatter their fragile happiness by speaking of reality.

After a time she lifted her head from his shoulder and he kissed her, and then let her go and wiped a stray tear from her cheek. She smiled wanly and sniffed back the rest of her tears.

'I'm sorry,' he told her, not sure why he was apologising.

'It's not your fault, my love,' Leila sighed.

'You know, I don't think I ever really lamented the fact that I was common-born until tonight, when I realised how far out of my reach you really are.'

'I'm here in your arms, aren't I?' she whispered, kissing him again.

'Yes,' he agreed. 'In secret. In the dark—'

'Shh!' she told him softly, placing her finger on his lips. 'Don't think like that. It wouldn't matter if you were a Warlord in your own right, Starros, you know that. My father wants to be the father-in-law of the next High Prince.'

'He's the brother-in-law of the current one,' Starros pointed out sourly. 'And uncle to the next. That would make most men happy.'

'But he's only Regent of Krakandar, my love, not her Warlord. He wants Damin to be High Prince, because it means he will have to surrender Krakandar Province, and who better to be Krakandar's new Warlord than the man who has ruled her so diligently as her regent all these years?'

'He can do that without you becoming Damin's wife, Leila.'

She shook her head. Leila might not agree with her father, but she understood his motives well enough. 'He can't be certain of it, though. If Damin married a woman with a suitable male relative, a man younger than my father, he might be tempted to appoint him Krakandar's Warlord when he becomes High Prince. It may even be a

434

condition of the marriage agreement. My father will not risk that happening.'

Starros kissed her again, to stop her reminding him of all the reasons they would never have more than this – nights of sneaking through the slaveways to each other's room, stolen kisses in a secluded garden nook, a few brief moments of happiness in the dead of night when the palace slept. They had been meeting like this for more than a year now and Starros couldn't help feeling that Damin's arrival meant, one way or another, things would be brought to a head. The feeling that his time with Leila was a finite and fragile thing was so strong it was almost a premonition.

'I wish I could have done something for you tonight,' he told her, holding her close. 'Your father was being so obvious. It must have been awful.'

She smiled and sat down on the edge of the bed. 'Actually, I think for the first time in my life, I felt a genuine rush of affection for that dreadful cousin of mine. I've never seen anybody handle my father the way he did.'

'Damin's not dreadful,' he objected. 'He can be a bit flippant, at times, I suppose, but—'

'Of course he's not dreadful to *you*,' she interrupted, with a smile. 'You're a man. You look up to him. He's rich, he's handsome, he's athletic . . . he's everything other men want to be. But he used to terrify me when we were children. All of them did, a little. Damin was always so damned sure of himself and everyone but you used to fall victim to his charm. Even Kalan used to make me feel small, and she was a year younger than me.'

Starros sat down beside her and pulled her into his arms. 'You make it sound like we tormented you deliberately.'

'It was torment,' she agreed, laying her head on his shoulder. 'But I know it wasn't deliberate. All the others just seemed to have so much more purpose in life than I did. I'm the ultimate useless accessory, Starros, groomed from birth to marry a man I don't want and who doesn't want me.' She looked up at him with that sad little smile that always worried him. It had a haunting look of utter finality to it, as if it was the last smile he was ever going to see from her. 'I was never really one of them. Neither were you.'

'Nobody ever treated me differently because I was the fosterling.'

'Not then, perhaps. It's a different story now we're grown. Damin's your best friend, but look at my father's reaction today when you rode at his right hand. We're both doomed to be forever clouded by Damin's shadow, I fear.'

'I don't think you're being fair to him or me,' Starros told her, wishing they could talk of something else. Even in Starros, there lurked the uncomfortable possibility that Princess Marla might just decide some day that Leila truly was the only safe consort for her son. He loved Damin like a brother, but the thought of him and Leila . . . well, it just didn't bear thinking about.

'I'm making you uncomfortable with all this talk of Damin, aren't I?'

He smiled and nuzzled her ear, slipping the thin straps of her nightdress off her shoulders. The silk whispered over her pale skin as it fell to reveal her small, perfect breasts in the candlelight. 'I could think of a few more useful ways to spend what little time we have together,' he said, bending to kiss them, 'than talking about Damin bloody Wolfblade.'

Leila threw her head back and moaned with pleasure, a sound that suddenly changed to a scream of terror as she froze in his arms.

Starros jumped to his feet and spun around, his heart in his mouth as Leila scrambled to cover herself, thankful they were in the servants' wing and not the main palace where her scream would have brought the guards running.

Behind them, his arms crossed, casually leaning against the doorframe leading to the dressing room, was Damin.

'Damin bloody Wolfblade, eh?' the young prince said. 'Nice one, Starros.'

'Oh gods, no . . . Damin, please . . .' Leila sobbed, reaching for Starros's hand. 'Please . . . please don't . . .'

'Damin . . . I can explain . . .' Starros began anxiously.

The prince pushed off the doorframe and crossed the room, stopping at the foot of the bed. He studied them for a moment, his expression unfathomable in the candle-light. He must have come through the slaveways, the same way Leila had. They used them so frequently as children, it probably never even occurred to Damin to knock. Starros had no idea what Damin was thinking. Or what he was planning to do.

'Damin?'

Suddenly, the young man's face split into a wide grin. 'Mahkas would have an apoplectic fit if he knew about this.'

'That's kind of why we haven't told anyone,' Starros said, putting his arm around Leila protectively.

'Are you going to tell my father?' Leila asked warily as she leaned into him, still clutching her nightdress across her breasts to cover herself.

'Dear gods, no!' Damin laughed, sitting himself down cross-legged on the end of the bed. 'What you two get up to after dark is none of my concern. Mind you, if you really *were* my fiancé, Leila, I'd probably have to kill Starros with a rusty spade or something for laying a hand on you, but as we both know there's more chance of a demon child showing up tomorrow than you and I ever getting married, we don't really have to worry about it, do we?'

Starros felt Leila relax against him at the news.

'I am curious about one thing, though,' the prince added.

'What's that?'

'Do you often use my name as a curse?'

Starros shook his head, smiling with relief. 'You didn't hear all of it, Damin.'

'Actually, I probably heard far more than you intended.' He turned to his cousin and looked at her curiously. 'Were we really so awful to you when we were children, Leila?'

'Damin, I didn't mean it the way it sounded.'

'Even so, I probably owe you an apology. I must have been a real little prick at times. I didn't mean to be.'

'Who *are* you?' Starros asked, as Leila sniffed back her tears through a wan smile. 'And what have you done with the real Damin?'

He grinned at them. 'Can't I have the odd moment of compassion for my poor cousin and my old friend? Doomed to be clouded forever by my shadow, as they are?'

'You should stop now, Damin,' Leila advised. 'You're about to ruin a beautiful apology by turning into a little prick again.'

'Then I'll change the subject,' the prince offered. His smile faded a little and he turned to Starros, confirming his friend's earlier suspicion that Damin was much more of a political creature than anybody realised. 'I assume when you told me today that you'd fill me in at a better time, this juicy little secret was at the top of the list?'

'Actually, I asked Starros not to say anything to you, Damin.'

'Why not?'

'I haven't seen you for four years. I didn't know if you could be trusted.'

'Let's just pretend I can be,' Damin suggested, a little put out, Starros thought, by Leila's accusing tone. 'What are you going to do about it?'

'There's nothing that can be done about it,' Starros shrugged. 'Even if Mahkas wasn't determined to have you marry Leila, I'm the last person in Hythria he'd consider as a consort for his only child. I'm a commoner. I'm a bastard.'

'I could always have the High Prince grant you some sort of title,' Damin offered. 'Make you Lord Starros, the Earl of Something.'

'You could make him a Warlord and it wouldn't matter to my father, Damin. You know that. The only bloodline good enough for his daughter is yours.'

'Haven't you ever found the idea of us marrying just a little bit icky?' Damin mused. 'I mean, we're first cousins. Our children might have three eyes, or an extra leg or something. It happens with chickens when you interbreed them too closely.'

'Our fathers were only half brothers, so, strictly speaking, we're only half first cousins, if there is such a thing. And I don't find the idea *icky*, as you so elegantly put it, Damin. I find it intolerable.'

'Then maybe the first step is to kill the notion once and for all.'

'What do you mean?' Starros asked, not sure if he liked the idea of stirring up such a hornets' nest with Mahkas. He was in enough trouble today for simply riding at his friend's side. And there was Leila to consider.

Damin didn't seem to have the same concerns, however. 'Mahkas still harbours the hope that Leila and I will marry because my mother has never actually told him outright that she won't allow it. Maybe it's time she did.'

'Would she do it, though?' Leila asked.

'If I ask her the right way, she might.'

Leila looked up at Starros and, for the first time, he saw a glimmer of true hope in her eyes. 'If my father knew there was no possibility . . .'

'Let's not count our chickens before they hatch, sweetheart.'

'They might be deformed,' Damin added.

Leila turned on him in annoyance. 'You know, you might have the veneer of civilisation, Damin Wolfblade, but you still really are that horrible little monster who used to call me names when we were children.'

'I'm sorry,' the prince sighed, almost sounding like he meant it. 'I don't take things seriously enough, I know. Mother's always at me about it. Elezaar's convinced it's my worst fault and that I'll bring Hythria to her knees because of it. Even Lernen tells me off about it, and coming from someone with his list of vices, that's really saying something. But it doesn't mean I won't try to help you.' He grinned again and added, 'It just means I'll drive you insane while I'm doing it.'

'Go away, Damin,' Leila ordered impatiently. 'And lock the door on your way *out*.'

Surprisingly, Damin did as Leila asked. He climbed off the bed and bowed elegantly to them. 'Your wish is my command, my lady. I shall leave now, and you two can pick up where you left off.'

'Get out.'

Starros was afraid Damin might argue the point, but the young prince did as his cousin bid and a few moments later they heard the door to the slaveways snick shut. Alone again, Starros sat down on the bed and held Leila tight, feeling her tremble against him as she allowed the shock of their exposure to overwhelm her for a moment.

'Damin won't betray us,' he assured her softly after a time, rocking her back and forth gently. 'He said he'd try to help us. And he will. It's no mean thing to have a prince of Hythria on our side.'

'That's the problem,' Leila replied, leaning back in his arms to study his face in the dying light of the candle. She seemed better now. More in control. 'I don't doubt his intentions are noble, but my well-meaning cousin's help may prove the most dangerous thing of all.'

'What do you mean?'

'In trying to help us, he may inadvertently expose us.'

'I think Damin's a lot smarter than you give him credit for, my love.'

'I hope so,' she replied with a thin smile. 'And at least I know where he stands on the matter of our betrothal.'

Starros smiled and pulled her close to him again, kissing the top of her head. Her hair was fragrant, smelling faintly of the rose-scented soap she used. 'Did you ever seriously think Damin wanted to marry you?'

'No.'

'Then you have nothing to fear, Leila. By helping you, Damin is helping himself.'

'Self-interest, eh? Now *that's* a motive I can ascribe to my cousin quite comfortably.'

He bent his head and kissed her again to stop her talking, sick of hearing about Damin and the danger they courted for being so foolish. It had been like this from the beginning, the threat of discovery an ever-present shadow that prevented them from being truly happy. *What would happen, would happen*, he decided fatalistically, and there was little either of them could do about it.

'Make love to me, Starros,' she murmured against his cheek.

Starros smiled. 'I thought you'd never ask,' he breathed in her ear, hoping that, at least for a little while, their love-making would keep the uncertainty of their future from suffocating them completely.

47

The false hope of spring that had blessed the city the day of Damin's arrival was nothing but a pleasant memory the next morning when Wrayan arrived at the palace for lunch, far earlier than required. He didn't think his hosts would mind. He had a lot of catching up to do, particularly with Rorin, so as soon as his spies reported Mahkas and his entourage were riding out of the third gate, heading for Walsark, Wrayan handed over the last of the day's business to Luc, ordered the stable boy at the Pickpocket's Retreat to saddle up his mount, and headed up to the palace through raindrops that felt like sharp needles driven by an icy wind, as if the God of Storms himself was determined to slow his progress.

Even though it was raining, Orleon met him at the top of the palace steps as usual, made a few snide remarks about ignorant criminals who couldn't tell the time, and then had him shown, with ill grace, into the dining room, where the family usually gathered for breakfast. When Wrayan got there, however, the only one present was Rorin, although it was clear the others were expected soon by the amount of food the slaves were loading up on the buffet, padding on silent bare feet in a constant line from the tables to the slaveways entrance concealed behind a screen at the back of the room that led directly down to the kitchens.

'Wrayan!' Rorin cried, jumping to his feet as soon as he spied the visitor. 'I thought you were coming to lunch, not breakfast!'

'The two seem to blur into each other in this place, by the look of that buffet,' Wrayan noted, crossing the room to shake Rorin's hand. He'd only seen the young Fardohnyan two or three times since Marla had sent him to the Sorcerers' Collective. He was a young man now, the same age as Damin, Wrayan realised. He wasn't particularly tall, but he was fair-haired and blue-eyed as any Hythrun. *If you didn't know he was Fardohnyan by birth, you'd never guess*, he thought. Dressed in the black robes of the Sorcerers' Collective, the young man looked quite distinguished. 'Where is everybody?'

'Down at the training yards,' Rorin told him, as he resumed his place at the table. Wrayan took the seat beside him. He felt the chill from his ride seeping from his bones as he was warmed by the heat of the two fires that filled the red-granite fireplaces at each end of the room. A slave hurried to his side to fill his cup with fragrant lemon tea. He accepted the tea but waved away the offer of food.

'In this weather?'

'Apparently nothing is permitted to stand in the way when the pride of the Wolfblades is at stake,' Rorin added. 'Something to do with Damin and Captain Almodavar. I'm not sure what it was exactly, but as it involved getting up at dawn in a freezing downpour to witness it, I decided to settle for letting Kalan fill me in on the details when it's done.'

Wrayan smiled. 'Ah, Almodavar's traditional welcome home for the Prince of Krakandar.'

'Some welcome! He takes him out and beats the living daylights out of him?' Rorin chuckled.

'Tries to. I'll wager you last night's Guild takings that

Damin's been training for nothing else since he learned he was coming home. Almodavar, too. It's been going on since Damin was about twelve or thirteen, I think. Ever since the captain gave Damin forty laps of the training yard for not killing him.'

'And to think, I used to wonder why they called the ruling lords of Hythria *Warlords*.'

Wrayan laughed in agreement. 'Dacendaran told me once the reason Hythria was such a favourite of Zegarnald is because we'd rather fight than eat.'

'Dacendaran?' Rorin asked with a raised brow. He was curious rather than sceptical.

'Long story,' Wrayan shrugged. 'If we get time, I'll tell you about it while you're here. I see you've graduated to the ranks of a full member of the Sorcerers' Collective,' he added, looking at Rorin's black robe. He admired the young man's willingness to wear it. Admittedly it was warm, but in Wrayan's experience they were damn itchy things.

'Last year,' Rorin confirmed, 'Kalan and I graduated at the same time. She suggested I make a point of wearing my robes while I'm here.'

'Because otherwise Lord Damaran looks at you like you should be out in the stables shovelling manure?' he guessed. Rorin nodded in agreement. 'You and Starros should get together and compare notes some time. Which brings up an interesting point, though,' Wrayan added thoughtfully. 'How can they test your ability as a sorcerer if there's nobody left in the Collective with any magical ability?'

'It's a written examination.'

'You're kidding me!'

Rorin shook his head. 'I don't think the word *magic* even got a mention. Mostly it was the history of the Harshini and Hythria and a stack of historical and geographical stuff with a bit of mathematics and a smattering of science. Damin could have passed it, if he tried. I just scraped through, incidentally. Kalan passed with flying colours. Naturally.'

'*That's* how they're testing for sorcerers these days?'

'Ironic, isn't it,' Rorin said with a grin. 'The only one in the whole damn place with any magical ability and I almost didn't get through.'

Wrayan studied the young Fardohnyan for a moment, wondering how he'd managed to keep his ability hidden all these years. 'Did nobody ever suspect *anything*?'

'Alija knew I had some sort of ability,' Rorin confirmed. 'There's no way to hide it completely. But she never suspected how much, and after a few futile attempts to have me demonstrate the limits of my power, I think she gave me up as a lost cause. As far as most people were concerned, I was Luciena Mariner's cousin and Kalan Hawksword's friend. Once they realised I couldn't even blow out a candle without taking a really deep breath, nobody cared who I was beyond that.'

'That's the difference between being an Innate and being able to wield true Harshini magic, I suppose. Alija always had trouble figuring out how much power I commanded, too.'

'She got the better of you once, didn't she?'

Wrayan frowned. He didn't like to think of it like that. 'She cheated. Anyway, Brak destroyed the scrolls she used to amplify her power. Since then, her ability is pretty much limited to what she was born with. She can read minds if she can establish physical contact, shield them rather obviously, and do a few other parlour tricks, but that's about it. The fact that she can't detect a mind shield I've created is a telling sign. She can brush over the source and feel it when someone is using magic in her vicinity, but unless she's witnessed it happen she can't recognise the residual effect for what it is, even when faced with it on a daily basis.'

'She's not bad at healing, when she concentrates on it,' Rorin told him, waving a barefoot slave over to refill his teacup. He waited until the slave was out of earshot before adding, 'I'll probably get hanged for saying this here, but she's actually not that bad as High Arrions go. She's quite dedicated to sorting the whole mess out. And she's desperate to find some real magical talent. I must have been a real disappointment to her, I think.'

Wrayan looked at him suspiciously. 'Rorin, you're not thinking about . . .'

He shook his head. 'Not a chance. I might applaud Alija's noble goals, Wrayan, but I know what drives her, and there's nothing noble about that. She's after real magicians for the Collective, but only because of what they can do for her plans to raise her own son to the throne. Besides, my loyalty is to the Wolfblades.'

'Are you sure?'

Rorin nodded, not offended by the question. 'Did I ever tell you what happened after you left me with Princess Marla?'

'Not really.'

'Well, on the way back to Greenharbour, she started asking me about my family – you know, who they were, where they were, what they did, if they'd miss me . . . that sort of thing.'

Wrayan nodded a little guiltily, thinking he probably should have done the same thing, but in his grief over Brak's apparent demise and everything else that had been happening at the time, he'd never thought to ask.

'My father's a sailor – did I ever mention that? So were my grandfather and my uncles. My family was poor, Wrayan, poorer than slaves, and I was the eldest of seven. I used to envy slaves when I was small because at least they had the benefit of knowing where their next meal was coming from. When that anvil came through the wall, it was just the last in a long line of bad luck for us.'

'I never understood why they didn't just put you on a ship bound for Greenharbour and have you jump ship when you got there.'

'Most Fardohnyan ships are crewed by slaves. That's one of the reasons we were always so poor. Why hire free men when you can buy slaves who'll work for nothing? I would've had to stow away – which meant death if I was caught – or sign on for a ten-year bond on an oceangoing trader. It was easier to go overland. And all we had time for, given the Palace Guard was hot on my heels when I left Talabar.' Rorin smiled at the irony. 'Not that it made much of a difference in the end, seeing as how I surrendered when I got to Westbrook anyway.'

'That's what you get for listening to a demon.'

'I learned that the hard way,' Rorin laughed. 'Anyway, to cut a long story short, I told the princess about my family and thought nothing more about it. I found out later that Princess Marla used her connections in Ruxton Tirstone's spice network to contact them. She let them know I was fine and she asked if they needed anything. And then she helped them out.'

'Helped them out how?'

'Princess Marla bought my father a river barge and Luciena arranged a shipping contract with her trading company. He and my uncles have their own boat now. They trade between Talabar and the ports along the Glass River in Medalon. Mostly wool, I think, and the odd pagan fleeing the Defenders. My father's doing very well for himself these days. They helped my cousin, too. She has her own shop now. Selling spices she gets from Ruxton's suppliers.'

'Have you been able to see your father?'

Rorin shook his head. 'No, but we write. It's easy enough to get a letter to him through the trading company. So you see, there's no need to fear my loyalty to the Wolfblades, Wrayan. Even if I wasn't related by marriage to them, my whole family owes them their livelihood. The debt I owe you for rescuing me can't easily be repaid, either. Or what I owe Princess Shananara.'

Wrayan felt his heart clench with longing, the mere mention of her name still enough to make him want her, even after all this time. 'You remember her, then?'

He nodded. 'A little. It seems like a dream most of the time.'

'What's it feel like?' Wrayan had always wanted to ask Rorin that. Although he'd been to Sanctuary, been taught to use his own power by the Harshini, Rorin had learned to use his power the way the Harshini were taught. Shananara had linked with his mind and deposited all the knowledge he needed in one fell swoop.

'It's hard to describe. It's just *there* . . . I think about it, and I *know*.' The young man shrugged self-deprecatingly. 'I wouldn't get too excited about it, Wrayan. I really don't have that much power compared to the Harshini. Not even as much as you, I suspect. Did *you* ever link with Shananara?'

'Yes,' he admitted. 'But she wasn't teaching me anything . . . well, that's not entirely true, she taught me . . . we were . . .' He threw his hands up, a little embarrassed. 'Oh, never mind.'

Rorin smiled and seemed to understand. Wrayan was never quite sure what else Shananara had planted in the young man's mind, but he didn't seem curious. Wrayan wished he could tell if Rorin was just being polite or he knew that Wrayan and Shananara had once – and only once – been lovers. There was no point in trying to read the young magician's mind. The shield Shananara had placed on Rorin's mind to prevent Alija learning his secret was immune to even Wrayan's casual penetration.

'So, what happens now you've graduated?' he asked.

'Kalan's decided the Sorcerers' Collective should be more involved in charitable works,' Rorin explained. 'Because it meant us leaving Greenharbour for a while, not surprisingly Alija went along with her noble suggestion and even agreed to fund it. We were in Nalinbar in northern Pentamor when the plague hit the city, helping to set up a refuge for ailing slaves whose owners can't support them any longer.'

'This was *Kalan's* idea?' Wrayan asked, a little sceptically.

'I think it was Princess Marla's idea, actually.' Rorin smiled wryly. 'You know these people, Wrayan. They don't draw breath without thinking how it's going to affect Damin's accession to the throne.'

'What's that got to do with Kalan?'

'Think about it. The next High Prince's selfless little sister getting her hands dirty among the poor and hopeless – how many votes is that going to be worth in the Convocation of the Warlords some day?'

'I see you've managed to maintain a healthy dose of cynicism about it all,' Wrayan remarked.

'It's a survival tactic,' Rorin laughed. 'I'd go crazy otherwise.'

'I see. So what about you and Kalan?'

'What about me and Kalan?' the young sorcerer asked with a puzzled look.

'Are you two . . . ?'

Rorin laughed aloud at Wrayan's unsubtle suggestion. 'No. Why?'

'Starros thought you might be.'

'Then Starros doesn't know Kalan as well as he thinks. Or me. Anyway, even if she weren't my best friend, I still wouldn't go there. I have no intention of being one of young Lady Hawksword's cast-off lovers, thank you, and believe me, there's a growing list.'

Wrayan shook his head, uncomfortable with the very idea. 'Don't tell me that. Not about Kalan. She's still a little girl in my mind.'

'Take a *really* close look when she gets here, Wrayan,' Rorin said, as voices in the hall told Wrayan it wouldn't be long before he had the opportunity to do as the young man suggested. 'She's not a little girl any longer.'

Wrayan wasn't pleased at all with Rorin's attitude. 'Shouldn't you be protecting her from that sort of thing?'

'I promised to keep her safe from any magical harm, Wrayan. I can't do much about who she takes to her bed.'

No sooner had he finished talking than the rest of the family burst into the dining room. Damin was in the lead and had obviously come straight from the training yard. He was wearing muddy trousers, but his shirt was clean, and he was sporting a fresh cut over his left eye and a bruise on his chin that looked quite painful. His hair was damp but he looked fit and healthy and in fine spirits. There was a young woman with him, laughing over something the prince had said, whom Wrayan mistook for Leila initially. She was slender and fair, dressed in a pale blue robe with dark blue sleeves. But it wasn't Leila. This young woman only came up to Damin's shoulder . . .

'*Kalan?*'

As Leila and Starros followed them into the dining room, the young woman turned and looked at him, her face lighting up when she realised who he was.

'Wrayan!' she screeched in a most unladylike fashion. She pushed past her brother and ran around the table. Wrayan rose to greet her and Kalan threw herself at him, almost knocking him off balance, hugging him so tightly he could barely breathe.

Damin watched the entire spectacle with a shake of his head. 'Don't hold back on us now, Kalan. Tell us how you *really* feel.'

'Shut up, you fool!' Kalan ordered her brother, without taking her eyes off Wrayan. She released her death grip on him and leaned back in his arms, her eyes alight with pleasure at the sight of him. 'You look exactly the same, Wrayan. I swear you haven't aged a day since the first time we met. Is that because you're part Harshini?'

'Should you be saying that out loud?' Leila gasped, glancing at the slaves.

'Everybody here knows the truth, Leila,' Kalan shrugged, and then she turned her beaming smile on Wrayan again. 'You'll stay for a while, won't you?'

'Of course.'

'Good. Then let's have some breakfast. Or is it lunchtime already? I'm starving.'

'Who won the fight?' he asked as he resumed his seat, Kalan taking the chair on his left.

'Damin, of course,' Leila informed him, as Starros held her chair out for her. 'Naturally, Almodavar claims he let him win.'

'Well, by the look of Damin, the old man gave a good account of himself.'

Damin grinned as he took his seat and the slaves began to pile his plate with food. 'He says that to save face. Almodavar hasn't been able to get the better of me for years. I only let him land the odd blow now and then to make him feel better. I'll give him one thing, though,' he added, fingering his bruised jaw gingerly. 'The old bastard can hit hard.' The prince glanced at Starros, his smile fading as he spied the young man heading for the door. 'Where are you going? Aren't you joining us?'

'I'm not hungry.'

'Don't be an idiot! You've been up since before dawn. Come and eat something.'

Starros bowed and shook his head. 'Assistant chief stewards don't eat with the family, your highness, you should know that.'

'You are *part* of this family, Starros,' Damin replied, suddenly serious.

Starros smiled wistfully. 'Not any more. So, if you will excuse me . . . ?' He bowed again and walked briskly from the room, leaving them watching after him in an uncomfortable silence.

Wrayan glanced at the young prince curiously, wondering why Damin hadn't realised how difficult it must for a bastard fosterling to find a place in a world so clearly divided by birthright and bloodlines. Then again, Damin being Damin, maybe he hadn't thought about it at all. Wrayan glanced around the table at the others. Rorin, protected from his common-born status by his black sorcerer's robes, seemed unsurprised that Starros had departed, while Kalan looked down at her plate uncomfortably.

It was Leila, Wrayan noted, who inexplicably jumped to her feet and fled the room, leaving her cousins staring after her in confusion.

'What's wrong with her?' Kalan asked.

'Nothing,' Damin replied shortly.

'But why—?'

'Stay out of it, Kalan.'

He knows, Wrayan thought in surprise, watching the prince turn his attention to his meal, ignoring the puzzled look his sister gave him. *He knows about Leila and Starros. How the hell did he find out so quickly? Did Leila tell him? Did Starros?*

It didn't really matter, Wrayan supposed. If Damin Wolfblade knew about the affair, then the damage was already done.

The question now is, the thief mused silently, reaching for his teacup as he surreptitiously studied Damin out of the corner of his eye, *what's he going to do about it?*

Wrayan got no chance to worry about it further, however, because at that moment Orleon opened the dining room

452

doors rather dramatically to announce that Lady Lionsclaw of Sunrise Province, fleeing reports of the plague as far north as Izcomdar, had arrived unexpectedly, along with her four young children, and was seeking sanctuary in Krakandar.

48

It was strange, Alija Eaglespike decided, how quickly a potential disaster could turn into an advantage. Take this unfortunate plague, for instance. To the casual observer, it was a human disaster on an unprecedented scale. And yet, even though Alija's intended target had escaped infection, there was a bright side.

Her husband, Barnardo Eaglespike, had been one of the first to fall victim to it.

Being a widow suited Alija. With rank of her own as High Arrion of the Sorcerers' Collective, unlike Marla she had no need to take another husband to protect her interests. And the gods had been kind, too, by waiting until her eldest son came of age before they took his father away. The transition of power had been seamless after Barnardo died. Although the Convocation had yet to confirm Cyrus as his father's heir because of the plague, it was just a formality. In the meantime, Cyrus was safe back in Dregian Castle with his wife and daughter, ruling his province with skill and wisdom, proving to everyone who mattered that when it came to the question of the next High Prince, there was really only one viable contender.

Fortunately, nobody was sure where the plague that was ravaging Hythria had originated. She felt no guilt about any part she might have played in its spread. The Denikan sailor blamed for starting the plague was roaming the streets of Greenharbour for days before Tarkyn found him. All Alija had done was give the poor man directions.

Still, it was fortunate the population had a focus for their anger. *There's always the need to blame someone. And always a need to exact revenge, even when it really wasn't anybody's fault.*

If anything, the more helpless the victims felt, the more they hungered for vengeance, as if in the act of seeking retribution, they would somehow regain control over their lives.

That was what had happened here in Greenharbour as soon as the full realisation of the scope of the deadly disaster had become clear. The people had driven the few Denikans brave enough to venture from their homeland into the streets, as if spilling their blood might wash away the disease. Some were killed outright, others driven through the city by angry mobs until they fell – either from exhaustion or fear – and were beaten to death, their crime nothing more sinister than the colour of their skin and being born some-where other than Hythria. Aware that Marla had been making noises prior to the plague about making some sort of treaty with the Denikans, Alija had waited until most of them were dead before she ordered the Sorcerers' Collective Guard to put down the riot. Of course, by then it was too late to save anyone. By the time the Collective soldiers had arrived, there wasn't a Denikan left alive in the city and any hopes Marla had for a peaceful treaty with the distant southern continent lay in ruins.

But the disease remained, and death was everywhere. Alija had heard of whole families taken by the sickness; of mothers abandoning their children. Tales of healers barricading themselves in their own houses, for fear of catching the disease they had no way of treating. The few in the Sorcerers' Collective who hadn't escaped back to their own provinces were the only ones left to care for the sick – because Alija insisted on it. But even that small and ultimately futile effort had stopped now. One too many of her people had caught the disease themselves and the few remaining members of the Sorcerers' Collective still resident in the city were holed up in the Sorcerers' Palace, refusing to go out into the streets at all. The palaces and townhouses of the rich stood deserted, too, as their occupants either fled the city or were stricken by the disease.

The sickness struck with terrible speed. It killed so swiftly there was a cynical saying around the city: *Breakfast with your descendants – dinner with your ancestors*. And it was only going to get worse before the plague ran its course. It was still winter – such that it was in the warm, muggy climes of Greenharbour. When the weather warmed up, it was going to be much harder to control.

The plague had no respect for rank or birthright. Bodies were left in empty houses, rich and poor, because there was no one willing to give them a decent burial. At a meeting to discuss the crisis last week, Marla had talked of having the bodies loaded onto ships and setting them afire in the harbour, a sacrilege that Alija would have thought incomprehensible only a few weeks ago.

Now, as the hot, humid months of the rainy season approached, she was starting to think it might not be such a bad idea.

A low moan on the bed distracted Alija from her idle musings and she turned to her patient. Ruxton Tirstone stirred in his sleep, his body on the verge of giving in completely.

As a favour to Marla, Alija had come when she heard the news that Ruxton had been struck down. And he'd been struck hard. By Alija's estimate, about half the people who contracted the disease managed to survive, whether they were treated or not, but she doubted Ruxton would be one of them. There were large inflammations the size of grapefruits in his neck and groin that showed no sign of abating.

It won't be long now, she guessed. It was as if he was dead from the moment the high fever, the exhaustion, the headaches and the chills set in; his body just hadn't acknowledged it yet. He'd fallen into a coma several hours ago, his body wrung dry from vomiting and coughing up blood, which he seemed to have done in equal measure for days before finally settling into this uneasy coma. The dark lesions on his face and upper body that were visible above the silk sheets were so purple they were almost black and his breathing was becoming increasingly laboured.

She had little pity for the man, despite the fact that she had willingly risked her own life to come here. Ruxton could have been safe if he'd stayed in Marla's extensive and well-guarded town house, secure and isolated from the disease-ravaged city.

But no, you had to carry on as if it was business as usual, didn't you, Ruxton?

He'd been down on the wharves, trying to protect his spice cargoes, when he succumbed to the disease. With plague rampant in the city, Hythria's ships were being turned away from ports all over the world. Ruxton Tirstone stood to lose a fortune if he couldn't get his spices delivered. He'd sent his youngest son, Adham, north into Medalon several weeks ago to try to find somewhere to store his precious cargoes until the plague abated, but even that wasn't enough for him, apparently.

Serves him right, she thought unsympathetically. *That's what you get when you put profit ahead of common sense.*

But Alija wasn't here to help Ruxton. She was here because Marla believed she was a friend and Alija wasn't ready, just yet, to reveal how wrong the princess was about that.

They enjoyed a strange relationship, Alija Eaglespike and Marla Wolfblade. Although she showed every indication of being an astute and intelligent woman, even after more than a quarter of a century it astonished Alija that Marla never once suspected how she truly felt about her. The princess had never guessed that her beloved second husband, Nash Hawksword, had been Alija's lover. She continued to rely on Alija's counsel, with no clue her supposed friend was behind several attempts on the life of her precious son, Damin.

It never occurred to Alija to think Marla's ignorance arose out of anything other than her own skill at deception. She scanned the minds of the princess and those closest to her every opportunity she got, but not once had she detected even a glimmer of concern about the High Arrion. Their thoughts were always of ordinary, mundane things. There were no dark thoughts of vengeance or hunger for power in the minds of Marla or her staff.

Alija had been particularly concerned about the dwarf. If anybody knew the truth about the murder of Ronan Dell and his household all those years ago, it was Elezaar. But the dwarf *court'esa's* mind was as mediocre as his mistress's, his thoughts just as bland. If he knew the truth, he had forgotten about it, or buried it so deep he would never remember.

Ruxton moaned again, even the oblivion of a coma not enough to block his pain. *Oh, for the gods' sake*, she thought impatiently. *Will you hurry up and die?*

The door opened and she turned to see who it was, not surprised to find Marla standing there, hesitating on the threshold. *You don't mind sharing your bed with a peasant when there's a profit to be made, do you, Marla? But it's a different story when he's dying of the plague.*

'How is he?' Marla asked softly, as if she was afraid her mere words might wake him from his coma.

Alija shook her head sadly. 'I'm sorry, cousin. But it won't be long now.'

Marla nodded, dry-eyed and in control. That always surprised Alija about Marla. She seemed to be able to contain her feelings far more than Alija would have expected, given what she was like as a girl. Perhaps it was the result of four calculated and emotionless marriages. Perhaps it wasn't control at all. Perhaps Marla's outward calm was just a total lack of feeling.

'You should get some sleep, Alija,' the princess said, looking at the High Arrion with concern. 'It's bad enough to think I'm soon to lose another husband. I can't bear the thought of losing you, too.'

Alija smiled. 'Thank you, Marla. You don't know what it means to me to hear you say that.'

'Can I have something sent up for you?'

Alija shook her head. 'No. I'm fine.'

Marla spared Ruxton one last long, meaningful look, before closing the door behind her.

Idiot.

The High Arrion crossed the room and stopped at the foot of the bed, looking down on this commoner who had been married to Marla Wolfblade for over sixteen years. *What did he have*, Alija wondered, *that would make Marla want him?* She was the High Prince's sister. *Nobody* in Greenharbour doubted greed was the reason she'd married a common-born sailor, but after Jarvan Mariner died, Marla could have had any man in Hythria. She'd refused every offer for her hand from those of her own class and married another commoner instead.

The reason had always bothered Alija, but she had never been able to fathom it. Marla and Ruxton got on well enough, Alija could attest to that. Ruxton was an intelligent man and more than able to hold his own among his betters. But there had to be more to it. Marla didn't need his wealth. Between the fortunes left to her by her first three husbands, Marla's wealth was bordering on obscene. Ruxton brought her no alliances Alija knew of, no strategic benefit at all, really. And it wasn't love, Alija was certain of that. She had seen Marla in love and there was no hint of emotional turmoil in the self-contained woman who had dutifully arrived at the palace each morning for the past twenty-odd years to aid her wastrel brother in holding the country together.

What have you got, Ruxton Tirstone, Alija wondered, *that makes her want you so?*

Ruxton's breathing grew ragged, as if her silent question had upset him.

He'll be gone in a matter of minutes, Alija decided, coldly assessing his chances, hoping the end would come quickly. She had things to do and places to be.

But when you're gone, the secret of what Marla saw in a common spice trader goes with you.

It was too tempting. Too puzzling. Cautiously, Alija moved around the bed and sat down beside her patient. In order to read his thoughts she would have to touch him, something she'd managed to avoid until now. She hesitated for a time, until curiosity won out over fear, and laid her hand on Ruxton's limp arm, wondering if, in the last jumbled thoughts of an unconscious man, lay some insight as to how a common-born merchant had won the hand of the only sister of the High Prince of Hythria and managed to stay married to her for as long as he had.

Ruxton's breathing was deteriorating rapidly as she entered his mind. Even the large bunches of lavender placed strategically around the room could no longer smother the stench of death he exhaled with every tortured breath.

Ruxton's mind was blank, Alija discovered, disappointed. She thought *something* must be going on behind that veil of unconsciousness, but there was nothing. His mind was vacant, like the inside of an empty sphere, the walls slippery and smooth as coloured glass, opaque to her probe and any last residual thoughts that might struggle to find their way into his consciousness.

His last thoughts were of you, Alija murmured silently. She would tell Marla that to keep her happy. Or maybe she would tell her the truth. *His last thoughts weren't of you, my dear . . . they were of absolutely nothing at all . . .*

Another burst of coughing tore through Ruxton as his bleeding lungs tried vainly to find air. He was very close to death. So close that Alija would be a fool to remain in his mind any longer. She didn't know if she would die along with the spice trader if she was still linked to his mind in the moment of death and didn't fancy putting the theory to the test. Carefully, Alija unhooked the tendrils of her thoughts from Ruxton's mind as his breathing turned to weak, strangled gasps. A little concerned that she had left it too late, Alija hurried to extract her mind from that of the dying man. Somewhere in the background, she heard him draw his last, desperate breath . . .

And then an explosion seemed to go off in Alija's mind. She screamed, clutching her hands to her head as she fell off the bed and collapsed to her knees.

Even though the physical contact had been broken, the link remained in place as the smooth glass wall that she thought was Ruxton Tirstone's unconscious mind shattered into myriad, crystalline pieces, overwhelming Alija. Her skin prickled, itched and burned, the familiar, terrifying touch of true Harshini magic washing against her skin as a mind shield she hadn't even known was there disintegrated on the death of its owner.

It was instantaneous and blinding, unleashing a flash flood of Ruxton's memories and thoughts held back by the subtle shield – a work of such mastery she couldn't even conceive of it. The tirade washed over her like a crashing wave. It was too much to understand, too much to deal with, too much to bear.

Alija's last coherent thought before she lost consciousness was a name she had thought long passed into history. It jumped out at her from the maelstrom of Ruxton's final dying thoughts, flaring like a beacon in a storm. A threat she had believed dealt with and destroyed more than twenty-five years ago.

A ghost come back to haunt her.
Wrayan Lightfinger.

49

Orleon had already shown Tejay into Mahkas's study by the time Damin arrived downstairs. There was no sign of the children – presumably Orleon had made arrangements for their care – and the Warlord's wife was looking tired and travel-weary. Her riding habit was stained with mud splatters, her damp hair even more unruly than usual.

As far as Damin knew, Tejay Lionsclaw hadn't been back to Krakandar since Rielle and Darvad Vintner's wedding. He'd not seen her since about halfway through the third year of his fosterage in Natalandar, when, in keeping with their long-standing arrangement, Tejay had finally married Terin, the only son of Chaine Lionsclaw, Warlord of Sunrise Province. That was almost nine years ago. He had fond memories of his foster-sister, however. A skilled swordsman, she had delivered a sound beating to Damin on more than one occasion in the first few years he was fostered with her father.

'*Tejay?*'

She turned when she heard the door open. Motherhood and nine years had added a little bulk around her hips and a few crinkles around her eyes when she smiled, but other than that she was still the strong, forthright young woman that Damin remembered from his childhood.

'Is that *you*, Damin?' She smiled tiredly at him, looking him up and down with a critical eye 'My, didn't you grow into a big strong boy.'

He crossed the room, taking her hands in his and kissing her palms affectionately. 'What in the name of the gods are you doing here, Tejay? Where's Terin?'

'It's a long story.'

'You look exhausted. Sit down,' he urged, offering her a seat. There was a low table with cushions around it in the centre of the room, but Tejay gladly sat in the chair facing the desk.

'Can I get you anything?'

She shook her head. 'Orleon's got everything under control, as usual. I was so relieved when I heard you were here. I didn't know where else to go.'

'What are you talking about? Go where? Why aren't you in Sunrise with your husband?'

'I was,' she informed him. 'Until I got word Father was ill. Terin was having trouble with the Fardohnyans closing the borders, so I took the children and headed for Natalandar to see my father.'

'Is everything all right, Tejay?' he asked with concern. 'With you and Terin, I mean?'

'That's hardly the point, Damin,' Tejay said, shrugging off his question. 'And why would you automatically assume that there's something wrong with my husband? Or my marriage?'

'I didn't mean there was,' Damin assured her, surprised by her defensive reaction. 'It just seems a little odd that he'd let you go alone, that's all.'

Tejay bristled at the implied insult. 'Why? You think I can't look after myself?'

'No, of course I don't think that!' he assured her hastily. 'I just think I wouldn't let my wife traipse all the way across

464

the country, on her own, with plague on the loose and four small children in tow.'

'Good thing I'm not your wife, then,' she replied tartly.

Damin let the comment pass. 'Why not leave Chaine to deal with the Fardohnyans?'

Tejay shook her head, her face etched with weary sorrow. 'You haven't heard, then, I suppose.'

'Heard what?'

Tejay took a deep breath. 'Chaine Lionsclaw is dead, Damin. My husband is the Warlord of Sunrise Province now.'

Damin sank down on the edge of the desk in stunned surprise. 'When . . . when did this happen?'

'About a month ago. Chaine was killed in the Widowmaker Pass trying to get through to Fardohnya to convince the Plenipotentiary of Westbrook to keep the borders open. It was bandits, we think.'

'Then the news would have reached Greenharbour just after I left.'

She nodded in agreement. 'We were still reeling from that news when we got the word about my father within a day of Chaine's death. There was no way Terin could leave Sunrise after that. So I took the children and headed for Izcomdar without him.'

Damin did a quick mental calculation in his head and frowned. 'You haven't had time to get from Cabradell to Natalandar and then back here to Krakandar in a month.'

'I didn't even try. Rogan had a messenger waiting for me on the Pentamor border, telling me to turn back. The plague had reached Natalandar before me and our father was already dead. Apparently, he was so ill, he was one of the first to go when the disease hit the city. So we turned back the way we came, only to learn that Grosburn in Pentamor was starting to report the first cases of plague there, too. So I turned around again and headed north for Krakandar. I didn't know what else to do. I have my children with me, Damin. This is the last place in Hythria that seems to be immune from this dreadful blight.'

Tejay's tale was worrying for more than news the plague was spreading. Old Rogan Bearbow, the Warlord of Izcomdar, was dead. That alone was enough to make Damin want to weep. And for Chaine Lionsclaw, too – a good and loyal friend to the Wolfblades. He was sure there were going to be political ramifications from this unexpected turn of events that he'd not had time to figure out.

'I think we're more lucky than immune, Tejay. Rorin claims it's the weather that keeps us safe here in the north. Something to do with rats breeding, he says. It's much colder here than Greenharbour and it's still winter, which seems to keep the problem in check. And I'm so sorry about Chaine and your father. Chaine was a good man. Your father was a *great* one.'

She smiled wanly. 'He was very fond of you, too.'

'You're welcome to stay as long as you need, of course,' he promised. 'Just speak to Orleon. He'll arrange a message to be sent to Terin to let him know where you are. And that you and the children are safe.'

'I knew I could rely on you, Damin. Thank you.'

Damin crossed his arms, frowning thoughtfully. 'You present me with another dilemma, though.'

'What's that?'

'The plague is on your very heels, Tejay. At what point do we seal the city to keep us safe from it?'

'Now. Before the refugees and the warmer weather arrive,' Tejay advised. 'They'll bring this nightmare with them sure as the sun will rise tomorrow.'

'I think it's a bit late to start turning refugees away,' he said with a smile and then looked up as the door opened and a slave wheeling a small cart laden with fruit and fresh pastries and a pot of lemon-scented tea entered the room, followed by Starros, who ordered the slave to park the cart next to Tejay. The young man did as Starros bid, then bowed silently and left the room, leaving Starros to pour the tea.

Tejay looked over the cart with a frown. 'I appreciate the thought, young man, but haven't you got anything stronger than tea?'

Starros glanced at Damin, who shrugged. 'Get the lady a drink, Starros.'

'My lord,' Starros replied with a courtly bow. He walked to the side-board and returned with a cut-crystal decanter of dark, fortified wine, which he poured into the teacup in lieu of the tea, and then handed it to Tejay with another bow.

She studied him for a moment as she accepted the wine. 'Starros? I remember you. You were a fosterling here, when we visited Krakandar when Damin's stepsister, Rielle, married my kinsman Darvad, weren't you?'

'Yes, my lady. I was.'

'And you're Krakandar's assistant steward now?'

'Assistant *chief* steward,' he corrected with a faint smile.

Tejay nodded approvingly. 'You've done well for yourself, haven't you? Most fosterlings wind up in the Palace Guard. You must be very pleased to have attained such a high position in the household.'

Starros glanced at Damin for a moment. It wasn't hard to guess what he was thinking. But he did nothing more than incline his head towards Tejay in appreciation of the compliment. 'Indeed, my lady. What more could a lowborn bastard want out of life, I often ask myself.'

Tejay didn't miss the mockery in his tone. Damin frowned. 'Starros, can you ask Kalan and Rorin to join us?'

'Of course, your highness,' he replied with a slightly

insolent bow, and then left the room, closing the door softly behind him.

Tejay looked at Damin in confusion. 'Did I miss something there?'

'Don't worry about it. Starros just forgets himself sometimes.'

She shook her head and drained the teacup full of wine, then held it out to Damin for a refill. He did as she asked, and watched her drink that one down in three gulps as well.

'It's not lunchtime yet,' he reminded her.

'Good, that means I can have another one at lunch. Did you say Kalan was here?'

He nodded. 'She and Rorin were in Nalinbar when the plague started to get out of hand. I met up with them on the way here and convinced them they'd be safer in Krakandar. They'd closed the city gates in Greenharbour by then anyway, so there was no point in trying to go south.'

'Who is Rorin?'

'Rorin Mariner,' he explained. 'He's Luciena's cousin.'

The door opened again and Kalan entered the room with Rorin on her heels. Tejay rose to her feet wearily, but Kalan waved her back into her seat. 'Please, don't get up on my account, my lady.'

The Lady of Sunrise smiled gratefully and resumed her seat. 'Gracious, I thought Damin had grown, but you were just a little girl the last time we met, Kalan. And now look at you! A full member of the Sorcerers' Collective, no less!'

'It's all right, my mother has trouble coping with the notion, too,' Kalan laughed. 'This is Rorin Mariner, my lady.'

The young sorcerer bowed politely. Tejay looked him up and down and then glanced at Damin. 'You've got it made, haven't you?'

'What do you mean?' he asked innocently.

'A couple of sorcerers in your pocket already. Your younger brother set to inherit Elasapine when old Charel Hawksword finally passes on. One of the Taranger brothers is married to your stepsister, isn't he? The one who owns half the shipping in Hythria? The gods help us by the time you become High Prince, Damin.'

'Actually, I think Luciena only owns about a third of the shipping,' Damin corrected with a grin.

Kalan wasn't nearly so amused. Her smile faded as she stared at the Warlord's wife suspiciously. 'Do you have some sort of problem with my brother becoming High Prince, my lady?'

Tejay shook her head, a little taken aback by Kalan's ferocity. 'You have a feisty advocate there, Damin.'

'Pay no attention to her, Tejay,' Damin advised. 'She doesn't bite if you don't tease her.' Before his sister could object he turned to her and added, 'Tejay is suggesting we seal the city.'

'Is that necessary?' Kalan asked.

'The plague is already showing up in Izcomdar and Pentamor,' Tejay warned. 'It won't be long before it gets here. And if the Medalonians close their border . . .'

'Easier said than done,' Damin remarked, rubbing his bruised chin without thinking. The pain shot through his jaw and he hastily pulled his hand away. 'The border with Medalon is a couple of hundred miles long. There's no way to seal it effectively.'

'Why the urgency?' Rorin asked.

'My father is already dead,' Tejay told him. 'And my father-in-law. This is the only major city in Hythria free of the plague. If you can't stop it reaching Krakandar, there's no telling how many people it will kill before it's done with us.'

As she spoke, Rorin walked around the desk thoughtfully, until he was standing before the map of Hythria that

469

hung on the wall behind them. It was a beautiful piece of work, six feet high and twice that in length; it had been hand-sewn by Damin's great-great-grandmother as a wedding present to her husband almost a hundred years ago. Each province was sewn in a different coloured silk, the borders worked in real gold thread. Damin watched the young sorcerer curiously, the voices of Kalan and Tejay fading into the background as they discussed the implications of the plague.

Rorin studied the map in silence for a time and then turned to Damin. 'You've got more than the plague to worry about, Damin.'

'What do you mean?'

Rorin pointed at the map. 'Barnardo Eaglespike is dead. His son – or more importantly, *Alija's* son – Cyrus, is now Warlord. Effectively the High Arrion has control of Dregian Province.' He pointed at the next province, lying to the south of Dregian. 'Greenharbour Province. Currently under the administration of the Sorcerers' Collective, and has been ever since Graim Falconlance and his two sons were killed in that idiotic border skirmish with Pentamor a couple of years back. Remember? They were fighting over some worthless piece of land they both claimed was theirs because some fool announced he'd found gold in a stream that ran through it. After the dust settled and they realised both the Warlord of Greenharbour and his heir were dead, there was quite a bit of trouble over who should inherit. Finally, they settled on a distant cousin, I believe.'

'I remember,' Damin said with a nod. 'The gold they wre fighting over turned out to be pyrite, didn't it?'

'Fool's gold, indeed.'

Damin studied the map for a moment and then looked at Rorin. 'The cousin . . . that's Conin Falconlance. I know him. He's only a year or two older than me.'

'So he can't rule in his own right for years yet.' Rorin then pointed to Izcomdar and turned to look at Tejay. 'And now you tell us Lord Bearbow is dead. How old is your brother, my lady?'

Tejay looked up from her conversation with Kalan, obviously puzzled by the question. 'Rogan is twenty-seven.'

'And you have no other male relatives who might act as his regent until he comes of age?'

Tejay shook her head, a little worried about what Rorin was driving at.

'Then, for the next three years at least, Izcomdar is going to fall under the governance of the Sorcerers' Collective, too.' Rorin then pointed to Sunrise Province. 'Terin Lionsclaw is now the Warlord of Sunrise. His eldest child is . . . how old, my lady?'

'Four,' Tejay told him.

Rorin nodded and pointed to Elasapine. 'Then we have Charel Hawksword's province. He's an old man and he's been failing for years, so much so that he keeps Narvell with him all the time now, for fear he won't have taught his young heir everything he needs to know before he dies. But Narvell is only twenty-two. The twins have an uncle, by marriage at least, but if anything were to happen to Lord Hawksword, I can promise you they won't let the Regent of Krakandar govern Elasapine as well.'

'And if anything should happen to Mahkas,' Damin said with a frown, beginning to understand what Rorin was getting at, 'Krakandar would also fall into the hands of the Sorcerers' Collective until I come of age.'

Rorin nodded and studied the map again for a moment before turning to look at the others. 'Get Mahkas back here and seal the city,' the young sorcerer advised. 'And send a message to Narvell in Elasapine to keep Charel safe. You should warn your husband, too, my lady.'

'Warn him of what?' Tejay asked, still a little confused.

'To take care of himself,' Damin told her, staring at the map with deep concern. 'Because this plague means that, right now, we're one Warlord's death away from Alija Eaglespike having majority control of the Convocation of Warlords.'

50

'Your majesty,' Lecter Turon announced, closing the sandal-wood doors of King Hablet's office behind him. 'I've been having some thoughts on the issue of your heir.'

Hablet looked up from the report he was reading and scowled. 'Really? I think of little else.'

The eunuch smiled, wiping his damp forehead with a silk kerchief as he crossed the floor to stand before the king's gilded worktable. Even though the humidity was relatively low at this time of year, it seemed to have little effect on how much the man sweated. *Perhaps that's how he's always able to wheedle out of things so well,* Hablet thought with a private little chuckle. *The constant perspiration must make him slippery as an eel.*

'Invading Hythria is rather a convoluted way of going about solving the problem, your majesty.'

'What other choice do I have?'

'That's what I've been thinking about.'

'And?'

'I have a plan.'

'A plan?' the king scoffed, turning his attention back to the report. He cared little for the state of the flax crops in southern Fardohnya, but it wouldn't do to give the eunuch the idea his king was ready to drop everything to listen to the opinion of a mere slave. 'The last time I listened to one of your *plans*, Lecter, it cost me four million gold rivets.'

'Actually, it was only three and a half million,' the eunuch corrected. 'And you've collected easily twice that in tolls in the twenty-odd years since the Widowmaker was paved.'

Hablet couldn't argue with that. He pushed aside the blindingly dull report he'd been reading and leaned back in his gilded chair. 'What's your plan, then?'

'Correct me if I'm mistaken,' the eunuch began with the assurance of a man quite certain he wasn't, 'but you are currently massing our troops at Westbrook and Tambay's Seat, because with the plague ravaging Hythria, you have a legitimate reason to close the borders, and with the borders closed, the Hythrun have no idea about the armies gathering on the other side of the mountains.'

Hablet nodded, wondering what Lecter's point was. It was a perfectly wonderful plan as far as he was concerned. The problem with invading Hythria had always been those damned mountain passes. *That, and the fact it was obvious to anybody with one eye and half a brain what troop movements in the foothills of the Sunrise Mountains meant.*

In the normal course of events, it would have been a futile waste of time, money and manpower trying to attack Hythria over the mountains. There were only two navigable passes. A handful of determined adolescent girls could probably hold off the entire Fardohnyan army, if they set their minds to it. A naval invasion would have been just as futile. Although the Fardohnyans were better shipbuilders than the Hythrun, their neighbour's ports were too well defended to make it worth the trouble.

Hythria's only vulnerable point, really, was her border with Medalon. *If the Medalonians had had the will to move south*, Hablet thought, *with their tightly disciplined Defenders, Hythria would have been overrun a century ago.*

In fact, if Hablet could have found a way to keep the Defenders occupied elsewhere, sailing up the Glass River and crossing into Hythria at Bordertown would have been his first preference. Privately, he doubted if the Medalonians cared if Fardohnya invaded Hythria or not. They would care a *great* deal, however, if he tried to disembark his vast army in Medalon on his way to the conquest. The Sisters of the Blade would probably interpret his uninvited punitive force crossing their southern plains as an act of war.

Fortunately – for Hablet, at least – the plague in Hythria had changed everything. For the first time in decades, Hythria had its attention focused inwards. Hablet had no need to think about ways of getting across Medalon's southern plains, or the reaction of the Sisterhood to his territorial ambitions.

Originally, Hablet had closed the borders out of fear – a desperate attempt to protect Fardohnya from the sickness ripping Hythria apart – only afterwards realising what a marvellous opportunity the gods had handed him. He would not open the borders again until his troops were in place and his army could pour through the passes into Hythria.

The unsuspecting Hythruns, weakened and demoralised by the plague, would be powerless to stop him.

'What's wrong with my plan?' Hablet asked. 'I think it's brilliant.'

'And it *is* brilliant, sire,' Lecter agreed, then he added with a fawning smile, 'However, as your ultimate goal is the annihilation of the Wolfblade family, it might be viewed as . . . containing an element of danger, perhaps.'

'How is it dangerous? We go to war with Hythria. They call up every able-bodied man to fight us. The two nephews of Lernen the Lecher – Daniel and Narmin, isn't it? – rush to the front—'

'Damin and Narvell,' the eunuch corrected.

Hablet shrugged. 'Whatever. The point is, Lecter, the only two living males who can reasonably claim to be of the Wolfblade bloodline, who pose any sort of military threat and who are liable to outlive me, will be at the head of Hythria's army. They'll be dead before we reach the eastern border of Sunrise Province.'

'How can you be certain?'

'Trust me. It's a Hythrun thing. Honouring Zegarnald is more important to a Hythrun than breathing. They'd rather fight than take a willing woman to bed!' He glanced down at where the eunuch's manhood would have been located, had he still been in possession of it, and smiled nastily. 'A sentiment I'm sure you're familiar with.'

Lecter was too smart to rise to the taunt. 'Even so, sire . . .'

'You mark my words, Lecter,' he said dismissively. 'Those boys will rush to the front line to prove their worth to the God of War. And when they do, we'll kill them. What could be more straightforward than that?'

'But what if they *don't* rush to the front?'

Hablet laughed at the very notion. 'A Hythrun male with a heartbeat and two sound legs not going to war when he has the chance? Don't be ridiculous!'

'Even so, your plan to get past Winternest in particular relies on the engineers mastering the secrets of making a cannon work,' the eunuch reminded him, conceding Hablet might be right about the absurd Hythrun love of war. 'That day seems further away than ever.'

Hablet shrugged, unconcerned. 'They're just having a few . . . technical difficulties.'

'*Technical* difficulties, sire? My spies tell me the weapons explode without warning. Even when they do work, it's sporadically at best. And they still haven't found an alloy that won't split after a few shots and kill the men manning the guns.'

'Keep your voice down, Lecter,' the king warned. 'There's

no need to let everybody from here to Westbrook in on our little family problems.'

'The truth is, your majesty, you'd be safer with something a little less . . . overt.'

'I like overt,' Hablet informed his chamberlain.

'But you're using an invasion to cover what are, essentially, a couple of political assassinations.'

'And for a very good reason, Lecter. If I make any attempt on the Hythrun throne that can be traced back to me, people will start to wonder why. Once they start wondering why, somebody may stumble across that rather awkward twelve-hundred-year-old statute you discovered that passes my throne to the Wolfblades if I die without a male heir. Or had you forgotten about that?'

'Of course not, your majesty.' Lecter mopped his brow again, as it beaded with perspiration. 'I just think we could do this a little more subtly than a full-scale invasion.'

'What does that mean?' the king asked suspiciously.

'Your guests,' he began, wringing his damp kerchief as if it pained him to suggest such a thing. 'They are both closely related to the two young men you need to dispose of. Either one of them could get close to Damin Wolfblade or Narvell Hawksword without raising suspicion.'

'You think one of them might undertake the assassinations for me?' the king asked with withering scorn. 'What a brilliant idea! Recruit a member of his own family to assassinate Lernen's nephews! Now why didn't *I* think of that?'

'You mock the notion too hastily, sire,' Lecter objected. 'Without giving it any thought.'

'That's because such a stupid idea doesn't deserve any thought!' Hablet snapped. 'How, in the name of all the Primal Gods, do you propose to make either Luciena Taranger or her husband agree to turn around, go home and assassinate two members of their notoriously close-knit family?'

'By taking their children hostage,' the eunuch replied calmly.

Hablet hesitated for a moment. He hadn't thought of that. Those boys of theirs were noisy little brats, too. The younger one had already ruined the carpet in one of the guest rooms and broken a marble bust, and only yesterday, the older boy had got into a fistfight with two of the king's baseborn children that resulted in several bloody noses and a couple of screeching women demanding he have the eight-year-old Jarvan Taranger thrown into the harbour for daring to hurt their precious babies. Hablet didn't have a problem with the fight. Boys did that sort of thing all the time. It was good for his sons to learn to stand up for themselves. He could have done without the screeching women, though.

Scratching at his beard thoughtfully, Hablet tried to find fault with the notion, certain it couldn't be that easy. 'Wouldn't they just go back to Hythria, gather an army and come back here in force to retrieve the children?'

'What army, sire?' Lecter asked. 'Hythria is in disarray. All the Warlords have retreated to their strongholds, a third of their armies are dead from the plague, another third are dying of it and the remainder are too afraid to step outside for fear of catching it.'

'What about afterwards? Don't you think somebody in Hythria might think to question why a member of the family suddenly upped and killed one or both of their precious heirs? The whole point of this invasion is to arrange the death of the Hythrun heir and his half brother in a way that can't be traced back to me. Don't you think the first thing Xanda Taranger would say when they find him standing over his cousin's body with a dagger in his hand is: "Hablet made me do it"?'

'Experience has taught us that no assassination attempt against a member of the Wolfblade family, successful or otherwise, leaves the assassin alive to implicate the instigators afterwards, your majesty. They are cut down without mercy.'

'A fact both Captain Taranger and his wife are probably well acquainted with, Lecter.' He shook his head. 'No. I can't see it happening. It's a bad idea.'

'Won't you at least let me sound out the possibility?'

'How?'

'I only wish to make a few subtle enquiries, your majesty. Just to establish what the Tarangers value more: their children or their princes.'

Hablet shrugged, not seeing the harm in a few subtle enquiries. 'Just do it quietly, Lecter. I don't want them thinking we're up to something. Luciena spoke of purchasing another five ships at dinner last night, to replace some of their fleet's older vessels.'

The king smiled in remembrance of the conversation, thinking it was at that point he had really started to warm to the young Hythrun woman and her overly protective husband, despite their irritatingly boisterous children. Up until Luciena Taranger had announced her intention to buy Fardohnyan ships, rather than waste money purchasing inferior Hythrun or Karien vessels, Hablet had found her company quite dull. And more than a little offensive. It was wrong for a woman to be involved so blatantly in commerce. Although her husband was clearly an active partner in the business, she seemed to make far more decisions than he would have deemed reasonable, and certainly more than Hablet would have tolerated had she been one of his wives.

But nothing endeared a person to Hablet more than the notion of a tidy profit. The bribes alone, from the various shipbuilders in Talabar wanting to buy a slice of the action, would pay for the upkeep of his harem for the better part of a year. He frowned at the eunuch.

'Five ships, Lecter. That's an awful lot of money we'd be throwing away if she gets offended.'

'I'll be the soul of discretion, sire,' the chamberlain promised with a bow.

In a whisper of expensive silk, he turned and headed for the door. Hablet waited until he had almost reached it before calling after him, 'Was Balkar terribly upset when he learned Adrina had rejected him?'

Lecter hesitated, obviously quashing his irritation, before he turned and smiled at his king. 'He wasn't too put out. He may have even been relieved. He found Adrina's personality a little . . . grating, I think.'

'Did you have to give back the whole bribe?' Hablet asked with a malicious grin.

'A portion of it,' the eunuch agreed cautiously. 'Naturally, there was a fee for my services.'

'That's the fourth one you've had to return recently, isn't it?'

'The fifth, actually.'

'That little girl of mine must be costing you a fortune.'

Lecter Turon smiled unpleasantly. 'Never fear, your majesty. I will continue, with unwavering devotion, to seek suitable husbands for all your daughters. For Adrina, however, I will take special care to find somebody whom I believe will treat her in the manner she truly deserves.'

'I'm quite sure you will,' Hablet agreed, thinking there was nothing more amusing than watching Lecter Turon trying to be polite about the king's beloved daughter when inside the slave was eaten up with anger and humiliation and there was nothing he could do about it.

51

It was days before Alija's headache faded enough for her to think coherently again, even longer before she was able to come to grips with everything she had learned in that one brilliant starburst of jumbled thoughts and memories she had snatched from Ruxton Tirstone's mind at the moment of his death.

Fortunately, with the plague having put an end to all but the most necessary social intercourse, nobody really noticed the High Arrion was locked in her room with the curtains drawn, hiding in the darkness from the pain and the threat of impending insanity that linking with a dying mind had unleashed upon her.

Only Tarkyn Lye was allowed to wait on his mistress, but even the blind *court'esa* knew something was seriously amiss. He didn't question her, for which she was grateful. Alija wouldn't have known what to say, in any case. It would take her months, she guessed, to sort through the haphazard images that bombarded her waking thoughts and haunted her nightmares. Perhaps she would never truly understand them.

What Alija *did* understand, though, and what frightened her to the very core of her being, was that Ruxton's mind had been shielded so effectively that she hadn't even suspected it was there.

And it was her long-forgotten nemesis, Wrayan Lightfinger, who had wielded the spell.

It was more than just the knowledge that Wrayan lived that frightened Alija, when she could bring herself to think about it, several days after Ruxton died. She had always known, somewhere in the back of her mind, that he was still alive. Brakandaran the Halfbreed had told her that much when he visited her the day Nash Hawksword died, almost twenty years ago. That was the day the Halfbreed had destroyed the irreplaceable Harshini scrolls she had removed from the Sorcerers' Collective library.

It was the day Alija had learned the Harshini weren't nearly as extinct as everyone believed.

Strange that she should forget something so important.

Wrayan survived your attempt to cauterise the inside of his skull, and he's none the worse for it, Lord Brakandaran had told her. *He's no concern of yours any longer. Wrayan won't be back to bother your ambitions. The gods have another fate in mind for him.*

Why had she never tried to find Wrayan? Alija wondered. Was it something Brakandaran had done to her? Had he placed some magical inhibition on her curiosity that prevented her from remembering the Harshini still survived? Or even that she had been visited by the Halfbreed? Why had she never tried tracking the young man down?

Only Wrayan wouldn't be a young man any longer, she realised. *He would be in his forties by now.*

If Wrayan Lightfinger had shielded Ruxton Tirstone's mind, she reasoned through the pounding pulse that filled her aching head, he must have done it because Ruxton knew something he didn't want Alija to know. And it could *only* have been there to prevent her learning his secrets. There was no other person alive with the ability to read minds that she knew of . . . although for some disturbing reason, young Rorin Mariner's face suddenly loomed large in her mind.

She pushed the thought away, trying to concentrate on what she knew to be fact. Ruxton's mind had been shielded. Wrayan had done it.

Why?

To protect something, obviously. Or someone.

Logically, the answer to that was Marla Wolfblade. There was simply no other person in the world who impacted so critically on both Alija's world and Ruxton's.

But was the shield there to hide something specific? Or was it there as a general precaution?

Alija tried to recall that glassy smooth surface she had assumed was the outer limits of Ruxton's dying mind and realised how familiar that feeling was. She had seen it before; so many times, she assumed it was normal. *How many other minds around me are shielded from my touch?*

Marla's mind?

It would almost have to be, she decided, although how the princess had managed to locate Wrayan and convince him to perform such a service for her remained a mystery, as did the former apprentice's willingness to undertake the job. And where had he learned such skill? The young man who had placed the pretty lights in Tarkyn's mind had left an unavoidable trail a mile wide for her to follow the last time he'd challenged her. This shield had been so subtle, so seamless, that she would still be ignorant of its existence had she not been there at the moment of Ruxton's death.

Had the Harshini shown him how? The Halfbreed, perhaps?

And even more puzzling, if Wrayan Lightfinger was so skilled, so powerful now, where was he? Why had he never come back to the Sorcerers' Collective to challenge Alija? Or even to seek vengeance for what she'd done to him? In Wrayan's place, that was the first thing Alija would have done.

Holding her head in her hands against the agony, Alija

cursed the darkness loudly, bringing Tarkyn to her side to ask if there was something wrong. She pushed him away, certain she was close to working this out and not wanting the distraction of another human voice to break her train of thought.

How many more? That wretched dwarf Marla keeps as a pet? Almost certainly. There was Corian Burl at the palace, the seneschal whose thoughts had never seemed to dwell on anything more important than the weather. Marla's children, whom she'd always assumed were simply shallow creatures with no real ambition, because whenever she brushed their minds there was nothing there for her to see – *Damin, Kalan, Narvell, the Tirstone brothers . . .*

The list seemed endless. All of them shielded from her sight. All of them able to think what they liked; hide whatever secrets they chose; and for years now, she'd been none the wiser.

And Luciena. Of course.

The reason for the failure of her plan, all those years ago, to use Luciena as an assassin suddenly became clear. The Mariner girl had attacked Damin and the whole thing had been covered up to prevent Alija learning the greater secret – that Wrayan Lightfinger lived and Marla Wolfblade had known all along about Alija's plans to kill her son and take the throne with Nash Hawksword by her side. Wrayan had simply healed the girl's mind and let Alija think her attack had failed, just because Marla was willing to bide her time until Damin reached his majority.

Physical pain aside, the realisation severely shook Alija's faith in her own ability. The knowledge that for more than twenty-five years she had been operating under the false assumption that Marla knew nothing of her activities or her ambitions, that the princess's mind and the minds of those around her were simply open books laid out for Alija to peruse at her leisure, was completely wrong.

They had known, all of them, that they were vulnerable to me.

And they had taken precautions.

Alija was forced to reconsider everything she believed about the princess. All these years she had thought Marla little more than a misguided, easily deluded woman over-burdened with a sense of duty. She had convinced herself that Marla felt compelled to compensate for her brother's inadequacies by aiding him in the execution of his royal duties. All these years, Alija thought Marla simply a tool in the hands of wiser, more astute advisors. How wrong must that assessment be?

Suppose it is actually Marla leading the way? Suppose she's the one responsible for keeping Hythria together these past twenty-odd years?

Even more shocking was the notion that Marla might be aware of some of Alija's more treasonous activities, particularly among the Patriots.

But how *much* did she know? And how long had she known it? Why was she biding her time? Was she waiting for the opportune moment to take her vengeance?

Was Marla aware who the spies in her household were? Had she been feeding Alija nothing but a carefully orchestrated litany of lies and misdirection all this time?

Marla's barefaced, brazen gall was staggering. The princess had placed her own daughter in the Sorcerers' Collective, under Alija's care. It didn't seem nearly so foolish now, in hindsight. There was nothing Alija could have done to harm her, because Kalan was protected by forces beyond the High Arrion's comprehension.

When had the Wolfblades become so favoured by the gods?

Rorin's face pushed its way forward into her conscious-ness again. This time she stopped to consider why. Luciena's allegedly talented cousin, who'd proved to be such a disap-pointment. There was something elusive yet significant in

485

Ruxton's memories about that young man. Something connected with Wrayan and, improbably, the Harshini themselves.

Was that Rorin's secret? Was the faint hint of talent she could feel in him just an illusion? In reality, did he wield far more power than Alija had been able to detect?

Was he like Wrayan, perhaps? Nash Hawksword had told her of Kagan Palenovar's suspicion that Wrayan was a descendent of one of the many mixed-blood relationships the Harshini were so careless of back in the days of old; back before the Sisters of the Blade destroyed them all.

Is that why Marla insisted the boy study with Kalan? Because he was a *real* magician? Someone capable of protecting Marla's precious daughter from Alija's power? The haphazard memories tormented Alija, tantalisingly close to providing answers to everything she wished to know, yet so insubstantial, it was like trying to net a fog.

And her head felt as if it had been cleaved in two.

She had to figure this out – use reason where the gaps in a dying man's memory failed her. She *had* to know. Before she took another step. Before she made another move, Alija had to know how much Marla knew.

And really, when all was said and done, there was only one sure way to find out.

She forced her eyes open and turned to look at Tarkyn Lye in the dim light. The blind *court'esa* kept a vigil over his mistress, with a blue scarf tied across his mouth and nose to filter out the evil vapours of death. He must have feared her delirium was the onset of the plague. But he had stayed with her through her long, tortured days and nights of near madness, wiped her brow with a cool compress, and kept her covered when the sweat turned to chills. She appreciated his dedication, but it wasn't necessary.

There were other ways for Tarkyn Lye to prove his loyalty to her.

'What day is it?' Her voice was dry and cracked, her throat parched.

'It's the evening of Fourthday, my lady,' the *court'esa* informed her, rising to his feet. 'You've been delirious for six days now.'

'Who knows that I've been ill?'

'Nobody, my lady,' he assured her, silently counting the steps to her bedside. With unerring certainty, the blind man picked up the water jug by her bed and filled her cup, listening to the sound of the liquid to tell when the cup was nearing full. 'I told everyone you had taken to your room to mourn the late husband of your dear cousin, Princess Marla.'

Alija smiled weakly and accepted the cup, glad of the chance to quench her thirst, even if it was only water. She felt like she needed something much stronger. 'That was clever.'

Tarkyn bowed gracefully. 'I live only to serve, my lady.'

'Then serve me, Tarkyn.'

'How?'

'Who is the one person who might know the inner workings of Princess Marla's devious little mind?'

'Her pet dwarf,' Tarkyn answered without hesitation. 'The Fool. Elezaar.'

'I want him.'

'My *lady*?' he asked, a little alarmed by her request.

'Bring me Elezaar, Tarkyn Lye,' Alija ordered. 'I don't care how you do it or what it costs. Bring him to me. Just be sure he is alive and able to talk. And Marla mustn't know that I have him.'

'It won't be easy, my lady. With the plague abroad, I doubt he'd be allowed out of the house.'

'But you will find a way to get him out, Tarkyn. And you will bring him to me.'

The *court'esa* seemed reluctant to do her bidding. 'My lady, even if you were to torture the dwarf, I doubt you would get much useful information from him. He is truly dedicated to his mistress.'

'*I* will make him talk,' she said confidently, to herself as much as Tarkyn. Then sensing his scepticism, she smiled and added, 'You see, Tarkyn, I have the only thing in this world Elezaar the Fool cares about more than Marla Wolfblade.'

'What's that, my lady?'

'I have Crysander,' she said. 'His brother.'

52

Mahkas Damaran, Regent of Krakandar, returned from Walsark well pleased with the condition of the estate and the responsible manner in which his nephew was caring for the borough. Travin Taranger would be thirty next year, old enough to assume the title of his late father, the Earl of Walsark, and to officially take over the estate. The crops were healthy, the cattle fat, the lambs plump and numerous, and a new kiln was being added to the porcelain works in the town, which – Travin had boasted proudly – meant more jobs for the townsfolk who created the porcelain and worked in the pits, digging out the unique white clay that made the town's porcelain so valuable.

Something of an anomaly in a country where slaves were the norm, the Walsark porcelain works were almost entirely manned by freeborn workers and the town attracted craftsmen from all over the country. It made the porcelain expensive, but it was highly prized and Walsark's prosperity would have a flow-on effect to her neighbouring boroughs, too, Mahkas thought with satisfaction. The quartz, feldspar and mica needed to blend with the white clay – the elements that differentiated Walsark porcelain from mere pottery – were all imported from the surrounding boroughs. Their kiln output would be doubled in a year or two, Travin estimated, and the much sought-after Walsark porcelain could be made in sufficient quantities to consider exporting to Fardohnya or Medalon. Perhaps even Karien. He thought it unlikely they would bother with any markets beyond the continent. Sea voyages and porcelain were not happy travelling companions and, by all accounts, the nations across the vast reaches of the Dregian Ocean weren't civilised enough to appreciate fine porcelain anyway.

Mahkas was very happy with everything he'd seen in Walsark. It was important to him that all went well with Travin. He wanted the world – and specifically Marla – to know what a good job he'd done with the boy. He'd been like a father to Travin and his younger brother, Xanda, just as he'd been to Damin. It was important people recognised that. It was important that people looked at his nephews, smiled and remarked how lucky they were to have an uncle like Mahkas Damaran.

It helped assuage the guilt a little for having been responsible for their parents' deaths.

Not that he *really* blamed himself. Darilyn was a wicked, self-centred, shallow creature with no real appreciation of the sacrifices she must make to raise her boys. And Laran? Well, Damin's father had been an ungrateful, power-hungry fool, Mahkas had long ago convinced himself. Letting him die at the hands of a Medalonian Defender was the kindest thing he could have done for his nephew. At least Damin had grown up with some sort of stability and moral guidance in his life.

What sort of role model for a future High Prince was a man who would risk a civil war to manipulate the succession? Mahkas often asked himself, forgetting his own ready participation in the same venture. *What sort of man would Damin have grown into with Laran's distant affection the only warmth the boy might ever have known?*

I did Damin a favour, Mahkas reminded himself, whenever he started feeling guilty about it. He would rub at the sore spot on his arm and say it to himself over and over. *I did them a favour. I did them a favour. I did them a favour.*

'Leave it be!' Bylinda told him impatiently.

Mahkas's head jerked up and he realised he was doing it again – rubbing the tiny scar on his right arm as the carriage trundled along the road towards Krakandar City. He snatched his hand away and pulled his cloak a little closer around him. 'It's getting warmer, don't you think?'

'Warmer?' Bylinda asked, smiling at him as if she could tell he was simply making conversation to draw attention away from his obsessive worrying at that one little spot on his arm. 'Compared to what?'

'Compared to the last few days. I think perhaps spring is on the way.'

'I hadn't really noticed.'

Mahkas looked out of the carriage window at the brown fields rolling past, divided by tall green hedgerows. There were even a few hopeful vineyards along the Walsark road, roaming over the lower slopes in pleasantly symmetrical lines. They were quite pretty, too, with a native Krakandar rosebush planted at the end of each row. It was for more than just aesthetics that the roses grew alongside the vines. Not nearly as hardy as their neighbours, the roses would always wilt first, warning the vintners there was trouble with the vines.

'Do you think Leila and Damin will have had time to get to know each other a little better while we were gone?' he asked, as casually as he could manage.

'I don't know,' his wife shrugged. To her credit, Bylinda made no comment about it being the only thing on his mind for the past four days. Then she ruined it by adding, 'You won't be too disappointed if you get home and we don't catch them in bed together, will you?'

'I wish you wouldn't joke about this, Bylinda.'

'I wish you wouldn't push them so hard. If Damin is

meant to marry Leila, it will happen whether they love each other or not. For that matter, if Marla wants them to marry, it won't matter if they despise each other. But there's no point hoping they'll fall in love, Mahkas. Marla won't let that sway her decision.'

'It shouldn't *be* her decision. I'm Damin's uncle. His regent.'

'But the High Prince is *also* his uncle, and his legally adopted father, as well. It will be his decision about who Damin marries.'

'Which means it will be Marla's,' Mahkas complained.

'Yes, which means it will be Marla's.'

Mahkas shook his head, trying to deny the doubt that kept creeping up like a shadow on his dreams. 'Damin seemed quite keen for Leila's company the day he got home. He said he wanted to talk with her. In private.'

'That's a good sign then,' Bylinda agreed, more to keep him happy, he suspected, than any real belief that Damin's suggestion he speak with Leila alone was a sign of much deeper affection.

'Should I let him know I don't mind, do you think?'

Bylinda looked at him, puzzled. 'That you don't mind what?'

'Well, you said it yourself. Damin may be afraid of my reaction if I were to catch them in bed together. And you know how cautious Marla is. She's probably filled his head with all sorts of tales of woe about the consequences of an affair with a woman of his own class. Do you think I should take him aside, perhaps, and let him know – subtly, of course – that, in light of their pending engagement, if he wants to . . . how should I say this? . . . *taste the fruit before he buys it . . .* that I wouldn't mind?'

Bylinda stared at her husband in shock. 'You would whore your own daughter for the sake of your ambition?'

Mahkas was appalled that she should misunderstand him

492

so deliberately. 'How dare you even suggest such a thing? I would never do anything to harm Leila. Or degrade her. I am simply saying that I understand what it is to be young and in love and that I want my nephew to know I won't be angered if he feels the need to express his affection for Leila in a more . . . intimate way, before the betrothal is formalised.'

'You want to force Marla's hand, is what you really mean,' she accused. Bylinda turned her head away to look out of the carriage window for a moment, as if she was too angry to speak of it. When she turned to him again, her eyes were cold and she stared at him as if he were a complete stranger. 'Do you hear yourself, Mahkas? Do you know what your ambition is doing to your only child?'

'My ambition is for all of us.'

'Your ambition is for *you*, Mahkas Damaran, nobody else.' She wiped away an angry tear before she continued in a cold voice that he didn't think his wife capable of. 'And you may tell your nephew anything you want. But let him know that if *I* catch him laying a finger on my daughter without the benefit of a formal betrothal, I'll have him castrated, because I know for certain she doesn't love or want him, so any attempt by Damin to act on your disgusting suggestion would be rape.'

Mahkas was shocked beyond belief by his wife's defiance. And alarmed by her words. 'What do you mean that you know for *certain* Leila doesn't love Damin?'

But Bylinda shook her head and refused to answer him, turning to stare at the countryside as it rolled by.

She remained like that for hours, staring out of the window in stony, hostile silence, until the carriage came to a halt outside the walls of Krakandar and Mahkas learned that in his absence, his beloved nephew – the young man he was willing to give his only daughter to without the benefit of so much as a promise of a betrothal – had sealed his own city against him.

'What in the name of all the *gods* do you think you're doing?' Mahkas demanded of Damin when he was finally able to force his way into the city by threatening to have every man on the gate hanged for treason. It had taken him the better part of three hours until they had finally managed to get through to the palace. His fury was a palpable, living thing.

To rub salt into the wound, Damin appeared to have set up an informal council of war in Mahkas's own study. When he burst in, demanding an explanation, it was to find Damin, Almodavar, Kalan and Rorin Mariner poring over a map of the city, making plans for the gods alone knew what other mischief.

Damin looked up and frowned when he saw Mahkas, but instead of greeting his uncle or offering any sort of excuse for his actions, he turned to Almodavar. 'We've got a discipline problem if your Raiders let people through the gate the first time someone raises their voice at them. You'd better fix that.'

To Mahkas's astonishment, Almodavar took the criticism seriously and nodded in agreement with the young prince. 'I'll see it doesn't happen again.'

'Damin, I demand to know what is going on! The guards on the gate refused to let me in when I arrived. They claim you've sealed the city!'

'Not very effectively,' Damin pointed out, with a sudden grin. 'Seeing as how you're standing here telling me off about it.'

'It's because of the plague, Uncle Mahkas,' Kalan explained, giving her brother a look that spoke volumes. 'It's reached Natalandar already. And Grosburn. We'll be next if we don't take precautions.'

'What precautions?' he scoffed. 'There's nothing you can do against the plague.'

'Actually, that's not entirely true, my lord,' Rorin informed him. 'The Harshini knew what caused it, which is why the plague was never a problem when they were among us. We just need to—'

'The Harshini?' Mahkas cut in sceptically, not fooled by the young man's black sorcerer's robes. He was still a peasant in Mahkas's mind and all the trappings of civility in the world wouldn't change that. 'What would you know about the Harshini, boy?'

'More than you or I know,' Damin said, coming to Rorin's defence in the same way he defended Starros every chance he got. Marla had made a grave mistake in Mahkas's opinion, allowing her son to mix with commoners so readily. The young prince was quite inappropriately familiar with his lowborn companions and gave their opinions much more weight than they deserved. 'And I, for one, believe him. Rorin says it's all to do with keeping the rat population down.'

'Not just rats,' Kalan corrected. 'Cats. Dogs. Anything with fur. The plague is carried by fleas. If we can keep the city clean, if we can clean out all the places rats like to congregate, and have a way of isolating any cases that do occur, we might be able to stop it devastating the whole city.'

'But we have to do it *now*,' Damin emphasised. 'Before the weather really warms up and the fleas start to breed again.'

'Even if I agreed with this, you're asking the impossible!' Mahkas objected. 'You can't get rid of all the rats in the city. The grain store alone probably feeds ten thousand of them.'

'I know. So I've put out a bounty on them,' Damin announced. 'One copper rivet for every dead rat. Raek Harlen is already down in the city with a troop of Raiders, organising a way to dispose of the bodies. We thought the glassworks were probably the best place. They have the biggest furnaces in the city, at any rate.'

'You can't be serious! Who is going to pay for this?'

'It's not as if we can't afford it, Uncle Mahkas,' Kalan said, looking a little wounded that he wasn't applauding their foresight. 'And I'd be happy to bankrupt Krakandar if it means we don't die of the plague.'

'That's all right for you to say, young lady,' he snapped, 'but—' Mahkas stopped abruptly. The four of them – Damin, Almodavar, Kalan and Rorin – were staring at him as if he was completely ignorant of the danger, with no concept or ability to deal with this threat to his city. *How dare they think that? Krakandar has never had a better lord than Mahkas Damaran.* But it was clear rage would accomplish nothing here. He consciously bit back his anger, forcing himself to breathe deeply.

'Damin,' he said, in the calmest tone he could manage, 'you have no authority to order the city sealed. Or any of the other actions you've set in motion in my absence. However, I appreciate that you and Kalan were trying to do the right thing, so I'll overlook your disrespect and treat it as merely youthful enthusiasm.'

Damin looked at him oddly, and for a dreadful moment, Mahkas thought he actually meant to defy him.

'Youthful *enthusiasm*?' the young man repeated, as if he couldn't quite believe his ears.

Mahkas ignored the question. 'You can take me through your plans and I'll see if they have any merit, and implement them if they prove sound. I'm sure you've got some excellent suggestions about how to manage this dreadful situation and I'll be happy for you to assist me in dealing with it, if that is what you want.'

He waited, not sure what he was expecting Damin to do. This was the first time Damin had ever tried to exert any kind of authority in Krakandar and Mahkas wasn't sure what would happen if he forced the issue. Whether he was legally old enough to rule or not, Damin was Krakandar's prince. *Hell, they turned out in droves just to welcome him back to the city.* If Damin wanted to dig his heels in, Mahkas faced a much greater crisis than simply finding the city sealed in his absence.

But the young prince smiled and stepped back from the table. 'We were just trying to help, Uncle.'

Mahkas's knees almost gave way with relief. 'I know. And I do appreciate your efforts. You might have warned the gate about letting me back in when I arrived, however. It wouldn't have been quite such a shock.'

Damin grinned, suddenly back to the rakish young man Mahkas remembered. 'I promise, the next time I seal the city with you on the outside, Uncle Mahkas, I'll do it much more effectively.'

Mahkas laughed politely, not sure if he liked the way Damin had phrased that, but then he dismissed his own foolishness and glanced around the room. 'Is Leila not here helping you take over my city?'

'She's with Tejay Lionsclaw in the nursery, I think,' Kalan informed him.

'Lady Lionsclaw is here?'

'She and her children arrived the same day you left for Walsark, my lord,' Almodavar said. 'It was Lady Lionsclaw who brought the news of the spreading plague.'

'Then I'd best speak to her myself. Would you fetch her for me, please, Kalan?'

It was an unsubtle dismissal and his niece knew it. She nudged Rorin and the two of them left the room together. Almodavar also took the hint, pleaded other duties to attend to, and departed with a sharp salute, first to Damin and then – almost as an afterthought – to Mahkas.

Once they were alone, Mahkas felt a little easier. 'You

should be careful, Damin. Actions like the ones you took in my absence might be misconstrued.'

'I'm sorry. I didn't think.'

Mahkas nodded with relief. 'I know. Just think it through a little more carefully the next time, eh? Besides, I don't know how you found the time to organise any of this.' *You should have been with Leila*, he added silently, despairing to think Damin had found the time to plan the city's defence against the plague when he should have been wooing his future bride.

'What else is there to do?' the young man asked with a frown. 'Almodavar says you flatly refuse to let me accompany any of the raiding parties into Medalon.'

'Your father was killed while on a raiding party into Medalon.'

'It doesn't automatically follow that I will be, Uncle.'

'No,' he agreed. 'But it does mean your mother is rather touchy on the subject. I thought it would be better if we just didn't go there.'

Damin's eyes lit up mischievously. 'But if I'm on a raiding party into Medalon, I won't be here trying to take over your city. And I'd be much safer from the plague out there in the wilderness. It would be good practice for me. And if Almodavar or Raek Harlen came along to keep an eye on me, I could get in some much needed command experience. And it would be—'

'All right!' Mahkas cried, throwing his hands up to halt Damin's undoubtedly endless list of justifications. 'I'll think about it!'

He grinned happily. 'That's all I ask, Uncle Mahkas.'

'And *while* I'm thinking about it, you must do me a favour.'

'Name it.'

'Spend some time with your cousin, would you? She's missed you desperately while you've been gone.' He hesitated,

498

suffering a moment of guilt as he recalled Bylinda's harsh words in the carriage this morning about whoring his daughter for the sake of his ambition – and then he pushed his wife's foolish fears aside and added, 'The slaveways don't get the same traffic they used to when you were children.'

Damin stared at him in confusion. 'The slaveways?'

'You're only young once, Damin. Make the most of it.'

He was a bright boy. It took very little time for Damin to work out exactly what Mahkas was implying.

'You wouldn't mind?' he asked, as if making absolutely certain he understood.

'I already think of you as the son I never had, Damin.'

He was hoping, of course, that Damin would respond in kind and assure Mahkas that he was the father he'd never had, but the young prince simply nodded his understanding, looked at Mahkas oddly for a moment, and then, as if he had a sudden urge to be elsewhere, took his leave as quickly as he was able.

Mahkas smiled as the door closed behind Damin, thinking Bylinda was completely wrong. Damin was obviously so thrilled with his suggestion that he couldn't wait to find Leila and tell her there was nothing standing in the way of them finding happiness in each other's arms, and that they wouldn't have to wait for the betrothal to consummate their union.

Filled with a deep sense of satisfaction, he walked around the desk and glanced down at the map of the city sewers Damin and the others had been examining, without really seeing it. All Mahkas could think of was the brilliant future that lay ahead for his family. *Once Damin has come of age, and Lernen is dead, our daughter is married to the High Prince, and our own grandson the heir to the throne . . . then Bylinda will see things differently.* Leila would probably be a little more grateful, too, for all his efforts on her behalf.

He only hoped Leila had the sense to ignore the lessons

about taking precautions against an unwanted pregnancy she would have received from both her mother and her *court'esa*. Mahkas frowned when he caught himself thinking that. He was no better than all the others, he realised, recalling his greatest fear when Damin had left Krakandar to be fostered was that some minor lord's daughter would find her way into his nephew's bed, get herself knocked up and force Marla into agreeing to a totally inappropriate union. There was nothing inappropriate about Leila, he consoled himself. It was just that time was against him. Leila wasn't getting any younger. None of them was. He was doing this for the good of Hythria, he reminded himself.

And if it meant arranging to have his own daughter impregnated with a bastard sired by the next High Prince of Hythria to force Marla into making the right decision about her son's future, that was a sacrifice Mahkas was more than willing to make.

53

Ruxton Tirstone's death hit Marla harder than she had expected. Although she had never loved any man the way she once burned for Nashan Hawksword, sixteen years of marriage couldn't fail to leave its mark on her. Her grief was real, even if it was more for the loss of a companion than a lover.

Ruxton had been a good man – intelligent, reliable, trustworthy and enjoyable company. As marriages went, he was probably the best husband a woman in Marla's position could hope for. He never interfered in her affairs and expected her never to interfere in his. They had raised their children together in remarkable harmony and lived to see all of them grow into young men and women they could be proud of. It wasn't a bad tally, when all was said and done.

As usual, grief drove Marla into a bout of ruthless practicality. A public funeral was out of the question in these trying times, so they had to settle for a small family gathering in her townhouse, which Marla organised with her usual efficiency, and which even Lernen agreed to attend, in honour of his common-born brother-in-law. With Travin and Damin safe in Krakandar Province, Kalan missing in northern Pentamor somewhere with Rorin, Luciena and Xanda in

Fardohnya, Ruxton's daughter, Rielle, up north at Dylan Pass with her husband and children, and Adham wandering about Medalon somewhere, it was left to just Rodja and Marla to bid farewell to Ruxton.

Rodja was twenty-eight now, and had been married to a young woman named Selena Sorenn for the past four years. Selena was the daughter of Ruxton's main rival in the spice trade – a thin, bitter, disagreeable old man, who, after years of fighting Ruxton at every turn, had finally succumbed to the inevitable and allowed his only daughter to marry the son of his worst enemy. By contrast, Selena was like a ray of sunshine everywhere she went, her cheerful demeanour barely even dented by the devastation of the plague.

It never ceased to amaze Marla that old man Sorenn had fathered such a child, although the young woman's eternal optimism could be wearing at times. They had two children, both girls, on whom Rodja doted, and Selena was pregnant already with a third. Despite the fact Selena had effectively been traded by her father for spice route concessions from Ruxton, she and Rodja seemed happy enough together. With both their fathers now taken by the plague, however, they would inherit an effective monopoly on the spice trade, which Marla scolded herself for even thinking about at a time like this.

Ruxton deserved to be mourned as a good man and a loving father, not tallied and calculated for his final monetary worth. Then she smiled thinly and thought Ruxton would probably have appreciated the irony and that a monopoly on the spice trade was just the way he'd like to be remembered.

Adham Tirstone, like his brother Rodja, had followed his father into the family business, but it was proving much harder to make marital arrangements for the younger Tirstone boy. Rodja was the more business-minded of the brothers; the one with a head for figures and his father's ability to negotiate his way into or out of anything he pleased. Adham, on the other hand, was far more reckless and not the least bit interested in settling down. Ruxton had jokingly blamed Almodavar for Adham's restlessness, claiming that in the process of training the boys to defend themselves, the Krakandar Raider had filled his younger son's head with wild notions of battle and glory in honour of Zegarnald, the God of War. Marla didn't think Ruxton was that far off the mark, considering her own sons suffered the same inexplicable male need to constantly prove themselves by putting their lives in danger. Adham spent much of his time working with the caravans, arranging their protection from bandits both in Hythria and across the border into Fardohnya, and had, on more than one occasion, arrived back in Greenharbour proudly bearing the scars of a serious confrontation with them.

Marla fretted about Adham sometimes, trying to tell herself he was just young and would settle down when he got older, but he was twenty-six and showed no sign of it yet. He was a bad influence on Damin, too, she tried to convince herself, knowing full well it was, and always had been, Damin who instigated most of the trouble the boys had got into when they were children. When Adham was in town, the stepbrothers were constant companions and they seemed able to find more mischief in one week together than either of them could manage in a year alone.

Marla sighed as she thought about them, staring at her reflection in the mirror as she unpinned her white mourning veil. It seemed to be the only colour she wore these days. The funeral was done, Ruxton laid to rest in a temporary grave Marla had arranged to have dug in the small garden, until it was safe to relocate his remains to a more permanent home once the plague had run its course. There were still thousands of bodies out there in the city, she knew, not nearly as fortunate as Ruxton, and if they didn't do

503

something about them soon the city would never be free of this miserable disease.

But that was a problem for later. She was tired and still had to host a dinner for the family this evening and she certainly didn't feel like eating. But she owed it to Rodja and Selena. And to Ruxton's memory.

She was still sitting at her dressing table when Elezaar tapped her on the shoulder some time later, making her jump with fright.

'I'm sorry, your highness,' the dwarf said. 'But I did knock.'

'I was just daydreaming,' she shrugged, wondering how long she had been sitting there, staring into space. It was almost dark outside, she noted, the last traces of sunset fading into the velvet darkness of night.

'You look tired,' Elezaar told her with concern, bringing the flickering silver candlestick he was holding closer to the dressing table. 'You should rest.'

'We're all tired, Elezaar. It never seems to end.'

'I saw you speaking to Corian Burl after the funeral. Were you able to solve your other little problem?'

She nodded. Marla's 'other little problem' was much more potentially dangerous than the mere death of her fourth husband. She'd managed, with great difficulty and over a period of years, to finally convince the Denikans to send an envoy to meet with Hythria's High Prince in order to secure a treaty with the vast southern nation. The majority of Hythria's population considered the distant southerners across the Dregian Ocean as nothing but ignorant barbarians, aided by the ridiculous stories spread about by visitors to their country – her third husband included. But if Jarvan Mariner had taught Marla anything in the two short years they'd been married, it was not to underestimate the Denikans. Marla was determined to see such a treaty in place before Damin took the throne.

Unfortunately, the arrival of the Denikan envoy (their crown prince, no less) had coincided with the outbreak of the plague and the unfortunate belief it was the Denikans who had brought the disease to Hythria. Unable to get the young man on a ship out of the plague-cursed port, Marla had sent him to Sunrise Province masquerading as a *court'esa*, in the guise of a gift to Tejay Lionsclaw, Rogan Bearbow's daughter and Chaine Lionsclaw's daughter-in-law. Fully aware of who the young man really was, Chaine had promised to arrange to get the Denikan prince over the border and onto a ship for home out of Fardohnya. The relief Marla felt, now that Prince Lunar Shadow Kraig of the House of the Rising Moon was out of the city and out of danger of being stoned for the crime of being Denikan, she was able to breathe much easier. She glanced at the dwarf, and noticed he was holding a small scroll in his other hand. The type favoured by Ruxton's spies.

'What do you have there?'

'It's from Damin in Krakandar.'

Marla snatched the scroll from him and broke the seal anxiously, all thoughts of Denika and her prince forgotten. She had made Damin promise to write to her every day. Naturally, he'd done nothing of the kind. This was the first communication she'd had from him since he'd left the city. She held it closer to the light Elezaar was holding, squinting a little in the gloom.

Elezaar used his own candle to light the lamp on the dresser for her, so she turned towards it and examined the letter in the brighter light. It was dated a little over ten days ago, which meant it must have been delivered by a speeded courier – a rider with the ability to change horses at almost every stop, who would then pass on the scroll to another courier as soon as he crossed the border into the next province. Using speeded couriers, it was possible to get a letter from Greenharbour in the south to Krakandar, eight hundred miles to the north, in a little over six days. But they were expensive and Marla was surprised they were still running, with the plague spreading the way it was.

Mother, the letter began, written in Damin's own hand. *I trust this finds you and the rest of the family well – an optimistic hope, under the circumstances, but one I wish for nonetheless.*

'*We arrived in Krakandar without mishap,*' Marla read aloud, realising that Elezaar was also bursting from curiosity to know what was in the letter. '*I stumbled across Kalan and Rorin on my way through Nalinbar and brought them back with me, so you'll be relieved to know we are safe and sound and being coddled to death by Mahkas and Bylinda as if we were all still ten years old. The plague has not reached here yet, although it's spread as far as Pentamor and Izcomdar. Rogan Bearbow has fallen victim to it, and Tejay Lionsclaw and her children have taken refuge here with us until it's safe for her to return home.*'

The relief Marla felt was indescribable. All her efforts to locate Kalan since the plague took hold had proved fruitless. 'Thank the gods, Kalan and Rorin are safe.'

'And that they had the wit to head for Krakandar and not attempt to return here,' Elezaar added, almost as relieved as his mistress. 'It's not good news about the Warlord of Izcomdar, though.'

'*I assume you've heard by now,*' Marla continued reading, '*that Chaine is dead (another victim of the Widowmaker) and that Terin Lionsclaw is now Warlord of Sunrise? I wish I could say the idea makes me happy, but I fear something is amiss in the west and if not for this damn plague, I would return to Sunrise with Tejay to find out what it is. I have no proof of this, mind you, it's a gut feeling with no basis in fact, and Tejay insists all is well, but how much of that is truth and how much is simple loyalty to her husband, I cannot guess.*

'*It is moot at present, in any case. I'm not in a position to go anywhere. We have sealed the city against refugees bringing the plague in from the southern provinces and have set about purging the city of any likely carriers of the disease.'*

'Damin sounds as if he's learned a thing or two from me, after all, your highness,' Elezaar remarked, with a hint of paternal pride. Marla thought the dwarf's attitude quite amusing, given he had been appalled by the notion of becoming Damin's tutor at one time, and now he was obviously patting himself on the back for it. 'Do you think he's right to be concerned about Sunrise?'

Marla shrugged, wondering much the same. 'I don't know, Elezaar. Unfortunately, even if he is, I'm in no better position to investigate the matter at present than he is. I hope Chaine was able to get the Denikans across the border before he died, though.' She returned her attention to the letter and read on.

'On a slightly more hopeful note, Rorin says to have someone check the library. According to him, the Harshini believed the disease to be transmitted by fleas, and that clearing the city of all possible breeding grounds before they start to breed again in the warmer weather is the only way to control it. He's certain there are records of prior outbreaks still in the archives somewhere, which may be of some help to you. Perhaps Bruno Sanval will know where to look. Doesn't he know the contents of the Sorcerers' Collective library down to the last dead cockroach? Anyway, with Wrayan's help, we've enlisted the cooperation of every person here in the city, noble and commoner alike, even in the Beggars' Quarter. There's not a rat safe from capture and death in Krakandar. I wish I could claim this sterling effort is being driven by loyalty to their city, but I suspect fear of a painful death and the rat bounty, rather than civic pride, is their motivation. Still, as Elezaar would say, ask help only from those in whose best interest it lies to aid you. I think that's Rule Number Twenty-five, isn't it? Or is it Twenty-four, perhaps? Don't tell him I can't remember. I'll never hear the end of it.'

Marla glanced at the dwarf and smiled. 'Perhaps your teaching wasn't as thorough as you think, Elezaar. He's quoting Rule Number Twenty-three, as I recall.'

'He's applying the rules, madam. I think, given your son's somewhat mercurial nature, in the long run that may prove more useful than him remembering the order in which they're written.'

'Do you think Rorin is right about the rats?'

'He'd know, my lady, if anybody would.'

'I'll speak to Bruno then,' she said. 'If we could get this damned thing under control before the really hot weather hits us . . .'

'It's probably worth looking into.'

She nodded, deciding to pursue the matter tomorrow, and then returned to the letter, frowning as she read the next paragraph.

'Lastly, Mother,' the letter continued, *'I have a favour to ask – no, demand – of you. Will you please write to Mahkas and make it clear, in no uncertain terms, that you will never permit me to marry Leila? I know you've had your reasons for not putting an end to his speculation in the past, but the situation here is beyond awkward. It is untenable. Mahkas is throwing her at me like a cheap* court'esa *and it's tearing Leila to pieces, because, unlike her father, she can see his hopeless ambition for what it is. She doesn't love me and doesn't want me, nor I her, but I am fond enough of my cousin to wish her every chance at happiness. I know you care about Leila, too, so if you won't do it for me, do it for her, otherwise I will be forced to tell Mahkas myself, and we both know I won't do it nearly as tactfully as you will.*

'He finishes off the letter with *Please give my respects to Ruxton, and the boys, and tell Elezaar I beat Almodavar – again – although the old fossil insists he let me win. Damin.* And there's a postscript,' she noted, with a shake of her head. *'By the way, Mother, would it be terribly difficult to*

make Starros the lord of something when he finishes his appren-
ticeship with Orleon? With all these people dropping like flies
from the plague, there must be a vacancy somewhere?'

'Actually, that last suggestion about Starros may not be
a bad idea,' the dwarf said.

'It's his first one that bothers me. Should I do as he asks,
do you think?'

'Tell Lord Damaran there's no chance you'll allow his
daughter to marry Damin? You should have done it years
ago, your highness.'

'If I do it now, there will be speculation that I have
chosen a bride for my son.'

'If you do it now,' Elezaar countered, 'most people are
so concerned with the plague, that the betrothal of your
son, or the lack of it, will barely rate a mention.'

'Perhaps you're right,' she mused. 'I can just imagine
how uncomfortable it must be for both Damin and Leila.'

'Then put them out of their misery. Write the letter.'

She nodded, thinking the time had probably come to
do just that. Mahkas would understand. 'I'll do it in the
morning. In the meantime, I suppose I'd better be getting
down to dinner.'

'They'll wait for you, your highness.'

'Did we ever get a message from the Sorcerers' Collective
explaining why Alija didn't come to the funeral?'

'Not a word,' Elezaar confirmed. 'Perhaps the High
Arrion has succumbed to the plague herself? She didn't look
well when she left here the other day after Master Tirstone
passed away. In fact, she fled the house like all the demons
of the Harshini were on her tail.'

'I could never be that lucky,' Marla sighed, thinking how
convenient it would be if the plague removed Alija and a
few other enemies she'd dearly like to be rid of before it was
done. Pity there wasn't a way to select whom it killed. 'Go
downstairs and let them know I'm on my way, would you?'

'Are you sure you're feeling well enough for dinner, your highness?' Elezaar asked again, clearly worried about her. It wasn't an idle concern. They'd had plague in the house now. Despite all the precautions she had taken to keep Ruxton isolated, there was no telling how many of them would fall victim to it.

'I'm not ill, Elezaar,' she assured him. 'Just weary.'

'It's all right to grieve for him, you know,' the dwarf told her gently.

She turned to him sharply, angered by his presumptuousness. 'Don't try to second-guess me, Fool.'

'I'm sorry, your highness,' he said, instantly contrite. 'I will deliver your message. Was there anything else?'

'No. Just leave me be.'

'As you wish, your highness.'

Marla heard the door close behind the dwarf and turned to look at her reflection again. She hadn't cried much when Laran died, too overwhelmed with guilt at the thought that his death might be some sort of punishment for her infidelity. She'd not cried when Nash died, either. The hypocrisy of weeping for a man she had arranged to have assassinated was too much, even for Marla. She barely even noticed when Jarvan Mariner passed on, too involved in securing his vast wealth and furthering her ambitions for her son.

But Ruxton was different. They'd been married sixteen years. He was a friend, not a lover. *One should be allowed to weep for lost friends.*

So she did. For one small instant in time, Marla let down her walls, put her head in her hands and wept for Ruxton Tirstone.

54

From the moment Luciena mentioned she was interested in purchasing ships from the Fardohnyans, King Hablet's entire demeanour changed towards his reluctant house-guests. It made her very suspicious, but Xanda seemed unsurprised. According to her husband, trade was such a fundamental part of the Fardohnyan makeup the king probably didn't even realise he was doing anything differently now he'd smelled a whiff of profit on the wind.

As Xanda predicted, after the restrictions of a sailing ship, the children had run riot through the palace. Luciena couldn't blame them. After being confined on board for weeks, and trapped in a city riddled with plague prior to that, they were thrilled to finally have the illusion of freedom. Every time she tried to scold them for their unruly behaviour, however, Xanda stopped her. *Let them go*, he advised. *They're only children.* Xanda claimed Hablet wasn't that bothered by the children, anyway. Oddly enough, the Fardohnyan king seemed rather fond of them. But her riotous offspring drove that slimy little eunuch, Lecter Turon, quite insane. And that, Xanda claimed, made it all worthwhile.

Luciena was inclined to agree. There was something about the chamberlain that set her teeth on edge.

She was not the only one who thought that way about the eunuch, Luciena soon discovered. Hablet's eldest daughter, Adrina, had a similar opinion of her father's closest advisor and made no secret of the fact.

The princess had shared her dislike of the chamberlain with the entire dinner party a few days after they first arrived at the palace, making some rude comment across the table about Lecter that had her father guffawing with laughter and the chamberlain shooting her venomous looks that did not augur well for her future.

Adrina appeared unconcerned. She was a dusky, exotic, green-eyed creature with some indefinable quality about her that made men stop and take a second look. She wasn't pretty the same way her younger sister Cassandra was. Luciena wasn't sure what it was about the young princess, but even Xanda remarked on it.

Striking, he called her, not beautiful.

Of course, the fact that she usually dressed in the traditional Fardohnyan manner, which left her midriff bare – from just below her ample breasts to just below her jewelled navel – may have had something to do with the reason every man in the room followed her with his eyes whenever she graced them with her presence.

Adrina had a reputation for being rather difficult. Luciena had found her quite the opposite. She was charming, spoke Hythrun with barely a trace of an accent, and was frighteningly well educated. She had a sharp wit and a clever sense of humour and wasn't afraid to speak her mind, even when she knew her father wouldn't approve of her opinions. Confined to the harem unless granted permission by the king to leave, however, Luciena usually only saw her at dinner on the nights Hablet desired her company.

But today Luciena was visiting Adrina and had been allowed, for the first time, to step into Hablet's legendary harem.

Luciena wasn't sure what she was expecting. A room crammed with terrified women, she imagined, all primping and preening themselves, waiting to be chosen by their king for a night of desperate pleasure, hoping their performance was enough to catch his interest so they might be asked back for a return visit, perhaps. But to her surprise, the harem, as it turned out, wasn't even a room.

It was more a palace within a palace. Behind the harem walls were extensive gardens, a number of large buildings that housed the living and sleeping areas of the complex, a separate nursery and school for the children, their own kitchens, entertainment areas, even stables and a round yard where the royal children learned to ride. Nor was the harem confined to women. There were male slaves everywhere she looked (all eunuchs, Luciena suspected), a number of Loronged male *court'esa* who probably doubled as entertainment for the women and tutors for the children, depending on their area of expertise. Along the high walls, a contingent of Palace Guardsmen patrolled the wall-walk, although whether they were there to stop anybody breaking in or to prevent the residents from escaping, Luciena couldn't say for certain.

Across the lawns, the laughter of several children chasing hoops around a larger pavilion caught her attention.

'Luciena!'

She turned as Adrina hailed her from a small, silk-shaded pavilion set amid a flower-filled grotto on her left. The male slave leading her through the gardens bowed silently and walked away. Adrina indicated Luciena should sit on the small chair by the table.

'Good morning, your highness,' she said, taking the proffered seat. Adrina's slave stepped forward and proceeded to pour wine for them both. When the slave was done, the princess waved her away. 'Leave us, Tamylan.'

The slave bowed and silently withdrew, leaving Luciena alone with the princess.

'Do you have harems in Hythria?' she asked Luciena, taking a sip of her wine.

Luciena shook her head, quite certain the princess already knew the answer to her own question. One didn't learn to speak a language so well without knowing something of a nation's customs.

'No, your highness,' she replied with a smile. 'The men of Hythria find it hard enough to handle one wife, although it's not uncommon for a married couple to keep a number of *court'esa* on staff.'

'Does your husband keep *court'esa*?'

'We have two,' Luciena confirmed. 'One of them is a singer of some renown. She was a gift from Princess Marla on our tenth wedding anniversary. The other is a delightful young man, who, I have to admit, I bought for his accounting skills rather than his sexual prowess.'

'Is your husband in love with his *court'esa*?'

Luciena looked at the princess oddly, thinking it a very strange question. 'Not that I'm aware of.'

'You're lucky, then. My father is always falling in love with his *court'esa*. Never his wives.'

Luciena thought it very sad that Adrina should have such a gloomy outlook on life. 'I'm sure your mother and father love each other very much, your highness.'

Adrina laughed sourly. 'My father had my mother beheaded when I was two months old, Luciena. She tried to poison the *court'esa* he was in love with.'

'Oh,' Luciena said, not sure how else to respond to a revelation like that.

'Tell me about Hythria,' the princess ordered abruptly. 'Is it true the Sorcerers' Palace was built by the Harshini?'

'I believe it was.'

'And is it true your High Prince spends most of his time

having lavish orgies in his roof garden where he engages in a wide range of perverted sexual practices involving young boys, animals and sick blood rites?'

Luciena almost choked on her wine. 'I couldn't really say, your highness,' she replied evasively.

Adrina smiled. 'It's all right, Luciena, you're not giving away any state secrets. Everybody knows what the Wolfblade family is like.'

'And what exactly *are* they like, do you suppose?' she asked, rather taken aback by the young woman's obvious contempt for Hythria's royal family.

'Wasteful, perverted, irresponsible . . . we have competitions, sometimes, to see who can think of the most adjectives.'

'Are you aware, your highness, that I am an adopted member of this family you so casually malign?'

'Of course I am,' the princess shrugged. 'But you want to buy ships from us, so, in my father's mind at least, that cancels out any negative feelings he may entertain towards you regarding your family ties.'

'And what about in *your* mind?'

Adrina thought about her answer for a moment. 'I worry for Hythria.'

'That's very generous of you, your highness.'

The young woman smiled at Luciena's tone. 'Look north sometime, my lady. Karien is full of the Overlord's fanatics and Medalon is ruled by an atheist cult. It is left to Fardohnya and Hythria to ensure the Primal Gods are worshipped in the proper manner. Without us, the Harshini will never be able to return. I worry for Hythria, because if your nation gets much weaker, either Medalon or Karien might decide the apple is too ripe to leave hanging on the tree unattended.'

'You judge us far too harshly, your highness.'

'I don't think so,' Adrina said. 'Or can you give me

reason to hope? Is Lernen's successor going to do any better? I hear he's rather fond of horse racing. Definitely a sign that he's a serious and thoughtful ruler in the making.'

Luciena shook her head, unsure what she was supposed to say. Such cynical contempt was quite unexpected from one so young. 'Did you invite me here just to point out the failings of my family?'

Adrina bowed her head apologetically, perhaps realising she might have overstepped the mark. 'I'm sorry, I really didn't invite you here to upset you. Or insult you. In fact, my reasons are quite the opposite. I invited you here to warn you.'

'About what?'

'About the danger you and your family are in. I'm not the only one in the Summer Palace who thinks this way about the Wolfblades, Luciena.'

'Do you know of a specific danger, or are you just cautioning me to be on my guard?' she asked warily.

'Oh no, the danger is very real and quite specific. If I were you, I'd be making arrangements to get out of here, my lady, and I'd be doing it today.'

Luciena stared at the young woman suspiciously. 'And why should you want to warn me? Particularly if you think so little of the Wolfblades?'

The princess smiled. 'Because in helping you, I hinder Lecter Turon. Any small thing I can do to thwart that devious little worm's plans is a win for me. And trust me, Luciena, when I warn you that he *has* plans for you and your husband. And your children. Take my advice. Get out of the palace. Today, if you can arrange it. Just get out of Talabar while you still can.'

Luciena rose to her feet, putting aside her wine. 'I must thank you for the warning, your highness.'

'I want your word, though,' the young woman added, 'that you'll never reveal it was me who tipped you off.

My father tolerates me interfering with Lecter's plans because it amuses him, but there's a fine line between interference and treason. Betray me, and I'll be executed.'

She was quite serious. There was no trace of humour in Adrina's remarkable green eyes. They were outlined in kohl this morning, making them even more striking than usual.

'I'll not reveal your involvement, your highness. You have my word.'

'Not to your husband. Not to anybody. Not ever. Not even when you're back in Hythria, congratulating yourself on your narrow escape. You have no idea how easily these things get back to my father.'

Luciena nodded. 'Not to anyone, your highness. I give you my word. As a woman. And as a Wolfblade.'

'Then I will look forward to having you prove the word of a Wolfblade can be trusted.' Adrina smiled a little sceptically. 'Good luck, Lady Taranger.'

'And to you, your highness.'

Luciena curtseyed as politely as she could manage and then fled the harem, wishing she'd listened to her instincts and turned the ship around the moment they'd spotted Hablet's Palace Guard waiting for them on the docks. That it would have meant sailing away in a ship dangerously low on food and fresh water seemed insignificant now, because if Adrina was to be believed – and Luciena could think of no reason why the young princess would lie – her family was in danger.

They had to get out of there.

And they had to do it now. Today.

Before whatever sinister plan that evil little eunuch, Lecter Turon, had in mind for her family could be put into action.

55

With Krakandar's rat extermination drive in full swing, Wrayan had little chance to conduct any normal business for the Thieves' Guild in the weeks following the young prince's orders to seal the city. For the first time in years, he had precious little to do and plenty of time in which to do it.

The population had got right behind the effort to keep their city free of the plague. Even Mahkas's obsessive record-keepers had given up counting the number of rats they had trapped and killed and incinerated in the vast furnaces of the glassworks, but the common belief was that the number ran into the hundreds of thousands.

Rat catching was turning into a thriving business for some. There were even miracles attributed to this grand effort to clean up the city. Wrayan had witnessed one such miracle himself when old Ronlin, the blind beggar who regularly worked the street outside the Pickpocket's Retreat, discovered how much more profitable rat catching was than begging. His sight had been miraculously restored about three heartbeats after the beggar did the sums in his head. Wrayan had watched him take in the news, work out the profit margin, tear off the filthy rags that covered his supposedly blind eyes, and scurry away down the street in search of rats.

He wasn't sure what was more disturbing about that particular miracle: that Ronlin had so readily abandoned his career as a beggar, or that Wrayan found himself explaining to Fee (very slowly and more than once) that it really hadn't been magic that restored the beggar's sight because Ronlin had never been blind in the first place. Fyora was quite miffed to discover she'd been duped and was even talking about demanding a refund of the few copper rivets she'd thrown the poor man out of pity over the years. Wrayan was still shaking his head over the idea that in the twenty-odd years Ronlin had been begging outside the tavern, Fee had never woken up to the fact he was a fraud.

'Deep in thought?'

Wrayan started a little at the unexpected voice and looked up from the tally sheet he was working on in the booth by the window that he had long ago claimed as his own. Sitting in the previously unoccupied seat opposite him was a fair-haired boy of about fourteen, dressed in the worst collection of cast-off clothing Wrayan had ever seen. He stared at the lad in shock, then quickly looked around the tavern to see if anyone else had noticed his sudden appearance.

'Can anyone else see you?' he hissed.

'Of course not,' Dacendaran shrugged, and then he leaned forward and added in a theatrical whisper, 'Why are you whispering like that?'

'What are you *doing* here?' Wrayan pushed the tally sheets aside – not that there had been much to tally. With the city sealed and everyone's attention on rats, there wasn't much in the way of theft going on in Krakandar at present.

The boy-god shrugged and leaned back in the booth, surveying the tavern with a curious grin. 'Just thought I'd drop in and say hello.'

Wrayan snorted sceptically, certain there was much more

to Dacendaran's sudden appearance than him just dropping by to say hello. 'I didn't think the gods made house calls.'

'Shows how much you know. What's happening?'

Wrayan looked around the tavern warily, but nobody seemed to be paying the head of the Thieves' Guild and the God of Thieves any attention. 'Not much.'

'I noticed,' the boy remarked, his grin turning into a petulant scowl.

Wrayan smiled. 'Aha! So that's it! Business is a bit slow at the moment, eh, Divine One? What with everyone dropping dead from the plague and all.'

Dacendaran assumed an air of contrived innocence. 'I'm sure I don't know what you mean.' Then he added in a rather peeved tone, 'Anyway, even if that was the reason nobody's stealing much at the moment, what's your excuse? There's no plague here in Krakandar.'

'We've been rather busy keeping it that way,' Wrayan informed him. 'I'm sorry that doesn't quite fit with your plans for world domination, Divine One.'

The God of Thieves was not amused. 'You're supposed to be the greatest thief in all of Hythria, Wrayan. That's what you promised me.'

'And most of the time I am, Divine One. What's more, I rule all your other worshippers in Krakandar with an iron fist and keep them loyal to you and only you. But I'm not going to be much good to you if I die from the plague. So, just accept that things are going to be a little slow until this disease has run its course. Better yet,' he added as an afterthought, 'why not speak to whichever one of your brother or sister gods is responsible for this mess and get them to back off. Then we can all go back to business as usual.'

Dacendaran thought about that for a moment, and then nodded. 'All right,' he said, and abruptly vanished.

Wrayan stared at the suddenly empty seat, shaking his head.

'Isn't talking to yourself the first sign of delirium?'

Startled for the second time in almost as many minutes, Wrayan looked up to find Starros and Damin Wolfblade, the young Prince of Krakandar himself, standing beside his table, without the usual contingent of bodyguards that seemed to follow the young man around. Maybe with the city sealed against outsiders, Almodavar was satisfied the danger to his prince was scant enough to risk dispensing with them for a while. And Damin would be making the most of this unexpected freedom, Wrayan guessed, which was probably why he was here in the Pickpocket's Retreat. Wrayan glanced past the two young men to discover there were already murmurs racing through the tavern about the prince's presence in the Beggars' Quarter. It wouldn't be long before the place was packed to the rafters, once word got out that Damin was here.

And then he wondered how much the young men had heard of his conversation with Dace.

'I was just asking Dacendaran to do something about ridding us of this damn plague,' he explained with a smile, figuring the truth was probably more unbelievable than any story he could invent. 'Won't you join me?'

The two young men slid into the booth, occupying the seat so recently vacated by the God of Thieves. Fyora had spotted them and was already hurrying over with fresh tankards of ale. 'So tell me, to what do we owe this great honour, your highness?' he asked, as Fee arrived at the table. 'It's not often we catch you down here slumming it in the Beggars' Quarter with us poor peasants.'

'Rats,' Damin explained. 'Rats, rats and more rats. My uncle thinks we're crazy, but it seems to be working so far.'

'We've been down at the glassworks checking on the disposal of the carcasses,' Starros added.

'And the idea of coming all this way without paying a visit to the lovely Fyora was simply unthinkable,' Damin declared, with a winning smile at the *court'esa*. She blushed furiously and looked about ready to faint with happiness that Damin had remembered her name.

Wrayan shook his head at her foolishness. 'There's people waiting to be served, Fee.'

Forcing her attention away from the prince, whose mere presence seemed to have turned her into a puddle on the floor, Fee stared at Wrayan blankly. 'What?'

'You have *other* customers,' the thief reminded her, pointing at the bar where the inevitable crowd was starting to gather, every man and woman there trying to give the impression they hadn't noticed who was sitting in the corner booth with Wrayan Lightfinger.

Fyora glanced over her shoulder and sighed heavily, before turning back to Damin. 'Will there be anything else, your highness? Anything at all? More ale? Wine? Food?'

'Thank you, Fee, but this ale and your smile are all I need. Take care of your other customers.'

Still blushing an interesting shade of crimson, Fyora curtsied awkwardly and, with a great deal of reluctance, left the booth and headed back to the counter. Wrayan frowned at Damin disapprovingly. 'I wish you wouldn't do that.'

'Do what?' he asked, full of wounded innocence.

'Flirt with her like that. She's old enough to be your mother.'

'Actually, she's probably older than my mother,' Damin noted. 'And, excuse me, but I wasn't flirting with her! I was just being nice, that's all.'

Wrayan looked at Starros for help. 'You explain it to him.'

Starros put down his ale, wiped his mouth on the sleeve of his shirt and nodded in agreement. 'Wrayan's got a point, Damin.'

'*What* point?'

'You're Krakandar's prince. You shouldn't get too familiar with the working *court'esa*.'

Damin stared at Starros in horror. 'This from the man who stopped me in the middle of the Beggars' Quarter to introduce me to a couple of them! Gods, Starros! Don't frighten me like that! For a moment there, I thought you were Mahkas. And, if you don't mind, just exactly what's so wrong with getting to know the working *court'esa* of my city?'

Wrayan laughed delightedly. 'Oh, please, can you ask us that again, Damin? When your uncle is around to answer it? And can I watch?'

Damin grinned, knowing it would be worth selling tickets to see Mahkas's reaction. 'Think I might, now you mention it. Should liven up the conversation at dinner tonight, at the very least.' His grin faded a little then and he took another swig from the tankard, adding sourly, 'It might even get the topic off a few other things I'm getting rather tired of hearing about.'

Wrayan studied the two young men curiously for a moment. 'Trouble up in paradise?'

'Lord Damaran is just being . . . Lord Damaran,' Starros explained.

By the defeated tone of his voice, Wrayan guessed it had something to do with Leila. 'So you and your cousin aren't exactly . . . falling in love?' he asked Damin.

When the prince hesitated before answering, Starros shrugged. 'It's all right, Damin. Wrayan knows.'

'Then you can understand how little I want any part of this,' Damin said, the first time Wrayan could recall ever seeing him so serious. 'I've written to my mother and asked her to clear up the situation, but I don't hold out much hope that her answer will get here before Mahkas has Leila escorted naked into my room like some sacrificial lamb and tied hand and foot to the bed to await my princely pleasure.'

'It can't be that bad, surely?'

Starros nodded in agreement with the prince. 'He as good as told Damin he could have Leila if he wanted her.'

'Any *way* I wanted her,' Damin added unhappily.

Wrayan felt for both young men, knowing how awkward it must be for them. That their friendship seemed to be weathering the storm so well was a good sign, though. This could easily have destroyed it, had either young man doubted the other's integrity. 'I wish I could offer some useful advice, boys, but I think you're right, Damin. Mahkas is only going to believe your mother.'

'Can't *you* do something to him?' Damin asked hopefully.

'What do you mean?'

'You're a magician, aren't you? Can't you put a spell on him, or something like that? Make him stop believing I'm ever going to marry his daughter?'

'What you're asking for is called *coercion*,' Wrayan explained. 'Even if I had the skill to work one, I wouldn't attempt it. You can't make someone believe something they fundamentally disagree with, Damin, and expect it to hold for long. Besides, the Harshini really frown on that sort of thing.' Seeing that Damin wasn't totally convinced, he warned, 'And don't even think of asking Rorin to do it. He'd have less chance than me of making it work.'

'It was just a thought.'

'Make sure it stays that way.' Wrayan glanced around the tavern, noting it was almost filled to capacity by now, the crowd starting to edge a little closer to the booth. 'And unless you're planning to fight your way out of here, my lad, I suggest you get going while you can still find the door.'

Damin looked at the rapidly swelling crowd and nodded. 'I suppose we should. Thanks for the drink.'

'My pleasure,' Wrayan assured him, rising to his feet, thinking the only way Damin was going to get out of the Pickpocket's Retreat now, without being mobbed, was if Wrayan physically elbowed a path for him through to the door. 'I imagine you don't get served ale too often in the palace.'

'It's not Mahkas's vintage of choice, no,' Damin agreed with a chuckle. They slid off the bench and Starros automatically fell in on the other side of the prince as he stood up. Wrayan and Starros turned for the door.

Damin, however, did quite the opposite.

Unexpectedly, the young prince walked across to the nearest table, where several rough-looking workmen sat, nursing their ales and watching this highborn interloper warily. Damin smiled and introduced himself to the shocked commoners, which immediately precipitated exactly what Wrayan had been hoping to avoid. The young man was mobbed by the scores of people who'd come to gape at him, all wanting to say they'd met the young Prince of Krakandar, or shaken his hand, or even that they'd touched him.

'What the hell is he *doing*?' Wrayan asked Starros in annoyance. 'Damin should know better than to place himself in a situation so potentially advantageous to an assassin.'

'Securing his throne,' Starros replied, putting his arm out to prevent Wrayan interfering. 'Leave him be for a moment.'

'Are you mad?'

Starros smiled knowingly. 'Don't let Damin fool you, Wrayan. He's always been smarter than he pretends.

Underneath that jolly exterior, he's a smarter politician than his mother.'

Wrayan wasn't entirely convinced. 'I know what you mean . . . I've wondered the same, myself . . . but even so, Starros, Almodavar would kill Damin himself, if he saw him risking such close contact in a crowd like this without his bodyguard present.'

'And every man and woman in this place probably knows that, Wrayan,' Starros pointed out, looking around at the mob of thieves and beggars clamouring for the young prince's attention. 'Yet he does it anyway, and he's not afraid. You mark my word, news of this will get around the city before we're back at the palace. *The Prince of Krakandar isn't too scared or too proud to mix with his own people.* That's what they'll be saying. He couldn't make the citizens of Krakandar love him more if he paid them in gold.'

Wrayan looked at Starros for a moment and then shook his head. 'I'm not sure what's worse, Starros. That Damin might be so calculating, or that you actually admire him for it.'

'Damin's not being calculating,' Starros replied confidently. 'He's probably not even aware of what he's doing. Look at him, Wrayan. He's not faking anything. He really does like these people and he really isn't afraid of them.'

Wrayan watched Damin greet the patrons of the Pickpocket's Retreat, laugh and shake hands and even kiss a baby thrust into his arms for luck, and knew Starros was right. Damin was having the time of his life. It didn't make him any less nervous that something might happen to the prince in such close confines, but it was clear that Damin's popularity was more than just the hopeful wish by these people for their own prince in a city ruled for much of the past half century by caretakers and regents. These people finally had a lord of their own and they all wanted a little piece of him to keep for themselves, and Damin appeared happy to oblige them.

It took them the better part of an hour to make it from the table Damin had first stopped at to the door. By the time they got there, Wrayan was fairly certain that Damin Wolfblade owned every heart in the Beggars' Quarter.

56

Sealing the city and decimating the rat population might have slowed the advance of the plague in Krakandar, but it caused other problems that soon became apparent, the foremost of which was food. Although the grain store in the inner ring of the city held enough to keep the population fed for about a month and a half in an emergency, there was little else on offer and it was a delegation from the Krakandar Chamber of Commerce who suggested a cattle raid into Medalon to address the problem.

'Why a cattle raid into Medalon?' Mahkas asked, when the delegation consisting of the elected leader of the Chamber of Commerce, Hyreld Weaver, and several of his fellow members of the various trade guilds confronted the regent with the problem a few days after Damin and Starros had met with Wrayan in the Pickpocket's Retreat.

'Why not?' Damin asked in reply.

Mahkas glanced over his shoulder at Damin with a frown. Damin stood just behind his uncle's right hand, the fitting place for Krakandar's heir. Mahkas was sitting at his carved and polished desk, his gilded chair almost large enough to be called a throne. It was a recent acquisition, this almost-a-throne of his uncle's. Damin didn't remember it being here the last time he was home.

'I invited you to attend this meeting so that you may learn something of administering the province, Damin,' Mahkas scolded. 'Not to trivialise the importance of it with flippant comments like that.'

'Sorry, Uncle.' It was raining outside, the world grey and uninviting, but it was still preferable to being stuck here inside the palace discussing cows. Even rats were more interesting than this. Almodavar, Orleon and Starros waited behind the delegation from the Chamber of Commerce. Damin suspected they were as bored as he was, just better at not letting it show.

'If we're going to start cutting into our own herds, my lord,' the delegate from the Butchers' Guild explained patiently, 'we'll face problems later in the year that can easily be avoided by taking stock from over the border. Most of our cows are already with calf, ready to drop them in the spring. To slaughter them now would be detrimental to their numbers.'

'Won't the cows in Medalon be with calf, as well?' Mahkas asked.

'Certainly,' Hyreld Weaver agreed with a perfectly straight face. 'But they are *atheist* cows, my lord, and therefore their numbers are of no interest to us at all.'

Damin coughed to cover the laugh he just knew his uncle would disapprove of. He dared not look at Starros, who was probably on the verge of doing the same thing. *Atheist cows, for the gods' sake!*

'Something has to be done, my lord,' another fat little merchant urged. 'If you intend to keep the population confined, you must find a way to feed them.' The man looked as if he could miss quite a few meals and not suffer any detrimental effects.

'Perhaps you should discuss that with my nephew, Master Goldsmith. It was his idea, after all, to seal the city.'

The merchants all looked at Damin in surprise. '*Your* idea, your highness?'

'Guilty, I'm afraid.'

'You agreed with our proposal then?' the butcher asked.

'What proposal?'

'Why, the one in which we suggested the very same thing. The Chamber of Commerce drafted it not three days before you arrived.' Master Weaver beamed at him. 'You've no idea how relieved we were when we heard our suggestion had been acted upon.'

Damin glanced down at Mahkas, wondering why his uncle had mentioned nothing about it.

'Well . . . obviously, I . . . *we* . . . agreed with your assessment of the situation, Master Weaver,' he replied, a little uncertainly. *Had Mahkas just ignored the damn thing?*

'Then you will have read our recommendation that we should be raiding across the border, and will agree to that, too.'

'What if the Medalonians have closed their border against the plague?' Mahkas asked brusquely. It was hard to tell if he was angry or just being businesslike.

'Unlikely, my lord,' Almodavar replied. 'It's too long, too open and too impractical. If they're worried about plague spreading into Medalon, they'll be concentrating their efforts in the towns and cities. If anything, they'll be more vulnerable to attack than ever.'

'There!' the weaver declared. 'It is just as Captain Almodavar says. Safe as houses. And vital for the sake of the city.'

'That's not what he said,' Mahkas corrected, 'but I take your point. What do you think, Captain? Is it worth the risk?'

'I would think so, my lord.'

Mahkas thought about it for a moment and then nodded his approval. 'Very well then, I will issue the necessary orders. How many head of cattle do you want, gentlemen?'

'Four score would relieve our immediate problems,' the butcher told him. 'For now.'

'You heard the man, Almodavar. Bring us four score of fine Medalonian shorthorn so that Krakandar may eat beef.' Mahkas rose to his feet, which was obviously the signal that the audience was at an end. 'Good day, gentlemen.'

The delegates bowed to their lord, with varying degrees of elegance, and departed in a buoyant mood now they'd had their way about the cattle raids as well as sealing the city.

As soon as Orleon closed the door on the last of them, Mahkas turned on Damin. 'Please don't do that again.'

'Do what?'

'Contradict me in front of others.'

Damin stared at his uncle in confusion. 'All I said was that we agreed with their proposal. Which apparently we did, seeing as how they wanted the city sealed and we sealed it.'

'I had already sent a letter to the Chamber of Commerce before you arrived, denying their proposal, Damin. You made it look as if *you* overruled my decision. You made me look like a fool.'

'Well, if you'd told me that before the meeting, Uncle, I might have known better.'

Mahkas didn't seem to have an answer to that accusation, so he turned to Almodavar. 'Be ready to leave first thing in the morning, Captain.'

'Of course, my lord,' Almodavar said, saluting the regent sharply.

'Can I go with them?'

Mahkas shook his head without even stopping to consider the suggestion. 'Absolutely not, Damin.'

'Why not?'

'It's not safe.'

'Almodavar says it is,' Damin pointed out reasonably. 'He said the Medalonians will be concentrating their efforts on protecting their towns and cities. I probably won't even get to see a Defender, let alone pick a fight with one.'

'I could take along extra men, my lord,' Almodavar volunteered. 'To be on the safe side.'

Damin looked at his uncle hopefully. With Almodavar supporting him, he had a much better chance of being allowed to go on the raid. 'We'll only be gone for a few days. Eight or nine at the most. Right, Captain?'

'It shouldn't even take that long,' Almodavar agreed, 'if we raid the farms closest to the Border Stream.'

Mahkas glared at the captain, then turned to the chief steward for his opinion, which Damin considered a very good sign. It meant Mahkas's resolve was weakening.

'I suppose you think I should let him go, too, Orleon?'

'I think, my lord, that any constructive activity which keeps his highness occupied and out of the palace at such a trying time as this is an excellent suggestion,' the old steward replied solemnly. 'If you recall some of the previous . . . *incidents* we've been subjected to over the years, directly attributable to Prince Damin's efforts to relieve his boredom, I believe the most worthy recipients of his attention on this occasion should be our enemies.'

'He means yes,' Damin translated. He grinned at the old steward. *Good old Orleon.* Already he was going insane with Damin underfoot.

'I know what he means, Damin,' Mahkas informed him. 'And much as I hate to admit it, I'm inclined to agree with him. I heard about your little incident in the city the other day.'

'What incident?' he asked innocently.

'A near riot in the Beggars' Quarter? In a tavern?'

'Oh, that,' he said, wondering how Mahkas had learned of their visit to the Pickpocket's Retreat. 'And it wasn't a near riot. It wasn't even close, was it, Starros?'

Mahkas turned on Starros. '*You* were involved? I might have known. I suppose it was your idea.'

'It was *my* idea,' Damin said, annoyed at the way Mahkas constantly tried to find fault with Starros. He was so annoyed, in fact, that he added, 'There's a working *court'esa* down there I'm rather fond of, actually.' Damin knew Mahkas would be appalled to think he would even *know* any of the working *court'esa* in the Beggars' Quarter, let alone be on intimate terms with one of them.

'You try my patience, Damin.'

'Keep me cooped up in the city for another couple of weeks,' Damin suggested. 'Then you'll find out how really irritating I can be when I'm bored.'

It was blatant blackmail and Mahkas wasn't happy about it, but Damin could tell he was on the verge of giving in.

'If I agree to this, I want your promise that you'll be making no more visits to the Beggars' Quarter. We have *court'esa* in the palace for that sort of thing, Damin. And there's always . . .' Mahkas didn't finish the sentence, but Damin knew what he was thinking. *And there's always Leila.*

'I swear,' Damin said, dramatically placing his hand on his heart. 'If you let me go with Almodavar, Uncle Mahkas, I will give up my dear Fyora and never lay another hand on her.' This time it was Starros coughing to cover up his laughter. Fortunately, only Damin recognised the strangled noise the young man was making for what it was.

'I will hold you to that oath, Damin.'

'Then I can go?'

Mahkas shook his head, as if he was about to make the worst decision of his life. 'I suppose you might as well.'

'*Yes!*' Damin cried, and then quickly curbed his eagerness in the face of Mahkas's obvious disapproval of his unseemly enthusiasm.

'You'd better make certain he comes back in one piece, Captain,' Mahkas warned Almodavar.

'I'll keep him safe,' the Raider promised.

'You'd better,' Mahkas said. 'Because it won't be me you'll have to answer to if he comes to any harm. It will be Princess Marla.'

57

Three days later, Damin stood on the edge of the Bardarlen Gorge, the cool wind whipping the hair around his face, wishing he'd thought this through a little more carefully before demanding he be allowed to accompany the Raiders across the border into Medalon.

In front of him was a cutting, deep and treacherous, which could at its narrowest point – so Almodavar assured him – be cleared by a man on horseback. Almodavar and Raek Harlen stood either side of him, watching Damin survey the canyon, both of them veterans of many leaps over this gorge and both of them highly amused by Damin's reaction to his first sight of it. It wasn't that Damin wasn't expecting the gorge to be here. He'd heard tales of it all his life. He just hadn't expected it to be so . . . big.

'So how wide is this gorge, exactly?' Damin asked doubt-fully, putting one foot on the fallen log that lay just on the edge of the drop, so he could lean forward a little to look down. The bottom was far below them, two or three hundred feet at least. He could just hear the faintest sound of rushing water echoing off the steep, jagged walls of the canyon, where the Border Stream gathered speed over the rocks as it fell towards the lowlands of southern Medalon. The other side of the gorge was about three feet lower than the Hythrun side and fell away in a gentle, lightly forested slope.

It wasn't just that you had to clear the gorge, Damin realised. You then had to avoid hitting the trees on the other side when you landed.

'Eighteen, maybe twenty feet,' Almodavar told him with a shrug. 'Or thereabouts.'

'And if I'm terrified by the idea of jumping this thing on a borrowed horse, that just means I'm sane, right?'

'Better a borrowed horse who's done it before than that show pony you rode here from Greenharbour, lad.'

Raek nodded in agreement. 'If you're going to ride with the Raiders, Damin, we're going to have to find you a better horse.'

Seeing Damin was still not convinced about the likelihood of surviving this mad leap across the gorge, Almodavar smiled encouragingly. 'All Krakandar Raiders have to be able to clear the Bardarlen Gorge before they can truly call themselves a Raider.'

'And the ones that miss? They're all down the bottom of the gorge, I suppose?'

Raek Harlen laughed. 'We train the horses for it, Damin. And the riders.'

'You've been training for this your whole life,' Almodavar agreed. 'From the first time you were put in a saddle.'

Damin shook his head. 'My first riding lesson was on Elezaar's back, playing "horsey" around the nursery. I might have only been two or three at the time, but I don't believe we covered death-defying leaps that first day.'

'What would that damned dwarf know?' Raek shrugged. 'Besides, I've seen you jump this distance in the training yards plenty of times.'

Damin looked down again, unconvinced. 'There's quite a difference between six inches of water below you and a six-hundred-foot drop, Raek.'

'Actually, there's not,' the captain disagreed. 'The technique is the same, no matter what's beneath you. Anyway, *you* won't be jumping it, Damin, the horse will. Let the beast have his head and he'll decide on his own how much strength he needs to clear it. He's done it before. Just don't fall off.'

'And don't exaggerate, boy,' Almodavar scolded. 'It's no more than two hundred and fifty feet down there. Three hundred, tops.'

'Oh, well, that makes *all* the difference.'

'You're not scared, are you, Damin?'

He shook his head. '*Scared* seems far too inadequate a word, Raek.'

'Don't worry,' the younger captain assured him optimistically. 'We all felt like that the first time.'

'You'll be fine,' Almodavar added, clapping Damin on the shoulder. 'Mahkas would never have let you come if he didn't think you couldn't make it over the gorge.'

'As I recall, Captain, you told my uncle we were going to stay near the Border Stream. The Bardarlen Gorge didn't actually rate a mention.'

'We are at the Border Stream,' Almodavar replied, looking down at the thin silver ribbon of water tumbling over the rocks far below. 'Sort of.'

'Didn't we promise Lord Damaran we'd keep you safe?' Raek reminded him. 'We've got twice the men we need, twice the officers we'd normally take on a raid like this—'

'None of which will matter one iota, if I miss that damned jump.' Damin looked up suddenly and grinned at the two officers. 'Mahkas is going to kill both of you when he finds out you brought me here.'

'Only if you don't make it,' Raek pointed out reasonably.

He glanced down at the terrifying drop one last time and then turned away from it and gathered up the reins of his borrowed gelding. 'Guess I'd better not miss then, eh?'

The captains looked at each other and nodded with satisfaction. 'He's his father's son, all right,' Raek declared.

Damin appreciated the compliment, but wasn't sure what he'd done to deserve it. 'What do you mean?'

'It was Laran Krakenshield who first stood here, and looked across that gorge and decided it was the quickest way into Medalon,' Almodavar explained.

There was a hint of pride, and perhaps loss, in the captain's voice. He and Laran had been friends, Damin knew that, but it had never really occurred to him that the captain might still miss the Warlord of Krakandar after all this time. Damin had no memory of his father. He wasn't even two years old when Laran was killed in a border raid much the same as this one. To Damin, Laran was a legend. To Almodavar, he had obviously been a close friend.

'The best part about this crossing,' Raek remarked as he swung into the saddle of his own mount, 'is that to this day, they're so convinced it isn't possible to breach Bardarlen Gorge that it still hasn't occurred to those thickheaded Defenders how we manage to get across the border when they watch the known passes so closely.'

'Pity we can't come back this way,' Damin said, thinking no steer would attempt to jump the gorge. But it was a quick and (relatively) easy way into Medalon that allowed the Krakandar Raiders the chance to miss the Defender patrols and steal the cattle they wanted, and left them fresh and ready to fight their way back into Hythria at the ford which crossed the Border Stream some eighteen miles to the west. *And where the Defenders are undoubtedly lying in wait,* Damin feared, *if Almodavar's prediction about them guarding their towns and cities against the plague proves incorrect.*

Flanked by the two captains, Damin rode back to where the rest of the troop was waiting. There were sixty men in this raiding party, far more than was normally required for a simple cattle raid. But this was the young Prince of Krakandar's first official raid. Even if the men hadn't been going a little stir-crazy cooped up in a sealed city, this was a historic occasion they all wanted to be a part of.

'I'll send Axton and Helling across first,' Almodavar told him. 'Then Raek and his scouts. Then you.'

Damin nodded, knowing that Almodavar was letting the others go first to reassure him that it could be done. Deep down, Damin had no doubt that he could make it across the gorge. There was just that awkward veneer of reason and sanity that kept getting in the way.

'Whatever you do, don't hesitate,' Raek advised. 'Trust the horse. Windracer's done this before. He knows how to space his strides, how wide the jump is, and how to carry you over and stay balanced. Just keep focused on something in the distance roughly level with your eyes and make sure that when he jumps you grab the mane and don't pull on his mouth. It doesn't take many times jerking on a horse's mouth—'

'Before he starts to associate jumping with pain,' Damin finished, a little impatiently. 'And thinks he's being punished for something. I have jumped a horse before, Captain Harlen.'

'Just checking,' Raek said, obviously pleased that Damin seemed to know what he was about. He trotted up the slope a little further and then turned and waited for Almodavar to give the signal. The older captain scanned the slope on the other side of the gorge once again and then nodded.

They took the jump one at a time, the trooper Axton in the lead. The young man was a fearless horseman, no doubt the reason he'd been chosen to go first. He gave the mare her head and Damin held his breath as they galloped down the long slope and neared the edge of the gorge. At the very last minute, Axton leaned forward in the saddle and the horse launched herself over the log at the edge of the cliff and sailed across the gorge, stretching out to land on the other side without missing her stride, the momentum carrying both horse and rider into the trees.

Damin let out his breath and grinned. '*That* was impressive.'

'Wait until it's your turn,' Raek laughed. 'Watching it is nothing compared to doing it.'

Helling was already headed down towards the gorge at a gallop, as Raek and his scouts rode a little further up the slope to get as long a run-up as possible. Damin followed them, his heart pounding. He watched Helling land safely and then Raek Harlen and the two scouts, who would spread out as soon as they reached the other side, making sure the area was clear of Defenders.

And then, before he realised what was happening, it was his turn and Damin was thundering down the slope towards the Bardarlen Gorge and certain death if he misjudged the jump by so much as a single step.

Trust the horse, Raek had told him. There wasn't much else he could do. The gorge appeared in front of them far too soon, and he felt Windracer gathering beneath him for the leap. His heart in his mouth, the blood rushing through his veins so loudly it was all he could hear, Damin fixed his eyes on a thin sapling directly in front of them on the other side of the gorge, leaned forward and grabbed a handful of mane, letting the reins go loose. The horse leaped without faltering, and suddenly they were airborne. Damin had barely time to register that remarkable fact before the ground came rushing up to meet them and Windracer grunted, almost tossing him from the saddle, as they landed on the other side.

A faint cheer greeted his successful landing, but Damin had no time to savour his achievement, too intent on keeping his seat and avoiding the scattered trees that were suddenly in front of them. They plunged into the woodlands beyond the gorge. Whooping with glee, he let Windracer have his head for a few moments longer, and then gradually brought the beast under control.

With the blood singing through his veins so fast he was shaking from it, Damin turned the horse around and headed back towards the gorge.

By the time he got back to the others, Almodavar and several more Raiders had made the jump successfully, but they'd done this more often and were able to pull up their mounts long before they got lost in the trees as Damin had.

'Well done,' Almodavar told him with a grin when he saw Damin trotting up the slope through the trees.

Damin's pulse was pounding, his heart still banging against his ribs as if it wanted to burst clean out of his chest, but he was grinning so hard his face was aching. He leaned forward and patted Windracer's neck fondly. 'Windracer deserves most of the credit, not me, but by the gods, that was unbelievable!'

'You're a proper Raider now,' Raek assured him, as another man and horse sailed across the gap and landed safely.

'Does that mean we can do it again?' he asked, afraid he sounded like an excited child asking for a special treat. He was still exhilarated from his death-defying leap and doubted he'd be over it for some time yet.

'Provided your uncle doesn't find out about it,' Almodavar agreed, waving the next rider across.

Damin laughed. 'You're not even going to tell him we came this way, are you?'

'Actually, it's your mother I'm concerned about, more than your uncle,' Almodavar said.

Raek nodded in agreement. 'There's an old Harshini saying, Damin. *What the eye doesn't see, the heart doesn't grieve.*'

Almodavar looked at him, shaking his head. 'Mahkas could probably cope with the idea that you've jumped the Bardarlen Gorge – he jumped it himself more than once when he was younger – but your mother . . . Well, she has enough to worry about. If Mahkas doesn't know, then the Princess Marla isn't likely to learn of it, either. Not unless you tell her.'

'Are you kidding? She'd kill me herself.'

'Then it'll just be our little secret, won't it?'

'It's hardly a secret, Almodavar,' he laughed. 'Every man here just saw me do it.'

'But they're Krakandar Raiders, Damin,' Raek told him. 'And you're one of us now. They'd never tell.'

Another Raider landed safely and plunged into the trees, carried forward by the momentum of the jump. Damin watched the soldiers crossing the gorge one by one, filled with a deep sense of contentment at Raek's words; it was an even more intense feeling of homecoming, sneaking into Medalon on a cattle raid, than when he rode into Krakandar city and was greeted by a cheering mob.

This is what it is to be alive, he decided. This was more fun than anything he did in Greenharbour, more thrilling than the political games his mother played so expertly and insisted he master as well. Damin might have a natural gift for politics, but this was his legacy and his birthright. For all that he was Marla Wolfblade's son, he was Laran Krakenshield's son, too, and that part of him which hankered for action over rhetoric seemed suddenly fulfilled.

Damin had lived in Greenharbour for six years now; long enough to be under no illusions about his uncle, the High Prince. He saw how Lernen Wolfblade lived, he knew how confined his uncle was by his rank, and while he didn't agree with the way Lernen chose to keep himself amused, he could see how successive generations of High Princes had degenerated into overgrown children with nothing but their own pleasure to keep them occupied.

But this was real. This was dangerous, and exhilarating, and made him more aware than he had ever been that he was truly alive. The Krakandar Raiders were his to command some day and being Krakandar's Warlord when he came of age, six years from now, seemed more real to him, at that moment, than the idea that he would ever be Hythria's High Prince.

58

When the busy, raucous docks at Bordertown came into view, jutting haphazardly into the Glass River, Luciena wasn't sure if she should be relieved their hurried flight from Fardohnya was at an end or worried about what trouble they might have stepped into. Although their arrival in Medalon was not accompanied by the same intuitive feeling she'd had of something being badly amiss as in Talabar, Bordertown didn't particularly thrill her, either. It was foreign, strange, unfriendly and far, far from her home in Greenharbour.

'You look worried,' Xanda remarked, coming to stand beside his wife as Captain Drendik eased his shallow-draughted river barge into the chaotic wharves, looking for an empty berth. The *Melissa* was a trading boat; one Luciena's shipping company owned (although not according to its papers). It regularly plied the trade routes between Talabar in Fardohnya all the way to Brodenvale near the Citadel in northern Medalon. The *Melissa's* captain was a big, brusque man, with good reason to help Luciena and her family escape the Fardohnyan capital in the dead of night. He was Rory's father and Luciena's cousin.

'Escaping one unfriendly foreign country simply to land in another . . .' Luciena sighed, shivering as a chill breeze whipped the hair around her face. Bordertown was more east than north of Talabar, but here, where the Sanctuary Mountains tinted the northern horizon blue, the wind tumbling off their tall peaks had the smell of distant snow upon it. 'It isn't necessarily the best solution to our problem.'

Xanda nodded in agreement. 'I think I prefer the Sisterhood's indifferent hospitality, though, to Hablet's rather more personal interest in us.' He studied his wife closely for a moment. Luciena knew he was waiting for her to offer an explanation.

Things had been awkward between them since she'd returned from her meeting with Princess Adrina, refusing to say who'd she been with and demanding they leave Talabar that very day without offering any reason. Fortunately, Xanda trusted her enough to do as she asked without pressing her for an explanation at the time, but he wasn't happy with her continued silence on the issue.

Luciena had made all their escape plans alone.

For fear of being overheard, she was afraid to discuss anything more contentious than the weather with her husband while a guest in the Summer Palace. She had kept her own counsel and sent Aleesha with a sealed note to the only person in Talabar Luciena was sure she could trust and whom Lecter Turon would not have any reason to suspect. Then, under the pretext of taking the children to see a show by the famous Lanipoor Players, who were currently performing in the city, they had left the palace with nothing but the clothes on their backs.

It was only in the carriage on the way to Rorin's father's house that Luciena informed her husband they were leaving Talabar and it was a stroke of sheer good fortune that her cousin, her one trusted ally, was actually in port.

It would have been impossible to escape the city on the ship that had brought them to Talabar; it was under guard by Hablet's soldiers, supposedly to protect it from

Fardohnyan citizens concerned the Hythrun ship might have brought plague to the city. Normally, at this time of year, the *Melissa* should be heading up the Glass River to Brodenvale in Medalon with a cargo of fine Fardohnyan silks, ready to wait on the spring melt to speed her journey downstream, returning by the end of summer with a load of Medalonian wool and wines. They'd been delayed by a broken rudder, which was finally repaired, and Drendik had been preparing to sail that very day.

Had Luciena waited another hour, they would have missed him completely.

Her husband, however, was still a little annoyed at her refusal to divulge the source of her intelligence, or the reason why she had insisted they leave Talabar so abruptly.

'Of course,' he added cautiously, 'if I knew exactly *what* we were supposed to be escaping from . . .'

'I promised I wouldn't betray my source,' she reminded him. She'd been telling him the same thing for weeks.

'You sound like Ruxton Tirstone,' he complained. 'He says the same thing to Marla whenever she tries to find out where he gets his intelligence from.'

'I'm not trying to be mysterious, Xanda. I simply gave someone my word.'

'And your word to this mysterious someone is more important than your oath to me?'

'That's not fair. My marriage vows have nothing to do with my word to someone else.' She smiled, trying to lighten the tension a little. 'Besides, I thought we'd already established that I married you under duress? If that's the case, then my oath to someone else would be far more binding than my oath to . . . Adham *Tirstone*?'

'You made an oath to Adham Tirstone?' Xanda asked, obviously confused.

'No! He's here! Look!' she exclaimed, pointing to the

familiar figure standing on the dock scanning the cluttered boats for something. 'Adham!'

Damin's stepbrother looked up, searching for whoever had called his name. When he spied Luciena and the *Melissa*, he waved frantically to get their attention and then pointed to an empty berth a little further along the crowded dock. Luciena and Xanda both hurried along the railing in parallel with him as Drendik followed Adham's directions and, with his two brothers' help, eased the boat into the narrow berth.

'Welcome to Medalon!' the young man called, as the barge bumped against the wharf.

'What, in the name of all the Primal Gods, are you doing in Bordertown?' Xanda called down to him, impatiently waiting for the Fardohnyan crew to secure the boat.

'Long story!' Adham called back, looking around with a frown. Luciena could easily guess the reason for his concern. This was Medalon, home of the Sisters of the Blade. In this country, they conducted periodic purges to rid themselves of pagan worshippers. Even in Bordertown, probably the most tolerant place in the whole country, it was inadvisable to swear by the name of any god, let alone all of them. 'Are the children with you?'

'We're all fine!' Luciena assured him, yelling to be heard over the racket of the surrounding docks. She glanced around nervously, wondering if anybody was paying their shouted conversation any attention. 'What are *you* doing here?'

'Waiting for you,' he called up to her.

Too impatient to wait until the short gangplank was pushed out, as soon as the boat was tied up Xanda jumped the railing and landed on the dock beside Adham. Luciena couldn't hear what he was saying to Adham, though, because at that moment, against her explicit instructions, Emilie appeared from belowdecks.

'Why is it so cold here, Mama?'

Luciena looked down at her daughter with a frown. 'I thought I told you to stay below with your brothers.'

'They're fighting again. Is that Uncle Adham that Papa's talking to, Mama?'

'Yes, it is,' she replied, drawing Emilie to her for warmth. The children had no other clothes than those they'd fled Talabar wearing, and they were far too flimsy for Bordertown's chill winds. Although she'd been on deck for only a few moments, already the child was shivering.

'Why is Uncle Adham here?'

That was something Luciena was also anxious to learn. 'We'll find out soon enough, darling. Now go below, please, and tell Aleesha we'll be disembarking soon. And remind those boys that if I have to come down there and speak to them, neither of them will be able to sit down for the rest of the week.'

'You can thank Drendik's broken rudder that I'm here,' Adham informed them an hour or so later, after settling the family into one of Bordertown's better inns. The children were being bathed and fed in their rooms by Aleesha while the adults met in the taproom downstairs with a welcome cup of mulled wine and a loaf of fresh bread, baked so recently it was still warm from the oven. It was reasonably quiet so early in the day, with only a couple of women wearing the distinctive blue robes of the Sisterhood sitting at one of the tables on the other side of the room. Drinking tea and deep in conversation with each other, the Sisters paid the Hythrun newcomers little notice.

'As can we,' Luciena agreed. 'But what has Drendik's misfortune got to do with you?'

'I've been trying to unload a shipment of spices we had earmarked for Karien. They're turning us away at every port these days.'

'But why store your cargo here in Medalon?' Xanda asked. 'Aren't they just as sensitive about Hythrun ships carrying the plague?'

'The ship wasn't one of ours, it was a Karien trader.' Adham smiled apologetically. 'I know we have an unofficial agreement to use your ships wherever we can, Luciena, but the Kariens are much easier to deal with when it's their own people bringing the spices up the Ironbrook River, especially into Yarnarrow. We've had shipments held up for months at a time in the past, because they've supposedly been polluted by "heathen" handling. And it would cost too much to sail them back home, even if I could have found a way to cajole a terrified Karien crew to land in any port ravaged by plague.'

'So Ruxton arranged for the ship to offload in Medalon?'

Adham nodded. 'He sent me up here to sort the whole mess out just after you two left Greenharbour for Talabar. I eventually found some warehouse space in Testra where we could store the stuff until things settled down. Rodja contacted Drendik through our agent in Talabar while I was on the way here. He was supposed to pick up the spices here in Bordertown and move them up to Testra for us. Once I found the warehouse, I came back here and arranged for the Kariens to offload the cargo, paid them off and sent them on their way, thinking the *Melissa* would arrive any moment. That was a fortnight ago.'

'But, fortunately for us, Drendik's rudder broke,' Luciena said. 'What happened to your spice cargo?'

'It's still sitting on the end of the Bordertown wharves, while I go grey praying for it not to rain. Still, it's not a problem now,' he said, with obvious relief. 'The Primal Gods must have heard my prayers. Drendik promises me he can have my spices loaded and under cover by this evening. He'll be on the river again by tomorrow, heading for Testra. After that, Brehn can send us a deluge and I won't give a damn.'

'You're not going with the cargo to Testra?'

Adham shook his head. 'I've had enough of atheists and the Sisterhood's bureaucracy for a while. I trust Drendik. Besides, I've heard a few rather disturbing rumours about what's going on behind Fardohnya's closed borders on the other side of the Widowmaker. I think I'm going to be needed at home.'

'But Greenharbour is rife with plague,' Luciena reminded him.

'I meant home as in Krakandar. Rumour has it that's the only city in Hythria still free of the plague. At the very least, it's bound to be safer than Greenharbour, otherwise Damin wouldn't have been sent there.'

'Damin is back home in Krakandar?' Luciena glanced at Xanda in surprise before turning to Adham. 'But how will you get there? Surely the borders are closed?'

'You don't know our border with Medalon very well, do you?'

'He means it's miles and miles long,' Xanda explained in response to Luciena's questioning look. 'It's the reason there's no customs post on the border, either. It's impossible to police. Set up a roadblock in one place and everyone would just cross somewhere else. Fortunately, most of the trade between Hythria and Medalon happens on the Glass River with ships that sail out of Greenharbour.'

'I actually knew that, Xanda,' she told him, a little peeved by his lecture. She wondered if he was talking to her as if she was an ignorant tourist because he was still angry at her silence on the subject of their flight from Fardohnya. 'We own a good half of the ships doing the trading, remember?'

'I was just trying to point out that they couldn't close the border if they tried.'

'And they're *not* trying,' Adham assured them. 'The Defenders are only stopping people entering the town from the south to prevent the plague coming into Bordertown. They don't give a fig about people heading out in that direction.'

Luciena gasped as the possibilities dawned on her. 'But that means . . . why, we could be home in a couple of weeks!'

'That's certainly my plan,' Adham announced. 'You're more than welcome to join me, if you're heading that way.'

Xanda didn't even wait to check with his wife before nodding. 'Don't worry, we'll be joining you.'

Adham seemed unsurprised. 'Then you should take this opportunity to rest today, Luciena, and make certain the children know what they're in for.' He turned to Xanda and added, 'You'd better come with me. We'll need to purchase horses and enough supplies to get us home. Once we get out of here, I don't plan to stop until I'm across the border.'

Luciena nodded her agreement. Placing her hand over Xanda's, she smiled, hoping he'd take it as an unspoken apology. 'Go with him. Spend whatever it takes. Just make sure it includes warm clothes for the children. I want to go home.'

'So do I.' He leaned forward, kissed her lightly, and then smiled, squeezing her hand. He would forgive her eventually, she knew. The prospect of heading home was far more important than a silly squabble over keeping secrets from him.

Adham smiled, too, obviously just as anxious to be gone from Medalon. 'It'll be just like the old days, won't it? With nearly all of us gathered in Krakandar again.'

'And maybe this time, I won't try to assassinate Damin,' Luciena remarked dryly. Adham froze, staring at her, not sure if she was joking. She laughed softly. 'If you could see the look on your face, Adham.'

'I'm glad you can joke about it,' he remarked warily.

Her attempt to kill Damin when he was a boy was not a subject they spoke about often. Marla had sworn them all to secrecy so Alija Eaglespike would never learn that her interference with Luciena's mind – and Wrayan's subsequent shielding of it – had been discovered. It had also, for many years, been a memory filled with such extreme shame and humiliation for Luciena that nobody wished to remind her of it.

That had all changed six years ago when Damin finished his fosterage and arrived in Greenharbour. Expecting some residual resentment or mistrust, Damin had stunned Luciena by treating her as if nothing had happened. In fact, he'd been positively friendly towards her. Certain he hadn't forgotten the attack, she'd eventually asked him outright why he didn't seem bothered by what she'd done. The young prince had smiled and winked and said nothing more than, 'Rule Number Eleven'.

It had taken her weeks to find out that he was referring to Elezaar's notorious Rules of Gaining and Wielding Power. Rule Number Eleven: *Do the unexpected*. It told her more about Damin Wolfblade than any other single thing she had seen him do.

'It was Damin who started sidling up to me every time we bumped into each other at palace functions to ask me if I was planning to kill him again, Adham,' she explained with a shrug. 'I figured if my victim could find something in that entirely disastrous episode to laugh about, then perhaps I should, too.'

'I don't think Damin does it to put Luciena at ease, mind you,' Xanda added. 'I think he does it to frighten Elezaar, actually. That, or to irritate Marla.'

Adham shook his head. 'I wonder, sometimes, about that boy.'

'That's his intention, Adham,' Luciena replied, with a

flash of insight that made her realise something that up until now she had never really seen about Hythria's young prince. 'I think he *wants* to keep everybody wondering. I think Damin's deliberately keeping everybody in the dark about what he really thinks, or even what he's capable of. I doubt there's anybody in Hythria who could tell you what he's really like.'

Adham thought about Luciena's words for a moment and then nodded his agreement. 'You could be right, Luciena.'

'Pity we won't find out until he's High Prince,' Xanda remarked.

The conversation seemed to have suddenly turned serious. Luciena smiled, hoping to lighten things. And to get her husband and Adham moving. This pointless discussion about what Damin Wolfblade might or might not be like wasn't getting them over the border any faster.

'We could try asking him, you know. When we get to Krakandar,' she suggested. And then she added, tartly, 'Assuming, of course, that you two ever get around to arranging transport to get us there.'

Adham took the hint good-naturedly. He downed the last of his wine, rose to his feet and shook his head. 'I'm never going to get married.'

Xanda also rose to his feet, and smiled as he pulled his cloak around himself in preparation for the chill wind outside.

'No woman would have you anyway, Adham,' Luciena told him. 'Now go, both of you. And don't come back until you have everything we need. I want to take my children home.'

59

In twenty-five years of dedicated service, Elezaar the Dwarf had done much for his mistress. He had advised her, trained her, instructed and mentored her children, supported her, and sometimes even manipulated her, in his effort to keep himself safe by remaining under her royal protection.

Never once, in all those years, had he regretted his decision.

Marla Wolfblade had exceeded all his early expectations. He had latched onto an inexperienced and naive young princess, hopeful her position would protect him from Alija Eaglespike. He'd had no inkling she would one day rise far above even Alija's exalted station. It would have been nice to claim he'd had some insight, some premonition about Marla's potential. But in all honesty, he couldn't claim anything of the sort. The uncertain woman-child who had stood in Venira's Emporium all those years ago, shopping for her first *court'esa*, had given no hint of the future path she would take or the greatness she would achieve.

Nobody who knew Marla Wolfblade when she was fifteen would have believed she would eventually become the most powerful woman in Hythria. Arguably, she was even more than that now. One would be hard-pressed to name any man who wielded more power than the High Prince's sister.

But still, even after all this time, Elezaar had secrets he had never shared with his mistress. He had never divulged some of the more shameful details of his previous service, both in the House of Dell and a few other noble Hythrun Houses where the veneer of civilisation was barely skin-deep. Nor had he ever let her know he had witnessed the massacre of Ronan Dell and the rest of his household.

And he had never, in twenty-five years of loyal service, told Princess Marla that he had a brother.

Some of the information – such as the identity of Ronan Dell's killers – he had kept to himself as insurance. He had learned much about his mistress over the years and one thing that secretly surprised him was her ruthless decisiveness when the occasion called for it. Once, he had thought to keep some of his dangerous secrets to protect himself from Alija. Now, at the back of his mind, was the notion that if his beloved princess ever turned on him, he would need just as much insurance to protect himself from her.

There were other, less important things, too, that hadn't been worth sharing. That he had once had a younger brother had never seemed worth mentioning. After all, Crysander was dead by the time Elezaar entered Marla's service.

Or so Elezaar believed.

Until now.

For days, Elezaar had burned with the knowledge that his brother might still be alive.

The news had come in the form of a carefully worded message from the slave trader, Venira. Bekan, one of the slaver's statuesque doormen – all but unemployed with plague ravaging the city – had arrived at the kitchen entrance to Marla's townhouse, asking to see Elezaar. With plague on the loose, the cook wouldn't let him in the house, but she had called Elezaar down to speak to him through the barred gate in the high wall that had originally been designed to keep assassins out and which was, at present, keeping the sickness at bay. Marla had taken Damin's advice and had Bruno Sanval scour the libraries for information about past outbreaks of the plague, and subsequently instigated a drive to clean the city of rats and debris, employing plague survivors to do the work. She was paying them, too, even the slaves involved in the cleanup, and it finally seemed to be having an effect. They went whole days now with no new outbreaks reported. Marla was so optimistic that she was already starting to make tentative plans for the future, along with sending messages to every major province (in her brother's name, of course) with instructions to do as Krakandar and Greenharbour had done and cleanse their cities of disease-carrying vermin. If there was a way to rid Hythria of the plague, or even a chance it could be slowed down a little, Marla was determined to see it done.

But the welcome notion that the plague might be on the wane meant little to the dwarf because the news Bekan delivered left Elezaar faint with shock.

'My master has acquired some merchandise he thinks you may be interested in,' the slave announced, looking past Elezaar to ensure the cook wasn't hanging about in the yard, listening to their conversation.

'I've no interest in anything your master is selling,' Elezaar snorted contemptuously, turning to leave. This was probably a ploy of Venira's to unload excess stock he couldn't sell because the slave markets were closed. The dwarf wasn't interested in helping Venira show a profit during a plague. And he certainly didn't feel he owed the fat slaver any favours.

'He said to tell you the merchandise's name is Crysander.'

Keeping his shock well hidden, Elezaar hesitated and turned to look at the messenger, staring at him with his one good eye. 'What else did Venira say?'

'He said if you're interested in arranging a purchase, he'll hold off turning the merchandise out into the street.'

Elezaar shook his head sceptically, thinking how unlikely it was that Venira would discard anything likely to make him a profit. 'He threatened to turn him out, did he?'

The man shrugged. 'Times are tough, Fool. Venira can only afford to keep the stock that's likely to turn a profit and this one is well past his useful life.'

Could it be true? Elezaar was too afraid to hope. Crysander had been two years younger than Elezaar. Just past his twenty-third birthday the day Elezaar saw him fall on the blade of Alija Eaglespike's henchman in Ronan Dell's palace. Crys would be nearing fifty years old now, had he survived. Certainly well past his useful life as a *court'esa*.

And hadn't Ruxton once reported – years ago – that he'd heard a rumour about Elezaar's brother?

'Did Venira say how he acquired this . . . merchandise?'

The doorman shrugged. 'I think he was one of a batch of slaves purchased from someone in Dregian Province. I couldn't say who. I'm his doorman, not his bookkeeper.'

'*If* I was interested,' Elezaar had replied cautiously, 'and I'm not saying I am, mind you . . . but *if* . . . I would want to see what I was buying first.'

The doorman nodded. 'Venira expected as much.'

Torn with indecision, the dwarf hesitated for a long time before answering. 'Come back in three days. I'll tell you if I'm interested then.'

The three days had dragged, leaving Elezaar a nervous wreck. Trapped in Marla's townhouse, he could do nothing to investigate the possibility that his brother still lived. All he could do was torment himself worrying about it, trying to run various scenarios through his head in which Crys had somehow survived the mortal blow Elezaar was certain he'd watched his brother suffer. *The whole thing is probably just an elaborate lie*, he told himself, over and over. Venira undoubtedly had some other game afoot, some devious plan for showing a profit at a time when every other slaver in Greenharbour was in danger of going bankrupt.

But his dreams were haunted by visions of the past . . . *Ronan Dell's corpse laying across the blood-soaked silken sheets . . . Another body on the floor by his feet . . . he still couldn't remember her name. Just a child; her slender, broken body in the first bloom of womanhood . . .*

Elezaar was trapped in his nightmare, playing his lyre with desperate determination – a solo symphony to accompany the torment of Ronan Dell's pleasure . . .

Then the dream would change abruptly and Ronan Dell and his slave were dead once more and Crys was always there, with his handsome dark eyes and long dark hair and his slender, boyish physique, which even at twenty-three still retained a dangerous allure of adolescence for a man like Ronan Dell.

In his dream, Crys was unafraid. *He's not in any danger from the assassins,* Elezaar always realised at that point, amazed, even now, how much the revelation surprised him. *Crysander is one of them.*

'*You betrayed our master.*' The accusation echoed across time. Still shocking. Still terrifying to realise.

'*I've been faithful to my master all along . . . I have always belonged to the House of Eaglespike.*'

Then the sound of marching feet. A troop of soldiers rounding the corner . . . an overwhelming feeling of panic . . . Crysander shoving him back into the bedroom . . . turning to the captain of the troop . . .

Even in his dream, Elezaar's heart pounded against his ribs hard enough to break them. *In the hall, he could hear them talking . . . 'Did you find them all?'* Crys always asked as the soldiers stopped in front of him. And although he knew what was coming. Elezaar couldn't stop himself looking through the slit in the doorway . . .

'*Thirty-seven slaves,*' the man confirms. '*All dead. There* should be thirty-eight, counting the dwarf. We didn't find him.'

'And you won't,' Crys tells them. 'He's long gone.'

'My lady wanted nobody left alive,' the captain reminds him.

'No credible *witnesses*,' Crys says. 'The Fool could stand on a table at the ball tonight in the High Prince's palace, shouting out what he'd seen here, and nobody would believe him. You needn't worry about the dwarf.'

'I suppose,' the captain agrees doubtfully. 'What about you?'

Crys shrugs, still naively innocent of the fate that awaits him as he explains that he's already been sold to Venira's Emporium.

'Then we're done here.'

Elezaar tries to cry out a warning . . . the captain's hand moves from the hilt of his sword to the dagger at his belt . . . he clamps his mouth shut to save his own life . . . is almost drowned by the overwhelming guilt as he rationalises away what he knows must happen next . . .

The captain may simply be moving his hand to a more comfortable position, he remembers thinking.

And then the true nightmare begins . . . The captain's blade plunging into Crys without warning . . . the man — Alija's man — driving his dagger up under Crys's rib cage and into his heart . . . Crys falling . . . the creak of leather as the captain bends over to check Crys is dead . . . the fading stamp of booted feet . . . the scrape of his brother's sandals against the polished floors as the soldiers retreat, dragging Crysander's body behind them . . .

Elezaar sat upright with a jerk, bathed in perspiration, hating the dream and his own weakness for letting it torment him like this. It was still dark outside, the air cool and still in the pre-dawn silence. He took a deep breath, waiting for the pounding in his chest to subside.

At first, the nightmare had plagued him night after night.

But over the years, the dreams had faded until he was almost able to convince himself that he had put Ronan Dell's house of horrors behind him. The nightmares were back with a vengeance, however, and they wouldn't go away until he knew for certain if Crysander was still alive.

And if he is alive? What then?

Elezaar had no money of his own. To purchase Crysander from Venira would require Marla's cooperation. To gain that, he must tell her things he'd kept from her for twenty-five years. Just learning that he'd held back such valuable information from her would destroy the trust he'd spent almost a lifetime building.

And there was nobody else he could ask.

Had Ruxton Tirstone still been alive, Elezaar might have been able to prevail upon the spice trader to do him a favour simply out of friendship. Elezaar grieved his passing sorely, now more than ever. There was no point in asking Rodja Tirstone. Although the elder Tirstone son now ran his late father's spice empire, and certainly had the funds – and perhaps even the will – to help Elezaar, Rodja would consider the request unusual enough that he'd feel obliged to mention it to Marla, which put Elezaar right back where he'd started.

Anybody else in the family with the resources to purchase a slave from Venira was out of the city. Had Damin been here, Elezaar didn't doubt for a moment that he could have begged the young prince's assistance and received it, with Marla being none the wiser. Xanda and Luciena were fond of him, and their children adored him. They might have helped him, too, had he been able to ask for their aid. Adham Tirstone was reckless enough that he would have loaned Elezaar the funds without even asking why a slave needed so much money. Even Kalan might have come to his aid if he'd worded his request the right way.

But there was nobody he could turn to, which left Elezaar

with the untenable prospect of losing his brother a second time.

Or having to face Marla and ask for her help.

If he did that, it would mean admitting he'd kept the secret of Ronan Dell's killers from her, when she could have used the information to bring Alija down years ago, long before the Lady of Dregian Province ever rose to become the High Arrion.

Perhaps even before she plotted to kill Marla's son.

Elezaar didn't kid himself about his fate if Marla ever discovered he'd known something all these years which might have prevented any attack on Damin.

For that sin alone, I would be condemned.

And Marla wasn't exactly renowned for her mercy when it came to any threat to her children.

But it's only a problem if this slave really is Crysander, he reminded himself, desperately hoping it wasn't.

With a heavy sigh, Elezaar glanced out of the window. The faintest hint of pink was beginning to lighten the darkness. The three days were up and today he must tell Bekan if he was interested in the slave Venira wanted to sell him.

The slave named Crysander.

'I want to see him,' Elezaar told the doorman when he appeared at the barred gate a few hours later. 'I'll have to examine him, question him, before I decide if I'm interested or not.'

Bekan nodded. 'I'll come back tomorrow then.'

'No! Not here!' He thought frantically for a moment, wondering how he could get away from the townhouse. 'There's a tavern two streets from here. It's called the Lucky Harlot. I'll meet you there.' Their supplies of wine were getting low, Elezaar knew. With the plague showing signs of slowing down, it wouldn't be too difficult to convince Marla it was safe enough to make the short journey to the

Lucky Harlot to arrange some fresh supplies. 'Be there at noon. And bring the . . . merchandise.'

Bekan nodded and walked away, leaving Elezaar standing alone in the kitchen yard, his heart pounding as hard as it had in his nightmare.

60

With Damin out of the city on a cattle raid and likely to be gone for the better part of two weeks, Starros breathed a huge sigh of relief. They could all relax for a while, Leila most of all. Mahkas couldn't keep pushing her at Damin if he wasn't in the palace and Starros was convinced the prince had volunteered to take part in the raid for that very reason.

In Damin's mind, Starros thought, *facing a battalion of Defenders is probably preferable to spending another night listening to Mahkas's unsubtle hints across the dinner table.*

Well, mostly that reason, he amended with a faint smile, as he headed down the long corridor of the main wing of the palace, towards the servants' quarters and his room. It was after midnight and Starros was looking forward to finding his bed. Most of the slaves were asleep, and only the guards, posted throughout the palace as a precaution against assassins, although Damin wasn't even in the city tonight, were still awake.

Starros was usually the last one to find his bed. He had long ago decided 'assistant chief steward' was merely a euphemism for 'working twenty-two hours a day to make Orleon look omnipotent'. Still, the old steward was generally a good man, and Starros had grown up in the palace.

He knew Orleon asked nothing of him he hadn't done himself.

As he walked past Lord Damaran's study, Starros noticed a light under the door. He hesitated for a moment, wondering if he should disturb Mahkas, and then decided he might as well. If he didn't, the chances were good he'd be called from his bed as soon as he fell asleep if the regent decided he wanted anything later.

Starros knocked and opened the door without waiting for an answer. Mahkas was sitting at his desk, bending over a letter he was writing, squinting a little in the candlelight. He glanced up at the interruption with a frown.

'Is something wrong, Starros?'

'No, my lord. I just wanted to check if there was anything you needed before I go to bed.'

Mahkas thought about it for a moment and then shook his head. 'No. I'm fine.'

'Good night then, my lord.' He bowed and turned to leave.

'Starros!'

'Sire?'

'That *court'esa* Damin was talking about the other day, the one from the Beggars' Quarter. Is there anything I should be concerned about?'

Starros smiled. 'I think Damin was just having a bit of fun with you, my lord. Fyora works at the Pickpocket's Retreat. She's a friend of Wrayan Lightfinger's and old enough to be his mother. He kissed her hand once, that's all. I don't think you need lose any sleep over it.'

'I should have realised he was just trying to scare me into letting him go with Almodavar.' Mahkas smiled thinly. 'He hasn't changed much, has he?'

'No, sire. Not much.'

The regent put down his quill and examined Starros for a moment, his face creased with concern. 'You do understand, 'don't you, lad,' Mahkas asked, uncharacteristically concerned about Starros's feelings, 'how . . . *inappropriate* it is that you still think of Damin as your best friend?'

'I understand he's Krakandar's prince, my lord,' Starros assured the regent. 'And that I'm only the chief assistant steward. It's Damin who doesn't care what people think.'

'Then I will have to rely on you to make sure he remembers who he is,' Mahkas said.

'Yes, my lord.' He turned to leave, wondering why Mahkas was in such a garrulous mood. Normally, he spared Starros little more than a grunted acknowledgement of his presence.

'You're still good friends with my daughter, aren't you?'

Starros froze, wondering if this was the beginning of an interrogation that could only end with him in serious trouble. He turned to Mahkas and nodded carefully. 'Well, yes, I suppose . . .'

'Can *you* tell me what it's going to take? The gods know nobody else seems able to!'

Starros shook his head in confusion. 'I'm not sure I follow you, my lord.'

'What's it going to take to make her understand that she needs to be more . . . I don't know . . . how should I put it . . . *accommodating* towards her cousin?'

'You mean Damin?'

'Of course that's who I mean! Do you think *you* could talk to her? Leila always listened to you when you were children. She respects your opinion. And I know you've always had her best interests at heart. Perhaps . . . if *you* spoke to her, as her friend, she might come to understand her duty in this matter.'

Dear gods, I can't believe he's asking me to do this!

'Er . . . my lord, I really don't think it would be appropriate for the assistant chief steward to speak to someone as exalted as Lady Leila about anything so . . . intimate.'

565

Mahkas sighed heavily. 'Perhaps you're right. The gods know it's taken me long enough to get her to treat you according to your status. It would undo everything I've been trying to teach her to have you suddenly become her best friend again.' He nodded approvingly. 'Your sense of propriety does you credit, Starros.'

'Thank you, sire.' Starros thought he might choke if he didn't get out of there soon. 'I'll see you in the morning?'

'Yes,' Mahkas replied absently. 'Good night, Starros.'

'Good night, my lord.'

Closing the door behind him, Starros leaned against it and took a deep, calming breath before taking another step, horrified by the direction of his conversation with Mahkas. He was still trembling from the fright a short while later as he turned into the hall where his room was located, holding the candle a little higher to light his way.

What's it going to take to make her understand that she needs to be more accommodating towards her cousin? No wonder Damin was so anxious to get out of the palace.

Starros wondered how Damin was faring, roughing it out in the wilderness with nothing but a thin travel blanket for warmth, the rocky ground for a bed and his saddle for a pillow. They'd be well into Medalon by now, Starros estimated, perhaps even on the way back if they'd encountered no resistance. Damin was probably having the time of his life. The young prince had talked of being a Raider for as long as Starros had known him, and he would have walked away from his own mother's funeral for a chance to join them on a raid across the border.

Looking forward to finally seeing the end of his day, Starros reached his own room and wearily opened the door, startled to find the room filled with light. Almost every flat surface was covered with short, fat candles, ablaze with soft, warm radiance.

Stretched out on his narrow bed was Leila, her long, fair hair unbound, wearing nothing but the emerald necklace she had worn to dinner this evening.

Starros slammed the door shut hurriedly and then leaned against it, staring at her in shock. 'Leila!'

'You were expecting someone else?' she asked, pushing herself up on one elbow with an elegantly raised brow.

'What are you *doing* here?' he gasped.

'Waiting for you, lover.'

He was flabbergasted by the risk she was taking. 'You just left the door *unlocked?* Suppose it wasn't me who walked in just now?'

'Then you'd have rather a lot of explaining to do, my love.'

He forced a smile, his heart still thumping at the danger. Then he looked around at the candles curiously. 'What's all this then?'

She lay back on the bed, folding her arms behind her head, which did nothing but draw his attention to her small, perfect breasts and make it very hard for Starros to concentrate on what she was saying. 'You told me how much you hated the fact that we only ever meet in the darkness, lover. I wanted there to be some light.'

He pushed off the door, added the candle he was carrying to the collection on the shelf, and crossed the small room to the bed. 'You still shouldn't have taken the risk, Leila. If someone had seen you . . .'

'I was careful. I came through the slaveways. Anyway, merely *thinking* of you the way I do is a risk for me, Starros,' she reminded him, a little sadly. 'Why should the degree matter?'

He sat down on the bed and gathered her into his arms, holding her for a moment just for the sheer joy of it. But touched as he was by her thoughtfulness, he was acutely aware of the danger she courted. 'I still don't want you taking stupid risks for me. If your father ever suspected anything . . .'

'He doesn't,' she promised, and Starros was inclined to agree with her. They wouldn't have had that bizarre conversation just now if Mahkas suspected for a moment that his daughter and Starros were lovers.

'He can't see past his own ambition,' Leila added. 'If I walked into his study right this minute and declared I was in love, he'd just assume I meant Damin. Gods! I so want to tell him how wrong he is! I want to tell him I love you. I want to tell the whole world I love you!'

Starros kissed her and then shook his head, looking at her sternly. 'You're not going to do anything of the kind, Leila.'

'Would you rather we continued like this for the rest of our lives?' She began to unlace his shirt, kissing the bare flesh on his chest as she exposed it.

'Of course not. But if we just let Damin—'

She shook her head. 'Damin be damned! I don't want to wait on my cousin's pleasure. Why don't we run away to somewhere new? Someplace where nobody knows us.'

He smiled at the unlikely notion, as she pulled the shirt over his head. 'How would we live?'

'You could get a job,' she told him.

'Doing what?'

'I don't know. Whatever it is you do.'

He leaned forward to kiss her shoulder and neck. 'Wrayan offered me a job as a thief once.' He nibbled her earlobe, making her laugh softly, and then bent forward to kiss her breast.

'There you go,' she murmured appreciatively. 'You could be a thief and I could be . . . a Missus Thief.'

He stopped kissing her and looked at her oddly. 'A *Missus* Thief? You truly are uniquely unprepared for anything other than a career as a prince's wife, aren't you, my love?'

'Oh, I don't know. I could probably eke out a living as a *court'esa*,' she whispered against his neck, as she put her arms around him. '*You've* never complained about my skills, that I recall.'

'Why don't you refresh my memory?' he suggested.

Leila laughed softly and pushed him backwards. 'You want me to refresh your memory?'

'Then I'll be in a position to give you an accurate assessment of your skills.'

She laughed and climbed astride him, her skin the colour of spun gold in the candlelight. 'I'm going to *refresh your memory* into oblivion, my love.'

'You think so?' he asked with a smile, reaching for her breasts.

She caught his wrists before he could touch her and forced them back, holding his arms down on the bed above his head. Then she leaned forward so that her lips brushed his face like the whisper of silk. 'Tell me you love me, Starros,' she demanded, almost desperately.

'I love you.'

'Would you fight for me?'

'Of course.'

'Die for me?'

He smiled at her fierce expression. 'Is that a requirement of loving you?'

'Yes, damn you, it is.'

'Then, yes, I would die for you,' he promised heroically.

Leila was still holding his arms above his head, but was apparently satisfied with his answer. She gave him one of those sad, hopeless little smiles, let go of his wrists and sat back on her heels, still astride him. 'I would die without *you*, Starros,' she sighed. 'Don't ever leave me.'

'I won't.' He reached up gently to touch her face and noticed a tear on her cheek. 'Hey, silly girl. Don't cry. It won't always be like this. I promise.'

'With our luck, it'll just get worse,' she predicted grimly.

'You don't know that.'

After a moment of strained silence, Leila wiped her tears away with determined cheerfulness and began to work on the stiff leather of his belt, as if she refused to contemplate what the future might hold in case it ruined this moment for them. 'Don't you wish, sometimes, you could see the look on my father's face if he ever found out about us?'

Starros shook his head, looking at her strangely. 'No. I most certainly do not.' There was something inherently wrong with discussing Mahkas Damaran with his daughter while she sat astride him, wearing nothing but the family jewels as she tried to take his clothes off. 'And do you think we could talk about something else besides your father?'

'He's always going to come between us, Starros.'

'Not tonight, Leila,' he begged. 'And not in here.'

Leila finally managed to get the buckle undone. She leaned forward to kiss him seductively. 'All right then, my love, not tonight. Not in this room.'

Leila tossed the belt aside and set to work on his trousers, only instead of her hands she decided to use her teeth, which put an abrupt end to both the conversation and any thoughts Starros was having about . . . well, everything.

61

After Starros left his study, Mahkas sat for a while, wondering about what the young man had said. The lad showed remarkable maturity in his words. And he'd demonstrated wisdom beyond his years with his suggestion that it might be inappropriate for him to speak with Leila on such a delicate matter. He hadn't expected that from a bastard fosterling.

He should have suspected the young man was brighter than he appeared, Mahkas supposed. Marla hadn't wanted him appointed as Orleon's future replacement out of a sense of duty. Starros was capable and could be trusted, and Marla wasn't about to waste that sort of valuable resource in the Palace Guard.

And Starros was right, of course. It would be totally inappropriate for the assistant chief steward to discuss the intimate details of any affair of the heart with the daughter of the house. Under normal circumstances, they wouldn't even be on first-name terms.

But then, these weren't normal circumstances.

Mahkas rubbed at the scar on his arm absently, his correspondence forgotten. Leila's intransigence over Damin was beyond insubordination; it bordered on outright disobedience. Mahkas wasn't sure how much longer he could put up with the sulking, the heavy sighs and the sullen defiance Leila demonstrated every time Mahkas broached the subject. Much of the reason he had agreed to Damin joining Almodavar on the raid into Medalon was to give him an opportunity to straighten things out with his daughter. She had to understand. She had to stop this nonsense and start doing something about seducing her fiancé, not driving him away.

How many other daughters got such an offer? How many other girls lay awake at night, dreaming of a chance to wed – or even bed – Damin Wolfblade?

Yet Leila wanted no part of it all – as far as Mahkas could see – because of some silly resentment from her childhood that she should be well and truly over by now, considering she was twenty-three.

Her ingratitude was beyond his understanding. Mahkas could have arranged any number of marriages for his daughter and not even bothered to consult her. What more did she want from him? He wasn't selling her to a complete stranger for a few acres of land and a few head of cattle. He was letting her marry a man who loved her. A man she had grown up with. A man who would one day be High Prince of Hythria. How many daughters got even a fraction of that sort of consideration from their parents?

And what more could she want in a husband anyway? Damin had wealth beyond the dreams of avarice. He was young, good-looking, had no unbearable bad habits that Mahkas knew of. Admittedly, he never seemed to take anything seriously, but he was only young. No doubt he'd grow out of that eventually.

Leila should thank the gods her father had found her someone so agreeable. When she was seventeen, old Lord Snowden of Narrawn, in Elasapine Province, had made a very attractive offer for Leila that he'd rejected out of hand. Had Mahkas accepted the offer, Leila would be living in a draughty old fortress in the foothills of the Sunrise Mountains outside of Byamor by now, stepmother to Snowden's eight children from his five previous wives.

And yet she still had the temerity to scorn his choice.

Mahkas rubbed at his arm even harder, only noticing what he was doing when it really began to hurt. He pushed up his right sleeve and examined the small lump with concern. It seemed to bother him more and more lately. It was such a tiny little thing, too. The physicians he'd consulted about it – at Bylinda's insistence – all agreed that it was the legacy of some long-forgotten war wound. According to the healers, it was not uncommon for a shard of metal, too small to find or even notice when the wound was first inflicted, to work its way to the surface many years after the original injury. It would come out eventually, they assured him, of its own accord. Digging around for the shard before it was ready to exit the body would merely increase the likelihood of infection, with no guarantee they would find anything so small.

So he itched and scratched and suffered the irritation, because a small lump was vastly preferable – and much less painful – to having a gangrenous arm amputated.

Mahkas cursed the itching and fingered the long scar beside the lump to distract himself. He'd collected that one defending Riika the day she was kidnapped by the Fardohnyans just before they'd killed her. It ran almost the full length of his arm and had come close to ending his career as a soldier.

A stupid risk to have taken considering he was the one who'd arranged the kidnapping.

Mahkas pushed that thought away hurriedly. He had long ago convinced himself he was innocent of any involvement in Riika's death. It had been Darilyn's idea. Darilyn had forced him to take part. And Darilyn had paid for her treachery. Mahkas had told himself that so often now, he actually believed it was true.

He pulled his sleeve down and made himself concentrate on the problem of Leila and Damin. His sisters were long dead and nothing could be done to alter that. But he could alter Leila's fate. He could ensure the daughter of Mahkas Damaran lived as a princess. Not for his daughter the fate of a penniless wife, trying to hold together the appearance of prosperity because she suffered a noble name with no fortune or land behind it.

It still irked Mahkas that, even after all this time, he had no independent wealth of his own. His fortune was Krakandar's fortune; Damin's fortune. Everything he earned and anything he spent came from his nephew's coffers, not his own.

The ultimate irony, Mahkas thought. *Any money I receive when Damin marries my daughter will be money I've made for him, watching over his lands, his inheritance.*

But how was he going to make Leila understand this?

How was he going to make her do the right thing, not just for herself, but for her whole family?

Perhaps, Mahkas thought, *Starros should talk to her, after all.*

It was right of the young man to say that it might be inappropriate, but even Mahkas knew that Leila had been closer to Starros than any of the other children when they were growing up. He'd always stood up for her, even against Damin. Maybe Leila would listen to Starros. His opinion was objective. He wasn't a member of the family. He had no vested interest in the decision. It mattered little to Starros who Leila married.

For a moment Mahkas stopped worrying about Leila long enough to wonder what Starros did for female companionship. While officially a fosterling, he'd been allowed access to the palace *court'esa*, but, strictly speaking, they were out of bounds now he was considered staff rather than family. No doubt the fosterling was entertaining himself with some of the younger household slaves. Maybe even the housemaids. With a warm and rare feeling of paternal generosity, Mahkas promised himself he would find Starros a suitable match when the time came. Someone who might be able to serve Leila as a handmaiden, perhaps. There might even be a girl in Bylinda's entourage the fosterling already had his eye on. There were certainly one or two Mahkas had fondled surreptitiously, when he was certain his wife wasn't looking.

Mahkas shook his head. He was getting distracted. The question wasn't who Starros was sleeping with. The question was, could Starros finally make Leila see the error of her ways?

Mahkas had no doubt that Starros would do as he asked, if only because he must be anxious to make amends for his gross breach of protocol the day Damin arrived. And he must see the logic in the match; probably even welcome it. Fond as Starros was of both Leila and Damin, Mahkas could well imagine his delight at the prospect of Leila married to his good friend. *And maybe, if Starros explains things to her, as her friend – as Damin's friend, too – Leila will begin to understand.*

Mahkas leaned back in his seat and smiled. *Yes. It's a good idea. Quite a brilliant idea, actually.*

He glanced at the water clock on the mantel. It wasn't that long since Starros had announced he was going to bed. He'd still be awake. Now that Mahkas had settled on doing this, he didn't want to wait. Damin might be home any day, Starros had to talk to Leila as soon as possible. The sooner she understood, the sooner she would start to do as her father wished and the sooner Damin would come to realise that his cousin loved him. Once that happened, Damin would start to pressure his mother to make the arrangement formal, Mahkas reasoned.

Mahkas rose to his feet, picking up the candelabrum on the desk, and headed for the door.

It was chilly in the corridor leading to the staff quarters. As a free servant rather than a slave, Starros's room was on the same level as the family suites, although in a different wing. Slightly larger than the average staff bedroom, and boasting a small dressing room as well as its own entrance to the slaveways, Starros had been well favoured when he took on his apprenticeship with Orleon, as his accommodation indicated.

A draught in the hall made the candle gutter and flare as Mahkas strode along the corridor. When he finally reached Starros's door he hesitated, smiling to himself as he heard the obvious sounds of passion coming from inside the room.

Well, the question about who Starros is sleeping with is about to be answered, Mahkas chuckled to himself, wondering if it was that new girl Bylinda had bought last year in Byamor when they'd gone to visit Charel Hawksword and Kalan's twin brother, Narvell, to celebrate the young man's twenty-first birthday.

Leena, that was her name. She was the daughter of two slaves from the Warlord of Elasapine's own household and Charel had vouched for her personally. She was a buxom young thing, Mahkas recalled, of about eighteen or nineteen. And very attractive. So attractive that even Mahkas had cornered her once or twice, just to take a nibble out of what was, essentially, forbidden fruit. He'd never slept with her, though. He was too good a husband for that. Bylinda didn't mind him sleeping with the palace *court'esa* – that's what they were there for – but she took a very dim view of him spoiling her handmaids. It was a well-known fact that as soon as the lord of the house started sleeping with the handmaids, they got all uppity and full of their own importance and it was impossible to get a decent day's work out of them after that.

The cries from Starros's room grew louder, more intense, as his partner urged him on. Leena was certainly an enthusiastic and uninhibited lover, by the sound of it. Mahkas smiled as he turned the door handle, thinking that at the very least – in addition to embarrassing poor Starros – he'd finally get a good look at Leena naked, something he'd fantasised about on more than one occasion.

Mahkas hesitated for a moment longer and then threw open the door, half erect himself both from the voyeuristic delight of listening to their love-making and in anticipation of seeing Leena in all her voluptuous glory . . .

He blinked in the sudden and unexpected light as the door slammed back against the wall, blowing out a good half of the countless candles that seemed to cover every flat surface in the room.

A scream filled the room as Mahkas's brain took a moment or two to realise what he was witnessing; to register that it wasn't the voluptuous and dark-haired Leena who sat astride the bastard fosterling, her head thrown back, as she demanded *more, harder, faster* . . .

It was his own daughter.

He bellowed a wordless cry of anguished, horrified fury that echoed throughout the sleeping palace.

Leila screamed again as he lunged at her, grabbing her by the arm, dragging her off the bed, off *him* . . .

'*Guards!*'

Mahkas wasn't just angry. He was beyond rage. Beyond reason.

'*Leila!*' Starros cried, reaching for her desperately.

Mahkas put himself between them, twisting Leila's arm with such ferocity that her screams were as much from the pain of his grasp as they were from their discovery. Instead of cowering in shame, Starros clambered over the bed, desperate to tear Leila from her father's grasp, but the regent swung his elbow savagely up into the bastard fosterling's face, throwing him across the rumpled bed and against the wall.

A red veil of rage danced before his eyes as Mahkas dragged Leila into the hall. By now, the guards on duty had responded to his cries. Naked as a whore, struggling like a wild animal, Leila begged to be let go. A dozen Raiders pounded along the hall with drawn swords in answer to Mahkas's shout. Leila lashed out at him with her foot, connecting with his shin, making Mahkas grunt with the pain and momentarily lose his grip. On her hands and knees, sobbing like a child, she tried to crawl away from him. Furiously, he reached down, grabbed a handful of her long blond hair and dragged her back to his side.

'Arrest him!' Mahkas bellowed, pointing to Starros, who was trying to push himself up against the wall. His face was broken and bloody, his expression more dazed than defiant. 'He tried to rape my daughter!'

Starros barely had time to stand before his room was full of Raiders. Although he was unarmed, he tried to fight them off with no chance of succeeding. Mahkas, his hands still tangled in Leila's long hair, began dragging her along the hall, naked, humiliated and terrified, kicking and screaming in protest.

Starros cried out to her again, but he had no hope of reaching Leila as the guards overwhelmed him and the bastard fosterling's illicit love affair with Leila Damaran – along with his career as the chief assistant steward of Krakandar Palace – came crashing down in an abrupt and bitter end.

62

The Lucky Harlot was a much more salubrious establishment than its name implied. As a slave, Elezaar would not normally have been permitted in the main taproom unless he was attending his mistress, but the owners knew he was Princess Marla's personal slave and for her they were willing to bend the rules. Besides, there was plague in the city and any customer in good health was welcome.

Located in the better part of Greenharbour, the tavern boasted snowy white tablecloths, chairs upholstered in soft, pliable leather, a large cushioned seating area surrounding a low dining table overlooking a small paved courtyard and, most importantly, a number of discreet alcoves where one could discuss business in private.

His palms sweaty with anticipation, Elezaar limped along behind the silent slave who led him to the alcove where Bekan – and maybe Crysander – were waiting. When the slave indicated they had reached their destination he bowed and walked back to the taproom.

Taking a deep breath, the dwarf pushed aside the woven curtain. Waiting for him, seated on the cushions around the low table, were Venira's doorman, Bekan, an old man Elezaar didn't know and a slave he knew very well indeed.

'Tarkyn Lye,' he said, shaking his head. 'I should have known you'd be mixed up in this somehow.'

The blind *court'esa* turned his head in the direction of Elezaar's voice and smiled coldly. He wore a scarf over his eyes, to hide his scarred face, and a rich brocaded jacket over his well-fed belly. 'Well, well . . . if it isn't the Fool. And to think, Bekan and I were just laying odds on whether or not you'd actually show up.'

'Who were you backing?'

'Bekan was willing to risk his money on you. I thought you too much a coward to leave the safety of Marla Wolfblade's skirts.' The blind *court'esa* spoke with obvious contempt. Then he laughed and turned his head in the direction of Bekan. 'It just occurred to me why she's kept him around all these years, Bek.'

'Why's that?' Bekan asked.

'Well, look at the size of him. He's just the right height, when you think about it. Marla probably keeps him hidden under her skirts for pleasure. Elezaar was always particularly good at kissing arse, as I recall.'

For a moment, Elezaar almost forgot himself. The insult to his princess was enough to make him want to hurl himself across the low lacquered table and grab Tarkyn Lye by the throat. He wouldn't, of course. Even blind, Tarkyn was strong enough to brush him aside like a bug. And Bekan could break him in half, if he was so inclined.

So Elezaar simply swallowed hard and trusted no hint of his anger was betrayed by his voice. 'At least I can *see* what I'm kissing. Which makes me wonder, Tarkyn? How do you know where to find Alija's arse when she wants you to kiss it?' He laughed then, at his own foolishness. 'Of course! Silly me! I've heard blind men compensate for their disability. Your other senses must be much more acute. You can probably smell her slit from across the room!'

That struck a nerve. Tarkyn's expression darkened but,

like Elezaar, he apparently had no intention of letting his opponent know how much the remark insulted him. 'I can smell the stink of your *fear* across the room,' Tarkyn replied. 'That's for certain.'

'I'm not afraid of you, Tarkyn Lye.'

'Then more fool you, Fool.'

Affecting a bored sigh, Elezaar shrugged. 'Where's this slave you're claiming is my brother?'

'You mean you didn't recognise him the moment you laid eyes on him,' Tarkyn asked, sounding quite surprised. 'I'm appalled! So much for brotherly love.'

Elezaar's gaze fixed on the slave seated on the cushions against the back wall. If Tarkyn was appalled, Elezaar was shocked beyond words. This creature was nothing like the slender, handsome young man Elezaar remembered. He was old, although his exact age could have been anywhere between forty-five and ninety. Dressed only in ragged canvas trousers, his skin was the texture of orange peel, tanned from a lifetime of overexposure to the sun, and it hung on his emaciated frame as if it belonged to a larger man. His hair was long, thin and lank, and it was impossible to tell what colour it might once have been.

'*Crysander?*'

The man looked up slowly when Elezaar spoke his name. There was no light of recognition in his eyes. Just a blank stupor. It was the kind of look a slave wore when he'd had his spirit broken. It was the look of a man beaten down so many times he'd lost the will to get up again.

'That's not my brother.'

'Be very certain about that, Fool,' Tarkyn warned. 'If you deny him, he'll die. As you can see, he's hardly worth feeding now. Unless he has some other, more intrinsic value . . .' The blind man turned his head in the direction of Bekan. 'Stand him up. Make sure the dwarf gets a good

581

look at him. I'd hate for him to have second thoughts later. *After* we've killed him.'

Bekan pulled the slave to his feet. The man didn't resist. He was chained hand and foot, his body covered in old scars that looked to be the work of a lash or a thin cane. Elezaar was filled with pity at the sight of him, but nothing else. There was nothing in this shell of a man that reminded him of his brother.

But as he swayed on his feet, Elezaar noticed a faint white scar on the man's belly. It ran lengthwise from the base of his ribcage to just above his navel. Elezaar's mind suddenly filled with those horrifying images from his nightmare: *the captain's blade plunging into Crys without warning . . . the man – Alija's man – driving his dagger up under Crys's rib cage and into his heart, with businesslike efficiency . . . Crys falling . . . the creak of leather as the captain bends over to check Crys is dead . . .*

He shook his head to push the memories away and stared at the slave. It couldn't be Crysander. Not this broken husk.

But that scar . . .

'Come on, Fool!' Tarkyn urged with an edge of impatience. 'It can't be that difficult, surely, to recognise your own brother?'

Elezaar ignored the blind *court'esa*. 'Do you know who I am?' he asked the slave.

The old man nodded. 'Elezaar the Fool.'

That didn't prove anything. Anybody could have told him that. He could have worked it out just from the discussion they'd been having here in this room. Elezaar needed to ask something nobody but he and Crysander would know. Something that only two brothers might have shared. If he was an impostor – some helpless dupe roped into pretending he was Crysander because of a convenient scar – he would have no memories of their childhood together. Tarkyn Lye, or Alija, or whoever was behind this transparent plot to subvert him, couldn't possibly know everything the brothers had shared as children. They might have been able to find out what happened once they'd both been taken to be trained as *court'esa*, and may have even coached the slave to respond accordingly. But the years before then, the ten precious years of relative happiness the brothers shared as slave children in the household of a minor Pentamor nobleman were beyond their reach. If Crysander had hoarded those memories as Elezaar had, then he would know the answer to Elezaar's question.

'We had a game, my brother and I, when we were children. Something that meant a great deal to me. Do you know what it was?'

Elezaar waited anxiously for the slave to reply, his drawn-out silence convincing the dwarf he had no memories of a shared past the longer it went on.

'Horsey,' the slave said softly, as Elezaar was on the verge of turning to leave. His voice was gravelly and rough, as if he'd spent the last twenty-five years screaming at the top of his lungs and finally worn out his throat. 'Your legs were too short and you were never going to be able to ride a real horse. You wanted to know what it felt like . . .'

The voice faded away, as if that was all he could recall, and the slave hung his head, as if he expected punishment for speaking out of turn. Elezaar stood frozen in shock. And indecision. All his fears about what he should do next came crashing down on top of him.

Walk away, a small voice in his head urged. *Say they're wrong. Tell them it's not Crysander. Walk away. Now.*

'How much?' Elezaar heard himself asking, even though the voice of reason in his head was shouting at him, telling him he was a fool. *Crysander brought this on himself! He betrayed Ronan Dell! If he's suffered all these years, it's not your fault!*

'He's not for sale.'

Elezaar turned to Tarkyn. *So that's their game. Betrayal.* 'What do you want from me?'

The blind *court'esa* chuckled. 'You used to be such a self-centred little thing, didn't you? Too much of the good life has weakened you, Fool, softened your resolve. There was a time you cared for nobody but yourself. Look at you now. All pampered and favoured like a fat, neutered house cat and with just as much balls.'

'Just tell me what you want, Tarkyn.'

'Nothing too difficult. Just some information, that's all.'

'I won't betray my mistress.'

Tarkyn leaned back on the cushions and smiled confidently. 'Yes, Elezaar. I think you will.'

'You'll have to kill me first.'

'I don't think that will be necessary.' The blind slave reached beneath the table and brought out something that chilled Elezaar's blood. He placed it on the lacquered surface with a sinister smile. 'Remember this? You should. It's a souvenir from Ronan Dell's palace.'

Elezaar stared at the nightmare Tarkyn had placed on the table, feeling his bowels turn to water at the sight of it. Carved from a single piece of polished horn, the instrument was about a foot long, tapered at the point, which was barbed and serrated, sculpted to inflict as much damage as possible on whatever orifice it was inserted into. Wrapped around its length was a twist of jagged wire, the barbs sharpened to deadly points, a modification Ronan Dell had added himself when the instrument's initial novelty had begun to wane.

'He used it on all those young slaves he was so partial to, didn't he?' Tarkyn asked in a conversational tone, leaning forward to pick it up. He turned it over in his hands, holding the dreadful tool with extreme care for fear of slicing his own fingers open on its wickedly sharp surface. 'And you watched every blood-soaked moment of it, didn't you, Fool, playing the lyre for your master like a good little pet, while Ronan Dell got his kicks making his victims suffer. Did it ever bother you, Fool, that you just stood there while those poor children screamed and cried and eventually bled to death?'

Elezaar said nothing.

Tarkyn Lye pushed the instrument across the lacquered surface of the table leaving a long scratch in its wake. The resulting screech set Elezaar's teeth on edge. Venira's doorman ominously pulled on a familiar thick leather glove, similar to the one Ronan Dell used to wear when he—

Oh gods! No! He can't mean to . . .

'Bekan,' Tarkyn ordered, relaxing back against the cushions. 'Tell Crysander to bend over. I want to see how much fun we can have with Ronan's special little toy.'

'NO!' Elezaar cried desperately, as Bekan reached for the deadly instrument with one hand, forcing Crysander face-first onto the table with his ungloved hand. 'For the gods' sake, Tarkyn! *No!*'

'But you just told me you'd never betray your mistress,' the blind *court'esa* reminded him, apparently unconcerned.

Bekan picked up the instrument with the hand protected by the leather glove. Crysander lay there, unresisting, waiting with the fatalistic acceptance of a man who had been tortured so often he no longer understood why; only that he must endure.

'I respect your loyalty, Fool. You can go, if you like. We'll just have a bit of fun for a while, and then we'll probably be off, too. Not a good idea to be out after slave curfew at the moment. Not with plague in the city. Carry on, Bekan.'

'Call him *off*, Tarkyn!' the dwarf begged, unable to think of any other way to stop the torment these men had planned for his brother. The vacant, accepting look on Crysander's face was the worst of it. His eyes stared blankly at Elezaar.

He was beyond shame, beyond humiliation. Even beyond normal human emotions, perhaps.

Sensing he was on the brink of victory, the blind *court'esa* held up his hand to halt Bekan. 'Give me a reason, Fool.'

So relieved Tarkyn had stopped Bekan before it was too late, Elezaar wanted to cry. He hung his head in shame. 'I'll tell you whatever you want to know.'

I am betraying my princess. For the sake of a man who may or may not be my brother. I am betraying my princess. The tragedy was, Elezaar knew in his heart that he probably would have given Tarkyn what he wanted even if the old slave had been a total stranger. The days when he could witness such evil and remained untouched by it were long past.

'That's better,' Tarkyn said, smiling triumphantly. He waved his arm and Bekan put the instrument down.

With a shove, the doorman sat Crysander back down on the cushions and began to take off the leather glove. The slave's expression didn't change. Fear didn't meld into gratitude. Crysander simply didn't care.

'I had a feeling you'd get my point. If you'll pardon the pun. Have a seat, Fool. We have a lot to talk about. At least, you do, at any rate.'

Twenty-five years. I am throwing away twenty-five years of faithful service to a woman I love. A woman who has protected me, respected me and trusted me so much that she let me teach her children.

And for what? A sick slave Alija probably found in the markets a month ago.

But try as he might, Elezaar couldn't bring himself to leave. He couldn't walk away while that damned thing sat on the table and another innocent victim waited on the pleasure of a sadistic bastard like Tarkyn Lye. Not again. He could never go through that again.

Not even for Marla Wolfblade.

'What do you want to know?' Elezaar asked in a flat, defeated voice.

'Let's start with what really happened to Wrayan Lightfinger,' Tarkyn Lye suggested.

63

A strange sort of calm descended on Mahkas Damaran after he got over the initial shock of finding Leila sitting astride The Bastard Fosterling, moaning like a cheap whore. The Bastard Fosterling no longer had any other name, in Mahkas's mind. The being who was once Starros no longer existed.

He was The Bastard Fosterling now. The ungrateful whelp, who had first seduced, then corrupted Mahkas's beloved daughter. He'd replayed the scene in his mind over and over, adjusting it until it fitted with his preferred version of events and it was now much easier to recall.

It was fortunate, Mahkas told himself as he rubbed at the little scar on his arm, *that I arrived before The Bastard Fosterling could actually penetrate my daughter*, having now accepted this new and far more palatable memory as the truth. It would have been most regrettable if Damin had come home to find a baseborn servant had spoilt his prize. The gods must have been on his side, Mahkas knew, otherwise he would never have had second thoughts about asking The Bastard Fosterling to speak with Leila about Damin and followed him into the servants' wing, a place Mahkas rarely visited in the normal course of events.

Well, he was speaking to her, all right! Fortunate that

Mahkas had arrived in time, before anything worse could happen.

There was a knock on the door which he ignored, too busy pacing the rug in his study, rubbing at his arm, making sure he had all the facts clear in his head before he faced either Leila or The Bastard Fosterling. He was a fair man, he reminded himself. A good man. Nobody would be unjustly accused of anything in *his* city. The Bastard Fosterling would have to die, of course, that was a given, and Leila would have to be shown the error of her ways, but Mahkas was certain this whole thing could be cleared up quite easily.

He would talk to her, he decided. He would explain to her how wrong she was to allow herself to be so easily beguiled by that slick-tongued scoundrel, and how there was no real harm done. Damin was away – thank the gods – and with luck might never even learn anything about this awkward little incident. Leila needed to be punished, just a little, to make sure the lesson was well learned, but once that was done and The Bastard Fosterling was dead . . . well, everything could go back to the way it was before.

'Mahkas!' a muffled shout came through the door. 'I insist you let me in, this instant!'

He sighed. Bylinda was out there, all upset for no good reason. Perhaps the fact that she was a merchant's daughter gave her an unhealthy empathy for the common man which, even after more than twenty-four years of marriage, she'd never been able to shake entirely.

He would explain it to her, too, he decided. After he'd spoken to Leila.

Mahkas picked up the riding crop from his desk and walked to the door. He unlocked it and opened it, ignoring his wife who was still pounding on the carved panelling, demanding entry. She stepped back in shock as he emerged from the room. She wasn't alone, he noted with a slight frown. His niece, Kalan, was with her, and Tejay Lionsclaw. Typical of the women not to understand what it was like for a father placed in this regrettable position. And that common-born sorcerer friend of Kalan's was with them, too. *Was there no escaping them?*

'Uncle Mahkas?' Kalan ventured cautiously as he walked into the hall. 'Are you all right?'

'Mahkas!' Bylinda called after him, when he simply walked straight past them. 'Where are you going?'

He paid them no attention, ignoring everyone as he headed for the grand staircase, slapping the riding crop against his thigh as he walked.

'Mahkas!' Bylinda yelled, on the edge of hysteria. He was really going to have to speak to her later about making a scene in front of the servants. She was screeching like a fishwife.

He took the stairs two at a time, filled with a deep sense of righteousness. This could all be sorted out so easily, he was certain. He just had to make sure Leila understood her position. Once he'd made that clear to her – and killed The Bastard Fosterling – all would be well.

They followed him up the stairs, Bylinda openly sobbing now, as he headed along the hall. There were guards on Leila's door – for her own protection, of course – who saluted sharply as he approached. Mahkas stopped in front of them and addressed the four men calmly.

'You will guard this door,' he announced. 'You will not permit anybody other than me to enter this room. Not Lady Bylinda, nor any other man or woman in this house, highborn or low, unless it is with my express permission. Is that clear?'

The four Raiders nodded, a little uncertainly. Bylinda was running up the hall behind him, sobbing, calling his name. Mahkas continued to ignore his distraught wife, removed the key from his pocket and unlocked the door, stepping through and relocking it before Bylinda could reach him. He heard the guards moving to block her way. He heard her calling to him, desperately. To Leila.

Her pleas fell on deaf ears.

Instead, he turned to confront his daughter.

Leila was in the bedroom, still naked, still in the state he found her several hours ago when he had torn her from the arms of her lowborn lover . . .

No, he told himself sternly. *She's not to blame. The Bastard Fosterling did this to her. It was his fault. Leila is innocent, too naive for her own good. She just needs to learn what she did was wrong, that's all.*

She needed to understand how much she'd displeased him, however, so he'd had everything but the bed linen and the furniture removed from her room; neither had he allowed any fire to be lit against the cold night, not even a candle. It was important Leila contemplate the foolishness of her actions without any distractions.

Leila must understand that the most important lessons in life are always the hardest to learn.

In the dim dawn light breaking over the city, Leila pulled up the sheet she'd taken from the bed to cover her nakedness, and glared at him, unrepentant. She was curled up on the window seat, as far from him as she could get. Her arm was badly bruised, he noticed. A reminder of how selflessly he had saved her from certain damnation in the arms of that treacherous, baseborn pig.

'Are you feeling better, dear?' he asked sympathetically.

'Where is Starros?' she demanded. 'What have you done with him?'

'The Bastard Fosterling is no longer your concern, Leila.'

'I demand to see him!'

'You don't need to see him. He'll be taken care of. It's you I'm worried about, dearest.'

'You don't care about *me*!' she accused, turning to look out of the window. 'You only care that I'm available to marry your precious nephew.'

'Is that what's worrying you, darling? Please! Don't let it concern you! With luck, Damin will never even hear of this unfortunate incident. But if he does, then we'll deal with it. I'll explain everything to Damin. I'll make sure he knows nothing happened between you and . . . *him*. Everything will be fine.'

Leila turned to stare at her father. She looked horrified. 'Have you completely lost your mind? You think nothing *happened*? Gods, don't you see it even *now*? I've been sleeping with Starros for more than a year, you deluded fool! Did you hear me! A year! And everyone in the whole damn palace knows about it except you!'

Mahkas shook his head, smiling. He walked towards her, the riding crop tapping his thigh in time with his denials. 'No, no, no, of course nothing happened. I'll explain to Damin—'

'Are you *deaf*?' she shouted, climbing to her feet to face him defiantly. 'Starros is my lover, Father! And what's more, even Damin knows about it. He's known about it since the first day he arrived home!'

Mahkas kept shaking his head, tapping his thigh with the riding crop, refusing to listen to her lies. 'You need to understand, that's all, dear. I'll show you where you went wrong, and then we'll explain it all and Damin will forgive you. You're only a woman, after all, so you can't be expected to understand these things.'

He was almost at the window now, and for the first time, Leila seemed to notice the riding crop. She hesitated and backed up a little. 'Papa? What are you doing?'

'If you can't see the truth then I'll have to *show* you,

Leila,' he told her, pleased to see the dawning light of fear in her eyes. Fear was the first step in discipline. If she feared him, she would obey him.

I must remember to tell my nephew that . . .

'Papa!'

She screamed as he pulled the sheet away to reveal her naked whore's body – the body she had used to betray him with The Bastard Fosterling, the body she gave so carelessly without any consideration of what it might do to his plans.

No, it's not her fault, he reminded himself sternly. *She just needs to learn, that's all. She just needs to understand.*

He looked at his daughter dispassionately, knowing what he had to do, certain it was motivated by love and no other emotion – not rage or vengeance – just pure, untainted love. Leila had an arm across her breasts, the other over her mound, in a pitiful attempt to cover her nakedness in front of her father, trembling as she tried to back away from him.

'Don't try to fool me with false modesty, Leila. You weren't afraid to show yourself to The Bastard Fosterling. Am I not entitled to see what you appear to be willing to let every lowborn servant in the palace take a look at?'

Leila was clearly revolted by his accusation. 'Do you even *know* what you're saying, Father? Or have you completely lost your mind?'

He smiled again, taking pity on her. It must be hard to confront the idea that you had so badly let down a father who loved you so much. No wonder tears were already spilling down her cheeks, and he hadn't laid a hand on her yet. He raised the riding crop and slapped it into his left hand. Leila stared at it for a moment and began shaking her head in denial.

'Oh, gods, papa . . . *no* . . .'

'This is going to hurt me much more that it's going to

hurt you,' he told her as he advanced on her. 'You know that, don't you, darling?'

'Papa . . . *please* . . . no . . . you can't mean to . . .'

'It will be better if you turn around,' he advised, not wishing to mark that lovely face. Damin wouldn't like it if he left a scar.

'Papa, *please* . . .'

'Perhaps if you lay across the bed?' he suggested helpfully. 'Then you'll have something to hold on to.'

'You can't be serious!'

'Don't make me hurt you more than I have to, Leila.'

Somewhat to his disappointment, instead of doing as he asked, Leila sank down onto the floor and screamed for her mother as if she was five years old again. He could hear the ruckus going on outside the door as Bylinda tried to get past the guards. It would do her no good, of course. They were men. They understood the need for a father's discipline.

Leila continued to scream and call for her mother, whose frantic cries from the other side of the door grew even more hysterical. Losing his patience with his daughter now, Mahkas grabbed Leila by the hair and dragged her across to the bed, throwing her facedown on it. He ignored her cries for mercy, her pathetic cries for her mother; she even had the gall to cry out for The Bastard Fosterling.

Full of righteous calm, he raised the riding crop and brought it down sharply across her back, a large red welt appearing almost immediately. She screamed, sobbing like a child, begging him to stop. He raised it again. And again. Each stroke was a blow for honour, each welt a sign of his love.

Mahkas beat her until his arm ached. He didn't know how long he'd been at it, but Leila had stopped crying by then. She just lay there, unresisting, making small whimpering noises, like a kitten looking for its lost mother. He looked down at her semi-conscious form with satisfaction. Her back, from her shoulders to her buttocks, was a bloodied mess, but she'd no doubt learned her lesson.

It would be a long time before Leila Damaran defied her father again.

Mahkas opened the door, a little surprised to find Bylinda, Kalan and Tejay still waiting outside. Bylinda rushed at the door but he pushed her back and turned to the guards. 'I said nobody goes in there and I meant *nobody*. Disobey my orders and I will have you hanged for treason.'

He pushed Bylinda aside, ignored the dismayed look his niece and Lady Lionsclaw gave him, and continued down the hall, thinking that now he'd taken care of his daughter, it was time he did something about The Bastard Fosterling.

64

Helpless to do anything for her cousin, Kalan watched her uncle striding down the hall, tapping his riding crop against his thigh, appalled by his cruelty. Bylinda was hysterical, desperate to get inside the room to tend to her daughter, but there was no chance of getting past the guards, who were clearly as disturbed as she was by Lord Damaran's brutal behaviour.

'Please, Aunt Bylinda,' she urged, trying to get her aunt to stand. Tejay was on the other side of her, but Bylinda was so distraught her knees had given way. 'Let's get you to your room. There's nothing we can do here.'

'We can't leave her!' Bylinda sobbed. 'Please! You must do something!'

Tejay looked questioningly at Kalan over the top of Bylinda's head. 'Is there nothing you can do? No other way into the room?'

Kalan glanced over her shoulder at the guards before responding in a low voice, 'We might be able to get in through the slaveways.'

'The slaveways?'

'There are tunnels connecting all the rooms in the palace,' Kalan explained to Tejay.

'He's locked them, too,' Bylinda sobbed. 'There's no way into her room. Oh, gods, my poor baby . . .'

'Maybe there is a way in,' Kalan said thoughtfully, wondering what had happened to the master key the boys had secretly copied when they were children. If nobody knew of its existence, it might still be hidden above the ledge over the concealed door into Damin's room. 'But here is not the place to discuss it. Please, Aunt Bylinda, can you try to walk?'

With some difficulty, they got Bylinda to Kalan's room, where Rorin was waiting for them. He helped them put Bylinda on Kalan's bed, gave her a draught to calm her down and then came out to join Kalan and Tejay in the outer room.

'I was just explaining to Tejay that we might be able to get into Leila's room through the slaveways.'

'Surely the first thing Mahkas did when he confined Leila was to lock that door?'

'There's a master key,' Kalan told him. 'I just need to find it.'

'Which may solve your immediate problem, Kalan,' Tejay said, 'and allow us to tend to your cousin, but not the larger one.'

'What do you mean?'

'I *mean*, someone needs to put a stop to Mahkas,' she declared. 'You saw what he just did to his own daughter. What fate do you think lies in store for the young man he found her with?'

'Dear gods! Starros! With everything that was happening to Leila, I never even thought about him. What do you suppose Mahkas plans to do to him?'

'I'm guessing he plans to kill him,' Rorin suggested. 'As many times as he can.'

Tejay nodded her agreement. 'And that's today.

Tomorrow he might decide everyone who knew about the affair needs to be silenced, and from what I gather, that's a fair slice of the entire population of Krakandar City.'

'But how do we stop him?' Kalan asked. 'He's the Regent of Krakandar. He holds absolute power over everyone in the province. Even being a member of the Sorcerers' Collective means almost nothing compared to that here.'

'We need your brother,' Rorin concluded. 'He's the only one I can think of who Mahkas might listen to.'

'Damin?' Kalan scoffed, thinking it a good thing he *wasn't* here. 'What good would it do having him home?'

'He's Krakandar's prince,' Tejay reminded her. 'And the reason Mahkas seems so frantic about Leila. If he was here and perhaps able to convince your uncle that things aren't as desperate as Mahkas believes . . .'

'I suppose,' Kalan agreed, a little doubtfully. 'But he's not due back for days, maybe more than a week.'

'Is there no way to get a message to him?' Tejay asked.

Kalan shook her head in despair. 'He's in Medalon somewhere. He could be anywhere between the Border Stream and the Citadel.'

'Maybe we *can* get a message to him,' Rorin suggested thoughtfully.

'How?' Tejay demanded.

'Wrayan.'

'Who?'

'Wrayan Lightfinger,' Kalan told her, looking at Rorin hopefully. 'Can he do that?'

Rorin shrugged. 'I don't know. I'm not really a telepath like Wrayan. He might be able to do it, I suppose. In theory. Although he might need to know exactly where a person is to reach them. At least he knows the touch of Damin's mind, so he should be able to search for him. Then again, with the shield in place, even Wrayan might not be able to get through to him—'

'What *are* you babbling on about, young man?' Tejay cut in.

'We have a friend,' Kalan explained, wondering how much she should tell Lady Lionsclaw about Wrayan's magical ability. 'He lives in the city. He has certain . . . gifts.'

'Then why are you still standing here, lad?' she demanded of the young sorcerer. 'Off you go. If this friend of yours can get Damin Wolfblade back here even an hour earlier than he originally intended, it's worth a try.'

Rorin didn't need any further encouragement. He was gone a few moments later, leaving Kalan to stare at Tejay, shaking her head with the immensity of their task.

'Do you really think Damin can do anything, Tejay? Mahkas is Damin's regent. He has the power of life and death over Damin, too.'

Tejay leaned forward and patted Kalan's hand comfortingly. 'I think you underestimate your brother, dear. And the power behind his title. Regent or no, I wouldn't like to be Mahkas if the Prince of Krakandar decides to challenge him.'

'I hope you're right.'

'So do I,' Lady Lionsclaw agreed. 'Now let's see if we can find this master key of yours and go and tend to your cousin, eh? That will give us something constructive to do while we wait.'

'You don't have to get involved in this, you know, Lady Lionsclaw. It really is a family matter.'

'Damin was fostered with my father for five years, Kalan. I think of him as family. That makes you and Leila my family also.'

'He says the same of you,' Kalan told her, grateful for such a level head at a time like this. And one that Mahkas had no direct influence over. She smiled and placed her hand over Tejay's, squeezing it gratefully. 'Thank you, my lady.'

'There's no need to thank me, dear,' Tejay replied. 'I get a kick out of cutting arrogant, self-important little tyrants down to size.' And then she smiled and added, 'Just ask your brother.'

The master key to the slaveways was right where the boys had left it, sitting above the ledge over the door that led into Damin's room. It was caked with dust and spider webs and Kalan had never seen anything more wonderful in her life. With Tejay close behind her, carrying a basket filled with bandages, a salve for Leila's wounds made of chickweed, yarrow and wormwood, and a willowbark tonic for the pain, the two women hurried through the dimly lit slaveways until they reached the door that led into Leila's rooms.

Not surprisingly, it was locked. Kalan held her breath as she inserted the key, silently praying that it really was the master key the boys had copied all those years ago. The key caught on something and refused to budge. Cursing, Kalan tried again. The second time, it jagged again.

'Do it slowly,' Tejay whispered, in response to Kalan's even more savage curse.

Kalan did as Tejay suggested and, much to her relief, this time the key turned without resistance. Wincing as the door slid open with a squeal of metal upon metal that sounded preternaturally loud in the narrow corridors of the slaveways, the two women entered the main room of Leila's suite. There was no sign of her in the outer room, so they hurried through to the bedroom.

'Dear gods!' Tejay gasped.

Leila was unconscious, lying across the bed like a broken doll, her entire back a bloody canvas of welts, bruises and open cuts. It was more than an hour since Mahkas had emerged from his daughter's room. Kalan doubted if Leila had done anything in the intervening time except pass out.

As gently as they could, they tried to move her. She moaned faintly, the pain registering even in unconsciousness. On the verge of throwing up, Kalan hurried to the bathroom to fetch some water so they could bathe her wounds. She came back with the washbowl full of water and placed it on the floor beside the bed. Tejay was examining Leila's injuries with the critical eye of a woman who had seen more than her share of blood and open wounds in her time.

'This is a mess,' the Warlord's wife remarked with a frown.

'Should I get Bylinda?' Kalan asked in a whisper, afraid the guards outside might hear them speaking.

Tejay shook her head. 'The first thing she'd do if she saw Leila in this state is scream the house down. That would bring the guards, which would bring Mahkas, and then none of us will be able to help her. Better we do this quietly.' Tejay gently lifted away a few strands of Leila's long hair that were caught in the coagulating blood on her back. 'It's a good thing she's unconscious. I doubt I'd be able to stop screaming if it was me in this condition and someone tried to bathe my wounds.'

With infinite care they treated Leila's back, washing away the blood to reveal the full extent of the damage. Kalan let Tejay do most of the work. She seemed to know what she was doing. The extent of Leila's injuries was almost incomprehensible. It didn't seem possible that one human being could inflict such damage on another.

It was beyond belief that a father could do this to his own daughter.

'Poor Leila,' Kalan remarked as she watched Tejay work, handing her a towel when she needed it, or the jar of antiseptic.

'Poor Leila indeed,' Tejay agreed grimly. 'Can you get me some clean water, Kalan?'

The bowl was red with blood and loose bits of skin. Kalan took the bowl, emptied it down the garderobe, and then refilled it from the stopcock over the deep tiled bath that took up much of the spacious bathroom. She hurried back to Tejay and placed the water on the floor beside her again.

'She was always the quietest one of us,' Kalan remarked, sitting on the bed beside her cousin, gently stroking her blood-matted hair away from her face. 'And the most put-upon, I think. Starros always tried to look out for her. I'm not in the least bit surprised to learn they were lovers.'

'She'd have been better off using a *court'esa*,' Tejay said unsympathetically, 'if a quick roll in the sack was all she was after. Nobody gets beaten like this for being found with a *court'esa* in their bed.'

Kalan shook her head. 'It's not the same. I'd rather have a lover than a *court'esa*.'

Tejay looked up from her ministrations. 'Are you speaking from experience?'

Kalan shrugged, but avoided answering the question directly. 'I'm a member of the Sorcerers' Collective, Lady Lionsclaw. The same rules don't apply to us.'

'So are you and the young cutie lovers then?' she asked, wringing out the cloth again, staining the fresh water red.

'Young *cutie*? Oh, you mean Rorin? Good gracious, no! He's my friend.'

'And you think you can't be friends with your lovers?'

'I think most of my lovers don't want to be my friend,' Kalan corrected.

Tejay seemed amused by her philosophy. 'Well, I hope you know what you're doing, Kalan. Here, help me move her up the bed a little further.'

Kalan helped Tejay lift Leila's dead weight until she was lengthwise on the bed with her head on the pillow. She was still on her stomach – there was no way they could move her onto her back without causing her agonising pain. As gently as she could manage, Tejay began to apply the salve. Kalan flinched as she watched, thinking it was a very good thing Leila was still out cold. Any sound from this room was liable to bring the guards running.

'Are you going to bandage her?'

'No, for two reasons. The first is that it will instantly give away that we've been here if Mahkas comes back to find her all trussed up and taken care of, which will result in either the guards dying or him coming after you, or me, or Bylinda. The second reason is far more practical. Some of those cuts are still weeping. If we were to cover them now, the bandages would dry on the wounds and it would rip what's left of the skin on her back to remove them.'

Kalan cringed at the very thought of it.

'We'll need to get back in here when she's awake,' Tejay added, as she wiped her hands on a towel once she had finished with the salve. 'I've got some willowbark for the pain, but we'll never get it into her while she's unconscious.'

'I wish we could stay with her,' Kalan said, looking at Leila with concern. It didn't seem right to just walk away and leave her like this. She glanced out of the window, surprised to see the sun was completely risen. They needed to get a move on, or breakfast would be served and their absence questioned.

Tejay looked down at Leila, shaking her head in disgust. 'Your uncle should be hanged for doing this. I wouldn't whip a dishonest slave this savagely, let alone one of my own children.'

Kalan agreed with her, but she was also acutely aware that Leila was only half the problem. 'Do you think Starros will be all right?'

'Do *you*? Mahkas did this to his own daughter, Kalan. What do you think he's going to do to the man he believes seduced her?'

603

Kalan had never felt so helpless in her entire life. 'Maybe we can find a way to get in to see him? One of the guards told me they're holding him out in the cells behind the Raiders' Barracks—'

'Don't even consider it, Kalan,' Tejay warned, as she stoppered the jar of salve and placed it back in the basket. 'You have a way to help Leila of which your uncle is ignorant. Be grateful for that small gift. Don't risk it by trying to save a young man who might well be dead already.'

65

As Almodavar had predicted, there were no Defenders watching the ford at the Border Stream. Damin and his troop of sixty Raiders crossed the border into Hythria at a leisurely pace in broad daylight, driving a hundred head of stolen cattle before them, and encountered no resistance at all.

Damin was extremely disappointed. He was hoping for some action. Once he'd gotten over his leap across the Bardarlen Gorge, stealing cattle had proved to be quite the most boring thing he'd ever done. The Medalonian farmsteaders were so used to the frequent cattle raids from their Hythrun neighbours they rarely offered any resistance, and with rumours of plague on the loose, at the first sight of Hythrun Raiders they had simply run away and hidden in their houses and let the Raiders take their pick of the cattle.

'You know, some of us don't mind the idea we're going to arrive home in one piece,' Raek remarked when he saw Damin's crestfallen expression.

Damin reined in his mount beside Raek and waited with the captain as their stolen cattle splashed through the shallow ford, driven on by the Raiders behind them and the occasional encouragement of a stock whip. It was late afternoon and he was forced to squint into the sun slowly setting on the western horizon.

'Am I being that obvious?'

Raek smiled. 'Not really.'

'This is where my father died, isn't it?' Damin asked, as the significance of this place suddenly struck him.

'Yes.'

'Weren't you on the same raid?'

The captain nodded. 'It was over that way a bit, I think,' Raek told the prince, pointing to the right, a little further into Medalon. 'Although I could be wrong. It was pretty chaotic at the time.'

'Do you remember much of what happened?'

Raek Harlen shook his head. 'Lord Krakenshield took an arrow in the shoulder. I do remember seeing him fall. It knocked him off his horse. Didn't stop him for long, though.' He smiled. 'It took more than one Defender's arrow to bring Laran Krakenshield down. He was on his feet again, his sword in his other hand, before the Defenders could get near him.'

'But he still fell in the end.'

The captain nodded sadly. 'The last I saw of your father, Damin,' Raek said, 'he was on his feet, fighting off a couple of Defenders, his sword in his left hand, his wounded arm hanging by his side. I relaxed a little when I saw your Uncle Mahkas riding in to aid him and then someone attacked me from behind. For a while there, I was too worried about keeping my own head on my shoulders to see what happened to your father. It wasn't until after we'd driven the Defenders back that I learned Lord Krakenshield was dead.'

Medalon's grassy southern plains stretched away to the horizon on his right. On his left was Hythria and the ford and beyond it the safety of the tree line. Damin tried to imagine what it must have been like for his father, caught in the heat of battle: the dust, the smell of blood, the clang of metal on metal, the war cries, the squealing horses . . . but it was beyond him. The peaceful ford echoed with nothing more dangerous than the lowing of lazy cattle – *atheist* cattle, Damin reminded himself, with a faint smile.

'Am I anything like my father, Raek?'

The captain thought about his answer for a moment. 'Yes and no.'

Damin smiled. 'Just so long as you're not in any doubt about it, Captain.'

'In some things you're just like him,' Raek explained with a shrug. 'You're as tall as he was, and as broad across the shoulder. You have his sense of humour, too, I think, although he was more serious than you by nature. In other things, you favour your mother. You have her colouring, and more than your fair share of her skill for making people do as you want. But mostly, I think you're uniquely Damin.'

'I could probably convince myself that was a compliment, Captain, if I didn't think about it too closely.'

'And if I don't think about it too closely,' the Raider laughed, 'I could probably convince myself I meant it as one.'

Damin looked up and noticed Almodavar riding back towards the ford from the tree line on the Hythrun side of the border. He'd gone ahead with the scouts an hour or so earlier, to make certain the Defenders hadn't slipped over the border and were lying in wait on the other side. Damin splashed across the ford to meet him, wondering what had brought the captain back. The plan was for them all to meet up at the permanent camp site several miles across the border where a small corral had been built to hold the cattle. That was one of Mahkas's ideas. He was very efficient in everything he did. Even stealing cattle.

'Is something wrong?' Damin asked, as he rode up to meet the old captain.

'We found some fresh tracks,' Almodavar told him. 'Medalonian tracks. About half a dozen of them.'

'How can you tell they're not ours?'

'Their smiths work differently to ours. And their horses tend to be smaller.'

'Six of them, you say? A raiding party perhaps?'

'Don't know,' Almodavar shrugged. 'But I thought you might like to be in on the action.'

Damin grinned. 'Yes, please!'

'Come on, then,' the captain said. 'Raek can handle this.'

Damin didn't need to be asked twice. He urged his horse into a canter and was riding off in pursuit of a troop of Medalonian interlopers before anybody had a chance to change their mind and tell him he couldn't go.

The small Medalonian troop they pursued into Hythria made no attempt to conceal their presence, nor did they seem to have any doubt about where they, were heading. Almodavar's face became more concerned with every mile they rode in pursuit of the invaders, obviously worried about what this tiny but barefaced invasion squad was up to.

Their destination, it seemed, was the Raiders' own camp some ten miles from the Border Stream. Damin wasn't sure what was more worrying about that idea – that the Medalonians would so blatantly attack their enemy's position, or that they knew where the camp was in the first place.

That their purpose was to destroy the Hythrun base camp was obvious. In Almodavar's opinion, a small, probably handpicked strike force had been sent across the border to dismantle the corral in an attempt to make it harder to hold stolen cattle after any future raids. They undoubtedly had orders to burn whatever supplies and shelter they found, too, a fact that seemed to be borne out as the Raiders approached the camp. Damin could taste wood smoke on the air long before the camp itself came into view.

It was dark by the time Almodavar halted Damin and his small squad of pursuers about a mile from the camp to give them their orders. The Defenders probably didn't number more than half a dozen, the old captain estimated, and they would have come upon a Hythrun camp that hadn't been occupied for months. With luck, they would have let their guard down a little. The chance the Defenders would have sent a sortie of this nature over the border if they'd known there was a sixty-strong party of Raiders on their heels was highly unlikely. They were far too intelligent to make that sort of mistake.

'We'll attack from all sides at once,' Almodavar informed his men, after he'd allocated each Raider a position. Damin was to come at the camp from the western side, near the edge of the corral, spooking the Defenders' horses into fleeing if he had the opportunity. The Medalonians may have decided to make use of the corral while they destroyed the camp at their leisure.

'Try not to kill them if you can avoid it,' the captain added, almost as an afterthought. 'I want to know what they're doing here. Besides, the Sisterhood doesn't have much of a sense of humour when it comes to dead Defenders and we can't afford a war with Medalon right now.'

'We can't afford a war with *anybody* right now,' Damin pointed out grimly, thinking of the dire state of Hythria's defences with the plague running rampant through the country.

Almodavar nodded his agreement, then slapped Damin on the shoulder with an encouraging smile as the other four scouts slipped away into the darkness to take up their positions for the attack. 'The God of War will smile on you some day, Damin. Don't be too hasty to ask for Zegarnald's blessing.'

'It's all right, Almodavar. I do understand that the chance for glory in sneaking up on a handful of unsuspecting Defenders is limited, you know. I can live with that. To be honest, I'm just glad of a chance to do something to relieve the boredom.'

'Ah, now *that*,' Almodavar declared, 'is the true enemy of any warrior. Boredom. When you get down to it, most battles are ten per cent action and ninety per cent waiting around for something to happen.'

'You mean all those years you spent making me practise with a sword were wasted, when in fact I should have been learning needlework or some other skill that would keep my hands busy?'

Almodavar shook his head with a sigh. 'You've obviously been doing something to keep your hands busy, my lad. You're not going blind, too, are you?'

Damin sighed mournfully. 'You wound me, Almodavar.'

Almodavar grinned at the prince in the darkness. 'I'll do more than wound that precious royal hide if you're not in place by the time I give the signal, my lad.'

'I'm going,' Damin assured him with a grin, swinging up into his saddle. 'And never fear. I'll be there when you signal the attack.'

'Make sure you are. And while you're at it, try not to get yourself killed, either. I'd have far too much explaining to do to your mother and your uncle if you do.'

They left their horses some distance away from the base camp, so that no betraying nicker or rattle of tack would reveal their presence. Damin rounded the camp in the darkness and stepped carefully through the low scrub to ensure no snapped twig or startled rodent scurrying through the undergrowth betrayed his approach. Finally, after almost an hour of nerve-racking silence working his way forward, he was close enough to see the corral and a cloaked figure distributing hay (*Hythrun hay – our hay*, Damin thought in annoyance) to the horses confined within.

He hesitated, waiting to see what the trooper would do once the animals were fed. Perhaps he would come this way, giving Damin a chance to take him down silently, without alerting his companions to the presence of the Raiders. In the distance, Damin heard one of the other scouts give the hooting owl signal to indicate he was also in place and ready to attack. At the sound, the cloaked figure in the corrals looked up, pushing the hood back to reveal a distinctly feminine and disturbingly familiar profile.

Damin stared at the figure for a moment, not sure he believed his own eyes, then hurried forward, no longer paying any attention to the noise he might be making. The woman in the corral didn't notice him anyway. She turned back to the horses, completely unaware of the danger approaching until she felt the cold touch of steel upon her cheek from Damin's sword.

The woman screamed and spun around to face him.

'Hello, Luciena.'

She stared at him in disbelief. '*Damin?*'

Shocked and clearly stunned to find her adopted brother appearing out of nowhere in the darkness, she stared at him for a moment longer and then punched him angrily in the shoulder. 'For the gods' *sake*!' she snapped at him furiously. 'Don't sneak up on a person like that! You scared me half to death!'

Damin sheathed his sword and smiled broadly. 'Almost killed you did I, Luci? Well then, I guess that just about makes us even.'

66

The rest of the troop had caught up with them by the time Adham, Luciena and Xanda had finished bringing Damin and Almodavar up to date on their travels through Fardohnya and Medalon. Emilie and Geris had fallen asleep, but Jarvan was too excited to rest and had ingratiated himself into the small gap between Damin and his father, probably hoping his royal uncle would overrule any notions his parents had of sending him to bed.

Damin sat with Almodavar and Raek as they listened to Xanda and Luciena tell of their voyage to Talabar, their reception when they arrived, and Luciena's firm belief that Lector Turon was planning something dire against the family and that it had involved some sort of danger to her children. She wouldn't tell Damin who had warned her about the threat, and she obviously hadn't shared the information with her husband, either, which clearly irked Xanda. However, while Luciena's tale of Hablet's treachery was concerning, it was hardly surprising. It was Adham's unconfirmed news that Fardohnya was massing troops behind her closed borders that really worried Damin.

The stepbrothers left the group around the fire some time later, after Luciena and Aleesha had finally managed to get Jarvan to sleep. They walked towards the corral, away from any danger of being overheard. The Medalonian horses Adham and Xanda had purchased in Bordertown to get them back to Krakandar had been put with the Raider's horses and the corral was now filled with their stolen Medalonian cattle.

'How reliable is this rumour about Hablet's troops?' Damin asked, stopping to lean on the rough bark-covered rails of the corral. The cattle stood quietly in the chilly darkness, sleeping on their feet, a handy skill Damin had occasionally wished he owned.

Adham shrugged. 'I couldn't really say, Damin. I first heard it from one of our spice agents in Testra. His daughter was visiting relatives in Talabar but when she tried to book a passage back to Medalon, she found it next to impossible to get a berth home. Supposedly, one of the booking agents in Talabar told her all the ships were busy shifting troops to Tambay's Seat in southern Fardohnya.'

'The perfect staging area if you're planning to invade Hythria through the pass near Highcastle,' Damin pointed out with a frown.

Adham nodded in agreement. 'Normally, I wouldn't have paid the rumour much attention. I've heard some fairly outrageous tales by shipping clerks trying to cover their own inadequacies in my time. But when I paid off the Karien crew in Bordertown, after they dumped my spices on the wharf, I asked them if they were heading home. The captain said he was, but the mate disagreed. They ended up having quite a heated argument about it. The captain wanted to head back to Yarnarrow. The first mate seemed to think they could recoup some of the cost of the journey by transporting Fardohnyan troops south.'

'It starts to make you wonder what's happening behind the closed borders at Winternest, too, doesn't it?'

'Can't you contact Chaine Lionsclaw when we get back to Krakandar and ask him to investigate? If anybody in

Hythria can find out what's happening on the other side of the Widowmaker, it's him.'

'Chaine's dead,' Damin told Adham, realising how much news his stepbrother would have missed, due to his travels in the north. 'So is Rogan Bearbow. Terin is Warlord of Sunrise now. Tejay Lionsclaw is a guest at Krakandar, actually, waiting for things to settle down a bit before she attempts the journey home.'

Adham absorbed that information silently for a moment, before he raised another point that Damin had desperately been trying not to dwell on ever since his stepbrother had told them of his suspicions about the Fardohnyan troop movements. 'We're in serious trouble, you know, if Hablet really is planning to invade us as soon as he reopens the borders.'

'We can hold him off,' Damin shrugged, not willing to admit the unpalatable truth of what Adham was trying to tell him.

'And if we can't?'

'Then we'll fight him, Adham, and drive the greedy old bastard back over the Sunrise Mountains where he belongs.'

'Nice idea in theory, Damin. Who's going to fight him, exactly?'

'We have seven Warlords and close to a hundred thousand troops if we call up every reserve in the nation,' Damin replied optimistically. 'I'm sure we'll find someone to do the job.'

'Don't kid yourself, my friend. Hythria doesn't have anywhere near that many troops,' Adham warned. 'Our fighting capability's been decimated by the plague. And you don't have seven Warlords you can count on, either. You have three provinces administered by the Sorcerers' Collective, a regent ruling Krakandar and an untried, unconfirmed Warlord guarding the only two navigable passes into Hythria. Charel Hawksword's all but bedridden these days. And the only reason Cyrus Eaglespike and Dregian Province would ever agree to stand behind you, Damin, is because that's the best place to be if he's planning to stab you in the back.'

'And we're one Warlord away from Alija Eaglespike gaining majority control of the Sorcerers' Collective,' Damin added, thinking of Rorin's equally gloomy assessment of their current situation. He frowned at his stepbrother in the darkness. 'You're just a regular little ray of sunshine, aren't you, Adham?'

His stepbrother smiled humourlessly. 'If you think that's bad, consider this. Who normally leads Hythria's combined troops in battle?'

Damin had to stop and think about that one. Such a situation hadn't arisen in living memory. 'It's been so long since it happened last . . . I don't know . . . the High Prince, I suppose.'

'So that renowned tactical genius we all know and love, the brilliant Lernen *Wolfblade*, is going to lead us into battle against Hablet of Fardohnya, eh? Now there's something to look forward to. Good thing I already know how to speak Fardohnyan.'

Damin shook his head; like Adham, he couldn't imagine anything worse than Hythria's incompetent High Prince let loose with an army at his back . . . in the unlikely event, of course, that any Hythrun army would actually follow him to war in the first place.

Damin found it a little unsettling, however, to have Adham Tirstone point this out to him. These were all things he should have considered. He consoled himself with the thought that his stepbrother might be a trader rather than a soldier, but he'd had much longer to reflect on all the ramifications of this news.

The young prince was neither slow nor ignorant of the politics of his nation, however. He knew what needed to be done. 'We need to find ourselves a general.'

'Marla won't allow it.'

'She may not have a choice, Adham.'

'Your mother will never willingly invest that much power in someone who isn't a member of the family.'

'Then who does she think is going to . . .' Damin's voice trailed off as the awful truth dawned on him. He pulled his cloak tighter around himself, but the chill he felt didn't come from the still, clear night.

Adham nodded as he saw Damin's expression. 'And now you see the problem, don't you?'

Damin sighed heavily. 'If the High Prince can't lead the Hythrun to war, then they'll expect to follow his heir.'

'There goes your precious "Let's Convince Everybody Damin's an Idiot Until It's Too Late For Them to Do Anything About It" plan, I suspect,' Adham pointed out with a faint grin.

Damin cursed savagely for a moment, which did nothing to solve the problem, but did make him feel marginally better. 'Why couldn't this damn plague have hit Fardohnya instead of us?'

'Maybe the gods want to give you a chance to prove yourself.'

'Almodavar said much the same thing earlier. I thought he was just trying to keep my spirits up. I didn't realise he was being prophetic.' He turned and leaned his back against the railing, scuffing at the loose dirt with his boot. 'You realise, of course, that my entire practical experience of battle consists of capturing Luciena tonight? There hasn't been a decent war in Hythria since I was born. Everything I know is just theory.'

'I sat in on those same theory lessons, Damin,' Adham reminded him. 'I know what you were taught. Trust me, if you remember even half of it, you should be able to muddle through without losing Hythria to the Fardohnyans.'

'You think I can muddle through without losing the

country, do you? Thanks for the resounding vote of confidence, Adham.'

'Well, I'll follow you to war, brother,' Adham assured him, clapping his shoulder encouragingly. 'And so will Almodavar, I daresay.'

'Oh, well . . . that thought should keep Hablet awake at night. You, me and Almodavar.'

Adham shrugged. 'Like I said, I already speak Fardohnyan. If you lose . . . well, I'm adaptable. I'm sure I can learn to shout "Long Live Hablet" with the same forced enthusiasm that I shout "Long Live Lernen Wolfblade"!'

Damin smiled thinly, appreciating the sentiment. It was hard sometimes to get excited about the idea that Lernen was the rightful High Prince of Hythria when they all knew Marla was the actual ruler and that without her steady hand at the helm, Hythria would have descended into anarchy a long time ago.

But he couldn't let Adham get away with a remark like that without some sort of comeback. 'You damn traders are all alike, aren't you? You'd sell your own grandmother if you thought you could show a profit.'

'Why do you ask?' Adham shot back with a hopeful grin. 'Are you in the market for one?'

Damin laughed. 'Ruxton must be so proud of you.'

'I think he's more proud of Rodja than me. He's the one who likes to sit up all night going through the books, looking for another rivet to squeeze out of somebody. And both Rodja and Rielle have given him grandchildren, which makes them seem so much more considerate than me. I suspect my father thinks Almodavar corrupted me when we were children and turned me from Patanan, the God of Good Fortune, and into a follower of the God of War.'

'He may not be far off the mark,' Damin agreed. 'Given half a chance, Almodavar would turn Aunt Bylinda into a follower of Zegarnald, if he could.'

'It'll be good to see her again when we get back to Krakandar,' Adham said. 'Nobody ever spoiled us the way Bylinda did when we were children. Which reminds me, with all this talk of your new career as Hythria's saviour, I forgot to ask after Leila and Starros.'

'Ah . . . Leila and Starros. Now there's a battle yet to be fought.' Damin had done a rather good job of not dwelling on that particularly awkward situation for the past few weeks. But he couldn't put it off much longer. They were only a few days from home.

Adham looked at him curiously, obviously wondering at Damin's odd tone. 'I take it that means you and Leila still aren't formally betrothed?'

'Nor are we ever going to be, Adham. And I'm probably going to have the monumentally unpleasant job of breaking that sad fact to Mahkas when we get back home.' He smiled sheepishly. 'It's half the reason I'm out here stealing cattle with the Raiders, actually. I'm starting to think running away is a valuable and oft-maligned battle tactic that should be used much more often than it is.'

'I know I'm not a soldier, Damin,' Adham advised solemnly. 'But if I could make a suggestion? If it comes to war . . . if you do happen to find yourself leading Hythria's army . . . when you're looking across a battlefield at a hundred thousand Fardohnyans and trying to think of something to rally the troops, keep that little bit of wisdom to yourself, eh?'

67

One of the disadvantages of beating a man repeatedly with a mailed fist, Mahkas Damaran discovered, was that after a time he stopped looking like the man you wanted to punish and began to resemble nothing so much as a large black, red and purple hanging sack that had, miraculously, sprouted arms.

The Bastard Fosterling had passed out again, so Mahkas eased the chain-mail glove from his hand, a finger at a time, and stepped back from the limp body hanging from the chains suspended from the ceiling of the cold cell. The young man was too weak to stand, even when he was conscious; his wrists were raw around the metal cuffs, bloody and bruised from holding his entire weight.

It was six days now since Mahkas had found The Bastard Fosterling attempting to violate his daughter. He had come to visit him every one of those six days. Come to punish him for his temerity. Each day he vented a little more of his wrath on the hanging carcass that had once been The Bastard Fosterling and it would be a long time yet, Mahkas was determined, before he would allow the foul brute the blessed release of death.

'Call me when he wakes again,' Mahkas ordered the guard standing watch over The Bastard Fosterling's cell.

'Sir,' the man replied, clasping his fist over his heart in a perfectly correct salute.

Mahkas frowned, sensing the man's unspoken disapproval. It was a problem he had with all the Krakandar Raiders. Mahkas had told them what had happened. He had explained to them that The Bastard Fosterling had tried to rape his only daughter, but it seemed to have made little difference. At best, they seemed sceptical.

Mahkas knew exactly what the problem was. The Bastard Fosterling had grown up around these men. Many of them had trained him as a boy. They liked him. Trusted him, even. To make matters worse, he wasn't just any old bastard – he was Almodavar's bastard, and most of these men would have given their lives for their captain.

Perhaps it was better this way. There wasn't a bruise, a cut, not so much as a mark on The Bastard Fosterling that Mahkas hadn't put there. That, in itself, made him feel as if he'd in some way redressed the ill done to him and his kin.

But if the Raiders thought he didn't notice who was slow to obey his commands, who was a little too quick to rush to The Bastard Fosterling's aid when they thought Mahkas was gone from the cells, they were sadly mistaken.

Mahkas knew who was secretly defying him behind his back. He knew the mercenaries he would send on their way when their contracts came up for renewal on the Feast of Zegarnald, a few months from now. He knew the men who would find themselves on night watch for the next year without relief. The worst punishment, however, he decided, would be reserved for those traitors who whispered to each other when they thought Mahkas couldn't hear them. The ones who spread the vicious rumours that Leila and The Bastard Fosterling had been lovers for more than a year. The ones who smirked behind his back, claiming everyone in Krakandar had known about it except her father.

The ones who sniggered and leered and whispered behind their hands, '*I hear she was the one on top when he found them . . .*'

They were the ones Mahkas intended to silence permanently. Perhaps a raid over Krakandar's southern border to steal some of Rogan Bearbow's precious sorcerer-bred horses? The Warlord of Izcomdar crucified poachers who tried stealing his stock and left them hanging by the roadside (a tactic Mahkas had borrowed, and used himself, to great effect, on more than one occasion in Medalon). Mahkas could always claim his Raiders were on an unauthorised mission. He could deny any knowledge of the raid and even *thank* Rogan for putting the miscreants to death.

The more he thought about it, the better an idea it seemed. Old Rogan might be dead, but his son was cast in the same mould as his father. And his sister was currently sheltering here in Krakandar from the plague. He'd have no reason to suspect Mahkas of any wrongdoing at all. For that matter, Tejay would probably champion her host as being an honest and upstanding man. She must have been impressed with the way he'd dealt with this awkward situation.

No daughter of Rogan Bearbow's, Mahkas was certain, would even question the need for discipline.

Mahkas sighed as he turned for the door, wishing he'd been half as successful with Leila as old Rogan had been with Tejay. No one heard so much as a whimper of protest when her father arranged her marriage to Terin Lionsclaw. And look at her, the mother of four healthy sons, waiting in the safest place possible during the plague before she could return them to their home and their father.

What secret of parenting did Rogan Bearbow know that has eluded me? Was I too soft on Leila as a child? Should I have whipped her before this? Should I have restricted the contact she had with her mother?

Maybe that was the secret. Perhaps this was Bylinda's fault. Tejay's mother, as far as Mahkas could recall, had died giving birth. She'd not been corrupted by a whining woman's touch.

I will forbid Leila to see her mother, Mahkas decided, relieved to think that none of this might be his fault, after all. *It's too late to undo the damage, perhaps, but at least I can prevent the rot from spreading.*

Satisfied that he finally had an answer to his failure as a parent – one that left him blameless – Mahkas looked back at the pitiful, unconscious thing hanging from the chains. *Not feeling quite so romantic now, are we, old son?*

'He's to have no food or water,' Mahkas added, as an afterthought. No point in making it too easy on him.

'If those are your orders, my lord.'

Mahkas glared at the Raider. 'You disapprove, Sergeant?'

'I was just thinking—'

'I don't pay you to think, man.'

The sergeant squared his shoulders before replying. 'I was just thinking, my lord, that if you wish to keep the prisoner alive, to enable you to punish him sufficiently for his . . . *crime*, then you should at least allow him some water. He'll be dead from dehydration soon if he keeps on like this.'

That was actually quite a valid concern, but Mahkas was reluctant to admit this self-important sergeant might have a point. 'Water him then, if you must,' Mahkas ordered after a moment, with ill grace. 'Just don't let him die.'

'Sir?'

'He'll die when I decide he's repented sufficiently, Sergeant. And when I'm here to witness it. Not a moment before then, do you hear?'

'As you wish, my lord.'

Mahkas turned and headed for the stairs that would take him to the upper level of the cells, past another half-dozen disapproving Raiders on guard duty. *Perhaps the sergeant should be one of the men sent to Izcomdar on the horsestealing raid,* he thought. *That should take care of his insolent attitude.*

Mahkas emerged from the barracks, a little surprised to find it was almost sundown. He must have been down in the cells for hours. The wind was icy as he walked across the plaza towards the palace, the promise of spring a distant hope yet to be realised. As he approached the palace steps, he was a little annoyed to be met by a delegation of two, consisting of his wife and his niece, both of whom were refusing to accept that his way of handling this terrible situation was the only possible way to deal with it.

'Uncle Mahkas,' Kalan began, in her very best, most reasonable tone, as he reached the top step.

He appreciated his niece's efforts to avoid turning into the screeching harpy his wife had become this past week, but remained unmoved. 'Please, Kalan. See your aunt back to her room and leave me be. I have work to do.'

'You must let me see her, Mahkas!' Bylinda cried, falling to her knees, clutching at the hem of his cloak. 'She hasn't been allowed food, even warmth, for over a week! You're killing her!'

'If your daughter is dying, it is by her own choice, my lady,' Mahkas replied, shaking his wife off disdainfully. 'Now please, get a hold of yourself before the servants see you in such a state! Remember who you are!'

'Perhaps if I spoke to her, Uncle Mahkas? As her cousin and her friend, I might be able to point out the error of her ways, you know . . . woman to woman? Explain to her that life must move on.'

Mahkas shook his head sadly. 'If only it was that simple, Kalan. But Leila refuses to admit the truth. Until she does, she will suffer as she chooses.'

Not wishing to discuss the matter further, Mahkas

pushed past his wife and niece and headed into the palace. He left the two women standing on the top step, staring at him in despair, but paid them no further mind. And then he stopped abruptly. In a sudden flash of inspiration, Mahkas knew what he must do to bring Leila around. Kalan had just given him the clue.

It was so simple; he couldn't understand why he hadn't thought of it sooner. He turned and beckoned his niece to him.

'Uncle Mahkas?'

'Perhaps your cousin does need your help, after all, Kalan.'

'Anything,' the young woman promised.

'Come with me then,' he said. 'And we shall set this matter to rights, once and for all.'

'The Bastard Fosterling is dead,' Mahkas announced, standing at the door to Leila's bedroom. Kalan stood beside him. She knew his declaration was a lie. However, in keeping with the promise she had made on the way up here, Kalan did not contradict him.

Leila didn't react immediately. She was curled up on the mattress, the thin bloodstained sheet he'd left on the bed her only protection against the cold. And it was icy in here. The room had been without a fire for six days now and the weather was still cold enough outside that she would be feeling it acutely. Her back was scabbed over, the worst of the bruises already starting to yellow at the edges. He pitied her now, his anger more about her ongoing stubbornness than her original crime.

'Did you hear me, Leila? The Bastard Fosterling is dead. Even if you still imagine you feel something for him, there's no point now. He's nothing more than a soon-to-be-forgotten memory.'

'I would know if Starros was dead,' she muttered after

624

a time, so softly that Mahkas thought he might have imagined she spoke. They were the first words he had heard from her in days.

'Did you want proof?'

That got her attention. She raised her head to stare at him. Her eyes were puffy and bloodshot, red-rimmed from crying. Always a slender girl, she was thin to the point of being haggard. He'd allowed her no food, but she was able to drink from the stopcock in her bathroom, Mahkas supposed.

'What proof?'

Mahkas hesitated, then turned to Kalan. 'Your cousin Kalan is here to swear that what I tell you is true. You'll believe her, won't you, even if you won't take my word for it?'

Kalan glared at him, making no effort to hide her disgust at the lie he was telling his daughter. Mahkas shook his head warningly. He'd explained to his niece – in quite explicit detail – what would happen if she uttered so much as a sound that threw his word into question. *If you want your aunt to be allowed to visit Leila, you will do as I say*, he'd told her. *If you want your cousin to be clothed and warm and fed, then you'll make her believe what I wish her to believe.*

Kalan treated him to a hateful glower and then pushed past him, kneeling beside the bed to comfort her cousin. She took Leila's hand in hers and squeezed it gently. 'I'm so sorry, Leila.'

Not exactly the ringing endorsement he was asking for, but perhaps it was better than an outright declaration. It certainly got a reaction from his daughter. She began to cry, shaking her head in denial.

'It can't be true . . .'

'You have to hold on, Lee,' Kalan told her. 'You have to be strong.'

'Please, Kalan . . . tell me it's not . . .' She was sobbing too hard to finish the sentence.

'My lord,' Orleon said behind him in the outer room, after coughing politely to make Mahkas aware of his presence.

The regent turned impatiently, wondering how the old man had got past the guards. 'What?'

'You asked to be advised as soon as the raiding party returned from Medalon.'

'Yes?'

'We've just had word that Prince Damin, Captain Almodavar and the rest of the troops have entered the city, sire. And they appear to have some additional refugees with them.'

'Thank you, Orleon. That will be all.'

The old steward bowed and left the room with no further comment. Mahkas turned back to Leila and Kalan and smiled at them. 'There! You see! Didn't I tell you everything is going to be all right? Damin is home. The Bastard Fosterling is dead. All this terrible nonsense can be put behind us! There's nothing for you to worry about, dearest, not any more.'

'I hate you,' Leila sobbed, in too much pain even to raise her head again.

'Leila, you have to hold on a little longer,' Kalan urged gently. 'Starros would want you to do that. He'd *want* you to hang on until Damin gets here.' Kalan was sounding quite desperate. She leaned a little closer to her cousin's ear and added in a low, urgent voice, 'Damin will make things right, Lee, don't you see that?'

Mahkas unconsciously nodded his approval. That was good, reminding her of who she really loved. Knowing her fiancé was due home any time should encourage Leila to pull herself together.

And it seemed as if it worked. At the mention of Damin's

name, Leila lifted her head from her pillow and slowly turned to look at Mahkas; the first time she had willingly looked him in the eye since the day he'd beaten her. He didn't flinch from her accusing stare. He had nothing to feel guilty about.

'Damin will be home soon,' she said. Her voice was ethereal, yet determined. She appeared to have suddenly made a decision about something.

Kalan stood up and looked down at Leila with concern. 'Yes, he will.'

Leila smiled distantly and swung her legs around until she was sitting on the edge of the bed. Mahkas was filled with relief. This obvious sign that Leila was emerging from her listless, defiant depression was most encouraging. He should have thought about telling her The Bastard Fosterling was dead days ago.

'I should get ready for him,' Leila said, rising to her feet. She stumbled and fell against Kalan, seemingly unaware of her nakedness.

Mahkas smiled with relief. 'There you go! I knew things would be better as soon as you realised where your priorities lay! I'll have someone sent in to re-lay the fire. And run a bath for you. And clothes. You'll need something nice to wear to greet your fiancé.'

Leila struggled to hold herself upright against Kalan, who looked far from pleased at this inexplicable change in her cousin's demeanour. 'Just a bath will do for now,' she said, with a wan, remote smile. 'A nice, warm bath. Damin's barely at the outer gate, Father. I have time yet to make myself ready for him.'

'Did you want me to stay and help, Lee?' Kalan asked worriedly.

She shook her head. 'Just send someone in to run the bath. I'd like to soak in peace for a while.'

Mahkas yelled for a slave, beaming with relief. This was

far better than he could have hoped for and vindicated his belief that the only way to deal with his errant daughter was to force Leila to see the truth. Now that she believed The Bastard Fosterling was dead, there was obviously nothing standing in the way of her recognising where her true duty lay.

At his summons, several slaves hurried into the room to arrange Leila's bath. Another he sent to retrieve her wardrobe and another to light a fire and take the chill off the air. It would take Damin some time to get through the city to the inner ring and the palace. As Leila said, she had time.

One of the slaves helped Leila towards the bathroom, leaving Kalan staring after them, clearly unhappy. Mahkas thought he understood why, and smiled as he approached his niece to thank her for her assistance. Kalan was obviously uneasy with her part in the deception about Starros's death, despite his assurances.

'You did the right thing, Kalan.'

'You made me lie to her, Uncle.'

'Good lies that make her see the truth can never be a bad thing.'

He watched Leila stumble into the bathroom and heard the rush of water coming from the stopcock. It would take a while to heat the water, Mahkas guessed, and fill the huge tiled pool. Time enough for all of them to get ready for Damin's return.

'Are you going to let Aunt Bylinda in to see her now?' Kalan demanded of him suddenly.

'Later, perhaps,' he conceded. 'When I've had time to explain things to her.'

'In that case, would you excuse me, please, Uncle Mahkas? I'd like to get ready to greet my brother, also.'

'Of course. You may go.'

'Thank you, sire,' she said politely with a small curtsey and left the room. Mahkas smiled, thinking that perhaps twelve years in the Sorcerers' Collective had taught Kalan some dignity along with whatever else they taught there these days. She had handled herself very well indeed.

All Mahkas had to do now was wait for Damin to come home and inform him of the changes that had taken place in the Krakandar Palace while he was gone. Mahkas was certain there was nothing now standing in the way of the fulfilment of all his ambitions for his daughter.

68

As soon as Kalan could escape her uncle, she fled Leila's room, horrified by what she had done. Telling Leila that Starros was dead was the cruellest blow she could have delivered to her cousin, short of physically beating her.

But what choice did I have?

How else could she explain to Leila, with Mahkas standing there watching and listening to every word, that there *was* hope? How could she tell her cousin that far from adding to her woes, Damin might be her only chance to restore some semblance of sanity to this madhouse into which the palace had been transformed in his absence? Not that Kalan really believed Damin could do much. But there was always the slim hope that Tejay and Rorin were right.

There had been no time to explain anything, however, and no chance to slip through the slaveways. Kalan could only hope that Leila understood what she was trying to say to her. That she had somehow given her cousin something to cling to.

Kalan paced the balcony near the staircase, tormented by the possibilities, waiting for some sign that Damin was through the inner ring of the city, hoping Tejay was right about his ability to end this nightmare. Kalan didn't have quite as much faith in her brother as the Warlord of Sunrise's wife. She had seen him infrequently in Greenharbour. She and Rorin had been busy with their studies and Damin had been in Natalandar in Izcomdar Province until six years ago, when he finished his fosterage and Marla had finally sent for him. Whenever she did see her brother, Damin wasn't doing anything responsible, or noble, or even particularly important. Mostly, he seemed just to enjoy himself.

People scoffed at her brother, she knew, even dismissed him as shallow and not very bright. He had a reputation the length and breadth of Greenharbour for never taking anything seriously. Kalan hoped it was an act. The Damin that Tejay seemed to believe in was far more astute than Kalan had ever seen. Maybe he was just very good at applying Elezaar's Thirteenth Rule – *never appear too bright or too clever*. Maybe it was a survival tactic. A way of concealing who he really was from the many forces in Hythria who might not like what they saw, if the High Prince's heir was ever foolish enough to reveal his true nature.

If it wasn't, then both Leila and Starros were doomed.

A steady stream of people – slaves, free servants and a change of guard – passed Kalan as she waited. About ten minutes after she'd left Leila's room, Mahkas appeared, walking along the hall deep in discussion with the slave responsible for his daughter's wardrobe. He was telling her what he wanted Leila to wear: something elegant, yet alluring – something to let her fiancé know she was happy to have him home. He nodded absently to Kalan as he passed. Too intent on his plans for his daughter, he didn't ask why she was still waiting around in the hall.

A few moments later Rorin appeared and hurried towards her. He was wearing his sorcerer's robes, extremely conscious they were the only thing that protected him from Mahkas's snobbish scorn.

'I heard Leila's been let out,' he said, glancing past Kalan towards the room further along the hall that was still conspicuously guarded.

'It was awful, Rorin. He made me tell her Starros was dead.'

'What did she do?'

Kalan shrugged, at a loss to explain Leila's odd reaction. 'That was the worst part. It's like she grieved for him for all of about two heartbeats and then put it all behind her and said she had to get up and get ready for Damin.'

Rorin seemed as puzzled as Kalan. 'That doesn't sound right. Do you think your aunt will be allowed in there now? I've just come from her room. She sent me along to find out what's happening.'

'How is she?'

'She's frantic. But Tejay's with her.'

Kalan shook her head. 'I don't think Mahkas will let her in yet. Leila's having a bath anyway. Maybe he'll let Bylinda see her when she's dressed.'

'What if I get Tejay to tell her about the master key to the slaveways entrance?'

She looked down over the balcony into the hall, watched her uncle dismiss the wardrobe slave at the bottom of the grand staircase and stride across the hall out of sight along the corridor that led to his study. There was another slave lighting the candles downstairs against the approaching twilight, and when Kalan glanced out of the windows she noticed the sky was already fading into darkness.

'We can probably risk it now. The city guards have just sent word. Damin's back. He should be here soon.'

Rorin took her trembling hands in his and smiled at her, no doubt in an effort to stop her wearing a hole in the carpet. 'It'll be all right, Kalan.'

'You think Tejay's right, don't you?'

'Yes. I think you underestimate your brother.'

She snatched her hands away and crossed her arms

defensively. 'You're only saying that because he lets you hang around with him and his friends in Greenharbour.'

'And you have dinner with your brother on feast days, *occasionally*, at your mother's table and usually end up arguing with him about really stupid little things until Princess Marla gets so irritated that she threatens to have you both thrown out of the palace.'

'Once,' Kalan corrected, and then she smiled sheepishly. 'And I'll have you know I was *winning* that argument.'

'My point is, Kal, I probably know him better than you do these days. Damin's not as silly as he looks.'

'Well, there's something to be grateful for.'

She glanced down into the foyer and noticed Orleon heading out the main doors of the palace with a torch in his hand. With a start, Kalan realised what it meant. Someone was arriving at the palace. Given the hour and the news they'd just received about Damin's pending arrival, there was little doubt in her mind about who the steward had gone out to meet.

'He's here!'

Pushing Rorin aside, Kalan picked up her skirts and broke into a run, flying down the stairs in a way she hadn't dared since she was ten years old with her brothers and cousins in hot pursuit. She cleared the last three steps in a single jump and skidded on the polished granite floor, before coming to a halt as she hit the doors. Dragging them open, she ran towards Orleon, who was standing on the broad landing, his torch held high against the gathering gloom.

To Kalan's intense relief, Damin and the rest of the Raiders were riding across the plaza. She waited impatiently as they rode towards the palace. When they arrived, the troop milled about in front of the palace, waiting to be formally dismissed by Almodavar. To Kalan's astonishment her stepbrother, Adham Tirstone, rode at Damin's side.

'I spoke to Tejay about the slaveways,' Rorin told her, coming to stand beside Kalan as the troop dismounted. 'Isn't that Xanda and Luciena?'

Kalan nodded as she realised with growing amazement that her cousin Xanda and Rorin's cousin Luciena, along with their three children, were also part of the troop. Between her parents, Emilie rode her own mount, but Jarvan and Geris were doubled up with two of the Raiders riding in front of them. Their slave, Aleesha, rode another mount just behind them. Kalan couldn't imagine how their family managed to be riding with Damin, and although the children were clearly exhausted, the atmosphere among them seemed quite jovial.

Which meant all Wrayan's attempts to contact Damin had been in vain.

Picking him out of the crowd, hearing him laugh at a joke Adham must have made, Kalan knew with terrifying certainty that her brother had no inkling of what awaited him inside the palace.

'Damin!' she cried, yelling at the top of her voice to be heard over the sound of sixty-odd men and their horses preparing to dismount.

Her brother and stepbrother immediately turned towards her as the men around them fell silent. There was a note in Kalan's cry, a plea of desperation, that couldn't be ignored. Damin dismounted and pushed his way towards the steps as she ran down to meet him.

'Kalan?' he asked, obviously puzzled to find her awaiting his return so anxiously. 'What's wrong?'

'Mahkas found out about Leila and Starros.'

Every person in the courtyard heard her. Silence descended over the plaza, as if some mischievous god had suddenly robbed each man of the ability to speak. She looked at her brother expectantly. Now, when it really counted, Kalan prayed silently that he wouldn't let her down.

He didn't. It took less than a heartbeat for Damin to work out what Mahkas's reaction must have been to such news. She watched her brother's demeanour alter subtly, as if he intuitively understood what Tejay had predicted – that only the Prince of Krakandar could hope to confront her regent and have any chance of prevailing.

Kalan could have cried with relief.

'Where is Starros?' Damin asked Orleon in a voice Kalan had never heard her brother use before.

The old man barely even hesitated before answering. 'In the cells behind the Raiders' barracks, I believe, your highness.'

'Captain!'

Both Almodavar and Harlen responded to the authority in Damin's tone, almost instinctively. 'Your highness?'

'Raek, dismiss the men. Almodavar, you might like to come with me.'

The crowd of men and horses parted to let Damin and Almodavar through. Leaving Rorin to greet his cousin and her husband, Kalan hurried in her brother's wake, anxious to fill him in on all that had happened since Mahkas discovered the affair. She was hard-pressed to keep up with him, however. Damin lengthened his stride as if to accommodate his fury at the thought of his friend being confined like a common criminal, leaving Kalan more than a little concerned.

Even she was not sure what they would find.

The cells were guarded by half a dozen men who closed ranks across the entrance as the prince approached.

'Stand aside!' Almodavar barked impatiently.

The men didn't budge.

Damin walked up to the sergeant, a seasoned Raider in his mid-thirties named Pakin Clayne, who'd trained with Damin any number of times when the prince was a boy.

'I'm sorry, Prince Damin, but Lord Damaran left quite specific orders—'

'What are you going to do, Clayne?' he asked, stepping into reach of the man's sword arm. 'Kill me?'

'Please, your highness—'

'I will be Krakandar's Warlord and the High Prince of Hythria for a whole lot longer that Mahkas Damaran is going to be regent of this province, Sergeant Clayne,' Damin reminded the man in a voice that frightened Kalan a little. 'So you can either stand aside or you can run me through. Decide now. I'm in a hurry.'

Kalan was reasonably certain no man in Krakandar's army would dare draw a weapon in anger against her prince, but for a moment she had a bad feeling Clayne was seriously contemplating the idea. Although it couldn't have been more than a few seconds, it seemed a frighteningly long time before the sergeant signalled his men to fall back. Once past that hurdle, however, she forgot about him. Lifting a torch from the wall bracket, she hurried along the corridor and down the stairs to the lower level with Damin and Almodavar, past the mostly empty cells until they reached the very end.

'Unlock it!' Damin demanded, pushing Clayne out of the way before he'd barely turned the key.

When she saw Starros – if indeed the battered, broken thing hanging from the chains was their childhood companion – Kalan gasped and covered her mouth with her hand, afraid she was going to lose the contents of her stomach.

The human wreckage that hung limp and lifeless from the ceiling chains looked barely alive. He wore only a pair of thin linen trousers in the freezing cell and every inch of his exposed skin seemed to be either bruised or bleeding.

'Cut him down!' Damin growled. There was a brittle, sharp edge to Damin's words, as if each syllable was a cutting tool of its own.

The sergeant released the chains and lowered Starros to the floor. Almodavar caught him gently, cradling the young man in his arms, his expression so shocked, so shaken, he seemed incapable of speaking. Kalan held the torch high in her left hand and bent down to feel for a pulse behind Starros's bloody, swollen ear. It was there, faint and surprisingly regular.

'Who did this?' Damin demanded of the sergeant.

'Lord Damaran, your highness,' Clayne replied, this time without hesitating. 'With a chainmail gauntlet and an iron bar. He's been at him for days.'

'Will he live?' This time Damin directed his question to Kalan.

'Maybe. If he gets help. But we need to get him out of here, Damin. Now.'

'My lady,' the sergeant began, distraught at the idea that he might have to stand between the Prince of Krakandar, his sorcerer sister, Krakandar's most senior captain and a jail-break. 'Please . . . don't place us in the position of having to stop you.'

She ignored his plea and stared up at Damin. In the flickering torchlight, he seemed much older than his twenty-four years. And angrier than she had ever seen him. Damin looked down at Almodavar, who was holding the unconscious young man in his arms, tears coursing freely down his cheeks.

'We'll get him out of here,' he promised.

Almodavar looked up, seemingly oblivious of his tears. 'Remove Starros from the palace and he will become outlaw.'

'Better outlaw than dead,' Damin pointed out, his rage still contained, but Kalan wasn't sure for how much longer.

'You're asking me to defy your uncle?'

'Who is more important, Almodavar?' Damin responded in a low voice meant only for the captain. 'Krakandar's regent or your own son?'

The old captain looked down at the boy he had never

once acknowledged as his child and nodded slowly. 'Where can we take him?'

'Your highness, if you attempt to remove the prisoner . . . ,' the sergeant began again, clearly torn between his duty and his desire.

'You chose which side you were on when you stood aside, Sergeant,' Damin pointed out, glancing over his shoulder at the men gathered in the hall outside the cell. 'Don't go changing your mind on me now.'

'But Almodavar's right. Where *can* we take him, Damin?' Kalan asked. 'The city is sealed. And there's nowhere inside the walls of Krakandar where Starros is safe.'

'Take him to Wrayan.'

Almodavar looked shocked. 'You'd hand your best friend over to the Thieves' Guild?' Significantly, Kalan thought, even now Almodavar still hadn't actually acknowledged that Starros was his son.

'I'd hand my best friend over to the care of the one man in Krakandar who might have some hope of keeping him hidden.' Damin smiled, briefly, humourlessly. 'Don't worry, Almodavar. I'm sure he won't turn into a thief for spending a few days in a Guild safe house.'

Almodavar nodded reluctantly and then looked up at the sergeant. 'Clayne has a point, though, Damin. Your uncle is still regent here. Any man who aids you in removing Starros from the palace risks death.'

'As does any man who stands in my way,' Damin replied.

There was a moment of tense silence as Damin forced every man present to decide whose side he was on.

Kalan didn't let out her breath until the sergeant snapped his fingers and ordered one of the troopers to fetch a stretcher to carry Starros.

Obviously relieved that he wouldn't have to fight his way out of the cells with an escaping prisoner, Damin turned to Kalan and drew her away from the men so that he could speak to her out of their hearing. 'I want you to go with him, Kal. Tell Wrayan—'

'It's all right, Damin. I know what to tell him.'

He glanced across at the men. One of them hurried in with the stretcher Clayne had sent him for and laid it on the floor. Several of the other men gathered round and gently lifted Starros onto the canvas. 'I can't help feeling this is my fault.'

'Why? You didn't do anything.'

He nodded grimly. 'That's exactly my point, Kal.'

She didn't like the sound of that. 'What are you going to do now?'

'Have words with Mahkas,' he replied, in what Kalan considered to be the understatement of the decade.

'He hurt Leila, too. Not as bad as this, but—'

'It's all right. I'll see she's taken care of.'

'And she thinks Starros is dead. Mahkas made me tell her he was. It's been a nightmare, Damin. It's as if he's lost his mind. He won't let Aunt Bylinda in to see her. Leila's half-starved and sick with grief, and—'

'It's all right, Kalan,' he assured her, putting his hand on her shoulder. 'I'll straighten everything out. I know I said I'd wait until Mother wrote to him to clear this idiocy up, but it's too late for that now. I'll speak to Mahkas. I'll make certain he knows there's no future for me and Leila, and maybe then we can start working out a way for everyone to get what they want.'

'Just don't do anything foolish, Damin.'

He smiled, but it was forced and there was no hint of humour in his eyes. 'You know me.'

'Which is precisely *why* I feel the need to tell you not to do anything foolish, Damin.'

'Trust me,' he said, but he was watching them manhandle Starros onto the stretcher, rather than giving her warning the attention Kalan felt it deserved.

'You always claimed you hated people who said that.'

'Not as much as I hate people who hurt my friends,' he replied.

Four troopers took an end each of the two poles threaded through the canvas loops and carefully lifted Starros off the floor. Carrying another torch, Clayne took the lead and Almodavar fell in behind them. With the other two troopers leading the way, they headed out into the hall.

'Be careful,' she warned, standing on her toes to kiss her brother's cheek. She wasn't sure why she felt the need to make such a gesture. It just seemed the right thing to do. 'Mahkas is still regent here, Damin. You have no real power other than your name.'

'Then perhaps it's time Mahkas learned the power in the name of Wolfblade. I'll send word to the Pickpocket's Retreat when I've spoken to my uncle,' he said, turning to Almodavar, as if it would take nothing more than a few simple words to clear up this unfortunate misunderstanding. 'And I won't forget your loyalty,' he added to the Raiders who had just chosen to follow the orders of their young prince rather than the rightful ruler of Krakandar.

'Damin . . .' Kalan began, certain there must be something more she should say, but he didn't answer her. He turned away instead and suggested to Almodavar and Sergeant Clayne that they tell the guard on the inner gate that the man they carried had fallen victim to the plague, which should ensure no one examined the body on the stretcher too closely.

Then, without another word, Damin turned on his heel, pushed past the men and the stretcher and headed out of the cells to confront Mahkas.

69

Orleon was on the landing with Rorin when Damin returned to the palace. Luciena, Xanda and Adham, along with the children and most of the Raiders, were gone. As he walked, Damin went over in his mind all the things he wanted to say to his uncle, discarding those involving curses and impossible threats. It seemed hours since he'd bluffed his way past Sergeant Clayne, when in fact it probably wasn't much more than ten or fifteen minutes.

The two men looked up at his approach. Orleon bowed, his expression grave.

'What happened?' Damin demanded, as he reached the top step.

'Your uncle discovered Lady Leila and Starros together in his room,' the old steward explained. 'They were in a somewhat . . . compromising . . . embrace. That was six, nearly seven days ago.'

'He had Starros arrested,' Rorin added. 'Accused of rape. He locked Leila in her room, worked himself into a frenzy, and then beat her like a dog. In between times, he's been trying to extract a confession from Starros. At least, that's what he's calling it.'

Almost overwhelmed by the need to lash out at something, Damin slammed one gauntleted fist into the other, appalled that such a situation had been allowed to continue. 'Didn't somebody try to stop him?'

Orleon looked away, unable to answer him, but Rorin – nowhere near as shy of his common-born rank as the steward – wasn't as reticent. 'How, Damin? Your uncle is the ultimate authority in this city. Just who exactly was supposed to walk up to him and point out the error of his ways?'

Damin's expression darkened ominously. 'Well, never fear, Rorin. I intend to point out more than the damned error of his ways, I can promise you that.'

The young man nodded his agreement, but laid a restraining hand on his arm. 'Just don't lose your temper with him.'

'I'll be fine.'

'I know,' Rorin agreed. 'But look at you, Damin. You're already shaking with fury. You can't achieve anything by—'

Rorin's warning was cut off by a scream. A cry of pure anguish tore through the night like a sharp sword through a silk scarf. Orleon and Rorin glanced back towards the palace at the sound, puzzled by its source. Damin suffered no such uncertainty. That was his Aunt Bylinda screaming and there was only one thing that would evoke such an extreme reaction in his aunt.

'Leila!'

Damin was through the palace doors and pounding up the staircase before the first screams subsided. He heard someone behind him and guessed it was Rorin. There was a moment of abrupt silence and then, as if she had gained a second wind, the screams began again, even more tormented than the first round. Everyone in the palace seemed frozen in place by the sound, even the Raiders standing watch at the door to Leila's room. They stood looking at the closed door uncertainly, as if they didn't understand how such a dreadful sound could be coming from inside.

Damin's approach seemed to galvanise the men into action. One of them turned and began banging on the door. The screams were unrelenting. Damin reached the door and turned the knob, only to discover it locked.

He bashed on it with his gauntleted fist, the metal spikes on his gloves gouging the woodwork. '*Leila! Bylinda!*'

The tormented screams kept on, but there was no other answer.

'Open the damn thing!'

'I'm sorry, your highness, but Lord Damaran has the key.'

The door was solid oak and wouldn't give way easily, Damin thought, even if they tried to kick it down.

'What about the slaveways?' Rorin asked breathlessly, as he caught up with Damin.

'It would take too long,' he replied, looking for anything that might aid them. He spied a granite pedestal in the alcove between Leila's door and the next suite. The sergeant in charge of the guard detail saw it at almost the same time and looked at Damin questioningly.

'Break it down!' Damin ordered, wishing he could put his hands over his ears to block out Bylinda's cries of anguish. A priceless vase smashed to the floor as two of the Raiders picked up the pedestal, turned and rammed the door with it at a run. It didn't budge. They backed up and ran at it again. And again. On the third hit, the wood around the lock splintered and they could finally kick the door open.

Damin overtook them before they were through the outer room. The bedroom was empty, but the screams were louder, coming from the bathroom. In the time it had taken Damin to get there, it seemed as if Bylinda had barely drawn breath.

It took a moment or two for Damin to take in the sight that greeted him as he burst through the bathroom door.

The stopcock was still open and the deep pool had over-flowed, splashing onto the blue tiled floor. Bylinda stood just inside, her hands on her face, the screams coming from her as if she'd tapped some wellspring of anguish that might never be staunched.

But it was the bath that drew Damin's eye and tore the screams from his aunt. The water that splashed onto the tiles was red with blood. Leila floated facedown in the water, her hair splayed out around her battered, naked body that slapped against the side of the bath as the overflowing stop-cock created tiny waves in the deep pool. Around each of her wrists the water ran a darker red, the blood from Leila's open veins feeding the pool, adding her life essence to the overflowing bathwater that escaped the confines of the tub with careless disregard.

It must have been only a moment between Damin bursting into Leila's bathroom and him plunging into the tepid water to drag her free, but he had time to notice the shattered mirror over the washstand. And the broken foot-stool. She must have smashed the glass with the stool and then used the shards to slit her wrists. Bylinda had probably come in through the slaveways to tend to her daughter, only to find Leila had already taken matters into her own hands.

Rorin was right behind him as Damin dragged Leila from the water, his leather armour weighing him down as it became waterlogged. The young sorcerer pulled Bylinda away as Damin lifted Leila out of the tub, holding the distraught mother back forcibly to allow Damin a chance to lift Leila clear.

Rorin was trying to calm her, without much success. There was nothing to be said that would make this ghastly scene any easier to bear. Nothing anybody could do that would make this awful thing better.

'No . . . please, Leila, no . . . not this . . . ,' Damin whis-pered desperately to his cousin, over and over, oblivious of the soaking he received in the process from both the bath-water and her blood. She weighed nothing, as if her soul had taken all the weight of her body with it when it departed.

Dripping and distraught, he lowered Leila's body to the tiled floor, looking for some sign of life, but his cousin had been both determined and efficient. This was no feeble attention-grabbing exercise, no fake suicide attempt to let people know the depth of her despair. Leila had wanted to die and meant to succeed. She'd gone to meet her lover, slicing the veins on both arms lengthwise, halfway to the elbow. Her body was already cooling, the blood no longer spurting from her veins.

Damin stared at Leila in numb disbelief, holding her against him as if his mere presence might do something to restore her blue lips to a more life-like sheen, as if he held her long enough, she might gain from his strength. Her sightless eyes might flutter and blink and she would smile at him and say, 'Ha! That got you, didn't it?'

But there was nothing. Leila was probably dead before Bylinda found her and no amount of wishing, hoping or praying on Damin's part was going to bring her back.

'Damin?'

It was Rorin who spoke. There was a strange edge to his voice, the mere mention of Damin's name a question laden with caution.

Damin looked up at him, with no concept of the menacing spectre he presented, kneeling there on the floor, Leila's life-less body in his arms, dripping with the bloody water of his cousin's final bath. Bylinda tore herself free from Rorin's hold and threw herself at them. Numb with shock, Damin let her take Leila from him without resistance.

'Leila! Oh, my baby! What have you done?' Bylinda wailed. 'Leila! Leila!'

'Damin?' Rorin repeated, clearly concerned about some-thing, but the words seemed distant, somehow, as if the blood rushing through Damin's veins and pounding in his ears filtered out the sounds of the real world.

In all his life, Damin Wolfblade had never lost his temper. He'd been angry on occasion, riled, irritated, even furious. But never had he stepped across the threshold into true rage. And even now, he wasn't sure if the icy calm he felt was rage or grief. Whatever it was, Damin knew it needed an outlet. It needed a focus, and the focus was the man who had beaten his best friend to a pulp, the man who had driven his own daughter to suicide.

'*Damin!*'

Rorin's voice followed him from the room, clearly panicked by the thought of what the young prince intended to do next. The outer room had filled with people – slaves, more Raiders and Tejay Lionsclaw. Damin strode straight past them all, without even registering they were there. His mind was filled with nothing but the need to confront Mahkas. To make his uncle answer for what had been done to his cousin and his friend. He wasn't driven by any of the noble, rational arguments Kalan had been hoping he'd use to convince their uncle that he was being unreasonable.

Damin wanted vengeance.

Blood for blood. He intended to open Mahkas up from neck to navel, to watch his life spill out the way Leila's had done.

Poor Leila, whose only crime was the misfortune of having a father who couldn't see past his own ambition.

They had all laughed about it so many times when they were children. And it *had* seemed funny, because never had two children desired a union less than Damin and his cousin. They all knew what Mahkas expected and thought it was hilarious, because even when they were small children, they understood how unlikely it was that Marla would ever permit such a marriage to go ahead.

It had gone beyond a joke, however. There was nothing

to laugh about now. For Leila, there would be nothing to laugh about ever again.

Rorin was still calling after him urgently when he reached the bottom of the grand staircase and headed along the hall to the east wing, where he knew Mahkas would be waiting to welcome him home.

70

As Damin had expected, Mahkas was waiting for him in his study, sitting behind his desk engrossed in his work, apparently unconcerned by his wife's desperate screams. Admittedly, they had stopped now, but when he looked up from the papers he was working on, the Regent of Krakandar was smiling warmly, as if nothing was amiss. The candles flickered and the fireplace flared in the draught as the door slammed open against the wall.

'Damin! You're home!'

In reply, too full of vengeful rage to speak, Damin drew his sword and advanced on his uncle, dripping wet with Leila's blood and bathwater, consumed only by the need to do something – *anything* – to right the terrible wrong that had happened in this place.

Mahkas's smile faded as he rose cautiously to his feet, staring at the naked steel in his nephew's gauntleted hand. He seemed only then to notice that Damin was soaked to the skin and that there was as much blood as there was water staining his nephew's leather armour. '*Damin*? Is something wrong?'

His feigned ignorance infuriated Damin, that he had sat here, unmoving, listening to the tormented screams of his own wife echoing through the palace, that he had done nothing while his daughter bled to death in despair, shredded what little reason Damin had left.

With a wordless cry of fury, he drew back his arm ready to drive the sword through his uncle's heart and pin Mahkas by the chest to his damned gilded would-be throne. He saw the shock in his uncle's eyes as Mahkas realised what Damin intended, saw the miserable, black-hearted coward draw back in fear . . . and thrust the blade forward . . .

Only to discover his hand suddenly empty.

Stunned, Damin spun around with a furious cry to discover Rorin standing behind him, his eyes black with the power he was drawing, the sword intended for Mahkas's heart now firmly and inexplicably embedded in the panelling near the door by Rorin's head.

'*Damin!*' Rorin cried warily, taking a step backward, as if he'd just realised that in saving Mahkas by ripping the sword magically from Damin's furious grasp and sending it harmlessly into the panelling, he'd brought the young prince's wrath down on himself. 'Think about this!'

Still too enraged to form a coherent sentence, Damin let out a yell of frustration and turned back to face his uncle. He was angry with Mahkas, not Rorin. Besides, Rorin may well have done him a favour. It would be far more satisfying to rip Mahkas's black heart out with his bare hands, than the quick, relatively painless release a sharp blade offered.

His eyes full of fear, Mahkas had scrambled clear of the desk and his heavy, throne-like chair and backed up against the wall, against the beautifully embroidered map of Hythria. In three strides, Damin was on him. He slammed Mahkas backwards with his forearm pressed across his uncle's throat, the sharp metal scales of his gauntlet cutting into the soft skin of the older man's neck.

Mahkas gasped for breath, unable to speak because of the pressure on his throat, blood beading around the tips of the spiked scales of Damin's gauntlet where they cut his flesh. Damin could smell his uncle's fear, although it was clear, even now, that Mahkas could not quite comprehend the reason for it.

'Damin, *no*!' another voice cried desperately, female this time.

Damin glanced over his shoulder. Tejay had burst into the room, followed by a clutch of Raiders who crowded behind her in the doorway, torn with indecision. These men were sworn to protect Krakandar's regent, but, more importantly, they lived to serve Krakandar's prince. The men hesitated on the threshold, unsure about whom they should be protecting. Tejay solved their dilemma for them by the simple expedient of slamming the door on the Raiders with her foot and then she turned to confront Damin.

'This is none of your concern, Tejay,' he told her, surprised at how icily calm he sounded. A few moments ago, he'd been too angry to speak. But now, with Mahkas pinned against the wall and the breath slowly being squeezed out of him by the sharp spikes that encircled Damin's forearm, the young prince found his voice, unaware of the chilling, terrible timbre of his words. 'This is a family matter.'

'Damin,' Tejay repeated, taking a step closer, speaking in a voice that sounded as if she was fighting to keep a level, reasonable tone. 'Let him go. Please.'

He didn't answer her. Instead, he turned back to glare at Mahkas, to breathe in the stench of his fear. Leila must have felt something of the same fear. What else would have driven her to suicide? And Starros? Had he hung in those dreadful chains, awaiting the next blow, never sure where it would fall, or when? Had Mahkas revelled in their fear the way Damin was drinking in his uncle's terror now?

Mahkas's eyes were wide, he was gasping for breath and his face was turning blue.

Damin's eyes never left his uncle's suffocating face as he answered Tejay. 'He killed Leila, my lady. He damn near killed Starros. Give me one good reason why I *shouldn't* kill him.'

'One Warlord,' Tejay said.

Those two simple words struck a note somewhere in Damin, something that pierced his veil of rage. He eased the pressure on Mahkas's throat a little and turned to her. '*What?*'

'We're one Warlord away from Alija Eaglespike gaining control of the Convocation of Warlords, Damin,' Rorin reminded him in a voice devoid of all emotion.

Damin glared at them both. The young sorcerer's eyes were still dark, the whites consumed completely, as if he held onto his magical power as some form of protection against Damin's fury.

Tejay nodded her agreement. 'No matter how satisfying it might feel, Damin, kill Mahkas now, while you're still six years away from inheriting your seat, and Krakandar will be in the hands of the Sorcerers' Collective before the sun rises tomorrow morning.'

Damin turned to stare at Mahkas, knowing Rorin and Tejay were right. That one reason alone was enough for him to spare his uncle's life. The fact that he could see their point, and appreciate its significance, infuriated the young prince even more. He wanted blood. That he could hesitate on the brink of wreaking righteous vengeance for Leila's death and Starros's brutal torture, for something as cold and impersonal as politics, made Damin disgusted with himself.

But it stayed his hand.

Slowly, he lifted his forearm from Mahkas's throat and took a step back. His uncle collapsed against the wall, barely able to stand, his fear abating a little as it occurred to him that his nephew didn't plan to kill him after all.

'Damin . . . ,' Mahkas gasped. 'I don't know what you've been told, but Leila's waiting for you . . .'

'Leila's *dead*!' Damin yelled at him, making his uncle flinch. 'And it might as well have been *you* who wielded the blade!'

Mahkas looked past Damin to Tejay and Rorin in confusion. 'Dead? What's he talking about?'

'Leila has killed herself, Mahkas,' Tejay informed him. 'That's what all that screaming was about, in case you were wondering.'

He shook his head, denying Tejay's words, smiling patronisingly at her ignorance, as he stood a little straighter. 'No, no, no . . . you must be mistaken, Lady Lionsclaw. Bylinda's just being hysterical, that's all. Leila's fine. She's waiting for Damin. They're to be married, you know—'

'This is *her* blood I'm wearing, you bastard!' Damin exploded. 'She killed herself because you wouldn't let it go! You couldn't let her be happy. Leila is dead because of your pathetic ambition!'

Mahkas backed away from him in shock, but it seemed more for his nephew's ingratitude than grief at the loss of his only child. 'But Damin, I don't understand. Why are you saying these things? I did all of this for you! I've kept Krakandar safe, made her more prosperous than she's ever been. Everything was for you. All of it. Even my own daughter . . .'

It was more than Damin could stand, to listen to his uncle justify Leila's death by claiming it was done on his behalf. He grabbed Mahkas again, slamming him against the wall once more, this time with his gauntleted hand around his uncle's throat. 'You did this for *yourself*, you miserable prick! Don't you *dare* try to shift the blame onto me for your sorry delusions.'

'*Damin! No!*' Tejay cried, as she sensed what little self-control he had left beginning to slip.

Damin ignored her. Instead, he focused all his anger and rage on his uncle, his grip tightening inexorably. When he spoke, his voice was steel dipped in icy rage. 'So let's clear this up, once and for all, shall we? There is not now, or *ever*, going to be a wedding between me and Leila. Do you *get* that yet?' He slammed Mahkas's head against the wall to emphasise his point.

'When your mother hears of this . . .' Mahkas managed to gasp weakly.

'My mother already *knows*, you stupid bastard! I wrote to her weeks ago, demanding she finally set you straight. She should have done it years ago. She told me that herself, but she didn't want to hurt your feelings. Well, I don't give a pinch of shit about your feelings, *Uncle* Mahkas, so let's see if I can state this clearly enough so that even *you* will get it through your thick, brainless skull. There never *was* going to be a wedding. You just seem to be the only person in the whole damned world who doesn't understand that! And now,' he added, slamming his uncle's head against the wall once more, just because it felt so damned good, 'thanks to you and your sad delusions, Leila is dead and I'm going to rip out your miserable heart with my bare hands.'

'Damin,' Rorin warned anxiously. 'Don't do this.'

Mahkas was gasping for breath, choking again as Damin's fist closed on his windpipe. The desire to crush it completely was overwhelming.

'Don't give Krakandar away because of something your uncle did,' Tejay advised behind him.

He hesitated once more. Tejay was right, Damin knew it. In his mind, at least. But his heart wanted vengeance and it was proving an almost equal fight between the two warring factions inside him.

'Mahkas Damaran simply isn't worth Krakandar or the High Prince's crown, Damin.'

And that, Damin realised, was the crux of it. Mahkas *wasn't* worth it. He was nothing – a deluded fool who couldn't see past his own ambition. With a disgusted shove, he let Mahkas go, unable to look at him any longer.

He turned away and found himself face to face with Tejay.

She nodded her approval. 'Marla Wolfblade raised our next High Prince far too well to have him falter this close to the finish, Damin.'

Behind him, Mahkas staggered to his feet, grasping his bruised throat. He snarled at Tejay's words and then coughed painfully. 'Raised him well? That's a joke! Did you see what this ungrateful bastard just did? He . . . he tried to kill me! Guards!'

They were waiting outside the door for just such an order and burst into the study at Mahkas's shout. The room rapidly filled with armed men, but they hadn't drawn their weapons. Not yet, at least.

'Arrest my nephew!'

The sergeant stared at Mahkas in surprise. 'My *lord*?'

'You heard me! Arrest him! He just tried to kill me!'

'But . . . your nephew is the prince, my lord,' the sergeant pointed out nervously. '*Our* prince . . .'

'I know who he is, idiot. Now arrest him! Get him out of my sight!'

Damin faced the Raiders defiantly for a moment and then shook his head and held up his hands to show he intended no resistance. He could feel Tejay and Rorin relaxing at the gesture.

'It's all right, Sergeant,' he assured the Raider, taking a deep breath to calm his raging pulse. 'I'm done here. All the people who are going to die in this place tonight are already dead.'

'Perhaps, if you'd loved Leila the way she loved you, my daughter wouldn't have felt the need to take her own life,' Mahkas sneered behind him.

Damin had taken a bare two steps towards the door when his uncle spoke, and his derision sent Damin toppling over the edge of reason. He was on Mahkas before anyone could stop him.

It didn't take much to slake his need for retribution. He delivered one savage blow, one short, sharp jab with his gauntleted fist. Mahkas was quick enough to dodge the punch, but not quick enough to get out of its way completely. He turned his head at the last instant and the blow glanced off his chin and grazed his throat instead, dragging the gauntlet's sharp spikes across his windpipe. Blood gushed from the wound but when Mahkas opened his mouth to cry out, nothing came out but a wet, bubbling noise.

Damin stepped back, shaking off the Raiders who'd attempted to restrain him, satisfied that if he couldn't kill him, he had silenced Mahkas at least.

In stunned disbelief, everyone – even Tejay and Rorin – fell back out of his way as the Prince of Krakandar strode from the room, leaving the regent lying on the floor, covered in blood, fighting to draw breath through the hole in his windpipe, his severed vocal chords robbing him of the ability to give voice to his pain.

71

It was days before Elezaar could bring himself to return to Marla's townhouse. In the intervening time he wandered blindly through the plague-infected city, not caring about his own welfare; tempting fate, begging it to offer him a release. Unfortunately for Elezaar, just as the rat drive in Krakandar had kept the plague at bay, so it had begun to have an effect here in Greenharbour. It seemed as if the tide had turned and the first tenuous signs of recovery were already visible. He didn't catch the plague and no cutpurses attacked him and beat him to death. It was as if the gods wanted him to suffer, so they allowed him to roam Greenharbour's normally dangerous streets with impunity.

Denied even an accidental death as an avenue of escape, Elezaar eventually faced the fact that he could not walk away from the consequences of his betrayal so he made his way back home.

The least he could do for Marla – the *last* thing he could do for his mistress – was warn her of the danger he'd placed her and her whole family in.

It took him another day to gather the courage to do what must be done, but finally, after pawning the silver wolf's head brooch that held his cloak together, Elezaar was able to buy what he needed from an apothecary in the merchant quarter. The herbalist was one of the few who could see the first signs of recovery and he was anxious to sell his medicines and perhaps claim some credit for plague cures that he'd actually had nothing to do with. The man didn't question Elezaar as he made his purchase. He simply took the money, handed over the small vial to the dwarf, and went back to mixing his potions.

Elezaar drank the contents of the vial down before he turned and finally headed for home.

Marla hurried into the hall when she heard Elezaar was back. She was clearly worried about his disappearance and expected a satisfactory answer about where he'd been. Elezaar was ready for that. He intended to tell her the truth.

He'd told all the lies he was ever going to tell.

'Where have you been!' the princess demanded of him, as soon as she laid eyes on him. 'Look at you. Elezaar! You're filthy! I've been out of my mind with worry. We all thought you taken by bandits, or become a victim of the plague!'

And she would have been worried, he knew. She cared about him, perhaps even loved him, in her own way, although in all his years in her service nothing sexual had ever passed between them.

Nobody had ever cared about Elezaar the Fool before Marla Wolfblade came along. *Yet I betrayed her anyway . . .*

'I *am* a victim, your highness. But only of my own weakness.'

Marla looked at him oddly. 'Is there something you want to tell me, Elezaar?'

He nodded. 'Something I must tell you, your highness. I certainly don't want to do it.'

'You're being terribly cryptic. What's going on?'

He was starting to feel a little nauseous as the contents of the vial began to take effect. 'Can we sit, your highness? I'm not feeling well.'

Marla nodded her permission and allowed him to take a seat on the cushions around the low table normally reserved for visitors of her own class. She seated herself opposite, curious and a little concerned perhaps, but with no inkling of the devastating blow he was about to deliver.

'Now, out with it,' she ordered. 'Where have you been? And what is this thing you must tell me?'

'I have a brother.'

Marla smiled. 'Well, I can see I shall have to have you whipped for keeping that from me.'

She was still beautiful, he thought, as he studied her face. She had turned forty last year but still managed to look five years younger. A combination, the dwarf knew, of being able to afford the best, never having to work outdoors and picking the right mother. Marla came from a long line of women who aged well.

'You may wish more than that on me, your highness, by the time I've finished my tale,' he warned ominously.

'Are you drunk, Elezaar?' she asked, looking at him with concern. He was sweating profusely and feeling quite unwell.

He shook his head. 'No. Just . . . weary. Did I ever tell you I was born in Pentamor Province?'

'You mentioned it once, I think.'

'I was happy as a child. For a time. I mean, I was born a slave, but not all of us are doomed to a life of desperate helplessness. I had a brother. He was two years younger than me. His name was Crysander.'

'Elezaar—'

'Please, my lady, let me finish this.'

She nodded, clearly not happy with his request. Elezaar hoped he would have enough time to do what must be done.

'When Crysander was eight, our owner sold us to a *court'esa* school. My brother was always going to be handsome but I'm not sure why they wanted me. I think it was because they had plans to make Crys into a Loronged *court'esa* and thought they could try the poison on me first. Perhaps the logic was that if I survived it, Crys probably would too. So I trained as a *court'esa* and, when I was sixteen, they held me down and poured Loronge down my throat and, much to everybody's astonishment, I survived it. Two years later, so did Crysander.'

'Your brother is also a Loronged *court'esa*?' Marla asked, a little surprised.

'He was.'

'What happened to him?'

'He was sold to a man from Dregian who bought him as a wedding gift for Barnardo Eaglespike.'

Marla was silent for a moment. When she finally spoke, her voice was icy. 'Are you telling me, Elezaar, that all this time you've had a brother who is a *court'esa* in Alija's household and you didn't think it worth mentioning?'

'No, your highness, of course not!'

'Then you'd better finish your tale, Fool. Now that you have my undivided attention.'

Elezaar wiped his sweaty brow with his sleeve and blinked several times to clear his vision before continuing. 'We were separated after I was Loronged. I only heard much later that Crys was sent to Dregian Castle. My first owner was a woman in Greenharbour who thought I'd make an interesting conversation piece at dinner.' He shook his head, not wanting his last thoughts to be of that best-forgotten time. 'I was bought and sold a number of times after that – I was an accomplished musician, after all, as well as a novelty. But I never served in the same household as my brother until I was purchased by Ronan Dell.'

Marla frowned. 'I know that name . . . wasn't he the

friend of my brother's who was murdered all those years ago? It was around the time I first came back to Greenharbour, wasn't it? When Hablet made an offer for my hand? If I remember it correctly, Kagan Palenovar was convinced the Patriots were behind the assassination, but he could never prove it.'

'Ronan Dell and his entire household were slaughtered on the Feast of Kaelarn the year you arrived back in Greenharbour,' the dwarf confirmed.

'Not his entire household,' Marla remarked coolly. 'You escaped, obviously.'

'They killed everyone *except* me,' Elezaar continued, as if Marla hadn't spoken, his one good eye glazing over in dark remembrance as he related his tale. He could see it as if he was still standing in the room. He could hear the flies. Smell the blood . . .

'They killed Lord Dell first,' Elezaar said. For twenty-five years he'd told this tale to nobody. It astonished him how difficult it was to finally talk about it.

'I heard them coming. We were in his bedroom when they killed him. I hid behind the curtains.' He fixed his one good eye on Marla, his voice hardening as he relived the nightmare. 'I almost gave myself away, cheering for his assassins as they struck the killing blow. Ronan Dell was a monster, your highness. He made your brother's worst obsessions seem almost harmless by comparison. He had all these instruments, you see . . . scores of them . . . from all over the world. He collected them like other men collect insects or precious stones . . . And he used them, every chance he got; sometimes on his *court'esa*, sometimes on a random slave unfortunate enough to enter the room carrying a tray of drinks when Ronan was showing off to his friends.'

'Friends like my brother, you mean?' the princess asked frostily.

'Yes, my lady, the High Prince was a regular visitor to Ronan Dell's palace,' he agreed, knowing there was little about Lernen that would shock Marla after all these years. And this was a time for absolute truth. Trying to gild over the unpleasant parts of his story would defeat his purpose. 'His favourite toy, and the worst of them all, was a carved bull's horn wrapped in jagged wire . . .' Elezaar hesitated, not sure if he had the words to describe what he had seen, or how it had made him feel.

Marla could see he was distressed. Although obviously still angry with him, her face creased with concern. 'Oh gods, Elezaar! Surely, he didn't make *you* . . . ?'

The *court'esa* shook his head and forced himself to go on. 'I used to wish he had. Then I would have bled to death, too, after a while, and the torment would have stopped. But I was there to watch. I was there to play my instrument while he had his fun with his toys, because the sick bastard liked to do it to music. *Keep playing, Fool!* he'd shout, if I began to falter. He killed them in time to the tempo I set.' Tears filled Elezaar's eyes, blinding him to everything but the memories. 'It was up to me, you see . . . if I played fast, then they died at that speed, and if I slowed down, then the torment just went on for longer.'

Elezaar pulled at his own silver slave collar as his breathing became more ragged. He wasn't sure if it was reliving his time with Ronan Dell that made him short of breath. He thought he might be rambling and knew he should try to stick to the point. His time was running out. 'Did I mention that he had a particular fondness for virgins? He used to buy them from the slave markets. Really young, sometimes only twelve or thirteen. That way he was certain they were pure.'

Elezaar wiped his eyes, ashamed by his weakness. He'd never shed a tear about it before today. To have appeared even a tiny bit moved by what he was witnessing would have amused Ronan too much and urged him on to greater feats of torment. The dwarf fixed his gaze on Marla and attempted to pull himself together. 'I didn't have to suffer Ronan Dell's particular brand of perverse pleasure just once, your highness. I got to suffer it night after night after night.'

Disturbed as she was by his story. Marla was clearly puzzled by his sudden need to unburden himself. 'Why are you telling me this now, Elezaar?'

'Because Ronan Dell was murdered, your highness. He was betrayed and murdered. By my brother.' *He's not in any danger from the assassins. Crysander is one of them.* 'When I accused him of betraying our master, he told me he'd been faithful to his real master all along. He told me he'd always belonged to the House of Eaglespike.'

Marla sagged back against the cushions in shock. '*Alija* had Ronan Dell killed?'

The look on the princess's face tore Elezaar apart. It was as if he could see her trust, her belief in him, evaporating before his very eyes. And it was only going to get worse. His betrayal went far deeper than mere silence.

'And all this time you could bear witness to this crime, Elezaar? And you never uttered a word?'

'I told nobody what I witnessed, your highness. The day you found me at Venira's Slave Emporium, I was hiding from Alija. When you walked in with her, I was certain my life was over. And then I realised you were the High Prince's sister and that under your protection, I might escape her . . .'

'So you set out to make yourself indispensable to me,' Marla concluded, making no attempt to hide her bitter disappointment.

'I wanted to make certain you were strong enough to defy her if she ever demanded you hand me over to her.' He hung his head in shame. 'There was nothing selfless in my willingness to help you, your highness. In the beginning, I kept what I knew to myself because I thought I might need it as insurance some day. And then . . . well, after you came to rely on me and listen to my counsel, I was terrified of losing your trust. I knew how you'd react if you learned I'd known about this and not told you. And now I've just made things worse.'

Marla seemed too dumbstruck to be angry with him. She would find her voice soon, he figured. Elezaar had confessed much, but he'd yet to reveal his worst, and most recent, crime.

'I saw my brother fall in Ronan Dell's palace,' he continued while he still had the strength. 'I saw them take his body away. I believed my brother was dead. For twenty-five years I had no reason to think otherwise.'

'Are you telling me you think he might not be dead after all?'

'I got a message a few days ago. Venira's doorman came to the house. He told me they had a slave called Crysander. I arranged to meet him.'

'And never came back,' Marla reminded him.

He couldn't answer that accusation so he just kept on talking, feeling the heat from the poison infuse his body, warning him his time was growing short. 'We arranged to meet at the Lucky Harlot. When I got there, Bekan was waiting for me. With my brother. And Tarkyn Lye.'

Marla rose to her feet and began to pace the room, back and forth. She didn't need to be told what Tarkyn Lye's presence meant. It seemed as if she was trying to walk off her fury. After a while, the princess stopped pacing and turned to look at him.

'What *exactly* have you done, Elezaar?'

'They had my brother, your highness, and Ronan Dell's favourite toy.' His eyes filled with tears again and he could no longer stop them falling. 'Please, your highness . . .

understand . . . I . . . I couldn't watch it happen again. It almost destroyed me once before, standing by helplessly . . . I couldn't let them do the same to my brother. Not when I had it in my power to stop it.'

For a moment, a glimmer of sympathy flickered across the princess's face. 'What did you tell Tarkyn Lye, Elezaar?'

'Everything.'

Marla stared at him in shock. 'What do you mean, *everything*?'

'Exactly what I said, your highness. I told him everything. I told him about Wrayan Lightfinger. About the mind shields. About how you'd known Alija and your second husband were lovers since before Lord Hawksword died. I even told him how you found out Luciena's mind had been tampered with and why you'd kept the discovery a secret. By the time I was done, I was *looking* for things to tell him.' Elezaar no longer noticed his tears. He looked up at his beloved princess and shook his head sorrowfully. 'I'm so sorry, your highness. I know you deserve better than this, but I had to do something . . .'

Marla was stunned into speechlessness.

'In the end, for the secret about Rorin's magical ability and the reason you'd allowed Kalan to join the Sorcerers' Collective, they gave me a moment alone with Crysander.' The tears coursed freely down his face as he forced himself to finish his tale. It was an effort to sit upright now and it wasn't just the veil of tears that made his vision blur. 'It was too late by then to undo the damage I'd done to you, my lady. But I was able to ensure they would never use Crysander against me again.'

'Elezaar—'

'It was quick, my lady,' he assured her. 'I'm small, I know, but I'm stronger than I look. He didn't feel any pain.'

She stared at him, the pain of his betrayal replaced,

momentarily, with the shock of this latest confession. 'Are you saying you *killed* your own brother?'

'I made sure they couldn't use him against me. Not again.'

Unable to hold himself upright, he toppled sideways, feeling the spittle on his chin he no longer had the ability to contain. He heard Marla cry out as she realised something was terribly wrong, something far more serious than guilt or treachery. Dizzy and holding on to consciousness with the very last of his will, Elezaar felt the princess's cool hand on his burning forehead. It made the pain worse, because he knew he didn't deserve such consideration from the woman he had betrayed so heinously.

'By the gods, Elezaar . . .' She sounded desperate, rather than angry. 'What have you done to yourself? What have you taken?'

His vision had all but gone, fading into dimness. With his one good eye, he tried to focus on Marla's face. He wanted his last memory to be of her.

'I am my own judge, your highness,' he whispered, lacking the strength to speak any louder. 'And my own executioner.'

With the darkness closing in around him, Elezaar felt Marla gather him into her arms and hold him, rocking him like a small child. He was foaming at the mouth, his muscles twitching uncontrollably. She must realise by now that he'd poisoned himself. Marla wasn't a fool. She would know, just by looking at his pallid, clammy skin, that he was on the brink of death. And he knew she must despise him for his treachery.

In spite of that, she held him against her body, as if her shock, her disappointment and even her anger were unimportant matters she was willing to put aside simply because Elezaar the Fool was dying.

'Oh, Elezaar,' Marla murmured softly.

Strange, but she sounds like she's crying. He lost himself in her last embrace, his head resting on her breast, thinking that for this one tender moment, it had almost been worth it.

'Why try to face this alone, you little fool? Why didn't you come to me?'

He wanted to tell Marla that he was a coward. He'd been afraid. Afraid of losing her protection. Afraid of being cast back into the pit. Afraid of being sold by one high-born house after another, until he was worthless. Afraid he'd wind up as bear-bait when he was past his prime.

And he wanted to remind Marla he'd tried to warn her, time and again, not to place her trust in him. It was the Fourth Rule of Gaining and Wielding Power. *Trust only yourself.*

Most of all, Elezaar wanted to tell his beloved princess that he was afraid of never seeing her again. But he could feel his tongue swelling, making it impossible to speak.

Don't leave me, little man, he imagined he could hear her sobbing. *What will I ever do without you?*

Elezaar knew her words were merely his own wishful thinking. He understood what he had done and knew he was beyond redemption. Beyond forgiveness. But it was nice to dream. It was nice to think he would draw his last breath with her forgiveness on his lips.

With death so close he could reach out and touch it, the dwarf felt cool lips pressing on his forehead and wondered if he was dreaming again. Then he felt a soft cheek pressing against his face and tasted salty tears on his swollen tongue.

And then, when the effort to hold on became too much for him, he willingly let go. Wrapped in the embrace of the only woman he had ever loved, Elezaar let the darkness take him.

72

Wrayan Lightfinger and Kalan Hawksword worked through the night on Starros, but as dawn broke over Krakandar City, Wrayan still wasn't certain they'd be able to save him. The young man had been beaten more savagely than anything Wrayan had ever encountered before, and he was astonished that Starros was still able to draw breath.

Wrayan wished, not for the first time, that his magical ability included more healing. He knew a little. The Harshini had shown him a few things during his years with them, but having the knowledge of how to fix something and having the power to make it happen were two entirely different things. Starros was probably still alive because Wrayan had used what little power he wielded to keep him that way. To heal him completely, however, would take somebody with Brak's formidable power or the active co-operation of the gods, a step Wrayan was extremely reluctant to take unless it was their only option.

The last time Wrayan had begged a god for help, it had cost him his soul.

The door opened behind him and Kalan slipped into the dim room, holding a steaming mug of tea. She closed the door and handed it to Wrayan, then looked down at Starros's unconscious body with a frown.

'How is he?'

'Unchanged,' Wrayan told her, sipping the tea appreciatively. 'Any word yet about how much longer before Rorin gets here?'

'No.'

He glanced out of the dusty window and noticed it was lighter outside. He'd been up all night, watching over Starros. Kalan had stayed with him for much of the time and he was surprised by how much he'd enjoyed her company as they worked to use what skills they had – Kalan's quite-substantial medical knowledge (*they have to teach us something at the Collective, you know*) and Wrayan's limited Harshini healing skills – to keep Starros alive.

Wrayan had always had a soft spot for Kalan, and in between tending their wounded friend, they'd spent a lot of the night catching up. She kept him entertained with tales of her life in Greenharbour and her apprenticeship at the Sorcerers' Collective – an institution that seemed quite different and far more structured than the haphazard organisation Wrayan remembered.

He was amazed at how grown up Kalan seemed, how mature and in control of herself she was. He supposed he shouldn't really have been surprised. Princess Marla's youngest daughter was twenty-two years old now and had always been the brightest of the bunch. More like her mother than either Damin or Narvell – well-educated, a little cynical and accustomed to the viper-pit politics of Greenharbour – Kalan Hawksword was far removed from the child Wrayan remembered.

He stretched his shoulders to ease the stiffness a little, leaned forward, pinched out the candle stub beside the bed, and then glanced up at her. She looked remarkably fresh and alert for someone who'd been awake the better part of the night. She'd even had time to brush out her long fair hair and braid it loosely down her back. Only her rumpled green silk gown betrayed the fact that she'd not come straight from the palace.

'Shouldn't you be getting back home?'

'Not until I know he's going to be all right,' she said, looking down at Starros with concern. His breathing was shallow and laboured, but it was steadier than it had been when Kalan first brought him to the Beggars' Quarter last night. 'Did you want to get some sleep? I can sit with him for a while.'

He shook his head. 'I don't need sleep as often as—'

'Us poor humans?' she finished for him with a smile. 'Rorin says the same thing.'

Wrayan looked up at her. 'I wasn't going to say it quite like that, but yes, one advantage of having even a little bit of Harshini blood in your veins seems to be the ability to go for a long time without sleep. How about you?'

'I got a few hours. Fyora made up a pallet in the other room for me.'

The safe house where they had brought Starros was a couple of streets away from the Pickpocket's Retreat. Wrayan used it sometimes, when he wanted to be alone, or when he had business to conduct that he didn't want witnessed by the patrons of the Pickpocket's Retreat. Only Fyora, Luc North and a few other trusted lieutenants knew about it and he was certain they would never betray either Starros or the location of the house.

Kalan sat on the edge of the bed and took Starros's swollen hand in her own, stroking the splinted bandages gently. Two of his fingers were broken, and quite a few of the bones in his hand, as if Mahkas had deliberately laid his hands out and smashed them with his iron bar. 'He's not getting any better, is he?'

Wrayan shrugged, unable to answer her question. 'It's hard to tell. I think he's going to live. Unless he's bleeding internally. Rorin will be able to tell better than me.'

'And then what?'

'What do you mean?'

'Look at him, Wrayan. We've managed to keep him alive, but even with Rorin's help, some of these injuries are never going to heal properly. He'll be crippled, at the very least.' Kalan fell silent, but Wrayan got the impression she wanted to say something else.

'And . . . ?'

'I was just wondering . . . isn't there something else you and Rorin can do?'

'You mean magically, I suppose?'

She nodded.

'I've done everything I know how to, Kalan. Rorin should be able to do more. His power is more inclined towards healing than mine.'

'But he's not as strong as you.'

'But the Harshini taught him,' Wrayan reminded her. 'Shananara gave him the knowledge he needed to use his power. I know it included some healing. I'm just not sure how much.'

'I remember once, not long after we got to Greenharbour, we sneaked out of the Sorcerers' Collective during the Festival of Jashia to watch the fireworks. I slipped off the wall and hurt my ankle. Rorin fixed it without even knowing how he did it.' She smiled in remembrance. 'It drove him mad for weeks afterwards, trying to recall what he'd done. He said he just knew what he had to do, but afterwards he couldn't say what it was.'

'Then let's hope that when he gets here, he can help Starros, because the only other alternative is to ask the gods for help.'

Kalan looked at him in surprise. 'You can *do* that?'

He shook his head reluctantly. 'Don't get too excited about the idea, Kal. Calling on the gods for direct inter-vention comes at a very high cost.'

'What sort of cost?'

'Your soul, usually.'

She laughed at him, obviously thinking he was teasing her. 'Are you telling me you've sold *your* soul to a god, Wrayan Lightfinger?'

'Every last bit of it. To save your mother, actually.'

Kalan's smile faded. 'Are you serious?'

Wrayan nodded. 'It happened a long time ago. Before your mother was even married to Laran Krakenshield. I accidentally cast a spell on her and had to call on a god to lift it.'

'The God of Thieves,' Kalan guessed. 'Dacendaran.'

He smiled. 'I had to promise to become the greatest thief in all of Hythria.'

'And are you?' she asked.

'I like to think so,' he replied smugly.

She smiled. 'And if you call on Dacendaran again?'

'Then I suspect Starros is going to have to consider a career change.'

Kalan shrugged and looked down at her foster-brother. 'That may not be such a big deal, you know. I'm fairly certain he doesn't have a future waiting for him in Krakandar Palace any longer.'

'Even so, it's a big thing to ask of someone. My father was a pickpocket. I grew up worshipping the God of Thieves. I made my deal with Dacendaran fully aware of what it meant. Starros doesn't have that luxury, and I'm not sure, in his place, that I'd like to wake up to find my soul's been traded away on my behalf without being consulted.'

'Let's see what Rorin can do first then,' she agreed, 'before we start invoking divine intervention.' Kalan glanced up at the rapidly brightening day and frowned. 'Speaking of Rorin, I wish I knew what happened up at the palace last night. Damin looked pretty angry when I left.'

'Well, you can be fairly certain both your uncle and your brother are still alive.'

'How?'

'No bells,' he told her. 'If anything really awful had happened to either Krakandar's regent or her prince, the city would be ringing with them.'

'That's a really comforting thought, Wrayan.'

He grinned at her tiredly. 'I do try my hardest to help, you know.'

The sound of the front door opening put an end to any further speculation about the fate of her uncle or her brother. Wrayan put the tea down beside the smoking candle stub and together they hurried out into the main room to find Fyora carefully locking the door behind her. Rorin was with her, dressed in regular street clothes rather than his black sorcerer's robes – a wise move if one didn't particularly want to be noticed in the Beggars' Quarter.

'Where have you been?' Kalan demanded of Rorin, as soon as she saw him.

'I came as soon as I could,' Rorin replied. 'How's Starros?'

'Struggling,' Wrayan told him. 'It's time to find out how much healing knowledge Shananara left you with.'

The young man nodded. 'I'll do what I can. Have you seen Damin?'

'No,' Kalan replied. 'Why?'

Rorin seemed more than a little concerned. 'I thought he might have come down here last night, after he . . .' His voice trailed off, and he looked at Kalan as if he didn't have the words to tell her what he must.

Wrayan studied him for a moment, reading Rorin's unease simply from the way he was standing, the whole manner in which he spoke, rather than picking up on his thoughts. Whatever news the young man brought, it wasn't good.

'Fee, can you put the word out on the street that Damin might be somewhere in the city? See if anybody's seen him?'

Annoyed by the realisation that she was being sent away, Fyora nodded her agreement reluctantly and let herself out of the small house, muttering about ungrateful wretches who didn't deserve her aid or assistance.

Kalan waited until she saw Fyora's shadow pass by the window facing the narrow street before she demanded an explanation. 'After Damin *what*?' she asked suspiciously.

Rorin looked away uncomfortably. 'Damin and Mahkas had something of an *altercation*, I suppose you could call it.'

'What's that mean in reality?' Wrayan asked doubtfully.

'He damn near killed him.'

'Mahkas almost killed Damin?' Kalan gasped.

'Damin almost killed Mahkas,' the young sorcerer corrected. 'I've never seen anybody so furious in my entire life, Kal. I swear, if Tejay Lionsclaw hadn't been there to reason with him, Damin may have actually killed your uncle with his bare hands.'

'I'm not surprised,' Wrayan said. 'Damin and Starros were always close. He wouldn't have stood by and let what's been done to his best friend go unchallenged.'

Rorin shook his head. 'It wasn't about Starros . . .' He hesitated, obviously unsure about how to go on. 'I guess there's no easy way to break this to you. I'm so sorry, Kalan. Leila killed herself within minutes of Mahkas telling her Starros was dead.'

Kalan cried out in wordless despair and sagged against Wrayan with the shock of Rorin's news. He caught her in his arms and helped her sit down on the narrow wooden bench by the fire, where she put her head in her hands, sobbing for her cousin, muttering something about it being her fault. Squatting beside her, his arm around her shoulders, he glanced up at Rorin. 'And you don't know where Damin is now?'

'Nobody's seen him since last night when he left Mahkas bleeding on the floor of his study with a severed windpipe.'

673

'Will he live?' Wrayan wasn't particularly concerned for Mahkas Damaran, but he was acutely aware of what it would mean if Krakandar's regent died.

'He'll live,' Rorin confirmed. 'I healed it as best I could, but I doubt he'll ever speak in much more than a whisper again. Damin punched him in the throat.'

'That's got to hurt,' Wrayan grimaced.

Rorin nodded grimly. 'I imagine it did, given Damin was wearing a spiked battle gauntlet at the time.'

'Ouch,' Wrayan said, thinking of the pain and the damage a strong gauntleted fist could do to something as delicate as a human throat. 'And you say you can't find Damin now?'

'It's like he's vanished completely.'

'He won't have done that,' Wrayan said confidently. 'After you've seen to Starros, I'll see if I can sense him. Given enough time, I should be able to track him down. Failing that, Fee may have some luck. Damin Wolfblade won't get very far in Krakandar City without somebody recognising him.'

'I thought you couldn't find a shielded mind?'

'I said I had almost no chance of finding one shielded mind in the vastness of the southern Medalonian plains, as I recall,' he reminded the young sorcerer. 'Finding someone here in the confines of the city is a different matter entirely. I can't speak directly to Damin's mind, of course, because of the shield, but I should be able to pinpoint every shielded mind within the walls of the city if I try hard enough. There's not that many of them.' He turned back to Kalan who was still sobbing inconsolably. 'Come on, Kal,' he said gently. 'It's not your fault.'

She turned and buried her head into his shoulder. 'It *is* my fault, Wrayan,' she sobbed, her voice muffled by his coat. 'I made Leila believe Starros was dead. She killed herself because she thought he was gone. I *know* she did.

That's why she was so calm, so serene, when I left her. She'd decided to do it even then . . . Oh, gods, if only I'd stayed with her . . .'

'There, there, Kalan,' he murmured, like a mother comforting a small child. Wrayan held her close and let her cry, thinking Kalan was probably right. Leila adored Starros. He was the one bright spot in her life, the man who loved her simply for being Leila. 'Don't torment yourself. Leila made her own decision. And if anything, we're all at fault here,' he told her, holding her close. 'Not just you.'

Kalan lifted her head and stared at him in confusion, sniffing loudly. 'What do you mean?'

'Every one of us who knew about them, all of us who encouraged them, everyone who turned a blind eye to them . . . we're all to blame. There was no way this was ever going to end happily.'

'I should have done *something*,' Kalan insisted, wiping away a fresh round of tears. 'I should have told Mahkas to go to hell when he made me promise to back him up in his lie.'

'And if you had, the chances are Leila would still be dead,' Rorin said. 'Mahkas was planning to have his way or a funeral. You can't blame yourself for that.'

'I wish Damin *had* killed him,' she announced savagely.

'No, you don't,' Rorin told her. 'The problems that would have caused don't bear thinking about. Under the circumstances, he couldn't do much at all really. No more than you can.'

She glared at him. 'Care to wager on that?'

Wrayan shook his head in concern. 'Kalan, Rorin is right. Don't buy into this. Damin's taken enough vengeance for all of you and now you need to let it go. If not for your Aunt Bylinda's sake, then think of Starros.'

'I can't go back to the palace,' she warned, her eyes

dangerous. 'If I saw Mahkas now, the way I'm feeling, a punch in the throat with a metal gauntlet would seem the least of his problems.'

'You can stay down here.' Wrayan offered. 'I don't imagine you'll be missed at the palace for a while yet.' He glanced up at Rorin. 'You ready to try a bit of magic on our friend?'

Rorin nodded. 'I'll see what I can do,' he promised. 'But don't expect too much.'

'Do what you can,' Wrayan told him, jerking his head in the direction of the other room on the ground floor where Starros lay. Rorin took a deep breath and headed into the bedroom, leaving Wrayan alone with Kalan.

She was still sobbing, tormented by the thought that she might have contributed to Leila's suicide. He sat beside her on the bench, gathered her into his arms, and let her cry against him, whispering soothing nonsense words to her that did nothing but prevent the silence and her grief from completely overwhelming her.

73

Wrayan eventually found Damin down in the fens. After scanning the city for the telltale feel of a shielded mind that wasn't at either the palace or the safe house, he located the young prince amid the dense foliage and hidden pools of Krakandar's water supply.

Wrayan had never been to the fens in all the time he'd lived in Krakandar, and could quite easily have got lost when he went looking for the prince, but he had an unfair advantage.

Fixing on Damin's shielded mind and using it like a beacon in the early morning light, he sought him out with the unerring sureness of a man who had the benefit of supernatural assistance.

'You know, for a thief, you don't sneak about very well,' Damin remarked, stepping onto the path in front of Wrayan and making him jump with fright. 'I could hear you coming half an hour ago when you stumbled through the gate.'

The young prince obviously wasn't pleased to see him. Wrayan got the distinct impression he didn't particularly want to be found. He still wore his bloodstained leather armour. He had taken off the gauntlets, though, Wrayan was relieved to discover.

'Not my natural element down here among the wild

things,' Wrayan said with a cautious smile, wary about Damin's mood. The young man gave no obvious sign of his frame of mind. 'You can keep your bugs and spiders. Give me a roof to scramble over any day. Besides, I wasn't trying to sneak up on you.'

'You came looking for me, though.'

'The entire city is looking for you, Damin. Have you been down here all night?'

'It's the only place in the whole city I've ever been able to hide.'

Damin turned and walked back along the path a little until he came to a small clearing. Wrayan followed him, looking around curiously.

'Starros and I claimed this place as our own when we were children,' Damin explained. 'It seemed as good a place as any to get lost in for a while.'

Wrayan could well imagine how the still darkness of the fens would have felt like the only safe haven in Krakandar last night, when Damin had come down here. He would have needed time to calm the rage inside him, time to deal with what had happened.

And what he'd done. The murky darkness would have suited his mood.

'How's Starros?'

Wrayan shrugged. 'He's still alive.'

'You sound surprised.'

'To be honest, I am, a little. Rorin's with him now, but he's not very optimistic. We may find ourselves caught between two equally unpalatable choices.'

'What choices?'

'Letting him die or asking the gods to intervene.'

Damin looked horrified that he could even suggest such a thing. 'Surely it's not a question of choice? If you can prevail upon the gods to help, Wrayan, for pity's sake, why are you standing here? Do it!'

'Even if it costs Starros his soul?'

'Even that! Gods, I thought you were part Harshini! You can't just let him die!'

'Not even if he wants to?'

'Starros isn't the sort to throw his life away on a whim.'

'Neither was Leila, I would have thought,' Wrayan replied. 'But that was her choice when faced with the prospect of going on without Starros. Why do you imagine his reaction to going on without the love of his life would be any different to Leila's?'

Damin glared at the thief and, for a brief moment, Wrayan was reminded that this was Krakandar's prince, not just Starros the fosterling's best friend. 'Leila was doing more than giving up, Wrayan,' he said with unexpected insight. 'She was taking her revenge on Mahkas with the only weapon she had. Her own life. She might have felt she had nothing to live for once she believed Starros was dead, but it was the desperate need to get back at her father that gave her a reason to die.'

Wrayan studied him closely for a moment, and then shook his head. That wasn't the observation of a frivolous boy.

Whether he liked it or not, Damin couldn't go on hiding behind the veneer of light-hearted charm he worked so carefully to cultivate. And the older he got, the harder it was going to be. 'You're not going to be able to keep this up much longer, Damin.'

'Keep what up?'

'This act you put on for other people. Sooner or later, somebody is going to realise you're not nearly as shallow as you try to make people believe.'

'And it *will* be sooner, rather than later,' Damin agreed heavily, taking a seat on moss-covered log that had been slowly rotting away in the clearing for decades, by the look of it. 'Along with all the other joy the last few days have brought us, Adham Tirstone informs me there's a good chance Fardohnya is massing for an invasion behind the closed borders in the Sunrise Mountains. Chaine Lionsclaw is dead, half the provinces have lost their Warlords to the plague, the rest of our fighting capability is tenuous at best, and if we don't want dear Uncle Lernen leading what's left of our army into certain defeat, guess who's going to get *that* job? I imagine by the time I've called up our reserves in the name of the High Prince, trodden all over the tender egos of every remaining Warlord in Hythria and had a stand-up fight with the High Arrion to get her to release the troops we'll need from the provinces under the Collective's control, there won't be a soul left in Hythria who thinks I'm *anything* like the incumbent High Prince.'

Marla's son to the core, Wrayan thought. *His best friend is at death's door. His cousin just killed herself and he all but tore out his uncle's throat with his bare hands. And what is Damin Wolfblade doing? Hiding down here in the fens grieving? No. He's down here working out his battle plans because Hythria might be under attack.*

Damin shrugged, and added, 'There's a certain level of protection in being thought of as a fool, Wrayan. Elezaar taught me that.'

'You know, back when I was an apprentice, long before you were born, I had a discussion with old Kagan Palenovar about you. Or at least the idea of you.'

'The old High Arrion?'

Wrayan nodded. 'He was one of the men who arranged for your mother to turn down Hablet's offer and marry Laran Krakenshield instead.'

'You mean Hablet might have been my father if they hadn't? Gods, that's a scary thought.'

'The notion of placing two provinces in the hands of one man and breaking a signed marriage contract with Hablet of Fardohnya seemed quite a bit scarier at the time.

I can remember asking Kagan if he was entrusting a third of the country's military power and wealth to Laran Kraken-shield in the vague hope of an heir some day who'd be more than a pointless figurehead.'

'What did he say?'

'He offered me a wager. *If my nephew fathers him,* Kagan said, *I'll bet you any amount you want, the next High Prince of Hythria will be a man to be reckoned with.*'

Damin smiled thinly. 'I think I would have liked this Kagan Palenovar of yours.'

'Actually, he's more yours than mine. He was your grand-mother Jeryma Ravenspear's brother, so I guess that makes him your great-uncle, or something. But what I'm trying to say is, Damin, I think Kagan would have won the bet.'

'I appreciate the sentiment, Wrayan, but it's a bit misplaced. I haven't done anything to be proud of.'

'Don't be too sure of that. Mahkas is still alive because even in the depths of unconscionable rage you had the presence of mind to understand the ramifications of giving in to your desire for vengeance.'

Damin smiled sourly. 'You weren't there, Wrayan. There's no honour to be found anywhere in what happened last night. And you have *no* idea how close I came to giving in.' He shook his head and then ran his hands through his hair impatiently, as if it would somehow clear his head. 'Do you remember when I was a boy? Almodavar gave me forty laps of the training yard once because I didn't kill him. He took me to task again the night Luciena attacked me, because I didn't kill her, either. He used to tell me I was too sentimental. He told me I'd never be able to make the killing stroke if I stopped to think about it.'

'He was probably right.'

'No. He wasn't. I thought about it, Wrayan. And believe me, there is nothing I have ever wanted more than to kill Mahkas. I was ready, willing and able to do it.'

'But you didn't.'

He looked at Wrayan sceptically. 'Don't try to congratulate me on my honour or my presence of mind. I didn't choose not to kill Mahkas. I chose not to kill him *yet*.'

'And that makes you a bad person?'

'I don't know if I'm bad. But I'm pretty certain I've discovered a capacity for being a callous bastard I didn't know I had.'

'And that's why you're down here in the fens wallowing in self-pity, I suppose?'

Damin shook his head, almost amused by the idea. 'I'd be less of a callous bastard if I was. I haven't been grieving for Leila or worrying about Starros. I've been sitting here all night trying to figure out the best way to deal with Hablet.' Then he added with annoyance, 'For all the good it's done.'

Wrayan smiled at his obvious irritation. 'You mean, even with these previously untapped depths of callous bastardry to call on, you haven't thought up some invincible battle strategy in the space of a few hours? What good are you, Damin Wolfblade?'

The young man forced a smile. 'I've had military strategy forced down my throat with every meal since I was three years old. I *should* have been able to come up with something in about ten minutes.'

'How can you? You don't have any reliable intelligence to go on. For all you know, Adham's got it completely wrong and Hablet's just massing his harem behind the border. It's an easy mistake to make. I understand his daughters alone number close to his standing army.'

This time Damin's smile almost looked genuine. 'They're more dangerous, too, from what I hear. The eldest daughter is apparently a shrew of monumental proportions.'

'I've heard that, too. And that's my point, Damin. Don't lose any sleep over what you don't know. Find out what's really happening over the border. Then, if it turns out we are about to be invaded, by all means, lose all the sleep you want trying to figure out a way to stop it.'

'Will you help me, Wrayan?'

'Of course I will,' Wrayan replied, surprised that Damin had even felt the need to ask.

The young prince nodded and rose to his feet. 'Good. Then I want you to go to Greenharbour. I need you to speak to my mother. What I want of her will be less inflammatory if I don't commit it to paper.'

'What did you want me to tell her?'

'She needs to know what's happened here,' Damin said. 'She needs to know about Mahkas. And about Starros and Leila. And about Hablet's possible plans for us.'

Wrayan frowned, thinking that nothing of what Damin wanted him to tell Marla seemed particularly contentious. 'And?' he prompted, guessing there was more.

'And then I want you to have her make Lernen appoint me general of Hythria's combined armies.'

'Oh. Is that all?'

'Isn't that enough?'

'There's one problem you may not have considered, Damin. Even if you had the rank, you can't lead Hythria's armies anywhere if you've not come of age.'

'Then it's time we did something about that, too.'

'Don't even *think* of asking me to magically speed up time so you can reach your majority faster.'

Damin looked at him in surprise. 'Can you actually *do* that?'

'I don't know. And anyway, it's beside the point. Even if I could, I wouldn't. So how, in the name of all the Primal Gods, are you planning to get around the fact that your thirtieth birthday is six years away?'

'By making it irrelevant.'

'I don't follow you.'

He shrugged. 'We'll just change the age of majority to twenty-five.'

Wrayan stared at him in shock. 'Just like *that* . . . change the age of majority?'

'Works for me.'

Wrayan was silent for a moment as he thought about what it would mean to the whole nation if Marla was able to get Lernen to make such a radical change in the structure of Hythrun society. He shook his head, flabbergasted by the very notion. 'It would throw the whole country into turmoil.'

'Only for a little while. And in case you haven't noticed, Hythria's already in a fair bit of turmoil now. A little more will hardly be noticed in the general scheme of things.'

'But think of what it means . . . there are provinces—'

'Currently under the control of the Sorcerers' Collective – like Izcomdar and Pentamor – with living heirs capable of taking charge, that will suddenly find themselves with a Warlord again,' Damin finished for him with a smug little grin.

'And no longer under Alija's control. You really are a lot smarter than you look, Damin.'

'Well, I'm quite happy for Marla to get the credit for this one. I just want the control such a change will give me over our troops. If we're going to face Hablet across a battlefield, we can't do it with one hand tied behind our backs.' Damin glanced up through the canopy of trees and frowned. 'It's getting late. We should be getting back, I suppose.'

Without waiting for a reply, Damin headed along the path back towards the gate that led up to the palace. Wrayan watched the young prince leave, a little dumbstruck. He'd always suspected Damin was brighter than he pretended, but the proof far exceeded his expectations. Even Marla would have been hard-pressed to come up with such a drastic and surprisingly workable solution.

And then another thought occurred to Wrayan, which turned his faint smile into a deep frown. 'Damin!' he called.

The prince stopped and turned to look at him. 'Yes?'

'I don't suppose it escaped your notice that if Marla manages to convince Lernen to lower the age of majority, in a few months you'll be able to inherit Krakandar.'

'No, it didn't escape my notice.'

'Don't you think Mahkas might have something to say about that?'

'Go pay him a visit, Wrayan,' Damin suggested coldly. 'I think you'll find Mahkas Damaran is going to have a bit of trouble saying anything to anybody from now on.'

Without waiting for Wrayan to answer, the young prince turned and continued to walk back along the path towards the palace.

It was only then that Wrayan understood what Damin meant when he spoke of his previously unsuspected capacity for being a callous bastard.

74

If Alija Eaglespike thought the information she had accidentally gleaned from Ruxton Tirstone's dying mind was shocking, what she learned from Tarkyn Lye's meeting with the dwarf left her breathless.

Tarkyn brought her the information supplied by Elezaar several hours after she had dispatched him to Venira's Emporium to collect Crysander, and a week later she was still trying to digest it all.

Standing on the balcony of her bedroom as the sun set in the west, painting the white city pink and gold, Alija smiled at the irony.

The Fool really was a fool, after all.

A slight breeze blew in off the harbour, cooling the perspiration on her skin and making her shiver. She pulled her robe a little closer and glanced across at the bed where her latest lover lay sprawled across the covers, his breathing deep and even as he slept. Younger than Alija by a good ten years, his name was Galon Miar. He was a recent widower, his wife having fallen victim to the plague in the first wave some months ago. He was a commoner, too – a quaint little habit Alija had picked up from Marla. But he was a powerful man in his own right, despite his common birth. On his right hand, he wore a gold ring worked in the shape of a raven. The ring of the Assassins' Guild.

His advantage to Alija – besides the obvious sexual attraction of a handsome and athletic younger man – was the rumour rife in Greenharbour that Galon Miar would be the next Raven. With the head of the Assassins' Guild in her bed – quite literally – Alija didn't anticipate much resistance to anything she wanted to do, once her lover took over the guild.

It warmed her soul, simply thinking of the possibilities.

She was under no illusions about Galon. There was no love involved in this affair. Alija was almost fifty and it was dye and a lavish and expensive daily routine of cosmetics that kept the more obvious signs of ageing at bay. She didn't kid herself that Galon had taken her as a lover because he desired Alija more than he might a younger woman. He found her attractive (she'd been in his mind, so she knew that for certain), but what really attracted him wasn't her body, it was her power. He was in her bed because he was just as determined to have the Sorcerers' Collective in his pocket when he ruled his guild as she was to have him in hers.

And now . . . well, with what she now knew about the goings-on in the Wolfblade household, there was nothing standing in her way.

It was luck, or perhaps divine intervention, that had finally provided Alija with the edge she needed to bring the Wolfblades down. She had been at Venira's, looking for house slaves when she spied the old slave named Crysander. Normally, the High Arrion wouldn't have gone to anywhere as exorbitant as Venira's for simple house slaves, but with the markets closed, and her own staff depleted, she had no choice. Besides, with his slaves protected and isolated from the general population, they were much less likely to have been exposed to the plague.

Venira really had been planning to toss the slave onto the streets and let him starve when Alija first saw him. It was a comment the slaver made in passing about Crysander being a waste of food that made Alija stop and take a second look.

'What did you call him?'

'Crysander,' Venira had told her with a shrug.

'I had a *court'esa* once,' she said. 'His name was Crysander, too.'

'I remember him,' Venira had replied, with the distant look of a man reminiscing about a large amount of money. 'He was the Fool's brother, wasn't he? Didn't he die in that awful massacre at Ronan Dell's palace?'

Alija's eyes narrowed. 'I paid you rather a lot of money, Venira, to make certain our transactions that day remained confidential.'

The fat man had smiled obsequiously. 'Trust me, my lady. Your coin purchased my total amnesia on the subject.'

'Show him to me,' she ordered, curious to see if this Crysander was anything like the slender, handsome young man she remembered. As it turned out, he wasn't. Wizened and old, bent almost double by a lifetime of cruel physical labour, the slave was a walking human ruin.

Then Alija noticed the scar, thinking it strange that he would bear such a mark in almost exactly the same place her Crysander was stabbed. And he *had* been stabbed. She'd made certain of that; demanding they bring the *court'esa*'s body back to her. Alija wanted proof the slave was silenced, and nothing short of his dead body lying at her feet would have satisfied her.

'How did you get that mark on your belly?' she asked the old slave curiously.

'A plough blade, my lady,' the slave replied in his hoarse, rasping voice. 'I slipped and fell on it when I was a boy.'

'You're lucky to have survived,' she remarked.

'So they tell me, my lady,' the slave replied.

'Ironic, don't you think,' Venira chortled beside her, his multiple chins wobbling with mirth. 'Your Crysander would be almost this age by now, too, had he survived.'

Alija had thought no more about the man, until she'd woken up from the stupor brought on from being caught in Ruxton's dying mind and realised that she now possessed the information to make this poor imitation of Crysander the *court'esa* into a reasonable facsimile of the real thing.

Among the recollections she discovered in Ruxton Tirstone's thoughts were images of him and Marla's dwarf sitting in a dimly lit kitchen late at night (she supposed it was the kitchens at Marla's townhouse). Apparently, the two men shared ale quite often. Ruxton had been a common man, after all, and for all his outward veneer of civilisation, there were some things from his youth he'd still enjoyed, and a good dark ale was among them. The memory was so sharp, Alija actually found herself craving a tankard on occasion.

But more importantly, among the memories of those quiet ales shared in the small hours of the night were the stories the two men swapped, mostly about their younger days, when neither of them imagined they would one day find themselves living under the roof of the High Prince's sister, either as her husband or her slave. The memories in themselves were insignificant – just the idle ramblings of a couple of drunken fools – but they recalled intimate, tiny details of both men's lives that Alija would never have been able to discover on her own, even if she'd had an army of investigators searching for clues.

It had been a simple matter, really, to join her mind to the old slave's and fill it with those stolen memories. It was a risk, of course, but the chances were good Elezaar would require proof this slave was his brother. In his place, Alija would have demanded an answer to a question only the two of them might know. Perhaps, she reasoned, lost somewhere in those quiet, late-night conversations with Ruxton Tirstone, was the answer to whatever question the dwarf decided to pose.

It cost a great deal to purchase Venira's assistance – the Fool would never deal with Tarkyn directly, Alija knew. Elezaar had to be convinced this offer came from someone unconnected with the High Arrion, in the beginning at least.

Alija's gamble had paid off. Crysander had answered the vital question correctly. Elezaar had seen the scar – which also meant he must have witnessed his brother dying, which was another problem to be dealt with later – and to save his long-lost brother from unspeakable torture, the Fool had told Tarkyn everything he wanted to know.

Although she didn't doubt Tarkyn's ability to intimidate the dwarf, she was astonished at how easily he had capitulated. Once he began, it was as if a dam had burst inside him and the information couldn't spill out fast enough.

All the vague plans and plots Alija had only glimpsed during her contact with Ruxton suddenly snapped into sharp focus. Wrayan Lightfinger was alive and well and running the Thieves' Guild in Krakandar, Elezaar confirmed. The magical shields he had placed on the minds of Marla and her family were the result of the teaching he received from the Harshini themselves, because, according to the Fool, that was where Wrayan had disappeared to after their battle in the temple. He had been rescued, so the Fool claimed, by none other than Brakandaran the Halfbreed, who had taken him back to Sanctuary to be healed. There he had learned how to wield his power with a finesse Alija would have given her soul to achieve.

Alija might have scoffed at the tale, except she'd met Brakandaran and felt his power. She didn't doubt for a moment that every word of it was true.

She learned that her coercion hadn't failed, either. Luciena really *had* tried to kill Damin Wolfblade when he was just a boy. The plot remained undiscovered until the attack. Marla had ordered Wrayan to remove all traces of Alija's interference, shielded the girl's mind, and then chosen to let the incident go unremarked rather than tip anyone off to the fact that Marla was wise to Alija's plan.

Even more disturbing was the news that Rorin Mariner was not just Luciena's Fardohnyan cousin, but, like Wrayan, a genuinely gifted sorcerer and a human descendant of the magical lost race of the Harshini. He'd been taught to use his power in a Harshini mind meld – the same way they taught their own children – so the dwarf informed them, which accounted for why Alija had never suspected his ability. His skill made Wrayan look clumsy, which terrified Alija, because for twenty years she'd never detected a single mind shield Wrayan had set, and if she couldn't detect his handiwork, how was she ever going to protect herself from him?

And then, just when she had thought she couldn't be surprised, the Fool had shocked them all by announcing that Marla had known Alija was having an affair with Nash Hawksword twenty years ago, and that she suspected the High Arrion of being involved in the first of many attempts on her son's life.

The list seemed endless. Every word of the dwarf's testimony drove home, with brutal force, how dangerous Marla Wolfblade really was.

Alija cursed her own arrogance for not having seen it sooner.

And she cursed Tarkyn Lye for being a sentimental fool.

After several hours of startling revelations, Elezaar had begged a moment alone with his brother. Tarkyn, thinking a chance for further bonding would simply reinforce the power they had over the dwarf, had ordered Bekan from the alcove and taken the opportunity to relieve himself while the brothers had a moment of privacy. He wasn't gone more than a few minutes, he promised Alija, but when he came back, the dwarf was gone and Crysander lay back against the cushions with his neck at a very strange angle.

They still hadn't found him a week later. He wasn't back at Marla's townhouse. He was nowhere to be found. And that was a problem, because she knew for certain, now, that Elezaar the Fool could implicate the House of Eaglespike in the murder of Ronan Dell. Even this long after the fact, that one incident alone was enough to bring the Eaglespikes down.

She had to find the dwarf and she had to kill him.

Galon stirred on the bed. Alija looked over at him and smiled. *It shouldn't be too difficult*, she thought, pushing off the balcony and heading back towards the bed, *for a man of Galon's skill and connections to find one miserable dwarf and dispose of him for me.*

After all, what was the point of having a tame assassin if you didn't let him off the leash every now and then?

75

Damin took the time to bathe and change before he entered the dining room to meet with the rest of the family, mostly because he didn't want to upset his aunt. He could imagine her reaction if she happened to bump into him walking the halls of Krakandar Palace still drenched in Leila's blood. It gave Wrayan time, too, to fetch Kalan and Rorin from the safe house where they were watching over Starros.

Damin wanted to address the whole family (with the obvious exceptions of Mahkas and Bylinda, who would undoubtedly consider his intentions treasonous), and he was in no mood to repeat himself.

They were having a late breakfast when Damin arrived. As soon as Luciena spied him, she ordered Aleesha to take the children downstairs to the day nursery. The slave gathered the children to her and hurried them from the dining room with a nervous curtsey as she passed Damin by the door.

He closed the door behind the departing children and then glanced around the room, fixing his gaze on the two slaves standing watch over the buffet.

'Out!' he ordered abruptly.

The slaves did as the prince commanded without question and left the hall through the slaveways entrance behind the screen at the back of the room.

'Good morning, Damin,' Tejay said cautiously, apparently the only one present who wasn't afraid to address him directly.

'My lady.'

Damin glanced around the dining room. Xanda and Luciena sat together at the far end of the long table. Next to Luciena were the three empty places just vacated by her children. Tejay's four boys were too young to join the adults at meals and were probably down in the day nursery having breakfast. Next to the empty seats, Adham was sitting beside Tejay.

Kalan and Rorin were missing, but they should be here soon. He'd sent Wrayan to fetch them when they got back to the palace from the fens. That was just before Orleon had met him in the hall and handed Damin the letter he currently held in his right hand. It had arrived by speeded courier yesterday, but with the city sealed against travellers from the south, the guards on the gate had been reluctant to admit the courier. Finally, one of the officers on the gate had agreed to accept the letter, but he'd waited until he'd finished his watch before delivering the document to the palace.

'I have a letter from my mother,' he announced, holding it up for them to see. 'Ironic, don't you think, that she includes an apologetic note to Mahkas informing him she will not agree, under any circumstance, to a betrothal between Leila and me.'

Nobody was sure what they were supposed to say to that.

Adham broke the uncomfortable silence. 'Are you all right, Damin?'

'Is anybody here *all right*?' he snapped. Then he shrugged. 'I'm sorry. I'm not angry with you. I'm just a little annoyed at the notion that this whole damn mess might have been avoided if somebody had thought to deliver this letter yesterday.'

'It wouldn't have made a difference,' Tejay pointed out. 'Mahkas found Starros and Leila together more than a week ago. The damage was done long before you or that letter got here.'

The news didn't make Damin feel any better, but he forced himself not to dwell on it. There was too much to be done. 'Orleon's currently arranging to have the ballroom cleared so Leila can be laid out before the funeral. How's Bylinda faring?'

'Your aunt is far stronger than anyone gives her credit for, Damin. She'll come through this in one piece,' Tejay said.

'And Mahkas?'

There was a moment of awkward silence before anybody answered him. It was Xanda who finally found the courage to tell Damin what had happened after he left. 'He lives, Damin. Rorin healed his wounds as best he could, but I gather there was some residual damage beyond even a sorcerer's skill to mend.'

'That's good news. I really don't have time for him to die right now.'

His comment had them all staring at him in concern. Before anyone could respond to it, however, the door opened behind him and he turned to find Kalan, Wrayan and Rorin filing into the dining room. Both Rorin and Kalan looked as if they'd been up all night and Kalan's eyes were red-rimmed and swollen. She ran to her brother when she spied him and threw her arms around him. Damin hugged her silently, understanding her pain. Leila was dead because she thought Starros would be waiting for her in the afterlife. It would be a long time, if ever, before Kalan could forgive herself for her part in that lie.

After a few moments, Kalan stepped back and studied him warily. 'Are you all right, Damin?'

'I'm fine,' he assured her. 'Although I'm leaning towards ordering a lashing for the next person who asks me that.'

Kalan seemed to think he was serious. She took a seat at the table beside Adham, folded her hands in her lap and said nothing more.

'Marla sends other news in her letter,' Damin added grimly. 'The worst of which, I'm sorry to tell you, Adham, is the news that Ruxton Tirstone was taken by the plague.'

Every eye in the room fixed on the young trader, wondering how he might take the news of his father's death. Damin watched the colour drain from his face, but he remained in control of his emotions. Nobody else reacted to the news. Perhaps, with everything that had gone on this past day, they were all so emotionally wrung out there was nothing left in any of them to grieve for Ruxton Tirstone. *It's a pity, really*, Damin thought. *Ruxton was a good man. He deserved more than this.*

'I wish we had the time to do his memory justice,' Damin told his stepbrother sympathetically. 'But there are other things that demand our attention and, in the end, we're probably better off doing what we can for the living rather than the dead.'

Adham nodded silently in agreement. Kalan reached across and took his hand comfortingly, but said nothing.

'To that end,' Damin said, turning his attention to the two sorcerers, 'I need you two to do whatever you must to save Starros. Even if that means selling his soul to whatever god is willing to come to his aid.'

Wrayan and Rorin exchanged a worried glance, but it was Kalan who answered him. 'Damin, you can't make that sort of decision for Starros without—'

'I can and I have, Kalan,' Damin announced. 'I'll take responsibility for it.'

Wrayan shook his head. 'Damin, I think you should consider—'

He turned on the thief impatiently. 'You told me your only choice was to sell his soul or let him die, Wrayan. If you're not willing to do the latter, then speak to the gods and get it over with. There's a war coming. I can't afford to have the only two real sorcerers in Hythria tied up tending the former assistant chief steward of Krakandar Palace, even if he is my best friend.'

'What war?' Tejay asked suspiciously.

'We think Hablet is taking advantage of the borders being closed to gather his troops for an invasion,' Adham informed the Warlord's wife, before Damin had a chance to explain. His voice was dull and emotionless, but it was clear he wasn't incapacitated by his grief.

'You didn't get that intelligence from Sunrise Province, did you?' she asked.

'Mostly it came from the Fardohnyans,' Adham agreed, looking a little puzzled. 'Why do you ask?'

'Terin wouldn't know if his arse was on fire unless somebody was there to point it out to him,' she remarked sourly, confirming Damin's suspicions that all was not well in the Lionsclaw household. Tejay looked up at the young prince with a frown. 'That's where you're going, isn't it? To Sunrise?'

Damin nodded. 'With as many Krakandar troops as I can muster. I plan to swing past Byamor on the way and collect Narvell and all the Elasapine troops Charel Hawksword can spare us, too.'

'Then I'm coming with you,' Tejay announced.

'Is that really a good idea, Tejay?' Luciena asked with concern. 'If we really are facing a war—'

'It's a war that, more than likely, will be fought in my province,' Tejay pointed out. 'There's no way I'm going to let Terin deal with this on his own. Assuming he's capable of dealing with it in the first place.'

Damin studied her with concern. 'We're going to have to have a little chat about your husband fairly soon, aren't we?'

She nodded, looking resigned. 'Yes, Damin, I think we are.'

'What about your children?' Luciena asked.

'They can stay here. Krakandar's by far the safest place in Hythria, at the moment. Bylinda may even welcome the distraction.'

'Even if Aunt Bylinda's not up to it, you'll be here to keep an eye on them, Luciena,' Damin told his adopted sister. 'There's still too much plague about for you and Xanda to risk heading back to Greenharbour with your own children, and I want Xanda here to keep an eye on things while I'm gone.'

His cousin looked at him doubtfully. 'What exactly am I supposed to be keeping an eye on?'

'A month or so from now, Mahkas is probably going to get some news from the High Prince that will drastically affect the length of his tenure as regent here. I have a feeling he's not going to take it very well. I want someone in the palace I can trust – and someone who can take charge if need be – so that when we're through dealing with Hablet, I still have a province to come back to.'

Xanda glanced at Luciena to see if she had any objections before he nodded his agreement. 'We've been away from Greenharbour for so long now, a bit longer isn't going to make that much difference. We'll stay.'

'Thank you,' Damin said, greatly relieved his cousin hadn't balked at the suggestion. He turned to Adham with a questioning look. 'What about you?'

'Rodja will have everything under control in Greenharbour. I'll tag along with you, if you don't mind.'

Damin spared him a thin smile. 'Just the answer I expected from a man corrupted by Almodavar into following the God of War.'

'What did you want me and Rorin to do?' Kalan asked.

'I'm sending Wrayan back to Greenharbour. I want you and Rorin to go with him. Mother will need your help, and if ever there was a need to have a couple of insiders in the Sorcerers' Collective, it's going to be in the next few months as we prepare for war.'

'No,' Kalan said flatly.

Damin stared at her in surprise. 'What?'

'I'll go back to Greenharbour with Wrayan, but Rorin is going to Sunrise Province with you.'

'Why?' Damin and Rorin both asked at the same time.

'Because you're Hythria's heir, Damin, and we can't afford to lose you in battle. Rorin is the only magical healer in the world that we know of. The most useful place for him in any battle you're involved in is at your side.'

'She's actually got a very good point,' Wrayan agreed.

Damin hadn't thought about the advantage of having a sorcerer at his side in battle. The idea had a lot to recommend it. He glanced at Rorin, who shrugged. 'I'm fine with it if you are.'

'Then I guess you're coming to Sunrise with us, Rorin,' Damin said.

'When do we leave?' Adham asked.

'Tomorrow morning,' he informed them. 'At first light. As soon as we're finished here, I'm going down to the barracks to talk to Almodavar. I plan to leave for Elasapine with all the Krakandar troops we can spare now, which should be about twenty-six centuries, and have Raek Harlen follow with the rest of them in a couple of weeks.'

'Aren't you going to wait for Leila's funeral?' Kalan asked.

Damin shook his head. 'If I wait, Kalan, I may run into Mahkas.'

'I think, given the circumstances, Damin,' Xanda suggested carefully, 'you may find him willing to forgive you.'

'I'm not really interested in whether our uncle forgives me or not, Xanda,' Damin replied coldly. 'My concern is one of timing.'

'I don't understand,' Kalan admitted with a frown.

'It's quite simple, Kal. The next time I see Mahkas, I *will* kill him, and as I said earlier, it doesn't suit me for him to die just yet, so it's better for everyone if I just get out of his way until it does.'

His words left them speechless. Damin glanced around the room at his family and his most trusted friends – these people who thought they knew him so well – and was disturbed to realise they were looking at him like he was a complete stranger.

To hell with it, he thought. They were going to find out who I really am sooner or later.

Besides, it was Elezaar's final Rule of Gaining and Wielding Power.

Eventually, every true prince must step forward and take command.

And he should expect his people to follow him.

EPILOGUE

Marla Wolfblade had buried four husbands, but it had never occurred to her that she might one day be forced to carry on without Elezaar at her side. Watching them lower him into the child-sized grave, she felt the wrench of his death even more keenly than when he'd died in her arms. Losing Elezaar meant losing a part of herself. He had been by her side for so long, she felt incomplete without him. And afraid. Afraid of what the future might hold.

Afraid of what she had become.

It was still hard for Marla to accept that Elezaar had taken his own life. That his death was accompanied by unconscionable betrayal was almost beyond her comprehension. Nevertheless, even when she forced herself to confront the cruel reality of his final deed, somehow Marla couldn't find it in herself to hate him for it.

Because I am responsible for Elezaar's death, she acknowledged silently, *as surely as if I'd handed him a vial of poison and ordered him to drink it.*

It devastated Marla to realise Elezaar had killed himself rather than confront her fury and, along with her unbearable grief, it made her confront the truth about who she really was. Marla knew she'd hardened her heart over the years. She'd had to, simply to survive. She effectively ruled Hythria and nobody did that by showering hugs and kisses on the Warlords. Marla had no choice but to grow hard and unsentimental. It was toughen up or die. *But when did I become so heartless?* she wondered. *Was it the night I arranged to have Nash killed?*

Was that the beginning or the end of my journey into the abyss?

Am I now so terrible? she asked herself. *So cold? So ruthless that Elezaar would willingly taken his own life rather than face my wrath?*

As the slaves settled Elezaar's small, twisted body in the temporary grave Rodja had ordered dug in the small garden of her townhouse, Marla remembered the first time Luciena had accused her of being ruthless. It had come as a shock to her then to learn that people thought of her that way. It was devastating to realise even those closest to her obviously believed the same about her. *Do my children fear me as Elezaar must have? Do they quail at the mention of my name? Does the whole of Hythria tremble when I speak?*

Does the world fear me now, the way I once feared it? Am I the despot I so desperately tried to prevent my sons from becoming?

And how did it happen? Marla asked herself, trying to pinpoint the exact moment in time when her concern for her family had turned into a callous disregard for anyone else. *At what point did I let my fear take over and turn me into this terrifying, hard-shelled monster?*

No closer to an answer than she had been when she first asked herself the same question as she sobbed over Elezaar's dying body in her arms, Marla watched, dry-eyed and rigid with self-control, as they buried the dwarf next to Ruxton Tirstone. A light rain fell, warm and sticky as blood, but she barely noticed. As the slaves covered over his small linen-wrapped body with the freshly turned earth, the princess sank down onto the wrought-iron garden seat. Only Marla and her stepson, Rodja Tirstone, had attended the burial. Nobody else understood the significance of Elezaar's death, and even Rodja, perhaps, didn't fully comprehend her loss. Or her part in it.

And even if anybody did understand what his loss means to me, who is left in Greenharbour to grieve for the Fool?

The family was spread across Hythria. She'd had no word from Krakandar since sending Damin the letter containing the note to Mahkas her son had requested regarding his uncle's futile hopes for a betrothal. There had been a message from Adham, though. Unaware of his father's death, he had sent a letter through one of Ruxton's agents in Medalon, advising him of his success in finding somewhere to store their precious cargo of spices and containing the news that Xanda and Luciena were headed for Bordertown and that he intended to meet up with them there and then head home via Krakandar. Rodja came by to tell her about the letter the same day Elezaar returned home. He was the one who had found her with the dwarf, holding his long-dead body to her breast, tears streaming down her face, rocking him back and forth, unaware of how long she had been there, holding him, cursing him, begging him not to abandon her . . .

Fortunately, Rodja had inherited much of his father's common sense, along with his genial temperament. He'd taken care of everything for Marla. He'd arranged for the *court'esa* to be laid out in the main hall – a signal honour for a slave – arranged for candles to be lit around the house and the gardens to guide his soul to the underworld, organised for the grave to be dug and then stood with her while they sent him on his way.

'Will you be all right, your highness?'

Marla forced down her self-doubt, her guilt, even a little

of her grief, before she looked up at him from the garden seat and frowned. 'I've been your stepmother since you were eleven years old, Rodja. How is it you never call me Mother?'

'I never realised you wanted me to.'

'I'm not sure I ever did,' she replied, thinking this was just another symptom of the woman she had become. The Tirstone children respected her, but they had never warmed to her the way her own children had warmed to Ruxton. 'And I'm quite certain I don't deserve the moniker. If anyone mothered my children, and Ruxton's, it's Bylinda Damaran. All of you should probably call her by that name.' She smiled wanly, hoping Rodja just thought her in a reflective mood, not tearing herself apart with guilt and self-recrimination. 'It's just . . . you've been such a great help since your father died . . . "your highness" seems far too impersonal.'

'What do you want me to call you?'

She thought about it for a moment. 'I think, given the nature of our relationship, I wouldn't be offended if you addressed me by name.'

'As you wish,' he said, and then added awkwardly, 'Marla.'

'It'll get easier with practice, I'm sure.'

'You're not going to stay out here in the rain, are you?'

Marla looked up, a little surprised to realise it was still spitting. 'I suppose I shouldn't waste time sitting here doing nothing. I have a lot to do. And you have a wife about to give birth any moment. I shouldn't keep you any longer, Rodja. But I do appreciate you being here. Elezaar would have appreciated it, too.'

'Elezaar meant a lot to all of us, Marla.' He didn't seem to have nearly as much difficulty using her name this time. 'The others will be devastated when they learn he's gone.'

'I should write to them about it. Along with everything else on my desk that I must deal with today.'

'Hythria won't fall apart if you take the day off, you know.'

'I'd not be too certain of that.' She fell silent for a moment. Was her grand notion that Hythria would fall apart if she relaxed her guard for a day simply another symptom of her ruthless megalomania?

Stop it, she scolded herself impatiently. *You're going to drive yourself insane if you keep thinking like that!*

She looked up at Rodja, squaring her shoulders a little, as if that small act would drive away her doubts. 'Should I tell the others the truth about how he died?'

'As I've no more idea of the truth than anyone else, I couldn't really say.'

Marla wasn't so far gone in her grief that she missed his censure. 'Elezaar poisoned himself, Rodja, because he feared me. That's the truth you seek.'

The rain suddenly forgotten, Rodja sank down beside Marla on the garden seat, shocked to the core by her revelation. 'He *killed* himself? I don't understand. Why would Elezaar take his own life? Why did he fear you?'

'He feared my anger, because he betrayed me to Alija.'

Rodja shook his head in disbelief. 'No. I don't believe it.'

'You'd better get used to the idea. Things are going to change around here, now that Alija knows all our innermost secrets.'

'You must be mistaken . . .'

'If only I was,' she sighed.

He studied her warily for a moment. 'You appear to be taking this news remarkably well,' he said, clearly concerned that she was sitting serenely in the rain, not pacing up and down, or throwing things, or ranting with fury at Elezaar's treachery.

'I think that's because, oddly enough, in his own way, Elezaar has done me a favour.'

'By betraying us? That's a kinder way of putting it than I'm thinking, right now.'

'He's finally forced my hand, Rodja. There'll be no more dancing around with Alija. No more pretending. No more hiding. No more suffering her smug superiority or acting like a simpering fool, thanking her for her advice, calling her a friend.'

'I can see how that might appeal to you, Marla, but with everything going on . . . the plague . . . Gods! Could he have picked a worse time to do this?'

'There was never going to be a good time.'

'I still don't get it,' Rodja said, shaking his head. '*Why?* Why would he betray you? Or any of us, for that matter?'

'Elezaar betrayed us to save his brother.'

'I didn't know he had a brother. Still, it's no excuse.'

'You think not?' she asked with a slightly raised brow. 'What would you do to save Adham from being tortured before your very eyes?'

'That's different.'

'How so?'

'Well, for one thing, Adham's not—'

'A slave?'

'I didn't mean it like that.'

'I know,' she assured him, patting his arm. 'And I know what Elezaar did seems unforgivable. But when I think of some of the things I've done these past twenty years that are just as questionable, simply to save my brother from the consequences of his own foolishness, I find it hard to condemn Elezaar for the same crime. And that's the tragedy of Elezaar's death, Rodja. I never got the opportunity to tell him that. He was so certain I would turn him out once I learned of his treachery, he killed himself without giving me a chance to prove him wrong.'

Rodja fell silent. As his father's right-hand man these past few years, her stepson was more familiar than most with some of the things she'd done. He'd even aided her on occasion, when she required the resources of his father's intelligence network and Ruxton was unavailable.

'Do you fear me too, Rodja?' she asked, when he offered no reply.

'A little bit,' he admitted.

'It's a very lonely feeling, knowing you're feared.'

'You're not alone, Marla.'

'I am now that Elezaar's gone,' she replied. They were both getting soaked by the rain neither of them seemed to notice.

'What are you going to do?' he asked after a while, when the silence began to get uncomfortable.

'Bring Alija down. I have no choice now.'

'That's not going to be easy.'

'I'll need your help.'

'What do you want me to do?'

'Knowledge is power, Rodja.'

Her stepson smiled thinly, which made him look disturbingly like Ruxton. 'Elezaar's Tenth Rule, if I remember his lessons correctly.'

Marla nodded. 'And I intend to apply Elezaar's rules like never before. I want information. I want to know everything Alija does, Rodja, and who she does it with. I want to know who she speaks to and who she doesn't speak to. I want to know who she's sleeping with. I want to know what she eats for breakfast. I want to know what undergarments she wears. I want to know everything that happens in her household right down to the colour of her bowel movements.'

Rodja nodded and then frowned a little. 'That's going to cost a lot of money.'

'I can afford it.'

'Then I'll arrange it for you.'

'Thank you, Rodja.'

He hesitated, and then looked at her with concern. 'Are you *sure* you'll be all right, Marla?'

She paused before she replied and then nodded. 'Oddly enough, yes, I think I'm going to be fine,' she said.

Rodja left her in the garden after a time, the gently falling rain like a heavy mist around her. Marla sat by the fresh grave, her own guilt slowly giving way to anger as she pondered the motives behind Elezaar's willing betrayal. She thought she understood, now, some of his reasons at least. And she intended to make it up to him. She would give Elezaar in death the one thing he had craved in life and she had been too preoccupied to notice. She owed him that much at least.

For years, Elezaar had urged Marla to be more overt in her dealings with the High Arrion. Marla had resisted, determined not to do anything to force the issue until Damin would safely come of age. Her reticence frustrated the dwarf, Marla knew that, but the decision was hers to make and she had chosen to preserve the status quo.

Marla no longer had that luxury. In death, Elezaar had managed to manipulate her into doing what he hadn't been able to make her do in life.

Well, you'll get your wish, Elezaar, she promised him silently. *I will bring Alija down. You've left me with no other choice.*

Fortunately, even with everything Alija now knew about Marla's plans for the future, with all she would have learned about Marla's actions in the past, one thing she couldn't know – because Elezaar hadn't known it, either – was just how far Marla was willing to go to get what *she* wanted.

Alija is probably still patting herself on the back for being so clever, Marla realised. *I wonder if she has any idea how far I'm willing to go to make this country a safe place for my son to rule?*

Or just how far, Marla admitted silently to herself, *I'm willing to go to unburden myself of this intolerable guilt.*

It might be lonely, knowing you were feared, but Marla consoled herself with the idea that vengeance was an all-consuming pastime. It should keep the loneliness at bay. Because it was vengeance that began to fill Marla's thoughts, pushing away the guilt and the grief.

Alija had forced Elezaar to betray his mistress, something he would never have done willingly. For that, as much as anything else, Marla decided, Alija Eaglespike must die. The murder of Ronan Dell and his household, her attempts on Damin's life, stealing Nash from her, the plots Alija stirred up against the High Prince every chance she got, her plans to raise first her husband and now her son to the throne – there were plenty of reasons to bring Alija down, but Marla had always been able to convince herself that waiting until the right time was better than taking action at the wrong time.

But Alija had crossed the line when she made Elezaar betray Marla, and for that she would die – Marla was determined about that. The dwarf was the sad casualty of a battle between two powerful women who were about to step out from behind their civilised façades to face each other down.

Alija had drawn first blood. This wasn't a battle of wits any longer. It was war.

EXTRAS

www.orbitbooks.net

About the Author

Jennifer Fallon lives in Alice Springs, in central Australia, and writes anywhere she can get her hands on a computer. She writes full-time and moonlights in business training and IT as a consultant. Visit her website at www.jenniferfallon.com for more information.

Find out more about Jennifer and other Orbit authors by registering for the free Orbit newsletter at www.orbitbooks.net

If you enjoyed
WARRIOR,
look out for

MEDALON

also by

Jennifer Fallon

I

The funeral pyre caught with a whoosh, lighting the night sky and shadowing the faces of the thousands gathered to witness the Burning. Smoke, scented with fragrant oils to disguise the smell of burning flesh, hung in the warm, still air, as if reluctant to leave the ceremony. The spectators were silent as the hungry flames licked the oil-soaked pyre, reaching for Trayla's corpse. The death of the First Sister had drawn almost every inhabitant of the Citadel to the amphitheatre.

R'shiel Tenragan caught the Lord Defender's eye as she pushed her way through the green tunics of the senior Novices to take her place past the ranks of blue-gowned Sisters and grey-robed Probates. Feeling his eyes on her, she looked up. The Mistress of the Sisterhood would have her hide if he reported she'd been late. She met the Lord Defender's gaze defiantly, before turning her eyes to the pyre.

Out of the corner of her eye she saw the Lord

Defender take an involuntary step backwards as the flames seared his time-battered face. Surreptitiously, she glanced at the ranks of women and girls who stood in a solemn circle around the pyre. Their faces were unreadable in the firelight. For the most part they were still, their heads bowed respectfully. Occasionally, a foot shuffled on the sandy floor of the arena. *How many were genuinely grieving*, she mused, *and how many more had their minds on the Quorum, and who would fill the vacancy?*

R'shiel knew the political manoeuvring had begun the moment Trayla had been found in her study, the knife of her assailant still buried in her breast. Her killer was barely out of his teens. He was waiting even now in the cells behind the Defenders' Headquarters to be hanged. Rumour had it that he was a disciple of the River Goddess, Maera. The Sisterhood had confiscated his family's boat – and with it, their livelihood – for the crime of worshipping a heathen god. He had come to the Citadel to save his family from starvation, he claimed, to beg the First Sister for mercy.

He had killed her instead.

What had Trayla said to the boy, R'shiel wondered? What would cause him to pull a knife on the First Sister – a daunting figure to an uneducated river-brat? Surely he must have known his plea would fall on deaf ears? Pagan worship had been outlawed in Medalon for two centuries. The Harshini were extinct and with them their demons and their gods. *If he wanted mercy, he should have migrated south*, she thought unsympathetically. They still believed in the heathen gods in Hythria and Fardohnya, R'shiel knew, and the whole of Karien to the north was fanatically devoted to the worship of a single god, but in Medalon they had progressed beyond pagan ignorance centuries ago.

A voice broke the silence. R'shiel glanced through the firelight at the old woman who spoke.

'Since our beloved Param led us to enlightenment, the Sisters of the Blade have carried on her solemn trust to free Medalon from the chains of heathen idolatry. As First Sister, Trayla honoured that trust. She gave her life for it. Now we honour Trayla. *Let us remember our Sister.*'

She joined the thousands of voices repeating the ritual phrase. It was uncomfortably warm this close to the pyre on such a balmy summer's eve and her high-necked green tunic was damp with sweat.

'*Let us remember our Sister.*'

Small and wrinkled, Francil Asharen was the oldest member of the Quorum and had presided over this ceremony twice before. She was Mistress of the Citadel, the civilian administrator of this vast city-complex. Twice before she had refused to be nominated as First Sister and R'shiel could think of no reason that would change her mind this time. She had no ambition beyond her current position.

Harith Nortarn, the tall, heavily-built Mistress of the Sisterhood, stood beside her. R'shiel grimaced inwardly. The woman was a harridan and her beautifully embroidered white silk gown did nothing to soften her demeanour. Generations of Novices, Probates, and even fully qualified Blue Sisters lived in fear of incurring her wrath. Even the other Quorum members avoided upsetting her.

R'shiel turned her attention to the small, plump woman who stood at Harith's shoulder: Mahina Cortanen. The Mistress of Enlightenment. Her gown was as elaborate as Harith's – soft white silk edged with delicate gold embroidery – but she still managed to look like a peasant in a borrowed dress. She was R'shiel's personal favourite of all the Quorum members, her own mother included. Mahina was only a little taller than Francil, and wore a stern, but thoughtful expression.

Next to Mahina, Joyhinia Tenragan wore exactly the right expression of grief and quiet dignity for the occasion. Her mother was the newest member of the Quorum and, R'shiel fervently hoped, the least likely to be elected as the new First Sister. Although each member of the Quorum held equal rank, the Mistress of the Interior controlled the day-to-day running of the nation, because she was responsible for the Administrators in every major town in Medalon. It was a position of great responsibility and traditionally seen as a stepping-stone to gaining the First Sister's mantle.

R'shiel watched her thoughtfully then glanced at the man who was supposed to be her father. Joyhinia and Lord Jenga were coldly polite toward each other – and had been for as long as R'shiel could remember. He was a tall, solid man with iron-grey hair, but he was always unfailingly polite to her and had never, to her knowledge, denied he was her father. Considering the frost that seemed to gather in the air between her mother and the

Lord Defender whenever they were close, R'shiel could not imagine how they had ever been warm enough toward each other to conceive a child.

The fire reached upward, licking at Trayla's white robe. R'shiel wondered for a moment if the fragrant oils had been enough. Would the smell of the First Sister's crisping flesh sicken the gathered Sisters? *Probably not*, she noted darkly.

Behind the members of the Quorum and the blue-gowned ranks of the Sisters, the Probates and Novices were ranked around the floor of the amphitheatre, their eyes wide as they witnessed their first public Burning. Some of them looked a little pale, even in the ruby light of the funeral pyre, but tomorrow they would cheer themselves hoarse with glee when the young assassin was publicly hanged. *Hypocrites*, she thought, stifling a disrespectful yawn.

The vigil over the First Sister continued through the night. The silence was unsettling. Another yawn threatened to undo her, so R'shiel turned her attention to the first ten ranks of the seating surrounding the Arena. They were filled by red-coated Defenders who stood to attention throughout the long watch. Lord Jenga had not spared them a glance all night. He did not have to. They were Defenders. There was no shuffling of feet numbed by standing all night. No bored expressions or hidden yawns. She envied their discipline.

As the night progressed, the crowd in the upper levels of the tiered seating gradually thinned. The civilians who lived at the Citadel had jobs to do and other places to be. They could not afford the luxury of an all-night vigil. In the morning, the Sisters, Probates and Novices would still expect to be waited on. Life went on in the Citadel, regardless of who lived or died.

The night dragged on in silence until the first tentative rays of daylight announced the next and most anxiously awaited part of the ceremony.

As a faint luminescence softened the darkness, Francil raised her head. 'Let us remember our Sister!'

'Let us remember our Sister,' the gathered Sisters, Probates, Novices and Defenders echoed in a monotone. Every one of them was tired. They were beyond being reverent and wished only that the ceremony were over.

'Let us move forward toward a new future,' Francil called.

'Let us move forward toward a new future,' R'shiel repeated, this time with slightly more interest. Finally, the time had come to announce Trayla's successor, a decision that affected every citizen in Medalon.

'Hail the First Sister, Mahina Cortanen!'

'Hail the First Sister, Mahina Cortanen!' the crowd chanted.

R'shiel gasped with astonishment as Mahina stood forward to accept the dutiful, if rather tired, cheers of the gathering. She couldn't believe it. *What political scheming and double-dealing had the others indulged in? How, with all their intrigues and plotting had the Quorum actually elected someone capable of doing the job well?* R'shiel had to stop herself from laughing out loud.

As the cheers subsided, Mahina turned to Jenga. 'My Lord Defender, will you swear the allegiance of the Defenders to me?'

'Gladly, your Grace,' Jenga replied.

He unsheathed his sword and stepped forward, laying the polished blade on the sandy ground at the feet of the new First Sister. He bent one knee and waited for the senior officers down on the arena floor to follow suit. The Defenders up in the stands placed clenched fists over their hearts as Jenga's voice rang out in the silent arena.

'By the blood in my veins and the soil of Medalon, I swear that the Defenders are yours to command, First Sister, until my death or yours.'

A loud, deep-throated cheer went up from the Defenders. Jenga rose to his feet and met Mahina's eyes. R'shiel watched her accept the accolade. Never had a woman looked less like a First Sister.

Mahina nodded to Jenga, thanking him silently, then turned to the gathering and opened her arms wide.

'I declare a day of rest,' she announced, her first proclamation as First Sister. Her voice sounded rasping and dry after the warm night standing before a blazing bonfire. 'A day to contemplate the life of our beloved Trayla. A day to witness the execution of her murderer. Tomorrow, we will begin the next chapter of the Sisterhood. Today we rest.'

Another tired cheer greeted her announcement. With her dismissal, the ranks of the Sisterhood dissolved as the women turned with relief toward the tunnel that led out of the arena to make their way home. They muttered quietly among themselves, no doubt as surprised as R'shiel was to learn the identity of the new First Sister. The Defenders still did not move, would not move, until every Sister had left the arena. Mahina led the exodus. R'shiel studied Joyhinia and the other members of the Quorum, but they gave no hint of their true feelings.

The sky was considerably lighter as the last green-skirted Novice disappeared down the tunnel and Jenga finally dismissed his men. R'shiel waited for the others to leave, hoping for a moment alone with the Lord Defender. The pyre collapsed in on itself with a sharp crack and a shower of sparks as the Defenders broke ranks with relief. Many simply sat down. Many more flexed stiff knees and rubbed aching backs. Jenga beckoned two of his captains to him. The men rose stiffly, but saluted sharply enough for the Foundation Day Parade.

'Georj, keep some men here and keep the pyre burning until it is nothing but ashes,' he ordered the younger of the two wearily.

'And the ashes, my Lord?' Georj asked.

'Rake them into the sand,' he said with a shrug. 'They mean nothing now.' He turned to the older captain. 'Tell the men they may only rest once their mounts are fed and taken care of, Nheal. And then call for volunteers for the hanging guard. I'll need ten men.'

'For this hanging guard you'll get more than ten volunteers,' Nheal predicted.

'Then pick the sensible ones,' Jenga suggested,

impatiently. 'This is a hanging, Captain, not a carnival.'

'My Lord,' the captain replied, saluting with a clenched fist over his heart. He hesitated a moment longer then added tentatively, 'Interesting choice for First Sister, don't you think, my Lord?'

'I don't think, Captain,' Jenga told him stiffly. 'And neither should you.' He frowned, daring the younger man to laugh at his rather asinine comment. 'I am sure First Sister Mahina will be a wise and fair leader.'

R'shiel saw through his polite words. Jenga was obviously delighted by Mahina's appointment. That augured well for what she had in mind.

'The expression "about bloody time" leaps to mind, actually,' Nheal remarked, almost too softly for R'shiel to make it out.

'Don't overstep yourself, Captain,' Jenga warned. 'It is not your place to comment on the decisions of the Sisterhood. And you might like to tell your brother captains not to overindulge in the taverns tonight. Remember, until tomorrow, we are still in mourning.'

Jenga turned from the pile of embers, and noticed R'shiel for the first time. As day broke fully over the amphitheatre, bringing with it a hint of the summer heat to come, he walked stiffly toward the exit tunnel where she was standing.

'Lord Jenga?' she ventured as he approached.

'Shouldn't you return to your quarters, R'shiel?' Jenga asked gruffly.

'I wanted to ask you something.'

Jenga glanced over his shoulder to ensure his

orders were being carried out, then nodded. R'shiel fell into step beside him as they entered the cool darkness of the tunnel that led under the amphitheatre.

'What will happen now, Lord Jenga?'

'The appointment of a new First Sister always heralds a change of direction, R'shiel, even if only a small one.'

'Mother says Trayla was an unimaginative leader, lacking in initiative. Actually, she used to refer to her as "that useless southern cow".'

'You, of all people, should know better than to repeat that sort of gossip, R'shiel.'

She smiled faintly at his tone. 'And what about Mahina? Joyhinia calls her an idealistic fool.'

'Sister Mahina has my respect, as do all the Sisters of the Blade.'

'Do you think her elevation means a change in the thinking of the Sisterhood?'

The Lord Defender stopped and looked at her, obviously annoyed by her question. 'R'shiel, you said you wanted to ask me something. Ask it or leave. I do not want to stand here discussing politics and idle gossip with you.'

'I want to know what happens now,' she said.

'I will be called on to witness the Spear of the First Sister swear fealty to Mahina. It will undoubtedly be Lord Draco.'

'He's supposed to be the First Sister's bodyguard,' R'shiel pointed out. 'Yet Trayla died at the hand of an assassin.'

'The position of First Spear is a very difficult

one to fill — the oath of celibacy it requires tends to discourage many applicants.'

'So he gets to keep his job? Even though he didn't do it?'

Jenga's patience was rapidly fading. 'Draco was absent at the time, R'shiel. Trayla fancied she was able to deal with a miserable pagan youth and ordered him out of the office. Now, is that all you wanted?'

'No. I was just curious, that's all.'

'Then be specific, child. I have other business to attend to. I have an assassin to hang, letters to write and orders to issue . . .'

'And banished officers who offended Trayla to recall?' she suggested hopefully.

Jenga shook his head. 'I can't revoke the First Sister's orders, R'shiel.'

'The First Sister is dead.'

'That doesn't mean I can rearrange the world to my liking.'

'But it does mean you can rearrange the Defenders,' R'shiel reminded him. She turned on her best, winning smile. 'Please, Lord Jenga. Bring Tarja home.'